THE WORLD'S CLASSICS

FYODOR DOSTOEVSKY

Devils

Translated and edited by
MICHAEL R. KATZ

Oxford   New York
OXFORD UNIVERSITY PRESS
1992

Oxford University Press, Walton Street, Oxford OX2 6DP

Oxford New York Toronto
Delhi Bombay Calcutta Madras Karachi
Petaling Jaya Singapore Hong Kong Tokyo
Nairobi Dar es Salaam Cape Town
Melbourne Auckland

and associated companies in
Berlin Ibadan

Oxford is a trade mark of Oxford University Press

Devils (Besy) first published 1871

First published as a World's Classic paperback 1992

British Library Cataloguing in Publication Data
Data available

Library of Congress Cataloging in Publication Data
Dostoevsky, Fyodor, 1821–1881.
[Besy, English]
Devils / translated and edited by Michael R. Katz.
p.   cm.—(The World's classics)
Translation of: Besy.
Includes bibliographical references (p.   ).
I. Katz, Michael R.   II. Title.   III. Series.
PG3326.B6   1992   891.73'3—dc20   91-25225
ISBN 0-19-281850-3

Typeset by Pure Tech Corporation, Pondicherry, India
Printed in Great Britain by
BPCC Hazells Ltd.
Aylesbury, Bucks

DEVILS

FYODOR MIKHAILOVICH DOSTOEVSKY was born in Moscow in 1821. His mother died of consumption in 1837 and his father was murdered on his estate two years later. In 1844 he left the Engineering Academy in Petersburg and devoted himself to writing. *Poor Folk* (1846) met with great critical success. In 1849 he was sentenced to death on account of his involvement with a group of utopian socialists, the Petrashevsky circle. The sentence was commuted to penal servitude and exile, but the experience radically altered his political and personal ideology and led directly to *Memoirs from the House of the Dead* (1861–2). In 1857, while still in exile, he married Maria Dmitrievna Isaeva, returning to Petersburg in 1859. In the early 1860s he founded two new literary journals, *Vremya* and *Epokha*, and proved himself to be a brilliant journalist. He travelled in Europe, which served to strengthen his anti-European sentiment. During this period abroad he had an affair with Polina Suslova, the model for many of his literary heroines. Central to their relationship was their mutual passion for gambling—an obsession which brought chaos to his financial affairs. Both his wife and his much loved brother, Mikhail, died in 1864, the same year in which *Notes from the Underground* was published; *Crime and Punishment* and *The Gambler* followed in 1866 and in 1867 he married his stenographer, Anna Snitkina, who managed to bring stability into his frenetic life. His other major novels, *The Idiot* (1868), *Devils* (1871), and *The Brothers Karamazov* (1879–80) met with varying degrees of success. In 1880 he was hailed as a saint, prophet, and genius by the audience to whom he delivered an address at the unveiling of the Pushkin memorial. He died six months later in 1881

MICHAEL R. KATZ is Professor of Russian, Chairman of the Department of Slavic Languages, and Director of the Center for Soviet and East European Studies at the University of Texas at Austin. He has published books on the literary ballad and on dreams in fiction, and has translated works by Herzen, Chernyshevsky, Dostoevsky, and Tolstoy.

CONTENTS

DEVILS

PART ONE

PART TWO

INTRODUCTION

IN a letter written from Dresden, dated 8 October 1870, addressed to his publisher, Fyodor Dostoevsky described the difficulty he was having with the new novel he'd begun writing:

For a very long time I had trouble with the beginning of the work. I rewrote it several times. To tell the truth, something happened with this novel that had never happened to me before: week after week, I would keep putting aside the beginning and work on the ending instead ... What I can guarantee is that, as the novel progresses, it will hold the reader's interest. It seems to me that the way I have it now is for the best.

That novel was *Besy* (1871-2), or *Devils*, although it has also been translated into English as *The Possessed*. It was the third of Dostoevsky's five major works—preceded by *Crime and Punishment* (1866) and *The Idiot* (1868), followed by *A Raw Youth*, or *The Adolescent* (1875), and *The Brothers Karamazov* (1879).

Dostoevsky wrote *Devils* at a particularly painful time in his life. He was living in Western Europe and was not only short of money, but kept losing at the gambling tables. His health had taken a turn for the worse: he was suffering an increase in the frequency of epileptic attacks and finding his strength ebbing as a result. His wife was ill, his baby daughter fretful. He had disturbing encounters with a number of West European radicals and revolutionaries and was desperately eager to return to Russia. In his intense longing, he devoured Russian newspapers and journals to keep informed of events and trends back home.

Devils is first and foremost a crucial link in a chain of ideological Russian novels written in the middle of the nineteenth century, each responding to its predecessor in several interesting ways. Alexander Herzen's *Who is to Blame?* (1841-6) initiated the series with its penetrating examination of the question of culpability for the unhappy fate of its attractive but superfluous aristocratic hero and the talented young woman he comes to love. Ivan Turgenev replied to Herzen in his best-known work, *Fathers and Sons* (1862); there he shows a man of the younger generation, a self-styled nihilist, brought low by his involvement with an intelligent but unworthy society woman when he is forced to confront 'the abyss of romanticism within himself'. In a novel with a more emphatic interrogative title, *What is to be Done?* (1865), Nikolai Chernyshevsky rewrites Turgenev's novel, but presents a more sympathetic portrait of the 'new people', the younger generation of nihilist men and women, who manage to conduct their personal relationships in a manner consistent with their ideological convictions. In *Devils* Dostoevsky not only refers directly to the authors, characters, and themes in all of the above, but re-examines the fundamental questions raised and the agonizing answers offered by each work.

The title of Dostoevsky's novel and its first epigraph are borrowed from Alexander Pushkin's splendid literary ballad 'Devils' (1830). The poem combines visual images, repetition, parallelism, and refrains to create a haunting atmosphere in which external folkloric spirits are compared to internal demons tormenting the lyrical hero of the work. The novel's second epigraph, the story of the Gadarene swine from St Luke's Gospel, recounts a great miracle, a dramatic exorcism performed by Jesus in which devils are transferred to swine and promptly self-destruct, thus leaving the sick man restored to his right mind, sitting at the feet of Jesus. In a letter to his friend A. N. Maikov written in October 1870, Dostoevsky explained the relevance of this miracle to the meaning of his novel:

Exactly the same thing happened in our country: the devils went out of the Russian man and entered into a herd of swine, i.e. into the Nechaevs ... *et al.* These are drowned or will be drowned, and the healed man ... sits at the feet of Jesus. It couldn't have been otherwise. Russia has spewed out all the filth she's been fed and obviously there's nothing Russian left in those spewed-out wretches.

Devils is at once both a political pamphlet and a religious tract. It emerges from two quite separate inspirations, one narrowly ideological and programmatic, the other broadly spiritual and moral. In 1869, while still abroad, Dostoevsky learned the details of the notorious Nechaev case from his reading of Russian newspapers. A young student named Ivanov, a member of a secret revolutionary committee or cell called a 'group of five', had been murdered by Sergei Nechaev (1847–83), revolutionary and conspirator, disciple and friend of the anarchist Bakunin, co-author with him of the extraordinary *Catechism of a Revolutionary* (1866). Why was Ivanov murdered? Most likely because he'd begun to suspect Nechaev was nothing more than an impostor and con-man, and was threatening to expose them all to the authorities. Nechaev was afraid (or pretended to be so) and managed to persuade his co-conspirators to participate in the murder. Their victim's body was disposed of in a pond. Afterwards Nechaev left Russia for Switzerland; he later returned, was quickly arrested, tried, convicted, and imprisoned in the Peter-Paul Fortress in Petersburg. He died in 1883. Both the transcript of Nechaev's trial and the text of the *Catechism* were published in Russian newspapers.

Dostoevsky read the shocking account and was provoked to write a counter-revolutionary political pamphlet, a tendentious anti-nihilist tract, to expose the 'new men' once and for all, to explain the origin of their mistaken ideology, and to assign blame for their misguided activities. In February 1873 he went so far as to send a copy of his latest novel to the heir to the Russian throne, the future Tsar Alexander III. The letter accompanying the work stated the author's intention in no uncertain terms:

It's almost a historical study, in which I've sought to account for the possibility of such monstrous phenomena as the Nechaev movement occurring in our strange society ... Our Belinskys and Granovskys would never have believed it if they'd been told they were the direct spiritual fathers of the Nechaev band. And it's this kinship of ideas and their transmission from fathers to sons that I've tried to show in my work.

The other major source of inspiration for *Devils* was religious. For some time Dostoevsky had been working on a huge project called 'Atheism', the story of a character's loss of faith. The author's plans for the work were sketchy: after falling from grace the hero was to undergo intense spiritual suffering and conduct a thorough investigation of all religious faiths. This *magnum opus* was never written, but it provided fuel for Dostoevsky's last three novels.

In 1869 the main theme of 'Atheism' became intertwined with and then engulfed by a related idea. Dostoevsky began writing 'The Life of a Great Sinner': the main character was to be, sequentially, an atheist, a believer, a fanatic, a sectarian, and then an atheist again. Opposed to this fictional hero was a figure based on a real monk, Father Tikhon Zadonsky, who would reside in a monastery and represent true faith. The work was intended to resolve once and for all the question of God's existence.

Dostoevsky's *Devils* is a fusion of these two sources: it is on the one hand a powerful political pamphlet, an attack on nihilism, an investigation of its origins, a dire warning about future consequences if nothing is done to halt its spread. On the other hand it is a far-reaching spiritual quest, a search for God in the face of pervasive doubt, an examination of human behaviour in the absence of God, and an attempt to find the ultimate solution to the problem.

The political pamphlet has as its centre the young revolutionary Peter Verkhovensky and his motley band of conspirators, the 'group of five', in a squalid little provincial town in Russia. Early versions of this main character in the notebooks depict him as having neither faith nor programme; his only aim is to achieve power over others. He is obviously modelled on the historical figure of Nechaev, but emerges as a caricature of that iron-willed revolutionary. In the end he manages to escape all consequences of his actions and seek refuge in the West.

The spiritual quest has as its centre the mysterious figure of Stavrogin. At one point in the notebooks Dostoevsky writes: 'Stavrogin is everything.' Indeed, almost all characters in the novel can be defined in terms of their relationship to him: Varvara Stavrogina—his birth mother; Stepan Verkhovensky—his spiritual father; Tikhon—his father-confessor; Peter Verkhovensky—his idolater; Shatov and Kirillov—his 'disciples'; Virginsky, Liputin, Lebyadkin, Lyamshin, Erkel and Fedka—his 'devils'; and Liza, Dasha, Marya Lebyadkina, Matryosha and Marie Shatova—his 'mistresses'.

There are few characters who don't fit the scheme: Peter Verkhovensky's 'disciple' Shigalyov, governor von Lembke and his wife Yulia Mikhailovna, the 'great writer' Karmazinov, and the narrator of the chronicle, Mr Govorov. But for the most part all the actions of other characters are organized around the presence, even the absence, of Stavrogin. When Dostoevsky maintains that 'Stavrogin is everything' perhaps what he really means is that 'Stavrogin is nothing'—a cosmic 'black hole' at the centre of the novel's moral universe. After his attempt at confession to Father Tikhon is aborted, and he fails to establish genuine relationships with any of his 'mistresses' (suggesting both his moral and sexual impotence), Stavrogin's squalid, unheroic, 'lukewarm' implosion is inevitable.

Many characters spout ideological convictions expounded by Stavrogin at some previous stage in his life. The landscape is strewn with disciples and devils clinging to vestiges of his thought who distort and parody them beyond recognition. Shatov, for example, is an arch-Slavophile, who elevates the nation to godhood; his fanatic messianic nationalism knows no bounds. Kirillov, the arch-Westernizer, elevates man to godhood and his absurd individualism leads to self-annihilation.

Only Stepan Trofimovich Verkhovensky, a character based on the Russian historian T. N. Granovsky, the 'direct spiritual father' of Nechaev's band (as Dostoevsky instructed the future Tsar), and Stepan's bizarre last journey and absurd confession—of his lifelong love for Varvara Stavrogina and his genuine faith in God—bring to final synthesis both the novel's political theme and its spiritual quest. It is Stepan Trofimovich who ultimately interprets the story of the Gadarene swine from Luke, the one that serves as the second epigraph and that Dostoevsky himself had explained to Maikov in the letter quoted above. That letter continues:

And bear this is mind, my dear friend: a man who loses his people and his national roots also loses the faith of his fathers and his God.... Well, if you really want to know—this is the theme of my novel in essence. It's called *Devils*, and it describes how the devils entered into the herd of swine.

Certain aspects of Dostoevsky's literary technique deserve particular attention. Mr Govorov, who combines the roles of objective narrator and eyewitness chronicler is quite extraordinary. At times he seems omniscient, at others, he claims or displays only limited knowledge of events and motives. His own ideological stance is problematic, as is his personal life (e.g. his frustrated affection for Liza). His speech is riddled with qualifications, hesitations and negations, combined with an infuriating reluctance to say all that he knows or thinks.

Devils is without doubt Dostoevsky's most humorous work. It has more irony, more elements of burlesque and parody, more physical comedy and buffoonery, more exaggerated characterizations and ambiguous use of language than any of his other works. It has often been claimed that humour is 'one of the things that gets lost in translation'. This new version attempts to capture some of the author's comic devices and find suitable equivalents for them in English.

In the letter to Maikov quoted above Dostoevsky described his work on *Devils*:

There's no doubt that I'll write it badly; being more a poet than an artist, I've always tackled themes beyond my powers. And so I'll make a mess of it, that's for sure. The theme is too powerful. But, inasmuch as none of the critics who've thus far passed judgement on me has failed to accord me some talent, the chances are that this long novel won't be too bad in spots. And that's all I can say.

Surely that's not all that can be said!

I would like to express my gratitude to Neill Megaw for supplying the poetry, Dina Sherzer for helping with the French, Sidney Monas and Bill Wagner for checking the footnotes, Russell Richardson for entering changes in the draft, my research assistants Julie Swann and Pete Smith for their help with the text, Sally Furgeson for her excellent proof-reading, and Oxford University Press's copy-editor for numerous suggestions, corrections, improvements and the translation of Lebyadkin's poem in Part 3.

MICHAEL R. KATZ
The University of Texas

NOTE ON THE TEXT

DOSTOEVSKY'S novel *Devils* (*Besy*) was first published in the journal *Russian Messenger* (*Russkii vestnik*) in 1871 (nos. 1, 2, 4, 7, 9–11) and 1872 (nos. 11–12). It was issued as a separate volume in 1873. The text of this latter edition was included in the most recent edition of Dostoevsky's *Complete Collected Works in Thirty Volumes* (*Polnoe sobranie sochinenii v tridtsati tomakh*), Leningrad: Nauka, vols 10–12, 1974–5. It is this text that was chosen for a new translation of the work.

The chapter entitled 'At Tikhon's' or 'Stavrogin's Confession' appears where the author originally intended it, rather than as an Appendix. Dostoevsky's publisher Katkov refused to print it because he found it too shocking. The author accepted this decision and the chapter never appeared during Dostoevsky's lifetime. It was discovered in 1921 among the author's papers and published a year later.

TRANSLATOR'S NOTE

CERTAIN characters in the novel, according to the habit of aristocratic Russians of the period, mix French with their Russian. It would be distracting to provide English translations of every French phrase, especially when used repetitively and/or meaninglessly, by Stepan Trofimovich, for example, with his *cher ami* (dear friend), *passons* (let's leave that), *voyez-vous* (you see), and so on. Those phrases necessary for comprehension are translated at the foot of the page.

SELECT BIBLIOGRAPHY

1. BIOGRAPHY

Frank, Joseph, *Dostoevsky*, 3 vols to date, Princeton, 1976– .
Grossman, Leonid, *Dostoevsky. A Biography*, London, 1974.
Kjetsaa, Geir, *Fyodor Dostoyevsky. A Writer's Life*, New York, 1987.

2. GENERAL STUDIES

Anderson, Roger B., *Dostoevsky: Myths of Duality*, Gainesville, Florida, 1986.
Bakhtin, Mikhail, *Problems of Dostoevsky's Poetics* (trans. Caryl Emerson), Minneapolis, 1984.
de Jonge, Alex, *Dostoevsky and the Age of Intensity*, London, 1975.
Fanger, Donald, *Dostoevsky and Romantic Realism*, Chicago, 1967.
Frank, Joseph, *Through the Russian Prism*, Princeton, N.J., 1990.
Frank, Joseph and Goldstein, David (eds), *Selected Letters of Fyodor Dostoevsky*, New Brunswick, N.J., 1987.
Holquist, Michael, *Dostoevsky and the Novel*, Princeton, 1977.
Ivanov, Vyacheslav, *A Study in Dostoevsky: Freedom and the Tragic Life*, New York, 1968.
Jones, John, *Dostoevsky*, Oxford, 1983.
Jones, Malcolm V., *Dostoevsky: The Novel of Discord*, London, 1976.
Kabat, Geoffrey C., *Ideology and Imagination: The Image of Society in Dostoevsky*, New York, 1978.
Leatherbarrow, William, *Fedor Dostoevsky*, Boston, 1981.
Mochulsky, Konstantin, *Dostoevsky: His Life and Work*, Princeton, New Jersey, 1967.
Peace, Richard, *Dostoevsky: An Examination of the Major Novels*, Cambridge, 1971.
Steiner, George, *Tolstoy or Dostoevsky*, New York, 1967.
Wasiolek, Edward, *Dostoevsky: The Major Fiction*, Cambridge, Massachusetts, 1973.

3. ON *DEVILS*

Wasiolek, Edward (ed.), *The Notebooks for The Possessed* (trans. Victor Terras), Chicago, 1968.

CHRONOLOGY OF FYODOR DOSTOEVSKY

Italicized items are works by Dostoevsky listed by year of first publication. Dates are Old Style, which means that they lag behind those used in 19th century Western Europe by twelve days.

1821	Fyodor Mikhailovich Dostoevsky is born in Moscow, the son of an army doctor (30 October).
1837	His mother dies.
1838	Enters the Engineering Academy in St Petersburg as an army cadet.
1839	His father dies, probably murdered by his serfs.
1842	Is promoted second lieutenant.
1843	Translates Balzac's *Eugénie Grandet*.
1844	Resigns his army commission.
1846	*Poor Folk* *The Double*
1849	*Netochka Nezvanova* Is led out for execution in the Semyonovsky Square in St Petersburg (22 December); his sentence is commuted at the last moment to penal servitude, to be followed by army service and exile, in Siberia.
1850–4	Serves four years at the prison at Omsk in western Siberia.
1854	Is released from prison (March), but is immediately posted as a private soldier to an infantry battalion stationed at Semipalatinsk, in western Siberia.
1855	Is promoted corporal. Death of Nicholas I; accession of Alexander II.
1856	Is promoted ensign.
1857	Marries Maria Dmitrievna Isaeva (6 February).
1859	Resigns his army commission with the rank of second lieutenant (March), and receives permission to return to European Russia.

Resides in Tver (August–December).
Moves to St Petersburg (December).
Uncle's Dream
Stepanchikovo Village

1861   Begins publication of a new literary monthly, *Vremya*,
founded by himself and his brother Mikhail (January).
The emancipation of the serfs.
The Insulted and the Injured
A Series of Essays on Literature

1861–2 *Memoirs from the House of the Dead*

1862   His first visit to Western Europe, including England and
France.

1863   *Winter Notes on Summer Impressions*
Vremya is banned, for political reasons but through a
misunderstanding, by the authorities.

1864   Launches a second journal, *Epokha* (March).
His first wife dies (15 April).
His brother Mikhail dies (10 July).
Notes from the Underground

1865   *Epokha* collapses for financial reasons (June).

1866   Attempted assassination of Alexander II by Dmitry Ka-
rakozov (April).
Crime and Punishment
The Gambler

1867   Marries Anna Grigorievna Snitkina, his stenographer, as
his second wife (15 February).
Dostoevsky and his bride leave for Western Europe
(April).

1867–71 The Dostoevskys reside abroad, chiefly in Dresden, but
also in Geneva, Vevey, Florence, and elsewhere.

1868   *The Idiot*

1870   *The Eternal Husband*

1871   The Dostoevskys return to St Petersburg. Birth of their
first son, Fyodor (16 July).

1871–2 *Devils* (also called *The Possessed*)

1873–4 Edits the weekly journal *Grazhdanin*.

1873–81 *Diary of a Writer*

1875   *A Raw Youth*

1878   Death of Dostoevsky's beloved three-year-old son Alyosha (16 May).

1879–80   *The Brothers Karamazov*

1880   His speech at lavish celebrations held in Moscow in honour of Pushkin is received with frenetic enthusiasm on 8 June, and marks the peak point attained by his reputation during his lifetime.

1881   Dostoevsky dies in St Petersburg (28 January). Alexander II is assassinated (1 March).

Devils

A NOVEL IN THREE PARTS

Strike me dead, but I can't see the track,
We've lost our way, what are we to do?
A devil seems to be leading us unto the field,
And making us go around in circles.

   . . .   .

So many of them, where are they being driven?
And why are they singing so mournfully?
Are they burying a house-spirit,
Or celebrating a witch's wedding?

A. PUSHKIN*

And there was there an herd of many swine feeding on the mountain: and they besought him that he would suffer them to enter into them. And he suffered them. Then went the devils out of the man, and entered into the swine: and the herd ran violently down a steep place into the lake, and were choked. When they that fed them saw what was done, they fled, and went and told it in the city and in the country. Then they went out to see what was done; and came to Jesus, and found the man, out of whom the devils were departed, sitting at the feet of Jesus, clothed, and in his right mind: and they were afraid.

LUKE 8: 32–5

PART ONE

By way of an introduction: some details from the biography of the highly esteemed Stepan Trofimovich Verkhovensky

I.

IN setting out to describe the recent and very strange events that occurred in our hitherto completely undistinguished little town, I am compelled by my own lack of talent to begin from some time back, that is, with a few biographical details about the talented and highly esteemed Stepan Trofimovich Verkhovensky. Let these details serve merely as an introduction to the present chronicle; the actual story I intend to relate will follow later.

I can state forthwith that Stepan Trofimovich always played a rather special role among us, a civic role so to speak, and he loved this role so passionately that it seems to me he couldn't have existed without it. It's not that I'd compare him to an actor on stage: God forbid, all the more since I myself respect him. Perhaps it was all a matter of habit, or, more precisely, his constant and noble tendency since childhood to indulge in pleasant fantasies about his own splendid civic standing. For example, he enjoyed his position as a 'persecuted' man, even, so to speak, an 'exile'. There's a certain traditional glamour contained in these two little words that had seduced him once and for all, and, over many years, gradually elevated him in his own estimation, and finally placed him on a pedestal that was highly gratifying to his vanity. In an English satirical novel of the last century a certain Gulliver, returning from the land of the Lilliputians where the people were only a few inches tall, had grown so accustomed to thinking of himself as a giant that, as he walked along the streets of London, he kept shouting at passers-by and carriages to be careful and get out of his way so he wouldn't trample them, imagining that he was still a giant and they were very tiny. People laughed at him and made fun of him, and rough coachmen even lashed him with their whips. But was that fair? What is habit not capable of? Habit had driven Stepan Trofimovich almost as far as that, but in a more innocent and inoffensive way, if one can put it like that, because he was such a splendid man.

I'm actually inclined to think he was entirely forgotten in the end; on the other hand, it can't be said that he was completely unknown earlier on. There's no doubt that at one time he belonged to our famous galaxy of illustrious men of the last generation; at one time, though only for a brief moment, his name was uttered by many impulsive people of the day almost in the same breath with Chaadaev, Belinsky, Granovsky, and Herzen* (who was then just embarking on his activities abroad). But Stepan Trofimovich's activity ended almost as soon as it began as a result, so to speak, of a 'whirlwind of concurrent circumstances'. And what do you think? It turned out later there had been neither 'whirlwind' nor 'circumstances', at least not in this instance. Only a few days ago I learned to my great amazement, but from a most reliable source, that Stepan Trofimovich had been living in our province not as an exile, as we'd been led to believe; nor had he ever been under police surveillance. Such is the power of imagination! All his life he devoutly believed that in certain spheres he was regarded with apprehension, that his every step was being watched, and that three successive governors in the last twenty years arrived to take over the administration of our province with a certain preconceived notion about him inculcated from above and handed down with their appointment as governor. Had anyone tried to persuade the honourable Stepan Trofimovich with irrefutable evidence that he really had nothing to fear, he would certainly have been highly offended. And yet he was a very intelligent and talented man, even, so to say, a scholar, although, in fact, his scholarship... well, in a word, his scholarship had accomplished very little, in fact, it seems, it had accomplished nothing at all. But then that happens all the time with men of learning in Russia.

He returned from abroad and distinguished himself as a university lecturer towards the end of the 1840s. He managed to deliver only a few lectures, on the Arabs, I believe; he also succeeded in defending a brilliant dissertation on the potential civic and Hanseatic significance of the little German town of Hanau between 1413 and 1428, including the peculiar and obscure reasons why that significance never materialized. His dissertation was a clever and painful dig at the Slavophiles* of the day and immediately made him many bitter enemies. Later on, after he lost his university position, he managed to publish (as a form of revenge, so to speak, just to show them what sort of man they'd lost) in a progressive monthly journal* which translated the works of Dickens and advocated the ideas of George Sand, the beginning of some very profound piece of research; I believe it was about the causes of the extraordinary moral nobility of certain knights at some time or other, or something of that sort. In any case it expounded some lofty and exceptionally noble idea. It was said afterwards that the continuation of his research had been hastily forbidden and that even the progressive journal suffered as a result of having published the first part. That may very well have been so, since all sorts of things were possible in those days. But in this case it was more likely that nothing of the kind occurred and the author himself was simply too lazy to complete the work. He curtailed his lectures on the Arabs because somehow someone (obviously one of his reactionary enemies) had intercepted a letter to someone else which contained an account of certain 'circumstances', as a result of which someone was demanding some kind of explanation from him.

I don't know whether it's true, but it was also asserted that at the same time in Petersburg an enormous, unnatural, and subversive organization of some thirteen members was uncovered, one that had almost shaken the foundations of society. It was said that they were planning to translate the works of Fourier himself.* As bad luck would have it, at the same time in Moscow a poem written by Stepan Trofimovich was confiscated, a work he'd written six years earlier in Berlin, during the first flowering of his youth, which had circulated in manuscript among two admirers and one student. This poem lies before me now on the table; I acquired it about a year ago from Stepan Trofimovich, recopied by the author himself quite recently, bearing his signature and bound in sumptuous red morocco. It isn't lacking in poetry, moreover, and actually reveals some talent. It's strange, but in those days (that is, to be more precise, during the thirties) people frequently wrote like that. I find it difficult to describe the subject, since, to tell the truth, I can't understand a thing. It's some sort of allegory in lyrical-dramatic form, reminiscent of the second part of *Faust*.* The scene opens with a chorus of women, followed by a chorus of men, then a chorus of forces of some sort, and finally a chorus of human souls who have not yet lived, but who would very much like a chance to do so. All these choruses sing about something very obscure, primarily about someone's curse, but with a hint of supreme humour. Then the scene suddenly changes and a 'Festival of Life' begins during which some insects sing, a turtle appears to chant sacramental Latin words, and even, if I remember correctly, a mineral (that is, a completely inanimate object) bursts into song about something or other. In general everyone is singing all the time, and if they speak, it's simply to abuse one another in the vaguest of terms, but always with an element of higher meaning. Finally the scene changes once more to some wild place; a very civilized young man wanders among the rocks picking and sucking herbs of some sort. In reply to a fairy who asks why he's sucking herbs, he says that, aware of an abundance of life within him, he's searching for oblivion and finds it in the juice of these herbs. But his principal desire is to lose his mind as soon as possible (a desire that may be quite superfluous). Then suddenly a youth of indescribable beauty rides in on a black horse followed by a huge crowd of people from many nations. The youth represents Death, which all peoples yearn for. Last but not least, in the final scene, the Tower of Babel suddenly appears; athletes of some sort are finishing it off, singing a song of new hope. When at last they reach the top, the lord, perhaps of Olympus, runs away in comic fashion; then mankind, grasping the situation, assumes his place and immediately begins leading a new life with fresh insight into all things.

So, this was the poem that was considered so dangerous at the time. Last year I proposed to Stepan Trofimovich that he publish it, since nowadays it would be considered perfectly innocuous; he rejected my suggestion with obvious displeasure. He didn't appreciate my view of the poem's complete innocuousness; I'm even tempted to ascribe to this a certain coolness on his part towards me which lasted for two whole months. And what do you think? Suddenly, almost at the same time I was proposing to publish it here, the poem was published over there, that is, abroad, in a revolutionary anthology, entirely without Stepan Trofimovich's knowledge. At first he was alarmed, ran to the governor and wrote the most noble letter of self-justification to Petersburg, which he read to me twice, but never sent off because he didn't know how to address it. In short, he was upset about it for one whole month; but I'm convinced that in the innermost recesses of his heart he was extremely flattered. He practically slept with the copy of the journal procured for him; during the day he kept it hidden under his mattress, and wouldn't even allow the maid to make his bed. Although he daily expected to receive a telegram, he viewed the matter with disdain. No telegram ever came. At the same time he made peace with me, which testifies to the extreme goodness of his gentle and unresentful heart.

2.

Of course, I'm not claiming that he didn't suffer for his convictions; it's just that now I'm absolutely convinced he could have carried on writing about those Arabs of his to his heart's content, if only he'd provided the necessary explanations. But at the time he was carried away by pride, and with notable haste managed to convince himself that his career had been shattered once and for all by a 'whirl-wind of circumstances'. But if truth be told, the real reason for the change in his career was the extremely delicate proposition made previously and brought up once again by Varvara Petrovna Stavrogina, the wife of a lieutenant-general and a woman of wealth and importance. This was to be responsible, in the capacity of head tutor and friend, for the education and intellectual development of her only son, not to mention a handsome salary. This proposal was first made to him in Berlin, at the very time he was first widowed. His first wife was a rather frivolous girl from our province whom he'd married in his early, impetuous youth. I believe he endured much sorrow with that young woman, attractive though she was, as a result of having insufficient means to support her, as well as other, somewhat more delicate considerations. She died in Paris after living apart from him for three years; she left him a five-year-old son, 'the fruit of our first, joyous, as yet unclouded love', as the grief-stricken Stepan Trofimovich once declared to me.

From the start the fledgling had been sent back to Russia where he was to be brought up by some distant aunts in a remote region. Stepan Trofimovich had declined Varvara Petrovna's proposal at that time, and, in less than a year, swiftly married a taciturn German girl from Berlin, without any need to do so. But, in addition, there turned out to be other reasons for declining the position of tutor: he was fascinated by the resounding fame of a certain professor at the time; he, in turn, hastened back to the department where he'd studied, hoping to put his own eagle's wings to the test. And then, when his wings had been singed, he naturally recalled the proposal which had previously given him pause.

The sudden death of his second wife, who'd lived with him for less than a year, decided the matter once and for all. I can state quite candidly: everything was resolved by the passionate sympathy and precious, so to speak classical friendship of Varvara Petrovna, if such an expression may be used to describe friendship. He threw himself into the embrace of that friendship, and the matter was settled for over twenty years. I use the expression 'threw himself into the embrace', but God forbid anyone should jump to unwarranted and frivolous conclusions; this embrace must be understood only in the loftiest possible moral sense. The most subtle and delicate of ties united these two extraordinary human beings for ever.

Stepan Trofimovich also accepted the position as tutor because the property left him by his first wife was very small indeed and was located next to Skvoreshniki, the Stavrogins' magnificent estate on the outskirts of town in our province. Besides, it was always possible, in the quiet of his own study, no longer distracted by the weight of university affairs, to devote himself to the cause of learning and enrich the literature of his country through his most profound scholarship. No scholarship ever materialized; on the other hand, it did prove possible to spend the rest of his life, more than twenty years, as a 'reproach incarnate', so to speak, to his native land. In the words of the people's poet:*

> A reproach incarnate
> ...   .
> You stand before your fatherland,
> A liberal idealist.

However, the person to whom that poet of the people was referring may have had the right to assume that pose for his entire life, if he so desired, boring though it might be. But our Stepan Trofimovich, to tell the truth, was merely an impostor compared with such figures; he grew tired of standing, and frequently preferred to lie down for a while. But, to do him full justice, though lying down, he remained a 'reproach incarnate' even in this recumbent position,

which was certainly good enough for the inhabitants of our
province. You should have seen him at our club when he
sat down to play cards. His whole demeanour proclaimed,
'Cards! Imagine me sitting down to play a game of whist
with you! Is it fitting? Who's responsible for this? Who's
destroyed my career and turned me to whist? Ah, perish
Russia!' Then he'd majestically trump with a heart.

To be perfectly honest, he was very fond of a game of
cards, as a result of which, especially during his later years,
he had frequent and unpleasant squabbles with Varvara
Petrovna, particularly since he always lost. But more about
this later. I shall merely mention that he was a man with a
conscience (sometimes, that is), and therefore was often
depressed. Throughout his twenty-year friendship with Varvara Petrovna he regularly, three or four times a year, sank
into a state of 'civic grief', as it was known among us, that
is, into depression, but our much esteemed Varvara Petrovna
preferred the former phrase. Later on, in addition to civic
grief, he began sinking into champagne; but all his life the
vigilant Varvara Petrovna strove to protect him from all such
petty proclivities. As a matter of fact, he really needed a
nanny, because there were times when he became very
strange indeed: in the midst of the most sublime grief, he
would suddenly start laughing in a very uncouth way. There
were even moments when he would start making humorous
remarks about himself. There was nothing Varvara Petrovna
feared as much as humour. She was a woman of the classical
type, a female Maecenas,* who acted only with the loftiest
of intentions. The twenty years of influence this superior
lady had on her poor friend were of the greatest consequence. It will be necessary to talk about her separately,
which I will now proceed to do.

3.

There are some very strange friendships: both friends are
practically ready to devour one another; they live their whole
lives like that, yet are unable to part. In fact, there's
absolutely no way they can part: the one who, in a fit of
petulance, decided to end the relationship would in fact be

the first to fall ill and perhaps even die, if this should ever happen. I know for a fact that Stepan Trofimovich, on several occasions, and sometimes following the most intimate, tête-à-tête sessions with Varvara Petrovna, would jump up from the sofa immediately after her departure and begin pounding the wall with his fists.

There was nothing in the least allegorical about this; once he even knocked some plaster off the wall. Perhaps you'll ask how I could have discovered such intimate details. Well, what if I witnessed it with my own eyes? What if on more than one occasion Stepan Trofimovich sobbed on my shoulder, depicting in vivid colours every last circumstance of the affair? (The things he said at such times!) But here's what used to happen after almost every one of these sobbing fits of his: by the following day he was fully prepared to crucify himself for his own ingratitude. He would summon me hastily or else come running over, simply to tell me that Varvara Petrovna was 'an angel of honour and delicacy, while he himself was the complete opposite'. Not only did he come running to me, but very often he would describe all this to her in the most eloquent letters, confessing over his full signature, that, for example, only the day before he'd told a third party that she was supporting him merely out of vanity; that she envied his learning and talents; that she hated him and was simply afraid to reveal that hatred openly, for fear he'd leave and thus damage her literary reputation; that as a result of all this, he despised himself and had decided to die a violent death; that he was waiting for a final word from her to settle everything, once and for all, and so on and so forth, much in the same vein. After all this one can well imagine the pitch of hysteria reached on occasion by the nervous outbursts of this most innocent of fifty-year-old babes! Once I myself read one of his letters after some quarrel between them trivial in its cause, but venomous in its conduct. I was horrified and implored him not to send it.

'Impossible... it's more honest... my duty... I'll die if I don't confess everything to her, absolutely everything!' he replied, almost in a fever, and sent the letter off anyway.

That was the difference between them: Varvara Petrovna would never have sent such a letter. It's true he was passionately fond of writing and wrote even though he lived in the same house with her, and in moments of hysteria he even wrote twice a day. I know for a fact that she always read these letters with the most careful attention, even when she received two in one day; after she read them, she always folded them up and stored them away in a special drawer, all sorted and labelled. Furthermore, she stored them away in her heart. But then, after keeping her friend waiting all day for a reply, she'd greet him as if nothing at all had happened, as if nothing special had transpired the day before. Little by little she trained him so well that he himself would never dare remind her of what had occurred, but would merely gaze into her eyes for a while. But she never forgot a thing, while he sometimes forgot all too soon, and, emboldened by her serenity, would often be found laughing and joking over a glass of champagne if friends arrived. How venomously she must have glared at him at such moments, but he didn't notice a thing! Only afterwards, a week later perhaps, or a month, or even six months, at some particular moment he'd accidentally recall a phrase from one of his letters, then the whole letter with all its attendant circumstances, and suddenly he'd be overwhelmed by shame; he'd be so tormented that he'd fall ill with one of his bilious attacks. These kind of bilious attacks were peculiar to him, often the regular outcome of nervous distress, and constituted a curious constitutional idiosyncrasy.

Indeed, Varvara Petrovna must have hated him on numerous occasions; but the only thing about her he failed to notice until the very end was that he'd finally become like a son to her, her own creation, one might even say, her invention. He'd become flesh of her flesh; she supported and maintained him not only because she 'envied his talents'. How offended she would have been by such suppositions! In her heart there lay hidden unmitigated love for him, amidst the constant hatred, jealousy, and contempt. She protected him from every speck of dust and fussed over him for twenty-two years; she would have endured nights without sleep if anything had threatened his reputation as a poet, scholar, or public figure. She had invented him and she herself was the first to believe in her own invention. He was like a daydream of hers... But in return she demanded a great deal from him, sometimes amounting to servitude. She was incredibly unforgiving. Now I'll relate several episodes about that.

4.

Once, when the first rumours* about emancipation of the serfs began circulating, and all Russia was suddenly rejoicing and preparing to be completely reborn, Varvara Petrovna was visited by a baron from Petersburg, a man of the best connections who was intimately involved in the reforms. Varvara Petrovna valued such visits very highly because since the death of husband her own connections in high society had weakened and finally dissolved altogether. The baron sat with her for about an hour and had tea. No one else was present, but Varvara Petrovna had invited Stepan Trofimovich to show him off. The baron had actually heard something about him, or else pretended he had, but during tea paid him very little attention. Naturally, Stepan could keep his end up and his manners were elegant. Although, I believe, of modest origin, he had in fact been raised from childhood in an aristocratic household in Moscow and consequently was very well brought up; he spoke French like a Parisian. Therefore the baron was supposed to realize from the outset the sort of people Varvara Petrovna surrounded herself with, even though she lived in provincial isolation. However, things turned out differently. When the baron positively confirmed the absolute truth of the first rumours circulating about the great reform, Stepan Trofimovich couldn't restrain himself: he suddenly cried, 'Hurrah!' and even made a gesture expressing his delight. His cry was not very loud, was even quite graceful; the expression of delight may even have been premeditated, the gesture carefully rehearsed in front of a mirror half an hour before tea. But somehow it failed to come off, and the baron permitted himself the faintest of smiles, though he did so with extraordinary politeness, and ventured some phrase or other about the universal and proper emotion shared by all true Russian hearts on such a great occasion. He soon left, and in doing so, didn't forget to extend two fingers for Stepan Trofimovich to shake. On returning to the drawing-room Varvara Petrovna remained silent for a few minutes, apparently looking for something on the table. Then she suddenly turned to Stepan Trofimovich and with pale face and flashing eyes hissed at him in a whisper:

'I'll never forgive you for this!'

The next day she greeted her friend as if nothing had happened; she never referred to the incident again. But thirteen years later, at a certain tragic moment, she recalled it and reproached him for it, and grew very pale in the same way she had some thirteen years before when she'd first reproached him. Only twice in her entire life did she say to him, 'I'll never forgive you for this!' The episode with the baron was the second time, but the first was so typical, and, I believe, so relevant to Stepan Trofimovich's fate, that I've decided to relate it as well.

It was in the spring of 1855, in May, just after news of Lieutenant-General Stavrogin's death had reached Skvoreshniki; the foolish old man had died of a stomach disorder as he was hastening to the Crimea on active service. Varvara Petrovna was left a widow and went into full mourning. It's true she couldn't grieve very much, since she'd been separated from her husband for the last four years on account of the incompatibility of their temperaments, and had been providing him with an allowance. (The Lieutenant-General himself had only about a hundred and fifty serfs and his salary, apart from his social position and connections; all the wealth and Skvoreshniki itself belonged to Varvara Petrovna, the only daughter of a very rich tax-farmer.*) Nevertheless she was shaken by the unexpected news and withdrew into total seclusion. Of course, Stepan Trofimovich was constantly at her side.

May was in full splendour; the evenings were marvellous. The wild cherry trees were in bloom. Every evening the two friends would stroll in the garden and sit in the summer-house until nightfall, pouring out their thoughts and feelings to each other. These were poetic moments. Under the influence of the change in her position, Varvara Petrovna talked more than usual. She seemed to be clinging to her friend's heart, and this went on for several evenings. A strange thought suddenly occurred to Stepan Trofimovich: 'By any chance was the inconsolable widow relying on him and expecting him to make her a proposal at the end of her year of mourning?' It was a cynical thought; but then the loftiness of man's nature sometimes actually contributes to his propensity for cynical thoughts, if for no other reason than the complexity of his development. When he considered the idea more carefully, he found that it was just as he suspected. He pondered: 'True, she's enormously wealthy, but she's so...' Indeed, Varvara Petrovna couldn't exactly be described as a great beauty: she was a tall, bony woman with a sallow complexion and an extremely long face, somewhat resembling a horse. Stepan Trofimovich hesitated more and more; he was plagued by doubt. Once or twice he even shed a few tears in his indecision (he wept rather frequently). In the evenings, in the summer-house, that is, his face involuntarily began to assume a kind of capricious and ironical expression, somewhat flirtatious, yet arrogant at the same time. This occurs unintentionally, involuntarily; and in fact, the nobler the man, the more noticeable it is. Goodness knows what to make of it all, but it's most likely that nothing was stirring in Varvara Petrovna's heart such as fully to have justified Stepan Trofimovich's suspicions. Besides, she would never have exchanged the name Stavrogin for his, no matter how famous it was. Perhaps it was all merely feminine wiles on her part, a manifestation of some unconscious female need, entirely natural in certain extreme feminine situations. I can't swear to it, however; the depths of a woman's heart are uncharted territory to this very day! But I'll proceed.

It must be supposed that soon she guessed the meaning of the strange expression on her friend's face; she was sensitive and observant, while he was all too often innocent.

But their evenings continued just as before, and their conversations were just as poetic and interesting. Then once, at nightfall, after a most animated and poetic conversation, they parted amicably, pressing each other's hands warmly as they stood near the steps of the annexe in which Stepan Trofimovich resided. Every summer he used to move from the large manor-house at Skvoreshniki into this little annexe which stood virtually in the garden. He'd just returned to his apartment and, in a state of agitated meditation, had taken out a cigar, though not yet lit it, when he stopped, exhausted, motionless, by the open window, looking out at some white clouds that drifted light as a feather near the bright moon, when suddenly a light rustle caused him to shudder and turn around. Before him stood Varvara Petrovna, whom he'd left only a few minutes ago. Her rather sallow face had turned almost blue; her lips were pressed together tightly and trembled at the corners. She looked him right in the eye for ten full seconds with a firm, implacable glare; then all of a sudden she whispered rapidly:

'I'll never forgive you for this!'

Ten years later, when Stepan Trofimovich related this gloomy episode to me in a whisper, after first closing his door, he swore that at the time he was so dumbfounded that he'd neither seen nor heard Varvara Petrovna leave his room. Since she never once alluded to the incident afterwards, and everything went on exactly as it had before, he'd been inclined ever since to consider it a hallucination preceding sickness, particularly since that very evening he really did fall ill and remained so for two whole weeks, which, by the way, put an end to their evening meetings in the summer-house.

But in spite of his suspicion that it was merely a hallucination, every day of his life he waited, as it were, for what might be the continuation and, so to speak, the denouement of this episode. He didn't believe that would be the end of it! That being so, at times he must have given his friend some very strange looks.

5.

It was she herself who had designed the clothes he was to wear for the rest of his life. This outfit was elegant and very characteristic: a long black frock-coat, buttoned almost to the neck, but very stylishly cut; a soft hat (in summer, a straw hat) with a wide brim; a white cambric cravat tied in a large bow with dangling ends; a cane with a silver knob; in addition, hair hung to his shoulders. He had dark brown hair which had only recently begun to turn a little grey. He was clean-shaven. He's said in his youth to have really been quite handsome. But in my opinion, he was an unusually impressive figure even in old age. Besides, what sort of old age is fifty-three? However, in keeping with a certain civic coquetry, he made no effort to appear younger, but even seemed to take pride in the respectability of his years; and in his appearance–tall, lean, with shoulder-length hair, he resembled a patriarch perhaps, or rather, a lithograph of the poet Kukolnik* in an edition of his works published in the thirties, especially when he sat in summer on a bench in the garden beneath a flowering lilac bush, with both hands resting on his cane, a book open beside him, lost in poetic reverie over the setting sun. As far as books are concerned, I must note that towards the end he seemed to give up reading. But that was only towards the very end. He would always read all the newspapers and journals to which Varvara Petrovna subscribed. He was also always interested in the achievements of Russian literature, although he never lost a sense of his own worth. Once he actually became involved in the study of our contemporary internal politics and foreign affairs, but soon he gave all that up. Here's what else used to happen: he'd set out for the garden with a volume of de Tocqueville in his hands,* while in his pocket he'd have hidden a copy of Paul de Kock.* But that's all by the way.

I must mention in parenthesis that picture of Kukolnik: Varvara Petrovna had first come across it as a young girl while attending the gentry boarding school in Moscow. She fell in love with the picture at once, as is usual for girls in boarding schools who fall in love with anything that comes their way, including their instructors, especially those who teach calligraphy and drawing. But the odd thing here is not the nature of the young girls, but that even at fifty Varvara Petrovna kept this picture as one of her most treasured possessions; it may very well have been solely because of this that she designed Stepan Trofimovich's apparel to have some resemblance to that shown in the picture. But this, too, is a mere detail.

During the early years, or, to be more precise, during the first half of the time he spent at Varvara Petrovna's, Stepan Trofimovich was still thinking about producing some great work and every day was about to begin in earnest. But during the second half of his time there he seemed to have forgotten everything he'd ever known. More and more frequently he told us, 'It seems I'm ready to begin work. All the materials have been collected, but I just can't get started! Nothing ever gets done!' And his head would droop in despair. Undoubtedly this was meant to endow him with even greater dignity in our eyes, as if he were a martyr to scholarship; but he himself wanted something entirely different. 'They've forgotten me; no one needs me any more!' he'd exclaim on more than one occasion. This intense depression really took hold of him towards the end of the fifties. Varvara Petrovna finally realized it was a very serious matter. Besides, she too couldn't bear the thought that her friend had been forgotten and was no longer needed. In order to distract him and, at the same time, revive his fame, she took him off to Moscow where she still had a number of distinguished literary and learned acquaintances; but as it turned out, Moscow also proved to be unsatisfactory.

It was a peculiar time; something new was in the air, quite unlike the previous tranquillity, something very peculiar indeed, and it was perceived everywhere, even in Skvoreshniki. All kinds of rumours were circulating. In general the facts were more or less known, but it was also apparent that in addition to facts, there were certain ideas accompanying them; the main thing was that there was a large number of these ideas. And this is what was most perplexing: in no

way was it possible to orient oneself or be certain what these
ideas meant. Varvara Petrovna, as a consequence of her
feminine disposition, was always suspicious that they concealed some secret. She took to reading newspapers and
journals, prohibited publications from abroad, and even
political pamphlets which were just beginning to appear then
(she had access to everything); but this merely made her
head spin. She set about writing letters to which she
received very few replies; and as time went on, the replies
she did receive became more and more incomprehensible.
Stepan Trofimovich was solemnly invited to explain 'all
these new ideas' to her once and for all; but she remained
decidedly dissatisfied with his explanations. Stepan Trofimovich's view of the entire movement was arrogant in the
extreme; according to him, it all came down to the fact that
he'd been forgotten and was no longer needed. At last they
remembered even him, at first in periodicals published
abroad as a martyr in exile, and then later in Petersburg, as
a former star in an illustrious constellation; for some reason
they even compared him to Radishchev.* Then someone
published a notice that he was dead and promised to write
his obituary. Stepan Trofimovich was immediately resurrected and became even more dignified than before. All
disdain for his contemporaries vanished at once, and his
daydream was rekindled: to join the movement and demonstrate his power. Varvara Petrovna regained all her old faith
in everything and became terribly active. They decided to
leave for Petersburg without delay to witness everything on
the spot, to investigate it all personally, and, if possible, to
participate jointly in the new activity with all their heart
and soul. Meanwhile, Varvara Petrovna declared that she
was prepared to establish her own journal and devote the
rest of her life to it. Seeing it had gone that far, Stepan
Trofimovich became even more arrogant; along the way he
began to treat Varvara Petrovna almost patronizingly, a fact
which she promptly stored away in her heart. However, she
had another very important reason for making this trip,
namely, the renewal of her former connections. She thought
it necessary to remind society of her existence, or at least

to attempt to do so. The stated pretext for her journey was a meeting with her only son who was then completing his studies at a Petersburg lycée.

6.

They went to Petersburg and spent almost the entire winter season there. But by Lent everything had burst like a rainbow-coloured soap bubble. Their dreams were shattered, and the confusion, instead of being resolved, became even more repugnant. In the first place, high social connections were not established, except perhaps on the most microscopic level and with humiliating effort. The offended Varvara Petrovna threw herself into the 'new ideas' wholeheartedly and began hosting soirées. She invited writers, and large numbers of them were produced almost immediately. Then they began to come of their own accord, without invitation; each one brought someone else. Never before had she seen such writers. They were unbelievably vain, though quite open about it, as if by being so they were fulfilling some obligation. Some of them (although by no means all) even showed up drunk, and appeared to see some new, recently discovered beauty in their condition. They were all curiously proud of something or other. It was written on every face that they had just come upon some extremely important secret. They abused each other, but considered it to their credit that they did so. It was rather hard to determine precisely what they wrote, but they included critics, novelists, playwrights, satirists, and investigatory journalists. Stepan Trofimovich penetrated into the very highest circle where the movement itself was directed. It was an incredibly long climb to reach that circle, but once there he was given a hearty welcome, although, of course, no one knew anything about him and no one had heard of him except that he 'stood for some idea'. He manœuvred among them so successfully that he even managed to get them to attend Varvara Petrovna's salon once or twice, in spite of their Olympian grandeur. They were very serious people, very polite and well-behaved. The others were afraid of them, but it was clear they had no time to waste. Two or three former literary celebrities, who happened to be in Petersburg and with whom Varvara Petrovna had long maintained the most refined contacts, also showed up. But, to her surprise, these genuine and indubitable celebrities were as quiet and humble as church-mice; some of them simply attached themselves to this new rabble, ingratiating themselves disgracefully. At first Stepan Trofimovich was very lucky; they took him up and began showing him off at public literary gatherings. When he appeared on stage the first time as a reader at one of these gatherings, he was received with tempestuous applause lasting a full five minutes. Nine years later he still recalled this fact with tears in his eyes; however, he did so more on account of his artistic temperament than out of gratitude. 'I swear to you and I'm ready to wager', he once said to me (but to me alone and in confidence), 'that not one person in the audience knew even the first thing about me!' That's a remarkable admission: it indicates what keen intelligence he had if, then and there, right on stage, he could have perceived his own predicament so clearly, in spite of his exalted mood. But it also indicates what keen intelligence he lacked, if nine years later he was unable to recall these events without feeling offended. They made him sign two or three collective letters of protest (against what he hadn't the slightest idea); he signed them. They also made Varvara Petrovna sign to protest against some 'disgraceful act'; and she signed too. However, even though the majority of these new people continued to visit Varvara Petrovna, they considered it necessary for some reason to regard her with contempt and unconcealed ridicule. Afterwards, in moments of bitterness, Stepan Trofimovich hinted to me that it was from then on that she came to envy him. She understood, of course, that she couldn't really associate with these people; nevertheless, she received them eagerly, with all her hysterical feminine impatience; and above all, she still seemed to be expecting something from them. She spoke very little at her soirées, although she certainly might have said more; for the most part she listened. They talked about the abolition of censorship and a superfluous letter in the alphabet,* the

replacement of cyrillic letters by roman ones, someone who
was exiled the day before, about a scandal in the Shopping
Arcade, the advantage of dividing Russia up into national
communities united in a voluntary federation, about the
abolition of the army and the navy, the restoration of Poland
as far as the Dnieper, the emancipation of the serfs, political
pamphlets, about abolishing inheritance, the family, children, and priests, the rights of women, about Kraevsky's
splendid house (no one would ever be able to forgive Mr
Kraevsky*), and so on and so forth. It was clear that among
this rabble of new people there were quite a few scoundrels,
but undoubtedly there were also a number of very honest,
even extremely attractive people, in spite of their rather
astounding differences of opinion. The honest people were
much less intelligible than the coarse, dishonest ones, but
it was impossible to discern who was controlling whom.
When Varvara Petrovna declared her intention to establish
a new journal, an even larger crowd rushed to her, but
straight away she was showered with accusations that she
was a capitalist and exploiting labour. The bluntness of these
accusations was matched only by their unexpectedness. Once
the venerable General Ivan Ivanovich Drozdov, a former
friend and colleague of the late General Stavrogin, a most
worthy fellow (in his own way), known to all of us, an
extremely obstinate and irritable man who had an enormously large appetite and was terribly afraid of atheism, quarrelled with one of the illustrious young men at one of
Varvara Petrovna's soirées. The young man was quick to
reply, 'You must be a general if you talk like that', that is
to say, he could conceive of no worse term of abuse than
'general'. Ivan Ivanovich flew into a terrible rage: 'Yes, sir,
I am a general, and a lieutenant-general at that, and I've
served my sovereign, while you, sir, are just a boy and an
atheist to boot!' An unconscionable scandal ensued. The
next day the episode was ventilated in the press; signatures
were collected for a collective letter of protest against
Varvara Petrovna's 'disgraceful conduct' in not throwing the
general out of her house at once. A caricature appeared in
an illustrated journal, caustically depicting Varvara Petrovna,

the general, and Stepan Trofimovich in one picture as three reactionary friends; the caricature was accompanied by some verses written specially for the occasion by the people's poet. I'll just put in that many of those reaching the rank of general have indeed acquired the absurd habit of saying: 'I've served my sovereign...', that is, as if they had their own special sovereign, apart from the one who rules over us ordinary mortals.

Naturally it was impossible to remain in Petersburg any longer, the more so since Stepan Trofimovich was soon overtaken by an incredible fiasco. Unable to restrain himself, he began making declarations about the rights of art; they began laughing even louder at him. At his last reading he decided to impress them all with his civic eloquence, imagining that he could touch their hearts, relying on their respect for the years he spent 'in exile'. He accepted without question the uselessness and absurdity of the word 'fatherland'; he concurred with their views on the harmfulness of religion; but he loudly and firmly declared that Pushkin was more important than a pair of boots, and very much so. They hooted at him so mercilessly that he burst into tears right there on stage before the public. Varvara Petrovna carried him home more dead than alive. '*On m'a traité comme un vieux bonnet de coton!*'[1] he babbled senselessly. She looked after him all night, gave him laurel water to drink, and repeated to him until dawn, 'You're still useful; you'll make another appearance; they'll learn to appreciate you... in some other place.'

The next day, early in the morning, five of the writers came to see Varvara Petrovna, including three total strangers she'd never seen before. With stern expressions they informed her that they'd considered the matter of her journal and had come to the following conclusion. Varvara Petrovna had never authorized anyone to consider her journal or come to any conclusions. They decided that, after establishing the journal, she should turn it over to them at once with the capital to run it as a free, co-operative association; she

---

[1] They treated me like an old night-cap!

should leave for Skvoreshniki, not forgetting to take Stepan Trofimovich with her, who was now 'out of date'. As a matter of courtesy they agreed to recognize her right of ownership and every year would send her one sixth of the net profit. What was most touching of all was that out of these five men, undoubtedly four had no motive of personal gain, and were merely acting on behalf of the 'common cause'.

'We left in a complete daze,' Stepan Trofimovich said afterwards. 'I couldn't understand a thing. I remember muttering to the rumble of the train:

> Vek and Vek and Lev Kambek,
> Lev Kambek and Vek and Vek...*

The devil knows what else I mumbled all the way to Moscow. It was only there I recovered my senses, as if expecting to find something different. Oh, my friends,' he would sometimes exclaim in a moment of inspiration, 'you can't imagine what grief and bitterness envelop your entire soul when a great idea that you've long regarded as sacred is suddenly seized upon by ignorant people and dragged into the street before other fools, just like themselves, and you suddenly encounter it in the market-place in an unrecognizable form, covered with mud, presented from an absurd angle, without proportion or harmony, a mere plaything in the hands of stupid children! No! It was not like that in our day; that's not what we were striving for. No, no, not at all for that. I don't recognize a thing... Our time will come and once again we'll restore everything that's now tottering to a firm footing. Otherwise, what will happen?...'

7.

Immediately upon their return from Petersburg Varvara Petrovna sent her friend abroad 'for a rest'; besides, she felt it necessary for the two of them to be apart for a while. Stepan Trofimovich departed enthusiastically. 'I'll revive there,' he exclaimed. 'There at long last I'll get to work!' But in his very first letters from Berlin he struck the usual note. 'My heart is broken,' he wrote to Varvara Petrovna,

'I can't forget a thing! Here in Berlin everything reminds me of my past, my first raptures and first torments. Where is she? Where are they both? Where are you, you two angels of whom I was never worthy? Where is my son, my beloved son? And where, last of all, am I, I myself, my former self, strong as steel, steadfast as a rock, when now some *Andrejeff*, *un* Orthodox clown with a beard, *peut briser mon existence en deux*',[1] and so on and so forth. As for Stepan Trofimovich's son, he'd seen him only twice in his entire life, first, when he was born, and second, recently in Petersburg where the young man was about to enter university. As stated above, all his life the boy had been brought up by aunts in a remote province (at Varvara Petrovna's expense), some seven hundred miles from Skvoreshniki. And as for *Andrejeff*, that is, Andreev, he was simply a local merchant, a shopkeeper, a great eccentric, a self-taught archaeologist, a passionate collector of Russian antiquities, who would sometimes cross swords with Stepan Trofimovich on scholarly topics, but more often on political ones. This worthy shopkeeper, with a grey beard and large silver-rimmed glasses, still owed Stepan Trofimovich four hundred roubles for a few acres of timber he'd bought from Verkhovensky's little estate (near Skvoreshniki). Although Varvara Petrovna had provided her friend with ample funds when she sent him off to Berlin, Stepan Trofimovich had really been counting on having those four hundred roubles before his departure, probably to cover his secret expenses, and he almost cried when *Andrejeff* asked him to wait another month; the latter, however, had every right to request such a delay since he'd paid the first instalment almost six months in advance when Stepan Trofimovich claimed special need at that time. Varvara Petrovna read his first letter eagerly; she underlined in pencil the exclamation, 'Where are they both?' She noted the date on the letter and locked it away in a drawer. He was referring to his two deceased wives, of course. The second letter she received from Berlin contained a variation on this theme: 'I'm working twelve hours a day.' ('I'd settle

[1] can break my life in two

for eleven,' Varvara Petrovna muttered.) 'I'm rummaging in libraries, collating, copying, running about; I've visited several professors. I've renewed my acquaintance with the wonderful Dundasov family. What a charming woman Nadezhda Nikolaevna remains even now! She sends you her regards. Her young husband and all three nephews are in Berlin. I spend my evenings with young people talking until dawn; we hold almost Athenian parties, but only in regard to refinement and splendour. Everything is very noble: lots of music, Spanish airs, dreams of human regeneration, ideas of eternal beauty, the Sistine Madonna, light alternating with darkness, but then, there are spots even on the sun! Oh, my friend, my noble, faithful friend! My heart is with you and I am yours, yours alone, *en tout pays*, and even *dans le pays de Makar et de ses veaux*, about which, you recall, we spoke so often with fear and trembling in Petersburg before my departure. I recall it with a smile. Only after crossing the border did I feel safe—a strange, novel sensation, the first time in so many years...', and so on and so forth.

'Oh, what nonsense!' decided Varvara Petrovna as she folded his letter. 'If he's up until dawn at Athenian parties, he's certainly not sitting over his books twelve hours a day. Was he drunk when he wrote that letter? How dare that Dundasova woman send me her regards? Oh well, let him have a good time...'

The phrase '*dans le pays de Makar et de ses veaux*' was a reference to the popular Russian saying: 'Where Makar never drove his flock'. Sometimes Stepan Trofimovich intentionally translated Russian proverbs and popular sayings into French in the most absurd way; without doubt he understood them and was able to translate them correctly, but he did it as a way of showing off and because he thought it witty.

But his good time didn't last very long; he stayed there less than four months and hurried back to Skvoreshniki. His subsequent letters consisted merely of outpourings of the most sentimental love for his absent friend and were literally soaked with tears over their separation. There are certain natures which are extremely attached to home, just like lap-dogs. The reunion of the two friends was ecstatic. A few days later everything was back to normal, even more boring than before. 'My friend,' Stepan Trofimovich said to me some two weeks later in secret, 'my friend, I've discovered something terrible, for me, that is... *je suis un* ordinary hanger-on, a parasite, *et rien de plus*! *Mais r-r-rien de plus*!'[1]

8.

A lull followed lasting almost nine years. The hysterical outbursts and sobbings on my shoulder recurring at regular intervals in no way interfered with our well-being. I'm amazed that Stepan Trofimovich didn't put on weight during this period. His nose got a little redder and his equanimity increased; that was all. Little by little a circle of acquaintances formed around him, although it was never very large. Even though Varvara Petrovna had little contact with this circle, we all still acknowledged her as our patroness. After the lesson she'd received in Petersburg, she settled down once and for all in our town. In winter she lived in her town house; she spent the summers on her nearby estate. Never did she enjoy such importance and influence in our provincial society as during the last seven years, that is, up to the time our present governor was appointed. The former governor, the unforgettable and mild-mannered Ivan Osipovich, was a close relative of hers; she had once done him a very great favour. His wife trembled at the very thought of displeasing Varvara Petrovna, and the worship accorded her by our provincial society at times bordered on idolatry. Naturally, this meant that things were good for Stepan Trofimovich as well. He was a member of the club; he lost magnanimously at cards; and he was respected, even though many regarded him as a mere 'scholar'. Subsequently, when Varvara Petrovna allowed him to live in a separate house, we enjoyed even more freedom. We gathered at his place twice a week; it was very merry,

---

[1] I'm just a . . . and nothing more. Absolutely nothing more!

especially when he was generous with the champagne. The
wine came from a shop belonging to that same Andreev.
Varvara Petrovna paid the bill every six months, and the
same day Stepan Trofimovich almost always suffered one
of his bilious attacks.

The oldest member of the circle was Liputin, a provincial
official, middle-aged and an avowed liberal with a reputation
in our town of being an atheist. He was married to his
second wife, an attractive young lady with a large dowry;
besides that, he had three grown-up daughters. He kept his
entire family under lock and key, in fear of God; he was
extremely stingy and had managed on his salary to purchase
a house and acquire some capital. He was an anxious sort
of person, who had not risen far in the service; he was not
very well respected in town and not received at all in the
best circles. In addition he was a notorious gossip who'd
been punished for it more than once, severely, once by an
officer, and another time by a landowner and respected
father of a family. But we loved his sharp wit, enquiring
mind, and distinctive malicious gaiety. Varvara Petrovna
didn't like him, but somehow he always knew how to play
up to her.

Nor did she like Shatov, who'd become a member of the
club only during the last year. Shatov had been a student
and was expelled from the university after a scandal. In his
childhood he'd been a pupil of Stepan Trofimovich; he was
born a serf on Varvara Petrovna's estate, the son of her late
former valet Pavel Fyodorov, and was greatly indebted to
her. She didn't care for him because of his pride and
ingratitude, and could never forgive the fact that he failed
to return to her immediately after his expulsion from the
university. Quite the contrary: he never replied to the urgent
letter she wrote him at the time, preferring instead to
enslave himself to some cultivated merchant as a tutor to
his children. He went abroad with this merchant's family,
more in the role of nursemaid than tutor; but at the time
he was extremely eager to travel. The children had a
governess, a lively young Russian lady, who'd also joined
the household on the eve of their departure, chiefly because

she came so cheap. Two months later the merchant dismissed her for 'free thinking'. Shatov set out after her, and soon married her in Geneva. They lived together for three weeks and then separated as free and unfettered individuals; of course, their poverty was also a factor. He wandered around Europe alone for a long time after that; goodness knows how he managed to live. It's said he used to shine shoes on the street and worked as a stevedore in some port. Finally, about a year ago, he returned home to his native town and settled down to live with an old aunt whom he buried a month later. He had very little contact with his sister, Dasha, who'd also been brought up by Varvara Petrovna and who was a favourite of hers and was even treated as an equal. With us, he was always gloomy and taciturn; but occasionally, whenever his convictions were called into question, he'd get extremely irritated and his tongue would loosen up. 'Shatov has to be tied up before you can argue with him,' Stepan Trofimovich would remark on occasion; but he was actually quite fond of him. During his time abroad some of Shatov's former socialist convictions had radically altered, and he had embraced the opposite extreme. He was one of those idealistic Russian personalities who are suddenly struck by some compelling idea and seem overwhelmed by it immediately, sometimes even for ever. They're never really able to cope with the idea, but they profess it passionately, and they spend their whole lives as it were writhing desperately under the weight of the stone that's fallen on them and already half-crushed them to death. In appearance Shatov closely resembled his convictions: he was clumsy, fair-haired, dishevelled, short, broad-shouldered, thick-lipped with very heavy, overhanging pale blond eyebrows, a furrowed brow, and an unfriendly, stubbornly downcast gaze that seemed ashamed of something. There was always one tuft of hair on his head that refused to be smoothed down and stood straight up on end. He was about twenty-seven or twenty-eight years old. 'I'm not surprised his wife ran away from him,' Varvara Petrovna declared once, after looking him over thoroughly. He attempted to dress neatly, in spite of his extreme poverty.

Once again he did not ask Varvara Petrovna's assistance, but managed to get by somehow or other. He used to work for various merchants. At one point he was employed in a shop; then he was about to set off on a steamer as an assistant clerk with some merchandise, but fell ill before departure. You can't imagine the poverty he was capable of enduring without giving it a single thought. After his illness Varvara Petrovna sent him a hundred roubles anonymously, in secret. He discovered the secret, however, thought about it, accepted the money, and went to thank Varvara Petrovna. She received him warmly, but then he disappointed her expectations disgracefully; he stayed only five minutes and sat there in silence, staring blankly at the floor and smiling stupidly. Then suddenly, without allowing her to finish her sentence, and at the most interesting part of the conversation, he stood up, made a clumsy, sort of sideways bow, became terribly embarrassed, accidentally brushed against and knocked over an expensive inlaid table, which broke in pieces, and walked out, nearly dead with shame. Afterwards Liputin reproached him severely for not giving back those hundred roubles with contempt, since they'd come from his former despotic landowning mistress; instead, he'd not only accepted the money, but had even gone to thank her for it. He lived alone, on the outskirts of town, and didn't like it when anyone, even one of us, dropped in on him. He regularly turned up at Stepan Trofimovich's parties and borrowed newspapers and books from him to read.

Another young man who used to appear at these parties was named Virginsky, a local official, who bore some resemblance to Shatov, although he was obviously his complete opposite in all respects. But he too was 'a family man'. He was a pathetic, extremely quiet young man, although already thirty years old, and well educated, though chiefly self-taught. He was poor, married, worked in the civil service, and supported both an aunt and a sister-in-law. His wife and these other ladies shared the most liberal convictions, but it all assumed a rather crude form, like, 'some idea that's landed in the streets', as Stepan Trofimovich had once expressed it in another context. They derived it all from books, and at the first hint of a rumour from our progressive circles in the capital, they were ready to throw everything out of the window, if they were but told to do so. Madame Virginskaya practised as a midwife in town; as a girl she'd spent a long time in Petersburg. Virginsky himself was a man of remarkable purity of heart; rarely have I encountered more genuine spiritual fervour. 'I'll never, never give up these bright hopes,' he used to tell me with sparkling eyes. He always talked about his 'bright hopes' quietly, sweetly, in a half-whisper, as if in confidence. He was rather tall, but extremely thin and narrow-shouldered, with unusually sparse reddish hair. He meekly accepted all Stepan Trofimovich's condescending remarks about his views, though sometimes he objected with great seriousness and often left him confounded. Stepan Trofimovich treated him affectionately; in general, he behaved like a father to us all.

'You're all only "half-baked!" ' he jokingly observed to Virginsky, 'They're all like you, though I haven't noticed the same nar-row-mind-ed-ness in you, Virginsky, that I've encountered in Petersburg *chez ces séminaristes*;* still, you're all only "half-baked"! Shatov would love to have been fully-baked, but even he's only half-baked.'

'And what about me?' asked Liputin.

'Why, you're simply the golden mean that gets along everywhere... in your own way.'

Liputin was offended.

It was said about Virginsky, and, unfortunately, it was all too true, that his wife, after spending less than a year with him in legal wedlock, suddenly announced that he was redundant and that she preferred a certain Lebyadkin. This Lebyadkin, a stranger to our town, later turned out to be an extremely suspicious fellow, and actually not the retired staff-captain he claimed to be. He merely knew how to twirl his moustache, drink, and spout the most absurd nonsense imaginable. In the most indelicate manner this fellow moved immediately into Virginsky's house, glad to partake of another man's bread; he ate and slept there, and eventually began to slight the master of the house. It was also reported that on hearing his wife's announcement that she was finished with him, Virginsky replied, 'My dear, up to this point I've only loved you, but now I respect you.'* I doubt whether such an ancient Roman pronouncement was ever really uttered. On the contrary, they say he wept profusely. Once, two weeks after his dismissal, all of them, the whole 'family', went to have tea in the woods outside town along with some acquaintances. Virginsky was in a feverishly excited mood and took part in the dancing; but suddenly, without any provocation, he grabbed hold of the giant Lebyadkin who was doing a solo can-can, seized his hair with both hands, pushed him over, and began dragging him around with all manner of screeches, shouts, and tears. The giant was so cowardly that he put up no defence, and all the while he was being dragged around he hardly uttered a squeak. But afterwards he took offence with all the ardour of a man of honour. Virginsky spent the whole night on his knees begging his wife for forgiveness; but he didn't obtain it because he steadfastly refused to apologize to Lebyadkin. Moreover, he was attacked for the poverty of his convictions and his stupidity; the latter charge was based on the fact that he'd knelt while explaining himself to a woman. The staff-captain disappeared soon afterwards and reappeared in town only quite recently, together with his sister and some new goals to accomplish; but more about him later. It's no wonder the poor 'family man' unburdened his heart to us and was in such need of our society. However, he never spoke about his domestic affairs. Only once, returning from Stepan Trofimovich's house with me, he was about to make some roundabout reference to his own situation, when all of a sudden, grabbing my hand, he declared passionately:

'It's nothing; it's merely a private matter; in no way, no way whatever will it affect our "common cause".'

Occasional visitors would turn up in our circle; a Jew named Lyamshin, as well as a Captain Kartuzov. At one time an inquisitive old man used to attend, but he died. Liputin brought along an exiled Catholic priest named Slonczewski; for a while we received him on principle, but later stopped doing so.

9.

At one time it used to be said in town that our circle was a hotbed of free-thinking, depravity, and atheism; this rumour circulated for some time. And yet, all that we did was indulge in the most innocent, pleasant, typically Russian, cheerful liberal banter. 'Higher liberalism' and the 'higher liberal', that is, a liberal without goals, are possible only in Russia. Stepan Trofimovich, like every witty man, needed an audience; besides that, he needed the sense that he was fulfilling some higher obligation in propagating ideas. Finally, he needed someone to drink champagne with and someone with whom, over a glass of wine, he could exchange pleasant ideas of a certain kind about Russia and the 'Russian spirit', about God in general and the 'Russian God' in particular; to repeat for the hundredth time the same scandalous little anecdotes known to everyone and repeated over and over again. We were not averse to hearing local gossip, after which we sometimes arrived at stern and highly moral judgements. We even fell into talking about humanity in general, making stern pronouncements about the fate of Europe and all mankind. We predicted categorically that after Caesarism* France would immediately decline to the rank of second-rate power; we were absolutely convinced that this could happen very easily and quite soon. We'd predicted long ago that the pope would assume the role of a simple archbishop in a unified Italy; we were completely convinced that this thousand-year-old question was a mere detail in our age of humanitarianism, industry, and railways. Then again, that's the only way 'higher Russian liberalism' can treat such matters. Sometimes Stepan Trofimovich would talk about art, always very eloquently, though rather abstractly. He'd sometimes recall the friends of his youth, names that had left their mark on the history of our development; he would recall them with tender emotion and reverence, though sometimes with a tinge of envy. And, if things really got too boring, the Jew Lyamshin (a little post-office clerk), a real virtuoso on the piano, would sit down to play; in the intervals he'd imitate a pig, a thunderstorm, or childbirth (including the baby's first cry), and so on and so forth. That was the only reason he was invited. If we'd had a great deal to drink, and that sometimes happened, but not too often, we'd go into raptures; once we even sang the *Marseillaise* in chorus to Lyamshin's accompaniment, but I don't know how well it came off. The great day, the 19th of February,* we celebrated enthusiastically and began drinking toasts in its honour way in advance. This was a long time ago, before Shatov and Virginsky joined us, and Stepan Trofimovich was still living in the same house with Varvara Petrovna. Some time before the great day Stepan Trofimovich had fallen into the habit of muttering to himself some well-known, though rather bizarre verses, probably composed by some former liberal landowner:

> The peasants are coming and bringing their axes,
> Something terrible is about to happen.*

It went something like that, I don't remember exactly. Varvara Petrovna overheard him once and cried, 'Nonsense! Nonsense!' and went away in a rage. Liputin, who happened to see this, observed rather sarcastically to Stepan Trofimovich,

'What a shame it would be if during the celebration the serfs really do create some unpleasantness for their former owners.'

And he drew his forefinger across his neck.

'*Cher ami*,' Stepan Trofimovich remarked good-naturedly, 'believe me, this' (he repeated the gesture across his own neck) 'will yield no benefit whatever either to our landowners or anyone else. We'll never be able to organize anything without our heads, even if it's our heads more than anything that prevent us from understanding.'

I should observe that many people assumed something unusual would occur on the day of the proclamation, something of the sort predicted by Liputin; all these were our so-called experts on the people and the government. It seems that Stepan Trofimovich also shared their views, to such an extent that almost on the eve of the great day he began asking Varvara Petrovna's permission to go abroad; in short, he'd begun to worry. But the great day came and went, more time elapsed, and once again an arrogant smile appeared on Stepan Trofimovich's face. He uttered some noteworthy thoughts* on the character of Russians in general and Russian peasants in particular.

'Like all people in a hurry, we've been too hasty with our peasants,' he concluded his series of noteworthy thoughts. 'We've made them the rage; for several years a whole branch of our literature has fussed over them as if they were some newly discovered treasure. We've crowned their lice-ridden heads with laurel wreaths. During the last thousand years the Russian village has given us nothing more than the Komarinsky dance. One wonderful Russian poet, who wasn't short on wit, upon seeing the great Rachel* on stage for the first time, exclaimed in ecstasy, "I wouldn't trade Rachel for a single peasant!" I'm prepared to go even further: I would trade all the peasants in Russia for one Rachel. It's time to see things in a sober light and no longer confuse our own rough home-made pitch for *bouquet de l'impératrice*.'

Liputin agreed at once, but observed that it was still necessary to act against the dictates of one's own conscience and praise the peasants for the sake of the cause; even high society ladies dissolved in tears upon reading *Anton Gore-myka*,* and several even wrote letters from Paris to their stewards back home in Russia, directing them to treat their peasants as humanely as possible.

It so happened, as if on purpose right after the rumours concerning Anton Petrov,* that in our very own province, only a few miles from Skvoreshniki, there occurred a certain misunderstanding, as a result of which a detachment of soldiers was dispatched in the heat of the moment. This time Stepan Trofimovich was so upset that he even managed to scare the rest of us. He shouted in the club that more troops were necessary and should be requested by telegraph from another district; he ran off to the governor to assure him that he had absolutely nothing to do with the affair; he asked that his name not be linked to it in any way as a result of his previous associations; and he urged that word of his declaration be sent to the proper authorities in Petersburg at once. It's a good thing it all blew over fairly quickly and went nowhere; but at the time I was surprised at Stepan Trofimovich's behaviour.

Three years later, as is well known, people began talking about nationalism and then 'public opinion' came into being. Stepan Trofimovich was highly amused.

'My friends,' he instructed us, 'if our nationalism has really "come into being", as they now assure us in the press, it's still at school, in some German *Peterschule*,* poring over a German textbook, repeating its endless German lessons, and some German teacher makes it go down on its knees whenever necessary. I can vouch for the German teacher; but it's much more likely that nothing at all has happened, nothing of the sort has come into being, and everything is going along just as it did before, that is, under God's protection. In my opinion, that should be enough for Russia, *pour notre sainte Russie*. Moreover, all this Pan-Slavism* and nationalism is much too old to be considered new. Nationalism, if you like, has never existed among us except as a form of amusement in a gentlemen's club, and only in Moscow at that. Of course I'm not talking about the age of Igor.* And, last of all, it's the consequence of idleness. With us everything is the consequence of idleness, including what's fine and what is good. Everything is the consequence of our nice, aristocratic, well-educated, whimsical idleness. I've been saying that over and over for the last thirty thousand years. We don't know how to live by our own labour. And as for this fuss they're making now about some "engendering" of public opinion, where has it come from all of a sudden, just dropped from the sky? Don't they understand that in order to have such public opinion, first of all work is required, our own work, our own initiative, our own experience! You can't get something for nothing. If we work, we'll have our own opinions. But since we'll never work, our opinions will be formulated by those who've worked instead of us up to now, that is, by the same old Europe, the same old Germans—our teachers for the last two hundred years. Besides, Russia is too great a problem for us to solve alone without the Germans and without work. For the last twenty years I've been sounding the alarm and summoning people to work! I've given my life to this task, and, fool that I am, I myself believed in it! Now I no longer believe, but I can still call and will continue to do so right up to the end, to the grave; I'll pull the bell-rope until it tolls my own requiem!'

Alas! We could only agree. We applauded our teacher, and with such enthusiasm! In fact, gentlemen, one can still hear this kind of 'nice', 'clever', old 'liberal' Russian nonsense all over the place!

Our teacher believed in God. 'I don't understand why everyone around here says I'm an atheist!' he would declare on occasion. 'I believe in God, *mais distinguons*,[1] I believe in Him as a being who is conscious of Himself only through me. I can't believe as my servant Nastasya does, or as some gentleman landowner does, "just in case", or as our dear Shatov does, but Shatov doesn't count. Shatov *makes* himself believe, like a Muscovite Slavophile. And as far as Christianity is concerned, in spite of my sincere respect for it, I'm not a Christian. I'm more like an ancient pagan, like the great Goethe or a classical Greek. The fact that Christianity doesn't really understand women is enough, as George Sand has splendidly shown in one of her brilliant novels.* And as for genuflections, fasting, and all the rest of it, I don't understand why it matters to anyone else what I do. However busy our local informers are, I don't want to become a hypocrite. In 1847 Belinsky sent his famous letter to Gogol* from abroad; in it he strongly reproached him for believing "in some kind of God". *Entre nous soit dit*,[2] I can imagine nothing more comical than the moment Gogol (Gogol as he was at that time) read that expression and... the entire letter! But, joking apart, since I still agree with the heart of the matter, I declare and maintain, "They were real men!" They knew how to love the people, they knew how to suffer for them, they knew how to sacrifice

---

[1] but let's distinguish
[2] Just between ourselves

for them, and they knew how to stay away from them when necessary, how not to pander to them in certain matters. Could Belinsky really have sought salvation in lenten oil or radishes and peas?'

But at this point Shatov intervened.

'Those characters of yours never really loved the people, never suffered for them, never sacrificed for them, no matter what they thought up to console themselves!' he muttered gloomily, lowering his eyes and twisting in his chair impatiently.

'How can you say they never loved the people?' cried Stepan Trofimovich. 'Oh, they loved Russia!'

'Neither Russia, nor the people!' cried Shatov, his eyes gleaming. 'It's impossible to love something you don't know; they understood nothing about the Russian people! All of them, and that includes you, and especially Belinsky, have closed your eyes to the Russian people; that's obvious even from Belinsky's letter to Gogol. Belinsky is just like the inquisitive fellow in Krylov's fable* who didn't even notice the elephant in the museum of curiosities, but directed all his attention to French social insects; he never saw anything else. Yet he may have been smarter than all the rest of you! Not only have you overlooked the Russian people, but you've treated them with scornful contempt, all because you couldn't conceive of any people except for the French, and then only the Parisians, and you were ashamed that Russians were not just like them. That's the naked truth! He who has no people has no God! You can be certain that all who cease to understand their own people and lose contact with them, immediately and to that same extent lose the faith of their forefathers; they become either atheists or indifferent. I'm telling the truth! It's a fact that will prove to be true. That's why all of you, and all of us now, are either vile atheists or apathetic, dissolute rubbish, nothing more! And you too, Stepan Trofimovich, I don't exclude you one bit, in fact, I want you to know that I've had you in mind as I said all this!'

Normally, after delivering a monologue like this (as he very often did), Shatov would grab his cap and rush to the door, absolutely convinced that now everything was at an end and he'd severed friendly relations with Stepan Trofimovich once and for all. But the latter always managed to stop him just in time.

'Hadn't we better make it up, Shatov, after exchanging all these pleasantries?' he'd say good-naturedly, extending his hand from his armchair.

The awkward but bashful Shatov didn't care for displays of affection. The man's exterior was coarse, but inside, it seems, he was extremely sensitive. Although he often went too far, he was always the first to suffer as a result. Muttering something under his breath in response to Stepan Trofimovich's offer, and shuffling his feet about like a bear, he would suddenly and unexpectedly grin, take off his cap, and sit down again in his former place, staring stubbornly at the floor. Of course some wine would be brought in and Stepan Trofimovich would propose an appropriate toast, to the memory of some social activist from the past, for example.

CHAPTER 2

Prince Harry. Matchmaking

I.

THERE was one other person in the world to whom Varvara Petrovna was just as attached as she was to Stepan Trofimovich: this was her only son, Nikolai Vsevolodovich Stavrogin. It was to serve as his tutor that Stepan Trofimovich had first been employed. The boy was eight years old at the time, and his father, the frivolous General Stavrogin, was already living apart from his mother, so that the boy grew up entirely under her care. One must do justice to Stepan Trofimovich: he managed to win his pupil's affection. His whole secret lay in the fact that he was a child himself. I wasn't around in those days, and he felt in constant need of a true friend. He didn't hesitate to make a friend of so small a creature, as soon as the child had grown a bit older. Somehow it happened quite naturally that the distance between them disappeared. More than once he would awaken his ten- or eleven-year-old friend in the night, simply to pour out his own wounded feelings, through tears, or to reveal some domestic secret, without ever realizing it was the wrong thing to do. They'd throw themselves into each other's arms and weep. The boy knew that his mother loved him very much, but he hardly loved her at all. She spoke to him very little and rarely interfered with him in any way, but somehow he was always morbidly aware of her intense gaze fixed on him. Moreover, his mother entrusted his entire education and moral development to Stepan Trofimovich. At that time she still believed in him absolutely. It must be assumed that the tutor upset his pupil's nerves to some extent. When at the age of sixteen he was enrolled in a lycée, he was pale and fragile, unusually quiet and pensive. (Later on he was distinguished by remarkable physical strength.) One must also suppose that the two friends' nocturnal weeping in each other's arms was not solely a consequence of domestic difficulties. Stepan Trofimovich had succeeded in touching his young friend's deepest heart-strings and evoking in him an initial intimation, as yet undefined, of that eternal, sacred yearning which some chosen souls, once they've tasted and known it, never ever exchange for any cheap pleasure. (There are some devotees who value the yearning even more than the most radical satisfaction of it, if such a thing were to be believed.) In any case it was a good thing the tutor and his fledgling were separated and dispatched in different directions, even though it came a bit late.

For the first two years the young man used to come home from the lycée during vacations. When Varvara Petrovna and Stepan Trofimovich were in Petersburg, he'd sometimes attend his mother's literary evenings, to listen and observe. He said very little and remained quiet and shy, as before. He treated Stepan Trofimovich with tender affection, but already with (somewhat) increased reserve: apparently he wasn't eager either to discuss lofty matters with him or to reminisce about their past. After completing his course he entered military service in accordance with his mother's wishes; soon he was enrolled in one of the most distinguished regiments of the Horse Guards. He never came home to show off his uniform to his mother, and began writing her less frequently from Petersburg. Varvara Petrovna sent him money without stinting, in spite of the fact that after the reforms the income from her estate had fallen so low as to leave her at first with less than half of what she had been getting. She had however managed to put aside a considerable sum through years of economizing. She was very interested in her son's successes in Petersburg high society. Where she had failed, he, a young officer, both wealthy and with expectations, could succeed. He renewed some contacts which she could no longer even dream of, and was received everywhere with great delight. But soon rather strange rumours reached Varvara Petrovna: the young man had suddenly plunged into mad dissipation. It wasn't that he was gambling or drinking too much; there were just reports of wild recklessness, running down people in the street with his horses, bestial behaviour towards a woman of high society with whom he was having an affair, and whom he publicly insulted afterwards. There was something even a bit too obviously sordid about the whole business. It was said, moreover, that he'd become a bully who went around pestering people and offending them for the sheer pleasure of it. Varvara Petrovna was worried and depressed. Stepan Trofimovich assured her that all this was merely the first, violent outburst of a nature too richly endowed, that the seas would soon be calmed, and that it closely resembled the youth of Shakespeare's Prince Harry who'd caroused with Falstaff, Poins, and Mistress Quickly. This time Varvara Petrovna didn't cry, 'Nonsense, what nonsense!' as she was so accustomed to do lately with Stepan Trofimovich; on the contrary, she listened to him very carefully, demanded that he explain himself in greater detail, and even picked up her Shakespeare and perused the immortal chronicle with great attention. But the play did nothing to soothe her, nor did she find much of a resemblance. Meanwhile, she was waiting feverishly for answers to several of her letters. She didn't have long to wait; soon she received the fateful news that Prince Harry had been involved in two duels almost simultaneously. He was entirely to blame for both, had killed one of his opponents outright and maimed the other, and as a result of these activities, he was now awaiting trial. The affair later came to an end with his being reduced to the ranks, deprived of his rights, and exiled to service in an infantry regiment; he escaped harsher punishment as a special favour.

In 1863* he managed somehow to distinguish himself; he was awarded a cross and promoted to the rank of non-commissioned officer. Soon afterwards he regained his commission. During all this time Varvara Petrovna sent maybe as many as a hundred letters to the capital, full of requests and entreaties. In an extreme situation such as this she permitted herself a degree of humiliation. After his promotion the young man suddenly resigned his commission; once again he didn't return to Skvoreshniki, and he stopped writing to his mother altogether. It was learned from roundabout sources that he'd returned to Petersburg, but he was no longer encountered in the society he'd been frequenting; now he appeared to be hiding somewhere. It was discovered that he was keeping somewhat strange company; he was associating with the dregs of Petersburg's population, penniless civil servants, retired army officers who begged for charity, and drunkards; he was visiting their sordid families and spending his days and nights in dismal slums and God knows what kind of low haunts; he'd let himself go, went about in tatters, and apparently liked it that way. He didn't ask his mother for any money; he had his own small estate—formerly belonging to his father, General Stavrogin, which provided him with some income at least, and which, according to rumour, he'd rented to some German or other from Saxony. At last his mother pleaded with him to visit her, and Prince Harry appeared in our town. This was the first time I got a good look at him, never having set eyes on him before.

He was a very handsome young man, about twenty-five years old, and, I must confess, I was most impressed. I'd been expecting to meet some filthy ruffian, wasted by debauchery and reeking of vodka. On the contrary, he was the most elegant gentleman I'd ever met, extremely well dressed, and behaving as only those long accustomed to the most refined nobility behave. Nor was I the only one to be so surprised: the whole town was amazed, especially since, of course, everyone knew Mr Stavrogin's entire biography, in such detail furthermore, that it was inconceivable how this knowledge had been acquired. Most astonishing of all, half of it turned out to be true. Our ladies were all mad about the new arrival. They were sharply divided into two groups—in one they adored him, in the other they were out for his blood; but both groups were mad about him. Some people were particularly fascinated by the idea that his soul might harbour a fatal secret; others positively relished the notion that he was a murderer. It also turned out that he was extremely well educated, even considerably knowledgeable. Of course, it didn't take much knowledge to impress us; but he could form opinions about current and extremely interesting topics, and, what was even more valuable, he had a great deal of good sense. I must mention this as something of a peculiarity: all of us, from the very first day, found him to be an extremely sensible man. He wasn't very talkative; he was elegant without affectation, surprisingly modest, but at the same time bold and self-assured as no one else among us was. Our dandies regarded him with envy and were eclipsed by him. His face also impressed me: his hair was just a bit too black, his bright eyes a bit too clear and serene, his complexion a bit too fair and delicate, his colour a bit too fresh and pure, his teeth like pearls, his lips like coral—he seemed to be a paragon of beauty, yet at the same time there was something repulsive about him. His face was said to resemble a mask; there was also, by the way, talk of his extraordinary physical strength. He was quite tall. Varvara Petrovna regarded him with pride, but with constant worry. He spent about six months among us, and was languid, quiet, rather gloomy; he appeared in society and observed all the rules of our provincial etiquette with meticulous attention. He was related to the governor on his father's side and was received in his house as a close relative. But after a few months the wild beast suddenly unsheathed its claws.

By the way, I should mention parenthetically that our kind, gentle Ivan Osipovich, the former governor, was a bit of an old woman, although he came from a good family and had connections; this explains why he remained in office so many years, constantly avoiding any and all obligations. Judging by his generosity and hospitality he really should have been a marshal of the nobility* in the good old days, not a governor in such tumultuous times as ours. It was constantly alleged that our town was administered not by the governor, but by Varvara Petrovna. Of course, this was sarcasm but none the less it was a flagrant lie. Indeed, a great deal of wit had been wasted on this subject. On the contrary, in recent years Varvara Petrovna had deliberately and consciously withdrawn from any position of authority, in spite of the extraordinary respect she enjoyed in our society, and she voluntarily restricted herself to severe, self-imposed limits. Instead of loftier responsibilities, she suddenly began to manage her own estate; in two or three years she succeeded in restoring its income to its former level. Instead of her previous poetic impulses (trips to Petersburg, plans to establish a journal, etc.), she began to economize and save money. She even separated herself from Stepan Trofimovich, allowing him to occupy an apartment in another house (something he'd been pestering her about for some time under all sorts of pretexts). Little by little Stepan Trofimovich began to refer to her as a prosaic woman or even in jest as 'my prosaic friend'. Naturally, he only allowed himself to make such jokes in the most respectful manner and he chose his occasions very carefully.

All of us within her intimate circle, and Stepan Trofimovich more than anyone, understood that her son had now appeared before her almost in the guise of some new hope, or even in the aspect of some new dream. Her passion for him dated from the time of his success in Petersburg society and particularly intensified from the moment he'd been reduced to the ranks. Yet she was obviously afraid of him and behaved like a slave in his presence. It was clear that she feared something ill-defined and mysterious, something she herself couldn't explain; many times she'd stare at her Nicolas* unnoticed, pondering, trying to comprehend something... And then the wild beast suddenly unsheathed its claws.

2.

Suddenly, for no reason at all, our prince perpetrated two or three impossible outrages against various persons; the point being that these outrages were absolutely unheard of, quite beyond the pale, utterly out of the ordinary, completely ridiculous and very childish. The devil knows why he did it: there was no good reason. One of the most respected senior members of our club, Pavel Pavlovich Gaganov, an elderly gentleman with a fine record of service, had the innocent habit of adding to almost every phrase the passionate exclamation, 'No, sir, I won't be led around by the nose!' Well, what harm was there in that? But one day at the club when he uttered these words in the context of a heated

discussion among a small group of members who'd gathered
around him (all persons of some consequence), Nikolai
Vsevolodovich, who was standing alone apart and not participating in the discussion, suddenly went up to Pavel
Pavlovich, seized him suddenly but firmly by the nose with
two fingers, and proceeded to drag him several paces around
the room behind him. He couldn't have had any grudge
against Mr Gaganov. One might conclude that it was merely
a schoolboy's prank, quite unforgivable, of course; however,
it was later reported that in the midst of his action Nikolai
Vsevolodovich was almost in a trance, 'as if he were out of
his mind'. But this circumstance was recalled and analysed
only much later. In the heat of the moment all they recalled
was the next instant, when he certainly was well aware of
everything that was going on, and was not only not embarrassed but on the contrary wore a cheerful, malicious grin,
'not seeming the least bit sorry'. There was a terrible
commotion; he was surrounded at once. Nikolai Vsevolodovich kept turning to look around, without responding to
anyone, and gazing with curiosity at the people who were
shouting at him. At last all of a sudden he seemed to become
aware once again; at least that's how it was reported. He
frowned, went up to the insulted Pavel Pavlovich decisively,
and in obvious irritation muttered very quickly:

'You must forgive me, of course... I really have no idea
why I suddenly felt like doing such a stupid thing...'

This casual apology was equivalent to a fresh insult. The
outcry got even worse. Nikolai Vsevolodovich shrugged his
shoulders and left.

All of this was very stupid, not to say outrageous—a
calculated and premeditated outrage, as it appeared at first
glance, and therefore constituting a deliberate and absolutely
impudent insult directed at our whole society. That was how
everyone took it. To begin with, Mr Stavrogin was immediately and unanimously excluded from membership of the
club; next, it was decided to appeal to the governor on the
club's behalf to ask him (without waiting for the case to be
heard officially in court) instantly to restrain this injurious
ruffian, this 'bully from the capital, by the administrative

powers entrusted to him, and thereby guarantee the rights of all decent citizens in our town against breaches of the peace'. It was maliciously and disingenuously suggested that 'perhaps some law could even be invoked against Mr Stavrogin.' This phrase had been inserted to irritate the governor because of his relations with Varvara Petrovna, an amplification accomplished with great delight. It just so happened that the governor wasn't in town at the time; he'd gone off a little way away to act as godfather to the child of an attractive lady, recently widowed, who'd been left by her husband in an interesting predicament; but he would be back soon. Meanwhile, they paid tribute to the esteemed and insulted Pavel Pavlovich: he was hugged and kissed. The whole town called on him. They even planned a subscription dinner in his honour, and only abandoned the idea at his insistence, perhaps finally realizing that the man had, after all, been led around by the nose, and therefore there wasn't much reason to celebrate.

And yet, how did it happen? How could it have happened? What's so remarkable about it is the fact that no one in the whole town attributed this savage act to insanity. In other words, they were inclined to expect such behaviour from Nikolai Vsevolodovich even in his right mind. As for me, to this very day I can't explain it, in spite of ensuing events, which really should have explained everything and satisfied everyone. I'll also add that four years later, in answer to a carefully worded question about this episode in the club, Nikolai Vsevolodovich replied, 'Well, I wasn't feeling quite well at the time.' But there's no reason to get ahead of my story.

I also found rather curious the outburst of universal hatred with which we all fell upon that 'ruffian and bully from the capital'. We were prepared to imagine some insolent scheme and deliberate intention to insult the whole of society at once. It was apparent that no one cared for the fellow; on the contrary, everyone was against him. Why was that? Up until this most recent incident he'd never quarrelled with anyone and had never insulted anyone; on the contrary, he'd been as polite as a gentleman in a fashion plate, had such a character been able to speak. I suppose he was hated for his pride. Even our ladies, who'd started off adoring him, now denounced him more vociferously than the men.

Varvara Petrovna was terribly shaken. She later confessed to Stepan Trofimovich that she'd been expecting something unusual for quite some time, every day for the last six months or so, even something 'of this sort'—a remarkable confession on the part of his own mother. 'It's begun!' she thought with a shudder. The morning after the fateful episode at the club, she brought up the subject with her son cautiously but resolutely, and trembling all over, poor dear, in spite of her resolution. She hadn't slept a wink the whole night and had gone so far as to consult with Stepan Trofimovich early that morning; there she wept, something that had never occurred in anyone else's presence before. She wanted Nicolas to say something to her at least, to be so good as to provide some explanation. Nicolas, always so polite and respectful to his mother, listened to her for some time frowning, but very seriously; then he suddenly stood up and, without uttering a single word in reply, kissed her hand and went out. That very same day, in the evening, as if on purpose, another scandal took place, though much milder and more ordinary than the first; nevertheless, as a result of the general mood, it greatly intensified the clamour in town.

It was then that our friend Liputin turned up. He appeared before Nikolai Vsevolodovich immediately after the conversation with his mother, and earnestly entreated him to do him the honour of attending a party to celebrate his wife's birthday that very evening. For some time Varvara Petrovna had shuddered at her son's predilection for such low acquaintances, but she never dared say anything to him about it. Besides, he'd already made several acquaintances among the third estate of our society and even lower—but such was his propensity. He hadn't yet been to Liputin's house, although he'd met him before. He guessed that Liputin was inviting him now in response to yesterday's scandal at the club, and that, as one of the local liberals, he was ecstatic about it, sincerely believing that one should behave in precisely that way with senior members of the club, and that this was all to the good. Nikolai Vsevolodovich laughed and promised to attend.

There was a large number of guests at the party; the crowd wasn't much to look at, but very lively. Liputin, vain and envious as ever, entertained only twice a year, but on these occasions spared no expense. The most honoured guest, Stepan Trofimovich, couldn't come on account of illness. Tea was served, and there was plenty of vodka and appetizers. They played cards at three tables; the young people, while waiting for supper, danced to piano accompaniment. Nikolai Vsevolodovich invited Madame Liputina to dance; she was an extremely pretty young woman who was terribly shy with him. He danced a few turns, sat down next to her, entered into conversation and began entertaining her. Noticing at long last how very pretty she was when she laughed, suddenly, in front of all the assembled guests, he grabbed her around the waist and kissed her on the lips, three times in a row, with great gusto. The poor frightened woman fainted. Nikolai Vsevolodovich picked up his hat and went up to her husband who was standing dumbfounded amidst the general confusion; looking at him, he too became embarrassed, muttered rapidly, 'Don't be angry', and then left. Liputin followed him into the hallway, handed him his coat, and accompanied him downstairs bowing. But the next day there was a rather amusing sequel to this essentially harmless incident, one that has since raised Liputin in the general esteem, and which he was able to turn to his own advantage.

About ten o'clock in the morning Liputin's servant, Agafya, an easy-going, lively, rosy-cheeked peasant woman about thirty years old, appeared at Mrs Stavrogina's house; she'd been sent by Liputin with a message for Nikolai Vsevolodovich and insisted on 'seeing the master himself'. He had a bad headache, but came out to receive her. Varvara Petrovna managed to be present as the message was delivered.

'Sergei Vasilich' (that is, Liputin), Agafya declared boldly, 'first of all ordered me to pay you his respects and then enquire about your health. He wants to know how you slept after the party and how you feel now after what happened last night.'

Nikolai Vsevolodovich grinned.

'Give him my regards and thank him. And tell your master from me, Agafya, that he's the most intelligent man in the whole town.'

'And he ordered me to reply', Agafya blurted out, more boldly still, 'that he knew as much already without your telling him and wishes he could say the same about you.'

'Indeed! But how could he possibly know what I'd say to you?'

'I can't say for sure how he knew, but after I left and had gone about one block, I saw him running down the street after me without his cap. "And, Agafya," he said, "if in despair he says to tell your master that he's the most intelligent man in town, don't forget to reply at once that the master knows as much himself and wishes he could say the same about you."'

3.

At last the interview with the governor took place. Our dear, kind Ivan Osipovich had only just returned and had time to hear all the complaints from angry club members. There was no doubt that something had to be done, but he was at a loss. The hospitable old fellow also seemed somewhat afraid of his young relative. He decided, however, to prevail upon him to apologize both to the club and the offended party, but in a satisfactory manner, and, if need be, even in writing. Then he'd gently persuade him to leave town, to set off to Italy for example and satisfy his curiosity, or indeed, travel anywhere abroad. In the room where, on this occasion, he'd decided to receive Nikolai Vsevolodovich (at other times the young man, as a relative, had moved freely about the house), sat Alyosha Telyatnikov, a well-mannered civil servant who was treated almost as a member of the governor's family; he was sitting in the corner opening packets of post. And in the next room, at the window closest to the door, sat a visitor, a heavy-set, healthy-looking colonel,

Ivan Osipovich's friend and former colleague; he was reading a copy of *The Voice*,* paying no attention, of course, to what was going on next door. He even sat with his back to the door. Ivan Osipovich began in a roundabout way, almost in a whisper, but became confused. Nicolas looked very unfriendly, not at all like a relative; he was very pale and sat with downcast eyes, listening with a frown, as if trying to overcome an acute pain.

'You have a kind heart, Nicolas, and a generous one,' said the old man among various other things. 'You're an extremely well educated man, you've moved in high society, and even here you've behaved in an exemplary way up to now, and by so doing you've been a great consolation to your mother, whom we all cherish... But now, once again, everything appears in such an enigmatic and threatening light! I'm speaking as a friend of your family, as an older man who sincerely loves you and who's related to you, at whose words you cannot take offence... Tell me, what impels you to commit such lawless acts against all accepted rules of behaviour? What can be the meaning of these outbursts that seem like the actions of someone in a state of delirium?'

Nicolas listened in annoyance and impatience. Suddenly a sly and mocking expression seemed to flash across his face.

'I might as well tell you what impels me,' he replied gloomily, and with a glance around the room, bent down close to Ivan Osipovich's ear. The well-brought-up Alyosha Telyatnikov moved a few steps closer to the window, and the colonel began coughing over his copy of *The Voice*. Poor Ivan Osipovich hurriedly and trustfully inclined his ear; he was exceedingly curious. Then something absolutely inconceivable occurred; on the other hand, it was all too clear in one respect. All of a sudden, instead of hearing Nicolas whisper some interesting secret into his ear, the old man felt him suddenly seize the upper part of his ear between his teeth and bite down on it quite hard. He shuddered and his breath failed him.

'Nicolas, is this some kind of a joke?' he moaned mechanically in a strange voice.

Alyosha and the colonel didn't have time to realize what was happening; besides, they couldn't really see and to the very end it appeared to them as if the two men were whispering to one another. But at the same time the desperate expression on the old man's face alarmed them. They stared at each other, not knowing whether to rush to his assistance as had been previously agreed, or to wait a little longer. Nicolas may have noticed this and bit the ear even harder.

'Nicolas, Nicolas!' moaned the victim once again, 'come now... you've had your joke! Enough is enough.'

In another instant the poor old man would surely have died of fright; but the monster took pity and released his ear. The old fellow's mortal terror had lasted one full minute, and immediately afterwards he suffered some kind of fit. Half an hour later Nicolas was arrested and confined, for the time being, to the guardroom, where he was locked in a special cell with a special guard posted at the door. This was a harsh decision, but our gentle governor was so angry that he resolved to accept full responsibility even if he had to answer to Varvara Petrovna. To everyone's amazement, when the lady arrived at the governor's residence at speed and in a state of great agitation to demand an immediate explanation, she was refused an audience at the front steps, whereupon she set off home again, without even getting out of her carriage, unable to believe what was happening.

Finally everything became clear! At two o'clock in the morning the prisoner, who'd been remarkably quiet up to then and had even dozed, suddenly began making a commotion. He beat his fists furiously against the door; with unnatural strength he wrenched off the iron grating; he shattered the window, cutting his hands very badly. When the officer of the guard arrived with his men and the keys and ordered the cell to be unlocked so they could overpower and restrain the maniac, it turned out that he was suffering from an acute attack of brain fever. They took him home to his mother. Everything became clear at once. All three of our doctors expressed the opinion that for the three days previous to this incident the patient could have been in a delirium, and that although he seemed to be fully aware and capable of acting with great cunning, he was not actually in his right mind or in control of his actions; moreover, all this was supported by the facts. Thus it turned out that Liputin had guessed the truth before anyone else. Ivan Osipovich, a gentle and sensitive man, was deeply embarrassed; but it's worth noting that even he must have considered Nikolai Vsevolodovich capable of an insane action when in his right mind. The members of the club were also contrite and couldn't understand how they'd overlooked the obvious and missed the one possible explanation of all these strange events. Naturally, there were some sceptics, but they didn't maintain their views for long.

Nicolas was an invalid for more than two months. A well-known specialist was summoned from Moscow for a consultation; the whole town called on Varvara Petrovna. She forgave them all. When, in the spring, Nicolas had completely recovered, and had accepted without demur his mother's proposal of a trip to Italy, she prevailed upon him to pay farewell visits to all the local people and, whenever possible, to offer appropriate apologies. Nicolas agreed with alacrity. It was known at the club that he'd held a very delicate conversation with Pavel Pavlovich Gaganov in his own home, and that the latter had been fully satisfied. As he paid these visits Nicolas was very serious, rather gloomy in fact. Everyone seemed to receive him with great sympathy, but for some reason everyone was embarrassed and glad he was leaving for Italy. Ivan Osipovich even shed a few tears, but for some reason or other decided not to embrace him even at their final farewell. It's true that among us some remained convinced that the scoundrel had simply made fun of us and that his illness was merely a pretext. He also went to see Liputin.

'Tell me', he said, 'how could you have known in advance what I'd say about your intelligence and how could you have provided Agafya with an answer?'

'Why,' answered Liputin with a laugh, 'it was because I consider you an intelligent man too and could guess what your answer would be.'

'Anyway, it was a remarkable coincidence. But, tell me this: you must have considered me an intelligent man, not a madman, when you sent Agafya?'

'The most intelligent and most rational of men; I merely pretended to believe you weren't in your right mind... And you yourself guessed at once what I was thinking and sent me back proof of your sharp wit with Agafya.'

'Well, there you're making a slight mistake; as a matter of fact I was... ill,' muttered Nikolai Vsevolodovich, frowning. 'Why!' he shouted, 'do you really think I'm capable of attacking people when in full possession of my senses? Why would I do a thing like that?'

Liputin backed down and didn't know what to reply. Nicolas turned rather pale, or at least so it seemed to Liputin.

'In any case, you have a very amusing way of thinking,' continued Nicolas. 'And as for Agafya, I know full well you sent her over to abuse me.'

'You didn't expect me to challenge you to a duel, did you?'

'Oh, right!' I've heard something to the effect, actually, that you're not very keen on fighting duels....'

'Why on earth should we borrow from the French?' Liputin backed down once again.

'So you support Russian nationalism, do you?'

Liputin backed down even further.

'Well, now! What's this I see?' cried Nicolas, suddenly noticing a volume of Considérant* in the most conspicuous place on the table. 'Surely you're not a Fourierist, are you? You might just be! And isn't that borrowing from the French as well?' he laughed, tapping the book with his fingers.

'No, that's not borrowing from the French!' Liputin cried spitefully, jumping up from his chair. 'It's borrowing from the universal language of mankind, not just the French! It belongs to the language of the universal social republic and the harmony of all mankind, that's what! And not just the French!...'

'Damn it, there's no such language!' Nicolas continued laughing.

Sometimes even a trifle can hold one's attention exclusively and for a long time. Most of what I have to say about Mr Stavrogin will come later; for now I'll just observe, as a matter of curiosity, that of all the impressions he received during the time spent in our town, the one most sharply etched in his memory was the unattractive and almost abject figure of this little provincial official, this envious man, this crass family tyrant, this miser and usurer who locked up leftovers and candle-ends after dinner, and who at the same time was a passionate advocate of God knows what kind of future 'social harmony', who revelled at night in ecstatic visions of some fantastic future phalanstery,* believing in its imminent realization in Russia, in our very own province, as firmly as he believed in his own existence. And that in the very place where he'd saved up to buy himself 'a little house', where he'd married for the second time and taken a dowry, where perhaps within a hundred miles there wasn't a single man, including himself, who had the least, even superficial resemblance to any future member of this 'universal social republic and all-embracing harmony'.

'God only knows where these characters come from!' Nicolas would wonder in disbelief, recalling on occasion this unexpected Fourierist.

4.

Our prince travelled for over three years and was almost completely forgotten in our town. We heard from Stepan Trofimovich that he'd been all over Europe; he'd even been to Egypt and Jerusalem. Then he managed to attach himself to some scientific expedition to Iceland and actually spent some time there. It was also reported that he spent a winter attending lectures at some German university. He rarely wrote to his mother—once every six months, even less; but Varvara Petrovna didn't get angry or take offence. Without complaining she submissively accepted the relationship established once and for all between her son and herself; of course, each and every day during those three years she worried over, yearned for, and dreamt about her Nicolas without fail. She shared neither her daydreams nor her complaints with anyone. She'd even become somewhat distant from Stepan Trofimovich. She was devising some plans of her own; she became stingier than before, began to save more than ever, and grew angry over Stepan Trofimovich's losses at cards.

Finally, in April of this year, she received a letter from Paris, from Praskovya Ivanovna Drozdova, a general's widow and childhood friend of hers. In the letter, Praskovya Ivanovna, whom Varvara Petrovna had neither seen nor corresponded with for eight years, informed her that Nikolai Vsevolodovich had grown very close to them, had befriended Liza (her only daughter), and intended to accompany them to Switzerland that summer, to Verney-Montreux; all this in spite of the fact that in the household of Count K. (a man of influence from Petersburg, now living in Paris), he was being received as if he were the count's own son, so much so that he appeared to be living at the count's house. The letter was brief, and its object perfectly clear, although it merely stated the above-mentioned facts without drawing any conclusions. Varvara Petrovna didn't ponder long; she decided quickly what to do, made the necessary arrangements, took along her protégée Dasha (Shatov's sister), and left for Paris in the middle of April and then went on to Switzerland. She returned home alone in July, having left Dasha with the Drozdovs, who, according to the news she brought back, planned to arrive in our town at the end of August.

The Drozdovs were also landowners in our province, but the duties of General Ivan Ivanovich Drozdov (who'd been a friend of Varvara Petrovna and a former colleague of her husband), had always prevented them from spending much time on their magnificent estate. After the general's death the year before, the inconsolable Praskovya Ivanovna had gone abroad with her daughter, intending, incidentally, to try the grape-cure at Verney-Montreux during the latter part of the summer. On their return to Russia she intended to settle down in our province for good. She owned a large house in town which had stood empty for many years, its windows boarded up. They were wealthy people. Praskovya

Ivanovna, who in her first marriage had been Madame Tushina, was, like her schoolfriend Varvara Petrovna, the daughter of a tax-farmer from the good old days; she had also been provided with a large dowry when she married. Tushin, a retired cavalry captain, had been a man of means as well as some ability. At his death he left a considerable sum to his only daughter Liza who was then seven years old. Now that Lizaveta Nikolaevna was almost twenty-two, her fortune could easily be said to consist of two hundred thousand roubles of her own, not to mention the property she would inherit in due course after her mother's death, especially since she had no children from her second marriage. Varvara Petrovna was evidently very pleased with her trip. In her opinion she'd been able to reach a satisfactory agreement with Praskovya Ivanovna; she told Stepan Trofimovich all about it as soon as she returned. She was even effusive with him, something she hadn't been for quite some time.

'Hurrah!' cried Stepan Trofimovich and snapped his fingers.

He was in absolute ecstasy, all the more so since he'd suffered extreme despair throughout the separation from his friend. She'd gone abroad without even saying a proper goodbye and without telling 'that old woman' anything about her plans, fearing, perhaps, that he might blurt something out. At the time she'd been angry with him over a sizeable loss at cards which she had just discovered. But while still in Switzerland her heart told her that upon her return she'd have to compensate her forsaken friend, especially since she'd been treating him rather harshly for some time. The swift and mysterious parting had struck a blow to Stepan Trofimovich's timid heart, and, as if deliberately, it was shortly followed by other difficulties. He was tormented by significant financial obligations of long standing, which couldn't possibly be settled without Varvara Petrovna's assistance. In addition, in May of this year, the term of our good, kind governor, Ivan Osipovich, was finally coming to an end; he was replaced, under really rather unpleasant circumstances. Then, in Varvara Petrovna's absence, our new governor, Andrei Antonovich von Lembke arrived; at the same time, there occurred a noticeable shift in attitude throughout almost all our provincial society towards Varvara Petrovna, and consequently towards Stepan Trofimovich as well. At least, he'd already made some unpleasant, albeit valuable observations, and seemed to grow more timid during Varvara Petrovna's absence. In great anxiety he suspected that he'd already been identified as a dangerous person to the new governor. He'd learned for a fact that several of our ladies were intending to curtail their visits to Varvara Petrovna. It was said of the future governor's wife (who was not expected to arrive until autumn), that although reputed to be very proud, she was actually a genuine aristocrat, not at all like 'our poor old Varvara Petrovna'. For some reason or other everyone knew, down to the last detail, that the new governor's wife and Varvara Petrovna had met once in society and had parted on unfriendly terms; the result was that even the slightest mention of Mrs von Lembke would make a painful impression on Varvara Petrovna. But Varvara Petrovna's bold and triumphant expression and the contemptuous indifference with which she greeted both the opinions of our ladies and the agitation in our society, revived the timid Stepan Trofimovich's fallen spirits and cheered him up in no time at all. He began to describe for her the new governor's arrival with a particular kind of cheerfully obsequious humour.

'No doubt, *excellente amie*, you're aware', he said flirtatiously, in an affected drawl, 'what is meant by a Russian administrator in general, and a new Russian administrator in particular, that is, newly-baked, newly-placed... *Ces interminables mots russes*!... But you can hardly know in practice what's meant by administrative ecstasy*—precisely what sort of thing that is.'

'Administrative ecstasy? No, I don't know.'

'It's... *Vous savez, chez nous... En un mot*, appoint some insignificant nonentity to a position, say, selling stupid railway tickets, and this nonentity will immediately conclude that he has the right to look down upon you as if he were Jupiter when you come to him to buy a ticket, *pour vous*

montrer son pouvoir.[1] "Now then," he says, "I'll demonstrate
my power over you..." And it reaches the point of administrative ecstasy in these people... *En un mot*, I recently read
how a sexton in one of our churches abroad, *mais c'est très
curieux*, drove out of his church, I mean, literally drove out,
a distinguished English family, *les dames charmantes*, before
the beginning of a Lenten service, *vous savez ces chants et
le livre de Job...*[2] merely because "it wasn't right for foreigners to be wandering around a Russian church; they
ought to come at the proper time..." and he caused the
ladies to faint... This sexton was having a fit of administrative ecstasy, *et il a montré son pouvoir...*'

'Be brief, if you can, Stepan Trofimovich.'

'Mr von Lembke has left for a tour of the province. *En
un mot*, this Andrei Antonovich, even though he's a Russi-
fied German professing the Orthodox faith, and even
though, this I grant him, he's a remarkably handsome man,
still in his forties...'

'Where did you get the idea he's such a handsome man?
He has the eyes of a sheep.'

'Absolutely. But I must yield to the opinion of our
ladies...'

'Come to the point, Stepan Trofimovich, I beg of you!
By the way, since when have you started wearing a red
cravat?'

'I... I only put one on today...'

'And are you taking your constitutionals? Do you go for
a six-mile walk every day as your doctor prescribed?'

'No... not always.'

'I thought so! I suspected that even when I was in
Switzerland!' she exclaimed in irritation. 'Now you'll have
to walk ten miles a day, instead of six! You've let yourself
go terribly, terribly, ter-rib-ly! You've not just grown older,
you've become decrepit... I was shocked when I saw you
just now, in spite of that red cravat of yours... *quelle idée
rouge!*[3] Go on about von Lembke, if you really have some-

---

[1] to demonstrate his power over you
[2] you know those psalms and the Book of Job
[3] what a crazy idea!

thing to say, and get it over with soon, I beg you. I'm tired.'

'*En un mot*, I was only going to say that he's one of these men who at forty become administrators, having previously vegetated in some insignificant post, and then suddenly he becomes an important person by acquiring a wife or some other no less desperate measure... So, he's just left town... and I want to tell you that people have been whispering into both his ears, claiming that I'm a corrupter of youth and a sower of provincial atheism... And he started making enquiries at once.'

'Is that true?'

'I've even taken measures. When they "informed" on you and said you "controlled the province", *vous savez*, he allowed himself to use the expression "there'd be no more of that." '

'Is that what he said?'

' "There'd be no more of that," and *avec cette morgue*...¹ We'll see his wife, Yulia Mikhailovna, here at the end of August; she's coming straight from Petersburg.'

'From abroad. We met there.'

'*Vraiment?*'

'In Paris and then in Switzerland. She's related to the Drozdovs.'

'Related? What a remarkable coincidence! They say she's ambitious and... she's supposed to be very well connected.'

'Well connected? Nonsense! She was an old maid until the age of forty-five, without a kopeck to her name, and then she jumped at her von Lembke, and now her sole aim in life is to push him forward. They're both schemers.'

'They say she's two years older than he is.'

'Five. Her mother used to wear out her skirts on my doorstep in Moscow; when Vsevolod Nikolaevich was still alive, she'd beg to be invited to our balls as a special favour. And then her daughter, with a turquoise bow on her forehead, would sit in a corner all evening without ever being asked to dance, so around two o'clock I'd send over a partner simply because I felt so sorry for her. She was already

¹ with such arrogance

twenty-five at the time, but they used to dress her up like a little girl in short skirts. It became awkward to invite them.'

'I can imagine that bow of hers.'

'I tell you, I arrived and stumbled on their intrigue. You've just read Madame Drozdova's letter. What could be clearer? What did I find? That fool Drozdova, who was never more than a fool, suddenly looks at me as if to enquire, "Why have you come?" You can imagine how surprised I was! I looked around and there's that von Lembke woman scheming away, and with her that relative of hers, old man Drozdov's nephew, and then everything became clear! Naturally, I changed all that in an instant and Praskovya is back on my side once again. But the intrigue, the intrigue!'

'Which you overcame, however. Oh, you Bismarck, you!'

'I may not be Bismarck, but I'm still capable of recognizing hypocrisy and stupidity when I encounter them. Von Lembke is hypocrisy and Praskovya is stupidity. I've rarely met a more flaccid woman in my life; what's more, she has swollen feet; what's more, she has a kind heart. What could possibly be more foolish than a kind-hearted fool?'

'An evil fool, *ma bonne amie*, an evil fool is even more foolish,' Stepan Trofimovich protested nobly.

'You may be right. Do you remember Liza?'

'*Charmante enfant!*'

'But now she's no longer an *enfant*, but a woman, and a woman of character. She's generous and passionate, and what I like about her is that she stands up to her credulous fool of a mother. There was almost a scandal over that relative of hers.'

'Why, he's surely not really related to Lizaveta Nikolaevna at all... Does he have designs on her then?'

'You see, he's a young officer, not very talkative, rather modest as well. I always want to be fair. I think he himself is against all this intrigue and doesn't want anything, it's just that von Lembke woman who's been scheming. He had great respect for Nicolas. You understand, the whole affair depends on Liza, but I left her on very good terms with

Nicolas, and he himself promised to come home in November. The von Lembke woman must be scheming on her own, and Praskovya, merely blind. She suddenly told me that all my suspicions were only fantasy; I told her to her face that she was a fool. I'm prepared to swear to that on Judgement Day. And if Nicolas hadn't asked me to leave for a while, I wouldn't have left without discrediting that deceitful woman. She's been trying to use Nicolas to get into Count K.'s good graces, actually hoping to separate a son from his mother. But Liza is on our side, and I've got an understanding with Praskovya. Did you know she's related to Karmazinov?'

'What? He's a relation of Madame von Lembke's?'

'Yes indeed. A distant one.'

'Karmazinov, the novelist?'

'Why, yes, the writer. Why are you so surprised? Of course, he considers himself to be a great man. The conceited creature! She'll be coming with him; meanwhile, she's making a great fuss over him there. She plans to organize something here, too, a kind of literary gathering. He'll be coming for a month; he wants to sell his last piece of property here. I almost met him in Switzerland, although I wasn't very eager to. I hope, however, he'll deign to recognize me. In the old days he used to write me letters and visit my house. I'd appreciate it if you'd dress a little better, Stepan Trofimovich; you're becoming more slovenly every day... Oh, how you torment me! What are you reading these days?'

'I... I...'

'I understand. The same as always—friends, drinking-bouts, the club and cards, and a reputation as an atheist. I don't like that reputation of yours, Stepan Trofimovich. I'd prefer you weren't known as an atheist, I'd prefer it now especially. I'd have preferred it before too, because it's only idle chatter after all. There, it finally had to be said.'

'*Mais, ma chère...*'

'Listen to me, Stepan Trofimovich, as far as learning is concerned, of course I'm ignorant compared to you, but I thought about you a great deal on my way here. I've come to one conclusion.'

'What's that?'

'That you and I are not the cleverest people on earth; there are people who are even cleverer than we are.'

'That's witty and to the point. If there are people cleverer than we, then there are also people more correct; so, we can make mistakes, right? *Mais, ma bonne ami*, let's assume I make a mistake; won't I still have my universal, eternal, supreme right of freedom of conscience? Don't I have the right not to be a hypocrite or a bigot if I don't want to be, for which, naturally, I'll be despised by certain people to the end of my days. *Et puis, comme on trouve toujours plus de moines que de raison*,[1] and since I'm in complete agreement with this...'

'What, what did you say?'

'I said, *on trouve toujours plus de moines que de raison*, and since I'm in...'

'You can't have thought that up yourself. You must have borrowed it from somewhere.'

'Pascal said it.'*

'So it wasn't your own... just as I thought! Why don't you ever invent anything like that—so concise and to the point; you're always so long-winded. That's much better than what you were saying about administrative ecstasy just now...'

'*Ma foi, chère*, you ask why? In the first place, probably because I'm no Pascal, after all; *et puis*... in the second place, we Russians don't know how to say anything in our own language... At least, we haven't yet said anything...'

'Hmmm! That may not be true. At least you should make a note of such sayings and memorize them, you know, they'll come in handy in conversation... Ah, Stepan Trofimovich, I came to have a very serious talk with you!'

'*Chère, chère amie!*'

'Now that all these von Lembkes and Karmazinovs... Good Lord, how you've let yourself go! Oh, how you torment me!... I'd like these people to show you some

---

[1] And then, since one always encounters monks more frequently than common sense

respect, because they aren't worth a finger of yours, not even the little one. And how do you behave yourself? What do they see? What shall I show them? Instead of standing nobly as a testament, providing a model, you surround yourself with rabble, you've acquired impossible habits, you've grown decrepit, you can't do without your wine and cards, all you read is Paul de Kock and you never write a thing, while they're all busy writing. You waste all your time on idle chatter. Is it possible, is it permissible to associate with such scum as your inseparable Liputin?'

'Why do you call him "mine" and "inseparable"?' Stepan Trofimovich protested timidly.

'Where is he now?' continued Varvara Petrovna sternly and sharply.

'He... he has the utmost respect for you and has gone to S—k, to claim his inheritance from his mother.'

'All he ever seems to do is get money. And how's Shatov? Still the same?'

'*Irascible, mais bon.*'

'I can't stand your Shatov; he's evil and thinks too much of himself!'

'How is Darya Pavlovna?'

'Are you asking about Dasha? Why do you ask about her?' Varvara Petrovna looked at him inquisitively. 'She's well; I left her with the Drozdovs... In Switzerland I heard some news of your son, something bad, not at all good.'

'*Oh, c'est une histoire bien bête! Je vous attendais, ma bonne amie, pour vous raconter...*'

'Enough, Stepan Trofimovich, give me some peace; I'm exhausted. We'll have plenty of time to talk, especially about the bad things. You've begun to sputter when you laugh; that's a sure sign of senility! And how strange your laugh is now... Lord, you've acquired so many bad habits! Karmazinov will never come to see you! And people here take pleasure in anything, as it is... Now you've revealed your true self. Well, that'll do, I'm tired! You might finally spare me.'

---

[1] Oh, it's rather a stupid story! I was waiting for you, my dear friend, to tell you it

Stepan Trofimovich 'spared her', but left greatly perturbed.

5.

Our friend certainly had acquired not just a few bad habits, especially of late. He'd noticeably and swiftly let himself go; it was true he'd become slovenly. He drank more, became tearful more easily, and his nerves grew weaker; he'd become too sensitive to things of beauty. His face had acquired the peculiar ability to change extremely quickly, for example, from the most solemn expression to the most ridiculous, even stupid one. He couldn't stand solitude and constantly craved amusement. One had always to repeat bits of gossip to him, local anecdotes, and they had to be fresh every day. If no one came to see him for a long time, he'd wander disconsolately from room to room, approach the window, stand there chewing his lips pensively, sighing deeply, and end by almost whimpering. He was always full of foreboding, fearing something unexpected and inevitable. He became apprehensive and began to pay more attention to his dreams.

He was very gloomy all that day and evening; he sent for me, was very agitated, spoke at length, and told me everything, though rather incoherently. Varvara Petrovna had known for some time that he didn't keep anything from me. In the final analysis he seemed worried about something in particular, something which perhaps even he couldn't quite understand. Previously, when we'd get together alone and he'd begin to complain, after a little while a bottle would almost always appear and things would become a bit more cheerful. But this time there was no wine, and it was obvious that he had to suppress a desire to send for some more than once.

'Why is she so angry with me all the time?' he kept complaining like a little child. '*Tous les hommes de génie et de progrès en Russie étaient, sont et seront toujours des* gamblers *et des* drunkards, *qui boivent* [1] like fish... by no means am I

---

[1] All men of genius and progress in Russia were, are, and always will be gamblers and drunkards who drink

such a gambler or drunkard... She reproaches me for never writing anything. What a strange thought!... Why do I lie down? "You", she says, "should stand as a model and a reproach." *Mais, entre nous soit dit*, what else should a man do who's destined to stand as a "reproach" except lie down—doesn't she know that?'

At long last it became clear what was tormenting him so particularly persistently now. Many times that evening he went up to the mirror and paused before it for a while. Finally, he turned away from the mirror towards me and, with a strange sort of despair, he announced:

'*Mon cher, je suis un* man who's let himself go.'

Yes, indeed, up to then, up to that very day, he'd been absolutely sure of one thing, and one thing alone, namely, that in spite of Varvara Petrovna's 'new views' and 'changed ideas', he was still irresistible to her feminine heart, that is, not only as an exile or a famous scholar, but also as a handsome man. For twenty years this flattering and reassuring conviction had been rooted in him, and perhaps, of all his convictions, he found it the most difficult to part with. Did he have any foreboding that evening of the colossal ordeal he was to undergo in the near future?

6.

Now I'll proceed with a description of the rather amusing incident with which my chronicle really begins.

The Drozdovs finally returned at the very end of August. Altogether their arrival, which occurred shortly before the coming of their long-awaited relative, the wife of our new governor, created a notable stir in our society. But I'll discuss all these interesting events later; for now I'll say only that Praskovya Ivanovna presented Varvara Petrovna, who'd been expecting her so impatiently, with a most vexing riddle: Nicolas had parted with them back in July, and, having met Count K. on the Rhine, had set off with him and his family for Petersburg. (N.B.: The count's three daughters were all still unmarried.)

'I could learn nothing from Liza,' Praskovya Ivanovna concluded, 'because of her pride and obstinacy, but I could see with my own eyes that something had happened between her and Nikolai Vsevolodovich. I don't know what, but I think that you, my dear Varvara Petrovna, will have to find out from your Darya Pavlovna. In my opinion Liza was offended by something. I'm really delighted to have brought your protégée back at long last, and I hand her over to you now: good riddance.'

These venomous words were uttered with evident irritation. It was obvious that this 'flaccid woman' had rehearsed them in advance and had already relished their effect. But Varvara Petrovna wasn't the sort of person to be disconcerted by sentimental effects and riddles. She sternly demanded the most detailed and satisfactory explanations. Praskovya Ivanovna lowered her voice immediately, and ended up dissolving in tears and outpourings of deepest affection. This irritating but sentimental woman was, just like Stepan Trofimovich, constantly in need of true friendship; her main complaint against Lizaveta Nikolaevna was that 'her daughter was no real friend to her'.

Amidst all these explanations and outpourings the only thing that seemed certain was that a quarrel had taken place between Liza and Nicolas, but apparently Praskovya Ivanovna was unable to form a definite opinion of its nature. As for the charges levelled against Darya Pavlovna, she not only withdrew them completely in the end, but even particularly asked that no significance be attached to her words since she'd said them 'in irritation'. In brief, it was all extremely vague, even somewhat suspicious. According to her story, the quarrel had arisen from Liza's 'obstinate and sarcastic' character; 'the proud Nikolai Vsevolodovich, though deeply in love, couldn't bear her sarcasm and soon became sarcastic himself.'

'Soon afterwards we made the acquaintance of a young man, apparently the nephew of your "professor", with the same surname....'

'His son, not his nephew,' Varvara Petrovna corrected her. Praskovya Ivanovna could never remember Stepan Trofimovich's surname, and always referred to him as the 'professor'.

'Well then, his son, so much the better, it's all the same to me. He's an ordinary young man, very lively and easy-going, but there's nothing special about him. Well then, Liza did behave badly; she befriended the young man simply to make Nikolai Vsevolodovich jealous. I don't much blame her: it's typical female behaviour, even charming. Only instead of getting jealous, Nikolai Vsevolodovich befriended the young man himself, as if he didn't notice a thing or didn't really care. This made Liza furious. The young man soon left (he seemed on his way somewhere in a hurry), and Liza began to find fault with Nikolai Vsevolodovich on every possible occasion. She noticed that he would sometimes talk to Dasha, and she immediately flew into such a rage that it even made life difficult for me, her mother. My doctors had warned me not to get excited, and I was fed up with that lake they make such a big fuss about; it gave me toothache and brought on an attack of rheumatism. It's a published fact that Lake Geneva causes toothaches; it's a feature of the place. And then Nikolai Vsevolodovich suddenly received a letter from the countess and left immediately, packing up in one day. They parted friends; it was Liza who saw him off and she was very cheerful and relaxed, laughing quite a bit. But it was all for show. After he left she became pensive; she stopped talking about him and didn't let me either. I'd advise you, too, my dear Varvara Petrovna, not to bring up the subject with her; you'll only make it worse. But if you keep silent, she'll be the first to broach it with you; that way you'll find out more. I think they'll get together again, as long as Nikolai Vsevolodovich comes back soon, as he promised.'

'I'll write to him at once. If it's all just as you say, then it's a only little quarrel; it's all rubbish! Besides, I know Darya too well; it's rubbish.'

'I confess I was wrong about Dashenka. They had merely talked quite normally together, out loud, too. But as a mother, it all upset me very much at the time. Besides, I saw that Liza herself was also treating her with the same affection as before...'

That very day Varvara Petrovna wrote to Nikolai Vsevolodovich and implored him to return at least a month earlier than he'd originally planned. Nevertheless there was still something unclear and unexplained in all of this. She thought about it all evening and all night. 'Praskovya's opinion' seemed too innocent and sentimental to her. 'All her life Praskovya has been too sensitive, even as a schoolgirl,' she thought. 'And it's not like Nicolas to run away because of some young girl's sarcasm. There must be some other reason, if there really was a quarrel. But that officer is here; they brought him along too. He's moved in with them like a relative. And Praskovya was a little too quick to apologize about Darya; she's probably keeping something to herself, something she didn't tell me.'

By morning Varvara Petrovna had devised a plan to put an end to at least one of her quandaries—a plan remarkable for its originality. What was in her heart when she conceived it? It's hard to say, and I won't take it upon myself to explain all its contradictions in advance. As a chronicler I'll limit myself to describing events exactly, just as they came about; I'm not to blame if they seem implausible. However, once again I must testify to the fact that by morning she no longer suspected Dasha of anything whatever and, to tell the truth, she never really did; she was too sure of her. Moreover, she couldn't even admit the possibility that her Nicolas could've fallen for her... for 'Darya'. That morning, as Darya Petrovna was pouring tea at breakfast, Varvara Petrovna stared at her intently for a while, and, perhaps for the twentieth time since yesterday, muttered to herself with absolute conviction, 'It's all rubbish!'

She merely observed that Dasha looked somewhat tired and was even quieter than usual, more apathetic. After tea, following their long-established custom, they sat down together to do some needlework. Varvara Petrovna asked for a full account of her impressions of abroad, primarily about nature, the local peoples, the towns, customs, art and industry—everything she'd observed. Not one question about the Drozdovs or her life with them. Dasha, who was sitting beside her at the work-table and helping her embroider, talked for about half an hour in her even, monotonous, but rather feeble voice.

'Darya,' Varvara Petrovna interrupted her suddenly, 'do you have anything particular you'd like to tell me?'

'No, nothing,' Darya replied after thinking for a moment, looking at Varvara Petrovna with her pale eyes.

'Nothing in your soul, your heart, or on your conscience?'

'Nothing,' repeated Dasha quietly, but with a sort of sullen determination.

'I knew it! Be assured, Darya, I'll never doubt you. Now stay and listen. Move over here. Sit down opposite me. I want to see all of you. That's it. Now listen. Do you want to get married?'

Dasha answered with a long, questioning but not altogether astonished glance.

'Wait. Don't say a word. In the first place, there's a very great difference in your ages; but you know better than most that that's rubbish. You're a reasonable girl, and you mustn't make any mistakes in your life. Besides, he's still a handsome man... In a word, Stepan Trofimovich, whom you've always respected. Well?'

Dasha gave her an even more questioning look, this time not only in surprise, but blushing perceptibly.

'Wait. Don't say a thing. Don't be in such a hurry! Even though you'll get some money from my will, what will happen to you after my death, even if you do have money? People will deceive you and take your money, and you'll be ruined. But with him, you'll be married to a famous man. Now look at it from another angle: if I were to die now, what would become of him, even though I've provided for him, too? But I know I can rely on you. Wait. I haven't finished. He's frivolous, irresolute, cruel, egotistical, and has unseemly habits. But you must appreciate him, first of all because other men are much worse. After all, I'm not trying to get rid of you by unloading you on some scoundrel. You didn't think that, did you? But the important thing is, you'll appreciate him because I ask you to.' She broke off, suddenly irritated. 'Do you hear? Why don't you say anything?'

Dasha sat there in silence, listening.

'Wait, don't say a word. He's an old woman—so much the better for you. What's more, he's a pathetic old bag; he really doesn't deserve to be loved by any woman. But he deserves to be loved because he's defenceless, and you'll love him for that. Do you understand me? Do you?'

Dasha nodded her head affirmatively.

'I knew it. I expected no less of you. He'll love you because he has to, because he has to. He should adore you!' Varvara Petrovna shrieked as it were in particular irritation. But I know him; he'll fall in love with you even without any obligation. Besides, I'll be here myself. Don't worry, I'll always be here. He'll complain about you, start to slander you, whisper about you to the first person he meets; he'll whine, he always does; he'll write you letters and send them from one room to the next, two letters a day, but he still won't be able to live without you, that's the most important thing. Make him obey you; if you can't, you're a fool. He'll want to hang himself, he'll threaten to do so—don't believe him; it doesn't mean a thing! Don't believe him, but keep your eyes peeled all the same; you never know, one day he may really decide to hang himself. It can happen with people like that: they hang themselves because they're weak, not because they're strong. That's why you shouldn't push him too far—that's the first rule of married life. Also remember he's a poet. Listen, Darya, there's no higher pleasure than self-sacrifice. In addition, you'll be doing me a great favour, that's the main thing. Don't think I'm talking so much nonsense; I understand what I'm saying. I'm an egoist, and you can be an egoist, too. I'm not forcing you to do it; it's up to you. Whatever you say, that's what will be. Well, why are you sitting there like that? Say something!'

'It's all the same to me, Varvara Petrovna, if it's absolutely necessary for me to get married,' said Dasha firmly.

'Necessary? What are you hinting at?' Varvara Petrovna looked sternly and intently at her.

Dasha was silent, picking at the embroidery-frame with her needle.

'You may be clever, but you're talking nonsense. Even though it may be true that I've decided it's high time for you to get married, it's not out of any necessity; it's only because the idea has occurred to me, and it's only to Stepan

Trofimovich. If it weren't for Stepan Trofimovich, I'd never have thought of marrying you off now, even though you're already twenty... So?'

'As you wish, Varvara Petrovna.'

'Then you agree! No, don't say anything, what's the hurry? I haven't finished. According to my will you're to receive fifteen thousand roubles. I'll give them to you now, right after the wedding. You'll give him eight thousand, that is, not him, but me. He has debts of about eight thousand roubles; I'll pay them off, but he has to know it's with your money. You'll keep seven thousand, and you must never give him even one rouble. Never pay his debts. If you do it once, you'll never see the end of it. Besides, I'll always be here. You'll receive an allowance of twelve hundred roubles a year, with extras fifteen hundred, plus room and board which I'll also provide, just like he gets now. But you'll have to supply your own servants. I'll pay this annual allowance in one lump sum, directly to you. But you must also be kind: give him a little something and let his friends visit him once a week; if they come more often, chase them away. But I'll be here myself. And when I die, your allowance will continue until his death, do you hear, only until *his* death, since it's his allowance, not yours. As for you, in addition to the seven thousand I'll give you now, which you won't touch unless you're really stupid, I'll leave you another eight thousand in my will. You won't receive anything else from me; you must understand that. Well, do you agree or not? Will you say something at last?'

'I've already said something, Varvara Petrovna.'

'Remember you're completely free; as you wish, so it shall be.'

'May I enquire, Varvara Petrovna, whether Stepan Tro-fimovich has said anything to you yet?'

'No, he hasn't said anything and still doesn't know, but... he'll say something very soon!'

She jumped up instantly and threw on her black shawl. Dasha blushed a little once more and followed her with her enquiring gaze. Varvara Petrovna suddenly turned around, her face burning with anger.

'You fool!' she cried pouncing on her like a hawk, 'you ungrateful fool! What do you think? Do you really imagine I'd compromise you in any way, however small? He'll come crawling on his knees to ask you, he'll die from happiness, that's how it will all be arranged! After all, you should know I'd never let anyone hurt you! Or do you think he'll take you for those eight thousand roubles and that I'm in a hurry to sell you off? You fool, you fool, ungrateful fools the lot of you! Give me my umbrella!'

And she hurried off on foot along wet brick pavements and across wooden planks to see Stepan Trofimovich.

7.

It's true she wouldn't let anyone hurt her 'Darya'; on the contrary, she considered that she was acting now as Darya's benefactress. The most generous and irreproachable indignation flared in her soul when, as she put on her shawl, she caught sight of her protégée's embarrassed and mistrustful gaze fixed upon her. She'd genuinely loved the girl since she was a child. Praskovya Ivanovna was right in calling Darya Pavlovna her favourite. Long ago Varvara Petrovna had decided once and for all that 'Darya's character was unlike her brother's' (that is, unlike Ivan Shatov's); she was timid and gentle, capable of great self-sacrifice; she was set apart by her devotion, unusual modesty, rare reasonableness, and, chiefly, by her gratitude. Up to now, apparently, Dasha had lived up to all her expectations. 'There will be no mistakes made in her life,' said Varvara Petrovna when the girl was still only twelve; and since she was inclined to attach herself obstinately and passionately to any dream that attracted her, to every new scheme, every idea that caught her fancy, she decided promptly to raise Dasha as if she were her own daughter. In no time she had set aside a sum of money for her and engaged a governess, Miss Criggs, who lived with them until the girl was sixteen, but who was then suddenly dismissed for some reason. Teachers from the gymnasium came to give her lessons, including one genuine Frenchman who taught Dasha French. He was also suddenly dismissed, almost turned out of the house. An impoverished lady, a widow of good family, came to give piano lessons. But her principal teacher was really Stepan Trofimovich. In fact, it was he who 'discovered' Dasha: he'd begun tutoring the timid child even before Varvara Petrovna began thinking about her. Once again I repeat: it was astonishing how attached children became to him! Lizaveta Nikolaevna Tushina studied with him between the ages of eight and eleven (naturally, Stepan Trofimovich taught her without compensation, nor would he have accepted any from the Drozdovs). But he himself had fallen in love with that charming child and used to invent all sorts of stories about the creation of the world, the earth, and the history of mankind. His lectures about primitive peoples and ancient man were much more interesting than the Arabian Nights. Liza, who was in ecstasy over these stories, used to imitate Stepan Trofimovich in a most amusing way at home. He found out and once caught her at it. Liza was mortified; she threw her arms around him and burst into tears. So did Stepan Trofimovich, out of ecstasy. But soon Liza went away, leaving only Dasha. When teachers came to give her lessons, Stepan Trofimovich discontinued his, and gradually paid less and less attention to her. This went on for some time. Then, when she turned seventeen, he was suddenly struck by how attractive she was. This took place at Varvara Petrovna's table. He began talking with the young girl, was very pleased at her answers, and ended by proposing to give her a serious and comprehensive course on the history of Russian literature. Varvara Petrovna approved and thanked him for the excellent suggestion; Dasha was delighted. Stepan Trofimovich started preparing the lectures in earnest, and finally they began. He commenced with the ancient period; the first lecture was fascinating; Varvara Petrovna herself was in attendance. When Stepan Trofimovich concluded and announced to his pupil that next time they'd discuss *The Tale of Igor's Campaign*,* Varvara Petrovna suddenly stood up and declared that there would be no further lectures. Stepan Trofimovich winced, but said nothing. Dasha flushed crimson. But that was the end of the enterprise. This occurred exactly three years before Varvara

Petrovna's latest original scheme.

Poor Stepan Trofimovich was sitting at home alone and had no idea what was going to happen. Plunged in gloomy reflection, he'd been looking out the window for some time to see if any of his friends might be coming to visit him. But no one was going to come. It was drizzling outside and growing cold; the stove would have to be lit; he sighed. All of a sudden a terrible apparition flashed before his eyes: Varvara Petrovna, in this awful weather and at this ungodly hour, was coming to see him! Moreover, on foot! He was so astounded that he forgot to change his clothes and received her dressed just as he was, in his everyday pink quilted waistcoat.

'*Ma bonne amie!...*' he cried weakly and rose to greet her.

'I'm glad you're alone: I can't stand your friends! And you smoke all the time; good Lord, what foul air! You haven't even finished your tea and it's nearly twelve o'clock! Disorder is your idea of heaven! Filth is something you enjoy! What are all these scraps of paper doing on the floor? Nastasya, Nastasya! What's your Nastasya doing? Open the windows, my dear, open the transoms, the doors, open everything wide. We'll go into the drawing-room; I've something to discuss with you. And sweep up, my good woman, for once in your life!'

'He makes such a mess!' Nastasya whined in an irritable, plaintive voice.

'Well, you clean it up, fifteen times a day if you have to! What an awful drawing-room,' she exclaimed as they passed into that room. 'Shut those doors tight, or else she'll try to listen in. We absolutely must change this wallpaper. I sent the paper-hanger over here with samples. Why haven't you chosen anything? Now sit down and listen to me. Sit down, for goodness' sake, I beg you. Where are you going? Where are you going? Where *are* you going?'

'I... just a moment,' Stepan Trofimovich shouted from the other room, 'Here I am again!'

'Oh, you've changed your clothes!' she said sarcastically, looking him over. (He'd put a frock-coat on over his waist-coat.) 'Yes, now you're more appropriately attired for what

I have to tell you. Sit down, for goodness' sake, I beg you.'

She explained everything to him all at once, abruptly and persuasively. She even alluded to the eight thousand roubles which he so desperately needed. She described the dowry in great detail. Stepan Trofimovich's eyes bulged and he began to tremble. He heard everything, but couldn't take it all in. He wanted to make some reply, but his voice failed. He knew only that it would all turn out exactly as she wished; there was no point in objecting or disagreeing; he was already as good as married.

'*Mais, ma bonne amie*,' he said at long last, 'to marry for the third time, at my age... and to such a child! *Mais c'est une enfant*!'[1]

'A child who's twenty years old, thank God! Stop rolling your eyes, please, I beg you; you're not on stage. You're very clever and erudite, but you don't understand a thing about life; you need a nanny to look after you all the time. What will become of you after I die? She'll make you a good nanny; she's a modest girl, solid, and reasonable; besides, I'm not going to die right away, I'll still be here myself. She's a home-body, an angel of gentleness. The happy thought occurred to me back in Switzerland. Do you understand when I say she's an angel of gentleness?' she screamed at him furiously all of a sudden. 'You live in filth; she'll keep you clean and orderly; everything will shine like a mirror... Good Lord, do you really think I have to beg you to marry this treasure, list all the advantages, arrange the match? Why, you should go down on your knees... Oh, you shallow, shallow, faint-hearted man!'

'But... I'm already an old man.'

'What do your fifty-three years matter? Fifty isn't the end of life, it's only the mid-point. You're a handsome man, you know that yourself. You also know how much she respects you. If I die, what'll become of her? But if she's married to you, she'll be happy and I'll be content. You're a man of importance; you have a name and a loving heart; you receive a pension which I consider to be an obligation.

---

[1] But my dear friend ... But she's a child!

You'll save her, perhaps; you'll even save her! In any case, you'll be doing her an honour. You'll prepare her for life, further her emotional development, guide her thinking. How many people are there today who come to ruin because their thinking is misguided? By that time your book will have been completed, and you'll remind people of your existence.'

'As a matter of fact, I...' he muttered, already gratified by Varvara Petrovna's skilful flattery. 'As a matter of fact, I'm now planning to get to work on my *Tales of Spanish Life*...'

'Well, there you are, perfect.'

'But... what about her? Have you told her?'

'Don't worry about her; there's no reason you should be curious. Of course, you must ask her yourself, beg her to do you the honour, you understand. But don't worry, I'll be right here. Besides, you do love her...'

Stepan Trofimovich's head was spinning; the walls were going round and round. There was one terrible thought with which he couldn't be reconciled.

'*Excellente amie!*' he said, his voice suddenly trembling. 'I... I never imagined you'd want to marry me off... to another... woman.'

'You're not a young girl, Stepan Trofimovich; only girls are married off. You're taking a wife,' Varvara Petrovna hissed maliciously.

'*Oui, j'ai pris un mot pour un autre. Mais... c'est égal,*'[1] he said, staring at her with a lost expression.

'I see that *c'est égal*,' she muttered contemptuously. 'Good Lord, now he's fainted! Nastasya! Nastasya! Water!'

But water wasn't necessary. He recovered. Varvara Petrovna picked up her umbrella.

'I see there's no point in talking to you now...'

'*Oui, oui, je suis incapable.*'

'But by tomorrow you'll have rested and thought it over. Stay at home. If anything happens, even during the night, you must let me know. Don't write me any letters; I won't read them. Tomorrow I'll come to see you at the same time,

---

[1] Yes, I said the wrong thing. But . . . it makes no difference.

alone, for your final answer, and I trust it will be satisfactory. Try not to receive any of your friends, and make sure the place isn't filthy; as it is, it's a real disgrace. Nastasya! Nastasya!'

Needless to say, the next day he consented; he couldn't help it. There was a particular circumstance involved...

8.

Stepan Trofimovich's estate, as we used to refer to it (consisting of about fifty souls according to the old way of reckoning, and adjoining Skvoreshniki), was not really his estate at all; it had belonged to his first wife and consequently it now belonged to their son, Peter Stepanovich Verkhovensky. Stepan Trofimovich was merely acting as his trustee; therefore, when the nestling was fully fledged, he delegated formal authority to his father to run the estate. This arrangement was advantageous to the young man: he received as much as a thousand roubles a year from his father as income from the estate, while under the new regime it really didn't produce more than about five hundred (perhaps even less). God knows how such an arrangement had been arrived at. Moreover, it was Varvara Petrovna who sent the young man the whole thousand roubles; Stepan Trofimovich didn't contribute one single rouble. On the contrary, he kept all the income from the estate for himself; in addition, he ruined the estate completely, having rented it to some entrepreneur and having, unbeknown to Varvara Petrovna, sold off for timber the wood which had been its main asset. He'd been selling off the wood bit by bit for some time. In its entirety it was worth at least eight thousand roubles, but he received only five thousand for it. However, he sometimes lost a little heavily at the club and was afraid to ask Varvara Petrovna. She gnashed her teeth when she finally learned about it. And now, all of a sudden, his son had declared that he was returning and intending to sell his property for whatever price he could get, and he commissioned his father to make all necessary arrangements for the sale. It was clear that Stepan Trofimovich, being such a generous and unselfish man, felt ashamed before *ce cher enfant*[1] (whom he'd last seen as a student some nine years before in Petersburg). Originally the whole estate might have been worth thirteen or fourteen thousand roubles, but now it was unlikely to fetch even five. No doubt Stepan Trofimovich was fully entitled, by the terms of the formal agreement, to sell off the timber, and, taking into account the incredible thousand-rouble annual allowance he'd been dispatching promptly for so many years, he could have made a very sound case. But Stepan Trofimovich was generous and had noble intentions. An astonishingly beautiful thought flashed through his mind: when his Petrushka arrived, he would suddenly lay on ᵗhe table the maximum price, that is, the sum of fifteen thousand roubles, without any reference to the money he'd been sending every year; then, amidst tears, he'd press *ce cher fils* to his heart warmly, thus settling all accounts between them. Very cautiously and in abstract terms he began unfolding this picture to Varvara Petrovna. He hinted that it would even endow their friendship, their... 'idea', with some special, noble quality. It would reveal the unselfishness and generosity in fathers of the older generation, of that generation in general, compared to the frivolous and socialist younger generation. He said a great deal more, but Varvara Petrovna kept silent. At last she informed him tersely that she was willing to purchase the property and would even pay the maximum price for it, that is, six or seven thousand roubles (though it could've been had for four). As for the remaining eight thousand which had disappeared along with the wood, she said not one word.

This occurred a month before the proposed match. Stepan Trofimovich was staggered, and began thinking. Previously he could still have hoped that his dear son might never return—that is, a stranger, viewing it from the outside, might have expressed such a hope. As a father, Stepan Trofimovich would certainly have rejected with indignation the very notion. Be that as it may, strange rumours continued to circulate about his dear little Petrusha. At first,

[1] this dear child

after completing his course at the university about six years previously, he lounged around Petersburg with nothing to do. Then we suddenly received word that he'd participated in drafting an anonymous proclamation and was implicated in the affair. Afterwards, he suddenly turned up abroad, in Switzerland, in Geneva—he must have been running away.

'I find it surprising,' a very embarrassed Stepan Trofimovich said to us at the time, 'Petrusha *c'est une si pauvre tête*! He's kind, generous, and very sensitive; in Petersburg I was very happy to compare him to other modern young people, but *c'est un pauvre sire tout de même*...[1] And, you know, it's all a result of that same immaturity and sentimentality! They're all bewitched, not by realism, but by the emotional and idealistic aspects of socialism, so to speak, by its religious overtones, its poetry... all second-hand, of course. As for me, just think what that means! I have so many enemies here, even more *there*, they're sure to ascribe it to his father's influence... Good Lord! Petrushka, a revolutionary! What times we live in!'

Very soon, however, Petrushka sent his precise address from Switzerland so that he could continue receiving his allowance as usual: that meant he wasn't really an émigré. And now, having lived abroad for four years, he was suddenly about to appear again in his homeland and was informing us of his imminent arrival: that meant he wasn't really accused of anything. What's more, it even seemed as if there was someone in particular interested in his fate and protecting him. He wrote now from the south of Russia where he was carrying out some private but important commission, and was very occupied. All this was splendid, but where could Stepan Trofimovich find the remaining seven or eight thousand roubles to offer a decent price for his son's estate? And what if a scandal were to result, and, instead of the beautiful picture envisaged it turned into a lawsuit? Something indicated to Stepan Trofimovich that his sensitive Petrusha would never renounce his own interests. 'Why is it,' Stepan Trofimovich once asked me in a

[1] is not very bright! ... he's a poor creature all the same

whisper, 'why is it all these desperate socialists and communists are also so incredibly miserly, acquisitive, and proprietorial? In fact, the more socialist someone is, the further he's gone in that direction, the stronger his proprietorial instinct. Why is it? Could it also be out of sentimentality?' I don't know if there's any truth to Stepan Trofimovich's remark; I know only that Petrusha had received certain information about the sale of the wood and all the rest of it, and Stepan Trofimovich knew his son had that information. I also had the chance to read Petrusha's letters to his father; he wrote infrequently, once a year or even less. But lately he'd sent two letters, one right after another, informing his father of his imminent arrival. All his letters were short and dry, consisting entirely of instructions; and since, in accordance with the latest fashion, father and son had been using familiar forms of address since their time in Petersburg, Petrusha's letters closely resembled those injunctions of days gone by which former landowners used to send from the capital to the serfs left behind to manage their estates. Now suddenly the sum of eight thousand roubles which would settle the whole affair had turned up in Varvara Petrovna's proposition; moreover, she made it perfectly clear to him that this sum would never be forthcoming from anywhere else. It goes without saying that Stepan Trofimovich consented.

He sent for me right after she left, and refused to see anyone else all that day. Of course he wept a little, spoke eloquently and at length, frequently lost his train of thought, uttered several accidental witticisms and was pleased by them, then had a mild bilious attack—in short, everything took its usual course. After all this he picked up the portrait of his German wife who had died some twenty years earlier, and began to appeal to her plaintively: 'Will you ever forgive me?' In general he seemed very confused. We even had a little something to drink to drown our sorrow. Soon, however, he fell fast asleep. The next morning he tied his cravat in masterly fashion and dressed with great care, frequently going up to the mirror to have a look at himself. He sprinkled his handkerchief with cologne, only a few drops, but, upon catching sight of Varvara Petrovna through his window, he quickly took out another handkerchief and hid the perfumed one under his pillow.

'That's splendid!' replied Varvara Petrovna upon hearing his consent. 'In the first place, it shows noble determination; secondly, you've heeded the voice of reason which you rarely do in your personal affairs. But there's no reason to hurry,' she added, glancing at the knot of his white cravat. 'For the time being, don't say anything, and I'll keep quiet too. Your birthday is approaching; I'll bring her with me to see you then. Give us evening tea and, please, no wine or refreshments. I'll make all the arrangements myself. Invite your friends—no, we'll confer on the selection. The evening before you and she will talk it over if necessary; at your party we won't actually announce or publicize the betrothal, merely hint at it or indicate as much, without any formality. Then the wedding will take place about two weeks later, with as little fanfare as possible... In fact, you both might want to go away for a while after the wedding, even to Moscow, for example. Perhaps I'll go with you, too... The main thing is, keep quiet until then.'

Stepan Trofimovich was astonished. He tried to say that he couldn't behave that way, that he had to talk it all over with his fiancée, but Varvara Petrovna shouted at him in great irritation:

'What on earth for? In the first place, nothing may come of it...'

'What do you mean?' muttered the suitor, absolutely dumbfounded.

'It just may not. I still have to see... But it will all come to pass just as I've said, don't you worry. I'll prepare her myself. There's no reason for you to do it. Everything that needs to be said and done will be; there's no reason for you to meddle. For what purpose? In what role? Don't go and see her and don't write her any letters. And don't breathe a word about it, I beg you. I'll keep quiet too.'

She positively refused to explain it any further and left, obviously upset. Apparently Stepan Trofimovich's excessive willingness had startled her. Alas, he really didn't understand his situation, and the matter still didn't present itself to him from certain other points of view. On the contrary, he had adopted a new tone, sort of triumphant, even frivolous. He was swaggering.

'I like that!' he exclaimed, stopping in front of me, arms outspread. 'Did you hear that? She's trying to arrange it so I'm the one who refuses in the end. Why I can lose my patience too and... refuse! "Stay here," she says. "There's no reason for you to go and see her." But I ask you, why is it essential that I marry? Simply because this ridiculous fantasy has occurred to her? I'm a serious man, and may choose not to submit to the idle fantasies of an eccentric woman! I have responsibilities to my son and... and to myself! I'm making a sacrifice—doesn't she realize that? I may even have consented because I've become bored with life and it's all the same to me. But she can irritate me and then it may no longer be all the same; I'll get offended and refuse. *Et enfin, le ridicule...* What will they say at the club? What will... Liputin say? "Perhaps nothing will come of it"—what a thing to say! That's the limit! That's... what can one say? *Je suis un forçat,*[1] *un Badinguet,** un* man pushed to the wall!...'

And at the same time a kind of capricious complacency, something frivolously flippant could be discerned amidst all these plaintive exclamations. That evening we had a few more drinks together.

[1] I'm a convict

CHAPTER 3

Another man's sins

I.

ABOUT a week went by and things became rather more complicated.

I'll note in passing that during this unhappy week I had to endure a great deal of anguish while remaining in almost constant attendance on my affianced friend and serving as his closest confidant. He was oppressed by shame more than anything, even though we saw almost no one throughout the whole week and remained entirely alone; but he felt shame even in my presence, to such an extent that the more he revealed, the more annoyed he was with me afterwards. With his usual mistrustfulness he suspected that everyone in town already knew everything; he was afraid to show himself not only at the club, but even in his own circle. He even went out for a stroll, his regular constitutional, only during twilight hours, when it was already quite dark.

A week passed and he still didn't know whether or not he was betrothed; there was no way he could find out for sure, no matter how hard he tried. He still hadn't encountered his fiancée; in fact, he didn't know whether she was his fiancée. He didn't even know whether there was anything to the whole affair! For some reason Varvara Petrovna categorically refused to receive him. In reply to one of his first letters to her (and he wrote many), she asked him plainly to spare her from having to engage in any communication with him for a while, since she was so very busy. And, while she had so much important information to convey to him, she was deliberately waiting until such time as she was less busy; then 'in good time' she would let him know when to come and see her. She promised to return his letters unopened because it was 'mere self-indulgence'. I read this note myself; he showed it to me.

However, all this rudeness and vagueness were nothing compared to his chief worry. This worry tormented him exceedingly and relentlessly; he grew thinner and his spirits sagged. It was something he was more ashamed of than anything else, something he didn't even want to discuss with me; on the contrary, whenever it came up, he lied and prevaricated like a little boy. Meanwhile he sent for me every day; he couldn't stand to be without me for more than two hours; he needed me as one needs water to drink or air to breathe.

Such behaviour was somewhat wounding to my own pride. It goes without saying that I'd long since guessed this great secret of his and had seen right through it. It was my own most deeply held conviction at the time that the revelation of this secret, this chief worry of Stepan Trofimovich, wouldn't have redounded to his honour, and therefore, still a young man, I was somewhat indignant at the coarseness of his feelings and the ugliness of his suspicions. In the heat of the moment and, I must confess, as a result of feeling fed up being his confidant, I may have placed too much blame on him. In my callousness I forced him to make a complete confession to me, although I too recognized that it might be somewhat difficult for him to admit certain things. He also saw right through me, that is, he clearly realized that I understood him completely and was angry with him; and he was angry with me both because I was angry with him and because I understood him completely. My irritation may have been petty and ridiculous; but mutual isolation can sometimes be extremely detrimental to genuine friendship. From one point of view he had a clear understanding of several aspects of his situation and even expatiated rather precisely on those points he didn't think necessary to conceal.

'Oh, she wasn't always like this!' he used to say about Varvara Petrovna. 'She wasn't like this when we used to talk... Do you know, she could still talk in those days? Can you imagine that she used to have ideas, her own ideas? Now it's all changed! She says that was all old-fashioned nonsense! She despises the past... Now she might be some bailiff or steward, embittered and always angry...'

'Why on earth is she angry now, when you've agreed to her request?' I inquired.

He gave me a knowing look.

'*Cher ami*, if I hadn't consented, she'd have been terribly angry, ter-ri-bly! But still not so angry as she is now I have consented.'

He was very pleased with this turn of phrase and we finished off a bottle of wine between us that evening. But it lasted only a short time; by the next day he was more horrid and gloomy than ever.

But most of all I was annoyed at him because he couldn't even make up his mind to pay the requisite call on the Drozdovs who'd just arrived, in order to renew their acquaintance, which apparently they were eager for, since they kept asking after him; he too worried about it almost every day. He talked about Lizaveta Nikolaevna with a kind of ecstasy that I found totally inexplicable. Undoubtedly he remembered her as a child whom he'd loved at one time; but, besides that, he imagined for some reason that in her company he'd suddenly find relief from all his torments and would even resolve all his most salient doubts. In the person of Lizaveta Nikolaevna he expected to encounter some extraordinary being. But he still didn't go to see her, though he planned to do so every day. The point was that I myself desperately wanted to be presented and introduced to her, and I could only rely upon Stepan Trofimovich to do it. My frequent meetings with her at the time—only on the street, of course, when she was out for a ride, wearing her riding-habit, astride a handsome horse, accompanied by her so-called relative, a handsome officer, the late General Drozdov's nephew—had made an enormous impression on me. My infatuation lasted only a moment, and I soon came to realize the impossibility of fulfilling my dream; but even though it lasted only a moment, it was still real. So you can imagine how indignant I sometimes felt with my poor friend who stubbornly insisted on his isolation.

All the members of our circle had been officially warned from the start that Stepan Trofimovich wouldn't be receiving guests for some time and had asked to be left in peace. He insisted that a notice be circulated to that effect, even though I advised him against it. It was I, too, who made the rounds, visiting each one at his request and informing them that Varvara Petrovna had entrusted some urgent task to our 'old man' (as we used to refer to Stepan Trofimovich among ourselves), namely, to organize some correspondence stretching over many years; as a result, he'd locked himself up, I was assisting him with the task, and so on and so forth. Liputin was the only one I didn't get to see, and I kept putting it off—to tell the truth, I was afraid to see him. I knew in advance he wouldn't believe a word I said, and would certainly imagine there was a secret involved which was being concealed from him alone. And, as soon as I left, he'd immediately go running through town to find out what it was and spread rumours all around. Just as I was imagining all this, I happened to meet him on the street. It turned out he'd already found out about everything from someone else whom I'd just informed. But, strange to say, he wasn't at all curious about Stepan Trofimovich and asked no questions; on the contrary, he interrupted me as I was about to apologize for not visiting him sooner, and immediately switched to another topic. It's true he'd acquired quite a bit of news to share; he was in a state of extreme agitation and was overjoyed to hit on someone who'd listen to him. He began talking about recent events in town, the arrival of the new governor's wife 'with her fresh topics of conversation', the opposition that was already forming in the club, all the shouting about new ideas, and how it had infected all of them, and so on and so forth. He carried on talking for about a quarter of an hour and it was all so amusing I was unable to tear myself away. Although I couldn't stand him, I must confess he had the gift of making one listen to him, especially when he was very angry about something. The man, in my opinion, was a born spy. At any moment he knew the latest news and all the ins and outs of our town, especially the unsavoury bits, and one couldn't help being amazed at how he took to heart things that sometimes didn't concern him in the least. It always seemed to me that his main character trait was envy. That evening when I told Stepan Trofimovich about my meeting and conversation with Liputin earlier that morning, he grew very agitated and, to my great surprise, posed the following bizarre question: 'Does Liputin know or not?' I attempted to argue that there was no way he could have found out, and no one he could have found out from; but Stepan Trofimovich stood his ground.

'Well, believe it or not,' he concluded unexpectedly at last, 'I'm convinced that he not only knows all the details of our situation already, but that he even knows something more, something neither you nor I know yet, and perhaps will never find out, or if we do, it'll be too late, when there's no turning back!...'

I remained silent, but these words intimated a great deal. For five days afterwards we didn't say another word about Liputin; but it was clear to me that Stepan Trofimovich very much regretted having expressed such suspicions and having said so much.

2.

One morning—some seven or eight days after Stepan Trofimovich had consented to be married—around eleven o'clock or so, as I was hurrying over as usual to see my grieving friend, I had an adventure along the way.

I met Karmazinov, 'the great writer', as Liputin called him. I'd been reading Karmazinov since I was a child. His stories and tales are familiar to the whole previous generation, as well as to the present one. I'd delighted in them; they were the joy of my childhood and youth. Afterwards I cooled somewhat towards him; I didn't like his recent, more tendentious works as much as I did his early ones which contained so much pure poetry; as for his latest works, I really didn't like them at all.

Generally speaking, if I may be so bold as to express my own opinion on so delicate a matter, all these gentlemen of mediocre talent, usually hailed during their own lifetime as geniuses, not only vanish without trace and fade from human memory as soon as they die, but sometimes, even during their lifetime, as soon as a new generation emerges to replace theirs—these men are forgotten and neglected by everyone incredibly quickly. This seems to occur among

Russians all of a sudden, like a change of scenery on stage. Oh, it's not the same with all your Pushkins, Gogols, Molières, Voltaires—those who had something new to say! It's also true that the gentlemen of mediocre talent have usually written themselves out in the most pitiful fashion by the time they reach venerable old age, though often they themselves don't realize it. It frequently turns out that a writer who's said to have very profound ideas, and who's expected to exert a very serious influence on the development of society, in the end reveals such triviality and insipidity in his fundamental themes that no one regrets the fact that he managed to write himself out so soon. But grey-haired old men don't notice this and get angry. Their vanity, especially towards the end of their careers, sometimes takes on astonishing proportions. God knows who they begin to take themselves for—for gods, at the least. It was said of Karmazinov that he valued his connections with powerful people and with high society more than he did his own soul. They said he would meet you, treat you kindly, flatter you, charm you with his generosity, especially if he needed you for something, and, of course, if you came to him properly recommended. But at the first sight of a prince, a countess, or someone he held in awe, he'd consider it his sacred obligation to drop you with the most offensive disregard, like a splinter of wood or a fly, right then and there, even before you'd left his presence; and he seriously regarded this as the highest and most appropriate form of behaviour. In spite of his absolute restraint and total mastery of good manners, they say his vanity can easily reach a hysterical pitch and that he can never conceal his author's irritability, even in those circles of society where there's little interest in literature. If by chance someone were to surprise him by indifference, he'd be mortally wounded and try to take revenge.

About a year ago I read a journal article* of his that had terrible pretensions to the most naïve poetry as well as psychology. He was describing the loss of a steamer somewhere off the coast of England, which he'd actually witnessed; he watched people being saved from drowning and dead bodies being taken from the water. The entire article, rather long-winded and verbose, was written with the sole aim of showing off. Reading between the lines it declared: 'Take an interest in me; see what a fine fellow I was during these moments. What do you care about the sea, the storm, the cliffs, or the ship's wreckage? After all, I've described it all very well with my mighty pen. Why are you staring at this drowned corpse holding a dead child in its lifeless arms? Look at me instead; see how I couldn't stand this spectacle and had to avert my eyes. Look how I've turned my back on it; now I'm so horrified I can't look back at it; I'm even closing my eyes—now then, isn't this all very interesting?' When I shared my opinion of Karmazinov's article with Stepan Trofimovich, he agreed with me.

When rumours began circulating among us about Karmazinov's imminent arrival, of course I desperately wanted to have a look at him, and if possible, make his acquaintance. I knew I could arrange it through Stepan Trofimovich; they'd been friends at one time. And then all of a sudden I met him at the crossroads. I recognized him at once; he'd been pointed out to me some three days earlier when he drove past with the governor's wife in a carriage.

He was a rather short, prim old man, though no more than fifty-five, with a rather ruddy complexion and thick grey locks of hair that had strayed from beneath his round, cylindrical hat and curled around his small, clean pink ears. His clean little face was not all that handsome, with its thin, long, cunningly pursed lips, its somewhat fleshy nose, and its sharp, clever little eyes. He was dressed in somewhat outdated clothes, the kind of cloak that might be worn in Switzerland or northern Italy at that time of year. In any case, all his accessories—cuff-links, collars, buttons, a tortoiseshell lorgnette on a thin, black ribbon, a little ring—were those worn by people of irreproachably good taste. I'm sure that in the summer he wears colourful prunella shoes trimmed with mother-of-pearl buttons. When we met, he was standing at the crossroads, looking around very carefully. Noticing that I was regarding him with curiosity, he asked in a mellifluous, though rather shrill voice:

'Could you possibly tell me the shortest way to Bykova Street?'

'Bykova Street? Why, it's just here, very close by,' I exclaimed in great excitement. 'Go straight along this street and then take the second turning on the left.'

'I'm very grateful to you.'

Damn it all: it seems I came over shy and appeared servile! He noticed it immediately, and, of course, understood everything at once, that is, he understood that I knew who he was, that I'd read his works and had revered him since childhood, and that now I was shy and appeared servile. He smiled, nodded to me once again, and went off in the direction I'd indicated. I don't know why but I turned around and followed him; I don't know why but I trailed behind him for some ten paces. Suddenly he stopped again.

'And could you possibly tell me where the nearest cab stand is?' he shouted to me again.

A nasty shout; a nasty voice!

'Cab stand? The nearest cab stand... is over there by the cathedral; there's always a cab waiting,' I said and nearly turned to summon a cab. I suspect it's precisely what he expected me to do. Naturally I came to my senses at once and stopped, but he noticed my movement and followed me with that nasty smile of his. Then something happened that I'll never forget.

Suddenly he dropped a small bag which he was holding in his left hand. Actually, it wasn't a bag, but a kind of case, more like a small briefcase, or to be exact, a small handbag, like an old-fashioned lady's handbag; as a matter of fact, I really don't know what it was; all I know is, I rushed to pick it up.

I'm absolutely convinced I didn't pick it up, but I made an initial movement that was incontestable; I was unable to conceal it and blushed like a fool. That cunning man immediately exploited the situation for all it was worth.

'No, don't. Allow me,' he said charmingly, that is, when he realized I wasn't going to pick up his handbag; he picked it up, as though forestalling me, nodded once more, and set off on his way, leaving me feeling like an idiot. I might as

well have picked it up myself. For five minutes or so I felt
absolutely disgraced once and for all; but, as I approached
Stepan Trofimovich's house, I suddenly burst out laughing.
The encounter seemed so amusing that I immediately decided to entertain Stepan Trofimovich with the story and
even act the whole scene out for him.

3.

But this time, to my astonishment, I found him extraordinarily changed. It's true, he pounced on me with unusual
eagerness as soon as I entered, and began listening to me,
but with so absent-minded an expression that he seemed at
first not to understand a word I said. But as soon as I
mentioned the name Karmazinov, he flew into a terrible rage.

'Don't talk about him! Don't even mention his name!' he
cried, almost in a frenzy. 'Here, look at this! Read it! Go
on, read it!'

He opened a drawer and tossed three small pieces of paper
on to the table; they were written hastily in pencil and were
from Varvara Petrovna. The first note was dated two days
before, the second the day before, and the last had just
arrived, about an hour before. The contents were trivial;
they all concerned Karmazinov and reflected Varvara Petrovna's vain and ambitious apprehensiveness that Karmazinov might forget to pay her a visit. Here's the first note
written two days before (there was probably one three days
before, and perhaps another even four days before):

If he finally honours you with a visit today, don't say a word about
me, I beg you. Not the slightest hint. Don't start talking about
me and don't remind him of me.

V. S.

Yesterday's note:

If he finally decides to visit you this morning, it seems to me the
most dignified thing would be not to receive him at all. That's
what I think; I don't know what you think.

V. S.

Today's note, the last one:

I'm sure there's a cartload of rubbish in your room and that it reeks of tobacco smoke. I'm sending Marya and Fomushka over; they'll clean it all up in half an hour. Don't you interfere; sit in the kitchen while they're working. I'm sending you a Bukhara rug and two Chinese vases: I've been planning to give them to you for some time. I'm also lending you my Teniers* (for a while). Put the vases on the window-sill, and hang the Teniers to the right over the portrait of Goethe, where it'll be more conspicuous and it's always light in the morning. If he finally appears, receive him with utmost courtesy, but try to talk about trifles, something erudite, and behave as if you'd just parted yesterday. Not a word about me. Perhaps I'll look in on you this evening.

V. S.

P. S. If he doesn't come today, he won't come at all.

I read the notes and was amazed that he was so agitated over such nonsense. Looking at him enquiringly I suddenly noticed that while I was reading he'd managed to replace yesterday's white cravat with a red one. His hat and walk-ing-stick lay on the table. He was pale, his hands trembling.

'I don't care about her anxieties!' he cried furiously in reply to my enquiring glance. '*Je m'en fiche*! She has the gall to get excited about Karmazinov, while she doesn't even answer my letters! Here, here's one of my letters she sent back unopened yesterday; it's right here on the table under-neath that book, *L'homme qui rit*.* What do I care if she's worried about her darling Ni-ko-len-ka? *Je m'en fiche et je proclame ma liberté. Au diable le Karmazinoff! Au diable la Lembke!*[1] I've hidden the vases in the hallway, the Teniers in the chest of drawers, and demanded she receive me at once. Do you hear: demanded! I've sent her the same kind of note, written in pencil, unsealed, by Nastasya, and now I'm waiting. I'd like Darya Pavlovna to say it in her own words, before the face of God, or at least before you. *Vous me seconderez, n'est-ce pas, comme ami et témoin.*[2] I don't want

---

[1] I don't give a damn and I proclaim my freedom. The devil take Karmazinov! The devil take that Lembke woman!

[2] You'll support me, won't you, as a friend and a witness?

to blush; I don't want to lie; I don't want any secrets and I won't let there be any in this affair! Let them confess everything to me, openly, sincerely, nobly, and then... then, perhaps, I'll astonish their entire generation by my generosity!... Am I a scoundrel or not, my dear sir?' he concluded suddenly, looking at me menacingly, as if I were the one who considered him a scoundrel.

I suggested he take a drink of water; I'd never seen him in such a state. All the time he spoke he rushed from one corner of the room to another, and then suddenly stopped in front of me in an extraordinary attitude.

'Do you really think,' he began again with extreme hauteur, surveying me from head to toe, 'do you really suppose that I, Stepan Verkhovensky, won't be able to find sufficient moral strength to collect my belongings, my beggar's bundle, and, hoisting it on to my feeble shoulders, walk out of these gates and disappear from here for ever, when my own honour and my great principle of independence are at stake? It won't be the first time Stepan Verkhovensky has had to overcome despotism with magnanimity, even though it's the despotism of an insane woman, that is, the most offensive and heartless kind of despotism that can exist on earth, in spite of the fact that you, my dear sir, have just allowed yourself to smile at my words! Oh, so you don't believe I could summon sufficient magnanimity to end my life as a tutor in some merchant's house or die of starvation in a ditch! Answer me, answer me at once: do you believe me or not?'

I deliberately remained silent. I pretended that I couldn't offend him with a negative answer, yet couldn't answer in the affirmative. In all this irritation of his there was something that really did offend me, but not personally. Oh, no! But... I'll explain that later.

Then he grew pale.

'Perhaps you're bored with me, Mr G——v,'* (that's my name), 'and you'd like to... stop coming to see me?' he asked in the same tone of pallid composure that usually preceded some unusual outburst. I jumped up in alarm; at the same moment Nastasya entered and silently handed Stepan Trofimovich a piece of paper on which something was written in pencil. He glanced at it and tossed it to me. On the paper there were only three words written in Varvara Petrovna's hand: 'Stay at home.'

Stepan Trofimovich silently grabbed his hat and walking-stick and quickly left the room; I followed him automatically. Suddenly voices and sounds of someone's rapid footsteps were heard in the corridor. He stopped as if struck by lightning.

'It's Liputin and I'm lost!' he whispered, seizing my arm.

At that moment Liputin entered the room.

4.

I didn't know why he should be lost on account of Liputin, but I didn't attach much significance to his words; I ascribed it all to his nerves. Nevertheless, his alarm was extraordinary and I decided to keep a close eye on him.

But Liputin's appearance upon entering the room indicated that this time he had a genuine right to visit despite all prohibitions. He brought an unfamiliar person with him who must have been a new arrival in town. In response to a blank stare from the terrified Stepan Trofimovich, he immediately cried aloud:

'I've brought you a visitor, a very special one! I've taken the liberty to break in upon your solitude. Mr Kirillov, a most notable civil engineer. But the main thing is, he knows your son, the honourable Peter Stepanovich. They're very close friends, and he has a message from him. He's just arrived.'

'You added the part about a message,' the guest remarked sharply. 'There isn't any message, but it's true I know young Verkhovensky. I parted from him in Kh—v province about ten days ago.'

Stepan Trofimovich shook hands automatically and motioned to them to sit down; he looked at me, then Liputin, and suddenly, as if recovering his senses, sat down himself. He was still holding his hat and cane, but didn't notice that.

'Oh, but you were just about to go out! I was told you were indisposed as a result of your work.'

'Yes, I'm not feeling well and was just about to go out for a walk; I...' Stepan Trofimovich halted, rapidly tossed his hat and cane on to the sofa and—blushed.

In the meantime I hurriedly examined the visitor. He was a young man, about twenty-seven years old, decently dressed, well-proportioned, slender, with dark hair; he had a pale, somewhat slovenly cast to his face, and black lustre-less eyes. He seemed rather pensive and absent-minded; he spoke brusquely and rather ungrammatically; he ordered his words somewhat strangely, and became flustered if he had to compose a longish sentence. Liputin clearly noticed Stepan Trofimovich's extraordinary alarm and was apparently pleased. He sat down on a wicker chair which he placed almost in the centre of the room so that he could be the same distance away from both host and guest, who sat facing each other on two sofas. His sharp eyes darted inquisitively around the room.

'I... haven't seen Petrushka for some time... Did you meet him abroad?' Stepan Trofimovich muttered awkwardly to his visitor.

'Both here and abroad.'

'Mr Kirillov—Aleksei Nilych—has just come from abroad after an absence of about four years,' Liputin joined in. 'He was travelling to acquire advanced training in his speciality and has come here hoping to secure a position on the construction of our railway bridge; now he's waiting for an answer. He's acquainted with the Drozdovs and Lizaveta Nikolaevna through Peter Stepanovich.'

The engineer sat there as if bristling, and listened with awkward impatience. He seemed angry about something.

'He's also acquainted with Nikolai Vsevolodovich.'

'You know Nikolai Vsevolodovich too?' Stepan Trofimovich enquired.

'Yes, I do.'

'I... haven't seen Petrushka for a very long time and... hardly have the right to call myself his father... *c'est le mot*; I... how did you leave him?'

'I just left him... he'll be here soon,' Mr Kirillov replied in haste once again to be done with it. He was definitely angry.

'He's coming! At last I... you see, it's been so long since I've seen Petrushka!' said Stepan Trofimovich, and got bogged down in his own sentence. 'I'm now waiting for my poor son before whom... oh, whom I have wronged! That is, I mean that when I left him in Petersburg, I... in a word, I didn't think much of him, *quelque chose dans ce genre*. He's a nervous lad, you know, very sensitive and... timid. Before he went to bed he'd bow down to the ground and make the sign of the cross over his pillow, so he wouldn't die during the night... *je m'en souviens. Enfin*, he had no aesthetic sense whatever, that is, nothing sublime, nothing fundamental, no germ of any future idea... *c'était comme un petit idiot*.[1] But I seem to be all mixed up. Excuse me, I... you've come upon me at...'

'Are you serious about making the cross over his pillow?' the engineer enquired suddenly with a special kind of curiosity.

'Yes, he made the sign of the cross...'

'All right, I just wanted to know. Go on.'

Stepan Trofimovich looked enquiringly at Liputin.

'I'm very grateful for your visit, but, I confess, right now I'm not... in a state to... Allow me to ask where you're staying?'

'In Filippov's house on Bogoyavlenskaya Street.'

'Ah, that's also where Shatov lives,' I observed involuntarily.

'Precisely, in the very same house,' Liputin exclaimed, 'but Shatov lives upstairs, in the attic, while he's staying down below with Captain Lebyadkin. He knows Shatov and his wife, too. He became a close friend of hers abroad.'

'*Comment*! Do you really know anything about the unhappy marriage *de ce pauvre ami* and that woman?' cried Stepan Trofimovich, suddenly carried away by emotion. 'You're the first person I've met who knows her personally, if only...'

'What nonsense!' interrupted the engineer, flushing all over. 'How you exaggerate, Liputin! I've never seen Shatov's

---

[1] I remember. In short . . . he was like a little idiot.

wife—well, only once, at a distance, never close up... I do know Shatov. Why do you make up such things?'

He turned on the sofa sharply, grabbed his hat, then put it down again, and settled back as before; with some kind of challenge he fixed his flashing black eyes on Stepan Trofimovich. I couldn't understand such strange irritability.

'Excuse me,' Stepan Trofimovich observed imposingly, 'I understand that this may be a very delicate matter...'

'It's not a delicate matter at all, but somewhat embarrassing; I didn't say "nonsense" to you, but to Liputin, because he exaggerates so. Im sorry if you thought it was meant for you. I know Shatov, but I don't know his wife at all... not at all!'

'I understand, I understand, and if I insisted, it's only because I'm so fond of our poor dear friend, *notre irascible ami*, and have always been very interested... In my opinion that man has altered his former ideas too abruptly—perhaps they were a young man's ideas, but they were correct. Now he's shouting so many different things about *notre sainte Russie*, that for some time I've been attributing this change in his organism—I don't want to call it anything else—to some violent upheaval in his family life, that is, his unhappy marriage. Having studied my poor Russia, I know it like the back of my hand; I've devoted my entire life to the Russian people. I can assure you that he doesn't know the Russian people, moreover...'

'I don't know the Russian people either and... I've no time to study them!' the engineer interrupted again and turned sharply on the sofa. Stepan Trofimovich halted in the middle of his speech.

'He's studying, he's studying,' Liputin interpolated. 'He's already begun studying and is writing a very interesting article about the reasons for the increasing number of suicides in Russia, and the causes leading to an increase or decrease of suicides in society in general. He's reached some astonishing conclusions.'

The engineer became terribly agitated.

'You have no right whatever,' he muttered angrily. 'It's not really an article. I wouldn't do anything so stupid. I just happened to ask you about it in confidence. It's not an article at all; I won't publish it; you have no right...'

Liputin was obviously enjoying himself.

'I'm sorry, perhaps I made a mistake in calling your literary work an article. He's merely collecting observations; he's not dealing with the essence of the problem, or, so to speak, its moral aspect, at all; he even rejects morality completely, and supports the latest principle of total destruction on behalf of the ultimate good. He's demanding more than a hundred million heads for the establishment of good common sense in Europe, far more than were called for at the last peace congress.* In this sense Aleksei Nilych has gone further than all the rest.'

The engineer listened with a contemptuous and pallid smile. They were all silent for about half a minute.

'This is all so stupid, Liputin,' Mr Kirillov said at last with some dignity. 'If I happened to say a few things, and you seized on them, I can't help it. But you don't have the right, because I never say anything to anybody. I despise conversation... If one has convictions, it's clear to me... but what you did is stupid. I don't argue about those points when everything's been resolved. I can't stand such arguments. I never want to participate in them...'

'Perhaps you're right,' Stepan Trofimovich said, unable to restrain himself.

'I beg your pardon, but I'm not angry with anyone here,' the guest continued quickly and with feeling. 'For four years I've seen very few people... I've spoken very little for the last four years, and have tried not to meet people—for reasons which don't concern anyone—for four years. Liputin found out about this and is laughing. I understand and pay no attention. I'm not easily offended, only annoyed at his taking such liberties. But if I choose not to expound my ideas to you', he concluded unexpectedly, scanning us all with his resolute gaze, 'it's not because I'm afraid you'll inform on me to the authorities. That's not it. Please, don't imagine anything of the kind...'

No one made any reply to this. We merely looked at one another. Even Liputin forgot to snigger.

'Gentlemen, I'm very sorry,' Stepan Trofimovich said, getting up from the sofa resolutely, 'but I'm feeling unwell and upset. Excuse me.'

'Ah, he's telling us to leave.' Mr Kirillov caught on suddenly, picking up his cap. 'It's a good thing you said so because I'm very absent-minded.'

He stood up and with a good-natured expression went up to Stepan Trofimovich with his hand extended.

'I'm sorry I came when you weren't well.'

'I wish you every success here among us,' Stepan Trofimovich replied, shaking his hand generously and without haste. 'I understand that if, in your own words, you lived abroad for so long, shunning people for your own reasons, and—if you've forgotten Russia, then, of course, you must regard us genuine Russians with some astonishment, as we regard you. *Mais cela passera.*[1] There's only one thing that troubles me: you want to build a bridge here, yet at the same time you say you support the principle of universal destruction. They won't let you build our bridge!'

'What? What did you say? Oh, hell!' the astonished Kirillov cried and suddenly burst into a cheerful ringing laugh. For a moment his face assumed a most childlike expression that seemed to suit him very well. Liputin rubbed his hands in glee at Stepan Trofimovich's successful witticism. All the while I kept wondering why it was that Stepan Trofimovich had been so afraid of Liputin and why, when he first heard his voice, he cried, 'I'm lost!'

5·

We were all standing at the front door. It was the moment when host and guests hurriedly exchange their last, most cordial words, and then part happily.

'It's all because he's so gloomy today,' Liputin observed suddenly as he was leaving the room, and, so to speak, in passing. 'It's because of the row he had with Captain Lebyadkin earlier over his sister. Every day, morning and evening, Captain Lebyadkin thrashes that lovely little sister

---

[1] But that will pass.

of his, her that's deranged, with a whip, a real Cossack whip. That's why Aleksei Nilych has taken up residence in one wing of that house, so's to have nothing to do with it. Well, goodbye.'

'His sister? His sick sister? With a whip?' Stepan Trofimovich cried out, as if he himself had suddenly been thrashed with a whip. 'What sister? Which Lebyadkin?'

His previous alarm returned in an instant.

'Lebyadkin? Oh, he's a retired captain. He used to refer to himself only as a staff-captain before...'

'Oh, what do I care about his rank? What sister? My God... you say, Lebyadkin? There used to be a Lebyadkin living here...'

'That's the one, *our* Lebyadkin, you remember, over at Virginsky's?'

'But wasn't that one caught with counterfeit bills?'

'Now he's come back. He's been here almost three weeks and under the most unusual circumstances.'

'He's a scoundrel!'

'As if there weren't any other scoundrels among us?' Liputin grinned suddenly, as if scrutinizing Stepan Trofimovich with his furtive little eyes.

'Oh, my God, that's not what I meant... although I agree with you completely about that scoundrel, I agree with you. But then what? What were you going on to say?... Undoubtedly you were going to say something else!'

'It's all such nonsense... that is, the captain, to all appearances, left here not because of those counterfeit bills, but simply to find his little sister since she'd apparently taken refuge from him somewhere. Well, now he's brought her back here, and that's the whole story. What exactly are you afraid of, Stepan Trofimovich? Besides, I'm only repeating what he says when he's drunk; when he's sober, he doesn't say anything about it. He's an irritable fellow, and a sort of military aesthete, as it were, but with very bad taste. And this sister of his is not only insane, but lame as well. It seems she was seduced by someone, as a result of which for many years, Mr Lebyadkin has been receiving a yearly allowance from her seducer as compensation for the injury to his honour, at least that's what emerges from his chatter—but in my opinion, it's merely drunken talk. He's simply boasting. Besides, this sort of thing is usually settled much more cheaply. But it's absolutely certain he does have some money; a week and a half ago he was walking around barefoot, and now, as I myself have seen, he's got his hands on hundreds of roubles. His little sister suffers fits almost daily; she shrieks, while he "keeps her in line" with his whip. "You have to instil respect", he says, "in a woman." Well, I don't understand how Shatov can go on living near them. Aleksei Nilych stayed with them only three days; he'd known them in Petersburg. But now he lives in a separate wing because of the disturbance.'

'Is all this true?' asked Stepan Trofimovich, turning to the engineer.

'You talk too much, Liputin,' Kirillov muttered angrily.

'Mysteries, secrets! Why are there suddenly so many mysteries and secrets?' Stepan Trofimovich cried, unable to restrain himself.

The engineer frowned, blushed, shrugged his shoulders, and was about to leave the room.

'Aleksei Nilych even took away his whip, broke it, and threw it out the window; they had a big quarrel,' added Liputin.

'Why are you talking like this, Liputin? It's stupid. Why?' asked Aleksei Nilych, turning around in a flash.

'Why hide, out of modesty, the noblest impulses of one's soul, I mean your soul, since I'm not talking about myself.'

'How stupid this all is... and completely unnecessary... Lebyadkin is stupid and totally worthless—no use to the cause and—totally pernicious. Why do you carry on so about all these things? I'm leaving.'

'Ah, what a pity!' Liputin exclaimed with a blatant grin. 'Otherwise, Stepan Trofimovich, I'd have amused you with another little anecdote. I even came here with the intention of telling you it, but you've probably heard it already. Well, next time, perhaps, since Aleksei Nilych is in such a hurry... Goodbye. The anecdote concerns Varvara Petrovna. She did something very amusing the day before yesterday; she sent for me deliberately; it's simply a riot. Goodbye.'

But Stepan Trofimovich had seized hold of him: he grabbed him by the shoulders, pushed him firmly back into the room, and sat him down on a chair. Liputin was actually a little scared.

'What's all this?' he began, cautiously regarding Stepan Trofimovich from his chair. 'She summoned me suddenly and asked me to tell her "in confidence" what I thought: was Nikolai Vsevolodovich in his right mind or not? Isn't that astonishing?'

'You're out of your mind!' Stepan Trofimovich muttered, and all of a sudden flew into a rage. 'Liputin, you know all too well that you came here simply to tell me that despicable story and... something even worse!'

In an instant I recalled his previous assumption that Liputin not only knew more about this affair than we did, but knew something else which we'd never find out.

'For heaven's sake, Stepan Trofimovich!' Liputin muttered as if in mortal terror, 'for heaven's sake...'

'Silence! Now begin. I beg you, Mr Kirillov, to return and stay here. Please! Sit down. And you, Liputin, tell us straight and plainly... and no excuses.'

'Had I known this would upset you so, I'd never have begun... But I thought you already knew everything from Varvara Petrovna!'

'You didn't think that at all! Begin, begin at once, I tell you!'

'Just do me a favour, sit yourself down, otherwise I'll be sitting and you'll be... running around in such agitation. That wouldn't do.'

Stepan Trofimovich contained himself and sank majestically into an armchair. The engineer stared sullenly at the floor. Liputin looked at them with immense enjoyment.

'Well, how shall I begin? I'm so confused...'

6.

'Suddenly, the day before yesterday, she sent one of her servants asking me to come at twelve o'clock the next day. Can you imagine? I dropped everything and yesterday, at twelve o'clock sharp, I called on her. I was shown right into the drawing-room; I waited a minute or so—then she came in. She asked me to take a seat and then sat down opposite me. I sat there and could hardly believe it: you know how she used to treat me! She began at once without beating around the bush, like she usually does. "You recall", she says, "that four years ago when Nikolai Vsevolodovich was ill, he committed several strange acts which confounded the entire town until they were explained. One of these acts concerned you personally. Then, after he recovered, Nikolai Vsevolodovich called upon you at my request. I also know that he'd spoken with you several times before. Tell me frankly and openly how you..." (here she became a little confused)"—how you found Nikolai Vsevolodovich?... How did he strike you in general?... What opinion of him did you form at the time and... what opinion of him do you have now?..."

'Here she became completely confused; she even paused for one entire minute and flushed suddenly. I was alarmed. She began again, not exactly in an emotional tone of voice (that doesn't suit her), but in a very impressive one:

' "I want you", she says, "to understand me clearly and without any mistakes," she says. "I've sent for you because I consider you a perceptive and clever individual, capable of making accurate observations." (What compliments!) "Of course", she says, "you'll realize it's a mother speaking... Nikolai Vsevolodovich has experienced several misfortunes and numerous reverses in his life. All that", she says, "could have affected his state of mind. Naturally", she says, "I'm not talking about insanity; that could never be!" (This was said proudly and resolutely.) "But there might be something strange or unusual involved, a peculiar turn of thought, a tendency to a particular point of view." (These were her exact words. I was astonished, Stepan Trofimovich, at the precision with which Varvara Petrovna was able to explain the matter. She's a lady of great intellect!) "At least", she says, "I myself have observed in him a chronic anxiety and a propensity to certain moods. But I'm his mother, whereas you're a stranger; that means, with your intelligence, you're capable of forming a more independent judgement. Finally, I implore you" (that's the word she used, "implore") "to tell me the whole truth, without holding back anything, and if you give me your word never to forget all that I've told you in confidence, you may expect me to display my absolute and eternal gratitude to you on every possible occasion." Well, there you have it!'

'You... you've shocked me so...' Stepan Trofimovich muttered, 'I don't believe you...'

'No, observe, just observe,' Liputin cried as if he hadn't even heard Stepan Trofimovich, 'how great her anxiety and worry must have been, for a woman of such eminence to turn to a man like me with such a question, and to stoop to such an extent that she herself was asking me to keep it a secret. What on earth could it mean? Perhaps she's received some unexpected news about Nikolai Vsevolodovich?'

'I don't know... about any news... I haven't seen her for several days, but... I must observe...' muttered Stepan Trofimovich, obviously still trying to gain command of his thoughts, 'I must observe, Liputin, that if all this was conveyed to you in confidence, and now, in front of all these people, you...'

'In absolute confidence! May the Lord strike me dead if I... And as for talking about it here... well, what of it? We're not strangers, are we? Even if we include Aleksei Nilych?'

'I don't share your outlook; undoubtedly we three will keep it a secret, but it's you, the fourth, I'm afraid of. I don't trust you at all!'

'What do you mean by that? My interest is greater than anyone else's, since I've been promised eternal gratitude! As a matter of fact, I'd like to point to a very strange incident in this connection, more psychological, so to speak, than merely strange. Yesterday evening, under the influence of this conversation with Varvara Petrovna (you can just imagine the impression it made), I turned to Aleksei Nilych with a discreet question: "You", I say, "were previously acquainted with Nikolai Vsevolodovich both in Petersburg and abroad. What do you think", I ask, "of his intellect and abilities?" He replies in his usual laconic manner that he was a man of fine intellect and sound judgement. "Have you ever noticed", I ask, "during the course of years", I ask, "any tendency in his thinking, or peculiar cast of mind, or some kind of, so to speak, as it were, madness?" In a word, I repeated Varvara Petrovna's own question. Imagine: Aleksei Nilych suddenly became pensive and frowned, just as he's doing now. "Yes," he says, "sometimes I thought there was something strange about him." Note that if Aleksei Nilych thought it strange, there really must have been something to it, don't you think?'

'Is that true?' Stepan Trofimovich asked, turning to Aleksei Nilych.

'I'd prefer not to talk about it,' Aleksei Nilych replied, suddenly raising his head, his eyes flashing. 'I wish to contest your right, Liputin. You have no right to involve me in this matter. I didn't state my entire opinion. Although I was acquainted with him in Petersburg, that was a long time ago; and even though I met him again quite recently, I don't really know Nikolai Vsevolodovich very well at all. I ask you to leave me out of it... it's all so much like gossip.'

Liputin threw up his hands with a gesture of persecuted innocence.

'So, I'm a gossip! Perhaps even a spy? It's very well to criticize, Aleksei Nilych, when you want to be left out of it. But Stepan Trofimovich, you wouldn't believe this Captain Lebyadkin. Why, he seems so stupid... it's embarrassing to say how stupid he is. There's a certain Russian comparison for specifying degree. Yet he too considers himself offended by Nikolai Vsevolodovich, even though he admires his wit. "I'm struck", he says, "by this man. A wise serpent" (his own words). And I ask him (still under the influence of yesterday's meeting and after the conversation with Aleksei Nilych): "Well, Captain," I say, "what do you think about it? Is your wise serpent mad or not?" Believe me, it was just as if I'd suddenly struck him from behind with a whip, without his permission. He simply jumps up from his place. "Yes," he says... "yes," he says, "but that", he says, "can't affect his..." He didn't say what it couldn't affect.

Then he becomes sadly pensive, so much so that he sobers up. We were sitting in Filippov's tavern. Only half an hour later he suddenly strikes the table with his fist: "Yes," he says, "maybe he's mad, but that can't affect his...", and once again he didn't say what it couldn't affect. Of course, I'm merely conveying the gist of our conversation, but the meaning is clear; everyone you ask is struck by the same thought, even though it's never entered their minds before: "Yes", they'll say, "he's mad; very clever, but perhaps he's really mad." '

Stepan Trofimovich sat pensively, thinking hard.

'And how does Lebyadkin know?'

'Wouldn't you like to ask Aleksei Nilych about that, since he's just called me a spy. I'm a spy and—I don't know anything, but Aleksei Nilych knows all the details, and keeps his mouth shut.'

'I don't know anything, or very little,' the engineer replied with the same irritation. 'You got Lebyadkin drunk to find out. Then you brought me here to find out more and make me talk. Therefore, you must be a spy!'

'I still haven't got him drunk; he's not worth the money, even with all his secrets. That's what they're worth to me, I don't know about you. On the contrary, he's the one who throws his money about. Twelve days ago he came to ask me for fifteen kopecks; now he's treating me to champagne, not I him. But you've given me an idea; if I have to, I'll get him drunk, precisely to find out, and perhaps I will find out... all your little secrets,' snapped Liputin spitefully.

Stepan Trofimovich looked in bewilderment at the two combatants. They were both giving themselves away, and above all, they were making no bones about it. It occurred to me that Liputin had brought Aleksei Nilych for the express purpose of drawing him into some necessary conversation through a third person, his favourite manœuvre.

'Aleksei Nilych knows Nikolai Vsevolodovich very well,' he continued irritably, 'only he's concealing it. And, as for your question about Captain Lebyadkin, he made his acquaintance before the rest of us, in Petersburg, some five or six years ago, during that little-known period, if one can

express it thus, in Nikolai Vsevolodovich's life before he
decided to honour us with his presence. Our prince, one
must conclude, was surrounding himself at the time with a
rather strange set of acquaintances in Petersburg. That was
when he got to know Aleksei Nilych.'

'Be careful, Liputin, I warn you that Nikolai Vsevolodovich himself was intending to be here soon, and he knows
how to stand up for himself.'

'Why are you warning me? I'm the first one to say he's
a man of the most subtle and exquisite intelligence; yesterday I reassured Varvara Petrovna absolutely to that effect.
"But as for his character," I told her, "I can't vouch for
that." Lebyadkin told her the same thing yesterday: "He's
suffered", he told her, "because of his character." Eh,
Stepan Trofimovich, it's all very well for you to shout about
gossip and spying, but note, that was only after you got it
all out of me, and what's more with such extraordinary
nosiness. But now take Varvara Petrovna; yesterday she got
right to the point. "You", she says, "are an interested party
in this affair; that's why I'm turning to you." I should say
so! What kind of motives did I have for swallowing a
personal insult from his lordship in public? It seems to me
I have reasons apart from gossip to be interested in this
matter. One day he shakes your hand, the next, in return
for your hospitality, he slaps you across the face in front of
everyone, just because he feels like it. It's all due to his life
of ease! The most important thing for all these butterflies
and fighting cocks is the fair sex! These landowners with
their little wings, like cupids of old, these lady-killers *à la*
Pechorin!* It's all very well for you to talk, Stepan Trofimovich, a confirmed bachelor, and to accuse me of being a
scandalmonger before his lordship. But if you were to marry
some pretty young thing, for you're still a very handsome
man, then you too might bolt the door against the prince
and put up barricades round your own house! Here now,
let's suppose that *Mademoiselle* Lebyadkina, the one who
gets thrashed with a whip, were neither mad nor lame; then,
so help me, I'd have thought that she herself had fallen
victim to the passions of our young general, and as a result

Captain Lebyadkin had suffered "a blow to his family honour", as he himself expresses it. But that might contradict his own exquisite taste, not that it would have stopped him. Every berry is worth picking, as long as the mood is right. You talk about rumours I've been spreading; the whole town is talking about it. I merely listen and nod. Nothing wrong in that, is there?'

'The whole town is talking? What about?'

'Why, this Captain Lebyadkin shouts for the whole town to hear when he's drunk; well, isn't that the same as if the whole market-place were talking about it? Why am I to blame? I only take an interest in it among friends, since I still think of myself as being among friends here,' he said, casting us an innocent glance. 'Now something's happened; just listen to this. It turns out that his lordship seems to have sent Captain Lebyadkin three hundred roubles from Switzerland through a certain most honourable young lady, a modest orphan, so to speak, whom it is my privilege to know. But a little later Lebyadkin receives exact information, I won't say from whom, but also from a most honourable person, and consequently, a most reliable one, that a thousand roubles have been sent instead of only three hundred!... That means, Lebyadkin cries, the young lady has made off with seven hundred. He's practically about to summon the police, at least he threatens to do so and spreads it all around town...'

'That's despicable, despicable on your part!' cried the engineer suddenly, jumping up from his chair.

'You yourself are that most honourable person who assured Lebyadkin in Nikolai Vsevolodovich's name that a thousand roubles had been sent instead of three hundred. Why, the captain told me that himself when he was drunk.'

'That's... that's an unfortunate misunderstanding. Someone made a mistake and it seems as if... That's nonsense and you're despicable!'

'I'd like to believe it's nonsense; I listened with great sadness because, say what you will, that most honourable girl is implicated, first of all, in the matter of the seven hundred roubles, and secondly, in her apparently intimate relations with Nikolai Vsevolodovich. His lordship cares nothing about disgracing an honourable girl or dishonouring someone else's wife, as the episode in my own house demonstrated. If some very generous man were to turn up, he'd force him to cover up another man's sins with his own honourable name. That's just what I had to endure; I'm talking about myself...'

'Take care, Liputin!' Stepan Trofimovich said, getting up from his seat and turning pale.

'Don't believe it, don't you believe it! Someone's made a mistake, and Lebyadkin was drunk...' cried the engineer in indescribable anxiety. 'It will all be explained. I can't take any more of this... I think it's all so loathsome. Enough, enough!'

He ran out of the room.

'What are you doing? Wait, I'll go with you!' Liputin cried in alarm, jumping up and running out after Aleksei Nilych.

7.

Stepan Trofimovich stood there for a moment in deep thought, managing to look at me without seeing me; then he picked up his hat and cane and quietly left the room. I went out after him as I had before. As he passed through the gate he noticed that I was following him and said:

'Oh, yes, you can serve as a witness... *de l'accident. Vous m'accompagnerez, n'est-ce pas?*'[1]

'Stepan Trofimovich, are you really going there again? Think what may come of it!'

With a hopeless expression and a pathetic smile—one of shame and absolute despair, but at the same time, one of strange rapture—he stopped for a moment and whispered to me:

'I can't possibly marry to cover up "another man's sins"!'

I was just waiting for him to say that. Finally, those secret words so long concealed from me had been uttered after a whole week of evasion and prevarication. I was absolutely furious:

---

[1] of the incident. You'll accompany me, won't you?

'How can such a filthy, such a... despicable idea occur to you, Stepan Trofimovich—with your enlightened mind and kind heart and... even before you heard it from Liputin?'

He looked at me, but didn't answer; he simply continued on his way. I didn't want to be left behind. I wanted to have my own version to present to Varvara Petrovna. I'd have forgiven him if, in his womanish faint-heartedness, he merely believed Liputin. But now it was clear he'd thought of it himself before hearing it from Liputin; Liputin had merely confirmed his suspicions and thrown oil on the flames. He hadn't hesitated to suspect the girl from the start, even though he had no grounds, not even Liputin's rumours. He explained Varvara Petrovna's despotic actions to himself as a desperate desire to cover up the aristocratic misdeeds of her precious Nicolas by marrying the girl off to an honourable gentleman as soon as possible! I certainly wanted him to be punished for that!

'*O! Dieu qui est si grand et si bon!*[1] Oh, who can comfort me?' he cried, walking another hundred paces or so and then stopping suddenly.

'Let's go home at once and I'll explain it all to you!' I exclaimed, and forced him to turn towards home.

'It's him! Stepan Trofimovich, is it you? Is it?' a fresh, young, shrill voice rang out, like some kind of music close by.

We didn't see anything, but suddenly a young woman on horseback appeared alongside us; it was Lizaveta Nikolaevna Tushina, with her faithful companion. She stopped her horse.

'Come here, come here at once!' she cried loudly and cheerfully. 'I haven't seen him for twelve years, and I recognized him, but he... Don't you know me?'

Stepan Trofimovich took the hand extended to him and graciously kissed it. He looked at her as if he were praying and was unable to utter a word.

'He does recognize me and is pleased to see me! Mavriky Nikolaevich—Maurice—he's delighted to see me! Why

---

[1] Oh God, who is so great and so good!

haven't you been to see us these last two weeks? My aunt's been trying to persuade me that you were ill and were not to be disturbed; but I knew she was lying. I kept stamping my foot and swearing at you, but I wanted, I really did want you to call on us first; that's why I didn't send for you. Goodness, he hasn't changed one bit!' she said, leaning over to look at him. 'It's amazing how little he's changed! Oh, no, there are some wrinkles, lots of wrinkles around his eyes and on his cheeks, and his hair's gone grey; but his eyes are just the same! And have I changed? Have I? Why don't you say something?'

At that moment I recalled the story about how she'd been virtually ill when taken away to Petersburg at the age of eleven; she wept all during her sickness and kept asking for Stepan Trofimovich.

'You... I...' he muttered, his voice breaking with joy. 'Just now I cried, "Who will comfort me?"—and your voice rang out... I consider it a miracle *et je commence à croire*.'[1]

'*En Dieu? En Dieu, qui est là-haut et qui est si grand et si bon?*[2] You see, I remember all your lectures by heart. Maurice Nikolaevich, what faith he preached to me then *en Dieu, qui est si grand et si bon*! And do you recall those stories about how Columbus discovered America and everyone shouted, "Land! Land!" My nanny, Alyona Frolovna, says that for some time afterwards I used to cry out in my sleep, "Land! Land!" Do you remember telling me the story of Prince Hamlet? Do you recall describing how the poor emigrants were transported from Europe to America? And none of it was true; later I found out how they were really transported. But how well he told me those lies, Maurice Nikolaevich; it was almost better than the truth! Why are you staring at Maurice Nikolaevich? He's the best, most faithful man in the whole world, and you'll certainly come to like him as much as you do me! *Il fait tout ce que je veux*.[3] But, my dear Stepan Trofimovich, you must be unhappy again, if you're standing in the middle of the street

---

[1] and I'm starting to believe.

[2] In God? In God above, who is so great and so good?

[3] He does everything I want.

and wondering aloud who'll comfort you. You are unhappy, aren't you? Well?'

'I'm happy now...'

'Is my aunt being disagreeable?' she continued without listening. 'Is she the same wicked, unjust aunt, yet still so precious to us all? Do you remember how you threw yourself into my arms in the garden, and how I comforted you and wept. Why, don't worry about Maurice Nikolaevich! He knows all about you, absolutely everything, and has done for some time. You can cry on his shoulder as much as you like, and he'll still stand firm!... Raise your hat, take it right off for a moment, stick your head up and stand on tiptoe, so I can kiss your forehead, just as I did the last time we said goodbye. Look, that young girl is watching us from the window... Come on, come closer, closer. Good Lord, how you've gone grey!'

And she leaned over in her saddle and kissed him on the forehead.

'Come, let's go back to your house! I know where you live. I'm going there right now. You stubborn man, I'll pay you the first visit; then I'll drag you along home for the rest of the day. Run along and get ready to welcome me.'

And she galloped off with her cavalier. We returned home. Stepan Trofimovich sat down on the sofa and burst into tears.

'*Dieu! Dieu!*' he cried, '*enfin une minute de bonheur!*'[1]

Not more than ten minutes later she arrived as promised, accompanied by her Maurice Nikolaevich.

'*Vous et le bonheur, vous arrivez en même temps!*'[2] he said, rising to meet her.

'Here are some flowers for you. I just visited Madame Chevalier; she grows flowers all winter long for nameday celebrations. And here's Maurice Nikolaevich—let me introduce you. I wanted to bring you a meat pie instead of flowers, but Maurice Nikolaevich assures me that's not in the Russian spirit.'

This Maurice Nikolaevich was an artillery captain, about thirty-three years old, fairly tall, handsome, irreproachably

[1] God! God! ... at last, a moment of happiness!
[2] You and happiness both arrive at the same time!

correct in appearance, with an imposing, and at first glance rather severe countenance, notwithstanding the astonishing and supremely tactful kindness which everybody perceived in him almost from the first moment of acquaintance. He was reticent, however; he appeared rather cold, and didn't make friends easily. Afterwards many people said he wasn't too clever; that was not altogether fair.

I won't even try to describe Lizaveta Nikolaevna's beauty. The whole town was already talking about her, although some of our ladies and young girls disagreed heatedly with the prevailing opinion. There were even some who hated Lizaveta Nikolaevna, primarily because of her pride. The Drozdovs had scarcely begun paying their social calls—a fact that offended many people, even though the real reason for the delay was Praskovya Ivanovna's indisposition. Second, they hated her because she was a relative of the governor's wife; third, because she went riding every day. Up to then we hadn't seen any horsewomen in our town; it was only natural that Lizaveta Nikolaevna, riding her horse and having failed as yet to pay any social calls, should have offended our society. Besides, everyone knew she went riding on doctor's orders, and that occasioned many sarcastic remarks about the state of her health. She was in fact ill. The first thing one noticed was her sickly, nervous, incessant agitation. Alas! The poor girl was suffering a great deal; it would all be explained later. Now, recalling the past, I can no longer say she was the great beauty she seemed to be then. Perhaps she really wasn't that pretty at all. She was tall and slender, but supple and strong; her face was rather striking with its irregular features. Her eyes seemed to be set at a slant, rather like a Kalmuck's.* She looked pale, had high cheekbones, a dark complexion, and a thin face. Still, there was something about her that was both attractive and triumphant! There was a kind of power in the ardent gaze of her dark eyes; she looked like 'a conqueror come to conquer'. She seemed proud, sometimes even arrogant; I don't know if she ever managed to be kind, but I do know that she desperately wanted to and tried to make herself be kind. No doubt her character was composed of many fine impulses and the very best elements; but everything always seemed to be seeking, but not finding its own level; everything was in chaos, in a state of agitation, restlessness. Perhaps she made too many severe demands on herself, without finding the strength to satisfy them.

She sat on the sofa and glanced around the room.

'Why do I always feel so sad at moments like this? Can you explain it, with your learning? All my life I've thought I'd be so glad to see you again and recall so many things; but now I don't feel glad at all, despite the fact that I do still love you... Ah, good Lord, there's my portrait hanging on the wall! Let me see it! I remember it, yes I do!'

The splendid miniature water-colour of the twelve-year old Liza had been sent to Stepan Trofimovich by the Drozdovs from Petersburg about nine years ago. Ever since it had hung on his wall.

'Was I really such a pretty child? Was that really my face?'

She stood up and, with the portrait in her hands, looked in the mirror.

'Here, take it!' she cried, giving it back to him. 'Don't hang it up now; do it later. I don't want to look at it.' She sat down on the sofa again. 'One life ended, and another began; then that one ended, and a third began; and so on, without ceasing. All the ends seem to have been snipped off, as if by a pair of scissors. See what old tales I'm telling you, but they contain so much truth!'

She smiled and looked at me; she'd glanced at me several times before, but in his agitation Stepan Trofimovich had quite forgotten his promise to introduce me to her.

'Why has my portrait been hanging under those daggers? And why do you have so many daggers and sabres?'

As a matter of fact, he had two curved daggers crossed on his wall, I don't know why; above them was a genuine Circassian* sabre. When she asked, she was looking directly at me; I was going to reply, but stopped short. Stepan Trofimovich finally understood the problem and introduced me.

'I know, I know,' she said. 'I'm very glad to meet you. Mother's heard a great deal about you too. Let me introduce you to Maurice Nikolaevich; he's an excellent fellow. I've had an amusing idea about you already: you're Stepan Trofimovich's confidant, aren't you?'

I blushed.

'Oh, please forgive me. That wasn't what I meant to say. It's not at all amusing, it's just...' (She blushed and looked embarrassed.) 'But why are you ashamed of being such an excellent fellow? Well, Maurice Nikolaevich, it's time to go! Stepan Trofimovich, you must be at our house in half an hour. Good Lord, there's so much to talk about! Now I'm your confidante, in all regards, do you understand, *in all regards*!'

Stepan Trofimovich became alarmed at once.

'Oh, Maurice Nikolaevich knows everything; don't mind him.'

'What does he know?'

'What do you mean?' she cried in astonishment. 'Why, then it's true they're hiding it! I didn't want to believe it. And they're hiding Dasha. My aunt wouldn't let me see Dasha just now, she said she had a headache.'

'But... but how did you find out?'

'Oh, good heavens, just like everyone else. It wasn't very difficult!'

'Really?...'

'Well, what of it? Of course, Mother found out first from nanny, Alyona Frolovna; your Nastasya came running over to tell her. You told Nastasya, right? She says you did.'

'I... I mentioned it once...' Stepan Trofimovich muttered, blushing all over. 'But... I merely intimated... *j'étais si nerveux et malade et puis*...'[1]

She burst out laughing.

'Your confidante wasn't around at the time and Nastasya just happened to be there—well, that's all there is to it! The whole town is full of gossips! Well, never mind; it really doesn't matter. Let them all know, it's actually better that way. Come and see us as soon as possible; we dine rather early... Oh yes, I almost forgot,' she said, sitting down again.

[1] I was so upset and ill, besides

'Listen, tell me about Shatov.'

'Shatov? He's Darya Pavlovna's brother...'

'I know he's her brother! What a funny man you are, really!' she said, interrupting him impatiently. 'I want to know what sort of person he is.'

'*C'est un pense-creux d'ici. C'est le meilleur et le plus irascible homme du monde...*'[1]

'I've heard he's something of a strange fellow. But that's not what I meant. I've heard he knows three languages, including English, and that he can do literary work. If that's true, I have a great deal of work for him. I need an assistant, the sooner the better. Is he taking on work or not? He's been recommended to me...'

'Oh, absolutely, *et vous ferez un bienfait...*'[2]

'I'm not doing it as a *bienfait*; I really need an assistant.'

'I know Shatov fairly well,' I said. 'If you want me to send him a message, I'll go and see him at once.'

'Tell him to come and see me tomorrow at noon. Splendid! Thank you. Are you ready, Maurice Nikolaevich?'

They left. Naturally, I went straight over to Shatov.

'*Mon ami*!' Stepan Trofimovich said, catching me on the front steps. 'You must come and see me at ten or eleven o'clock, when I get back. Oh, I feel very guilty towards you and... towards everyone, everyone.'

8.

I didn't find Shatov at home; I dropped in on him again two hours later, but he still wasn't there. Finally at eight o'clock I went over, either to find him at home or leave a note, but once again he wasn't there. His apartment was locked; he lived alone, without servants. I considered enquiring about Shatov down below, at Captain Lebyadkin's, but there it was also locked, with neither light nor sound coming from inside, as if the place were deserted. Recollecting stories I'd heard earlier, I passed Lebyadkin's door with considerable curiosity. In the end I decided to call on

[1] He's a local dreamer. He's the best and most irritable man on earth.
[2] and you'll be doing a good deed

Shatov the next day, but a little earlier. I wasn't convinced a note would work; he might ignore it—Shatov was such a shy, stubborn fellow. Cursing my lack of success, I was just going out of the gate when suddenly I bumped into Mr Kirillov. He was on his way home, and he recognized me first. Since he began asking questions, I told him everything in general terms and said I wanted to leave a note.

'Come along,' he said. 'I'll arrange everything.'

I recalled Liputin's having said that Kirillov had rented the wooden annexe in the yard that very morning. Since the annexe was too big for him alone, an old deaf peasant woman lived there as his servant. The owner stayed in a different, newer house on another street and ran a tavern; this old woman, it seems, was his relative, and was left to look after his old house. The rooms in the annexe were fairly clean, but the wallpaper was soiled. In the room we entered the furniture consisted of various odds and ends, all rather worthless: two card-tables, a chest made of alder, a large deal table from a peasant hut or someone's kitchen, some chairs and a sofa with wicker backs and hard leather cushions. An ancient icon hung in the corner, in front of which the old woman had lit a lamp before we came in; two large, dark oil paintings were hanging on the walls—one of the late Emperor Nikolai Pavlovich,* done during the 1820s, to judge by its appearance, the other, of some bishop or other.

Upon entering the room, Mr Kirillov lit a candle; from his trunk in the corner, not yet unpacked, he took an envelope, some sealing-wax, and a glass seal.

'Seal your note and address the envelope,' he said.

I was about to reply that was unnecessary, but he insisted. After addressing the envelope, I picked up my cap.

'I thought you might like some tea,' he said. 'I bought some. Would you?'

I didn't refuse. The old peasant woman soon brought in the tea, that is, a large kettle of boiling water, a small teapot full of a very strong brew, two large, crudely decorated earthenware mugs, a loaf of white bread, and a plateful of sugar lumps.

'I like tea', he said, 'especially at night; I walk around and drink a lot of tea, until daybreak. It's not easy to get tea at night abroad.'

'You go to bed at daybreak?'

'Always... for some time now. I don't eat much; only tea. Liputin is cunning, but impatient.'

I was surprised he wanted to chat; I decided to take advantage of the opportunity.

'Some unpleasant misunderstandings occurred this morning,' I observed.

He scowled.

'It was stupid—nonsense! All because Lebyadkin was drunk. I didn't say anything to Liputin; I merely explained the nonsense, because he got it all wrong. Liputin has a vivid imagination and made a mountain out of a molehill. I trusted Liputin yesterday.'

'And me today?' I asked with a laugh.

'But you know everything already. Liputin's either weak impatient, malicious, or... envious.'

His last word astonished me.

'You listed so many traits it wouldn't surprise me at all if one of them fitted.'

'Or all of them.'

'Yes, that's true, too. Liputin—he's sheer chaos! It's true, isn't it, that he was lying earlier when he said you wanted to write something?'

'Why was he lying?' he asked, scowling again, looking down at the ground.

I apologized and began to assure him that I wasn't prying. He blushed.

'That was true, what he said; I am writing something. But it doesn't matter.'

We remained silent for a minute or so; he suddenly smiled at me with that same childlike smile.

'He invented all that stuff about the heads; it's from a book. First he told me himself, but he doesn't really understand it. I'm merely looking for the reason why people dare not kill themselves. That's all there is to it. It doesn't really matter.'

'What do you mean, dare not? Are there that few suicides?'

'Very few.'

'Is that really what you've found?'

He didn't answer, stood up and began walking around the room, lost in thought.

'What is it, in your opinion, that deters people from committing suicide?' I asked.

He looked at me absent-mindedly, as if trying to recall what we were talking about.

'I... I still know so little... Two prejudices deter them, two things; only two; one is very small, the other very large. But the small one is very large, too.'

'What's the small one?'

'Pain.'

'Pain? Is it really all that important... in such a case?'

'Most important. There are two kinds of people: those who kill themselves either in great sorrow or in anger, and those who are insane, or whatever you want to call it... and do it suddenly. They don't think very much about pain, they just do it all of a sudden. But those who do it from reason think about it a great deal.'

'Are there really people who do it from reason?'

'A great many. If it weren't for that prejudice, there'd be more; a great many; everyone.'

'Surely not everyone?'

He was silent.

'Is there really no way of dying without pain?'

'Just imagine,' he said, stopping in front of me, 'imagine a stone as big as a large house; it's hanging over you. If it falls on you, on your head, will it hurt?'

'A stone as big as a house? Of course, it would be terrifying.'

'I'm not talking about terror; would it hurt?'

'A stone as big as a mountain? Thousands of tons? Of course it wouldn't hurt.'

'But if you stood there with it hanging over you, you'd really be afraid that it would hurt. Everyone would be afraid—the greatest scholar, the best doctor, everyone. Everyone would know that it wouldn't hurt, but everyone would be afraid that it would.'

'Well, what's the second reason, the big one?'

'The next world.'

'You mean, punishment?'

'That doesn't matter. The next world; just the next world.'

'Are there really no atheists who don't believe in the next world?'

He was silent once again.

'You may be judging from yourself.'

'Everyone has to judge from himself,' he said, flushing. 'Absolute freedom will occur only when it doesn't matter whether one lives or dies. That's the goal for everyone.'

'The goal? But then no one might want to live?'

'No, no one,' he said decisively.

'Man fears death because he loves life—that's how I understand it,' I observed, 'and that's what nature decreed.'

'That's disgusting—it's where the whole deception lies!' he cried, his eyes flashing. 'Life is pain, life is fear, and man is unhappy. Everything is now pain and fear. Man loves life now because he loves fear and pain. That's how it's been. Life is given in return for pain and fear now, and that's the whole deception. But man is still not really man. There will come a new man, happy and proud. He who doesn't care whether he lives or dies—he'll be the new man. He who conquers pain and fear—will become God. And then the old God will no longer exist.'

'Doesn't that mean then, that you think God exists?'

'He doesn't exist, yet He does. There's no pain in the stone, but there's pain in the fear of the stone. God is the pain of the fear of death. He who conquers pain and fear—will become God. Then a new life will dawn; there'll be a new man; everything will be new.... History will be divided into two parts: from the gorilla to the destruction of God, and from the destruction of God to...'

'To the gorilla?'

'... to the physical transformation of the earth and of man. Man will become God and will be changed physically. The world will be changed, and things will be changed, all thoughts and all feelings. What do you think, will man be changed physically then?'

'If it's all the same whether man lives or dies, then everyone will kill himself—perhaps that's what the change will be.'

'It doesn't matter. They'll have killed deception. Everyone who wants absolute freedom will have to dare to kill himself. Everyone who dares to kill himself will have discovered the secret of deception. There's no freedom beyond that; that's everything—there's nothing more. He who dares to kill himself is God. Everyone is now capable of making sure there'll be no God and nothing else. But no one's ever done it.'

'There have been millions of suicides.'

'But all for the wrong reasons, all in fear, and not for that purpose—not to kill fear. He who kills himself simply to kill fear—will become God immediately.'

'Perhaps he won't have time,' I observed.

'That doesn't make any difference,' he replied softly, with serene pride, almost with contempt. 'I regret you find this so humorous,' he added after about half a minute.

'I find it strange that you were so irritable this morning, but you're so calm now, even though you're speaking with feeling.'

'This morning? But that was so amusing,' he replied with a smile. 'I don't like to abuse people and I never laugh,' he added gloomily.

'Yes, those nights of yours spent drinking tea don't sound very cheerful.' I stood and picked up my cap.

'Is that what you think?' he asked, smiling in some surprise. 'Why not? No, I... I don't know,' he said, suddenly becoming confused. 'I don't know how it is with others, but I feel I can't be like them. Everyone thinks about it, then immediately thinks about something else. I can't think about anything else; all my life I've been thinking about one thing. God has been tormenting me all my life,' he concluded suddenly, with astonishing expansiveness.

'Tell me, if you don't mind, why is it you don't speak Russian very well? Could you really have forgotten how in the five years you lived abroad?'

'Do I not speak properly? I don't know. No, it's not because I lived abroad. I've talked this way all my life... It doesn't matter.'

'Another question, even more delicate: I quite believe you when you say you're not inclined to meet people and talk with them very little. Why did you have this conversation with me?'

'With you? This morning you sat there quietly and... besides, it doesn't matter... You resemble my brother, very much so, to an extraordinary degree,' he said, blushing. 'He died seven years ago. He was older, very, very much so.'

'He must have had a great influence on your thinking?'

'N-no, he said very little; he didn't say a thing. I'll pass on your note.'

He accompanied me to the gate with a lantern, to lock it after me. 'He's insane, of course,' I decided. At the gate I had another encounter.

9.

Just as I lifted my foot over the high sill of the gate, someone's strong arm seized me around the chest.

'Who goes there?' roared a voice. 'Friend or foe? Speak up!'

'He's one of us, one of us!' squeaked Liputin's thin voice nearby. 'It's Mr G—v, a young man with a classical education and connections in the very best society.'

'Well, if he's in society, I like him. Clas-si... that means, very well ed-u-ca-ted... I'm Ignat Lebyadkin, retired captain, at the service of the world and my friends... if they're loyal, if they're loyal, the scoundrels!'

Captain Lebyadkin, a man over six feet tall, heavy, fleshy, curly-haired, ruddy, and extremely drunk, could hardly stand up in front of me and articulated his words with difficulty. I'd seen him before, but only from a distance.

'Aha, and this one as well!' he roared again after noticing Kirillov, who'd yet to go back inside with his lantern; he began to raise his fist, but lowered it again.

'I forgive you for your learning! Ignat Lebyadkin is—very well ed-u-ca-ted...

> Love's great grenade now burst apart,
> Fiercely ablaze in Ignat's heart;
> Armless, he wept in bitter pain
> For Sevastopol* again.

'Even though I've never been to Sevastopol and have both my arms, still—what fine poetry that is!' he cried, thrusting his drunken face into mine.

'He doesn't have time for this; he's on his way home,' said Liputin, trying to persuade him. 'He'll tell Liza Nikolaevna tomorrow.'

'Lizaveta!' he roared again. 'Stay here! Don't move! Here's another version:

> A star flashes by in its course
> Encircled by Amazons wild
> She smiles at me from her horse
> The aristo-crat-ic-al child.

"To an Amazon-Star". But it's a hymn, don't you see! It's a hymn, if you're not an ass! Those idlers don't understand! Stop!' he cried, grabbing hold of my coat, although I was trying to get away from him with all my might. 'Tell her I'm a knight of honour; as for Dashka... I'll crush that little Dashka... She's only a serf-girl and she'd better not...'

At this point he fell down because I'd managed to tear myself out of his arms and was running along the street. Liputin followed right behind.

'Aleksei Nilych will pick him up. Do you know what I just found out from him?' he muttered hurriedly. 'Did you hear those verses? Well, he just put those same lines, "To an Amazon-Star", into an envelope and tomorrow he's going to send them to Lizaveta Nikolaevna, signed with his full name. What a fellow!'

'I bet you put him up to it.'

'You'd lose your bet!' Liputin laughed. 'He's in love, he's in love like a cat. And do you know, it all began with hatred? At first he hated Lizaveta Nikolaevna so much for riding around on her horse that he nearly abused her aloud on the street; and abuse her he did! Only the day before yesterday he shouted abuse at her when she rode by. Fortunately, she didn't hear him. And now suddenly, these verses! Do you know he plans to propose to her? Seriously, seriously!'

'I'm surprised at you, Liputin. Wherever there's nasty business going on, you're sure to be right there directing it!' I said angrily.

'That's going a bit too far, Mr G—v. Perhaps your poor little heart is quaking at the thought of a rival, eh?'

'Wha-at?' I cried, stopping at once.

'Well then, to serve you right, I won't say another thing! But wouldn't you really like to know? For example: the mere fact that idiot is no longer simply a captain, but a landowner in our province, a substantial one at that, because Nikolai Vsevolodovich just sold him his former estate with two hundred serfs... So help me God, I'm not lying. I just found out from a very reliable source. Well, now you can discover all the rest for yourself. I won't say another word. Goodbye!'

10.

Stepan Trofimovich was waiting for me in hysterical impatience. He'd been home an hour. I found him in a state similar to intoxication; for the first five minutes or so I thought he was drunk. Alas, his visit to the Drozdovs had left him in complete confusion.

'*Mon ami*, I've lost the thread of my thoughts entirely... Lise... I love and respect that angel as before; yes indeed, just as before; but now it seems that both of them were waiting for me simply to find out something, that is, to drag something out of me, and then be done with me... That's how it was.'

'You ought to be ashamed of yourself!' I cried, unable to control myself.

'My friend, I'm completely alone now. *Enfin, c'est ridicule.* Just think, they're all absorbed in secrets, too. They simply pounced on me with questions about those noses and ears, and about some Petersburg secrets as well. They had both just found out about those incidents involving Nicolas that took place here some four years ago. "You were here," they said. "You saw it. Is it true he was mad?" I don't understand where that idea came from. Why is Praskovya Drozdova so eager that Nicolas prove to be mad? She's so eager, so very eager! *Ce* Maurice, or, what's his name, Mavriky Niko-laevich, *brave homme tout de même*, is it really for his sake? And later she herself was first to write to *cette pauvre amie* from Paris... *Enfin*, that Praskovya, as *cette chère amie* calls her, is a real character, just like Gogol's immortal Koro-bochka,* Mrs Box, but a wicked Korobochka, a provocative Korobochka, in grossly expanded form.'

'It's not a "box", but a trunk, if it's an expanded form.'

'Well, reduced form then; it doesn't matter. But don't you interrupt, because everything keeps going around in my head. They seem all to have fallen out with one another; except for Lise; she keeps on with her "Auntie, Auntie". But Lise is clever, and there's something more to it. Secrets. But she's quarrelled with the old woman. And *cette pauvre* Auntie, it's true, tyrannizes everyone... then there's the governor's wife, society's disrespect, and even Karmazinov's "disrespect". And suddenly this idea of madness, *ce Lipou-tine, ce que je ne comprends pas,*[1] and... and they say she's been applying vinegar compresses to her head, and here we are now with our complaints and letters... Oh, how I tormented her and what a time to choose! *Je suis un ingrat!*[2] Imagine, I return home to find a letter from her; here, read it, read it! Oh, how ungrateful I've been.'

He handed me a letter he just received from Varvara Petrovna. Apparently she regretted having sent him the note that morning directing him to 'Stay at home'. Her letter was polite, but positive none the less, and very brief. She invited him to come and see her at twelve noon on Sunday, the day after tomorrow, and was urging him to bring one of his friends with him (my name appeared in parentheses). For her part, she'd invite Shatov, as Darya Pavlovna's brother. 'You can receive her final answer; will that be enough? Isn't that the formality you so desire?'

'Note the irritability of that last sentence about for-mality. The poor woman, the poor woman, my lifelong

---

[1] this Liputin, that I don't understand
[2] I'm so ungrateful!

friend! I confess, this *abrupt* decision about my fate has been oppressing me... I confess, I was still hoping, but now *tout est dit*, and I now know that it's all over; *c'est terrible*. Oh, I wish this Sunday would never arrive and everything would continue as it's always been: you'd come to visit, I'd still be here...'

'You're confused by all those despicable things Liputin said, by all those rumours.'

'My friend, you've just put your well-meaning finger on another sore spot. Your well-meaning fingers are usually merciless, and sometimes stupid, *pardon*, but, believe it or not, I'd almost forgotten about all that, those despicable things; that is, I hadn't forgotten, but, in my own stupidity, all the time I was with Lise I tried to be happy and convince myself of that. But now... oh, now I'm thinking about that generous, humane woman, so tolerant of my abominable faults—that is, even though she's not entirely tolerant, who am I to talk with my worthless, rotten character? I'm just a capricious child, with all the egoism of a child, but without its innocence. For twenty years she's been looking after me like a nurse, *cette pauvre* Auntie, as Lise charmingly calls her... And suddenly, after twenty years, the child decides to get married: "Marry, marry, marry!" So he writes letter after letter, while she applies vinegar compresses to her head, and... now he's got what he wants. On Sunday he'll be a married man, strange to say... But why did I insist upon it? Why did I keep writing letters? Yes, I forgot: Lise idolizes Darya Pavlovna, at least so she says; she says, "*C'est un ange*,[1] only a bit secretive." They both advised me to marry, even Praskovya... no, Praskovya didn't advise me. Oh, there's so much venom concealed in that Korobochka! Besides, Lise herself didn't really advise me: "Why should you get married?" she asked. "Aren't intellectual pleasures enough for you?" and she laughed. I forgave her for laughing because she has her own heartache. But they told me I couldn't get along without having a woman around. The infirmities of old age are approaching, they said. "She'll

[1] She's an angel

tuck you in, or whatever..." *Ma foi*, all this time I've been here with you, I've been thinking to myself that Providence has sent her to me in the decline of my stormy days, and she'll tuck me in, or whatever... *enfin*, she'll be useful around the house. Look, there's so much rubbish around here; look, it's just lying all over. I asked for it to be cleaned up recently, but there's still a book on the floor. *La pauvre amie* was always annoyed that there was so much mess... Oh, now her voice will no longer be heard here! *Vingt ans!*[1] And now, apparently they've received some anonymous letters, just imagine, claiming that Nicolas sold his estate to Lebyadkin. *C'est un monstre; et enfin*, who's this Lebyadkin? Lise listens and listens, oh, how she listens! I forgave her for laughing; I saw her face as she listened; as for *ce Maurice*... I wouldn't want to be in his place now, *brave homme tout de même*, though somewhat bashful; but never mind about him...'

He fell silent; he was exhausted and confused. He sat with drooping head, staring motionlessly at the floor with weary eyes. I took advantage of the pause to tell him about my visit to Filippov's house; I curtly and dryly expressed the opinion that Lebyadkin's sister (whom I'd never seen) might well have been Nicolas's victim at some time, 'during some mysterious period of his life', as Liputin used to say, and it was very possible that Lebyadkin was getting money from Nicolas for some reason, but that was all there was to it. As far as rumours about Darya Pavlovna were concerned, it was all nonsense, distortions spread by that scoundrel Liputin; anyway, that was what Aleksei Nilych maintained with some fervour, and there was no reason to doubt him. Stepan Trofimovich listened to my assurances with an absent-minded expression, as if it didn't concern him at all. In passing, I also mentioned my conversation with Kirillov, remarking that he might well be insane.

'Kirillov's not insane,' he mumbled listlessly, as though against his will. 'He's one of those people who have little minds. *Ces gens-là supposent la nature et la société humaine*

---

[1] Twenty years!

autres que Dieu ne les a faites et qu'elles ne sont réellement.[1]
Some play up to them, but at least Stepan Trofimovich
doesn't try. I saw it in Petersburg that time, *avec cette chère
amie* (oh, how I offended her then!), and I wasn't afraid of
their abuse or even of their praise. I'm not afraid now either,
mais parlons d'autre chose... It seems I've done some terrible
things; imagine, yesterday I sent a note to Darya Pavlovna
and... oh, how I curse myself for that!'

'What did you say?'

'Oh, my friend, believe me, it was all done with noble
intentions. I informed her that I'd written to Nicolas about
five days before, also with noble intentions.'

'Now I understand!' I cried with some emotion. 'And
what right did you have to link their names?'

'But, *mon cher*, don't destroy me completely, don't shout
at me. I feel totally crushed already, just like a... a cockroach; after all, my intention was so noble. Suppose that
something had actually happened... *en Suisse...*[2] or that
something began there. Shouldn't I enquire of their hearts
beforehand, so as... *enfin*, not to interfere with them and
become an obstacle on their path... I'm acting solely with
noble intentions.'

'Good Lord, how stupid you've been!' I cried involuntarily.

'Stupid, stupid!' he replied even with some eagerness.
'You've never said anything more to the point than that,
c'était bête, mais que faire, tout est dit.[3] I'll get married
anyway, even to cover up "another man's sins", so why did
I have to write? Isn't that it?'

'You're back to that again!'

'Oh, you won't frighten me now by shouting at me; you
see before you now a different Stepan Trofimovich. The
old one is dead and buried; *enfin, tout est dit.* Why are
you shouting, anyway? Merely because you're not the one

---

[1] Those people imagine nature and human society different from the way
God created them and they really are.

[2] in Switzerland

[3] it was stupid, but there's nothing to be done, it's all decided.

getting married and you won't have to wear those notorious horns on your head. Does that upset you again? My poor friend, you know nothing about women, whereas I've been studying them all my life. "If you want to conquer the whole world, conquer yourself"—that's the only good thing ever said by that other romantic like you, Shatov, my betrothed's brother. I'm glad to borrow his phrase. Well, now I'm ready to conquer myself and I'm getting married; meanwhile, what will I conquer instead of the whole world? Oh, my friend, marriage represents the moral death of a proud soul, of all independence. Married life will corrupt me, drain my energy and my courage in service of the cause. Then children will follow, probably not my own, or rather, certainly not my own; a wise man isn't afraid to look truth straight in the eye... Liputin proposed earlier erecting barricades to defend myself against Nicolas; Liputin is stupid. A woman can deceive the all-seeing eye itself. In creating woman *le bon Dieu* knew in advance, of course, all the risks involved, but I'm convinced that she herself interfered with His work and demanded that she be created in just such a way... with just such traits. Why else would anyone have gone to so much trouble for nothing? I know Nastasya might get angry at me for such free-thinking, but... *Enfin, tout est dit.*[1]

He wouldn't have been himself if he'd been able to dispense with the cheap, witty free-thinking that had flourished in his day. Now at least he managed to console himself with wit, but not for very long.

'Oh, I wish the day after tomorrow, Sunday, would never come!' he exclaimed suddenly, already in total despair. 'Why couldn't this one week be without a Sunday—*si le miracle existe*? What would it cost Providence to eliminate just one Sunday from the calendar, if only to demonstrate its power to an atheist, *et que tout soit dit*! Oh, how I've loved her! Twenty years, these last twenty years, and she's never understood me!'

'What are you talking about? I don't understand you, either!' I said in astonishment.

[1] In short, it's all decided.

'*Vingt ans*! And not once did she understand me; oh, how cruel it is! Does she really think I'm getting married from fear, from necessity? Oh, the shame! Auntie, Auntie, it's for you I'm doing it!... Oh, let her find out, this Auntie, that she's the only woman I've adored these last twenty years! She must find it out; if not, there'll be no wedding, they'll have to lead me by force to *ce qu'on appelle le* altar!'

This was the first time I'd heard such a confession and so forcefully expressed. I won't hide the fact that I felt a desperate urge to laugh. I was wrong.

'He's all I have left now; he's my only hope!' he cried suddenly, clasping his hands as if struck with a new, unexpected idea. 'Now he alone, my poor boy, can save me and... Why hasn't he come? Oh, my son! Oh, my Petrushka!... Even if I'm unworthy of the name of father, tiger is more like it, still... *laissez-moi, mon ami*, I'll lie down for a little while to collect my thoughts. I'm so tired, so very tired, and it's probably time you got some sleep, too. *Voyez-vous*, it's twelve o'clock...'

CHAPTER 4

The cripple

I.

SHATOV did not prove obstinate and, following the suggestion in my note, he appeared at Lizaveta Nikolaevna's at noon. We arrived almost simultaneously; I was going there to pay my first call. All of them, that is, Liza, her mother, and Maurice Nikolaevich, were sitting in the large drawing-room arguing. Mamma was insisting that Liza play a particular waltz on the piano, and then, as soon as she began playing, mamma declared it wasn't the right piece. Maurice Nikolaevich, in his simplicity, sided with Liza and maintained that it really was the right piece; the old woman burst into tears of vexation. She was ill and even had difficulty walking. Her legs were swollen and for the last few days she'd done nothing but behave capriciously, finding fault with everything, even though she was a little afraid of Liza. They were delighted by our arrival. Liza flushed with pleasure and, having said *merci* to me, no doubt on account of Shatov, went over and began scrutinizing him with interest.

Shatov had paused awkwardly in the doorway. After thanking him for coming, she led him up to her mother.

'This is Mr Shatov—I've told you about him; and this is Mr G—v, a great friend of mine and of Stepan Trofimovich. Maurice Nikolaevich also met him yesterday.'

'Which one is the professor?'

'There's no professor here, mamma.'

'Yes, there is. You said that there'd be a professor. It's probably that one,' she said pointing at Shatov with disdain.

'I never said there'd be a professor. Mr G—v is a civil servant and Mr Shatov is a former student.'

'Student or professor, they're both from the university. You just want to argue. But the Swiss one had a moustache and a little beard.'

'Mamma always refers to Stepan Trofimovich's son as a

professor,' said Liza, leading Shatov over to a sofa at the other end of the room.

'She's always like this when her legs are swollen; you see, she's not well,' she whispered to Shatov, still examining him with the same curiosity, especially the tuft of hair on his head.

'Are you in the military?' the old woman asked, turning to me; Lisa had mercilessly abandoned me to her.

'No, ma'am, I'm in the civil service...'

'Mr G——v is a great friend of Stepan Trofimovich,' Liza chimed in at once.

'Do you work for Stepan Trofimovich? He's a professor, too, isn't he?'

'Oh, mamma, you must be seeing professors in your dreams,' Liza cried in annoyance.

'I see quite enough of them when I'm awake. Why do you always contradict your mother?' She turned to address me: 'Were you here four years ago when Nikolai Vsevolodovich arrived?'

I said I was.

'And was there an Englishman here with you?'

'No.'

Liza started to laugh.

'So you see there really wasn't an Englishman—it's all lies. Both Varvara Petrovna and Stepan Trofimovich are lying. Everyone's lying.'

'Yesterday my aunt and Stepan Trofimovich discovered a resemblance between Nikolai Vsevolodovich and Prince Harry in Shakespeare's *Henry the Fourth*; in response to this mamma insists that there was no Englishman here,' Liza explained to us.

'If there was no Harry, then there was no Englishman, either. It was only Nikolai Vsevolodovich playing tricks.'

'I assure you mamma is doing this on purpose,' Liza said, finding it necessary to explain everything to Shatov. 'She knows her Shakespeare very well. I read her the first act of *Othello* myself; but she's in great pain at the moment. Mamma, do you hear, it's striking twelve o'clock. It's time to take your medicine.'

'The doctor has come,' a maid announced at the door.

The old woman stood up and began to call her little dog: 'Zemirka, Zemirka, at least you come with me.'

The disgusting old dog Zemirka failed to obey and crawled under the sofa where Liza was sitting.

'You don't want to come? Then I don't want you, either. Goodbye, dear sir, I don't know your name,' she said, turning to me.

'Anton Lavrentievich...'

'Well, it doesn't matter; with me it goes in one ear and out the other. Don't come with me, Maurice Nikolaevich, I only called Zemirka. Thank God I can still walk by myself; tomorrow I shall go out for a drive.'

She left the room in anger.

'Anton Lavrentievich, have a talk with Maurice Nikolaevich in the meantime. I assure you that you'll both benefit if you get better acquainted,' said Liza, smiling amicably to Maurice Nikolaevich who beamed with delight when she looked at him. I had no choice but to stay and talk to him.

2.

To my surprise Lizaveta Nikolaevna's interest in Shatov really turned out only to concern literature. I don't know why, but I kept thinking she'd invited him for some other reason. We, that is, Maurice Nikolaevich and I, seeing that they were not trying to conceal anything from us and were talking quite loudly, began listening to their conversation; then they asked our advice. The matter concerned Lizaveta Nikolaevna's long-standing intention to publish what was in her opinion a very useful book, but, due to her complete lack of experience, she needed someone to assist her with the project. The seriousness with which she set about explaining her plan to Shatov astonished even me. 'She must be one of the "new people",'* I thought. 'She's not wasted her time in Switzerland.' Shatov listened to her attentively, his eyes fixed on the ground, without showing the least surprise that a flighty young society girl should be involved in what appeared to be such an inappropriate business.

Her literary enterprise was as follows. A large number of newspapers and journals are published in Russia both in the capital and the provinces, and every day they report count-less events. The year passes and these newspapers are stored in cupboards, or else torn up and discarded, or used for wrapping parcels and other things. Many of the facts that are published make an impression and remain in the public's memory, but are then forgotten over the years. Subsequently many people would like to look them up, but what a task it is to sort through a sea of paper, sometimes without knowing the day, place, or even year of the event in question. But what if all the facts for a whole year could be collected in one book, arranged according to a specific plan, with a definite object in mind, a table of contents, an index, and cross-referenced according to date and month? Such a compilation would constitute an outline of Russian life for that year, despite the small number of facts actually published compared to the events taking place.

'Instead of a vast quantity of pages, there'd be a few thick volumes—that's the only difference,' observed Shatov.

But Lizaveta Nikolaevna defended her project with con-siderable passion, in spite of her inexperience and some difficulty in expressing herself. It had to be published in one volume, not even a very thick one, she assured him. But, even granting a hefty tome, it must be well organized, since the point of the project was to be the arrangement of the facts. Of course, not everything would be collected and reprinted. Official decrees, government acts, local regula-tions, and laws, though very important, could be entirely omitted from the proposed volume. Many other things could be excluded; the selection of events would be limited to those that more or less expressed the personal, moral life of the people, the character of the Russian nation at a given moment. Naturally, anything could be included: unusual incidents, fires, public subscriptions, all sorts of good and bad deeds, various pronouncements and speeches, perhaps reports about the flooding of rivers, even certain government decrees—but only things that characterized the period would be selected. Everything should express a particular point of view, a certain direction, a well-defined intention, an idea that illuminates the whole, the totality. Last of all, the book must be entertaining, even for casual reading, apart from its value as a reference work! It should be, so to speak, a picture of the spiritual, moral, and inner life of Russia for an entire year. 'Everyone must buy it; the book must be found on everyone's table,' Liza declared. 'I know it all depends on the plan; that's why I'm turning to you for advice,' she concluded. She was very excited; in spite of the fact that her explanation was a little confused and incomplete, Shatov began to understand her.

'In other words, something with a definite tendency, a selection of facts to support a specific tendency,' he muttered, still not raising his head.

'Not at all. There's no need to make the selection tendentious; we don't want any tendency at all. The only tendency is to be complete impartiality.'

'There's nothing wrong with having a tendency,' Shatov said, beginning to stir. 'It's impossible to avoid if there's any selection to be made at all. The selection of facts will indicate how they are to be interpreted. It's not at all a bad idea.'

'So you think such a book might be possible?' Liza asked in delight.

'It will have to be gone into and considered carefully. It's an enormous task. You can't think anything up on the spot. You need experience. Even when we come to publish the book, I doubt we'll know how to do it. Perhaps only after several attempts; but the idea is certainly attractive. It's a useful idea.'

He finally raised his eyes; they were sparkling with pleasure, so interested was he in the plan.

'Did you think up this idea yourself?' he asked Liza kindly, as if a little embarrassed.

'To think up the idea was no trouble at all; the difficult part is the plan,' she said with a smile. 'I understand so little; I'm not very clever; I can pursue only what's clear to me...'

'Pursue?'

'Perhaps that's not the right word?' Liza enquired hastily.

'Perhaps it is—I didn't mean anything.'

'When I was living abroad it occurred to me that even I might be of some use. I have some money of my own but it's not doing anything; why shouldn't I work for the common cause? Besides, the idea came to me all of a sudden, of its own accord; I didn't really think it up and was very pleased with it. But I realized at once that I couldn't do it without someone to help me, because I don't know how to do anything myself. The collaborator, of course, would become the co-editor of the book. We'd go halves: your plan and work, my original idea and the means for carrying it out. Will the book sell?'

'If we come up with a good plan, it'll sell.'

'I must warn you that I'm not doing it to make a profit; but I would like the book to be read and would be proud if there was a profit.'

'But how does it involve me?'

'Why, I'd like to invite you to be my collaborator... to go halves. You'll work out the plan.'

'Why do you think me capable of working it out?'

'I've been told about you and I heard here... I know you're very clever and... involved with the cause and... you think a great deal. Peter Stepanovich Verkhovensky told me about you in Switzerland,' she added hastily. 'He's a very clever man, isn't he?'

Shatov stole a momentary, fleeting glance at her, but quickly dropped his eyes to the floor again.

'Nikolai Vsevolodovich also spoke about you a great deal...'

Shatov suddenly blushed.

'But here are some newspapers,' Liza said, hurriedly taking a bundle of wrapped newspapers from the chair. 'I've tried to mark facts for selection, sort them, number them... you'll see.'

Shatov picked up the bundle.

'Take them home and look at them. Where do you live?'

'In Filippov's house on Bogoyavlenskaya Street.'

'I know the place. They say that a captain lives there next to you, a Mr Lebyadkin?' Liza asked, still hurriedly as before.

Shatov sat there with the bundle in his outstretched arms for a full minute, without making any reply, staring at the floor.

'You'd better find someone else to do this work; I won't be any use to you,' he said at last, lowering his voice in a very strange way, almost to a whisper.

Liza blushed.

'What work are you talking about? Maurice Nikolaevich!' she shouted. 'Please bring me that recent letter.'

I followed Maurice Nikolaevich to the table.

'Look at this,' she said, suddenly turning to me, unfolding the letter in great agitation. 'Have you ever seen anything like this? Read it aloud, please; I want Mr Shatov to hear it, too.'

With considerable astonishment I read the following message:

To the paragon of maidens, Miss Tushina

Dearest madam,
    Yelizaveta Nikolaevna!

> Oh, the je-ne-sais-quoi
> Of la belle Tushina!
> She canters along with a cousin—one sees
> A sweet little curl play with the breeze!
> And, bowing deeply in church with her mother—
> The blushes of every pious brother!
> For marriage's lawful joys I die!
> I tag along after, tear in eye.
>> *Composed by an uneducated man during an argument.*

Dearest Madam!
I pity myself most of all because I didn't lose an arm for the glory of my country at Sevastopol, never having been there at all, instead, having served the entire campaign purveying paltry provisions, which I consider disgraceful. You are a goddess of antiquity, while I am nothing, but I've caught a glimpse of eternity. Look at these verses as such, but as nothing more, since poetry is after all only nonsense, and justifies what would be considered impudence if written in prose. Can the sun be angry with an infusorium, if the latter composes verses to it from a drop of water where they exist in a multitude if glimpsed through a microscope? Even the humane society for the protection of larger animals in

Petersburg high society, which rightly feels compassion for dogs and horses, despises the tiny infusorium, makes no mention of it whatever, because it's not big enough. I'm not big enough either. The idea of marriage may seem ridiculous, but soon I'll be the proprietor of two hundred former serfs thanks to a misanthropist you despise. I can reveal a great deal and produce documents that might mean Siberia for someone. Don't despise my proposal. The letter from the infusorium is in the verses.

> Captain Lebyadkin, your most humble friend,
> at your command.

'This was written by a drunkard and a scoundrel!' I cried in indignation. 'I know him!'

'I received this letter yesterday,' Liza said, blushing and hurriedly trying to explain it to us. 'I realized at once, of course, that it was sent by a fool. I still haven't shown it to *maman*, so as not to upset her even more. But if he persists, I shan't know what to do. Maurice Nikolaevich wants to go see him and tell him to stop. Since I regard you as my collaborator', she said, turning to Shatov, 'and since you live there, I want to ask you what else I can expect from him.'

'He's a drunkard and a scoundrel,' Shatov muttered, as if with reluctance.

'Is he always this stupid?'

'No, when he's not drunk he's not stupid at all.'

'I once knew a general who wrote the same kind of verses,' I said with a laugh.

'Even this letter shows he knows what he's doing,' the silent Maurice Nikolaevich remarked unexpectedly.

'They say he's living with his sister?' asked Liza.

'Yes, he is.'

'It's said he tyrannizes her. Is that true?'

Shatov glanced at Liza again, scowled and muttered, 'It's none of my business!' and made for the door.

'Oh, wait,' Liza cried anxiously. 'Where are you going? There's still so much we have to discuss...'

'What is there to discuss? I'll let you know tomorrow...'

'But it's the main thing—the printing press! Believe me, I'm not joking; I really want to undertake this project,' Liza assured him, growing more and more anxious. 'If we decide to publish, where will it be printed? This is a most important question, since we won't be going to Moscow and it's not possible to use a local press for such a publication. For some time I've been thinking about establishing my own printing press, perhaps in your name; mamma would allow it, I know, only if it were in your name...'

'How do you know I could do the printing?' Shatov asked gloomily.

'Peter Stepanovich told me in Switzerland that you knew how to run a printing press and were familiar with the business. He was even going to send you a note, but I forgot to get it.'

Shatov's face, as I now recall, changed completely. He stood there a few seconds longer, then suddenly left the room.

Liza was angry.

'Does he always just walk out like that?' she asked, turning to me.

I started to shrug my shoulders, but Shatov suddenly returned, went up to the table and placed the bundle of newspapers on it.

'I won't be your collaborator; I don't have the time...'

'Why not? Why not? Are you angry, or what?' Liza asked in an embittered and imploring voice.

The sound of her voice seemed to strike him; for a few moments he stared at her intently, as if wishing to penetrate her very soul.

'Never mind,' he muttered quietly. 'I don't want to...'

He left. Liza was completely flabbergasted, even beyond reasonable measure, or so it seemed to me.

'What an extraordinarily strange man!' Maurice Niko-laevich remarked aloud.

3.

Of course he was 'strange', but there was much that was unclear about all of this. There was some hidden meaning to it. I simply didn't believe in this publication; then, there was that stupid letter with its very clear implication of 'producing documents' to reveal information. No one said anything about that; they all talked about other things. Finally, there was the printing press and Shatov's sudden departure, just because the printing press had been mentioned. All this drove me to the conclusion that something had occurred before my arrival, something I knew nothing about; consequently, I was superfluous here and none of this was any of my business. Besides, it was time for me to go; I'd stayed long enough for my first visit. I went up to Lizaveta Nikolaevna to take my leave.

She seemed to have forgotten that I was even in the room; she was standing in the same place near the table, deep in thought, her head bowed, her gaze fixed on one spot on the carpet.

'Ah, you're leaving, too. Goodbye,' she murmured in her usual friendly tone of voice. 'Give my regards to Stepan Trofimovich and tell him to come and see me very soon. Maurice Nikolaevich, Anton Lavrentievich is leaving. I apologize that mamma is unable to say goodbye to you...'

I left the room and had almost reached the bottom of the stairs, when a footman suddenly caught up with me:

'The mistress would like you to come back...'

'The mistress or Lizaveta Nikolaevna?'

'The latter, sir.'

I found Liza not in the large room where we'd all been sitting, but in the reception-room. The door leading to the room where Maurice Nikolaevich had been left alone was closed.

Liza smiled at me, but looked very pale. She stood in the middle of the room obviously hesitating, apparently still struggling; but suddenly she took me by the arm and silently, quickly led me to the window.

'I want to see *her* at once,' she whispered, fixing her ardent, powerful, impatient gaze on me, one that wouldn't permit even the slightest opposition. 'I must see *her* with my own eyes and I'm asking you to help me.'

She was in an absolute frenzy and—in despair.

'Whom do you wish to see, Lizaveta Nikolaevna?' I enquired in alarm.

'That Lebyadkin girl, the cripple... Is it true she's a cripple?'

I was stunned.

'I've never seen her, but I've heard she's a cripple; I heard it only yesterday,' I mumbled in eager haste, also in a whisper.

'I must see her immediately. Can you arrange it today?'

I felt terribly sorry for her.

'That's impossible. Besides, I wouldn't know how to go about it,' I said, trying to dissuade her. 'I'll go and see Shatov...'

'If you don't arrange it by tomorrow, I'll go to her myself, all alone, since Maurice Nikolaevich has refused. I'm relying solely on you; I have no one else. I spoke stupidly to Shatov... I'm sure you're a totally honest man, perhaps even devoted to me. Arrange it for me.'

I felt a passionate desire to help her in any way possible.

'Here's what I'll do,' I said after a moment's thought. 'I'll go myself, today for sure, and I'll see her *for sure*! I'll see to it I get hold of her; I give you my word. But let me confide in Shatov.'

'Tell him what I want and that I can't wait any longer, but that I wasn't deceiving him just now. He may have left because he's such an honest man, and didn't like it when he thought I was deceiving him. But I wasn't; I really do want to publish that book and establish a printing press...'

'He is an honest man, a very honest man,' I agreed warmly.

'Moreover, if it's not arranged by tomorrow, I'll go there myself, whatever happens, even if everyone finds out about it.'

'I can't be here earlier than three o'clock tomorrow,' I said, coming back to my senses.

'Well then, three o'clock. Did I guess the truth yesterday at Stepan Trofimovich's? Are you—a little devoted to me?' she asked with a smile, hurriedly shaking my hand on parting and hastening back to the abandoned Maurice Nikolaevich.

I left weighed down by my promise, not really understanding what had taken place. I'd met a woman in genuine

despair, unafraid of compromising herself by confiding in a
man she hardly knew. Her feminine smile at a moment so
painful for her, and the hint that she'd already noticed my
feelings the day before, rent my heart. But I felt sorry for
her, very sorry—nothing more! Her secrets suddenly became
sacred to me; even if someone had wanted to reveal them
to me now, I'd probably have covered my ears and refused
to listen. But I had a strong foreboding... Besides, I didn't
understand in the least how I'd be able to arrange anything
at all. Moreover, I didn't even know what I was supposed
to arrange: a meeting? What kind of meeting? How could I
bring them together? My only hope was Shatov, although I
should have known in advance that he wouldn't help me at
all. Still I hurried to see him.

4.

It was only later that evening, sometime after seven, that I
found him at home. To my surprise he had visitors—Aleksei
Nilych Kirillov and another man I knew only slightly, a
certain Shigalyov, Mrs Virginskaya's brother. This Shigalyov had been staying in our town for two months or so; I
don't know where he came from. The only thing I'd heard
about him was that he'd published an article in some
progressive Petersburg journal. Virginsky introduced me to
him by chance, on the street. In my whole life I'd never
seen such gloom in a man's face, such dejection and despondency. He looked as if he were expecting the end of the
world, not at some indefinite time in the distant future
according to the prophecies (which might never come true),
but at some very definite time, let's say the day after
tomorrow, precisely at twenty-five past ten in the morning.
We hardly exchanged two words on that first occasion; we
merely shook hands, looking like two conspirators. I was
most of all struck by the unnatural size of his ears; they
were long, broad, and thick, and stuck out in a most peculiar
way. His movements were slow and clumsy. If Liputin had
sometimes dreamt of establishing a phalanstery in our province, this man certainly knew the day and hour when it
would come to pass. He made an ominous impression on

me; I was surprised to meet him now at Shatov's house, all the more so since Shatov didn't like to receive guests.

From the stairs I could hear them talking very loudly, all three at once, apparently arguing; but as soon as I entered, they all fell silent. They'd been arguing on their feet; now suddenly they all sat down, so I had to sit down, too. The absurd silence was unbroken for three full minutes. Even though Shigalyov recognized me, he pretended not to, probably not out of hostility, but for no special reason. Aleksei Nilych and I bowed slightly to one another, but in silence; for some reason we didn't shake hands. At last Shigalyov looked at me harshly and frowned, naïvely confident that I would immediately get up and leave the room. At last Shatov stood up from his chair; all the others suddenly jumped up too. They left without saying goodbye; only Shigalyov, standing in the doorway, turned to Shatov, who was seeing them out, and said:

'Remember, you're obliged to submit a full report.'

'To hell with your reports, and damned if I'm obliged to anyone,' Shatov said, seeing him out and locking the door behind them.

'Idiots!' he said, looking at me and smiling somewhat wryly.

He was angry and it seemed strange he should start talking. Previously, whenever I'd come to see him (which, by the way, happened very rarely), he would always sit in a corner scowling; he'd reply angrily, and only after a long time would he come to life and converse with any enjoyment. On the other hand, when saying goodbye, again every time he'd unfailingly scowl and show us out as if ridding himself of his mortal enemies.

'I had tea with Aleksei Nilych yesterday,' I remarked. 'He seems obsessed with atheism.'

'Russian atheism has never gone beyond a pun,' Shatov mumbled, replacing the burnt-out candle-end with a fresh new candle.

'No, this man doesn't seem to be a punster; he doesn't even know how to talk, let alone make puns.'

'Men made of paper—it's all due to the servility of their

thought,'* Shatov observed serenely, sitting himself down on a chair in the corner and resting his elbows on his knees.

'There's also hatred involved here,' he said after a moment's silence. 'They'd be the first to be terribly unhappy if somehow Russia were suddenly transformed, even according to their own ideas, and if it were suddenly to become immeasurably rich and happy. Then they'd have no one to hate, no one to despise, no one to mock! It's all an enormous, animal hatred for Russia that's eaten into their system... There are no tears unseen by the world, concealed beneath a smile! Never has a falser word been uttered in Russia than about those unseen tears!' he cried, almost in a fury.

'What on earth are you talking about?' I asked with a laugh.

'And you—you "moderate liberal",' Shatov said, also with a laugh. 'Do you know,' he went on abruptly, 'I may have been talking nonsense about "the servility of their thought". You'll probably say, "You're descended from a servile lackey, while I'm not".'

'That's not at all what I was going to say... Good Lord!'

'You needn't apologize. I'm not afraid of you. Once I was only the son of a lackey, but now I've become a lackey too, just like you. Our Russian liberal is first and foremost a lackey; the only thing he does is look for someone's boots to polish.'

'What boots? Is this some sort of allegory?'

'Allegory! I see you're laughing at me... Stepan Trofimovich was telling the truth when he said I was lying under a stone, squashed but not crushed, and I was only wriggling; it was a good comparison.'

'Stepan Trofimovich tells me you're obsessed with the Germans,' I said with a laugh. 'Still, we've managed to pick a thing or two from those Germans' pockets for our own use.'

'We took only twenty kopecks, but gave away a hundred roubles of our own.'

Both of us were silent for a minute.

'That sore comes from his lying there too long in America.'

'Who? What sore?'

'I'm talking about Kirillov. He and I lay on the floor in a little hut over there for four months.'

'Have you really been to America?' I asked in astonishment. 'You never said anything about it.'

'What's there to tell? Two years ago the three of us used our last kopecks to set out for the United States on an emigrant steamer, "to experience the life of American workers for ourselves and to learn through *personal* experience the fate of men living in the most arduous social conditions". That was our goal when we set out.'

'Good Lord!' I said with a laugh. 'You'd have been better off going to some place in our own province at harvest-time, instead of rushing to America "to learn through personal experience"!'

'We hired ourselves out as workers to an exploiter of labour; there were six of us Russians working for him—students, landowners from their estates, even officers—all of us with the same grand goal. Well, we worked, sweated, suffered, got exhausted; finally Kirillov and I left—we'd fallen ill and couldn't endure it. The exploiter, our boss, cheated us when he paid us off; he gave me only eight dollars, and Kirillov fifteen, instead of thirty dollars each, as he'd agreed. And he beat us there, too, more than once. Then, without any work, Kirillov and I spent four months lying on the floor in a hut in that awful little town, he thinking about one thing, I about another.'

'The boss beat you? That happened in America? You must really have cursed him!'

'Not at all. On the contrary, Kirillov and I decided at the time that "we Russians, when compared to Americans, are little children; one has to be born in America, or at least live among them for many years, to become their equal." Here's what happened: when they asked us to pay a dollar for something that was worth only a few kopecks, we paid it not only with pleasure, but even with enthusiasm. We praised everything: spiritualism, the lynch mob, the guns, the tramps. Once when we were travelling, a man put his hand into my pocket, took out my hairbrush, and started brushing his own hair; Kirillov and I exchanged glances and decided it was all right; in fact, we actually approved...'

'It's strange how we not only get these ideas, but also try to act on them,' I remarked.

'Men made of paper,' Shatov repeated.

'Nevertheless, to cross the ocean on an emigrant steamer, to an unknown land, even with the goal of "learning by personal experience", etc.—I swear there's a kind of noble resolve to it all... But how did you get away?'

'I wrote to someone in Europe and he sent me a hundred roubles.'

When he spoke, Shatov was in the habit of always keeping his eyes fixed on the floor, even when he became excited. But now he suddenly raised his head:

'Would you like to know the man's name?'

'Who was it?'

'Nikolai Stavrogin.'

He suddenly stood up, turned to his lime-wood writing desk, and began looking for something. We'd heard a vague, but reliable rumour to the effect that for some time his wife had been having an affair with Nikolai Stavrogin in Paris, precisely at the time, some two years ago, when Shatov was in America. Of course, that was long after she'd left him in Geneva. 'If that's true,' I wondered, 'what made him come up with that name now and make a point of it?'

'I still haven't paid him back,' he said, turning to me suddenly and staring at me intently; then he sat down again in his former place in the corner and asked abruptly in a completely different tone of voice:

'You've come for some reason or other. What do you want?'

I told him everything all at once, in precise chronological order, and added that even though I'd had time to think it over after the initial excitement, I was more confused than ever. I realized it was very important to Lizaveta Nikolaevna, and I dearly wanted to help her; the trouble was that not only didn't I know how to keep the promise I'd made, but I didn't even understand what I'd promised. Then I insisted three times that she'd never considered or intended to deceive him; there must have been some misunderstanding, and she was very upset by his extraordinary sudden departure.

He listened with rapt attention.

'Perhaps I acted stupidly this morning, as I sometimes do... Well, if she didn't understand why I left like that... so much the better for her.'

He stood up, went over to the door, opened it, and listened at the top of the stairs.

'Would you like to see that person yourself?'

'That's just what I'd like, but how can it be arranged?' I cried, jumping up in delight.

'We'll simply go there when she's alone. When he comes back, he'll beat her if he finds out we were there. I often go there in secret. I had a fight with him earlier today when he started beating her again.'

'What are you saying?'

'Just that! I dragged him away from her by the hair. He was going to beat me as well, but I scared him and that's how it ended. I'm afraid he'll come home drunk, remember what happened—and give her a sound beating for it.'

On that, we went downstairs.

5.

The door to Lebyadkin's apartment was closed, but not locked, so we walked right in. The entire apartment consisted of two nasty little rooms with grimy walls on which filthy wallpaper literally hung in shreds. For a while this part of the building had housed an eating establishment until the landlord, Filippov, moved to his new abode. The remaining rooms of the former establishment were now locked, with only two rented out to Lebyadkin. The furniture consisted of plain benches and deal tables, with the exception of one old armchair missing an arm. In the second room in a corner stood a bed with a cotton coverlet; this belonged to Mademoiselle Lebyadkina. The captain himself always slept on the floor, usually in whatever he was wearing. The whole place was littered and filthy; there were standing pools of water. A large, heavy, soaking-wet rag lay on the floor in the first room, and in the same puddle sat an old worn-out shoe. It was obvious that no one looked after the place; the stoves weren't heated, meals weren't prepared. They even lacked a samovar, as Shatov told me later. The captain and his sister had arrived there absolutely impoverished, and, as Liputin said, at first they really did go begging door to door. But, after receiving some money unexpectedly, the captain started drinking, and had become so fond of it that he no longer cared about looking after the place.

Mademoiselle Lebyadkina, whom I was so eager to see, was sitting quietly in a corner of the second room, on a bench at the deal table. She didn't speak to us when we opened the door and didn't stir from the spot. Shatov said that their door didn't lock and had once been left wide open all night. In the dim light of a slender candle in an iron candlestick I could make out a woman of perhaps thirty, painfully thin, dressed in an old, dark cotton dress, with her long neck uncovered, and with thin, dark hair twisted on the nape of her neck into a bun about the size of a two-year-old's fist. She looked at us cheerfully enough; in addition to the candlestick, on the table in front of her lay a small, old-fashioned mirror, an old deck of cards, a tattered song-book, and a roll of German white bread, from which a few bites had been taken. It was apparent that Mademoiselle Lebyadkina used powder and rouge, and that she painted her lips. She also pencilled her eyebrows, which were long, thin, and dark anyway. Three long wrinkles were sharply etched on her high, narrow forehead, in spite of all the powder. I already knew she was lame, but on this occasion she didn't stand up or walk around. At some time in her early youth her emaciated face might have been pretty; but her quiet, soft, grey eyes were even now still remarkable. There was something dreamy and genuine radiating from her peaceful, almost joyful expression. This peaceful, serene joy, also reflected in her smile, surprised me after all I'd heard about her brother's Cossack whip and other evidence of his brutality. It was strange, but instead of the painful and even frightening feeling of revulsion that one usually experiences in the presence of creatures so punished by God, I found it almost agreeable to look at her from the very first moment; afterwards it was a feeling of pity, rather than revulsion, that took hold of me.

'That's how she sits, literally for days at a time, all alone, without stirring, telling her fortune with cards or looking into the mirror,' said Shatov, pointing at her from the doorway. 'He doesn't bring her any food. The old woman who lives in the annexe sometimes gives her something to eat out of charity; how can they leave her all alone like this with only a candle?'

To my surprise, Shatov spoke out loud, as if she weren't even in the room.

'Hello, Shatushka!' Mademoiselle Lebyadkina said affably.

'I've brought you a visitor, Marya Timofeevna,' Shatov replied.

'Well, I'm pleased to see him. I don't know who it is you've brought. I don't recognize him,' she said, staring at me intently from behind the candle, then turning again to Shatov. (She took no more notice of me during the rest of the conversation, as if I weren't even there.)

'Did you get tired of walking up and down all alone in your attic, or what?' she asked with a laugh, showing two rows of magnificent teeth.

'Yes, and I decided to visit you.'

Shatov moved a bench up to the table, sat down, and bid me sit next to him.

'I'm always glad to have a little chat, but I find you such a funny person, Shatushka, just like a monk. When did you last comb your hair? Let me do it for you,' she said, taking a comb from her pocket. 'You probably haven't touched it since the last time I did it for you!'

'I don't even have a comb,' Shatov said with a laugh.

'Really? Then I'll give you mine; not this one, but another, only remind me.'

She set about combing his hair with a very serious expression; she even made a parting on one side, drew back a little, looked it over to see if it was right, and then put the comb back into her pocket.

'Do you know, Shatushka,' she said, shaking her head,

'you may be a sensible fellow, but you're bored. I find it strange to watch you all; I don't understand how it is people can be so bored. Melancholy isn't boredom. I'm very cheerful.'

'Are you cheerful living with your brother?'

'Are you asking about Lebyadkin? He's my lackey. It doesn't matter whether he's here or not. I shout, "Lebyadkin, bring me some water! Lebyadkin, fetch my shoes!" and he runs to fetch them. Sometimes I just can't help laughing at him.'

'That's exactly how it is,' Shatov said aloud to me again unceremoniously. 'She treats him just like her lackey. I've heard her shout, "Lebyadkin, bring me some water!" and then she laughs. The only difference is that he doesn't run to fetch it; he beats her instead. But she isn't the least bit afraid of him. She suffers some kind of nervous fits almost every day; they erase her memory so afterwards she forgets everything that happened and gets confused about the time. You think she remembers when we came in; perhaps, but most likely she's altered it somehow and thinks we're someone else, even though she knows I'm Shatushka. It doesn't matter that I'm talking out loud; she doesn't listen to people unless they're talking directly to her; instead she sinks into daydreams of her own—sinks, precisely. She's an inveterate daydreamer; for eight hours at a time, entire days, she sits in one spot. This roll here; she's probably taken only one bite all day, and she'll finish it tomorrow. Now she's begun to tell her fortune with cards...'

'I keep trying to tell my fortune, Shatushka, but it won't come out right,' Marya Timofeevna said suddenly, catching his last few words. Without looking she extended her left hand towards the roll (also, no doubt, because she heard him mention it). She finally picked it up, but after holding it for a while in her left hand, she was distracted once again by the conversation and put it down on the table without noticing, without having taken even one bite. 'It always comes out the same: a road, an evil man, someone's treachery, a death-bed, a letter from somewhere, unexpected news—I think it's all lies, Shatushka. What do you think? If people can lie, why can't cards?' she asked, suddenly mixing them together. 'I said the same thing once to Mother Praskovya, she's a venerable woman; she used to come to my cell and tell my fortune with cards, without letting on to the Mother Superior. And she wasn't the only one who used to come. They'd sigh and shake their heads and chatter about me, but I used to laugh: "Well," I said, "Mother Praskovya, how can you receive a letter, when you haven't received one for the last twelve years?" Her husband had taken her daughter away to somewhere in Turkey and she hadn't heard a word from them in twelve years. Well, the next evening I was having tea with the Mother Superior (she's a princess by birth, you know), and there was a lady-visitor there, too, a great daydreamer. There was also a monk from Mount Athos,* rather a funny little man in my opinion. What do you think, Shatushka, that very morning the same little monk brought the Mother Superior a letter from her daughter in Turkey—there's the jack of diamonds for you—unexpected news, you see! So, we were drinking our tea, and the monk from Mount Athos says to the Mother Superior: "Most of all, reverend Mother Superior, the Lord has blessed your convent inasmuch as you keep a great treasure hidden away within its walls." "What treasure is that?" the Mother Superior asked. "Why, mother Lizaveta the blessed," he replied. This same Lizaveta the blessed had been living in a cage seven feet long and five feet high that had been set into the convent wall; she'd been sitting there behind bars for the last seventeen years, summer and winter, in nothing but a hemp shift, constantly poking at it with a piece of straw or a little twig; all during these last seventeen years she never said anything, never combed her hair, and never washed. In winter they shove a sheepskin through the bars; every day they give her a crust of bread and a mug of water. Pilgrims stand there and stare, gasp, sigh, and leave a little money. "Some treasure that is," the Mother Superior replied. (She was angry; she disliked Lizaveta very much.) "Lizaveta sits there out of spite, sheer obstinacy; the whole thing is nothing but hypocrisy." I didn't like that very much; I'd been thinking about locking myself up just like that, too. "In my opinion",

I said, "God and nature are one and the same." They all cried in one voice, "Well, I never!" The Mother Superior laughed and began whispering to her lady-visitor about something or other; she called me over and caressed me, while the lady-visitor gave me a pink ribbon as a present. If you like, I'll show it to you. And the little monk began lecturing me, right then and there; he spoke very politely and modestly, with such intelligence, too. I sat there and listened to him. "Did you understand me?" he asked. "No," I replied, "I didn't understand a thing. Leave me in peace," I said. After that, Shatushka, they did leave me in peace. Meanwhile, one of the lay sisters, who was doing penance for having uttered prophecies, whispered as we were coming out of church, "What is the Mother of God, do you think?" "The great mother," I replied, "the hope of the human race." "Yes," she said, "the Mother of God is the great mother—the damp earth, and in that there's much rejoicing for men. Every earthly sorrow, each earthly tear is a joy for us; and when you've watered the earth with your tears a foot deep, you'll rejoice at everything all at once. And", she said, "you'll have no more sorrow. Such", she said, "is the prophecy." Those words sank into my heart at the time. Since then whenever I say my prayers and bow down, I kiss the earth; and every time I kiss it, I weep. This is what I can tell you, Shatushka: there's nothing bad about these tears. And even though you have no grief, your tears will still flow, for joy. Tears flow by themselves, that's for sure. I used to go out and stand on the shores of the lake: our convent stood on one side, Pointed Mountain on the other, that's what they used to call it, the Point. I used to climb this mountain, turn to face the east, fall down on the earth, and weep. I'd weep and never remember how long I wept; I didn't remember anything and didn't understand anything. Then I'd get up, turn back, and the sun would be setting— so large, splendid, glorious—do you like looking at the sun, Shatushka? It's nice, but sad. I'd turn back to the east, and the shadow, the shadow from our mountain, flies like an arrow across our lake; it's narrow, so very long—almost a mile long, stretching to the island in the lake, and it cuts that rocky island right in half; and just as it does so, the sun sets altogether and it suddenly becomes dark. Then I begin to feel miserable; my memory suddenly comes back. I'm afraid of the twilight, Shatushka. Most of all I used to cry about my little baby...'

'Did you really have a baby?' Shatov asked, nudging me with his elbow; all the while he'd been listening to her very attentively.

'Why, of course I did: a little, rosy baby with such tiny little toe-nails; my only misery is that I can't remember whether it was a boy or a girl. Sometimes I think it was a boy, other times, a girl. And when I gave birth to it, I wrapped it up in cambric and lace, tied pink ribbons on it, strewed it with flowers, got it ready, said a prayer over it, and carried the unbaptized child away, through the forest. I'm afraid of the forest and I felt frightened. But most of all I cry because I gave birth to that baby and I don't even know who its father was.'

'Perhaps you really did have a baby?' Shatov mused cautiously.

'I think you're so funny, Shatushka, with your reasoning. Perhaps I really did have a baby; so what if I did, if it really doesn't matter whether I did or not? Now that's an easy riddle for you! Well, guess it!' she said laughing.

'Where did you take your baby?'

'To the pond,' she sighed.

Once again Shatov nudged me with his elbow.

'And what if you really didn't have a baby and all this is just your imagination?'

'That's a hard question, Shatushka,' she replied thoughtfully, showing no surprise. 'I can't say any more about it. Perhaps I really didn't have one. I think it's just your curiosity; but I still won't stop crying over it. I couldn't have dreamt it, could I?' Large tears glistened in her eyes. 'Shatushka, Shatushka, is it true your wife ran away from you?' she asked, suddenly placing both her hands on his shoulders and looking at him pityingly. 'Don't be angry; I'm not feeling so well either. Shatushka, you know what I dreamt about: he comes to me again, beckons to me, calls to me: "Pussycat," he says, "my pussycat, come to me!" I was so pleased by his calling me "pussycat"; I think he loves me.'

'He may even come when you're awake,' Shatov mumbled in a low voice.

'No, Shatushka, it was just a dream... he won't come when I'm awake. Do you know the song:

> For me, no need of a tall new house.
> I'll stay in this little cell,
> I'll live on here to save my soul,
> And pray to God for thee.*

Oh, Shatushka, Shatushka, my dear, why don't you ever ask me anything?'

'Because you won't tell—that's why I don't ask.'

'I won't tell, I won't tell, even if you kill me, I won't tell,' she said quickly. 'Burn me, I won't tell. However much I suffer, I won't say a thing; people will never know!'

'There, you see, everyone does as he pleases,' said Shatov even more softly, his head drooping lower and lower.

'But if you ask, I might just tell; perhaps I will tell!' she repeated ecstatically. 'Why don't you ask? Ask me, ask me nicely, Shatushka, perhaps I'll tell you. Beg me, Shatushka, so I'll agree to it myself... Shatushka, Shatushka!'

But Shatushka remained quiet; the general silence continued for a minute or so. Tears rolled softly down her powdered cheeks; she sat there, her hands resting on Shatov's shoulders, but she was no longer looking at him.

'Oh, what do I care about you, anyway? For pity's sake!' Shatov said, suddenly standing up from the bench. 'Get up!' he shouted and angrily pulled the bench out from under me and put it back again.

'He'll be here soon; I don't want him to know we were here. It's time we left.'

'Oh, you're still on about my lackey!' Marya Timofeevna said suddenly with a laugh. 'You're afraid! Well, goodbye, my dear guests; but listen to me for one more minute. A little while ago that Nilych, Mr Kirillov, came in here with Filippov, the landlord with a big red beard, just as my lackey was coming after me. The landlord grabbed hold of him, hurled him across the room, while my lackey shouted: "I'm innocent! I'm suffering for another man's guilt!" Well, would you believe it, we all just burst out laughing...'

'Hey, Timofeevna, it was me, not him with the red beard; it was me who pulled him away from you by his hair this very morning. And the landlord was here the day before yesterday and fought with you then. You've got it all confused.'

'Wait, maybe I did confuse it; perhaps it was you. Well, why argue over details? It doesn't matter to him who pulls him away from me, does it?' she said with a laugh.

'Let's go,' Shatov said and yanked me all of a sudden. 'The gate's creaking. If he finds us here, he'll beat us up.'

But before we even had time to run out on to the stairs we heard a drunken shout and a string of oaths at the gate. Shatov let me into his room and locked the door.

'You'll have to stay here for a minute, if you don't want to create a scene. You see, he's squealing like a little pig; he must have stumbled over the gate again. He falls flat on his face every time.'

But we didn't get away without a scene.

6.

Shatov stood listening at the closed door of his room; suddenly he jumped back.

Someone's fist was heard thumping hard on the door.

'He's coming, I knew it!' he whispered furiously. 'Now there'll be no getting rid of him before midnight.'

'Shatov, Shatov, open up!' the captain cried. 'Shatov, my friend!...

> I have come to welcome you,*
> To say that dawn so warm and bright
> Trembles all the forest through,
> Stirring hopes of new delight,
> To say that I've awakened too... goddammit to hell...
> A-tingle with life, beneath the branches...

Just like beneath the birch-rods, ha, ha!

Each little bird awakening now... begs for a drink!...
To tell you... I'm dying for a drink.
What kind of drink? No matter, I'll drink it.

Well, the hell with stupid curiosity! Shatov, do you understand how good it is to be alive?'

'Don't say a thing,' Shatov whispered to me again.

'Open up! Do you understand that there are more important things among men than quarrels...; there are moments when an hon-our-able person... Shatov, I'm a good man; I forgive you... Shatov, to hell with those proclamations, do you hear?'

Silence.

'Do you understand, you ass, I'm in love. I've bought a frock-coat. Look, a lover's frock-coat, for fifteen roubles. A captain's love requires the social niceties... Open up!' he roared ferociously all of a sudden and began pounding on the door violently with his fists.

'Go to hell!' Shatov suddenly roared back.

'You s-s-slave! You s-s-serf! And your sister's a slave and a serf... and a th-thief!'

'You sold your sister.'

'Liar! I tolerate this slander, when with one word of explanation I could... Do you know who she really is?'

'Who is she?' Shatov asked, suddenly approaching the door out of curiosity.

'Don't you understand?'

'I'll understand once you tell me. Who is she?'

'I'm not afraid to say it! I'm never afraid to say anything in public!'

'Well, I doubt that,' Shatov said, taunting him, and signalled to me to listen.

'You think I'm afraid?'

'Yes, I do.'

'I'm afraid?'

'Well, go on and say it then, if you're not afraid of your master's birch-rods... Why, you're a coward, even though you're a captain!'

'I... I... she... she's...' stammered the captain in a trembling, agitated voice.

'Well?' Shatov asked, putting his ear to the door.

There ensued a silence lasting for at least half a minute.

'Sc-sc-scoundrel!' was heard from the other side of the door at long last, and the captain beat a hasty retreat downstairs, puffing like a samovar, stumbling noisily on every step.

'Well, he's a sly one! Even when he's drunk he won't give himself away,' Shatov said, moving away from the door.

'What's it all about?' I asked.

Shatov waved my question aside, unlocked the door, and began listening on the staircase once again. He listened for a long time, even going down a few steps quietly. At last he returned.

'I don't hear anything. He didn't quarrel with her. He must've slumped asleep at once. It's time you went.'

'Listen, Shatov, what am I to make of all this?'

'Oh, whatever you like!' he said in a tired and disgusted voice, and sat down at his writing-table.

I left. One improbable idea was taking firmer and firmer hold of my imagination. I contemplated the next day with anguish.

7.

The 'next day', that is, that very same Sunday on which Stepan Trofimovich's fate was to be irrevocably sealed, is one of the most momentous days in my entire chronicle. It was a day of unexpected events, a day on which riddles of the past were resolved and new ones set, a day of harsh clarification and even worse confusion. In the morning, as the reader is already well aware, I was obliged to accompany my friend to Varvara Petrovna's house, according to her own wishes; and at three o'clock in the afternoon I was supposed to go to Lizaveta Nikolaevna's to tell her—I didn't know what, and to assist her—I didn't know how. In the meantime everything turned out in a way that no one could have predicted. In a word, it was a day of the most extraordinary coincidences.

It began when Stepan Trofimovich and I arrived at Varvara Petrovna's house precisely at twelve o'clock, just as she'd indicated, but didn't find her at home; she hadn't yet returned from church. My poor friend was so disposed, or, to put it more accurately, so indisposed, that this circumstance immediately overwhelmed him: he sank into an armchair in the living-room almost in a state of collapse. I offered him a glass of water, but in spite of his pallor and trembling hands, he refused my offer with dignity. By the way, his apparel on this occasion was remarkable for its elegance: he looked as if he were going to a ball. He wore an embroidered lawn shirt, a white cravat, he had a new hat in his hand, new straw-coloured gloves, and he even smelled faintly of scent. No sooner did we sit down than Shatov arrived, ushered in by the butler; clearly it was also by official invitation. Stepan Trofimovich was about to get up and offer his hand, but Shatov, looking carefully at both of us, went over to one corner of the room and sat down without nodding to anyone. Stepan Trofimovich looked at me again in dismay.

Thus we sat for several minutes in absolute silence. Stepan Trofimovich suddenly started whispering something to me, but I couldn't make it out; he was so agitated that he didn't finish what he started to say and gave up. The butler came in again to arrange something on the table; more likely it was just to gawk at us. Shatov suddenly addressed a loud question to him:

'Aleksei Yegorych, do you know if Darya Pavlovna went with her?'

'Varvara Petrovna went to church alone, sir; Darya Pavlovna stayed behind because she wasn't feeling well, sir,' Aleksei Yegorych reported in an edifying and respectful manner.

Once again my poor friend shot me a fleeting, agitated glance, so that finally I had to turn away from him. Suddenly a carriage was heard rumbling up to the entrance; some distant commotion in the house indicated that the mistress had returned. We all jumped up from our chairs, but there was another surprise: we heard the approach of many footsteps, which meant that the mistress was not alone. This indeed seemed rather odd, since it was she who'd fixed the time for the meeting. At last we heard someone coming in with oddly rapid steps, as if running; Varvara Petrovna would not have come in like that. Suddenly she almost flew into the room, all out of breath and in a state of great agitation. Behind her, at some distance and at a slower pace, came Lizaveta Nikolaevna, and with her, arm in arm—Marya Timofeevna Lebyadkina! Even if I'd dreamt this scene, still I'd never have believed it!

In order to explain this completely unexpected turn of events, we must go back an hour and describe the extraordinary adventure that befell Varvara Petrovna in church.

In the first place, almost the entire town had gathered for the service, that is, of course, the upper stratum of our society. It was known that the governor's wife would make an appearance, her first since arriving among us. I must remark that rumours had been circulating to the effect that she was a free-thinker and a proponent of the 'new principles'. All the ladies also knew that she would come dressed magnificently and with unusual elegance; consequently, the apparel of our own ladies was also distinguished on this occasion by its splendour and refinement. Only Varvara Petrovna was dressed modestly in black, as always; she'd been dressing that way for the last four years. Upon arriving at the cathedral she took up her usual position, in the first row on the left, and a footman in livery laid a velvet cushion down for her to kneel on; in a word, everything was normal. But it was observed that on this occasion, throughout the service, she prayed with unusual fervour; afterwards, when people recalled these events, it was even reported that she had tears in her eyes. When the service was finally over, our archpriest, Father Pavel, came forward to deliver a solemn sermon. We all loved his sermons and valued them highly; some of us tried to persuade him to publish them, but he would never agree to do so. On this occasion his sermon was particularly long.

It was during the sermon that a lady drove up to the church in an old-fashioned horse cab, that is, one in which women had to sit sideways, holding on to the driver's belt, and swaying at every jolt of the carriage, like a blade of grass in the wind. There were still some of these cabs to be found in our town. Stopping at one corner of the cathedral—for there were quite a few carriages and even some mounted police at the gate—a lady jumped down from the cab and handed the driver four kopecks in silver.

'What? Isn't that enough, Vanya?' she cried when she saw his grimace. 'It's all I have,' she added plaintively.

'Well, so be it. I took you without fixing the price,' the driver said with a hopeless gesture; he looked at her as if thinking, 'It'd be a sin to take more from the likes of you.' Then, stashing his leather purse in his coat, he touched his horse and drove off, accompanied by jeers from other drivers nearby. Jeers and even astonishment accompanied the lady as well, as she made her way to the gates of the cathedral through the carriages and the lackeys waiting for their masters to emerge. There really was something extraordinary and unexpected for everyone in the sudden appearance of such a person among the people in the street. She was painfully thin, and limping; her face was thickly covered with powder and rouge; her long neck was completely exposed since she wore neither kerchief nor burnous; she wore only an old, dark dress, in spite of the cold, windy, though clear September day. Her head was bare, her hair gathered into a tiny bun at the nape of her neck, into which an artificial rose had been stuck on the right side, the kind used to decorate cherubs during Holy Week. I'd noticed the same kind of cherub in a wreath of paper roses in a corner under the icons in Marya Timofeevna's room yesterday. As a finishing touch, although the lady walked modestly with eyes downcast, she was still smiling merrily and playfully. If she'd waited a moment or so more, they might not have let her into the cathedral... But she managed to slip through, and once she entered, she pushed her way to the front unnoticed.

Although the sermon was only half over and the enormous throng filling the church was listening to it with rapt and hushed attention, nevertheless several pairs of eyes shot glances of curiosity and amazement at the new arrival. She knelt down on the church dais, her powdered face touching the floor; she stayed there a long time, evidently weeping; but after lifting her head and getting off her knees, she soon recovered and cheered up. Merrily and with obvious relish she let her eyes roam the faces in the crowd and the walls of the church; she stared at other ladies with particular fascination, rising up on tiptoe to get a better look; she even started laughing once or twice, emitting a very strange giggle. But the sermon ended and the cross was carried out. The governor's wife was first to approach the cross, but stopped about two steps in front of it, obviously wishing to yield to Varvara Petrovna. She for her part seemed to be heading straight for it, without taking notice of anything in front of her. The unusual courtesy of the governor's wife undoubtedly contained an obvious and clever snub; that's how everyone took it, and that's how Varvara Petrovna must have taken it, too. But she walked on as before, without taking notice of anyone; with a most invincible air of dignity, she kissed the cross and immediately turned to head for the door. The lackey in livery cleared the way for her, even though everyone was moving out of her path anyway. But at the door, on the church porch, a small crowd of people blocked her way for a moment. Varvara Petrovna stopped; all of a sudden a strange, unusual creature, a woman with a paper rose in her hair, pushed her way through the crowd, and fell on her knees right in front of her. Varvara Petrovna, who was not easily disconcerted, especially in public, glared at her sternly and solemnly.

Here I hasten to observe, as briefly as possible, that even though over the last few years Varvara Petrovna had become, it was said, excessively careful and even stingy, she sometimes contributed quite generously, especially for some charitable purpose. She was a member of a benevolent society in the capital. During the last famine* she sent to Petersburg the sum of five hundred roubles to the main committee in charge of relief for the victims, and this was much talked about in our town. Finally, and most recently, just before the appointment of our new governor, she was planning to establish a local ladies' committee to assist the poorest expectant mothers in our town and in our province. In town she was accused of being ambitious; but the well-known impetuosity of Varvara Petrovna's character, combined with her determination, triumphed over almost all obstacles. The committee was very nearly formed, and the original idea grew larger and larger in the founder's exalted imagination. She dreamt of establishing a similar committee in Moscow and of the gradual expansion of its activity throughout the provinces. Then, with the sudden change of governor, everything came to a halt; it was said that the new governor's wife had already uttered some biting and, what was worse, appropriate and sensible remarks in public concerning the impracticality of the basic idea of such a committee, which remarks were reported back to Varvara Petrovna, naturally with some embellishment. God only knows the depth of the human heart, but I suppose that now Varvara Petrovna stopped at the church gate with some considerable pleasure, knowing that the governor's wife would have to pass by there, followed by everyone else: 'Let her see for herself how little it matters to me what she thinks or what clever remarks she makes about the vanity of my charitable deeds. So much for the lot of you!'

'What is it, my dear? What do you want?' asked Varvara Petrovna, looking more attentively at the young woman kneeling before her. The supplicant looked up at her with an awfully timid, embarrassed, almost reverent expression, and suddenly burst out laughing with that same strange giggle.

'What does she want? Who is she?' Varvara Petrovna asked, surveying the crowd with an imperious and enquiring gaze. Everyone was silent.

'Are you unhappy? Do you need help?'

'I need... I've come...' muttered the 'unfortunate creature' in a voice breaking with feeling. 'I've come merely to kiss your hand...' she said, and giggled once again. With an expression which children use to cajole an adult into giving them something they want, she reached out to take Varvara Petrovna's hand, but suddenly drew back, as if afraid.

'Is that all you came for?' asked Varvara Petrovna with a compassionate smile; but promptly took a mother-of-pearl purse out of her pocket, removed a ten-rouble note, and handed it to the stranger, who took it. Varvara Petrovna was fascinated; apparently she realized that this strange woman was not just an ordinary beggar.

'Look, she gave her ten roubles,' said someone in the crowd.

'Your hand, please let me kiss it,' muttered the 'unfortunate creature', holding on tightly with the fingers of her left hand to a corner of the ten-rouble note which fluttered in the breeze. For some reason Varvara Petrovna frowned a little and extended her hand with a serious, almost stern, air; the young woman kissed it with reverence. Her eyes shone with gratitude and a kind of ecstasy. It was just at this moment that the governor's wife drew near, followed by an enormous crowd of ladies and senior officials. The governor's wife was forced to pause for a moment in the crush; many others stopped as well.

'You're shivering. Are you cold?' Varvara Petrovna asked suddenly, and removing her cloak, caught in mid-air by her footman, she took off her own black (by no means inexpensive) shawl, and with her own hands wrapped it around the exposed neck of the young supplicant who was still down on her knees.

'Stand up, get off your knees, I beg you!' The young woman stood up.

'Where do you live? Is it really possible that no one here knows where she lives?' Varvara Petrovna asked, once again looking around impatiently at the crowd. But the crowd was different now; all she saw were the familiar faces of society people observing the proceedings—some with stern astonishment, others with sly curiosity, and, at the same time, an innocent desire for a scene, and still others who'd even begun to chuckle.

'I think she's one of the Lebyadkins, ma'am,' some kind person offered at last in reply to Varvara Petrovna's question. It was our worthy and well-respected merchant Andreev, who had glasses and a grey beard, and wore Russian dress with a tall, cylindrical hat which he was now holding in his hands. 'She lives in Filippov's house on Bogoyavlenskaya Street.'

'Lebyadkin? Filippov's house? I've heard something...
Thank you, Nikon Semyonych. But who is this Lebyadkin?'

'He calls himself a captain. He's a man who's not too
careful in his behaviour. And this, I'm almost sure, is his
younger sister. She must have escaped from the house,'
Nikon Semyonych continued, dropping his voice and giving
Varvara Petrovna a meaningful look.

'I understand. Thank you, Nikon Semyonych. And you,
my dear, are you Miss Lebyadkina?'

'No, I'm not.'

'Then perhaps your brother's name is Lebyadkin?'

'Yes, Lebyadkin is my brother.'

'This is what I'm going to do. Right now, my dear, I
shall take you home with me, and then you'll be taken back
to your own house. Would you like to come home with me?'

'Oh, yes, I would!' Miss Lebyadkina cried, clapping her
hands.

'Auntie, Auntie! Take me home with you, too,' Lizaveta
Nikolaevna's voice rang out. I must note that Liza had
arrived at the cathedral with the governor's wife, while
Praskovya Ivanovna, on her doctor's orders, had gone for a
drive in her carriage, taking Maurice Nikolaevich along to
amuse her. Liza suddenly left the governor's wife and ran
up to Varvara Petrovna.

'My dear, you know I'm always glad to see you, but what
will your mother say?' Varvara Petrovna began grandly, but
she suddenly became confused, noticing Liza's extreme
agitation.

'Auntie, Auntie, you must take me with you,' Liza begged,
kissing Varvara Petrovna.

'*Mais qu'avez-vous donc, Lise!*'[1] the governor's wife enquired with significant surprise.

'Oh, forgive me, my dear, *chère cousine*, I'm going to visit
my aunt,' said Liza in passing to her unpleasantly surprised
chère cousine, and kissed her twice.

'And tell *maman* to come to Auntie's as well, at once.
Maman was very eager to call on you; she said so herself,

[1] But what's the matter with you, Liza!

but I forgot to tell you,' Liza said, rattling on. 'I'm sorry, don't be angry, Julie... *chère cousine*.... Auntie, I'm ready!'

'If you don't take me with you, Auntie, I'll run behind your carriage screaming,' she whispered quickly and desperately into her aunt's ear; it was a good thing no one heard her. Varvara Petrovna even took a step back to cast a penetrating glance at this crazy girl. Her glance decided everything: she resolved to take Liza with her!

'Let's put an end to all this!' she blurted out. 'Fine, I'll be glad to take you with me, Liza,' she added at once in a loud voice, 'that is, of course, if Yulia Mikhailovna agrees to let you go,' she said, turning directly to the governor's wife with a candid look and utmost dignity.

'Oh, I certainly don't want to deprive her of such pleasure, all the more so, since I myself...' Yulia Mikhailovna muttered suddenly with astonishing affability, 'since I myself... know full well what a fantastic, wilful little head she has on those little shoulders of hers...' (Yulia Mikhailovna gave a charming smile).

'I'm extremely grateful to you,' replied Varvara Petrovna with a polite and stately bow.

'And I'm all the more pleased,' Yulia Mikhailovna continued to murmur, now almost in ecstasy, even blushing from a sweet sense of agitation, 'since, in addition to the pleasure of being at your house, Liza is being carried away by such a splendid, I should say, noble feeling... such compassion...' (she glanced at the 'unfortunate creature')'... and... right here on the church porch...'

'Such a feeling does you honour,' Varvara Petrovna said, expressing her generous approval. Yulia Mikhailovna impulsively extended her hand, and Varvara Petrovna, without the slightest hesitation, touched it with her fingers. The general impression was magnificent; the faces of several people in attendance shone with pleasure; a few sweet and ingratiating smiles were to be seen.

In a word, it suddenly became clear to the entire town that it was not Yulia Mikhailovna who'd been ignoring Varvara Petrovna up to now by not paying her a visit, but Varvara Petrovna herself, on the contrary, who'd been 'keep-

ing Yulia Mikhailovna at a distance, when she might have
been willing to call on Varvara Petrovna even on foot, if
only she'd been sure the latter would have received her.'
Varvara Petrovna's prestige rose to great heights.

'Get in, my dear,' said Varvara Petrovna to Mademoiselle
Lebyadkina, indicating the carriage that had just pulled up.
The 'unfortunate creature' ran to the carriage door joyfully
and the footman helped her in.

'Good Lord! You're lame!' Varvara Petrovna cried, as
though really frightened and she blanched. (Everyone noticed at the time, but didn't understand...)

The carriage moved off. Varvara Petrovna's house was not
far from the cathedral. Liza told me afterwards that Lebyadkina laughed hysterically all during the three-minute ride,
while Varvara Petrovna sat there 'as if in a hypnotic trance',
to use Liza's own expression.

CHAPTER 5

The wise serpent

I.

VARVARA PETROVNA rang the bell and flung herself into an armchair near the window.

'Sit here, my dear,' she said, motioning Marya Timofeevna to a seat in the middle of the room near a large round table. 'Stepan Trofimovich, what do you make of her? Go on, have a look at this woman. What do you make of her?'

'I... I...' Stepan Trofimovich began mumbling...

But a footman appeared.

'Bring me a cup of coffee at once, as soon as possible! Don't unharness the carriage.'

'*Mais, chère et excellente amie, dans quelle inquiétude...*'[1] exclaimed Stepan Trofimovich in a faltering voice.

'Oh! French, French! You can tell at once we're in high society!' Marya Timofeevna said, clapping her hands, rapturously, expecting to hear a conversation in French. Varvara Petrovna stared at her almost in terror.

We all remained silent, waiting to see what would happen. Shatov kept his eyes down, while Stepan Trofimovich looked very embarrassed, as if he were to blame for everything; his temples were bathed in perspiration. I glanced at Liza (she was sitting in the corner, close to Shatov). Her sharp eyes darted from Varvara Petrovna to the crippled woman and back again; her lips were twisted into an unpleasant grin. Varvara Petrovna noticed it. Meanwhile Marya Timofeevna was thoroughly diverted: with enjoyment and without the least trace of embarrassment she examined Varvara Petrovna's splendid drawing-room—the furnishings, rugs, pictures on the walls, old-fashioned painted ceiling, large bronze crucifix hanging in the corner, porcelain lamp, albums, and knick-knacks on the table.

'So, you're here, too, Shatushka!' she exclaimed suddenly.

---

[1] But, dear and excellent friend, in what distress

'Just think, I noticed you some time ago, but I thought: no, it's not you! How could you be here?' she said and laughed gaily.

'Do you know this woman?' Varvara Petrovna asked, turning to him immediately.

'Yes, ma'am,' Shatov muttered. He seemed about to move from his chair, but remained seated.

'What do you know about her? Tell me, please, this instant!'

'Well...' he replied with an unnecessary smile, then hesitated. 'You see for yourself.'

'What do I see? Well, say something!'

'She lives in the same house as I do... with her brother... an officer.'

'Well?'

Shatov hesitated again.

'It's not worth talking about...' he mumbled and lapsed into determined silence. He even turned red in his determination.

'Of course, there's nothing more to be got out of you!' Varvara Petrovna said, cutting him short in indignation. Now it was clear to her that everyone knew something and was afraid, avoiding her questions, wanting to conceal something from her.

The footman entered carrying a small silver tray with the cup of coffee she'd specially ordered, but at once, on her signal he offered it to Marya Timofeevna.

'My dear, you were very cold just now; drink it quickly and warm yourself up.'

'*Merci*,' Marya Timofeevna replied taking the cup, and suddenly burst out laughing because she had said '*merci*' to a footman. But encountering Varvara Petrovna's threatening glance she grew timid and put the cup on the table.

'Auntie, you're not angry, are you?' she murmured with a kind of frivolous playfulness.

'Wha-a-at?' Varvara Petrovna said with a start, sitting straight up in her chair. 'I'm no aunt of yours! What do you mean by that?'

Marya Timofeevna hadn't expected her to be so angry;

she began shaking all over with slight tremors, as if she
were having a fit, and then fell back into her chair.

'I... I thought that's what I was supposed to call you,'
she babbled, staring at Varvara Petrovna. 'That's what Liza
calls you.'

'Which Liza is that?'

'Why, this young lady,' she said pointing her finger.

'Since when has she become Liza to you?'

'You called her that just now,' Marya Timofeevna said,
feeling a bit bolder. 'Once I saw a beautiful girl like her in
my dream,' she added, laughing as it were unintentionally.

Varvara Petrovna thought for a moment and then calmed
down; she even smiled ever so slightly at Marya Timofeevna's last remark. Marya caught her smile, stood up from
her chair, and limping, approached her timidly.

'Here, take it; I forgot to give it back to you. Don't be
angry with me for my discourtesy,' she said, suddenly
removing from her shoulders the black shawl Varvara Petrovna had placed there earlier.

'Put it on again this minute and keep it from now on.
Go and sit down, drink your coffee, and please, don't be
afraid of me, my dear, calm down. I'm beginning to understand you.'

'*Chère amie*...' Stepan Trofimovich allowed himself to
begin again.

'Ah, Stepan Trofimovich, this is barely making sense
without your help, so spare me... Please, ring the bell next
to you for the maid.'

Silence ensued. Her eyes suspiciously and irritably surveyed all our faces. Agasha, her favourite maid, came in.

'Bring me my checked kerchief, the one I bought in
Geneva. What's Darya Pavlovna doing?'

'She's not feeling well, ma'am.'

'Go and ask her to come in here. Say I'd really like her
to come, even if she isn't feeling well.'

At this moment an unusual noise of footsteps and voices
was again heard in the next room, just as before; suddenly a
panting and 'distraught' Praskovya Ivanovna appeared at the
door. Maurice Nikolaevich was supporting her by the arm.

'Oh, good heavens, I could scarcely drag myself out here; Liza, are you mad, or what, the way you treat your mother?' she shrieked, investing that shriek with all her pent-up irritation, as weak, irritable people tend to do.

'My dear Varvara Petrovna, I've come to fetch my daughter!'

Varvara Petrovna glanced at her sullenly, and half rose to meet her; scarcely concealing her annoyance, she said:

'Good day, Praskovya Ivanovna, pray sit down. I knew you'd come.'

2.

There was nothing surprising for Praskovya Ivanovna in such a reception. Varvara Petrovna had always, from early childhood, treated her former schoolfriend despotically, and, under the guise of friendship, almost with contempt. But the present situation was exceptional. During the last few days relations between the two households had been strained to breaking point, as I mentioned briefly earlier. The reasons for this incipient rupture remained a mystery to Varvara Petrovna; consequently, they were all the more offensive to her. But the main thing was that Praskovya Ivanovna had succeeded in adopting an extraordinarily overbearing attitude toward Varvara Petrovna. The latter, of course, felt wounded; meanwhile, certain strange rumours had begun to reach her, also very irritating, particularly on account of their vagueness. Varvara Petrovna's character was straightforward and proudly candid, inclined to attack head-on, if one may express it like that. Less than anything could she tolerate secret and mysterious allegations, and always preferred open warfare. Be that as it may, it was now five days since these two ladies had seen each other. Varvara Petrovna had paid the last call and had left that 'Drozdova woman's' house feeling offended and confused. I can state with certainty that Praskovya Ivanovna came now in the naïve conviction that Varvara Petrovna had some reason to be afraid of her; this was obvious from the expression on her face. But it was also clear that Varvara Petrovna was possessed by a demon of the most arrogant pride whenever she had even the least suspicion that she was supposed to feel humiliated. Praskovya Ivanovna, like many weak personalities who have allowed themselves to be insulted for some time without protesting, showed unusual zest for launching an attack at the first favourable opportunity. True, she was unwell, but she'd become even more irritable as a result of her illness. Let me add that the presence of all these people gathered in the drawing-room would have done nothing whatsoever to inhibit these two childhood friends, if indeed some quarrel had erupted between them; we were looked upon as friends of the family, almost as subordinates. I realized this at the time not without anxiety. Stepan Trofimovich, who hadn't sat down since Varvara Petrovna entered the room, lowered himself into a chair in exhaustion the moment he heard Praskovya Ivanovna's shriek, and desperately tried to catch my eye. Shatov turned sharply in his chair and began to mutter to himself. I think he wanted to get up and leave. Liza stood up, but immediately sank down again, without paying the requisite attention to her mother's scream, not because of her 'obstinate character', but because she was entirely preoccupied with another powerful impression. She was staring into space, almost absent-mindedly, and had even stopped taking any notice of Marya Timofeevna.

3.

'Oh, over here!' Praskovya Ivanovna said, pointing to a chair near the table; with some assistance from Maurice Nikolaevich, she sank heavily into it. 'I wouldn't sit down in your house, my dear, if it weren't for my legs!' she added in a hysterical voice.

Varvara Petrovna raised her head slightly, and, with a pained expression, pressed the fingers of her right hand to her right temple, obviously feeling a sharp pain (*tic douloureux*).

'What's this all about, Praskovya Ivanovna? Why can't you sit down in my house? I enjoyed your late husband's sincere friendship all his life; you and I played with our dolls together when we were little girls in boarding school.'

Praskovya Ivanovna dismissed her with a wave of her hand.

'I knew that was coming! You always start talking about school when you intend to reproach me. That's your little trick. In my opinion, it's only rhetoric. I can't stand you and your boarding school.'

'You seem to have come in a very nasty temper; how are your legs? Here now, have some coffee, please; drink it and don't be so angry.'

'My dear Varvara Petrovna, you're treating me as if I were a little girl. I don't want any coffee, so there!'

And she querulously waved away the servant bringing her a cup of coffee. (By the way, the others also declined coffee, except for Maurice Nikolaevich and myself. Stepan Trofimovich accepted a cup, but placed his on the table. Although Marya Timofeevna really wanted another cup and had even reached for it, she thought better of it and ceremoniously declined, obviously quite pleased with herself for doing so.)

Varvara Petrovna smiled wryly.

'Do you know, Praskovya Ivanovna, my dear, you must have been imagining something when you came in here. All your life you've been imagining things. You became irritated because I mentioned school; but don't you remember when you arrived and assured the whole class that that hussar, Shablykin, proposed to you, and how Madame Lefebure proved you were lying? But you weren't really lying; you'd simply imagined it all to amuse yourself. Well, tell me, what is it now? What are you imagining? What are you so upset about?'

'Well, you fell in love with the priest at school, the one who taught us Scripture. There's something for you, if you want to harbour such memories for so long! Ha, ha, ha!'

She burst out laughing spitefully and ended in a coughing fit.

'A-ah, so you haven't forgotten about that priest...' Varvara Petrovna said, staring at her malevolently.

Her face turned green. Praskovya Ivanovna suddenly assumed a more dignified air.

'Well, my dear, I'm really in no mood for laughter right now. Why have you dragged my daughter into your scandal in front of the whole town? That's really why I came here!'

'Into my scandal?' Varvara Petrovna said, suddenly drawing herself up menacingly.

'Mamma, I too would like you to be more moderate,' Lizaveta Nikolaevna said suddenly.

'What did you say?' her mother replied, about to start screaming again; but suddenly subsided, catching sight of her daughter's flashing eyes.

'How can you talk about a scandal, mamma?' cried Liza, flushing. 'I came here myself with Yulia Mikhailovna's permission to hear this poor woman's story and to help her.'

' "This poor woman's story!" ' Praskovya Ivanovna drawled with malicious laughter. 'Is it right for you to get mixed up in such "stories"? Oh no, my dear! We've had enough of your despotism!' she said, turning furiously to Varvara Petrovna. 'I don't know whether it's true or not, but they say you've got the whole town trained; it seems to me, however, that now your time has also come!'

Varvara Petrovna sat there taut as an arrow ready to fly from a bow. For ten seconds she stared sternly at Praskovya Ivanovna without stirring.

'Well, Praskovya, you can thank God that everyone here is one of us,' she said at last with sinister composure. 'You've said more than you needed to.'

'Well, my dear, I'm not so afraid of public opinion as some people are; it's you, in the guise of pride, who tremble before public opinion. As for everyone here being one of us, it's you who should be pleased, since it would've been worse if any strangers had been here listening.'

'Have you grown a little wiser this past week?'

'No, I haven't grown any wiser this past week, but obviously the truth has now come out.'

'What truth? Listen, Praskovya Ivanovna, don't annoy me any further. I insist you explain yourself this very minute: what truth has come out and what exactly do you mean?'

'Why, here it is, the truth is sitting right here!' Praskovya Ivanovna replied suddenly and motioned to Marya Timo-

feevna with that desperate determination that no longer
worries about consequences, as long as it can land a solid
blow. Marya Timofeevna, who'd been looking at her all
along with cheerful curiosity, burst into joyous laughter at
the sight of the visitor's angry finger pointed at her; blithely
she shifted her position in her chair.

'Jesus Christ, Our Lord, have they all gone mad, or what?'
Varvara Petrovna cried, turning pale and sinking back into
her armchair.

She became so pale there was even general consternation.
Stepan Trofimovich was first to rush over to her. I went up
to her as well. Even Liza stood up, although she remained
near her chair. But it was Praskovya Ivanovna who was most
frightened of all: she cried out, raised herself as far as she
could, and wailed in a mournful voice:

'Varvara Petrovna, my dear, forgive my wicked foolishness! Water, someone give her a drink of water!'

'Don't whimper, please, Praskovya Ivanovna, I beg you.
And get away, gentlemen, do me a favour. I don't need any
water!' Varvara Petrovna pronounced firmly, though not
very loudly, through pale lips.

'My dear!' Praskovya Ivanovna continued, a little more
composed. 'Varvara Petrovna, my friend, although I may be
wrong to have said more than I should have, I'm most upset
by all these anonymous letters that horrible people have
been bombarding me with. They really ought to be sending
them to you, since it's you they're writing about, while I,
my dear, have a daughter!'

Varvara Petrovna stared at her in silence with eyes wide-
open, and listened in astonishment. At this moment a side
door in the corner opened soundlessly and Darya Pavlovna
appeared. She stopped and looked around; she was struck by
our general consternation. She probably didn't see Marya
Timofeevna at first, since no one had warned her. Stepan
Trofimovich, the first to notice her, made a quick movement,
blushed, and then announced in a loud voice: 'Darya Pavlovna!' As a result all eyes turned to greet the new arrival.

'Oh, so this is your Darya Pavlovna!' cried Marya Timofeevna. 'Well, Shatushka, your little sister doesn't look at

all like you! How can my brother refer to such a beauty as "that serf-girl Dashka"?'

Meanwhile Darya Pavlovna was approaching Varvara Petrovna; but, struck by Marya Timofeevna's exclamation, she turned around quickly and stood in front of her chair, directing a long, penetrating glance at this 'holy fool'.*

'Sit down, Dasha,' said Varvara Petrovna with chilling composure, 'Nearer, that's right. You can still see this woman sitting down. Do you know her?'

'I've never seen her before,' Dasha replied softly, and fell silent. Then she added, 'She must be the sickly sister of that Mr Lebyadkin.'

'And it's the first time, my dear, I get to see you, although I've been wanting to meet you for a long time, because in your every gesture I can see your fine upbringing,' Marya Timofeevna cried with enthusiasm. 'As for what my lackey says about you, is it really possible that you, a nice, well-brought up girl, would take money from him? Because you're so nice, nice, nice—that's my very own opinion!' she concluded ecstatically, waving her hand in front of her.

'Do you understand anything?' Varvara Petrovna asked with proud dignity.

'I understand everything, ma'am...'

'You've heard about the money?'

'It must be the money which, according to Nikolai Vsevolodovich's request in Switzerland, I was supposed to hand over to her brother, Mr Lebyadkin.'

Silence followed.

'Nikolai Vsevolodovich asked you to hand it over?'

'He very much wanted to send the money to Mr Lebyadkin, three hundred roubles in all. But since he didn't know his address, and knew he'd be coming to our town, he asked me to hand it over if Mr Lebyadkin arrived.'

'What money was... lost? What was that woman talking about just now?'

'That I don't know, ma'am; I also have heard Mr Lebyadkin's been telling other people that I didn't hand over all the money to him; but I don't understand that. There were three hundred roubles and I handed over three hundred roubles.'

Darya Pavlovna had regained her composure almost completely. I should observe in general that it was difficult to astonish or confuse this young lady for very long—whatever she really felt. Now she gave all her answers without haste, replying at once to every question precisely, quietly, serenely, without a trace of her first, sudden agitation and without the least embarrassment, which might have indicated an awareness of some fault on her part. Varvara Petrovna kept her eyes fixed on her face all the while she spoke. Varvara Petrovna thought it over for a minute.

'If,' she said at last quite firmly, obviously addressing her audience, although she was looking only at Dasha, 'if Nikolai Vsevolodovich turned to you with his request rather than to me, he undoubtedly had some special reason. I don't consider I have any right to enquire into the matter, if it's meant to be kept secret. But your participation in this affair is enough to put my mind completely at ease; I want you to know that above all, Darya. But don't you see, my dear, that with all your ignorance of the world, you might have committed an indiscretion; you did so when you entered into dealings with a scoundrel. The rumours that rascal circulated confirm your error. But I'll find out about him and, as your guardian, I'll do what I can to defend you. But now we must put a stop to all this.'

'The best thing would be, when he comes to see you,' Marya Timofeevna broke in suddenly, leaning forward in her chair, 'to send him to the servants' quarters. Let him play cards with them sitting on a chest, while we sit here drinking coffee. I suppose we could send him in a cup of coffee, too, but I have nothing but contempt for him.'

She shook her head expressively.

'We must put a stop to all this,' Varvara Petrovna repeated, after listening attentively to Marya Timofeevna. 'Stepan Trofimovich, can I ask you to ring the bell.'

Stepan Trofimovich rang the bell and suddenly stepped forward in great agitation.

'If... if I...' he muttered in a feverish state, turning red, breaking off, and stuttering, 'If I too heard the most revolting story, or rather slander, then... it was in total indignation... *enfin, c'est un homme perdu et quelque chose comme un forçat évadé...*[1]

He broke off and didn't finish; Varvara Petrovna, screwing up her eyes, looked him over from head to foot. The respectful Aleksei Yegorovich came in.

'My carriage,' Varvara Petrovna ordered, 'now, Aleksei Yegorovich, you get ready to take Miss Lebyadkina home; she'll direct you.'

'Mr Lebyadkin has been waiting downstairs for some time, ma'am; he's asked me to announce him.'

'That's impossible, Varvara Petrovna,' Maurice Nikolaevich spoke up suddenly in alarm; he'd been sitting there all the while in unbroken silence. 'If you permit me, ma'am, he's not the sort to be received in society. He... he... he's an impossible person, Varvara Petrovna.'

'Ask him to wait,' said Varvara Petrovna, turning to Aleksei Yegorevich; he went out.

'*C'est un homme malhonnête et je crois même que c'est un forçat évadé ou quelque chose dans ce genre,*'[2] Stepan Trofimovich muttered once again, blushed again, and broke off again.

'Liza, it's time to go,' Praskovya Ivanovna announced in some disgust and stood up. Now she seemed to regret having called herself a fool in her recent fright. While Darya Pavlovna was speaking, she listened with a supercilious grin on her face. But most of all I was struck by Lizaveta Nikolaevna's demeanour since Darya Pavlovna had entered: her eyes gleamed with hatred and contempt, totally undisguised.

'Wait a minute, Praskovya Ivanovna, I beg you,' Varvara Petrovna said, stopping her with the same extraordinary serenity. 'Do me a favour and sit down; I intend to say all that I have to say, and your legs cause you pain. That's right, thank you. I lost my temper earlier and said some hasty things to you. Do me a favour and forgive me; I behaved foolishly and I'm the first to regret it, because I

[1] in a word, he's a lost soul and something like an escaped convict
[2] He's a dishonest man and I think he might even be an escaped convict or something like that

so value fairness in all things. Of course, you lost your temper, too, and mentioned those anonymous letters. Every anonymous communication deserves contempt precisely because it's unsigned. If you're of a different opinion, I don't envy you. In any case, if I were in your place, I wouldn't soil my hands in other people's trash. But you've soiled yours. But since you started it, I'll tell you that about six days ago I too received a ludicrous, anonymous letter. Some rascal wrote to assure me that Nikolai Vsevolodovich had lost his sanity and I should fear some lame woman, who "was going to play a decisive role in my life". I remember that phrase. Realizing that Nikolai Vsevolodovich has a great many enemies, I immediately sent for a certain person living near here, one of his secret, most vindictive and contemptible enemies, and my conversation with that person told me in a flash what the letter's despicable provenance was. If you, too, my poor Praskovya Ivanovna, have been troubled *because of me* by similar despicable letters, if you're being "bombarded" with them as you say, then, of course, I'm the first to regret having served as the unwitting cause. That's all I want to say by way of explanation. I'm sorry to see you so exhausted and upset now. Besides, I've made up my mind to "admit" this suspicious fellow now whom Maurice Nikolaevich just described as someone who couldn't possibly be "received". Liza, in particular, has no place here. Come here, Liza, my dear, and let me kiss you again.'

Liza crossed the room and stood silently in front of Varvara Petrovna. The latter kissed her, took her by the hand, held her at some distance, looked at her with considerable feeling, made the sign of the cross over her, and then kissed her again.

'Well, goodbye, Liza' (one could almost hear tears in Varvara Petrovna's voice). 'You should know that I'll never stop loving you, whatever fate holds in store for you... God be with you. I've always accepted His holy will...'

She wanted to add something else, but restrained herself and fell silent. Liza started back to her place in the same silent way, as if lost in thought, but suddenly stopped in front of her mother.

'Mamma, I'm not going home. I'll stay here a while longer with Auntie,' she said in a low voice, but in those soft words her iron will made itself heard.

'My God, what's this?' Praskovya Ivanovna wailed, throwing up her hands helplessly. But Liza made no reply; it was as if she didn't even hear her. She sat down in the corner as before and stared into space again.

A triumphant and proud look appeared on Varvara Petrovna's face.

'Maurice Nikolaevich, I have a very great favour to ask you. Be so kind as to go downstairs and take a look at that man, and, if there's even the slightest possibility of "receiving" him, bring him up here.'

Maurice Nikolaevich bowed and left. In a minute he returned with Mr Lebyadkin.

4.

I've already said something about this gentleman's outward appearance: he was a tall, curly-haired, solid fellow, about forty years old, with a ruddy, somewhat bloated, flabby face; his cheeks quivered with every movement of his head; he had smallish, bloodshot, sometimes rather sly eyes, a moustache, sidewhiskers, and a prominent Adam's apple of a rather unpleasant sort. But what was most striking about him was that he now appeared in a frock-coat, wearing clean linen. 'There are people on whom even clean linen looks indecent,' Liputin once said in reply to Stepan Trofimovich, who'd reproached him in jest for his slovenliness. The captain also had a pair of black gloves: he held the right one in his hand, the left, tightly stretched and still unbuttoned, covered only half his fleshy left hand, in which he held a brand new, shiny top hat, undoubtedly worn for the first time. It turned out, therefore, that the 'frock-coat of love' which he'd been crowing about to Shatov only yesterday really did exist. All this, that is, the frock-coat and linen, had been procured (I subsequently discovered) on Liputin's advice, for some mysterious purpose. There was no doubt that his arrival now (in a hired carriage) was also at the instigation and with the assistance of a third party;

it would never have occurred to him on his own, nor would he have managed to dress, get ready, and make his mind up in three-quarters of an hour, even assuming he'd heard about the scene on the cathedral porch right away. He wasn't drunk, but was in that heavy, oppressed, hazy condition of a man who's suddenly awakened after a long drinking-bout. He looked as though a couple of slaps on the back and, he'd be drunk again immediately.

He was about to rush into the drawing-room when he suddenly tripped over the rug in the doorway. Marya Timofeevna nearly died laughing. He cast a furious glance at her and suddenly took several hasty steps forward in the direction of Varvara Petrovna.

'I've come, madam...' he blared as if through a trumpet.

'Be so good, my dear sir,' Varvara Petrovna said, sitting up very straight, 'as to take a seat over there, on that chair. I'll still be able to hear you from there and can see you better from here.'

The captain stopped and stared blankly in front of him; then he turned and sat down on the chair next to the door just as directed. His expression revealed a dearth of self-confidence, but at the same time insolence and a sort of permanent irritability. He was terribly afraid, that was obvious. But he suffered, too, in his vanity, and one could surmise that irritated vanity might make him decide on occasion, in spite of his fear, to commit some insolent act. Apparently he feared every movement of his own clumsy body. It's well known that the primary cause of suffering in all such gentlemen, when by some miraculous circumstance they appear in society, is none other than their own hands and the impossibility of finding a suitable place for them—something which they themselves are constantly aware of. The captain sat absolutely still on the chair, hat and gloves in hand, without lifting his stupid gaze from Varvara Petrovna's stern face. He may have wanted to look around more carefully, but he hadn't made up his mind to do so. Marya Timofeevna, no doubt finding the figure he cut terribly amusing yet again, burst out laughing, but he didn't budge. Varvara Petrovna kept him in that position ruthlessly, for a long time, one entire minute, scrutinizing him mercilessly.

'First of all, I'd like to hear your name from you yourself,' she said in a measured and expressive tone of voice.

'Captain Lebyadkin,' the captain roared. 'I've come here, ma'am...' he said, twisting in his chair again.

'Allow me!' Varvara Petrovna said, stopping him once more. 'Is this pitiful person who's attracted my interest really your sister?'

'She is, ma'am. She's my sister and has escaped my control, and she's in such a condition that...'

He suddenly faltered and turned crimson.

'Don't misunderstand me, ma'am,' he said, becoming terribly confused. 'Her own brother won't soil... in such a condition—that is, not in such a condition... in the sense that it stained her reputation... lately...'

He broke off abruptly.

'My dear sir!' Varvara Petrovna said, raising her head.

'I mean this sort of condition!' he suddenly concluded, tapping the middle of his forehead with his finger. There followed a short pause.

'Has she been suffering from it very long?' drawled Varvara Petrovna.

'Madam, I've come to thank you for the generosity you showed us on the church porch—to thank you in the Russian way, in brotherly fashion...'

'In brotherly fashion?'

'That is, not brotherly, but in the sense that I'm my sister's brother, ma'am, and believe me, ma'am,' he said faster, turning crimson once again, 'I'm not so uneducated as might appear on first glance in your drawing-room. My sister and I are nothing at all, ma'am, compared to the splendour which we see here. Besides, there are those who slander me. But as for reputation, ma'am, Lebyadkin is proud, and... and... I've come to thank you... Here's the money, ma'am!'

He took out his wallet, pulled out a pile of bills, and started counting them, his fingers trembling in a violent fit of impatience. It was obvious he wanted to explain something as quickly as possible and counting bills made him look even more foolish; he lost his last ounce of self-control. The money refused to be counted, his fingers became tangled, and, to complete his embarrassment, one green three-rouble note slipped out of his wallet and zig-zagged down to the floor.

'Twenty roubles, ma'am,' he said, jumping up suddenly with a pile of bills in his hand, his face covered in perspiration; noticing the bill on the floor, he was about to bend over to pick it up, but then, for some reason embarrassed, dismissed it with a wave of his hand.

'That's for your servants, ma'am, for the footman who picks it up; let him remember the Lebyadkin girl!'

'I can't allow that,' Varvara Petrovna said hastily, and in some apprehension.

'In that case...'

He bent down, retrieved it, turned crimson, and suddenly went up to Varvara Petrovna and offered her the money he'd counted out.

'What's this?' she asked, now genuinely alarmed and shrinking back in her chair. Maurice Nikolaevich, Stepan Trofimovich, and I all took a step forward.

'Don't be alarmed, no don't; I'm not mad, I swear, I'm not mad!' the captain assured everyone excitedly on all sides.

'Yes, my dear sir, you certainly are mad.'

'Madam, it's not at all what you think! Of course, I'm an insignificant link... Oh, madam, your rooms are magnificent, unlike those of Marya the Unknown, my sister, *née* Lebyadkina, but whom we'll call Marya the Unknown for a while, ma'am, but only *for a while*, for even God Himself won't allow that for ever! Madam, you gave her ten roubles; she accepted them, but only because they were from *you*, ma'am! Listen, ma'am! This Marya the Unknown doesn't take anything from anyone on earth, or else her grandfather, an officer killed in battle in the Caucasus before the eyes of Yermolov* himself, would turn in his grave; but from you, ma'am, she'd take it all from you. But she takes with one hand, ma'am, while with the other she offers you twenty roubles, in the form of a contribution to one of the charit-

184 *Devils. Part One*

able societies in the capital, of which, ma'am, you're a member... since you yourself, ma'am, published an announcement in the *Moscow News** that you were eager to receive contributions here in our town, and that anyone could sign the subscription list...'

The captain suddenly broke off; he was breathing heavily, as if he had performed some tremendous feat. Everything he said about the charitable society had probably been composed beforehand, perhaps under Liputin's tutelage. He was perspiring even more profusely; drops of sweat literally trickled down his temples. Varvara Petrovna shot him a penetrating glance.

'The subscription list', she said sternly, 'is always available downstairs with the porter; there you can sign and indicate the amount of your contribution, if you so desire. Therefore I ask you to put your money away now and not wave it about in the air. Good. I also ask you to return to your previous place. Good. I very much regret, my dear sir, that I erred with regard to your sister, and gave her charity assuming she was poor, when in fact she's so rich. But there's one thing I don't understand: why can she accept alms from me alone, yet refuse them from anyone else? You so insisted on that point that I'd like a full explanation.'

'Madam, that's a secret I'll take to the grave with me!' the captain replied.

'Why on earth?' Varvara Petrovna asked, but now somehow not quite so firmly.

'Madam, madam!...'

He lapsed into gloomy silence, looking down at the ground and placing his right hand over his heart. Varvara Petrovna waited, without taking her eyes off him.

'Madam!' he roared suddenly, 'will you allow me to ask you one question, only one, but a frank one, direct, in the Russian style, from the heart?'

'By all means.'

'Have you suffered at all, ma'am, in your life?'

'You mean, simply, that someone has made you, or is making you suffer?'

'Madam, madam!' he said, suddenly jumping up again,

probably not even consciously. Beating his breast, he continued, 'Here, in this heart, so much has been stored away, so very much that on Judgement Day God Himself will be astonished!'

'Hmm, that's putting it strongly.'

'Madam, I may be speaking irascibly...'

'Don't worry about that. I'll know when to stop you.'

'May I ask you one further question, ma'am?'

'You may ask one more.'

'Can one die simply from nobility of soul?'

'I don't know; I've never asked myself that question.'

'You don't know! You've never asked yourself that question!' he shouted with bombastic irony. 'Well, if that's so, then: "Be still, my despairing heart!" '* And he beat his breast ferociously.

Once again he walked around the room. It's characteristic of such people that they're absolutely incapable of containing their desires; on the contrary, they have an irresistible impulse to exhibit them at once, in all their squalor, as soon as they're conceived. Finding themselves in unfamiliar surroundings, such gentlemen usually begin timidly; but if you yield even a hairsbreadth, they'll immediately rush to commit some impertinence. The captain was already quite agitated; he walked around, waved his arms, didn't hear anyone's questions, talked about himself very quickly, so quickly that his tongue sometimes got twisted, and, without finishing what he was saying, he'd gallop on to begin another sentence. True, he was probably not altogether sober. Lizaveta Nikolaevna was also sitting nearby, though he didn't glance at her even once; her presence, however, seemed to excite him a great deal. But that's merely a supposition. There must have been some reason why Varvara Petrovna, overcoming her disgust, had decided to hear such a man out. Praskovya Ivanovna simply shook from fear, in truth not fully understanding what was happening. Stepan Trofimovich trembled as well; but he, on the contrary, was inclined to understand things all too well. Maurice Nikolaevich stood looking like a man ready to defend anyone in need. Liza was very pale and stared steadily at the wild captain, her eyes wide open. Shatov stayed sitting where he was; but, what was strangest of all, Marya Timofeevna not only stopped laughing, but became terribly sad. She sat resting her right elbow on the table, following her brother's declamation with a long, sad gaze. Only Darya Pavlovna seemed composed.

'This is all nonsensical allegory,' Varvara Petrovna said, getting angry at last. 'You haven't answered my question, "Why?" I'm waiting for an answer.'

'Didn't answer your question, "Why?" You're waiting for an answer to "Why?" ' repeated the captain, winking. 'That little word "Why" has been scattered around the whole universe from the first day of Creation, ma'am. All nature cries out to its Creator every minute, "Why?"—and for the last seven thousand years there's been no answer. Do you think Captain Lebyadkin alone can answer that question, ma'am? Is that really fair?'

'That's nonsense and not what I mean at all!' Varvara Petrovna said, growing angry and losing her patience. 'That's allegory; besides, you are too grandiloquent, my dear sir, and I consider that to be impertinent.'

'Madam,' the captain replied without hearing her, 'I might have wanted to be called Ernest, but was forced to bear the vulgar name Ignat. Why, do you suppose? I may have wanted to be called Prince de Montbart,* but I'm only called Lebyadkin, from *lebyed*, meaning a swan, why? I'm a poet, ma'am, a poet in my soul, and could receive a thousand roubles from a publisher, but I'm forced to live in a pigsty. Why? Why? Madam! In my opinion Russia's nothing more than a freak of nature!'

'You can't say anything more definitive than that?'

'I could recite the poem "Cockroach" for you, ma'am.'

'Wha-a-at?'

'Madam, I'm still not mad! I shall go mad, yes, but I'm not mad yet! Madam, one of my acquaintances—the no-o-oblest of men—wrote a Krylov fable entitled "The Cockroach".* May I recite it for you?'

'You want to recite a fable by Krylov?'

'No, I don't want to recite a fable by Krylov, but my own

fable, my own composition! Believe me, ma'am, no offence, but I'm not so uneducated or depraved as not to realize that Russia possesses a great fable-writer in the person of Krylov, in whose honour the minister of education has just erected a monument* in the Summer Garden, where little children can play. Now then, ma'am, you ask "Why?" The answer is at the end of the fable, written in letters of fire.'

'Recite your fable.'

He began:

> 'A cockroach once, of cockroach size,
> Cockroach born and bred,
> Fell right into a glass of flies—
> Flies who eat their dead!'

'Good Lord, what's this?' Varvara Petrovna cried.

'It's that, in the summertime,' the captain hastened to add, waving his arms wildly with the irritated impatience of an author whose reading has just been interrupted. 'In the summertime flies enter a jar and eat the dead ones; any fool can understand that. Don't interrupt me, please. You'll see, you'll see...' (He kept waving his arms.)

> 'The cockroach took up lots of space;
> The flies made quite a fuss:
> To Jupiter they cried, "This place
> Was hardly enough for us!"

> But while their prayer winged its way,
> Nikifor came along,
> Noble old chap, or so they say...'

'I haven't quite finished it yet; never mind, I'll go on in my own words!' the captain prattled. 'Nikifor takes the jar and, in spite of all the shouting, dumps the whole mess, flies and cockroach, into a pigsty, which he should've done some time ago. But observe, ma'am, observe, the cockroach doesn't complain! That's the answer to your question "Why?" ' he shouted triumphantly. 'The cock-r-roach doesn't complain! And as far as Nikifor is concerned, he represents nature,' he added, speaking rapidly and walking around the room in a very self-satisfied manner.

Varvara Petrovna flew into a terrible temper.

'Now allow me to enquire about that sum of money which was supposed to have been received from Nikolai Vsevolodovich, but was not turned over to you in full. Are you daring to accuse a certain member of my household?'

'That's slander!' Lebyadkin roared, raising his right hand dramatically.

'No, it isn't slander.'

'Madam, there are certain circumstances that compel one to suffer disgrace to one's family, rather than proclaim the truth aloud. Lebyadkin won't let the cat out of the bag, ma'am!'

He seemed dazed; he was in ecstasy. He was aware of his importance; he'd probably fantasized something like this. He wanted to insult someone, play a nasty trick, show his power.

'Please ring the bell, Stepan Trofimovich,' Varvara Petrovna asked.

'Lebyadkin is cunning, ma'am!' he said, winking at her with a nasty smile. 'He's cunning, but he has a weakness, his portal to passion! And that portal is the old, military hussars' bottle, whose praises were sung by Denis Davydov.* Now, when he stands in this portal, ma'am, it sometimes happens that he'll send a letter in verse, a most splendiferous letter, but one he'd like to have taken back afterwards with all the tears he's shed in his life, for the sense of the beautiful is destroyed. But the bird has flown the coop, and you won't catch him by the tail! Well, in this portal, ma'am, Lebyadkin might've said something about an honourable maiden, under the influence of noble indignation aroused by insults inflicted on his soul, such as those aimed by his detractors. But Lebyadkin is cunning, ma'am! And the sinister wolf sits over him in vain, constantly filling his glass and waiting for the end: Lebyadkin won't let the cat out of the bag; every time at the bottom of the bottle, contrary to expectation, he'll find only—Lebyadkin's Cunning! But enough, enough! Madam, your splendid rooms could belong to the noblest of men, but the cockroach doesn't complain! Observe, ma'am, and take note of it: he doesn't complain. Recognize his great spirit!'

At this moment the bell rang downstairs in the porter's room, and almost simultaneously Aleksei Yegorych appeared somewhat belatedly in answer to Stepan Trofimovich's summons. The dignified old servant was in state of extreme agitation.

'Nikolai Vsevolodovich has just arrived, ma'am, and is coming in right away,' he said in answer to Varvara Petrovna's enquiring glance.

I remember her particularly well at that moment: at first she blanched, but suddenly her eyes began to gleam. She straightened up in her chair and assumed a look of unusual determination. Everyone was stunned. The wholly unanticipated arrival of Nikolai Vsevolodovich, who was expected a full month later, was strange not only in its suddenness, but also by its fateful coincidence at that very moment. Even the captain stood still as a post in the middle of the drawing-room, his mouth open wide, staring at the door with a ridiculous expression on his face.

Then from the next room, a large, long hall, we heard the sound of quickly approaching footsteps, small steps, exceedingly rapid; someone was coming, apparently at a run, and suddenly flew into the drawing-room—but it wasn't Nikolai Vsevolodovich at all; it was a young man totally unknown to everyone there.

5.

I'll permit myself to pause here and sketch this unexpected new arrival with a few hurried strokes.

He was a young man, twenty-seven or thereabouts, a little above average height, with rather long, thin fair hair, and a patchy, barely discernible moustache and beard. He was neatly, even fashionably dressed, but not foppishly so; at first glance he seemed somewhat round-shouldered and awkward, but, in fact, he wasn't round-shouldered at all, and was actually rather relaxed. He appeared to be an eccentric, but later everyone found his manners perfectly acceptable, his conversation always to the point.

No one could say he was unattractive, yet no one liked his face. His head was elongated at the back, and seemed flattened at the sides, so his face appeared pointed. His forehead was high and narrow, but his features were small; his eyes were sharp, his nose small and pointed, his lips long and thin. His expression was almost that of a sick man, but this was only superficial. He had a deep wrinkle near each cheekbone which gave him the look of someone convalescing after a serious illness. However, he was in perfect health, quite strong, and had never been ill.

He walked and moved about very hurriedly, yet was in no particular rush to get anywhere. It seemed that nothing could embarrass him; he remained exactly the same regardless of circumstance and society. He possessed great self-assurance, but wasn't in the least aware of it himself.

He spoke quickly, hastily, but at the same time with certainty, and was never at a loss for words. In spite of his hurried demeanour, his thoughts were orderly, distinct and definite—that was particularly striking. His articulation was wonderfully clear; words poured forth from him like large, smooth grains, always well-chosen and at your service. At first this was attractive, but later it became repulsive, precisely because of his excessively clear articulation, his stream of ever-ready words. One began to imagine that the tongue in his mouth had a special shape, unusually long and thin, very red, with an extremely pointed tip, flickering constantly and involuntarily.

Well, then, this young man now rushed into the drawing-room, and, to tell the truth, to this very day I believe he'd already begun talking in the next room, so that he was speaking as he entered. In a flash he was standing in front of Varvara Petrovna.

'...Just imagine, Varvara Petrovna,' he rattled on with a stream of words, 'I came in thinking he'd have been here a quarter of an hour ago; he arrived an hour and a half ago; we met at Kirillov's; he left half an hour ago to come right over here and told me to be here in a quarter of an hour...'

'But who? Who told you to come here?' Varvara Petrovna enquired.

'Why, Nikolai Vsevolodovich, of course! Did you really not know about his arrival until this moment? But his baggage should've arrived here earlier; why didn't they tell you? Well, let me be the first to bring you the news. Of course we could send someone to look for him, but he'll probably be here soon, at the precise moment best suited to his intentions and, at least as far as I can judge, his calculations.' Then he surveyed the room and his gaze rested on the captain with particular attention. 'Ah, Lizaveta Nikolaevna, I'm delighted to meet you so soon; I'm very glad to shake your hand,' he said, rushing quickly to grab the little hand offered by the gaily smiling Liza. 'And, as far as I can tell, Praskovya Ivanovna hasn't forgotten her "professor" and isn't angry at him any more, as she was in Switzerland. How are your legs holding up, Praskovya Ivanovna? Were your Swiss doctors right when they recommended that you return to your native climate? What? Fomentations? That must be very beneficial. But how sorry I was, Varvara Petrovna' (he turned back to her quickly), 'that I didn't manage to see you abroad and pay my respects in person; besides, I had so much to tell you... I sent word to my old man, but as usual, he probably...'

'Petrusha!' cried Stepan Trofimovich, snapping out of his stupor; he threw up his hands and rushed to his son. '*Pierre, mon enfant*, why, I didn't even recognize you!' he said hugging him, tears streaming down his cheeks.

'Now, now, don't carry on, no flourishes, enough, stop it, I beg you,' Petrusha muttered hurriedly, trying to free himself from the embrace.

'I've always wronged you, always!'

'Come on now, that's enough; we can talk about it later. I knew you'd carry on. Calm down a little, will you?'

'But I haven't seen you in ten whole years!'

'All the more reason to avoid a fuss...'

'*Mon enfant!*'

'Come on, I know you love me, but take your hands off me. You're embarrassing other people... Ah, here's Nikolai Vsevolodovich! Now don't carry on, I beg you!'

Nikolai Vsevolodovich was already in the room; he'd entered very quietly and for a moment stood in the doorway, casting a quiet look on the assembled company.

I was struck by his appearance at first glance, just as I had been four years earlier when I saw him for the first time. I hadn't forgotten him in the least; but there are certain countenances that always, every time you see them, convey something new that you hadn't noticed before, even though you've met them a hundred times in the past. To all appearances, he was exactly the same as he was four years ago: just as elegant and dignified. He entered in the same dignified manner; he even seemed almost as young. His faint smile was just as officially gracious and complacent, his look just as stern, pensive, almost absent-minded. In a word, it seemed we'd parted only yesterday. One thing struck me: previously he'd been considered quite handsome, even though his face 'resembled a mask', as a few sharp-tongued ladies in our society had put it. But now—now, I don't know why, but from the very first glance he seemed to me to be decidedly, indisputably beautiful; his face could no longer be said to resemble a mask. Wasn't it because he'd become a little paler than before, and, maybe, a bit thinner? Or perhaps it was some new idea gleaming in his eyes?

'Nikolai Vsevolodovich!' Varvara Petrovna exclaimed, sitting up straight, but not rising from her chair, and stopping him with an imperious gesture. 'Stop a moment!'

In order to explain the terrible question that suddenly followed her gesture and exclamation—a possibility I'd never have imagined from Varvara Petrovna—I ask the reader to recall what her character was like throughout her life, as well as her extraordinary impulsiveness at critical moments. I also want you to realize that, in spite of her unusual strength, considerable common sense, and the practical, so to speak, business acumen she possessed, nevertheless, there were still moments in her life when she suddenly surrendered herself completely, and, if one may express it thus, totally without restraint. Finally, I ask you to bear in mind that the present moment could really be one of those when suddenly, the entire essence of one's life is concentrated, brought into focus—the whole past, present, and perhaps even the future. I must also recall by the way the anonymous letter she'd received, which she mentioned earlier to Praskovya Ivanovna with such irritation, with nothing at all being said, I believe, about the content of the letter; perhaps it was the letter that contained the explanation for the terrible question she suddenly put to her son.

'Nikolai Vsevolodovich,' she repeated, emphasizing each word in a firm voice in which there sounded an ominous challenge, 'I ask you to reply at once, without stirring one step: is it true that this unfortunate cripple—there she is, over there, look at her!—is it true that she is... your lawful wife?'

I remember that moment all too well; he didn't bat an eyelid and stared straight at his mother; there wasn't the slightest change in his expression. At last he smiled slowly, a kind of condescending smile, and, without saying a word, approached his mother quietly, took her hand, raised it respectfully to his lips and kissed it. So great was his customary and irresistible influence over his mother that even at such a moment she dared not withdraw her hand. She merely looked at him, her whole being transformed into a question, her entire countenance signalling that she couldn't tolerate the uncertainty a moment longer.

But he remained silent. After kissing her hand, he cast another glance around the room and, as before, moved unhurriedly straight towards Marya Timofeevna. It's very hard to describe expressions on people's faces at certain moments. I recall, for example, that Marya Timofeevna, quite overcome with fear, rose to meet him and clasped her hands in front of her, as if imploring him; at the same time I can recall the ecstasy in her eyes, a mad ecstasy that almost distorted her features—such ecstasy as people find difficult to endure. Perhaps she experienced both those feelings: fear and ecstasy. But I recall moving towards her quickly (I was standing nearby), because she seemed about to faint.

'You shouldn't be here,' Nikolai Vsevolodovich told her in an affectionate, melodious voice, his eyes ablaze with extraordinary tenderness. He stood in front of her in a most respectful stance; every gesture reflected his sincerest esteem. The poor girl, gasping for breath, murmured to him in an impulsive half-whisper:

'May I... now... fall on my knees before you?'

'No, of course not,' he said, smiling at her so magnificently that she too suddenly grinned happily. Speaking to
her very tenderly in the same melodious voice as if she were
a child, he added gravely:

'You must remember that you're a young woman. Even
though I'm your most devoted friend, I'm still a stranger,
not your husband, nor your father, nor your fiancé. Give
me your hand and let's go; I'll escort you to the carriage
and, if you let me, I'll take you all the way home.'

She listened to him and lowered her head as if pondering.

'Let's go,' she said, sighing and giving him her arm.

Just then she had a minor accident. She must have turned
carelessly and stepped down on her shorter, lame leg—in
brief, she fell sideways on to the chair, and if it hadn't been
there, she'd have fallen to the floor. He caught hold of her
at once and supported her, took her firmly by the arm and
led her carefully and sympathetically to the door. She was
obviously upset by her fall. She was embarrassed; she
blushed and became terribly shy. Looking down at the floor
in silence, limping painfully, she hobbled out after him,
almost hanging on his arm. That was how they left. Liza,
I saw, suddenly jumped up from her chair as they were
leaving; her motionless gaze followed them to the door.
Then she sat down again in silence; but a spasm flickered
across her face, as if she'd touched something disgusting.

While all this was happening between Nikolai Vsevolodovich and Marya Timofeevna, everyone sat in stunned
silence; you could have heard a pin drop. But as soon as
they left, everyone suddenly began talking.

6.

Actually, they said very little; it was mostly just exclamation.
By now I've forgotten the order in which things happened
because of all the confusion. Stepan Trofimovich declaimed
in French and threw up his hands, but Varvara Petrovna
wasn't really interested in him. Even Maurice Nikolaevich
started mumbling abruptly and rapidly. But Peter Stepanovich was the most excited of all; he was desperately trying

to convince Varvara Petrovna of something with expansive gestures, but for a long time I failed to understand. He also turned to Praskovya Ivanovna and Lizaveta Nikolaevna; in his excitement he even shouted something in passing to his father—in a word, he was rushing all around the room. Varvara Petrovna, her face quite flushed, jumped up from her chair and shouted to Praskovya Ivanovna, 'Did you hear, did you hear what he just said to her?' But Praskovya was unable to reply; she merely muttered something, gesturing helplessly. The poor dear had her own problems: she kept turning her head to Liza, regarding her with inexplicable terror, but she no longer dared get up, or leave, or think, until her daughter did so. Meanwhile the captain undoubtedly wanted to slip away, as I observed. He'd been in a great panic from the moment Nikolai Vsevolodovich had come in; but Peter Stepanovich seized him by the arm and wouldn't let go of him.

'It's essential, absolutely essential,' he said, prattling on to Varvara Petrovna, still trying to convince her. He stood in front of her; she was sitting in the armchair again, and, as I recall, listening to him avidly. That was just what he wanted and he now commanded her full attention.

'It's essential. You can see for yourself, Varvara Petrovna, there's some misunderstanding here. There's much that seems strange, but it's all as clear as daylight, as plain as the nose on your face. I realize all too well that I haven't been authorized to talk about it and I must appear ridiculous intervening. But, in the first place, Nikolai Vsevolodovich himself doesn't attach any significance to this matter, and, in the last place, there are some cases in which it's difficult for a person to provide an explanation for himself; it's essential for a third person to assume that responsibility, one who finds it easier to discuss certain delicate points. Believe me, Varvara Petrovna, Nikolai Vsevolodovich is not in the least to be blamed for failing to answer the question you just put to him with a complete explanation, in spite of the fact that the matter is so trivial; I've known him since Petersburg. Besides, the whole story redounds to his honour, if it's absolutely necessary to use so vague a term as "honour"...'

'You mean that you witnessed some incident from which this... misunderstanding arose?' Varvara Petrovna asked.

'Witnessed it and participated in it,' Peter Stepanovich affirmed hurriedly.

'If you give me your word that this won't offend Nikolai Vsevolodovich's delicate feelings with regard to me, from whom he never conceals anything what-so-ever... and if you're sure that in doing so you'll even be affording him pleasure...'

'Pleasure, absolutely; therefore it'll also afford me particular pleasure to do it. I'm sure he'd ask me to do it himself.'

The insistent desire of this gentleman who had suddenly dropped from the sky to relate stories from other people's lives was rather curious, even contrary to the ordinary conventions of behaviour. But he'd caught Varvara Petrovna on his hook, having touched her most vulnerable spot. I as yet didn't fully understand this young man's character, not to mention his intentions.

'I'm listening,' Varvara Petrovna announced in a restrained and cautious way, somewhat annoyed by her own condescension.

'It's not very long; in fact, if you like, it's not really even a story,' he prattled on. 'But a writer with nothing better to do might cook up a novel from it. It's a rather interesting little affair, Praskovya Ivanovna; I'm sure Lizaveta Nikolaevna will listen with interest, because it contains much that's strange, if not actually fantastic. About five years ago, in Petersburg, Nikolai Vsevolodovich first encountered this gentleman—this very same Mr Lebyadkin who's standing here now with his mouth gaping, and who looks as if he was just hoping to slip away. Excuse me, Varvara Petrovna. I advise you not to run off, Mr Retired Official in the former commissariat department (you see, I remember you very well). Both Nikolai Vsevolodovich and I are familiar with your local activities, about which, don't you ever forget, you'll soon have to give account. Excuse me once again, Varvara Petrovna. At the time Nikolai Vsevolodovich referred to this gentleman as his Falstaff; that must be some old burlesque character' (he explained suddenly), 'whom everyone mocks and who allows everyone to mock him, as long as they pay him for it. At the time Nikolai Vsevolodovich was leading a life in Petersburg of "mockery", so to speak—I can't use any other word to define it, because he's not a man to give way to disillusionment, and he disdained to engage in any particular work at the time. I'm only talking about that one period, Varvara Petrovna. This Lebyadkin had a sister—the one who was just sitting here. The brother and sister didn't possess their own "corner"; they lived wherever they could. He wandered around under the arches of the Shopping Arcade, always wearing his former uniform and stopping better-dressed passers-by; whatever he got, he spent on drink. His sister lived like a little bird of heaven. She helped people in their own "corners" and worked as a servant when needed. It was a scene reminiscent of Sodom;* I'll pass over a description of life in those little "corners"—a life to which, in his eccentricity, Nikolai Vsevolodovich devoted himself at the time. I'm only talking about that one period, Varvara Petrovna; as regards his "eccentricity", well, that's his own expression. He doesn't conceal much from me. Mademoiselle Lebyadkina, who at one time happened to be meeting Nikolai Vsevolodovich rather too frequently, was struck by his appearance. He appeared, so to speak, as a diamond against the filthy background of her life. I'm not very good at describing human emotions, and therefore will pass over them; but the good-for-nothing people who lived there began to make fun of her and she became depressed. Even before that they used to mock her, but she would never notice it. She wasn't quite right in the head even back then, but that was nothing compared to what she is now. There's reason to believe that in her childhood she was provided with some education, thanks to a wealthy lady who took an interest in her. Nikolai Vsevolodovich never paid her the least bit of attention and spent his time playing preference with petty clerks using a greasy old pack of cards for quarter-kopeck stakes. But once when they were taunting her, without asking why, he seized one of the clerks by the collar, and tossed him out of a second-storey window. There was no question of chivalrous indignation at her injured innocence; the whole affair took place amidst general laughter, with Nikolai Vsevolodovich laughing more than anyone. When it all turned out satisfactorily, everyone made up and they all drank some punch together. But the innocent aggrieved party never forgot it. Naturally, it ended with the complete loss of her remaining mental faculties. I repeat, I'm not very good at describing feelings, but in this case the main point was her illusion. Nikolai Vsevolodovich fed that illusion of hers, as if on purpose; instead of laughing at her, he suddenly began treating Mademoiselle Lebyadkina with unexpected esteem. Kirillov (an extraordinary eccentric, Varvara Petrovna, and an extremely rude man—perhaps you'll get to meet him someday, since now he's back here), well, this Kirillov, who usually remains silent all the time, suddenly got very irritated and, as I recall, told Nikolai Vsevolodovich that he was treating this woman as if she were a marquise, and would finish her off altogether. Let me add that Nikolai Vsevolodovich had some respect for Kirillov. What answer do you think he gave him? "Do you suppose, Mr Kirillov, that I'm laughing at her? Disabuse yourself of that notion; in fact, I respect her because she's better than the rest of us." He said it, you know, in a very serious tone of voice. In the meantime, during those two or three months, apart from "Hello" and "Goodbye", he never really spoke to her. I was there, and well do I remember that it finally reached a point when she considered him her fiancé; he was unable to "elope" with her simply because he had so many enemies and family obstacles, or something of the sort. There was much laughter about it! It all ended when Nikolai Vsevolodovich had to leave; before his departure he made provision for her care, and, it seems, arranged to pay her a rather considerable annual allowance, at least three hundred roubles, if not more. In a word, let's suppose all this was mere indulgence on his part, the fantasy of a prematurely exhausted man—or even, in the last analysis, as Kirillov used to say, the latest experiment of a jaded young man eager to know to what lengths he could drive a poor, mad cripple. "You," he said, "deliberately chose the lowest creature, a cripple, mired in shame and covered with bruises—knowing, in addition, that this creature is dying of comical love for you—and suddenly set about hoodwinking her on purpose, just to see what will happen!" But how can a man be held responsible for the delusions of a mad woman with whom, mind you, he's hardly exchanged two words the whole time! There are things, Varvara Petrovna, about which it's not only impossible to speak sensibly, but not even sensible to begin speaking. Well, never mind, call it eccentricity—there's nothing more to be said about it. Meanwhile, they've gone and made a whole incident out of it... I'm partly aware, Varvara Petrovna, of what's been going on here.'

The speaker suddenly broke off and was about to turn to Lebyadkin, but Varvara Petrovna stopped him; she was in a state of extreme exaltation.

'Have you finished?' she asked.

'Not yet. To complete my story, with your permission, I'd like to ask this gentleman a few more questions... You'll see the point in a minute or two, Varvara Petrovna.'

'Enough; later. Stop for a moment, I beg you. Oh, what a good thing I allowed you to speak!'

'Just note, Varvara Petrovna,' Peter Stepanovich added hastily. 'Could Nikolai Vsevolodovich possibly have explained all this to you in response to your question—which was, perhaps, a bit too categorical?'

'Oh, yes, much too categorical!'

'And wasn't I right when I said that in certain cases a third party finds it easier to explain things, than one of the interested parties?'

'Yes, yes... But you were mistaken about one thing, and I see you continue to be mistaken.'

'Really? What about?'

'You see... But, why don't you sit down, Peter Stepanovich?'

'Oh, just as you wish; I am feeling a bit tired, thank you.'

In a flash he pulled up an armchair and positioned it so that he was sitting between Varvara Petrovna on one side and Praskovya Ivanovna on the other, near the table facing Mr Lebyadkin, from whose face his eyes hadn't shifted even for a moment.

'You're mistaken about what you call his "eccentricity"...'

'Oh, if only that were all...'

'No, no, no, wait a moment,' Varvara Petrovna said, stopping him, obviously ready to go on at some length and with feeling. As soon as he realized this, Peter Stepanovich gave her his full attention.

'No, this was something better than eccentricity, and, I can assure you, something holy! A proud man who suffered humiliation early in life, who reached the stage of "mockery", which you so accurately describe—in short, Prince Harry, as Stepan Trofimovich so splendidly dubbed him at the time, which would be absolutely perfect, if he didn't resemble Hamlet even more, at least in my opinion.'

'*Et vous avez raison*,[1] Stepan Trofimovich declared impressively and with feeling.

'Thank you, Stepan Trofimovich. I'm especially grateful to you for your unwavering faith in Nicolas, in the greatness of his soul and his calling. You even buttressed my own faith, whenever I started to lose heart.'

'*Chère, chère*...' Stepan Trofimovich said; he was about to step forward, but stopped, realizing it would be dangerous to interrupt.

'And if anywhere near Nicolas' (Varvara Petrovna was now virtually intoning) 'there'd been a gentle Horatio, great in his humility—another splendid expression of yours, Stepan Trofimovich—perhaps he might have been saved from the gloomy and "unexpected demon of irony" that's been tormenting him all his life. (That's your wonderful phrase, too, Stepan Trofimovich, "demon of irony".) But Nicolas had neither Horatio nor Ophelia. He only had his mother; but what can a mother do alone in such circumstances? You know, Peter Stepanovich, now it's perfectly understandable how a person like Nicolas could turn up even in such filthy haunts as you describe. This "mockery" of life (your astonishingly appropriate expression!) is so clear to me now, that insatiable desire for contrast, that gloomy background against which he sparkles like a diamond, again your comparison, Peter Stepanovich. Then he encounters a creature

___
[1] And you are right

whom everyone insults, a half-mad cripple, who, at the same time, possesses the noblest of feelings!'

'Hmmm, yes, let's suppose so.'

'Then can't you understand why he doesn't laugh at her like everyone else? Oh, you people! Don't you see how he's defending her from attackers, lavishing respect upon her as a "marquise" (that Kirillov must have an unusually profound understanding of people, even though he doesn't understand my Nicolas!). If you like, the trouble arose precisely from this contrast; if this unfortunate creature had been in a different setting, she might not have gone so far as to conceive so mad a delusion. A woman, only a woman can understand this, Peter Stepanovich, and what a pity you... I mean, it's not a pity you're not a woman, but at least on this one occasion, you'd understand so much better!'

'That is, in the sense the worse things are, the better. I understand, Varvara Petrovna, I do. It's a little like religion: the worse off a man is, the more downtrodden or impoverished an entire people is, the more stubbornly it dreams of reward in paradise. And if a hundred thousand priests are busy ministering as well, nurturing this dream and counting on it, then... I do understand, Varvara Petrovna, rest assured I do.'

'That's not exactly what I mean. But tell me, should Nicolas, in order to extinguish the illusion of this unfortunate organism' (I couldn't understand why Varvara Petrovna chose to use the word 'organism'), 'should he have laughed at her and treated her as all the other petty officials did? Do you really reject his great compassion, the noble tremor of his entire organism when he suddenly made Kirillov the stern reply: "I'm not laughing at her." What a noble, sacred reply!'

'*Sublime*,' muttered Stepan Trofimovich.

'Note, he's not nearly as wealthy as you think. I'm the one who's wealthy, not he; and at the time he was getting hardly anything from me at all.'

'I understand, Varvara Petrovna, I understand all this,' Peter Stepanovich said, now stirring in his chair with some impatience.

'Oh, that's my character! I recognize myself in Nicolas. I recognize youth, a propensity to formidable, tempestuous impulses... If you and I ever get to know each other better, Peter Stepanovich, and, for my part, I sincerely hope we do, especially since now I'm so obliged to you, perhaps you might come to understand...'

'Oh, believe me, for my part I hope so too,' Peter Stepanovich muttered curtly.

'Then you'll understand an impulse which, out of blind generosity, makes you respond to a person who's unworthy of you in all respects, a person who has no understanding of you, who's ready to torment you at every opportunity, and, in spite of everything, to turn that person all of a sudden into some sort of ideal, into an illusion, to invest all your hopes in him, to worship him, to love him your whole life without knowing why—perhaps precisely because he's so unworthy... Oh, how I've suffered all my life, Peter Stepanovich!'

With a pained expression Stepan Trofimovich tried to catch my eye, but I managed to turn away just in time.

'... And recently, very recently—oh, how I have wronged Nicolas!... You won't believe how they've tormented me on all sides: enemies, petty individuals, and friends—friends, perhaps, even more than enemies. When I received that first despicable anonymous letter, Peter Stepanovich, you won't believe it, but I actually hadn't contempt enough left to reply to that wickedness... I'll never, never forgive myself for that weakness!'

'I've heard something about these local anonymous letters already,' Peter Stepanovich said, suddenly growing more animated, 'I'll find out who wrote them, rest assured.'

'You can't imagine what sort of intrigues have been going on around here! Why, they've even been tormenting our poor Praskovya Ivanovna—now, why would they do a thing like that? I may have treated you rather badly today, my dear Praskovya Ivanovna,' she added in a generous outburst of tenderness, not without a hint of triumphant irony.

'Enough, my dear,' Praskovya Ivanovna muttered reluctantly. 'I think we should put an end to all this. Too much has been said already...' and she looked timidly at Liza, who was watching Peter Stepanovich.

'As for that poor, unfortunate creature, that insane young woman who's lost everything, but kept only her heart—I now intend to adopt her myself,' Varvara Petrovna suddenly exclaimed. 'It's a sacred duty I intend to fulfil. From this day on I shall take her under my protection.'

'That'll be a very good thing in a certain sense,' Peter Stepanovich said, now thoroughly animated. 'Excuse me, but I didn't quite finish just now. It was protection I was talking about precisely. You can imagine that when Nikolai Vsevolodovich went away (I'm picking up where I left off, Varvara Petrovna), that gentleman, the same Mr Lebyadkin, decided immediately that he had a right to appropriate the entire allowance provided to his sister; and so he did. I don't know many details about how Nikolai Vsevolodovich sorted it all out, but a year later when he was living abroad, he found out what had happened and was forced to make other arrangements. Once again I don't know all the details; he'll tell you himself. I know only that the interested party was placed in some remote convent, in extremely comfortable surroundings, but under friendly supervision—do you understand? What do you think Mr Lebyadkin decided to do then? First he makes every effort to discover where his source of income, that is, his sister, is being hidden; then, managing to do that only recently, he takes her away from the convent, asserting that he has a claim on her, and brings her back here. Now he doesn't feed her; he beats her and bullies her. And, after somehow receiving a considerable sum of money from Nikolai Vsevolodovich, he takes to drinking at once; instead of showing his gratitude, he ends up by issuing an insolent challenge to Nikolai Vsevolodovich, making ridiculous demands, threatening that if he refuses to pay the allowance in advance, he'll take him to court. Thus he mistakes Nikolai Vsevolodovich's voluntary gift for a required payment—can you imagine that? Mr Lebyadkin, isn't *everything* I've said here true?'

The captain, who'd been standing in silence staring at the floor up to now, took two quick steps forward and turned crimson.

'Peter Stepanovich, you've treated me very cruelly,' he said abruptly.

'How, cruel? Why so? But we'll talk about cruelty, or kindness, later. As for now, I ask you merely to reply to my first question: is *everything* I've said here true or not? If you think something is false, you can make your own statement right away.'

'I... you yourself know, Peter Stepanovich...' the captain muttered, but broke off and fell silent. It should be noted that Peter Stepanovich was sitting in an armchair with his legs crossed, while the captain stood in front of him in a highly deferential attitude.

Apparently Peter Stepanovich didn't care for Mr Lebyadkin's hesitation one bit; his face twitched with an angry spasm.

'Don't you want to say anything?' he asked, glaring intently at the captain. 'If you do, go right ahead. We're waiting.'

'You yourself know, Peter Stepanovich, that I can't say anything.'

'No, I don't know that; it's the first time I've heard that. Why can't you say anything?'

The captain remained silent, lowering his eyes to the floor.

'Let me go, Peter Stepanovich,' he said firmly.

'Not before you answer my question: is *everything* I've said here true?'

'Yes, sir, it is,' Lebyadkin said in a hollow voice, raising his eyes to his tormentor's face. Perspiration stood out on his temples.

'Is *everything* true?'

'Everything, sir.'

'Don't you have anything to add or note? If you feel we've been unfair to you, say so; protest, declare your dissatisfaction aloud.'

'No, I've nothing to say.'

'Did you recently threaten Nikolai Vsevolodovich?'

'That... that... that was due to drink, Peter Stepanovich.' (He raised his head suddenly.) 'Peter Stepanovich! If family honour and undeserved shame cry out among men, then, then—can a man be held to blame?' he roared, suddenly forgetting himself as before.

'Are you sober now, Mr Lebyadkin?' asked Peter Stepanovich, casting him a penetrating glance.

'Yes.'

'What do you mean by family honour and undeserved shame?'

'I didn't mean anyone, anyone in particular. I was talking about myself...' the captain said, collapsing once again.

'You seem to have been offended by what I said about you and your behaviour. You're very irritable, Mr Lebyadkin. But I haven't got on to your behaviour in its real sense. I'm going to talk about your behaviour in its real sense. I'm going to, that may well happen, but I haven't yet begun to talk about its *real sense.*'

Lebyadkin shuddered and stared wildly at Peter Stepanovich.

'Peter Stepanovich, I'm only starting to wake up now!'

'Hmmm. And is it I who've awakened you?'

'Yes, it's you, Peter Stepanovich; I've been asleep for four years with a cloud hanging over me. May I go now, Peter Stepanovich?'

'You may, unless Varvara Petrovna would like to...'

But she motioned him away.

The captain bowed and took two steps towards the door; he suddenly stopped, placed his hand over his heart, was about to say something, but didn't, and quickly left the room. But in the doorway he bumped into Nikolai Vsevolodovich who stepped aside; the captain shrank suddenly before him and froze on the spot, not taking his eyes off him, like a rabbit facing a boa constrictor. After a brief pause, Nikolai Vsevolodovich pushed him lightly aside and entered the drawing-room.

7.

He was cheerful and calm. Perhaps something very pleasant had just occurred that we hadn't yet heard about; but he did seem to be particularly pleased about something or other.

'Do you forgive me, Nicolas?' Varvara Petrovna asked, unable to restrain herself and rising to meet him.

But Nicolas just started laughing.

'So that's how it is!' he cried in a good-natured and light-hearted way. 'I see you know everything now. As I left here I thought in the carriage, "At least I should've told them the whole story, instead of just going off like that!" But then I remembered that Peter Stepanovich had been left behind, and I stopped worrying.'

As he said this he cast a quick glance around the room.

'Peter Stepanovich told us an old Petersburg tale about the life of an eccentric,' Varvara Petrovna put in enthusiastically, 'about a certain crazy and capricious person, but one who was always lofty in his sentiments, noble and chivalrous...'

'Chivalrous? Has it really gone that far?' Nicolas replied with a laugh. 'But I'm very grateful to Peter Stepanovich for his haste on this occasion' (he exchanged a rapid glance with him). 'You should know, *maman*, that Peter Stepanovich is a universal peacemaker; that's his role, his disease, his hobby, and I particularly recommend him to you on this count. I can guess what sort of tale he composed for you here. Compose he does, when he tells a story; he keeps an entire record office in his head. Observe that as a realist he's incapable of telling lies; truth is more important to him than the success of his tale... except, of course, for those particular circumstances when success is more important than truth.' (As he said this he looked around at everyone.) 'So, *maman*, you clearly see that you needn't ask my forgiveness; if there's something insane here, it's most likely connected with me; and, when all is said and done, I'm the one who's crazy—after all, I have to keep up my local reputation...'

He embraced his mother tenderly.

'In any case, the tale's been told, the matter's finished, and there's no need to discuss it further,' he added in a dry, resolute tone of voice. Varvara Petrovna understood this tone, but her exaltation didn't fade, quite the contrary, in fact.

'I didn't expect you for another month, Nicolas!'

'Of course, I'll explain it all to you later, *maman*, but as for now...'

He went up to Praskovya Ivanovna.

But she scarcely turned to look at him, in spite of having been so overwhelmed by his sudden appearance half an hour ago. Now she had other things to worry about: from the moment the captain had left, bumping into Nikolai Vsevolodovich in the doorway, Liza had suddenly begun laughing—at first quietly and intermittently, but then her laughter grew louder and more audible. Her face turned red. The contrast with her earlier air of gloom was extraordinary. While Nikolai Vsevolodovich was talking with Varvara Petrovna, she beckoned twice to Maurice Nikolaevich, as if wanting to whisper something to him. But as soon as he bent his head down, she immediately burst out laughing; one might have concluded that she was laughing at none other than poor Maurice Nikolaevich. However, she was evidently trying to regain control of herself, and put her handkerchief over her mouth. Nikolai Vsevolodovich turned to greet her with the most innocent and good-natured expression.

'You must please excuse me,' she said, speaking quickly. 'You... you, of course you've met Maurice Nikolaevich before... Good Lord, you're really inexcusably tall, Maurice Nikolaevich!'

And she laughed again. Maurice Nikolaevich was certainly tall, but by no means inexcusably so.

'Have you... been here long?' she mumbled, controlling herself once more and even becoming somewhat embarrassed, though her eyes were still flashing.

'A little over two hours,' Nicolas replied, staring at her intently. I must observe that he was unusually restrained and polite, but apart from that his expression was completely indifferent, even listless.

'Where will you be living?'

'Here.'

Varvara Petrovna was also watching Liza, but was suddenly struck by an idea.

'Where have you been up to now, Nicolas, up to now, for the last two hours?' she asked, going up to him. 'The train arrives at ten o'clock.'

'First I dropped Peter Stepanovich at Kirillov's house. I met him at Matveevo' (three stations away), 'and from there we travelled in the same carriage.'

'I'd been waiting in Matveevo since dawn,' Peter Stepanovich confirmed. 'The last few carriages of our train jumped the tracks during the night. I almost broke both my legs.'

'Broke your legs!' Liza cried. 'Mamma, mamma, last week you and I were going to go to Matveevo. We would have broken our legs, too!'

'Lord have mercy!' said Praskovya Ivanovna, crossing herself.

'Mamma, mamma, dear mamma, don't worry, even if I do break both my legs; it might happen, as you yourself say, since I go riding every day at breakneck speed. Maurice Nikolaevich, will you lead me about if I'm lame?' she asked, laughing again. 'If it does happen, I won't let anyone lead me except you; you can count on that. Well, let's suppose I break only one leg... Come on, be polite, say you'll consider it my good fortune.'

'Good fortune with only one leg?' Maurice Nikolaevich asked, frowning gravely.

'On the other hand, you will lead me about, won't you; only you, and no one else!'

'Even in that case it's you who'll be leading me about, Lizaveta Nikolaevna,' Maurice Nikolaevich said even more gravely.

'My God, he tried to make a joke!' Liza cried almost in horror. 'Maurice Nikolaevich, don't you dare do anything of the sort! What an awful egotist you are! I'm sure, to your own credit, you're slandering yourself. On the contrary: from morning till night you'll try to convince me that I've become more interesting without legs! There's only one problem, though—you're immeasurably tall, and without my legs I'll be so very small. How will you offer me your arm? We won't make a very good couple!'

She laughed frantically. Her witticisms and insinuations fell flat, but obviously she didn't care at all.

'Hysterics!' Peter Stepanovich whispered to me. 'Quick, a glass of water.'

He guessed right; a minute later everyone was fussing over her, and water brought. Liza kept embracing her mamma, kissing her passionately, and crying on her shoulder; then pulling back and looking her straight in the eye, she burst into laughter. Finally mamma began whimpering as well. Varvara Petrovna led them both away to her own room, out the same door through which Darya Pavlovna had come in earlier. But they stayed there only a little while, no more than a few minutes...

Now I'll try to recall every detail of the last few moments of that memorable morning. I remember that when we were left alone, without the women (except for Darya Pavlovna who didn't budge from her seat), Nikolai Vsevolodovich made his way around the room and greeted each and every one of us, except Shatov who was still sitting in the corner, and whose head hung even lower than before. Stepan Trofimovich began talking with Nikolai Vsevolodovich about something extremely clever, but Nikolai turned and went hurriedly up to Darya Pavlovna. On his way Peter Stepanovich grabbed him almost by force and led him over to the window, where he started whispering something to him quickly, obviously something very important, judging by the expression on his face and his accompanying gestures. For his part, Nikolai Vsevolodovich listened in a very lackadaisical and absent-minded way, with a formal smile, and, towards the end, even in some impatience; he kept trying to get away. He moved from the window just as the women were returning; Varvara Petrovna sat Liza down where she was before, insisting that they wait and rest another ten minutes, that the fresh air could scarcely do their frayed nerves any good just then. She was very concerned about Liza and sat down next to her. Peter Stepanovich, who was now free, promptly joined them and began a brisk and cheerful conversation. Then Nikolai Vsevolodovich finally went up to Darya Pavlovna in his unhurried way. Dasha trembled at his approach and jumped up quickly in obvious embarrassment; her face was very red.

'It seems you're to be congratulated... or not just yet?' he said, with a peculiar expression on his face.

Dasha made some reply, but it was difficult to hear.

'Forgive my indiscretion,' he said, raising his voice, 'but you do know I was expressly informed. Did you know that?'

'Yes, I know you were expressly informed.'

'I hope, however, that I've done no harm in congratulating you,' he said with a laugh. 'And if Stepan Trofimovich...'

'What for? Why are you congratulating her?' Peter Stepanovich asked, suddenly jumping up. 'Should I be congratulating you, Darya Pavlovna? Why, it's not for that, is it? Your blush indicates I've guessed right. Indeed, why else does one congratulate a lovely and virtuous young lady? And what kind of congratulations make them blush most of all? Well, then, accept my congratulations, too, if I've guessed right, and pay up! Don't you remember, we made a bet in Switzerland that you'd never get married... Oh, yes, speaking of Switzerland—what have I been thinking about? Can you imagine, it's half the reason I came, and I almost forgot all about it. Tell me,' he said turning quickly to Stepan Trofimovich, 'have you ever been to Switzerland?'

'Me? Switzerland?' Stepan Trofimovich asked, surprised and confused.

'Why? Aren't you going? You're getting married too, aren't you? You wrote...'

'Pierre!' cried Stepan Trofimovich.

'What do you mean, "Pierre"... Don't you see, if it gives you pleasure, I've come here to say I have nothing against it, since you undoubtedly wanted my opinion as soon as possible; if,' he rattled on, 'you really need to be "saved" as you wrote and implored in that letter, well, then, I'm at your service. Is it true he's getting married, Varvara Petrovna?' he asked, turning quickly to her. 'I hope I'm not indiscreet; he wrote that the whole town knows about it and is congratulating him, and that to avoid it he can only go out at night. I have his letter right here in my pocket. But would you believe, Varvara Petrovna, I can't understand a thing in it! Tell me something, Stepan Trofimovich, am I to congratulate you or "save" you? You wouldn't believe it, but he writes quite cheerfully, then suddenly he's full of despair. First of all, he asks my forgiveness; well, I suppose, that's just his way... But I have to say it: imagine, the man has seen me only twice in his life, and then accidentally, and now suddenly, about to embark on his third marriage, he thinks he's violating some parental obligation to me. He implores me at a distance of a thousand miles not to be angry and to permit him to remarry! Don't be offended, Stepan Trofimovich, it's characteristic of your generation. I'm broad-minded and I don't condemn you; let's assume it even does you honour, etc., etc. But again, the point is I don't really understand the point. There was something about "sins in Switzerland". I'm getting married, he said, for those sins or because of another man's sins, however he put it—in any case, because of "sins". "The girl", he said, "is a pearl and a diamond", and, of course, "he's un-worthy"—his own words. But because of another man's sins or some circumstances or other, "he's obliged to lead her to the altar and then go to Switzerland"; therefore I should "abandon everything and come rushing to save" him. Do you understand anything in all this? But... but, I can see from your expressions' (he turned around with the letter in his hands and looked them all straight in the eye with his ingenuous smile) 'in my usual way, I seem to have made a blunder... in my stupid candour or, as Nikolai Vsevolodo-vich says, my haste. Why, I thought I was among friends here, meaning your friends, Stepan Trofimovich, your own friends, and that I was the outsider. Now I see... I see that everyone knows something about it, and that is just what I don't know.'

He continued looking around the room.

'So Stepan Trofimovich wrote that he was getting married for "another man's sins committed in Switzerland" and you should come here "to save him", in those very words?' Varvara Petrovna asked, approaching him suddenly. Her face was bilious and distorted, her lips trembling.

'Well, I mean, don't you see, there may be something here I don't understand,' Peter Stepanovich replied, as if in alarm, and more hastily than ever. 'It's his fault, of course, for writing like that. Here's the letter. You know, Varvara Petrovna, his letters are interminable and incessant. In the last two or three months, he's sent letter after letter; I must confess, I don't always read them through to the end. Forgive me, Stepan Trofimovich, for my stupid confession, but you'll agree, won't you, that while the letter was addressed to me, it was really written for posterity, so you won't really mind... Come, come, don't be offended; after all, you and I are still friends! But this letter, Varvara Petrovna, this letter I did read. These "sins"—"another man's sins"—are probably some little sins of our own, and I bet they're thoroughly innocent ones. But because of them we've suddenly decided to devise this terrible story with a noble theme—precisely on account of the noble theme. Why, don't you see, there's a weakness in our financial position— it's finally necessary to confess. You know, we're rather too fond of a game of cards... but that's irrelevant, quite irrelevant. I'm sorry, I talk too much; so help me, Varvara Petrovna, he frightened me, and I really did come here partly to "save" him. Now, I feel ashamed myself. Am I holding a knife to his throat, or what? Am I some implacable creditor? He mentioned something about a dowry... But, do you mean to say you're really going to get married, Stepan Trofimovich? That's just like you—to talk and talk for the sake of your own voice... Oh, Varvara Petrovna, I'm sure you must be cross with me now for all this talk...'

'On the contrary, on the contrary, I can see your patience is quite exhausted, and you have good reason for that, of course,' Varvara Petrovna replied spitefully.

She'd been listening with malicious glee to Peter Stepanovich's whole "candid outburst"; he was obviously playing a part (what part I still didn't know, but it was obvious, even though played rather crudely).

'On the contrary,' she continued, 'I'm very grateful to you for having spoken; I wouldn't have known any of this but for you. For the first time in twenty years my eyes have been opened. Nikolai Vsevolodovich, just now you said you'd been expressly informed: was that Stepan Trofimovich writing to you in the same vein?'

'I did receive a perfectly harmless and... and... very generous letter from him...'

'You seem at a loss for words—enough! Stepan Trofimovich, I want you to do me a very great favour,' she said suddenly, turning to him with eyes flashing. 'Do me a favour: leave here at once and never set foot in my house again.'

I want you to recall her recent state of 'exaltation'—which still hadn't passed. True, Stepan Trofimovich was certainly at fault! But what really struck me most of all was that he withstood the accusations of his 'Petrushka' with utmost dignity, without trying to interrupt, as well as Varvara Petrovna's 'malediction'. Where did he find so much strength? I knew only one thing: he was unmistakably deeply wounded by his first meeting with Petrushka, particularly in view of all the embracing that had gone on. There was profound and *genuine* grief in his eyes and his heart anyway. He was conscious of another grief at the same time, namely, the poignant awareness of having acted despicably; he confided that to me later with total candour. And surely such unmistakable *genuine* grief, even in a phenomenally frivolous man, is capable of making him solid and resolute, if only for a very short time. What's more, real, genuine grief can sometimes make even fools smarter, though, of course only for a little while; it's characteristic of this kind of grief. If that's true, what can happen to a man like Stepan Trofimovich? A complete transformation—though, of course, only for a short time.

He bowed to Varvara Petrovna with dignity and didn't utter one word (it's true there was nothing else he could do). That was the way he wanted to leave the house; but he couldn't restrain himself and went up to Darya Pavlovna. Apparently she had a feeling he might do so because she began herself, all in a panic, to talk, as if trying to warn him:

'Please, Stepan Trofimovich, for God's sake, don't say anything,' she said rapidly and excitedly, with a pained expression on her face, hastily holding out her hand to him. 'Rest assured I respect you as much as ever... and value you just as highly... only think well of me, Stepan Trofimovich, I'll appreciate that very, very much...'

Stepan Trofimovich bowed very, very deeply to her.

'Just as you wish, Darya Pavlovna. You know you can do just as you wish in this whole affair. So it was, so it is, and so it will be in the future,' Varvara Petrovna concluded impressively.

'Why, now I understand everything!' Peter Stepanovich said, slapping himself on the forehead. 'But... but what an awful position all this puts me in! Darya Pavlovna, please forgive me!... Now look what you've done to me,' he said, turning to his father.

'Pierre, you could speak to me in a different tone, don't you think, my friend?' Stepan Trofimovich said very quietly.

'Don't shout, please,' said Pierre, waving his arms about. 'Believe me, it's all your sick, old nerves, and shouting doesn't serve any purpose. You'd better tell me why you didn't warn me, since you might have assumed I'd begin talking about it as soon as I came in.'

Stepan Trofimovich looked at him very intently:

'Pierre, you know so much about what's happening here. Can it really be you didn't know and hadn't heard a word about it?'

'Wha-a-at? What people these are! It isn't enough you're such a big baby, you're a spiteful baby as well! Varvara Petrovna, did you hear what he said?'

General commotion ensued; then suddenly an extraordinary event occurred that no one could have anticipated.

8.

First of all I must mention that during the last two or three minutes Lizaveta Ivanovna had been in the grip of some new impulse; she was whispering rapidly to her mamma and to Maurice Nikolaevich, who was bending over her. She looked agitated, but determined at the same time. At last she got up from her seat, obviously in a hurry to leave and hurrying her mamma, whom Maurice Nikolaevich was helping out of her armchair. But evidently they were destined not to leave before witnessing the entire scene to the end.

Shatov, who'd been completely forgotten by everyone in his own corner (not far from Lizaveta Nikolaevna) and, apparently, not knowing himself why he was still sitting there, suddenly got up from his chair and headed across the room towards Nikolai Vsevolodovich with a measured but decisive step, looking him straight in the eye. Nikolai noticed his approach at some distance and smiled faintly; but as Shatov drew nearer, he stopped smiling.

When Shatov halted silently in front of him, without taking his eyes off his face, suddenly everyone noticed and stopped talking, Peter Stepanovich last of all; Liza and mamma paused in the middle of the room. About five seconds elapsed; the expression of insolent bewilderment on Nikolai Vsevolodovich's face changed to anger; he knit his brows and all of a sudden...

All of a sudden Shatov swung a long, heavy arm and struck Stavrogin across the face with all his might. Nikolai Vsevolodovich staggered violently.

Shatov hit him in a peculiar way, not the way such slaps are usually given (if one can put it like that); in other words, not with the palm of his hand, but with his whole fist. His fist was large, heavy, bony, and covered with reddish hair and freckles. If the blow had landed on the nose, it would've been broken. But the blow fell on the cheek and struck the left corner of the lip and upper teeth; the blood began to flow at once.

I believe someone cried out immediately, perhaps it was Varvara Petrovna who screamed—I don't recall, because after that the room fell silent again. Moreover, the entire scene lasted no more than about ten seconds.

Let me remind the reader once more that Nikolai Vsevolodovich belonged to that category of people who know no fear. In a duel he could face his opponent's pistol with indifference, then shoot and kill with calm brutality. If someone struck him in the face, he wouldn't challenge the person to a duel; rather, he'd kill the offender on the spot. He was precisely that type of man, and he'd kill in full consciousness, not in rage. It seems he never experienced those blinding outbursts of anger when it's impossible to behave rationally. In the midst of a fit of rage that would sometimes overcome him, he could still maintain complete control of himself; therefore he understood that for committing murder except in a duel he'd certainly be sentenced to penal servitude. Nevertheless, he'd still have killed the offender without any hesitation.

I've been studying Nikolai Vsevolodovich for some time; and, given the special circumstances, as I write this now I know a great many facts about him. Perhaps I should compare him with other men of the past about whom our society has preserved certain legendary traditions. For example, it was said about the Decembrist L—n* that all his life he was searching for danger; he revelled in the sensation of it, and it became for him a physical necessity. In his youth he'd agree to fight duels for no reason at all; he went hunting bears in Siberia armed with only a knife; he loved to encounter escaped convicts in the forests of Siberia, who, I must observe in passing, are even more terrifying than bears. There's no doubt these legendary men were capable of feeling fear, perhaps even to an extreme degree—or else they'd have been a great deal more serene, and wouldn't have become so addicted to the sensation of danger. But what really fascinated them, of course, was overcoming their cowardice. The constant thrill of conquest and the awareness that no one could conquer them—that was what attracted them. Even before his exile L—n had struggled for some time with hunger and hard work as he earned his daily bread, merely because he didn't want to submit to the unjust demands of his wealthy father. Therefore, he had a many-sided concept of struggle; not only in bear fights and duels did he know the worth of his steadfastness and strength of character.

Nevertheless, many years have passed since that time, and the nervous, tormented, and dualistic nature of men in the present age is incompatible with the urgent need for those pure and immediate sensations so sought after by more active and restless men in the good old days. Nikolai Vsevolodovich might have looked down upon L—n, might even have called him a boastful coward, a crowing cock—

true, he wouldn't have said it aloud. Stavrogin would've shot his opponent in a duel, he'd have gone off on a bear hunt if necessary, and defended himself against a robber in the forest—just as fearlessly and successfully as L—n did, but without any sensation of enjoyment—merely out of unpleasant necessity—listlessly, languorously, even apathetically. As far as malice is concerned, some progress has been made compared to L—n, even compared to Lermontov.* There was more malice in Nikolai Vsevolodovich maybe than in both of them combined, but his malice was cold, calm, and, if I can put it this way, *reasonable*—consequently the most repellent and terrifying kind of malice imaginable. Let me repeat: at that time I considered him, and still do (now that it's all over), precisely the sort of man who, if he received a slap across the face or some other insult, would kill his opponent immediately, at once, on the spot, without challenging him to a duel.

And yet, in the present instance, something altogether different and quite strange occurred.

As soon as he'd regained his balance after the blow had almost knocked down in so humiliating a fashion, and the horrible, as it were sodden thud of the fist striking his face had died away in the room, Stavrogin immediately seized Shatov by the shoulders with both hands; but at once, almost the very same instant, he withdrew his hands and folded them behind his back. He was silent, glaring at Shatov, his face as pale as his shirt. But the strange thing was that the fire in his eyes seemed to go out. Ten seconds later his eyes looked cold and—I do not tell a lie—even tranquil. Only he was terribly pale. Naturally, I don't know what was going on inside the man; I saw only the exterior. I think that if the man existed who, shall we say, would grab a red-hot iron bar and squeeze it tight in his hand to test his fortitude, and then, in the course of ten seconds, could manage to conquer the unbearable pain, that man, it seems to me, would experience something similar to what Nikolai Vsevolodovich endured during those ten seconds.

Shatov was the first to drop his eyes, apparently compelled to do so. Then he turned around slowly and walked out of the room, but not at all in the way he'd entered earlier. He left quietly, in a particularly clumsy way, his shoulders hunched, his head hanging, as if he were debating something within himself. I think he was whispering. He walked to the door cautiously, without stumbling or knocking anything over; he opened the door a little and slipped out almost sideways. As he left, the tuft of hair sticking straight up on the back of his head was particularly noticeable.

Then, before all the screaming began, one terrible scream was heard. I saw Lizaveta Nikolaevna seize her mamma by the shoulder and Maurice Nikolaevich by the arm, and saw how she pulled them from behind two or three times, trying to make them leave the room; then all of a sudden she uttered a shriek and fell full length on the floor, unconscious. To this day I can still hear the sound of her head as it hit the carpet.

PART TWO

Night

I.

EIGHT days passed. Now that everything is over and I'm actually writing this chronicle, we know what it was all about; but at that time we knew nothing, and it's only natural that several things seemed strange to us. At any rate, Stepan Trofimovich and I shut ourselves up at first and observed things somewhat apprehensively from a distance. I was still venturing forth on occasion, and brought him back various bits of news, without which he'd never have survived.

Needless to say, all sorts of rumours were circulating in town, concerning the slap on the face, Lizaveta Nikolaevna's fainting fit, and everything else that had occurred that Sunday. But what most astonished us was this: who could possibly be responsible for divulging it all so quickly and accurately? No one present at the time, it seems, could have had any need or seen any advantage in exposing the secret of what had happened. There were no servants present; Lebyadkin was the only one who could have blurted it out, not so much in malice, because he'd left in great fear (and terror of one's enemy destroys any feeling of malice), but simply from his lack of restraint. But the following day Lebyadkin, together with his sister, disappeared without trace; he never went back to Filippov's house; he moved away to some other place, no one knew where, and seemed to have vanished. Shatov, from whom I'd hoped to find out about Marya Timofeevna, shut himself up in his own room and remained there for eight days, even interrupting his work in town. He wouldn't see me. I stopped by to see him on Tuesday and knocked at his door. There was no answer, but certain incontrovertible evidence convinced me he was at home, so I knocked again. He finally jumped up, probably from his bed, approached the door rapidly, and shouted as loud as he could: 'Shatov isn't at home.' On that, I went away.

Stepan Trofimovich and I, not without some alarm at the boldness of the supposition, but trying to encourage one another, finally arrived at one and the same conclusion: we decided that the only person who could have been responsible for the rumours was Peter Stepanovich, even though in a subsequent conversation with his father he assured him that the story was on everyone's lips, especially at the club, and that it was already known in great detail both to the governor's wife and her spouse. There's something else worthy of note: on the second day, Monday evening, I met Liputin, and he too knew everything right down to the last word; of course, he'd have been one of the first to find out.

Many ladies (including some from the highest society) were also curious about the 'mysterious cripple'—as they referred to Marya Timofeevna. There were even some who wished to see her in person and make her acquaintance, so that those people who had hastened to hide the Lebyadkins were obviously acting judiciously. But in the forefront stood the question of Lizaveta Nikolaevna's fainting fit; 'all society' was interested in it, not the least because it concerned Yulia Mikhailovna directly, as a relative of Lizaveta Nikolaevna and as her protectress. And what didn't they say about it! The mysteriousness of the circumstances intensified the gossip: both houses were sealed up tight. Lizaveta Nikolaevna, so people said, had taken to her bed with a very high fever; the same thing was said to be true of Nikolai Vsevolodovich, with the addition of several disgusting details, including one tooth knocked out and one cheek swollen from an abscess. It was even predicted in certain circles that a murder might soon take place in our town; that Stavrogin was not the sort of person to take such an insult; that he might kill Shatov, in secret, as in a Corsican vendetta. This idea was very popular; but most of the young people in our society listened to it all with contempt and an air of the most scornful indifference, feigned, of course. In general, our society's earlier hostility to Nikolai Vsevolodovich was strikingly in evidence. Even the most solid of our citizens began to accuse him, although they themselves didn't know of what. In whispers it was alleged that he'd compromised Lizaveta Nikolaevna's honour and there had been some intrigue between them in Switzerland. Of course the more cautious restrained themselves, but everyone listened with the greatest interest. Other conversations also took place, not in public, but in private, infrequent, almost in secret, very strange conversations, the existence of which I mention merely to warn the reader, and solely bearing in mind the future events of my narrative. Namely: some people said, knitting their brows, and God only knows on what basis, that Nikolai Vsevolodovich had some special business in our province, that in Petersburg through Count K. he'd established contact with certain highly placed people, that he might be in the service of the government, and might even have been commissioned by someone to carry out an assignment. When some very restrained and solid citizens smiled at this rumour, noting so reasonably that a person who thrived on public scandals and began life among us with a swollen face really didn't resemble a civil servant, they were told in a whisper that he wasn't officially in government service, but confidentially, so to speak, in which case such service required that the person serving resemble a civil servant as little as possible. This comment produced its effect; it was known that the zemstvo* in our province was regarded in the capital with considerable interest. I repeat, these rumours merely surfaced and then vanished without trace, for the time being, when Nikolai Vsevolodovich made his first appearance among us; but I must observe that many of these rumours resulted from the few but malicious words uttered in a vague and abrupt manner at the club by Artemy Pavlovich Gaganov, retired captain of the Guard who'd recently returned from Petersburg. He was a very wealthy landowner in our province and district, a member of Petersburg high society, and the son of the late Pavel Pavlovich Gaganov, the well-respected committee member of our club with whom Nikolai Vsevolodovich had had that extraordinarily crude and unexpected confrontation more than four years ago, which I described at the beginning of my story.

Everyone immediately found out that Yulia Mikhailovna paid an exceptional visit to Varvara Petrovna, and that on the porch of the house she was informed that 'for reasons of ill health she couldn't bè received'. It was also known that two days after this visit Yulia Mikhailovna deliberately sent to enquire about Varvara Petrovna's health. Finally, she came 'to the defence' of Varvara Petrovna everywhere, of course, only in the loftiest sense of the word, that is, in the vaguest possible way. Still, she listened sternly and coldly to the initial hasty insinuations about the incident on Sunday, so that in the days following such charges were no longer uttered in her presence. Thus the idea gained ground everywhere that Yulia Mikhailovna not only knew about this whole enigmatic episode, but also understood its entire mysterious significance to the last detail, not as an innocent bystander, but as a participant. I must observe, by the way, that among us she gradually started to assume that exalted influence which she undoubtedly aspired to and thirsted for; she'd already begun to see herself as 'surrounded' by admirers. Part of our society recognized her practical intelligence and tact... but more about that later. It was her patronage that partly explained Peter Stepanovich's extremely rapid success in our society—a success which greatly surprised Stepan Trofimovich at the time.

Perhaps he and I were both exaggerating. In the first place, Peter Stepanovich became acquainted almost immediately with everyone in our town in the first four days after his arrival. He turned up on a Sunday, and by the Tuesday I met him in a carriage with Artemy Pavlovich Gaganov, a proud, irritable and arrogant man, in spite of all his worldliness; his character was such that it was somewhat difficult to get along with him. Peter Stepanovich was also rather well received by the governor; in fact, so well received that he soon came to occupy the position of an intimate, so to speak, the favoured young friend of the family; he dined with Yulia Mikhailovna almost every day. He'd made her acquaintance in Switzerland, but there really was something very odd about his immediate success in his excellency's household. After all, he was still reputed to have been a revolutionary while abroad, whether true or not, who'd had a role in certain émigré presses and congresses, 'which facts could even be documented from newspaper clippings', as Alyosha Telyatnikov once maliciously observed to me (he's now retired, alas, a former low-ranking civil servant, who at one time was also a favoured young person in the old governor's household). But one fact was indisputable: this former revolutionary had returned to his beloved fatherland not only without interference, but almost at someone's urging; consequently, perhaps there was no substance to that story. Liputin once whispered to me that rumour had it Peter Stepanovich had apparently repented his actions and been pardoned, having provided the names of several other figures, and thus, perhaps, managed to expiate his own guilt and promised to make himself useful to his fatherland in the future. I conveyed this malicious story to Stepan Trofimovich who, in spite of the fact that he was hardly in a state to think clearly, became very thoughtful. Later it turned out that Peter Stepanovich had arrived with some extremely enthusiastic letters of introduction, at least one of which was addressed to the governor's wife by a very important old lady in Petersburg, whose husband was one of the most important old men in Petersburg. This old lady, Yulia Mikhailovna's godmother, mentioned in her letter that Count K. was very well acquainted with Peter Stepanovich through Nikolai Vsevolodovich, that he was very fond of him and thought him 'a worthy young man, in spite of his previous mistakes'. Yulia Mikhailovna valued highly her tenuous connections with 'high society' that were so difficult to maintain; she was naturally delighted with the letter from the important old lady. Nevertheless, there was still something peculiar about it all. She even put her husband on an almost familiar footing with Peter Stepanovich, such that Mr von Lembke actually complained to her... but more about that later. I must note for the record that even our great writer was extremely well-disposed towards Peter Stepanovich and invited him to visit at once. Such eagerness on the part of so arrogant a man wounded Stepan Trofimovich most of all, but I explained it to myself differently: in inviting a nihilist to his home, Mr Karmazinov undoubtedly had in mind his relations with the progressive young people in both our capitals. The great writer cowered in fear before the younger generation of revolutionaries, and, in his ignorance imagining that the keys to the future of Russia lay in their hands, he tried to ingratiate himself with them in a humiliating way, primarily because they paid him no attention whatsoever.

2.

Peter Stepanovich came to see his father twice, and, to my misfortune, I was present both times. The first time he visited him was on Wednesday, that is, four days after their meeting, and it was on business. By the way, the dispute over the value of the estate had somehow been resolved without much fuss and bother. Varvara Petrovna took it all upon herself and paid for everything, including the land, of course; she merely informed Stepan Trofimovich that it had all been settled. The butler, Aleksei Yegorovich, was authorized by Varvara Petrovna to bring him the papers to sign; he did so in silence, with the utmost dignity. I must observe, apropos of his dignity, that I could scarcely recognize our old man during these last few days. He behaved as never before; he became astonishingly taciturn, and had even refrained from writing Varvara Petrovna any letters since that Sunday, something I considered a miracle. But the main thing was, he became calm. Clearly he'd come upon some definitive and extraordinary idea that afforded him serenity. He'd found this idea and now was sitting and waiting for something to happen. Moreover, at first he was ill, particularly so on Monday; it was one of his bilious attacks. But he couldn't possibly remain without news during all this time; yet whenever I moved away from the facts and approached the heart of the matter, venturing theories, he would immediately start waving his arms about to get me to stop. But the meetings with his son left him with a painful impression, even though he remained unshaken. Afterwards on both occasions he lay on his sofa with vinegar compresses on his head; but he still remained calm underneath.

There were times, however, when he didn't wave his arms about to stop me. It also seemed that at times his newly acquired and mysterious determination abandoned him and he was beginning to struggle with a seductive new train of thought. This was only at certain times, but I took note of it. I suspected that he very much wanted to assert himself again, to come out of his isolation, to enter the fray, to fight one last battle.

'*Cher*, I'd demolish them!' he exclaimed on Thursday evening, after his second meeting with Peter Stepanovich, as he was lying on his sofa, his head wrapped in a towel.

Up to that moment he hadn't spoken one word to me all day.

' "*Fils, fils chéri*",[1] and so on; I agree that all these phrases are pure nonsense, the sort of vulgar language cooks use. All right, I can see it myself now. I provided him with neither food nor drink, I sent him away from Berlin to a distant province, a little baby, by post, and so forth, I agree... "You", he says, "didn't provide me with food and sent me away by post, and on top of that you robbed me here." "But, you wretch," I shout at him, "my heart has ached for you all my life even though I sent you off by post!" *Il rit.*[2] But I agree, I agree... I did send him off by post,' he concluded, almost rambling.

'*Passons*,' he began again five minutes later. 'I don't understand Turgenev. His Bazarov* is a contrived character who doesn't exist at all; the nihilists were the first to repudiate him because he bore no resemblance to anything.

[1] Son, dear son
[2] He laughs.

This Bazarov is a vague combination of Gogol's Nozdryov*
and Byron, *c'est le mot*. Look at them carefully: they turn
somersaults and squeal with delight like little puppies
playing in the sun; they're happy; they're victorious! What
sort of Byron is that?... Besides, it's all so humdrum! What
lowbrow and irritable vanity, what vulgar craving to *faire
du bruit autour de son nom*,[1] without noticing that *son nom*...
Oh, what a caricature! "Surely," I cry, "you don't mean to
offer yourself, just as you are, as a substitute for Christ?"
Il rit. Il rit beaucoup, il rit trop. He has a strange smile. His
mother didn't have that kind of smile. *Il rit toujours*.'[2]

Again there was silence.

'They're so clever; they planned everything in advance
for that Sunday...' he blurted out suddenly.

'Oh, undoubtedly,' I cried, pricking up my ears. 'It was
all arranged, absolutely transparent, and carried off very
badly.'

'That's not what I was talking about. Don't you know
that it was intentionally transparent, so that those who were
supposed to could tell? Don't you understand?'

'No, I don't.'

'*Tant mieux. Passons*. I'm very irritable today.'

'But why did you argue with him, Stepan Trofimovich?'
I asked reproachfully.

'*Je voulais convertir*. Of course, you'll laugh. *Cette pauvre*
aunt, *elle entendra de belles choses*![3] Oh, my friend, believe
me, I felt like a patriot that day! Moreover, I've always been
conscious of being a Russian... a genuine Russian can't be
anything different from you and me. *Il y a là-dedans quelque
chose d'aveugle et de louche*.'[4]

'Absolutely,' I replied.

'My friend, the real truth always strikes one as improbable, don't you know that? In order to make truth seem

---

[1] make himself noticed
[2] He laughs. He laughs a lot, he laughs too much . . . He's always
laughing.
[3] I wanted to convert him. . . . That poor aunt will hear some fine
things.
[4] There's something blind and suspicious in all this.

more probable, one must always mix it with some falsehood. That's what people have always done. This may be something we don't quite understand. What do you think, is there something we don't quite understand in their triumphant squealing? I wish there were. I do wish there were.'

I was silent. He was too, for a very long time.

'It's said', he began babbling suddenly, as if in a fever, 'that the French intellect is false, and it always has been. Why slander the French intellect? It's merely Russian indolence, our humiliating inability to produce an idea, our disgusting parasitism among the ranks of nations. *Ils sont tout simplement des paresseux,*[1] and it's nothing to do with the French intellect. Oh, all Russians should be annihilated like dangerous parasites for the good of mankind! We've been striving to achieve something different, altogether different; I don't understand anything. I've stopped understanding. "Don't you see?" I shouted at him. "Don't you see that if you place the guillotine in the foreground and are so enthusiastic about it, it's merely because it's so easy to chop off people's heads, while it's so much more difficult to have an idea! *Vous êtes des paresseux! Votre drapeau est une guenille, une impuissance.* Those carts, or how does it go: 'the rumble of carts carrying bread to mankind' is more useful than the Sistine Madonna,* or how do they put it: *une bêtise dans ce genre.*[2] Don't you understand?" I shouted at him. "Don't you understand, in addition to happiness mankind needs unhappiness just as much?" *Il rit.* "You", he says, "let fall your clever phrases while stretching your limbs out (he used a coarser expression) on a velvet sofa." Observe this habit of addressing one's father in familiar terms: it's fine, if both parties agree, but what if they're shouting abuse at each other?'

We remained silent for another minute.

'*Cher,*' he concluded all of a sudden, getting up quickly. 'You know this will absolutely end in something or other?'

'Of course,' I replied.

---

[1] They are simply lazy

[2] You're lazy! Your flag is an old rag, a symbol of impotence. . . . stupidity of that type

'*Vous ne comprenez pas. Passons.*[1] Things usually come to nothing in this world, but this will end in something, absolutely, absolutely!'

He stood up, walked about the room in great agitation and, reaching the sofa again, sank down on it exhausted.

On Friday morning Peter Stepanovich left for somewhere in our district and was away until Monday. I found out about his departure from Liputin; in the course of the same conversation, I also learned that the Lebyadkins, brother and sister, had moved across the river, into the Gorshechny quarter. 'I took them there myself,' Liputin added. Then, dropping the subject of the Lebyadkins, he suddenly informed me that Lizaveta Nikolaevna was soon to be married to Maurice Nikolaevich; and, even though it hadn't been announced, the engagement was now official and the whole matter was settled. The next day I met Lizaveta Nikolaevna, accompanied by Maurice Nikolaevich, out riding for the first time since her illness. She beamed at me from a distance, laughed, and nodded her head in a very friendly fashion. I relayed all this to Stepan Trofimovich; he paid attention only to the news about the Lebyadkins.

And now, having described our mysterious predicament in the course of those eight days when we still didn't understand anything, I'll go on to relate the following events of my chronicle, writing, so to speak, with full knowledge of the affair, and describing things as they became known and were explained subsequently. I'll start with the eighth day after that Sunday, that is, Monday evening, because in fact that's precisely when the 'new episode' began.

3.

It was seven o'clock in the evening and Nikolai Vsevolodovich was sitting alone in his study—a room he always liked. It had a high ceiling, rugs on the floor, and was full of heavy, old-fashioned furniture. He sat in a corner on the sofa, dressed as if he were going out, though apparently he wasn't planning to go anywhere. In front of him stood a

---

[1] You don't understand. Let's forget it.

lamp covered by a shade. The walls and corners of the large room remained in darkness. His expression was thoughtful and intense, not altogether tranquil; his face looked tired and somewhat drawn. He in fact was ill with an abscess; but the rumour about his having had a tooth knocked out was exaggerated. A tooth had merely been loosened, but was now firmly in its socket again. The inside of his upper lip had been cut, but now that too had healed. The swelling had lasted a week only because the patient was unwilling to see a doctor and have the abscess lanced properly; he was waiting instead for the swelling to burst on its own. Not only did he refuse to see a doctor, he hardly allowed his mother to visit him, and then only for few minutes once a day, just before nightfall, when it was starting to grow dark and the lamps hadn't yet been lit. Neither would he see Peter Stepanovich, who, however, dropped in to visit Varvara Petrovna two or three times a day while he lived in town. And now, at last, on the Monday, having got back that morning after an absence of three days, having rushed all around town and dined at Yulia Mikhailovna's, Peter Stepanovich arrived at Varvara Petrovna's in the evening; she'd been waiting for him very impatiently. The prohibition had been lifted, Nikolai Vsevolodovich was receiving visitors. Varvara Petrovna herself led the guest to the study door; she'd long been anxious for the two men to meet, and Peter Stepanovich had given her his word to drop in after he'd seen Nicolas and tell her all. She knocked timidly at Nikolai Vsevolodovich's door and, not receiving an answer, was bold enough to open it several inches.

'Nicolas, may I bring Peter Stepanovich in to see you?' she asked in a soft, restrained voice, trying to see Nikolai Vsevolodovich's face behind the lamp.

'You may, you may, of course you may!' Peter Stepanovich exclaimed loudly and cheerfully, pushing the door open with his hand and walking in.

Nikolai Vsevolodovich hadn't heard the knock at the door; he'd only heard his mother's timid question, but hadn't time to reply. He had in front of him a letter he'd been reading and was now pondering. He shuddered when he heard Peter

Stepanovich's unexpected voice, and quickly covered the letter with a paperweight that happened to be lying nearby. But he wasn't entirely successful: a corner of the letter and almost the entire envelope remained visible.

'I shouted as loud as I could so you'd have time to get ready,' Peter Stepanovich whispered hastily with astonishing innocence, approaching the table, his eye lighting instantly on the paperweight and the corner of the letter.

'And naturally you were able to see me trying to hide the letter I've just received under the paperweight,' said Nikolai Vsevolodovich calmly, without stirring in his seat.

'Letter? God bless you and your letter! What do I care?' the guest exclaimed. 'But... the main thing is', he said in a whisper again, turning towards the door which was already closed, and nodding his head in that direction.

'She never eavesdrops,' Nikolai Vsevolodovich observed coldly.

'Never mind if she did!' cried Peter Stepanovich in an instant, cheerfully raising his voice and getting comfortable in an armchair. 'I've nothing against it; I merely dropped in for a little private chat... Well, finally I've got in to see you! First of all, how are you? I can see you're fine. Perhaps you can come tomorrow. Well?'

'Perhaps.'

'Resolve their doubts once and for all and mine, too!' Peter Stepanovich said in a pleasant and jocular manner, gesticulating wildly. 'If you only knew what nonsense I had to tell them. But you do know.' And he laughed.

'I don't know everything. I've only heard from my mother that you've been... getting around.'

'I mean, I haven't said anything very definite,' Peter Stepanovich exclaimed suddenly, as if fending off a vicious attack. 'You know, I brought up the matter of Shatov's wife, that is, the rumours about your liaison in Paris, which of course explained the incident on Sunday... you're not annoyed, are you?'

'I'm sure you tried your best.'

'Well, that's the only thing I was afraid of. But anyway, what do you mean, "tried my best"? That's a reproach, isn't it? At least you get right to the point; I was afraid when I came here you wouldn't want to get right to the point.'

'I don't want to get to the point of anything,' Nikolai Vsevolodovich said in some irritation, but then immediately smiled.

'That's not what I'm talking about; that's not it, you're making a mistake, that's not it!' Peter Stepanovich said, waving his arms, scattering words like peas and suddenly enjoying his host's irritation. 'I won't bother you with *our* affair, especially in your present situation. I've come only about the episode on Sunday, and only to agree on the most essential steps, since it's impossible to do otherwise. I've come with the most candid explanations, which I need more than you do—that may flatter your vanity, but it's also the truth. I've come so as always to be frank with you from now on.'

'You mean you weren't always frank before?'

'You know that yourself. I dissembled many times... You're smiling. I'm grateful for that smile, as a pretext to explain. I provoked it deliberately by using the boastful phrase "dissembled" so you'd get angry right away—how could I presume to think I could dissemble?—and then I'd have the chance to explain myself. You see, you see how frank I'm being now? Well, sir, will you hear me out?'

Nikolai Vsevolodovich's expression, which was disdainfully serene and even ironic in spite of his guest's obvious desire to provoke him by a naïvety that was arrogant, premeditated and intentionally rude, finally revealed some uneasy curiosity.

'Listen to me,' said Peter Stepanovich, wriggling in his chair more than ever. 'When I came here (that is, in the general sense, meaning, to this town) ten days ago, of course I'd decided to play a role. The best thing would have been not to play one, to be myself, isn't that so? There's nothing more cunning than to be oneself, because no one ever believes you. To tell the truth, I wanted to act the fool, because that's an easier part than playing myself; but since acting the fool is still an extreme, and extremes provoke curiosity, I decided to stick with my own self after all. Well then, what is my own character? The golden mean: neither stupid, nor clever, rather untalented, "dropped from the moon" as sensible people around here say, isn't that so?'

'Well, that may indeed be the case,' Nikolai Vsevolodovich said with a faint smile.

'Ah, so you agree—I'm very glad; I knew beforehand that was what you thought... Don't worry, don't worry, I'm not angry; that wasn't why I described myself in that way, just to fish for compliments. "No," you say, "you're not un-talented. No," you say, "you're clever"... Ah, now you're smiling again!... I'm caught once more. Well then, let's suppose you wouldn't say, "You're clever." I can accept anything. *Passons*, as my papa says, and, in parenthesis, don't be annoyed by my verbosity. Look, here's an example for you: I always talk a great deal, that is, use a great many words, and I always hurry, but it never comes out right. Why do I use a great many words and why doesn't it come out right? Because I don't really know how to speak. Those who can speak well are those who speak briefly. So, I must be untalented, don't you think? But since this talent for being untalented is so very natural, why shouldn't I make good use of it? And I do use it. It's true that on my way here I thought about keeping silent at first; but being quiet is a very great talent, and, therefore, unbecoming to me, and secondly, it's dangerous to keep silent. Well then, I decided once and for all that it's better to speak, but precisely in my untalented way, that is, using very, very many words, and being in a terrible hurry to explain things, and finally, getting lost in my own explanations so my audience would leave without hearing me to the end, throw-ing up its hands, and, what would be best of all, saying to hell with it. Then it would turn out, in the first place, that you've convinced them of your ingenuousness, bored them to death, and you were incomprehensible—three good things in one! Tell me, after all that, who would suspect me of harbouring secret designs? Why, every last one of them would consider himself personally offended by anyone's saying that I was harbouring secret designs. What's more, sometimes I amuse them—and that's very valuable. They'd forgive me everything just because that clever lad who used to publish pamphlets has now turned out to be stupider than they are, isn't that so? I can see by your smile you approve.'

Nikolai Vsevolodovich, however, wasn't smiling in the least; on the contrary, he was frowning as he listened, and was somewhat impatient.

'What? Did you say, "It doesn't matter"?' Peter Stepanovich chattered on. (Nikolai Vsevolodovich had said nothing.) 'Of course, of course, I can assure you I didn't come here to compromise you by your association with me. You know, you're awfully touchy today; I came to see you with an honest and cheerful heart, but you're carping at every last word; I can assure you I won't mention anything too delicate today, I give you my word, and I'll agree to all your conditions in advance.'

Nikolai Vsevolodovich was stubbornly silent.

'What? Did you say something? Oh, I see, I seem to have said something stupid again; you haven't proposed any conditions, and you're not going to. I believe you, I believe you, don't worry. And I know very well there's no point in my proposing any, isn't that right? I'm answering for you in advance and—of course, because I lack talent, any and every talent... You're laughing? What is it?'

'Nothing,' said Nikolai Vsevolodovich, smiling at last. 'I merely recalled that I really did once refer to you as untalented, but you weren't there at the time, which means it must have got back to you... But I'd like you to get to the point.'

'I have got to the point. I'm talking about what happened on Sunday!' Peter Stepanovich prattled on. 'Well, how did I appear on Sunday, in your opinion? Exactly like a man in a hurry, an untalented mediocrity, and I barged in and took control of the conversation in a most untalented way. But they forgave me for everything because, in the first place, I dropped in from the moon; apparently everyone here's reached that conclusion. In the second place, I told them a nice little story and came to your rescue. That's true, isn't it?'

'Well, you mean you told it in such a way as to leave doubts in their minds and to suggest some collusion and conspiracy between us, when there really was none at all and I never asked you for anything.'

'Precisely, precisely!' Peter Stepanovich cried, as if in ecstasy. 'That's precisely what I did so you'd see the design behind it; it was for your sake, primarily, that I put on airs, because I'd caught you and wanted to compromise you. The chief thing was, I wanted to know how afraid you really were.'

'I'd like to know why you're being so honest now?'

'Don't be angry, please don't, and don't glare at me... But you're not glaring, are you? You'd like to know why I'm being so honest. Well, it's precisely because now everything's changed, of course, everything's past, covered up with sand. I've suddenly changed my mind about you. The old way is closed; now I'll never compromise you in the old way, only in a new one.'

'So you've changed your tactics?'

'It's not a question of tactics. Now you're completely free to do as you like, that is, say "yes" if you want to, or "no". That's my new tactic. And I won't say one word about "our" affair until you yourself want me to. You're laughing? Be my guest; I'm laughing too. But now I'm being serious, very, very serious, even though a person who's in such a hurry lacks talent, isn't that right? Never mind, I may lack talent, but I'm being serious, very serious.'

He really was speaking seriously, in a very different tone of voice and with unusual emotion, so that Nikolai Vsevolodovich looked at him with interest.

'You say you've changed your mind about me?' he asked.

'I changed my mind about you when, after Shatov hit you, you took your hands off him. Enough, enough, no more questions, please. I won't say another word now.'

He jumped up and waved his arms about as if he were fending off any questions; but since there weren't any and there was no reason to leave, he lowered himself into his armchair again, having calmed down a bit.

'Incidentally, in parenthesis,' he began jabbering right away, 'some people around here are saying you'll probably kill him and they're betting that von Lembke is intending to involve the police, but Yulia Mikhailovna won't let him... Enough, enough about that; I only said it to let you know. By the way, once again: you know I helped the Lebyadkins move that same day. Did you get my note with their new address?'

'Yes.'

'I didn't send it out of any "lack of talent"; I did it sincerely, because I'm eager to help. If it revealed my lack of talent, at least it was sincere.'

'Well, never mind, perhaps that's the way it has to be...' Nikolai Vsevolodovich said thoughtfully. 'But I must ask you not to send me any more notes.'

'It was unavoidable; and there was only one.'

'So Liputin knows?'

'That was unavoidable; but as you yourself know, Liputin wouldn't dare... By the way, it'd be a good idea if we went to see our group, I mean, *the* group, not *our* group, or else you'll start carping again. But don't worry, not right now, sooner or later. It's raining at the moment. I'll let them know; they'll gather and we'll go there one evening. They're waiting with gaping mouths, like baby rooks in a nest, to see what kind of treat we'll bring them. They're a hot-headed bunch. They've pulled out their little books and are all ready to argue. Virginsky's a universal humanitarian, Liputin's a Fourierist with a strong penchant for police work; he's valuable in one respect, but requires strict handling in all others; and finally, there's the one with long ears who'll expound his own system. And, you know, they're all offended I treat them so casually and throw cold water on them, ha, ha! We really must go and see them.'

'Have you presented me to them as some kind of leader?' Nikolai Vsevolodovich asked in as off-hand a manner as possible. Peter Stepanovich glanced at him quickly.

'By the way,' he replied, as if not hearing the question and eager to change the subject, 'I've come to see the much esteemed Varvara Petrovna two or three times now and was also obliged to tell her a great deal.'

'I can imagine.'

'No, don't imagine; I merely said you won't kill him and told her many other nice things. Just imagine: by the next day she'd found out I helped Marya Timofeevna move across the river. Did you tell her that?'

'I never thought to tell her.'

'I knew it wasn't you. But who could've told her besides you, I wonder.'

'Liputin, of course.'

'No-o, not Liputin,' Peter Stepanovich muttered, frowning. 'I know who. It looks like Shatov... But that's nonsense, let's forget about it! Although it really is terribly important... Incidentally, I kept waiting for your mother to come out with the real question all of a sudden... Oh, yes, the first few days she was awfully gloomy, but when I came today she's suddenly sparkling. What's it all about?'

'I gave her my word that within five days I'll have proposed to Lizaveta Nikolaevna,' Nikolai Vsevolodovich said suddenly with unexpected candour.

'Ah, well... yes, of course,' Peter Stepanovich muttered, somewhat embarrassed. 'You know, there're some rumours circulating about her engagement. They're probably true. But you're right; all you have to do is whistle and she'll come running to you right from the altar. You're not angry at my saying so?'

'No, I'm not angry.'

'I see it's extremely difficult to make you angry today and I'm beginning to be afraid of you. I'm tremendously interested to see how you'll behave yourself in public tomorrow. You've probably got a number of tricks up your sleeve. You're not angry at me for saying that, are you?'

Nikolai Vsevolodovich made no reply, which really irritated Peter Stepanovich.

'By the way, were you serious when you told your mother that about Lizaveta Nikolaevna?' he asked.

Nikolai Vsevolodovich looked at him intently and coldly.

'Ah, I see, it was only to reassure her, wasn't it?'

'And what if I was serious?' Nikolai Vsevolodovich asked firmly.

'Well, God bless you, as one says in these cases, it won't

interfere with the affair (note, I didn't say *our* affair; I know
you don't like the word "our"); as for me, well, as for me,
I'm at your service, you know that.'

'You think so?'

'I don't think anything, anything at all,' Peter Stepanovich
hastened to add with a laugh, 'because I know you've
considered all your own affairs beforehand, and have
thought everything through. I'm merely stating that I'm at
your service in all seriousness, at all times, in all places and
all cases, that is, in everything, do you understand that?'

Nikolai Vsevolodovich yawned.

'You've had enough of me,' Peter Stepanovich said suddenly, jumping up, grabbing his brand new, round hat, and
getting ready to leave, meanwhile staying put and talking
without interruption, though on his feet and from time to
time moving around the room, slapping his hat on his knee
at the livelier moments of the conversation.

'I also wanted to amuse you with stories about the von
Lembkes,' he cried cheerfully.

'No, thanks. Later, perhaps. But how's Yulia Mikhailovna's health?'

'What social conventions you and all the others go in for
around here! You don't care about her health any more than
a grey cat, yet you enquire about her. I admire that. She's
fine and has an almost superstitious respect for you, and
superstitiously has great expectations of you. She says nothing about the episode on Sunday and she's certain you'll
triumph just by making an appearance. I swear she imagines
you can do anything. But you're a mysterious and romantic
figure, now more than ever—an extremely advantageous
position to be in. Everyone is eager for you to appear. When
I left here—they were pretty keen, but now even more so.
By the way, thanks again for the letter. They're all afraid
of Count K. You know, I think they suspect you're a spy.
I don't say you're not, I hope you don't mind.'

'It doesn't matter.'

'It doesn't matter; it'll be useful in the future. They have
their own way of doing things here. Of course, I encourage them; Yulia Mikhailovna first of all, Gaganov as well...

You're laughing? Well, it's all a matter of tactics: I tell lies and more lies, and then suddenly I say something intelligent, just when they're all looking for it. They surround me and I start telling lies again. They've all given up on me by now; "he's capable," they say, "but he's dropped in from the moon." Von Lembke's invited me to join the civil service, to make me mend my ways. You know, I treat him very badly, I mean, I compromise him, but he just stares. Yulia Mikhailovna encourages it. Oh, incidentally, Gaganov is terribly angry at you. Yesterday in Dukhovo he said some nasty things about you. I told him the whole truth at once, that is, of course, not the whole truth. I spent the entire day with him in Dukhovo. It's a fine estate and a nice house.'

'So he's still in Dukhovo now?' Nikolai Vsevolodovich asked suddenly, almost jumping up and lunging forward.

'No, he drove me here this morning; we came back together,' Peter Stepanovich replied, as if unaware of Nikolai Vsevolodovich's momentary agitation. 'Oh, look, I've knocked a book off,' he said, bending over to pick up a splendid volume. '*Balzac's Women**—with illustrations,' he said, opening it suddenly. 'I haven't read it. Von Lembke also writes novels.'

'Really?' Nikolai Vsevolodovich asked, as if he were interested.

'In Russian, on the sly, of course. Yulia Mikhailovna knows about it and lets him. He's an idiot, but has a few tricks up his sleeve. They have it all worked out. Such strict form, such restraint! We could use something like that!'

'Are you praising the administration?'

'I should say so! It's the one thing in Russia that's natural and effective... I won't, I won't,' he cried suddenly. 'I'm not talking about that; not a word about that delicate subject. Well, goodbye; you look rather green.'

'I have a fever.'

'I can believe it. You'd better lie down. By the way, there's a sect of Castrates* here in the district, a curious lot... But more later. Here's a little anecdote, however: there's an infantry regiment in the district. On Friday evening I was in B—tsy drinking with some officers. We have three acquaintances there, *vous comprenez?* They were talking about atheism and, naturally, managed to cashier God. They were squealing with delight. Incidentally, Shatov maintains that in order to initiate a revolution in Russia, one must begin with atheism. That may even be true. One grey-haired old codger of a captain sat there silent the whole time, not saying a word, and then suddenly he stands up in the middle of the room and, do you know, as if talking to himself, he declares aloud: "If there's no God, then what kind of captain can I possibly be?" He picks up his cap, throws up his arms, and leaves the room.'

'He expressed a rather sensible idea,' Nikolai Vsevolodovich said, yawning for the third time.

'Really? I didn't understand him and wanted to ask you about it. Well, what else is there to tell you? The Shpigulin factory is quite interesting. As you know, there are five hundred workers employed there; it's a hotbed of cholera—it hasn't been cleaned out for fifteen years and the workers are underpaid; it's owned by millionaire merchants. I can assure you that a number of the workers have some idea of the *Internationale.** What, you're smiling? You'll see for yourself, but give me a little time, only a little! I've already asked you for some time, now I'm asking you again, and then... But I'm guilty, I won't, I won't, I'm not talking about that, you don't have to frown. Well, goodbye. Oh, good Lord!' he said, suddenly turning back. 'I completely forgot the most important thing: they just informed me that our box had arrived from Petersburg.'

'Meaning?' asked Nikolai Vsevolodovich, looking at him in incomprehension.

'I mean your box, your things, with frock-coats, trousers, and underwear. Did it arrive? Is it true?'

'Yes, they did mention something about it.'

'Ah, can we open it at once?'

'Ask Aleksei.'

'Well, tomorrow? What about tomorrow? Together with your things I have a jacket, a frock-coat, and three pairs of trousers—from Sharmer's,* on your recommendation, you remember?'

'I've heard it said you've been behaving like a gentleman here,' Nikolai Vsevolodovich said with a laugh. 'Is it true you're going to take lessons from the riding-master?'

Peter Stepanovich smiled his crooked smile.

'You know,' he said with extreme haste in a voice that quivered and faltered, 'you know, Nikolai Vsevolodovich, let's stop discussing personalities once and for all. Of course, you're entitled to despise me as much as you like, if it amuses you so much; still, it'd be better not to discuss personalities for a while, don't you think?'

'Fine, I won't do it again,' Nikolai Vsevolodovich replied. Peter Stepanovich laughed, slapped his hat on his knee, stood with one foot resting on the other, and assumed his former expression.

'Some people here even consider me your rival for Lizaveta Nikolaevna; so how can I ignore my appearance?' he said with a laugh. 'Who is it, by the way, who told you that? Hmmm. It's precisely eight o'clock. Well, I'll be off. I promised to drop in on Varvara Petrovna, but I think I'll pass this time. You should go to bed and tomorrow you'll feel better. It's raining outside and it's dark; I have a cab waiting because it's not too safe on the streets around here at night... Ah, by the way, here in town and in the vicinity there's a convict roaming around by the name of Fedya; he escaped from Siberia. Can you imagine, he used to be my serf; fifteen years ago my father sold him off as a recruit. A very interesting character.'

'Have you... spoken with him?' Nikolai Vsevolodovich asked, looking up at him suddenly.

'Yes. He's not hiding from me. He's prepared to do anything, absolutely anything, for money, of course; but even he has some convictions, of a sort, naturally. Oh, yes, here's something else: if you were serious before about your intention, you recall, concerning Lizaveta Nikolaevna, let me assure you once more that I too am prepared to do anything, of any kind, just as you like, entirely at your service... What's this, you're grabbing your stick? Ah, no, not your stick... Imagine, I thought you were looking for your stick.'

Nikolai Vsevolodovich wasn't looking for anything and didn't say anything, but he had in fact got up rather suddenly and had a strange expression on his face.

'If you also need anything with regard to Mr Gaganov,' Peter Stepanovich blurted out suddenly, now looking directly at the paperweight, 'I can arrange it, of course, and I'm sure you won't be able to manage without me.'

He left suddenly without waiting for an answer, but stuck his head in from the door once more.

'I said that', he shouted hurriedly, 'because Shatov, for example, had no right to risk his life on Sunday when he attacked you, did he? I'd be glad if you'd take note of that.'

He disappeared again without waiting for an answer.

4.

Perhaps as he disappeared he thought that Nikolai Vsevolodovich, left alone, would begin pounding the wall with his fists, and undoubtedly he'd have been glad to witness it, had it been possible. But he would have been deluding himself: Nikolai Vsevolodovich remained composed. For two minutes or so he stood at the table in the same attitude, apparently deep in thought; but soon a cold, listless smile appeared on his face. He sat slowly back down again on the sofa in the corner and closed his eyes, as if very tired. The corner of the letter was still peeking out from under the paperweight, but he didn't get up to hide it.

Soon he dozed off entirely. Varvara Petrovna, who'd worn herself out with worry these last few days, couldn't restrain herself; when Peter Stepanovich, who'd promised to drop in on her, failed to keep his promise and left, she decided to risk a visit to Nicolas herself, even though it wasn't her usual time. She was still hoping that he would tell her something definitive. Just as before she knocked quietly at the door; receiving no answer as before, she opened the door herself. Seeing Nicolas sitting there completely still, she cautiously approached the sofa, her heart beating. She was rather struck that he could fall asleep so quickly and could sleep sitting up so straight and still; it was almost possible to hear his breathing. His face was pale and stern, but seemed totally frozen and immobile; his brows were slightly knitted and frowning; he looked decidedly like a lifeless wax figure. She stood over him for about three minutes, scarcely daring to breathe, and was suddenly overcome by fear. She went out on tiptoe, stopped in the doorway, hurriedly crossed herself, and left unnoticed, carrying away a new oppressive feeling and a new anguish.

He slept for a long time, over an hour, still in the same stupor; not a muscle moved on his face, not the slightest motion could be observed in his whole body; his brows remained just as firmly knitted. If Varvara Petrovna had stayed there another three minutes, she would probably not have been able to endure the overpowering sensation of his lethargic immobility and would have woken him up. But he suddenly opened his eyes himself, and still without stirring sat there another ten minutes, as if stubbornly and curiously examining some object in the corner of the room that had caught his attention, even though there was nothing new or particular there.

At last the quiet, low chime of a large wall-clock, striking once, resounded in the room. In some unease, he turned his head to look at the clock-face, but the rear door leading into the corridor opened almost at the same time and the butler Aleksei Yegorovich came in. In one hand he carried a warm coat, a scarf and a hat, in the other, a silver tray with a note on it.

'Half past nine,' he announced quietly; having placed the coat on a chair in the corner, he held out the tray with the note, a small piece of paper, unsealed, with two lines written in pencil. After quickly reading these two lines, Nikolai Vsevolodovich took the pencil from the tray, wrote a few words at the end of the note, and placed it on the tray.

'Take it back as soon as I've gone out; now help me get dressed,' he said, getting up from the sofa.

Noticing that he had on a light velvet jacket, he thought for a moment, and asked for the cloth coat he used for more formal evening visits. Then, after dressing and putting on his hat, he locked the door through which Varvara Petrovna had entered and, removing the letter hidden under the paperweight, he went silently into the corridor, accompanied by Aleksei Yegorovich. They left by a narrow stone back staircase and descended into a passage that led straight into the garden. In the corner a lantern and a large umbrella were standing ready.

'With all this heavy rain the streets are really terribly muddy,' Aleksei Yegorovich reported, apparently making one last-ditch attempt to dissuade his master from going. But his master, opening the umbrella, silently went out into the damp, sodden old garden, dark as a cellar. The wind was howling and swaying the tops of the half-bare trees; the narrow, sandy paths were soggy and slippery. Aleksei Yegorovich went along dressed as he was, in a frock-coat without a hat, lighting the way three paces ahead with a lantern.

'Won't we be seen?' Nikolai Vsevolodovich asked suddenly.

'Not from the windows; besides, everything's been taken care of already,' the servant replied in quiet and measured tones.

'Is my mother asleep?'

'She retired at precisely nine o'clock, as she's been doing of late, and it's impossible for her to find out anything now. What time should I expect you?' he asked, daring to pose the question.

'At one o'clock, half-past, or two at the latest.'

'Very good, sir.'

After crossing the entire garden along winding paths which both of them knew by heart, they reached a stone wall; there, in the corner, they found a small door leading into a narrow and deserted lane; the door was almost always locked, but now the key appeared in Aleksei Yegorovich's hand.

'Won't the door creak?' Nikolai Vsevolodovich enquired again.

But Aleksei Yegorovich reported that it had been oiled yesterday 'as well as today'. By now he was soaking wet. After unlocking the door he handed Nikolai Vsevolodovich the key.

'If you're planning to go very far, sir, I should like to remind you to beware of people you meet, especially in deserted lanes, even more so on the other side of the river,' he couldn't refrain from warning him one more time. He was an old servant who'd taken care of Nikolai Vsevolodovich as a child and even bounced him on his knee; he was a stern and serious man who loved to listen to and read from devotional books.

'Don't worry, Aleksei Yegorovich.'

'May God bless you, sir, but only if what you're doing is righteous.'

'What?' Nikolai Vsevolodovich stopped as he was about to step out into the lane.

Aleksei Yegorovich repeated his wish resolutely; never before had he dared express himself aloud to his master in such words.

Nikolai Vsevolodovich locked the door, put the key in his pocket, and went along the lane, sinking into several inches of mud at every step. At last he emerged into a long, deserted street. He knew the town like the palm of his hand; but Bogoyavlenskaya Street was still a long way off. It was past ten when he finally stopped in front of the locked gates of Filippov's old, dark house. Now, after the Lebyadkins' departure, the lower floor was completely vacant, the windows boarded up, but there was a light burning in Shatov's room in the attic. Since there was no bell, he began knocking on the gate with his hand. A window opened and Shatov looked down into the street; it was terribly dark and very hard to make anything out. Shatov stared down for a long time—well over a minute.

'Is that you?' he asked suddenly.

'Yes,' replied the uninvited guest.

Shatov slammed the window shut, came down, and unlocked the gate. Nikolai Vsevolodovich stepped over a high threshold and, without saying a word, headed past him, straight to Kirillov's annexe.

5.

His place was left unlocked, the doors standing open. The passage and first two rooms were dark, but in the last room, where Kirillov lived and drank his tea, a light was shining and laughter could be heard, as well as an odd crying sound.

Nikolai Vsevolodovich walked towards the light, but stood on the threshold of the room without entering. Tea was on the table. The old woman, the landlord's relative, stood in the middle of the room; she was bareheaded, and had on only a petticoat, a hareskin jacket, and shoes on her bare feet. In her arms she carried an eighteen-month-old infant, wearing nothing but a little shirt, with bare legs, flushed cheeks, and ruffled flaxen hair, as if it had just been picked up from the cradle. It had probably been crying; there were still little teardrops under its eyes; but at that moment it was stretching out its little arms, clapping its hands and laughing the way babies laugh, with a sob in their voice. Kirillov was bouncing a red rubber ball on the floor in front of the child; the ball bounced up to the ceiling, and down again, and the child cried, 'Baw, baw!' Kirillov caught the 'baw' and handed it over; it took it in its clumsy little hands and threw it, while Kirillov ran to pick it up again. Finally the 'baw' rolled under the wardrobe. 'Baw, baw!' yelled the child. Kirillov lay flat on the floor and stretched out his arms, trying to retrieve the 'baw' from under the wardrobe. Nikolai Vsevolodovich entered the room; when the child saw him, it clung to the old woman and burst into prolonged childish wailing; the woman carried it out of the room immediately.

'Stavrogin,' said Kirillov, getting up from the floor with the ball in his hands, without showing any surprise at his unexpected visit. 'Would you like some tea?'

He rose to his feet.

'Very much. I won't say no, if it's still hot,' Nikolai Vsevolodovich said. 'I'm soaking wet.'

'It's warm, hot even,' Kirillov assured him with pleasure. 'Sit down: you're muddy, but that's all right. I'll wipe the floor later with a rag.'

Nikolai Vsevolodovich sat down and drank a cup of tea almost in one gulp.

'Would you like another?' asked Kirillov.

'No thank you.'

Kirillov, who still hadn't sat down, took a seat opposite him and asked:

'Why have you come?'

'On business. Here, read this letter from Gaganov. Remember I told you about it in Petersburg.'

Kirillov took the letter, read it, put it on the table, and looked at him expectantly.

'As you know', Nikolai Vsevolodovich began, 'I encountered this fellow Gaganov for the first time in my life a month ago in Petersburg. We met two or three times in the presence of other people. Without making my acquaintance or even speaking to me, he still took the opportunity to treat me with insolence. I told you about it at the time, but there's something you still don't know: after he left Petersburg, before I did, he suddenly sent me a letter, which, though not like this one, was highly improper; what was so strange about it was that it contained no explanation as to why it was written in the first place. I replied at once, also by letter, and wrote in all honesty that he was probably angry with me because of the incident with his father here at the club some four years ago. I said that for my part I was ready to offer him every possible apology on the grounds that my action was not premeditated and occurred in consequence of my illness. I asked him to take my apology into consideration. He didn't answer my letter and left; but now I find him here in an absolute rage. Several things he's said about me in public have been repeated to me—they're extremely abusive, full of astonishing accusations. Then this letter arrived today, the likes of which no one's ever seen, full of abuse and phrases such as, "your smashed up mug". I came here hoping you wouldn't refuse to act as my second in a duel.'

'You said a letter the likes of which no one's ever seen,' Kirillov said. 'But in a rage anything's possible; people do write them. Pushkin wrote one to Heeckeren.* All right, I will. Explain the form.'

Nikolai Vsevolodovich said that he wanted it to take place the next day and that he'd begin by renewing his offer of an apology, even with the promise of another placating letter, on condition that Gaganov, for his part, promise to write no further letters. He'd treat the letter already received as if it never existed.

'Too many concessions; he won't agree,' Kirillov said.

'I've come here to ask in the first place if you'd agree to offer him these terms.'

'Yes, I will. It's your business. But he won't agree.'

'I know he won't.'

'He'll want to fight. Tell me, how will you fight?'

'The point is I'd like to get the whole thing settled tomorrow. You should be at his place around nine in the morning. He'll listen to you and won't agree, but he'll set up a meeting between you and his second, let's say, around eleven. You'll settle the details, and we'll all agree to be there by one or two o'clock. Please try to arrange it. The weapons will be pistols, of course; and I'd particularly like you to set barriers at ten paces. Then you'll place each of us ten paces from the barrier; at a given signal we'll approach. Each of us must walk up to the barrier, but may fire sooner along the way. That's all, I think.'

'Ten paces between barriers is very close,' Kirillov observed.

'Well then, twelve, but no more; you realize he desperately wants to fight. Can you load a pistol?'

'Yes. I have a set of pistols. I'll give them my word you've never used them before. His second will also give his word about their pistols; two sets, and we'll toss to see which you use.'

'Fine.'

'Would you like to see the pistols?'

'Please.'

Kirillov squatted down in front of a suitcase in the corner; he still hadn't unpacked, but merely removed things as he needed them. From the bottom he pulled out a box made of palm-wood, lined with red velvet, and removed from it a set of fashionable, extremely expensive pistols.

'I've got everything: powder, bullets, cartridges. Wait, I also have a revolver.'

He dug into the suitcase again and pulled out another box with a six-chambered American revolver.

'You've a lot of weapons, very expensive ones, too.'

'Very. Extremely.'

The impoverished, almost destitute Kirillov, who, by the way, never noticed his own poverty, was apparently proud to display his valuable weapons, undoubtedly obtained at great sacrifice.

'Are you still of the same mind?' Stavrogin asked rather cautiously after a moment's silence.

'Yes,' replied Kirillov curtly, guessing at once by his tone of voice what the question was about. And he began removing the guns from the table.

'When?' Nikolai Vsevolodovich asked, even more cautiously, once again after a silence.

Meanwhile Kirillov put both boxes back in the suitcase and sat down again.

'As you know, it doesn't depend on me; it's whenever they tell me,' he mumbled, as if oppressed by the question, but at the same time obviously ready to answer any other questions. He looked at Stavrogin steadily with black, lustreless eyes, and a serene, but kind and friendly expression.

'Of course, I can understand your wanting to shoot yourself,' Nikolai Vsevolodovich began again with a slight frown, after a long, reflective silence that lasted a few minutes. 'I've thought about it myself sometimes, and always with this new kind of idea: if one were to commit some crime or, better still, some shameful act, that is, something disgraceful, very base and... absurd, so that a thousand years from now people would still remember it with disgust, and one were suddenly to think: "One blow in the temple, then nothing more." What would I care then about people or what they'll remember with disgust a thousand years from now, isn't that so?'

'You call that a new idea?' Kirillov said after a moment's thought.

'I... I don't call it that... But when it first occurred to me, I felt it was a totally new idea.'

' "You felt it"?' Kirillov repeated. 'That's good. There are many ideas that have always been around and all of a sudden become new ideas. That's true. I see a great deal now as if for the first time.'

'Let's suppose you had once lived on the moon,' Stavrogin broke in, without listening to him and continuing his own train of thought. 'And suppose you had committed there those sort of absurd crimes... Down here, you know for sure they'll be laughing at you there and remembering your name with disgust for a thousand years, for ever, as long as there's a moon. But right now you're here, and looking up at the moon: why should you care about what you did there and if they'll think of you with disgust for a thousand years? Isn't that right?'

'I don't know,' Kirillov replied. 'I haven't been to the moon,' he added without any irony, merely to establish the fact.

'Whose child was that in here earlier?'

'The old woman's mother-in-law was here; no, her daughter-in-law... it doesn't matter. For three days. She's lying ill, with the baby; she moans a lot at night—it's her stomach. The mother sleeps and the old woman brings the baby in here; I play ball with it. The ball's from Hamburg. I bought it there to throw and catch: it strengthens the spine. It's a little girl.'

'Do you love small children?'

'Yes,' Kirillov replied, rather indifferently, however.

'So you must love life, too?'

'Yes, I love life, too. So what?'

'But you've decided to shoot yourself.'

'What of it? Why put the two things together? Life is one thing, the other's something else. Life exists, but there's no such thing as death.'

'So you've begun to believe in a future everlasting life?'

'No, not in a future everlasting life, but in an everlasting here and now. There are moments, you reach moments, when all of a sudden time stops and becomes eternal.'

'And you hope to attain such a moment?'

'Yes.'

'That's hardly possible in our age,' Nikolai Vsevolodovich replied, also without irony, slowly, as if thoughtfully. 'In the Book of Revelation the angel swears* that time will cease to exist.'

'I know. That's very true; clear and precise. When all mankind reaches happiness, time will cease to exist because it'll no longer be necessary. It's a very true thought.'

'What will they do with it?'

'They won't do anything with it. Time is not an object, but an idea. It will vanish from men's minds.'

'Old philosophical clichés, the same as from the beginning of time,' Stavrogin muttered with disdainful pity.

'The same! The same as from the beginning of time, and never any others!' Kirillov cried, his eyes flashing, as if this idea heralded some great triumph for him.

'You seem very happy, Kirillov?'

'I am very happy,' he replied, as if answering the most ordinary question.

'But not so long ago you were still embittered, still angry at Liputin?'

'Hmmm... I've no quarrel now. Then I didn't yet know I was happy. Have you ever seen a leaf, a leaf off a tree?'

'Yes.'

'Not long ago I saw one that was yellow, slightly green, wilted around the edges. It was blowing in the wind. When I was ten years old I used to close my eyes on purpose and imagine a leaf—green, with bright veins on it, the sun shining. I would open my eyes and be unable to believe it because it was all so good, so I'd shut my eyes again.'

'Is this some kind of allegory?'

'No-o-o... why? I'm not talking about allegories, just a leaf, one leaf. A leaf is good. Everything is good.'

'Everything?'

'Everything. Man is unhappy because he doesn't know he's happy; that's the only reason. That's all! He who knows, becomes happy at once, that very moment. The mother-in-law will die, but the little girl will remain—that's good. I discovered it all of a sudden.'

'But what about a person who's starving to death or who abuses and violates a little girl—is that good?'

'Yes, it is. And if someone blows his brains out for that child, that's good, too; and if he doesn't blow his brains out, that's also good. Everything is good, everything. It's good for all those who know it's good. If they knew it was good, it'd be good; but as long as they don't know it's good, it isn't good. That's my entire idea, the whole thing; there isn't any more!'

'When did you find out you were so happy?'

'Last week, on Tuesday, no, Wednesday, it was Wednesday by then—during the night.'

'What was the occasion?'

'I don't recall; I was walking around the room... it makes no difference. I stopped the clock—it was thirty-seven minutes past two.'

'As a symbol of the idea that time must cease?'

Kirillov remained silent.

'They're bad,' he began again suddenly, 'because they don't know they're good. When they find out, they won't rape little girls. They must find out that they are good, and then they'll all become good at once, to the very last one.'

'And since you found out, are you good?'

'Yes.'

'Well, I agree with that,' Stavrogin said, frowning.

'He who teaches that everyone is good, will bring about the end of the world.'

'He who taught it was crucified.'

'He will come and his name will be man-God.'

'God-man?'

'Man-God, that's the difference.'

'Was it you who lit the lamp under the icon?'

'Yes, it was me.'

'Have you started believing?'

'The old woman likes the lamp lit... and she didn't have time today,' Kirillov replied.

'But you yourself don't pray, do you?'

'I pray to everything. Do you see that spider crawling along the wall? I look at it and feel grateful it's crawling.'

His eyes were gleaming again. He was staring straight at Stavrogin, with a resolute and unwavering expression. Stavrogin was frowning and watching him closely with distaste, but there was no trace of mockery on his face.

'I'll bet that by the time I come again, you'll even be believing in God,' he said, standing up and reaching for his hat.

'Why?' Kirillov asked, also getting up.

'If you found out you believed in God, then you'd believe;

but since you don't know you believe in God, you still don't
believe,' Nikolai Vsevolodovich said with a laugh.

'That's not right,' Kirillov said after some thought.
'You've twisted my idea. A worldly witticism. Remember,
Stavrogin, how much you've meant in my life.'

'Goodbye, Kirillov.'

'Come again, one night. When?'

'You haven't forgotten about tomorrow?'

'Ah, I had forgotten. Don't worry, I won't oversleep. Nine
o'clock. I know how to wake myself up when I want to. I
go to bed and tell myself, "seven o'clock", and I wake up
at seven o'clock, "ten o'clock", and I wake up at ten o'clock.'

'You have remarkable attributes,' said Nikolai Vsevolodovich, looking at his pale face.

'I'll go and open the gate.'

'Don't trouble, Shatov will unlock it.'

'Ah, Shatov. All right. Goodbye.'

6.

The front door of the empty house where Shatov lived was
not locked; but on entering the passage, Stavrogin found
himself in complete darkness and began to grope for the
stairs to the attic. Suddenly a door opened upstairs and a
light appeared; Shatov didn't come out, but merely opened
his door. When Nikolai Vsevolodovich reached the threshold
of the room, he could see him standing there, waiting by a
table in the corner.

'Are you willing to see me on business?' Stavrogin asked
from the doorway.

'Come in and sit down,' Shatov replied. 'Lock the door.
Wait, I'll do it myself.'

He closed the door and locked it, went back to the table
and sat down opposite Nikolai Vsevolodovich. He'd grown
thinner during the last week and now seemed feverish.

'You've worn me out,' he said in a low half-whisper,
lowering his eyes. 'Why didn't you come sooner?'

'Were you so sure I'd come?'

'Yes, but wait, I've been delirious... perhaps I still am...
Wait a moment.'

He stood and picked up something lying on top of three bookshelves near the wall. It was a revolver.

'One night in my delirium I imagined you were coming to kill me; early the next morning I spent the last of my money buying this revolver from that good-for-nothing Lyamshin. I wasn't going to let you kill me. Then I came to my senses... I have neither powder nor bullets; since then, it's been lying here on the shelf. Wait a moment...'

He stood up and started to open the window.

'Don't throw it away. What for?' Nikolai Vsevolodovich said, stopping him. 'It costs money, and tomorrow people will say there were revolvers lying around under Shatov's window. Put it back; that's right; now sit down. Tell me, why are you apologizing for thinking I'd come to kill you? I haven't come here to make peace with you now, but to discuss some important business. Tell me first of all if you struck me because of my involvement with your wife?'

'You know that wasn't the reason,' Shatov replied, dropping his eyes again.

'And not because you believed that ridiculous gossip about Darya Pavlovna?'

'No, no, of course not! What stupidity! My sister told me at the very beginning...' Shatov said harshly and impatiently, almost stamping his foot.

'Then my guess was right and yours was, too,' Stavrogin went on calmly. 'You're right: Marya Timofeevna Lebyadkina is my lawful wife; we were married in Petersburg about four and a half years ago. Was it because of her that you struck me?'

Shatov, totally astounded, listened in silence.

'I guessed it, but didn't believe it,' he muttered at last, looking at Stavrogin in a strange way.

'And you struck me?'

Shatov flushed and mumbled almost incoherently:

'It was because of your fall... for your lie. I didn't approach you to punish you; as I got close, I didn't know I'd strike you... It was because you meant so much to me during my life... I...'

'I understand, I understand, save your breath. I'm sorry you're feverish. My business is extremely important.'

'I've waited for you too long,' Shatov said, trembling all over and getting up from his seat, 'State your business, I'll speak too... later...'

He sat down.

'The business isn't of that sort,' Nikolai Vsevolodovich began, looking at him with curiosity. 'Owing to certain circumstances I've been compelled to choose this time today to warn you that you may be killed.'

Shatov looked at him wildly.

'I know my life may be in danger,' he said in measured tones, 'but how could you possibly find that out?'

'Because I'm also one of them, just like you; I'm also a member of their society, just like you.'

'You... you're a member of the society?'

'I can see from your eyes that you expected anything from me but that,' Nikolai Vsevolodovich said, smiling faintly. 'But does that mean you already knew there'd be an attempt on your life?'

'I didn't think so. And I don't now, in spite of what you're saying, although... although who can really be sure of anything with those idiots?' he suddenly cried in a rage, banging his fist on the table. 'I'm not afraid of them! I've broken with them. That fellow came running over here four times to tell me it was possible... but', he said, looking at Stavrogin, 'what is it, precisely, that you know?'

'Don't worry, I'm not deceiving you,' Stavrogin went on, rather coldly, with the air of a man who was merely doing his duty. 'You ask what I know? I know you joined the society when you were abroad, two years ago, at the time of the old organization, just before your trip to America, and, it seems, right after our last conversation, the one you wrote me so much about from America. By the way, forgive me for not answering your letter; I confined myself to...'

'Sending me money. But wait a moment,' Shatov interrupted, hurriedly opening a drawer in the table and taking out a rainbow-coloured banknote from under some papers. 'Here, take it, the hundred roubles you sent me; I would've perished over there but for you. It would've taken me a lot longer to pay it back, if it hadn't been for your mother:

nine months ago she gave me a present of one hundred roubles because I was so poor after my illness. But go on, please...'

He was out of breath.

'In America you changed your views and when you came back to Switzerland, you wanted to resign. They made no reply, but ordered you to take over someone's printing press here in Russia, to keep it, and then hand it over to someone sent by them to you. I don't know all the details, but that's the general plan, isn't it? And you agreed either in the hope or on the condition that it would be their last demand and afterwards they'd release you altogether. All this, whether it's true or not, I found out entirely by chance, not from them. But what you still don't know, it seems, is that these gentlemen have no intention whatsoever of breaking with you.'

'That's ridiculous!' Shatov howled. 'I declared in all honesty that I disagreed with them in everything! That's my right, my right of conscience and free thought... I won't stand for it! There's no power that could...'

'You'd better stop shouting, you know,' Nikolai Vsevolodovich interrupted him with utmost seriousness. 'That Verkhovensky is the sort of fellow who might be eavesdropping on us right now, using his own ears or someone else's, perhaps in your own passageway. Even that drunkard Lebyadkin was probably obliged to shadow you; perhaps you were supposed to follow him, too. Isn't that right? Tell me instead: has Verkhovensky agreed to accept your arguments or not?'

'Yes; he said it was allowed and that I did have the right...'

'Well, he's deceiving you. I know that even Kirillov, who scarcely belongs to the group at all, has been providing them with information about you. And they have many agents, some of whom don't even know they're working for the society. They've always kept an eye on you. Meanwhile, Peter Verkhovensky has come here to settle your case once and for all and he has full authority to do so; that is, to eliminate you at the first suitable opportunity, as someone who knows too much and could inform on them. I repeat, it's certain; let me add that for some reason they're absolutely convinced you're a spy, and that if you still haven't informed against them, you will soon. Is that true?'

Shatov's lip curled at such a question posed in so matter-of-fact a way.

'If I really were a spy, who would I report to?' he said angrily, without answering the question directly. 'No, leave me alone! Let me go to the devil!' he cried, suddenly seizing on his original idea, which, to all appearances, affected him much more than the news that his life was in danger. 'You, you, Stavrogin, how could you become involved in this shameful, inept, servile stupidity? You—a member of their society! What sort of an exploit is that for Nikolai Stavrogin?' he cried, almost in despair.

He even threw up his hands, as if he could make no more grievous or dismal discovery.

'Excuse me,' Nikolai Vsevolodovich said, genuinely surprised, 'but you seem to regard me as some kind of sun and yourself as some kind of insect compared to me. I noticed that even in the letter you wrote me from America.'

'You... you know... Ah, let's not talk about me any more, please!' Shatov broke off suddenly. 'If you can explain something about yourself, then do... in answer to my question!' he said heatedly.

'With pleasure. You ask how I could fall into that den of thieves. After what I've said, I'm obliged to be somewhat more open with you about this matter. You see, strictly speaking, I don't really belong to the society, I haven't ever belonged to it, and have far more right than you to leave them, since I never joined in the first place. On the contrary, from the very beginning I declared that I was not their comrade, and that if I happened to assist them, it was only because I had nothing better to do. In part I participated in the reorganization of the society according to the new plan, and that was all. But now they've changed their minds and decided it would be dangerous to let me go, and it seems that I've also been sentenced.'

'Oh, it's always the death sentence and always on official documents with seals, signed by three and a half men. Do you think they can bring it off?'

'On that point you're partly right and partly wrong,' Stavrogin continued in his previous indifferent, even flaccid manner. 'There's no doubt that much of it is fantasy, as it always is in these cases: a handful of people exaggerate their own size and significance. If you want to know, in my opinion all they really have is Peter Verkhovensky, and he's so good-natured that he considers himself merely an agent of the society. But their fundamental idea is no more stupid than others of this sort. They have their ties to the *Internationale*; they've managed to get their agents into Russia, and they've hit upon a rather original plan... but only in theory, of course. As far as their local intentions are concerned, the moves of our Russian organization are so obscure and almost always unexpected, they might really try anything. Note that Verkhovensky is a stubborn man.'

'He's a bedbug, an ignoramus, an idiot who understands nothing at all about Russia!' Shatov cried angrily.

'You don't know him well. It's true that in general they all understand very little about Russia, but only a little less than you and I do. Besides, Verkhovensky's an enthusiast.'

'An enthusiast?'

'Oh, yes. There's a point at which he stops playing the fool and becomes a... madman. I ask you to recall one of your own expressions: "Do you know how powerful a single man can be?" Please, don't laugh; he's fully capable of pulling the trigger. They're sure I'm a spy too. All of them, because they're so incapable of conducting their business, dearly love to accuse people of being spies.'

'But you're not afraid?'

'N-no... I'm not too afraid... But your case is completely different. I warned you so you'd keep it in mind. I think there's no reason to be offended if fools like these are a threat to you. The issue isn't their intelligence: they've struck at better people than you and me. But it's already a quarter past eleven,' he said, looking at his watch and getting up from the chair. 'I'd like to ask you one more completely extraneous question.'

'For God's sake!' Shatov exclaimed, leaping up from his chair.

'What do you mean?' Nikolai Vsevolodovich asked, looking at him enquiringly.

'Go on, ask your question, for God's sake,' Shatov replied in inexpressible agitation, 'but only if I can ask you one question. I beg you... I can't... go on, ask your question!'

Stavrogin paused and then began:

'I've heard you've had some influence here on Marya Timofeevna and that she likes to see you and listen to you. Is that true?'

'Yes... she listens...' Shatov replied with some embarrassment.

'In a few days I intend to make public my marriage to her here in town.'

'Is that really possible?' Shatov whispered, almost in horror.

'What do you mean? There's no problem about it; the witnesses to the marriage are here. It all took place in Petersburg in a completely legal and proper manner, and if it hasn't come to light until now, it's only because the two witnesses at the wedding, Kirillov and Peter Verkhovensky, and, in fact, Lebyadkin himself (whom I now have the pleasure of being related to) all gave me their word to keep silent.'

'That's not what I meant... You're talking so calmly... but, go on! Listen, you weren't forced into this marriage, were you?'

'No, no one forced me into it,' Nikolai Vsevolodovich replied, smiling at Shatov's provocative haste.

'What is she saying about that baby of hers?' Shatov asked hurriedly, as if in a fever, and incoherently.

'About a baby? Why, I've no idea, it's the first I've heard of it. She didn't have a baby and couldn't have: Marya Timofeevna is still a virgin.'

'Ah! That's what I thought! Listen!'

'What's the matter, Shatov?'

Shatov covered his face with his hands, turned around, then suddenly grabbed Stavrogin firmly by the shoulder.

'Do you understand, do you understand, at least,' he shouted, 'why you did all this and why you've decided on such punishment now?'

'That's a clever, nasty question, but I intend to astonish you, too. Yes, I do almost understand why I married her then and why I've decided on such "punishment" now, as you put it.'

'Let's leave that aside... let's wait and talk about it later; let's talk about the main thing now, the main thing. I've waited two years for you.'

'Really?'

'I've waited too long for you; I thought about you constantly. You're the only man who could... I wrote you all about it from America.'

'I remember your long letter very well.'

'Too long to be read right through? I agree: six sheets of notepaper. Silence, silence! Tell me: can you spare me another ten minutes, right now, this moment... I've waited too long for you!'

'By all means; I can spare you half an hour, but no more, if that's all right with you.'

'Only on condition', Shatov interrupted furiously, 'that you change your tone. Listen to me, now I'm demanding when I ought to be imploring... Do you understand what it means to demand when one ought to be imploring?'

'I understand that in so doing you're exalting yourself above everything commonplace in the pursuit of higher aims,' Nikolai Vsevolodovich said, almost laughing. 'And I'm also sorry to see that you're so feverish.'

'I beg you to respect me, I demand it!' Shatov cried. 'Not for my sake personally—to hell with that—but for something else; but I only have time for a few words about it... We're two beings who've met in infinity... for the last time in this world. Drop that tone of yours and speak to me like a human being. At least once in your life use a human tone of voice. And not for your sake, for mine. Do you understand you must forgive me for striking you in the face, if only because I provided you with an opportunity to realize your own unlimited power... You're smiling your disdainful, society smile again. Oh, when will you ever understand me? Do away with the young gentleman in you! Understand, I demand it, demand it, otherwise I don't want to talk to you. I won't stand for it!'

His frenzy was approaching delirium; Nikolai Vsevolodo-vich frowned and became somewhat more cautious.

'Since I'm staying here another half hour,' he said seriously and impressively, 'when my time is so valuable, believe me, I intend to listen to you at least with interest and... I'm sure I'll hear much that's new from you.'

He sat down on a chair.

'Sit down!' Shatov cried and then suddenly sat himself down.

'But let me remind you', Stavrogin put in once more, 'that I was about to ask a very great favour concerning Marya Timofeevna, at least one that's very important for her...'

'Well?' said Shatov, frowning suddenly with the look of a man who's been interrupted at the most important part of his speech, and who, though he's looking right at you, is still unable to grasp the meaning of your question.

'You didn't let me finish,' Nikolai Vsevolodovich added with a smile.

'Oh, well, that's nonsense. Later!' Shatov said, waving his hand with disgust, finally·understanding Stavrogin's grievance. And he turned straight to his principal theme.

7·

'Do you know,' he began almost menacingly, leaning forward in his chair, eyes flashing, and raising the index finger of his right hand (apparently unaware of this himself), 'do you know which nation is now the one and only "God-bearing" nation on earth, destined to regenerate and save the world in the name of a new God, and to whom alone the keys to life and the new word have been given... Do you know which nation that is and what its name is?'

'To judge from your method I must conclude and, it seems, conclude as soon as possible, that it's the Russian nation...'

'And you're laughing again. Oh, what a race!' Shatov burst out.

'Calm down, I beg you; on the contrary, I was expecting something of this sort from you.'

'Expecting something of this sort? Don't these words seem familiar to you?'

'Very familiar; I see all too well where you're heading. All you just said, and even the expression "God-bearing" nation, is merely the conclusion of a conversation you and I had abroad some two years ago, not long before you left for America... At least, that's as much as I can recall now.'

'They're your words entirely, not mine. Your very own, and not merely the conclusion of our conversation. "Our" conversation never took place: there was a teacher who uttered mighty words and a student who was raised from the dead. I was that student and you were that teacher.'

'But if I recall correctly, right after I spoke those words you joined the society and only then left for America.'

'Yes, and I wrote you about it from there; I wrote you about everything. No, I couldn't tear myself away from what I'd clung to since childhood, and lavished all my joyous hopes and tears of hatred on... It's hard to change one's gods. I didn't believe you at the time because I didn't want to believe, and I plunged into that filthy cesspool for the last time... But the seed remained in me and took root. Seriously, tell me seriously, did you ever finish reading my letter from America? Perhaps you never read it at all?'

'I read three pages, the first two and the last one; besides that, I skimmed the middle. But I always intended to...'

'Oh, it doesn't matter. Forget it! To hell with it!' Shatov said, waving his hand. 'If you've renounced what you said about the nation now, how could you have said it at the time?... That's what oppresses me now.'

'I wasn't joking with you then; in trying to convince you, I might've been more concerned about myself than about you,' Stavrogin said mysteriously.

'You weren't joking! In America I lay on a straw mat for three months next to... a poor wretch, and I found out from him that at the same time as you were sowing the seeds of God and motherland in my heart—at the same time, perhaps even the same day, you were poisoning the heart of that wretch, that maniac Kirillov... You were confirming lies and slander in him and you led his reason to the verge of

insanity... Go have a look at him now; he's your creation...
But you've already seen him.'

'In the first place, let me point out that Kirillov himself
told me just now how happy he is and how good. Your
assumption that all this occurred at one and the same time
is almost correct; what of it? I repeat, I wasn't deceiving
you, either one of you.'

'Are you an atheist? Are you an atheist now?'

'Yes.'

'What about then?'

'The same as I was then.'

'I wasn't demanding your respect for myself when we
began this conversation. With your intelligence, you
should've been able to understand that,' Shatov murmured
in indignation.

'I didn't stand up and leave at your first word, didn't end
the conversation, didn't walk out on you; I'm still sitting
here, calmly responding to your questions and your... shouting, which means that I still haven't lost my respect for
you.'

Shatov interrupted, waving his hand:

'Do you recall your formulation: "An atheist can't be
Russian; an atheist ceases at once to be Russian." Do you
remember that?'

'Yes?' Nikolai Vsevolodovich asked, as if asking him to
repeat it.

'You're asking? Have you forgotten? But that was one of
the most accurate formulations about one of the most
important characteristics of the Russian spirit that you
divined. You couldn't have forgotten? I'll remind you further: you also said at the time, "A person who isn't Orthodox can't be Russian." '

'I suppose that's a Slavophile idea.'*

'No. Today's Slavophiles reject it. Nowadays people have
become more intelligent. But you went even further: you
believed that Roman Catholicism is no longer Christianity;
you maintained that Rome proclaimed a Christ who'd suc-
cumbed to the Devil's third temptation, and, having announced to the entire world that Christ cannot survive on

earth without having an earthly kingdom, Catholicism had thereby proclaimed the Anti-Christ and had destroyed the whole Western world. It was you who pointed out that if France was in agony, it was solely the fault of Catholicism, for while it had rejected the stinking god of Rome, it had yet to find a new one. That's what you were able to say then! I remember our conversations.'

'If I were a believer, I'd undoubtedly say it again now; I wasn't telling lies, speaking as a believer,' Nikolai Vsevolodovich said very seriously. 'But I assure you this repetition of my former ideas is making an extremely unpleasant impression on me. Can't you stop?'

'If you were a believer?' cried Shatov, not paying the least attention to his request. 'But wasn't it you who told me that if mathematicians could demonstrate that truth lay outside Christ, you'd still prefer to remain with Christ rather than with the truth? Didn't you say that? Didn't you?'

'Let me ask you, once and for all,' said Stavrogin, raising his voice, 'where all this impatient and... malicious examination is leading?'

'Soon the examination will be over once and for all and you'll never be reminded of it again.'

'You keep insisting that we're outside time and space...'

'Silence!' Shatov cried suddenly. 'I'm stupid and clumsy, and may my name perish in ridicule! Allow me to repeat your own fundamental idea at that time... Oh, only ten more lines or so, only the conclusion.'

'Go on, repeat it, if it's only the conclusion...'

Stavrogin was about to glance at his watch, but restrained himself.

Shatov leaned forward in his chair and even for a moment raised his index-finger again.

'Not one nation,' he began, as if reciting line for line, and staring menacingly at Stavrogin, 'not one single nation has ever been established on principles of science and reason; there's never been an example of it, except for one brief moment, and then it was the result of stupidity. Socialism by its very nature must be atheism, because it has from the very beginning proclaimed itself an atheistic organization which intends to establish itself exclusively on principles of science and reason. Reason and science have always, now and from the beginning of time, played only a secondary and subordinate role in the life of nations; and so it will be until the end of time. Nations are formed and moved by some other force that commands and dominates them, whose origin is unknown and inexplicable. This force is the force of an insatiable desire to go on until the end, while at the same time denying that there is an end. It is the force of a continual and indefatigable affirmation of its own being and the denial of death. It's the spirit of life, "rivers of living water" as the Scriptures call it, the drying-up of which is threatened in Revelation.* It's the aesthetic principle, as philosophers say, or the moral principle, as they call it. I refer to it more simply as "the search for God". The goal of every national movement, in every nation at every period of its existence, is solely the search for God, for their God, their very own God, and belief in Him as the only true God. God is the synthetic personality of the entire nation, taken from its beginning to its end. It has never happened that all nations or even many nations shared one and the same God; instead, every nation has its own special one. It's a sign of the decay of nations when they begin to have gods in common. When the gods actually become common to nations they die, as does all faith in them, together with the nations themselves. The more powerful a nation, the more individual its God. There's never been a nation without religion, that is, without a conception of good and evil. Every nation has its own conception, and its own particular good and evil. When these conceptions become common to many nations, the nations begin to die and the very distinction between good and evil begins to fade away and disappear. Reason has never been powerful enough to define good and evil or to demarcate good from evil, even approximately; on the contrary, it's always confused them shamefully and pitifully; science has always provided solutions by brute force. This has been particularly characteristic of pseudo-science, that most terrible scourge of humanity, worse than pestilence, starvation, and warfare, and completely unknown until this century. Pseudo-science is a despot, the like of which has never been seen before. It's a despot possessing its own priests and slaves, before which everything else bows down with love and superstition hitherto inconceivable, before which science itself trembles and cringes shamefully. These are all your own words, Stavrogin, except for the part about pseudo-science; those are my words, because I myself am mere pseudo-science, and therefore I hate it particularly. I haven't altered anything in your ideas or words, not a single thing.'

'I don't think you've left them unaltered,' Stavrogin observed cautiously. 'You've accepted them ardently and modified them ardently, without even noticing. Just the fact that you reduce God to a mere attribute of nationality...'

He suddenly began to pay increased and particular attention to Shatov, not so much to his words, as to the man himself.

'Reduce God to a mere attribute of nationality?' cried Shatov. 'On the contrary, I elevate the nation to God. Has it ever been otherwise? The people is the body of God. Every nation is a nation only so long as it has its own particular God, excluding all other gods on earth without any possible reconciliation, so long as it believes that by its own God it will conquer and drive all other gods off the face of the earth. At least that's what all great nations have believed since the beginning of time, all those remarkable in any way, those standing in the vanguard of humanity. It's impossible to go against the fact. The Jews lived solely in expectation of the true God, and they left this true God to the world. The Greeks deified nature and bequeathed this religion to the world, that is, philosophy and art. Rome deified the nation in the state and bequeathed the state to other nations. France, in the course of its long history, was merely the embodiment and development of the idea of the Roman God, and if it finally hurled its Roman God into the abyss and embraced atheism, which, for the time being, they call socialism, it's solely because atheism is still healthier than Roman Catholicism. If a great nation doesn't believe that the truth resides in it alone (in it alone, to the exclusion of all other nations), if it doesn't believe that it alone is capable and chosen to resurrect and save everyone through its own history, then it immediately ceases to be a great nation and is at once transformed merely into ethnographic material. A genuinely great nation can never be content to play a secondary role in human history, not even a primary role; it must necessarily and exclusively be first. A nation which loses this faith is no longer a nation. But there is only one truth; consequently, only one nation can possess the true God, even though other nations have possessed their own particular great gods. The sole "God-bearing" nation is the Russian nation, and... and... and do you really think me such a fool, Stavrogin,' he shouted ferociously all of a sudden, 'that I can't see that what I say is either tired old platitudes, ground out of all those Slavophile mills in Moscow, or a totally new word, the last word, the sole word of regeneration and resurrection, and... what do I care if you're laughing at me this very moment! What do I care if you don't understand me at all, not one bit, not one word, not one sound!... Oh, how I despise your proud laughter and your expression!'

He jumped up from his chair; he was actually foaming at the mouth.

'On the contrary, Shatov, on the contrary,' Stavrogin said with utmost seriousness and restraint, without getting up from his seat. 'On the contrary, your ardent words have resurrected in me many extremely powerful recollections. I recognize my own mood of some two years ago in your words, and now I won't say as I did a moment ago that you're exaggerating the ideas I had at that time. I even think what I said was more exclusive, more absolute, and I can assure you for the third time that I'd very much like to confirm everything you've just said, down to the last word, but...'

'But you need a hare?'

'Wha-at?'

'It's your own foul expression,' Shatov said, laughing maliciously, sitting down again. ' "To make hare sauce, you need a hare; to believe in God, you need God." I'm told you used to say that in Petersburg, like Nozdryov,* who tried to catch a hare by its hind legs.'

'No, he used to boast, actually, that he had caught it. Incidentally, let me pose you a question, especially since I believe I have a right to do so now. Tell me: has your hare been caught or is it still running away?'

'Don't you dare use those words to ask me that; ask it in different words, different words!' Shatov cried, suddenly trembling all over.

'All right, in different words,' Nikolai Vsevolodovich replied, looking at him sternly. 'I merely wanted to know: do you yourself believe in God or not?'

'I believe in Russia, I believe in her Orthodoxy... I believe in the body of Christ... I believe that the Second Coming will take place in Russia... I believe...' Shatov mumbled in a frenzy.

'But in God? In God?'

'I... I shall believe in God.'

Not one muscle moved in Stavrogin's face. Shatov looked at him ardently and defiantly, as if wanting to scorch him with his gaze.

'I didn't say I don't believe at all!' he cried at last. 'I merely want you to know that I'm an unhappy, boring book and nothing more than that at the moment, at the moment... But to hell with me! You're the one that matters, not me... I'm a man without talent and can only offer my blood and nothing more, just like any man without talent. And to hell with my blood! I'm talking about you; I've waited here two years for you... Now I've been dancing around naked in front of you for half an hour. You, you alone could've raised the banner.'

He didn't finish; he sat there as if in despair, with his elbows on the table and head propped on his hands.

'I mention it to you in passing, as an oddity,' Stavrogin said, suddenly interrupting him. 'Why is it that everyone tries to foist some banner on me? Peter Verkhovensky is also convinced that I could "raise their banner", at least I'm told that's what he said. He's made up his mind that I could play the part of Stenka Razin* for them "because of my unusual aptitude for crime", also his words.'

'What?' Shatov asked. ' "Your unusual aptitude for crime"?'

'Precisely.'

'Hmmm. And is it true that you,' he asked, smiling maliciously, 'is it true that in Petersburg you belonged to a secret society that practised bestial sensuality? Is it true that the Marquis de Sade* could take lessons from you? Is it true you seduced and corrupted children? Tell me! Don't you dare lie,' he shouted, quite beside himself. 'Nikolai Stavrogin can't lie to Shatov who struck him across the face! Tell me everything, and if it's true, I'll kill you at once, this very moment, on the spot!'

'I did say those words, but I have not abused any children,' said Stavrogin, but only after a very long pause. He had turned pale and his eyes were burning.

'But you did say it!' Shatov went on imperiously, glittering eyes fixed on him. 'Is it true that you claimed not to see any aesthetic difference between a voluptuous, bestial prank and a heroic feat, even the sacrifice of one's own life for the benefit of humanity? Is it true that in both extremes you found identical beauty and equal enjoyment?'

'It's impossible to answer that... I don't want to reply,' Stavrogin muttered. He could very well have got up and left, but he didn't.

'I don't know either why evil is squalid and good is beautiful, but I do know why perception of a distinction between them is becoming blurred and lost in people such as Stavrogin,' Shatov persisted, trembling all over. 'Do you know why you made such a shameless, base marriage? Precisely because the shame and senselessness of that act bordered on genius! Oh, you never teeter on the edge; you hurl yourself boldly in head first. You married out of a passion for martyrdom, a craving for remorse, moral voluptuousness. It was a clear case of laceration of the nervous system... The affront to common sense was far too tempting! Stavrogin and a wretched, half-witted, destitute cripple! And when you bit the governor's ear, did you feel a sensual thrill? Did you? You idle, loafing, spoiled son of a nobleman, did you?'

'You're quite a psychologist,' Stavrogin replied, growing paler and paler, 'although you're partly mistaken about the reasons for my marriage... By the way, who could have provided you with all this information?' he asked, forcing a laugh. 'Could it have been Kirillov? But he didn't take part...'

'You've turned pale, haven't you?'

'What do you really want?' Nikolai Vsevolodovich asked, raising his voice at last. 'I've been sitting here taking your lashing for the last half hour; you could at least release me politely... unless you in fact have some rational motive for treating me this way.'

'Rational motive?'

'Absolutely. At the least you're obliged to reveal your motive to me. I've been waiting for you to do so, but all I get is frenzied malice. Be so good as to unlock the gate.'

He stood up from the chair. Shatov rushed after him furiously.

'Kiss the earth, bathe it in tears, beg for forgiveness!' he cried, grabbing hold of him by the shoulder.

'But I didn't kill you... that morning... I took my hands off you...' said Stavrogin almost in anguish, lowering his eyes.

'Come on, tell me everything! You came to warn me of danger, you allowed me to speak, and tomorrow you want to announce your marriage in public!... Can't I see from your face that some dreadful new idea is taking hold of you? Stavrogin, why am I condemned to believe in you for ever and ever? Could I possibly talk to any other person this way? I'm a modest person, but I was not ashamed of my nakedness because I was speaking with Stavrogin. I'm not afraid to make a caricature of a great idea by touching it because it was Stavrogin who was listening to me... Won't I kiss your footprints after you've gone? I can't tear you out of my heart, Nikolai Stavrogin!'

'I'm sorry that I'm unable to love you, Shatov,' Nikolai Vsevolodovich said coldly.

'I know you can't and I know you're not lying. Listen, I can make everything right: I'll catch you a hare!'

Stavrogin was silent.

'You're an atheist because you're a spoiled son of a gentleman, the last one there is. You've lost the distinction between good and evil because you no longer know your own people. A new generation is coming, straight from the heart of the people, and you won't recognize it at all, not you, nor the Verkhovenskys, father and son, nor I, because I too am a gentleman, I, the son of your serf and footman Pasha... Listen, find God through work; that's the essence of it all. Or else you'll vanish like rotten mould; find Him through work.'

'Find God through work? What kind of work?'

'Peasant's work. Go forth, cast off your riches... Oh, you're laughing; are you afraid I'm pulling your leg?'

But Stavrogin wasn't laughing.

'You assume that God can be found through work, peasant's work,' he repeated, after some thought, as if he'd really encountered something new and serious that merited consideration. 'Incidentally,' he said, suddenly switching to a new subject, 'you just reminded me. You know, I'm really not that rich, so there's nothing to cast off. I'm hardly in a position to guarantee even Marya Timofeevna's future.... There's something else: I came to ask you, if possible, not to abandon Marya Timofeevna in the future, since only you have any influence over her poor mind... I'm saying this just in case.'

'All right, all right, concerning Marya,' Shatov said with a wave of one hand, while holding a candle in the other. 'All right, afterwards, of course... Listen, go and see Tikhon.'

'Who?'

'Tikhon. Tikhon, him that used to be a bishop, and retired because of illness and lives here, on the edge of town, in the Efimovsky Monastery of Our Lady.'

'So?'

'Nothing. People come to see him. You should go. Why not? Well, why not?'

'It's the first I've heard of him and... I've never met that sort of person before. Thank you, I will go.'

'This way,' said Shatov, lighting the staircase. 'Go ahead,' he said, flinging the gate open into the street.

'I won't come to see you again, Shatov,' Stavrogin said quietly, as he stepped through the gate.

It was still dark and raining as before.

CHAPTER 2

Night (continued)

I.

HE walked along Bogoyavlenskaya Street; finally the road went downhill, he was walking in mud, and suddenly the wide, misty, as it were empty expanse of the river opened up in front of him. Houses gave way to hovels and the street vanished in a multitude of irregular alleys. Nikolai Vsevolodovich made his way along the fences for a while, not straying too far from the river bank, but resolutely finding his way without even thinking much about it. He was preoccupied by something else altogether and looked round in surprise when all of a sudden, coming out of a deep reverie, he found himself almost in the middle of our long, wet pontoon bridge. There wasn't a soul around, so it struck him as strange suddenly to hear, almost at his very elbow, a politely ingratiating and yet not unpleasant voice, with a saccharine drawl like that affected by our superior tradesmen or our curly-haired young shopkeepers in the Arcade.

'Would you allow me, kind sir, to share your umbrella?'

And, indeed, a figure of some sort crept, or pretended to creep, under his umbrella. A tramp was walking alongside him, almost 'rubbing elbows' as soldiers say. Slowing his pace, Nikolai Vsevolodovich bent over to have a look as best he could in the darkness: the man was not very tall and looked like a tradesman on a binge. He was neither warmly clad nor very well dressed; on his shaggy, curly head perched a soaking-wet cloth cap with its brim half torn off. He seemed to be a strong, lean, dark-haired man, with a swarthy complexion; his eyes were large, definitely black, with a bright gleam and a yellow tinge, like a gypsy's. This could be divined even in the darkness. He must have been about forty years old and he wasn't drunk.

'Do you know me?' Nikolai Vsevolodovich asked.

'Mr Stavrogin, Nikolai Vsevolodovich; you was pointed out to me last Sunday at the railway station, just as the train was pulling in. Besides, I've heard a lot about you.'

'From Peter Stepanovich? Are you... are you Fedka the convict?'

'They baptized me Fyodor Fyodorovich; my mother, she's still living in these here parts, sir; she's an old, God-fearing woman, growing more bent over all the time; she prays to God for us every day and night, so she don't waste her old age lying around on top of a stove.'

'Are you on the run?'

'I took fate into my own hands. I gave up books and bells and church affairs, sir, because they sentenced me to life in prison, and that's too long a time to wait.'

'What are you doing around here?'

'Well, day and night—I do the best I can. My uncle died here in the local prison last week, what was in for counterfeiting. So, in his memory, I tossed a few dozen stones at some dogs—that's all I've done so far. Besides, Peter Stepanovich promised to get me a passport, like what a merchant has, good for travel all over Russia, so I've been waiting for him to do me that favour. It's because, he says, his dad lost me in a card game at the English Club; and, he says, I consider that unjust and inhumane. And you, sir, would you be willing to give me three roubles for a little something to warm myself up?'

'So you've been waiting here for me; I don't like that. On whose orders?'

'As to whose orders, well, it wasn't anybody's; it was just that I knew you was generous, as does everyone else. You know how we get by: an armful of hay or a prod with a pitchfork. Last Friday I stuffed myself with meat pie, like Martin with soap,* but since then I ain't eaten a thing; next day I fasted, the third day I still had nothing to eat. I've had so much water from the river, there's a school of fish swimming in my belly... So perhaps you could give me something out of your generosity; I have a lady friend what's waiting for me not too far from here, but I can't go and see her without no money.'

'What did Peter Stepanovich promise you'd get from me?'

'He didn't promise nothing, sir, but said in so many

words, sir, I might be useful to you should occasion arise; but in what way, he didn't say exactly, because Peter Stepanovich wants to see if I have the patience of a Cossack, and he has no confidence in me at all.'

'Why not?'

'Peter Stepanych is an astrologer and knows all God's planets, but even he's not above criticism. I stand before you, sir, as before God Himself, because I've heard a lot about you. Peter Stepanovich is one thing, but you, sir, are another. When they say a man's a scoundrel, you know nothing more about him except that he's a scoundrel. And if they say he's a fool, then that man has no other calling except that of a fool. I may be just a fool on Tuesdays and Wednesdays, but on Thursdays I'm cleverer than what he is. Well, he knows I'm really looking for a passport now— since there's no way you'll get around Russia without documents—so now he thinks he's got his claws into my soul. Peter Stepanovich, I can tell you, sir, has an easy time of it because first he gets his own picture of a man and then that's what he always sees. Besides, he's very stingy. He fancies I won't dare disturb you without his permission, but I stand before you, sir, as before God Himself—why, I've been waiting for your honour on this bridge the last four nights, to show him I can make my own way quietly without the likes of him. After all, I think to myself, better to bow down to a boot than a bast sandal.'

'And who told you I'd be coming across this bridge at night?'

'Well, sir, truth be told, that came out by chance, mainly from Captain Lebyadkin's stupidity because he ain't got no control of himself... So, be generous and give me three roubles to pay me back for them boring last three days and nights of waiting. As for my soaking-wet clothes, well, that's a crying shame, but I'll say no more.'

'I'm turning to the left and you're going to the right; here's the end of the bridge. Listen, Fyodor, I like people to understand what I say once and for all: I won't give you a kopeck. Don't ever come to meet me on this bridge or anywhere else. I have no need for you and won't ever have, and if you don't listen to me—then I'll tie you up and take you to the police. Now, march!'

'Aha! Well, you give me something for my company at least. I've cheered you up a bit, ain't I?'

'Get away!'

'Do you know your way around here, sir? There're all sorts of alleys... I could guide you, for this town's so confusing, it's just like the devil had carried it around in a basket and shook it up.'

'Hey, I'll tie you up!' Nikolai Vsevolodovich said, turning threateningly.

'You might change your mind, sir; you don't want to harm a poor orphan like me.'

'Well, you're certainly sure of yourself!'

'I'm sure of you, sir, but not too sure of myself.'

'I said I have no need for you at all!'

'But I have need of you, sir, that's what. I'll wait for you on the way back. That's all there is to it.'

'I give you my word of honour: if I meet you here, I'll tie you up.'

'Well, then, I'd better get a belt ready for you, sir. All the best, sir. You've kept a poor orphan dry under your umbrella, and for that alone I'll be grateful to you until the day I die.'

He dropped back. Nikolai Vsevolodovich reached his destination feeling very anxious. This man who'd appeared like a bolt from the blue had been absolutely certain he was indispensable to him and altogether too bold in his hasty declaration of that fact. In general he felt people were being a bit casual with him. But it could very well be that the tramp hadn't been lying altogether, that he really had been trying to force his services on him on his own initiative, without Peter Stepanovich's knowledge; and that would be even more peculiar.

2.

The house Stavrogin arrived at stood in a deserted alley on the very edge of town between fences separating endless allotments. The little wooden house was isolated, newly built and still without cladding. The shutters on one of the windows had been intentionally left open and a lighted candle stood on the window-sill—apparently as a signal to a visitor expected late that night. Some thirty paces away Nikolai Vsevolodovich made out the figure of a tall man, probably the master of the house, standing on the porch; in his impatience he'd come out to look up the road. His voice could be heard as well, impatient and seemingly timid:

'Is that you, sir? Is it you?'

'Yes it is,' replied Nikolai Vsevolodovich, but not before he'd reached the porch and closed his umbrella.

'At last, sir!' said Captain Lebyadkin—for it was he—and began stamping his feet and fussing around him. 'Let me take your umbrella; it's soaking wet, sir; I'll open it up and put it here on the floor in the corner. Come in, sir, come in.'

The door was wide open from a passage leading into a room lit by two candles.

'If you hadn't given me your word you were definitely coming, I'd have given up hope.'

'It's a quarter to one,' said Nikolai Vsevolodovich, looking at his watch as he entered the room.

'It's pouring down, and so far to come... I've no watch and all I can see from my window is the allotments so... I lose track of things... but, I'm not really complaining. I wouldn't dare, I wouldn't; it's only because of the impatience that's been consuming me all week for it... finally to be resolved.'

'What?'

'My fate, Nikolai Vsevolodovich. Do come in.'

He bowed and indicated a place on the sofa near the table.

Nikolai Vsevolodovich looked around; the room was tiny with a low ceiling; the furniture consisted exclusively of essentials—wooden chairs and a sofa, also of recent construction without covers or cushions, two lime-wood tables, one near the sofa, the other in the corner covered with a tablecloth, set with dishes on which a clean napkin had been spread. In fact, the whole room was obviously kept very neat and clean. Captain Lebyadkin hadn't been drunk for the last eight days; his face looked bloated and bilious, his expression, restless, curious, and obviously bewildered: it was all too evident that he himself didn't know what tone of voice to use and what approach would be most advantageous.

'Here, sir,' he said, indicating his surroundings, 'I live like some Zosima. Abstinence, solitude, and poverty—the knights' vows in days of old.'

'You suppose that knights used to take such vows?'

'Have I made a mistake? Alas, I lack education! I've made a mess of everything! Would you believe, Nikolai Vsevolodovich, here for the first time I've recovered from my shameful proclivity—not one glass, not a single drop! I have a place to live and for the last six days I've felt the blessing of a clear conscience. Even the walls smell of resin and remind me of nature. What sort of man was I, what was I before?

> At night I'd wander without a home,
> My tongue hanging out by day...*

in the poet's inspired phrase of a poet! But... you're soaking wet... Wouldn't you like some tea?'

'Don't trouble.'

'The samovar's been boiling since eight o'clock, but... it's gone out... like everything else in the world. Even the sun, they say, will go out in its turn... But if necessary, I'll get it going again. Agafya's not asleep.'

'Tell me, is Marya Timofeevna...'

'She's here, indeed she is,' Lebyadkin interrupted him at once in a whisper. 'Would you like to see her?' he asked, indicating the closed door to the other room.

'She's not asleep?'

'Oh, no, goodness, no! On the contrary, she's been expecting you all evening; as soon as she heard you arrive, she went to dress up.' His mouth nearly twisted into a facetious smile, but he checked himself.

'How has she been in general?' Nikolai Vsevolodovich asked, frowning.

'In general? I don't have to tell you the answer to that,' he said with a shrug of pity, 'but now... now she's telling her fortune with cards...'

'All right, later; first let's finish with you.'

Nikolai Vsevolodovich sat down on a chair.

The captain didn't dare sit on the sofa, but quickly pulled up another chair, sat down, and leaned forward to listen in agitated expectation.

'What have you got there in the corner under the cloth?' Nikolai Vsevolodovich asked, suddenly noticing.

'That, sir?' Lebyadkin replied, also turning to look. 'That comes from your generosity, a sort of housewarming, so to speak, also taking into account the great distance you've come and your natural fatigue,' he said with an affecting snigger; then he got up from his seat and tiptoed over to remove the cloth very carefully and respectfully from the table in the corner. Under it there was an assortment of refreshments: ham, veal, sardines, cheese, a small green carafe and a tall bottle of claret; everything was neatly arranged, expertly, almost fashionably.

'Did you go to all this trouble?'

'Yes, sir. Been at it since yesterday, and everything I could, in your honour... Marya Timofeevna, as you know, doesn't care about this sort of thing. The most important point is, because of your generosity, it's all yours, since you're the master of this house, not me; I am, so to speak, your agent, though all the same, all the same, Nikolai Vsevolodovich, all the same, my spirit is still independent! You won't take that last thing away from me!' he concluded poignantly.

'Hmmm! I do wish you'd sit down again.'

'I'm so-o grateful, grateful and independent!' He sat down. 'Ah, Nikolai Vsevolodovich, so much has been brewing in this heart of mine I could hardly wait for you! Now you will decide my fate... and the fate of that unfortunate creature, and then... then, I'll pour my heart out to you, as I used to in the old days, four years ago! You did me the honour of listening then, you read my verses... So what if they called me your Falstaff, from Shakespeare? You meant so much to me in my own life! I'm in great fear now and awaiting advice and illumination from you alone. Peter Stepanovich is treating me abominably!'

Nikolai Vsevolodovich listened to him with interest and looked at him intently. Obviously, even though Captain Lebyadkin had stopped drinking, his state of mind was still far from serene. The speech of such inveterate drunkards always ends up a little incoherent, vague, somehow imperfect or insane, even though they still cheat, scheme, and deceive if necessary no worse than anyone else.

'I see you haven't changed in the least, Captain, during the last four years.' Nikolai Vsevolodovich spoke somewhat more politely. 'Apparently it's true that the second half of a man's life consists entirely of habits acquired during the first half.'

'Elegant words! You're solving the mystery of life!' cried the captain, half bluffing and half in genuine delight because he was a great admirer of clever sayings. 'Of all your sayings, Nikolai Vsevolodovich, I recall one in particular that you used back in Petersburg: "One must really be a great man to be able to go against common sense." So there!'

'Well, or else a fool.'

'All right then, or else a fool, but you've been dropping witticisms all your life, while they...? Let Liputin or Peter Stepanovich just try and say something like that! oh, Peter Stepanovich has treated me so cruelly!'

'But how about you, Captain, how have you behaved yourself?'

'It was the drink, and besides, I've a whole host of enemies! But now all, all of that's over with, and I've grown a new skin like a snake. Nikolai Vsevolodovich, do you know I'm writing my will and have already finished it?'

'That's interesting. What are you planning to leave and to whom?'

'To my fatherland, to humanity, and to students. Nikolai Vsevolodovich, I read the biography of a certain American in the newspapers. He left his enormous fortune to factories and to the exact sciences, his skeleton to students in the local academy, and his skin was to be made into a drum on which the American national anthem was to be pounded out day and night. Alas, we're mere pygmies compared to these flights of imagination in the States of North America; Russia is a freak of nature, but not of intellect. If I were to try and leave my skin to be made into a drum, to the Akmolinsky Infantry Regiment for example, in which I had the honour to begin my service, and if I were to specify that every day the Russian national anthem was to played on it in front of the whole regiment, they'd accuse me of liberalism and my skin would be banned... so for that reason I've confined myself to students. I want to leave my skeleton to the academy, but on condition, only on condition that a label be stuck on the forehead proclaiming for ever and ever: "Repentant freethinker". So there!'

The captain spoke heatedly and undoubtedly believed in the beauty of that American legacy; but he was also a rogue and very much wanted to amuse Nikolai Vsevolodovich, whom he'd served for a long time in the capacity of jester. But Stavrogin didn't even smile; on the contrary he enquired suspiciously:

'Of course you plan to publish your will during your lifetime and be rewarded for it?'

'And what if I do, Nikolai Vsevolodovich, what if I do?' Lebyadkin replied, looking at him closely. 'What sort of life have I had? I've even stopped writing poetry; at one time even you were amused by my verses, Nikolai Vsevolodovich, do you remember, over a bottle? But I've put down my pen. I wrote only one poem, like Gogol's "Last Story",* you recall, where he proclaims to Russia that the story had "poured forth from his heart like a song". I've sung my song as well and that's that.'

'What kind of poem?'

'It's called, "If she were to break a leg"!'

'Wha-at?'

That was just what the captain was waiting for. He had immeasurable respect and admiration for his own poems, but also, because of a certain roguish duplicity in his nature, he also liked the idea that Nikolai Vsevolodovich was always amused by his verses and would laugh at them, sometimes splitting his sides. In this way his two purposes were satisfied—the poetic and the subservient. But now he had yet a third, very delicate purpose in mind: in bringing his verses on to the scene, the captain hoped to justify himself on one point which he'd always felt extremely apprehensive and very guilty about.

' "If she were to break a leg", that is, while out riding. It's a fantasy, Nikolai Vsevolodovich, a delirium, but the delirium of a poet: once I was struck by meeting a lady on a horse and I posed a fundamental question: "What would happen if?"—I mean, if that happened. The answer's obvious: all her admirers would scurry away, all her suitors would desert her, saying "Goodbye for ever, my pretty lass." Only the poet would remain faithful to her, though his heart would be shattered in his breast. Nikolai Vsevolodovich, even a louse can fall in love; there's no law against it. But the lady was offended by the letter and the verses. They say even you were angry, isn't that so? That's sad; I didn't want to believe it. Well, what harm could I do with my imagination alone? Besides, word of honour, Liputin put me up to it: "Go on, send it. Every man has the right to send a letter." So I sent it.'

'Apparently you offered yourself as her suitor?'

'Enemies, enemies, enemies!'

'Recite your verse,' Nikolai Vsevolodovich said, interrupting him sternly.

'Ravings, it's ravings more than anything.'

But he stood up straight, stretched out his hand, and began to recite:

> 'Now that the fairest has broken her limb,
> She fascinates twice as much as before,
> And he whose heart was already a-brim
> Now twice as much the lady adores.'

'That's enough,' said Nikolai Vsevolodovich with a wave of his hand.

'I dream of Petersburg.' Lebyadkin switched to another subject as if no poem had ever existed. 'I dream of regeneration... Oh, my benefactor! Can I count on you not to refuse me money for the journey? I've waited for you all week as one waits for the sun.'

'No, I'm sorry, I have hardly any money left at all.

Besides, why should I give you any?'

Nikolai Vsevolodovich suddenly seemed to lose his temper. In dry, curt tones he enumerated all the captain's crimes: drunkenness, lying, wasting the money intended for Marya Timofeevna, taking her away from the convent, sending insolent letters threatening to reveal the secret, behaving badly with Darya Pavlovna, and so on and so forth. The captain cringed, gesticulated, began to object, but each time Nikolai Vsevolodovich stopped him peremptorily.

'And one more thing,' he said at last. 'You keep writing about "family disgrace". What kind of disgrace is it for your sister to be Stavrogin's lawful spouse?'

'But the marriage is kept secret, Nikolai Vsevolodovich, it's a secret, a fateful secret. I get money from you and all of a sudden I'm asked: what's this money for? I'm in a bind and unable to reply for fear of harming my sister or the honour of my family.'

The captain raised his voice: he loved this subject and relied upon it heavily. Alas, he didn't anticipate the blow in store for him. Serenely and precisely, as if he were talking about the most ordinary domestic arrangements, Nikolai Vsevolodovich informed him that in several days, perhaps as soon as tomorrow or the day after tomorrow, he was intending to announce his marriage publicly, "to the police, as well as to society", and by so doing, the question of his family honour would be laid to rest, likewise the question of any subsidies. The captain's eyes bulged; he didn't even understand; it was necessary to explain it all to him.

'But she's... a half-wit!'

'I'll make suitable arrangements.'

'But... what about your mother?'

'Well, she can do as she likes.'

'But will you bring your wife into your house?'

'Perhaps. But that's not really your business and it doesn't concern you.'

'What do you mean, it doesn't concern me?' the captain cried. 'What about me?'

'Well, you won't be brought into the house, of course.'

'But I'm your relative.'

'People flee from relatives like you. Why should I provide you with money, can you tell me?'

'Nikolai Vsevolodovich, this won't do, Nikolai Vsevolodovich. Perhaps you should think more about it. You don't want to lay hands upon... What will people think? What will they say in society?'

'Do you think I'm afraid of your society? I married your sister when I felt like it, after a drunken dinner, in a bet over a bottle of wine, and now I'll declare it all publicly... if it amuses me to do so now.'

He said this with particular irritation so the horrified Lebyadkin began to believe him.

'But what about me? Me? *I'm* the point here!... Maybe you're joking, Nikolai Vsevolodovich?'

'No, I'm not.'

'As you like, Nikolai Vsevolodovich, but I still don't believe you... If you do it, I'll lodge a formal complaint.'

'You're awfully stupid, Captain.'

'Maybe so, but it's all I have left!' the captain said, completely at a loss. 'Previously at least we used to get free lodging in exchange for housework my sister did in those places. But what will happen to us now if you just throw me out altogether?'

'You want to go to Petersburg and find a new career, don't you? By the way, is it true what I've heard, that you plan to inform on all the others in the hope of obtaining a pardon for yourself?'

The captain's mouth gaped wide open, his eyes bulged, and he made no reply.

'Listen, Captain,' Stavrogin suddenly began with utmost seriousness, bending close to the table. Up to now what he said had been as it were ambiguous, so Lebyadkin, who was used to playing the role of jester, was a little uncertain right up to the last moment: was his master really angry or merely fooling? Did he really have the crazy idea of announcing his marriage, or was he only teasing? Now Nikolai Vsevolodovich's unusually stern expression was so convincing that a shiver ran up and down the captain's back. 'Listen to me and tell me the truth, Lebyadkin: have you informed about something or not? Have you really managed to do anything? Have you sent off some stupid letter?'

'No, sir, I haven't done anything and... haven't even thought about it,' the captain replied, staring at him without moving.

'Well, you're lying when you say you haven't even thought about it. That's why you're wanting to go to Petersburg. If you didn't write anything, did you blurt anything out to someone around here? Tell me the truth; I've heard something about it.'

'When I was drunk I said something to Liputin. Liputin's a traitor. I opened up my heart to him,' whispered the poor captain.

'Opening your heart is one thing, but there's no reason to be an idiot. If you had an idea, you should have kept it to yourself; nowadays people with sense keep silent and don't talk.'

'Nikolai Vsevolodovich!' said the captain with a shudder. 'You've had no part in any of it, so it's not against you that I...'

'Surely you wouldn't inform against the cow that gives you milk?'

'Judge for yourself, Nikolai Vsevolodovich, judge for yourself!' And in despair, weeping, the captain began a hasty account of his life over the last four years. It was an idiotic tale of a fool who meddled in other people's affairs, the importance of which he hardly understood until the last moment because of his drunkenness and debauchery. He told how, while still in Petersburg, 'he'd been drawn in, at first simply out of friendship, like a true student, even though he wasn't really a student', and how, not knowing anything, 'not guilty of anything', he distributed various leaflets on staircases, left dozens of them on doorsteps and bell-handles, stuck them into letter-boxes instead of news-papers, brought them to the theatre, left them in people's hats, slipped them into pockets. Then he started to receive money from them, 'because I was hard up, sir, very hard up!' He distributed 'all sorts of rubbish' around districts in two different provinces.

'Oh, Nikolai Vsevolodovich,' he cried, 'what troubled me most was that it went against all civil laws and especially the laws of the fatherland! All of a sudden they printed that peasants should take up their pitchforks and march, bearing in mind that he who sallied forth poor in the morning might return home rich in the evening. Just think, sir! It made me shudder, but I kept distributing the stuff. Or else, suddenly five or six lines addressed to all Russia, without rhyme or reason: "Close down your churches at once, abolish God, dispense with marriage, do away with inheritance rights, take up your knives", and that's that, the devil only knows what else. With that scrap of paper, with its five lines, I was almost caught; the officers in the regiment gave me a beating, and then, God bless them, they let me go. Last year I was almost arrested again for passing off counterfeit fifty-rouble notes made in France on Korovaev; but, thank God, Korovaev was drunk and drowned in a pond just in time, and they didn't ever convict me. Here at Virginsky's house I proclaimed the freedom of a socialist wife. In June again I was distributing leaflets in a certain district. They say I'll have to do it again... Peter Stepanovich suddenly declares that I have to obey them; he's been threatening me for some time. You saw how he treated me that Sunday! Nikolai Vsevolodovich, I'm a slave, a worm, not God; that's what distinguishes me from Derzhavin.* I'm hard up, sir, very hard up!'

Nikolai Vsevolodovich listened to all this with interest.

'Much of what you say I didn't know,' he replied, 'of course, anything could've happened to you... Listen,' he said after a moment's thought, 'Tell them, if you like, well, you know who, that Liputin was lying and you were only trying to scare me by planning to inform, assuming that I was compromised too, and that you might've been able to get more money out of me that way. Do you understand?'

'Nikolai Vsevolodovich, my dear friend, do you really think I'm in such great danger? I've been waiting to ask you that question.'

Nikolai Vsevolodovich laughed.

'They wouldn't let you go to Petersburg, of course, even

if I gave you money for the trip... but now it's time I saw Marya Timofeevna,' he said and got up from his chair.

'Nikolai Vsevolodovich, what about Marya Timofeevna?'

'Like I told you.'

'Is it really true?'

'You still don't believe me?'

'Would you really cast me aside like an old, worn-out boot?'

'I'll see,' said Nikolai Vsevolodovich with a laugh. 'Well, let me go through.'

'If you wish, sir, I'll go and stand on the steps... so I don't overhear anything accidentally... the rooms are so tiny.'

'Fine; go and stand on the steps. Take my umbrella.'

'Your umbrella... do I deserve it, sir?' the captain asked in an ingratiating way.

'Everyone deserves an umbrella.'

'In one little phrase you've defined the minimum of human rights...'

But by now he was muttering automatically; he was too crushed by the news and completely at a loss. Moreover, almost as soon as he went out on to the steps and put up the umbrella, the usual reassuring thought that he was being deceived and lied to entered his frivolous, scheming head, and, if that was so, then he had nothing to fear since they were so afraid of him.

'If they're lying and deceiving me, what's the real point of it?' he wondered, and the thought gnawed away at him. The proclamation of the marriage seemed ridiculous to him: 'It's true this miracle-worker can make anything happen; he lives to harm other people. Well, and what if he's afraid himself since last Sunday's affront, more afraid than ever before? Now he's come to say that he'll announce it himself, because he's afraid I'll do it first. Hey, don't blow it, Lebyadkin! Why come at night, like a sneak, if he plans to make it public? And if he's afraid, it means he's afraid right now, this very minute, and has been for the last few days... Hey, don't mess it up, Lebyadkin!...

'He's using Peter Stepanovich to frighten me. Oh, this is scary, very scary; yes, it really is scary! Whatever possessed

me to blurt it all out to Liputin? The devil knows what
these devils are up to, I can't work it out. They're getting
busy again, just as they were five years ago. Honestly, who
could I have denounced them to? "Did I write anyone a
stupid letter?" Hmmm. Maybe I could write as if I was just
being stupid? Is he giving me advice? "That's why you're
going to Petersburg." The scoundrel—I've only dreamed
about it, while he's already planned it all! It's like he's
urging me to go. There's one of two things going on here:
either he's afraid himself again because he's been playing
tricks, or... or he's not afraid of anything and is merely
urging me to inform on all of them! Oh, Lebyadkin, it's
scary. Oh, don't mess it up!...'

He was so absorbed in thought he forgot to eavesdrop.
However, it was hard to listen at the door; it was solid,
made of one thick piece of wood, and they were speaking
softly; only muffled sounds could be heard. The captain
actually spat in disgust and went out again, lost in thought,
to whistle on the steps.

3.

Marya Timofeevna's room was twice the size of the one
occupied by her brother and was furnished in the same rough
style; but the table in front of the sofa was covered with a
pretty, colourful tablecloth; a lighted lamp stood on it; there
was a handsome carpet on the floor; the bed was separated
off by a long green curtain going right across the room; in
addition, there was one large, soft armchair near the table,
in which, however, Marya Timofeevna never sat. In the
corner, as in the previous apartment, there was an icon with
a lighted lamp hanging in front of it; on the table the same
essential articles were laid out: a deck of cards, a small
mirror, a song-book, even a bread roll. Moreover, there were
two small books with coloured illustrations, one excerpts
from a popular travel book adapted for young people, the
other a collection of light, edifying stories, for the most part
set in the age of chivalry, intended as a Christmas present
or for schoolchildren. There was also an album of photographs. Of course Marya Timofeevna was expecting a visitor,

since the captain had warned her; but when Nikolai Vsevolodovich entered, she was asleep, half-reclining on the sofa, her head resting on an embroidered worsted cushion. The guest quietly closed the door behind him, and from where he stood began to examine the sleeping woman.

The captain had been lying when he said she was dressing up. She was wearing the same dark dress she had had on that Sunday at Varvara Petrovna's house. Her hair was arranged in exactly the same way, gathered into a small knot on her nape; her long, thin neck was just as bare. The black shawl Varvara Petrovna had given her lay on the sofa, carefully folded. Just as before she was wearing too much powder and rouge. Nikolai Vsevolodovich hadn't stood there for more than a minute when she suddenly woke up, as if she'd felt his gaze fixed upon her; she opened her eyes and sat up quickly. But something strange must have happened to the visitor: he stayed standing on the same spot near the door; without moving, he continued staring into her face silently and steadily with his penetrating gaze. Perhaps his gaze was too severe; perhaps it expressed aversion, even a malicious pleasure in her fear—perhaps that was only the way it seemed to Marya Timofeevna as she emerged from her dream. But all of a sudden, after almost a minute's wait, a look of absolute terror came over the poor young woman's face; she shuddered, stood up, raised her trembling hands, and suddenly burst into tears, just like a frightened child; a moment longer and she'd have screamed. But the guest regained his composure; in an instant his face changed and he went over to the table with a most pleasant and affectionate smile.

'I'm sorry I frightened you, Marya Timofeevna, by arriving unexpectedly while you were asleep,' he said, extending his hand to her.

The sound of his affectionate words produced their intended effect; her fear vanished, although she continued to regard him apprehensively, obviously making an effort to understand something. Fearfully she extended her own hand. At last a timid smile appeared on her lips.

'Hello, Prince,' she whispered, looking at him strangely.

'You must have been having a bad dream,' he went on, smiling even more pleasantly and affectionately.

'How did you know I was dreaming *about that...*?'

Suddenly she began trembling again and took a step back, holding her hand up as though trying to protect herself, and about to cry once again.

'Calm down; that's enough. What are you afraid of? Don't you recognize me?' Nikolai Vsevolodovich asked, reassuring her, but this time it took much longer; she looked at him in silence with the same agonizing bewilderment, with some distressing thought in her poor head, desperately trying to grasp something. First she lowered her eyes, then suddenly threw him a swift, comprehensive glance. Finally, although she didn't really calm down, she seemed to have arrived at some conclusion.

'Sit down, please, here next to me, so I can get a good look at you later,' she said rather firmly, obviously with some new aim in mind. 'But as for now, don't worry, I won't look at you; I'll look down. And don't you look at me either until I ask you to. Sit down,' she added, even rather impatiently.

Some new feeling was evidently taking increasing possession of her.

Nikolai Vsevolodovich sat down and waited; a long silence followed.

'Hmmm. This is all very strange,' she mumbled suddenly, almost in distaste. 'Of course I was haunted by bad dreams; but why did I dream about you like that?'

'Well, let's leave your dreams alone for now,' he said impatiently, turning to look at her in spite of the prohibition, and for a moment that same expression may have come back into his eyes. He noticed she wanted to look at him several times, very much so, but she stubbornly restrained herself and kept looking down.

'Listen, Prince,' she said, suddenly raising her voice. 'Listen, Prince...'

'Why have you turned away? Why don't you look at me? What's this comedy all about?' he cried, unable to control himself.

But it was as if she didn't hear him at all.

'Listen, Prince,' she repeated a third time in a firm voice, with an unpleasant, troubled expression on her face. 'When you told me the other day in the carriage that our marriage would be announced, I was afraid because our secret would be out. Now I'm not sure any more; I've thought about it and I can see I'm not good enough. I'd manage dressing up, and might even be able to receive guests: it's no trouble inviting people in for a cup of tea, especially if you have servants. All the same, what will people say? That day, last Sunday, I noticed a great many things in your house. That pretty young lady was looking at me all the time, especially when you came in. It was you who came in then, wasn't it? Her mother is just a silly old society lady. My Lebyadkin also distinguished himself; I kept staring at the ceiling so I wouldn't laugh, they have a beautifully decorated ceiling there. *His* mother should really have been a Mother Superior; I'm afraid of her, even though she gave me the black shawl. All those people must have seen an unexpected side of me then. I wasn't angry, but I sat there thinking: what relation am I to them? Of course, only spiritual qualities are demanded of a countess—because she has so many servants to perform domestic tasks—and some social coquetry as well to be able to receive foreign visitors. Nevertheless, that Sunday they looked at me with despair. Dasha alone was an angel. I'm terribly afraid they might upset *him* by some careless remark about me.'

'Don't be afraid and don't worry,' Nikolai Vsevolodovich said, making a wry face.

'However, it doesn't matter to me if he's a little ashamed of me, because there's always more pity than shame, depending on the person, of course. He knows, after all, I should pity them more than they should pity me.'

'It seems you were really offended by them, Marya Timofeevna.'

'Who, me? Oh, no,' she said with a good-natured laugh. 'Not at all. I looked around at you all: you were all so angry and quarrelling with each other; you get together, but don't know how to have a good laugh. So much wealth, but so little mirth—I find it all so depressing. But I don't feel sorry for anyone now, except for myself.'

'I've heard you had a hard time with your brother when I wasn't there.'

'Who told you that? Nonsense; it's much worse now. Now I'm having bad dreams. I started having bad dreams because you came. I'd like to know why you've come. Tell me, please.'

'Don't you want to go back to the convent?'

'Oh, I just knew they'd suggest I go back to the convent! That monastery of yours is nothing special, you know! Why should I go back? What would I go back there with now? I'm completely alone! It's late for me to start a third life.'

'You're very angry about something. Could it be you're afraid I don't love you any more?'

'I'm not worried about you at all. I'm afraid I might fall out of love with someone.'

She laughed scornfully.

'I must have done *him* some great wrong,' she added suddenly, as if to herself. 'But I don't know what it is; that's always been my trouble. Always, always, these last five years, day and night I was afraid I had done him some wrong. I've prayed and prayed, and think constantly about the great wrong I've done him. Now it turns out it was true.'

'What turns out?'

'I'm only afraid there might be something on *his* side,' she went on, not answering the question, not even hearing it. 'And then again, he couldn't get along with such awful people. The countess would be glad to devour me, even though she let me ride in her carriage. Everyone's involved in a conspiracy—perhaps he is, too. Has he really betrayed me?' (Her chin and lips trembled.) 'You listen to me: have you ever read about Grishka Otrepiev* who was damned in seven cathedrals?'

Nikolai Vsevolodovich remained silent.

'Well, now I'll turn around and look at you,' she said, as if deciding suddenly. 'You turn around and look at me, too, but carefully. I want to make sure for the last time.'

'I've been looking at you for a while.'

'Hmmm,' Marya Timofeevna said, examining him closely. 'You've put on some weight...'

She was going to say more, but all of a sudden, for the third time, the earlier terror momentarily distorted her features; she took another step backwards, raising her arm to protect herself.

'What's wrong with you?' Nikolai Vsevolodovich cried, almost in a rage.

But her terror lasted only a moment; her face twisted into a strange, suspicious, unpleasant grin.

'I would ask you, Prince,' she said suddenly in a firm, insistent voice, 'to get up and come in.'

'*Come in*? Come in where?'

'For five years I've been imagining how *he* would come in. Now get up and go out of the door into the other room. I'll sit here, as if expecting nothing. I'll pick up a book. And all of a sudden you'll come in, after five years of travelling. I want to see what it'll be like.'

Nikolai Vsevolodovich ground his teeth and muttered something unintelligible.

'Enough!' he said, slapping his hand on the table. 'I want you to listen to me, Marya Timofeevna. Do me a favour, focus your entire attention, if you can. After all, you're not completely crazy!' he blurted out in impatience. 'Tomorrow I plan to announce our marriage publicly. You'll never get to live in a palace, rest assured. Would you like to spend the rest of your life with me, living far away from here? There's a place in the mountains in Switzerland... Don't worry, I'll never leave you and won't put you in a madhouse. We'll have enough money to live, without asking anyone's help. You'll have a servant; you won't have to work. Everything you desire that's possible you shall have. You'll say your prayers, go where you like, do what you wish. I won't touch you. I shan't go away anywhere for the rest of my life either. If you want, I won't even speak to you for the rest of my life; or, if you like, every evening you can tell me stories as you did in Petersburg in those places you lived. I'll read books to you, if you like. But only if you agree to spend your whole life in one place, and it's a grim place. Do you want to? Have you decided? You won't regret it, will you, or torment me with tears and curses?'

She listened to him with extraordinary interest and sat thinking in silence for a long time.

'It all seems so incredible to me,' she said at last ironically and with distaste. 'So I might spend forty years in those mountains.' She gave a laugh.

'So, we'll spend forty years there,' Nikolai Vsevolodovich said, frowning heavily.

'Hmmm. I won't go there for anything.'

'Not even with me?'

'Who are you that I should go there with you? Forty years sitting with him on top of a mountain—what a life! How very patient people have all become nowadays! No, a falcon can't have turned into an owl. My prince isn't like that!' she said proudly and triumphantly lifting her head.

An idea seemed to dawn upon him.

'Why do you call me "Prince" and... whom do you take me for?' he asked her hurriedly.

'What? Aren't you a prince?'

'I've never been one.'

'So then, you yourself admit, right to my face, you're not a prince!'

'I tell you I never was.'

'Good Lord!' she cried, clasping her hands. 'I expected anything from *his* enemies, but such insolence—never! Is he still alive?' she cried in a frenzy, turning on Nikolai Vsevolodovich. 'Have you killed him or not? Confess!'

'Whom do you take me for?' he cried, jumping up from his place, his face distorted. But it was no longer easy to frighten her. She said triumphantly:

'Who knows who you are and where you've come from! Only my heart, during these last five years, only my heart's been aware of the whole intrigue! I've been sitting here wondering, what kind of blind owl is this who's calling on me? No, my dear, you're a bad actor, even worse than Lebyadkin. Give my regards to the countess and tell her to send a better man than you. Tell me, did she hire you? Has she let you work in her kitchen out of charity? I can see right through your whole deception. I understand all of you, to the last man!'

He took firm hold of her arm just above the elbow; she laughed in his face:

'You look like him, very much like him; perhaps you're related to him—what a cunning lot! But my fellow is a bright falcon and a prince, while you're an owl and a shopkeeper! My man will bow down to God if he wants to and if he doesn't want to he won't, while Shatushka (he's my dear, sweet, darling!), slapped you across the face, so my Lebyadkin told me. And what were you so afraid of when you came in? Who was it who made you so scared then? When I saw your nasty face after I fell and you picked me up—it was as if a worm had crawled into my heart: it's not *he*, I thought, not *he*! My falcon would never have been ashamed of me in front of any society lady! Good Lord! The only thing that's kept me happy the last five years was the thought that my falcon was alive somewhere, beyond the mountains, soaring, gazing at the sun... Tell me, you impostor, how much are you getting for it? Was it for a great deal of money you agreed to do it? I wouldn't have given you half a kopeck. Ha, ha, ha!, Ha, ha, ha!'

'Oh, what an idiot!' Nikolai Vsevolodovich said, gnashing his teeth, still keeping firm hold of her arm.

'Go away, you impostor!' she cried imperiously. 'I'm my prince's wife. I'm not afraid of your knife!'

'My knife?'

'Yes, your knife! You have a knife in your pocket. You thought I was asleep, but I saw it: when you came in just now you took out your knife!'

'What are you talking about, you wretched creature? What kind of dreams are you having?' he cried and pushed her away from him with such force that she banged her shoulder and head against the sofa. He rushed out of the room, but she ran after him, limping and hopping, trying to catch up with him, and from the staircase, although the frightened Lebyadkin was restraining her with all his might, she managed to shout after him into the darkness, shrieking and laughing:

'Grishka O-tre-piev—a-na-the-ma on you!'

4.

'A knife, a knife!' he repeated in unquenchable rage, striding through mud and puddles, making no attempt to find the road. It's true that now and then he felt terribly like laughing, loudly and insanely; but for some reason he controlled himself and restrained his laughter. He came to his senses only on the bridge, on the very spot where he'd met Fedka earlier; the same Fedka was still there waiting for him now, and, upon seeing him, doffed his cap, grinned cheerfully, and began chattering boldly and merrily about something or other. At first Nikolai Vsevolodovich went on without stopping, for some time not even listening to this tramp who'd latched on to him again. He was suddenly struck by the thought that he'd forgotten all about him, forgotten him precisely as he was muttering under his breath, 'A knife, a knife.' He seized the tramp by the collar and, with all the force of his pent-up rage, hurled him against the bridge. For a moment Fedka thought of fighting back, but realizing almost at once that compared to his adversary, who had moreover caught him unawares, he was no more than a wisp of straw, he calmed down and fell silent, without resisting in the least. On his knees, pinned to the ground, his elbows twisted behind his back, the sly tramp serenely waited to see what would happen next, apparently without the least sense of danger.

He was right. With his left hand Nikolai Vsevolodovich had already removed his thick scarf to bind the prisoner's hands; but for some reason he suddenly released him and pushed him away. Fedka jumped to his feet at once, turned around, and a short, broad cobbler's knife, which seemed to appear from nowhere, gleamed in his hand.

'Away with that knife, put it away, put it away at once!' Nikolai Vsevolodovich commanded him with an impatient gesture, and the knife disappeared as quickly as it had appeared.

Nikolai Vsevolodovich resumed his way in silence, without turning round; but the persistent scoundrel kept after him, though, it's true, no longer chattering; he'd even dropped back one whole pace to maintain a respectful distance. They both crossed the bridge over to the other bank, this time turning to the left, and into a long, deserted lane that was a shorter route to the centre of town than the previous way along Bogoyavlenskaya Street.

'Is it true what they say, that you robbed a church somewhere in this district just the other day?' Nikolai Vsevolodovich asked suddenly.

'Well, I mean like, I first dropped in to say a few prayers, sir,' the tramp replied gravely and politely, as if nothing untoward had happened; his manner was not so much grave as almost dignified. There wasn't the least trace of his earlier 'friendly' familiarity. Here obviously was a serious and businesslike man, one who'd been gratuitously insulted, but who was capable of overlooking such insults.

'And when the good Lord led me there', he continued, 'I thought to myself, hey, what heavenly abundance! It all came about because of my helpless poverty, since the way we live, there's no way to get along without a little help from somewhere. And so, as God's my witness, sir, it was a total loss for me. The Lord punished me for my sins: for the censer, the pyx, and the deacon's strap I got all of twelve roubles. And for the chin-setting of St Nikolai, pure silver though it was, I got almost nothing: they said it was a fake.'

'Did you slit the watchman's throat?'

'Well, the watchman and I worked together to clean the place out, but later, the next morning, by the river, we had a little argument about who was going to carry the sack. There I did sin and lightened his load.'

'Go on killing, go on stealing.'

'That's just like what Peter Stepanovich advised me, the same thing, word for word, because he's ever so stingy and hard-hearted when it comes to helping out his fellow man, sir. Besides, he don't give a damn about the heavenly Creator what made us all out of earthly clay; he says it was nature alone what made us all, even down to the last of the beasts; and then, he don't understand that, our life being what it is, we can't possibly get along without some charitable assistance, sir. You try to tell him and he looks like a sheep staring at the water; you can't help but wonder. Now, believe me, sir, that Captain Lebyadkin, sir, where you just paid a visit, sir, when he was still living at Filippov's house, sir, once when the door stood wide open the whole night, sir, he lay asleep, dead drunk, with money spilling out of his pockets all over the floor. I got to see it with my own eyes, because, the way we live, we can't get along without some assistance, sir...'

'With your own eyes? Did you go there at night, or what?'

'Maybe I did, but nobody knows about it.'

'Why didn't you slit his throat?'

'I made some calculations, sir, and steadied myself. Once I made sure I could always steal a hundred and fifty roubles, why should I do a thing like that, when I could wait a bit, and pick up fifteen hundred roubles? Because Captain Lebyadkin (I heard it with my own ears, sir) has always relied on you, sir, when he was drunk, and there's not one drinking place around here, not even the lowest tavern, sir, where he ain't boasted about it when he was in that state, sir. So, having heard it said by lots of different people, I too decided to put all my hopes in your excellency. I'm speaking to you, sir, like you was my own father, my own brother, because Peter Stepanovich will never find out about it from me, nor will any other living soul. So, your excellency, will you let me have three roubles or not, sir? You might put my mind at ease, sir, so I'd know the real truth, like, because we can't get along without some assistance, sir.'

Nikolai Vsevolodovich laughed out loud; taking out his wallet, in which there were about fifty roubles in small bills, he tossed him one bill from a bundle, then another, a third, and a fourth. Fedka tried to catch them in mid-air, flinging himself forward, but the bills fluttered down into the mud. Fedka grabbed them and shouted, 'Oy, oy!' Finally Nikolai Vsevolodovich threw the whole bundle at him and walked on down the alley still laughing, this time alone. The tramp remained behind to hunt for the money, crawling around on his knees in the mud to retrieve the bills that were blowing away in the wind or sinking into puddles, and for an hour afterwards one could still hear through the darkness his fitful cries of, 'Oy, oy!'

CHAPTER 3

The duel

I.

THE NEXT DAY, at two o'clock in the afternoon, the duel took place as arranged. Artemy Pavlovich Gaganov's insistence on fighting no matter what helped facilitate a speedy resolution. He didn't understand his adversary's behaviour and was furious. He'd been insulting him for a full month with impunity, and still couldn't force him to lose patience. The challenge had to come from Nikolai Vsevolodovich himself, since Gaganov had no real pretext for issuing one. For some reason he was ashamed to admit to his own secret motivation, that is, simply his morbid hatred for Stavrogin because of the insult to his family some four years before. He himself considered such a pretext impossible, especially in view of the humble apologies offered twice by Nikolai Vsevolodovich. He'd concluded that Stavrogin was a shameless coward; nor could he understand how Stavrogin had tolerated that slap from Shatov. So at last he decided to send him an extraordinarily rude letter, one that finally compelled Nikolai Vsevolodovich to propose a meeting. Having dispatched this letter the day before, he was awaiting the challenge in feverish impatience, morbidly calculating the odds, one minute in hope, the next in despair. In any event, he'd secured himself a second the night before, to wit, Maurice Nikolaevich Drozdov, his friend, former schoolmate, and a man he respected highly. Thus, at nine o'clock the next morning when Kirillov arrived with his message, he found the ground already well prepared. All Nikolai Vsevolodovich's apologies and impossible concessions were rejected outright, from the very first word, with considerable passion. Maurice Nikolaevich, who'd been apprised of the course of events only the day before, nearly gaped in astonishment at such incredible proposals, and wanted to insist on a reconciliation; but observing that Artemy Pavlovich had guessed his intention and was almost trembling in his chair, he held his tongue and didn't utter a word. If it hadn't been for his word of honour to his friend, he'd have left at once; he stayed only in the hope of assisting in some way at the outcome of the affair. Kirillov transmitted the challenge; all the conditions of the encounter proposed by Stavrogin were immediately accepted, without any objection. There was only one addition, a very harsh one at that, namely: if nothing definitive were to come of their first shots, they would fire again; if the second round also ended inconclusively, there was to be a third. Kirillov frowned, negotiated a little about the third round, but having no success, agreed, saying however that 'a third round was possible, but a fourth was out of the question.' This was conceded. So, at two o'clock in the afternoon the meeting took place at Brykov, that is, in a little grove on the outskirts of town between Skvoreshniki on one side and the Shpigulin factory on the other. The previous day's rain had stopped, but it was damp, wet, and windy. Dark, low, ragged clouds sped across the cold sky; the tops of the trees rustled with a deep roar and their roots creaked; it was a very gloomy morning.

Gaganov and Maurice Nikolaevich arrived in a fashionable open carriage with a pair of horses driven by Artemy Pavlovich; they had a servant with them. Nikolai Vsevolo-dovich and Kirillov arrived almost simultaneously, not in a carriage, but on horseback, also accompanied by a servant. Kirillov, who'd never been on a horse before, sat straight upright in the saddle; in his right hand he held a heavy box with the pistols which he refused to entrust to the servant; with his left hand, in his inexperience, he constantly twisted and tugged at the reins, so that the horse kept tossing its head and showing an inclination to rear, which, however, didn't seem to frighten the rider in the least. Gaganov, who was a very suspicious fellow and quick to take offence, considered their arrival on horseback a fresh insult, in the sense that his enemies must have been counting too heavily on success if they considered a carriage unnecessary for transporting a wounded man back home. He emerged from his open carriage yellow with rage and felt his hands trembling, a fact which he communicated to Maurice Niko-laevich. Nor did he return Nikolai Vsevolodovich's bow, but turned away from him. The seconds cast lots: it fell to Kirillov's pistols. The barriers were measured, the combatants told to take up their positions, and the carriage, horses, and servants moved some three hundred paces away. The weapons were loaded and handed to the combatants.

It's a pity I have to tell the story so quickly and have no time to describe it all in detail; but it can't be done without at least a few asides. Maurice Nikolaevich was melancholy and preoccupied. Kirillov, on the other hand, was completely calm and unconcerned, very precise about the details of the duties he'd undertaken, but without the least fussiness and almost without interest in the fateful and imminent resolution of the affair. Nikolai Vsevolodovich was paler than usual and dressed rather lightly in an overcoat and white fur hat. He appeared very tired and frowned from time to time; he didn't find it in the least necessary to conceal his bad mood. But Artemy Pavlovich was the most remarkable of all at that moment, so it's impossible not to say a few words about him in particular.

2.

Up to now I haven't had the opportunity to describe his appearance. He was a tall man, fair, well fed, as the common folk say, almost fat, with thinning fair hair, about thirty years old, and perhaps even handsome. He'd retired with the rank of lieutenant; had he served long enough to become a general, he'd have been more impressive in that rank, and might even have made a good fighting general.

To characterize him one must mention the fact that the main reason for his retirement was the thought of the family disgrace which haunted him so long and painfully after the insult inflicted on his father at the club some four years ago by Nikolai Vsevolodovich. He felt it would be dishonourable to remain in the service and was convinced that he was tarnishing both his regiment and his comrades, even though not one of them knew anything about the incident. It's true he'd wanted to leave the service on one earlier occasion; but that was a long time ago, well before the insult, for an entirely different reason; he'd been hesitating up to now. As strange as it seems, the fundamental reason, or, rather, his original motive for retiring was the proclamation of the 19th of February emancipating the serfs. Artemy Pavlovich, the richest landowner in our province, who lost very little after the proclamation, and who was moreover capable of appreciating the humaneness of the measure and almost of understanding the economic advantages of the reform, suddenly felt personally offended by the publication of this proclamation. It was something unconscious, just a kind of a feeling, but the less he could account for it the stronger it grew. Until the death of his father he didn't take any decisive action; but he became known to several important figures in Petersburg for his 'noble' cast of mind, and he strenuously maintained contact with these people. He was a man who had retreated into himself, and very secretive. He had a further characteristic: he belonged to that strange but still intact group of Russian nobles who value too highly the length and purity of their lineage and maintain too serious an interest in the subject. At the same time, he couldn't bear Russian history, and considered all Russian customs as nothing more than swinishness. Even in his childhood, in a special military school for the sons of wealthy nobles where he had the honour both to commence and conclude his education, certain poetic views took root in him: he took a fancy to castles, medieval life in general, all the operatic side of it, and chivalry; he nearly wept from shame when he learned that the tsar had the right to inflict corporal punishment on Russian nobles during the Muscovite period, and he blushed at the comparison. This limited, extremely severe man, who understood military service and carried out his duties remarkably well, was a dreamer at heart. It was said he might be a good speaker at meetings and that he possessed a gift for words; but throughout his thirty-three years he'd never once opened his mouth to speak. Even in that important Petersburg circle to which he'd recently returned, he behaved with utmost arrogance. His meeting in Petersburg with Nikolai Vsevolodovich, who was just back from abroad, almost drove him out of his mind. At the present moment, standing at the barrier, he felt terribly distressed. He kept thinking the affair wouldn't come off; the least delay threw him into tremors. A pained impression registered on his face when Kirillov, instead of giving the signal to begin the duel, suddenly began talking, only for form's sake, it's true, as he declared for all to hear:

'I'm doing this for form's sake; now that the pistols are in your hands and I must give you the signal, I ask you for the last time, will you be reconciled? It's the duty of a second.'

As if on purpose Maurice Nikolaevich, who'd been silent up to this point, but suffering on account of his own compliance and indulgence, suddenly seized upon Kirillov's idea and also spoke up:

'I agree entirely with what Mr Kirillov said... the idea that one can't be reconciled standing at the barrier is a prejudice that suits only the French... And I must say, I really don't understand the nature of the insult; I've been wanting to say so for some time now... because all sorts of apologies have already been offered, haven't they?'

He blushed deeply. He rarely spoke so long and with such emotion.

'Once again I repeat my willingness to offer every possible apology,' Nikolai Vsevolodovich said extremely quickly.

'How is this possible?' cried Gaganov furiously, turning to Maurice Nikolaevich and stamping his foot in a rage. 'Explain to that man, if you're my second and not my opponent, Maurice Nikolaevich' (he jabbed his pistol at Nikolai Vsevolodovich) 'that such concessions merely serve to aggravate the insult! He finds it impossible to be insulted by me in return!... He doesn't consider it an insult to walk away from me at the barrier! What would he take me for afterwards, in your opinion... and you're my second, no less! You're simply irritating me so I'll miss.' He stamped his foot again; he was foaming at the mouth.

'Negotiations are over. Listen for the command!' Kirillov shouted with all his might. 'One! Two! Three!'

At the sound of 'three' the opponents started towards each other. Gaganov raised his pistol immediately and fired after his fifth or sixth step. He stopped for a second and, making sure he had missed, advanced quickly to the barrier. Nikolai Vsevolodovich advanced as well, raised his pistol, but much too high, and fired almost without aiming. Then he took out a handkerchief and wound it around the little finger of his right hand. Only then did it appear that Artemy Pavlovich hadn't entirely missed; his bullet had grazed the flesh of Stavrogin's finger, without hitting the bone; it was only a slight scratch. Kirillov announced that the duel would continue if the opponents were still not satisfied.

'I assert', cried Gaganov hoarsely (his throat had dried up), turning to Maurice Nikolaevich again, 'that this man' (he pointed at Stavrogin again) 'intentionally fired into the air... deliberately... That's another insult! He wants to make a duel impossible!'

'I have the right to fire as I wish, as long as I follow the rules,' Nikolai Vsevolodovich declared firmly.

'No, he doesn't! Tell him, tell him!' Gaganov shouted.

'I agree completely with Nikolai Vsevolodovich's point,' Kirillov announced.

'Why is he sparing me?' Gaganov raged, without listening. 'I despise his mercy... I spit on... I...'

'I give you my word I never meant to insult you,' Nikolai Vsevolodovich repeated impatiently. 'I fired into the air because I don't want to kill anyone else, neither you nor anyone; it has nothing to do with you. It's true, I don't consider myself insulted, and I'm sorry that angers you. But I won't allow anyone to interfere with my rights.'

'If he's so afraid of shedding blood, ask him why he challenged me,' roared Gaganov, still addressing Maurice Nikolaevich.

'How could he refrain from challenging you?' Kirillov interposed. 'You didn't want to listen; how could he be rid of you?'

'I have only one observation,' said Maurice Nikolaevich, making a painful effort to consider the matter. 'If an opponent declares in advance that he intends to fire into the air, then the duel cannot really continue... for delicate and... obvious reasons...'

'By no means have I declared that I'll fire into the air every time!' cried Stavrogin, now losing all patience. 'You have no idea what I have in mind and how I'll fire next time... I'm not obstructing the duel.'

'If that's so, let's continue,' Maurice Nikolaevich said to Gaganov.

'Gentlemen, to your positions!' Kirillov commanded.

Once more they approached the barriers; Gaganov missed again and Stavrogin fired into the air. One could argue about those shots fired into the air: Nikolai Vsevolodovich could have claimed he aimed properly, if he hadn't himself confessed to missing on purpose. He didn't aim up at the sky or into the trees; he seemed to point at his opponent, but the pistol was aimed several feet above his hat. The second shot was even lower, more persuasive; but it was now quite impossible to convince Gaganov.

'Again!' he cried, grinding his teeth. 'Never mind! I challenged him and I'll exercise my rights. I want to fire a third time... no matter what.'

'You have the right to do so,' Kirillov snapped back. Maurice Nikolaevich didn't say a thing. They parted for the third time; the command was given. This time Gaganov went right up to the barrier and there, only twelve paces away, started to take aim. His hands were trembling too much for a reliable shot. Stavrogin stood there, his pistol hanging down, awaiting the shot without moving.

'You're taking too long, too long to aim!' Kirillov cried impetuously. 'Fire! Fi-i-re!' The shot resounded; this time the white fur hat went flying off Nikolai Vsevolodovich's head. The shot was rather close; the crown of the hat was pierced very low above the head; a quarter of an inch lower and everything would have been all over. Kirillov picked up the hat and handed it to Nikolai Vsevolodovich.

'Fire! Don't detain your opponent!' cried Maurice Nikolaevich in a state of extreme agitation, seeing that Stavrogin, examining the hat with Kirillov, seemed to have forgotten about his turn. Stavrogin gave a start, looked at Gaganov, turned away, and this time, without the least tact, fired off to the side, into a grove of trees. The duel was over.

Gaganov stood there crushed. Maurice Nikolaevich went up to him and started saying something, but he seemed not to understand. As he left Kirillov doffed his hat and nodded to Maurice Nikolaevich; but Stavrogin had forgotten his former civility; after his shot into the grove, he didn't even turn towards the barrier; he handed his pistol to Kirillov and quickly headed for the horses. There was a look of malice on his face, and he remained silent. Kirillov was also silent. They mounted their horses and galloped away.

3.

'Why don't you say something?' he cried impatiently to Kirillov when they were not far from home.

'What do you want?' the other replied, almost slipping off his horse as it reared up.

Stavrogin restrained himself.

'I didn't want to insult that... idiot, but now I've done it again,' he said softly.

'Yes, you've insulted him again,' Kirillov snapped back, 'besides, he's not an idiot.'

'Still, I did everything I could.'

'No.'

'What should I have done?'

'You shouldn't have challenged him.'

'And accept another slap across the face?'

'Yes, accept another slap.'

'I don't understand a thing!' Stavrogin said angrily. 'Why does everyone expect more from me than from other people? Why should I have to put up with things that no one else does, bear burdens that no one else can bear?'

'I thought you were looking for a burden to bear.'

'Looking for a burden?'

'Yes.'

'Have you... observed that?'

'Yes.'

'Is it that noticeable?'

'Yes.'

They were silent for a minute. Stavrogin looked very troubled, almost stunned.

'I didn't fire because I didn't want to kill him; there was nothing more to it than that, I can assure you,' he said hurriedly and uneasily, as if justifying himself.

'You shouldn't have insulted him.'

'What should I have done?'

'You should have killed him.'

'Are you sorry I didn't kill him?'

'I'm not sorry about anything. I thought you really wanted to kill him. You don't know what you're looking for.'

'I'm looking for a burden to bear,' Stavrogin said, laughing.

'If you didn't want any bloodshed, why did you give him a chance to kill you?'

'If I hadn't challenged him, he'd have killed me anyway, duel or no duel.'

'That's none of your business. Perhaps he wouldn't have killed you.'

'And merely given me a beating?'

'That's none of your business. Bear your burden. Or else there's no merit in it.'

'I spit on your merit; I'm not looking for it from anyone!'

'I thought you were,' Kirillov concluded with terrible coldness.

They rode into the courtyard of the house.

'Do you want to come in?' Nikolai Vsevolodovich enquired.

'No, I'm going home, goodbye.' He dismounted and took the box under his arm.

'At least you're not angry with me, are you?' Stavrogin said, extending his hand.

'Not at all!' Kirillov replied, turning to shake hands. 'If my burden is light, it's because of my nature; perhaps your burden is heavier because of your nature. There's nothing to be very ashamed of, only a little ashamed.'

'I know I'm a worthless character, but I don't pretend to be a strong one.'

'Don't then; you aren't a strong person. Come and drink tea with me sometime.'

Nikolai Vsevolodovich went into the house very disturbed.

4.

He learned at once from Aleksei Yegorovich that Varvara Petrovna had been very pleased by Nikolai Vsevolodovich's decision to go out for a ride—his first after eight days of confinement. She'd ordered her own carriage and gone out on her own, 'according to her old custom, to breathe the fresh air, since in the last eight days she'd forgotten what it meant to breathe fresh air.'

'Did she go alone or with Darya Pavlovna?' Nikolai Vsevolodovich interrupted the old man with a quick question and frowned appreciably when he heard that Darya Pavlovna 'had refused to accompany her for reasons of ill health and and was now resting in her room'.

'Listen, old fellow,' he said, as if suddenly making up his mind, 'watch her all day today and if you observe that she wants to see me, stop her immediately and tell her I can't receive her for several days at least... I'll ask for her myself... and when the time is right, I'll let her know—do you hear?'

'I'll tell her, sir,' Aleksei Yegorovich replied with distress in his voice, dropping his eyes.

'But don't say anything until you observe that she really wants to see me.'

'Don't worry, sir, there'll be no mistake. All visits up to now have been arranged by me; you've always turned to me for assistance.'

'I know. Still, not before she wants to see me. Bring me some tea, as soon as you can.'

Just as the old man left, almost at the very same instant, the door opened again and there on the threshold stood Darya Pavlovna. Her expression was calm, but her face was pale.

'Where have you come from?' cried Stavrogin.

'I was standing here waiting until he left so I could come in. I overheard the order you gave him and hid around the corner on the right as he was leaving so he wouldn't see me.'

'For some time now I've been thinking of breaking off with you, Dasha... for a little while... for the present time.

I couldn't see you last night in spite of your note. I wanted to write to you myself, but I can't write,' he added in annoyance, almost in disgust.

'I thought we should break it off, too. Varvara Petrovna is very suspicious about our relations.'

'Well, let her be.'

'There's no need to worry her. So, now, until the very end?'

'You're still expecting the end, are you?'

'Yes, I'm sure.'

'In this world nothing ever ends.'

'This will end. Then call me and I'll come. Now, good-bye.'

'How will it end?' asked Nikolai Vsevolodovich with a laugh.

'You're not wounded and... you didn't lose any blood?' she said without answering his question about the end.

'It was stupid; I didn't kill anyone, don't worry. Anyway, you'll hear about it today from everyone. I'm not feeling too well.'

'I'll leave. Will there be an announcement of your marriage today?' she asked irresolutely.

'Not today; not tomorrow; the day after tomorrow, I don't know, we may all be dead, and so much the better. Leave me, please, leave me alone.'

'You won't ruin that other... that mad woman?'

'I won't ruin any mad women, neither one nor the other, but apparently I'll ruin a sane woman: I'm so vile and contemptible, Dasha, it seems that I really will call you "at the very end", as you say, and you, for all your sanity, will come. Why would you ruin yourself?'

'I know in the very end I'll be alone with you and... I'm waiting for that.'

'And what if at the very end I don't call you, but run away from you?'

'That can't be; you'll call me.'

'That shows great contempt for me.'

'You know it isn't just contempt.'

'Still there's some contempt?'

'I didn't express myself properly. As God is my witness, I've always wished you'd never have any need for me.'

'One good turn deserves another. I too never wished to ruin you.'

'You can never, in any way, be the cause of my ruin, and you know that better than anyone,' Darya Pavlovna said quickly and decisively. 'If I don't come to you, I'll join the sisters of mercy, become a nurse, and take care of people, or else become a book-pedlar and sell Gospels. That's what I've decided. I can't be anyone's wife; I can't live in a house like this. It's not what I want... You know everything.'

'No, I could never work out what you wanted; you seem to be interested in me the way some elderly nurses for some reason will take a greater interest in one particular patient relative to the others, or, more like it, the way some God-fearing old ladies who love to attend funerals find certain corpses more attractive than others. Why are you looking at me so strangely?'

'Are you very ill?' she asked with concern, looking at him in a peculiar sort of way. 'My God! And this is the man who hopes to get along without me!'

'Listen, Dasha, I see apparitions all the time now. Yesterday a little devil on the bridge offered to murder Lebyadkin and Marya Timofeevna to resolve the matter of my legal marriage once and for all and cover all traces. He asked me for three roubles in advance, but made it clear that the whole operation would cost no less than fifteen hundred roubles. Calculating devil, wasn't he! An accountant! Ha, ha!'

'But are you really sure it was an apparition?'

'Oh, no, it wasn't an apparition at all! It was merely Fedya the convict, a robber who's escaped from prison. But that's not the point; what do you think I did? I gave him all the money I had in my wallet, and now he's absolutely convinced that I've paid him an advance!'

'You met him at night and he made that proposal to you? Don't you see they've got you completely entangled in their net?'

'Well, let them. You know, I can tell by your eyes you have a question you're eager to ask me,' he added with a cross and irritable smile.

Dasha was frightened.

'I have no question at all and no doubts whatever. Be quiet!' she cried in alarm, as if fending off the question.

'In other words, you're sure I won't go to Fedka's shop?'

'Oh, God!' she cried, clasping her hands, 'why do you torment me this way?'

'Well, forgive my stupid joke; I must be adopting their bad manners. You know, since last night I've really felt like laughing, laughing all the time, a great deal, without stopping, for a long time, a great deal. It's as if I were infected with laughter... Hush! My mother's just arrived; I recognize the sound of her carriage stopping at the steps.'

Dasha seized his hand.

'May God keep you from your demon and... call me, call me very soon!'

'Oh, what sort of demon is it? It's only a disgusting, scrofulous little devil with a head cold, one of the failures. But, Dasha, isn't there something else you don't dare say?'

She looked at him in distress and reproach, then turned towards the door.

'Listen!' he cried after her, with a malicious, crooked smile. 'If... well, there, in a word, *if...* you understand, well, even if I went to his little shop, and then I were to call you afterwards, would you still come to me?'

She went out without turning back and without answering, covering her face with her hands.

'She'll come even after I've been to the shop!' he whispered to himself after thinking a little while, and a look of scornful contempt came into his face. 'A nurse! Hmmm!... But perhaps that's just what I need.'

CHAPTER 4

General expectation

I.

THE IMPRESSION produced in our society by the story of the duel, which quickly went round the town, was particularly noteworthy for the unanimity with which everyone hastened to declare himself unequivocally on the side of Nikolai Vsevolodovich. Many of his former enemies expressly announced that they were now his friends. The principal cause of this unexpected reversal in public opinion lay in a few unusually apt remarks uttered by a particular person who'd heretofore remained silent, but whose few words immediately lent significance to the event, which proved to be of great interest to the vast majority of us. This is how it happened: the day after the incident the entire town had gathered at our marshal of the nobility's house to celebrate his wife's name-day. Yulia Mikhailovna was there too; in fact, she presided there, together with Lizaveta Nikolaevna, who was radiant with beauty and a peculiar happiness that immediately struck many of our ladies as rather suspicious. I must state, by the way, that there was no doubt whatever about her engagement to Maurice Nikolaevich. In reply to a playful question posed by a retired, but still important, general (about whom more later), Lizaveta Nikolaevna openly declared that she was betrothed. And what do you think? Not one of our ladies was willing to believe her engagement. Everyone obstinately persisted in assuming that there'd been a romance, some fateful family secret precipitated in Switzerland, somehow with the willing connivance of Yulia Mikhailovna. It's hard to say why these rumours or fantasies persisted so stubbornly, and why Yulia Mikhailovna was seen to have had a hand in it. As soon as she came in everyone turned a curious, expectant gaze on her. I must note that since the event was still so recent, and, because of certain attendant circumstances, people talked about it that evening with a certain caution, in hushed tones only.

Besides, they still didn't know a thing about the position taken by the authorities. Neither combatant, as far as was known, had yet been disturbed. Everyone knew, for example, that early in the morning Artemy Pavlovich had returned home to Dukhovo without any interference. Meanwhile, of course, everyone was eager for someone else to be the first to speak out and by so doing open the door to the communal impatience. They rested their hopes on the above-mentioned general, and they were not disappointed.

This general was one of the most venerable members of our club; he was not a very wealthy landowner, but had a most original cast of mind. He was an old-fashioned ladies' man, and, by the way, was particularly fond at large gatherings of declaring aloud, with all the authority of a general, precisely what everyone else was whispering about. That was his special role, so to speak, in our society. In addition, he drawled and lisped in an affected way, no doubt having acquired this mannerism from Russians who'd travelled abroad or from those formerly wealthy Russian landowners who'd suffered the greatest losses after the emancipation reform. Stepan Trofimovich had once observed that the more a landowner lost, the more sweetly he lisped and drawled. Moreover, although he drawled and lisped so sweetly, he never noticed it in himself.

The general began speaking as one who knew what he was talking about. Besides being distantly related to Artemy Pavlovich, although on bad terms with him and even involved in a lawsuit against him, he had in addition once fought two duels and after one of them had been reduced to the ranks and exiled to the Caucasus. Someone mentioned Varvara Pavlovna, who had begun to drive out recently after her 'indisposition', not speaking of her precisely but of the magnificent matching of her four greys from the Stavrogin stud. The general suddenly remarked that he'd met the 'young Stavrogin' on horseback that very day... Everyone suddenly fell silent. The general smacked his lips and suddenly announced, fiddling with a gold snuff-box (given him by some important person):

'I deeply regret I wasn't here several years ago... that is, when I was in Karlsbad.... Hmmm. I'm very interested in that young man; I heard all sorts of rumours about him at the time. Hmmm. Tell me, is it true he's insane? Someone said it back then. I heard that a student here had insulted him in the presence of some of his cousins, and that he got away by crawling under the table; yesterday I heard from Stepan Vysotsky that Stavrogin had a duel with that... Gaganov fellow. And solely with the noble aim of offering himself as a target to that angry young man; merely to get shot of him. Hmmm. That sounds like what the Guards used to do in the twenties. Does he see anyone around here?'

The general fell silent, as if expecting an answer. The door to public impatience had been thrown wide open.

'What could be simpler?' cried Yulia Mikhailovna all of a sudden in a loud voice, irritated by the fact that all eyes in the room had suddenly turned to her as if by command. 'Is it really so surprising that Stavrogin fought a duel with Gaganov and didn't respond to that student? He couldn't very well challenge one of his own former serfs to a duel!'

Significant words! It was a clear, simple idea, but one that hadn't occurred to anyone else up to then. Words which had unusual consequences. Everything suggestive of scandal and gossip, everything petty and anecdotal was instantly shoved into the background; a different meaning came to the fore. A new personage appeared about whom everyone had been mistaken, one with almost ideally strict standards of behaviour. Having been mortally insulted by a student, that is, not by a peasant, but by an educated young man, he despises the insult because the offender was his former serf. Society had gossiped, and slandered him; frivolous people had regarded with contempt a man who'd been slapped across the face; but he despises the opinions of society, which had yet to rise to today's advanced standards, while being at the same time ready to make judgements about those standards.

'In the meantime, you and I, Ivan Aleksandrovich, sit here and talk about high standards, sir,' one old member of the club observed to another in a noble burst of self-reproach.

'Yes, sir, Peter Mikhailovich, yes, sir,' the other agreed enthusiastically. 'That's the younger generation for you.'

'It's not the younger generation, Ivan Aleksandrovich,' remarked a third who happened to turn up. 'It's not a question of the younger generation; this fellow is a star, sir, not simply one of the younger generation. That's how to look at it.'

'That's just what we need; we don't have enough people like that.'

The point of all this was that their 'new man', in addition to the fact that he turned out to be an 'indubitable nobleman', was also the richest landowner in the province and, consequently, couldn't help but be an asset and activist. But I've already referred to the attitude of our local landowners.

Some even got very excited:

'Not only did he refuse to challenge the student, he took his hands off him. Take special note of that, your excellency,' one of them pointed out.

'And, sir, they didn't haul him off to one of our new lawcourts either,' added another.

'In spite of the fact, sir, that in our new courts he'd have been awarded fifteen roubles in damages for the *personal* insult to a nobleman, ha, ha, ha!'

'No, I'll tell you a secret about our new courts,' a third cried in frenzy. 'If someone gets caught red-handed stealing or swindling and is convicted, he'd best run home quickly, while he still has time, and murder his own mother. He'll be acquitted instantly of all crimes and our ladies will wave their cambric handkerchiefs at him from the balcony; that's the absolute truth!'

'It's the truth, the absolute truth!'

There followed the inevitable anecdotes. They recalled Nikolai Vsevolodovich's connections with Count K. The count's severe, singular opinions on the latest reforms were well known. His remarkable public activities were also well known, though these had recently diminished somewhat. Now it suddenly became clear to everyone that Nikolai Vsevolodovich was engaged to one of the count's daughters, although there were no grounds whatever for that supposition. As far as some mysterious adventures in Switzerland and Lizaveta Nikolaevna were concerned, even our ladies ceased to mention them. By the way, let's add that by this time the Drozdovs had managed to pay all the obligatory visits they'd neglected at first. Everyone now considered Lizaveta Nikolaevna a most ordinary young woman, merely 'showing off' her weak nerves. Her fainting fit on the day of Nikolai Vsevolodovich's arrival was now explained by her alarm at the student's horrendous behaviour. They even emphasized the prosaic qualities of the very thing they'd previously invested with the most fantastic coloration. They forgot all about the little cripple and were even embarrassed to mention her. 'Even if there'd been a hundred little cripples—we were all young once!' They held up Nikolai Vsevolodovich's respect for his mother, pointed out his various virtues, and spoke admiringly of the education he'd acquired during four years at various German universities. Artemy Pavlovich's action was declared to be absolutely tactless: 'He didn't recognize one of his own kind.' Yulia Mikhailovna was now credited with extraordinary perspicacity.

Thus, when Nikolai Vsevolodovich finally appeared, everyone greeted him with the most innocent gravity; impatient expectation could be detected in every eye fixed upon him. Nikolai Vsevolodovich immediately lapsed into the strictest silence, which, of course, delighted everyone even more than if he'd talked his head off. In a word, he was a great success; he became the rage. In provincial society, once a person has appeared, he can never hide. Once again Nikolai Vsevolodovich began to perform all his social duties in the province as punctiliously as before. They didn't find him cheerful: 'This man has suffered; he's not like other people; he has good reason to be pensive.' Even the pride and supercilious inaccessibility for which he was so hated four years ago were now respected and appreciated.

Varvara Petrovna was the most triumphant of all. I can't say whether she was very upset about her shattered dreams concerning Lizaveta Nikolaevna. Of course, her family pride helped in this regard. One thing was odd: all of a sudden

Varvara Petrovna became absolutely convinced that Nicolas had 'made his choice' in Count K.'s household, but, strangest of all, she was convinced by the rumours which reached her as they did everyone else; she was afraid to ask Nikolai Vsevolodovich a direct question. Two or three times, however, she couldn't restrain herself, and reproached him in a discreet and good-natured way for not being very forthcoming; Nikolai Vsevolodovich smiled and kept silent. His silence was taken as a sign of consent. And yet, through it all she never forgot the cripple. The thought of her lay like a stone on her heart, a nightmare tormenting her with strange visions and premonitions—all this during and alongside her dreams about Count K.'s daughters. But more about this later. Naturally, people in society began to treat Varvara Petrovna with extreme and courteous respect once again, but she took little advantage of it and rarely went out.

She did, however, pay a formal call on the governor's wife. Of course, no one had been more enchanted and delighted by Yulia Mikhailovna's words at the name-day party for the marshal's wife: those words expunged much of the anguish from her heart and at once relieved most of what had been tormenting her since that unfortunate Sunday. 'I didn't understand that woman!' she declared; then, with her usual impulsiveness, she announced to Yulia Mikhailovna that she'd come to *thank* her. Yulia Mikhailovna was flattered, but maintained herself aloof. By that time she was beginning to be aware of her own importance, perhaps even a bit too much. For example, in the midst of the conversation she declared that she'd never heard anything about Stepan Trofimovich's activities or erudition.

'Of course I receive and pamper the young Verkhovensky. He's a little reckless, but he's still so young; and he's very well educated. Moreover, he's no old-fashioned retired critic.'

Varvara Petrovna hastened to observe that Stepan Trofimovich had never been a critic; on the contrary, he'd spent his entire life living in her house. He was famous as a result of circumstances surrounding his previous career, 'all too familiar to the entire world', and most recently because of his work on Spanish history; he was also planning to write about the current state of German universities and, it seems, something about the Dresden Madonna. In a word, Varvara Petrovna refused to surrender Stepan Trofimovich to Yulia Mikhailovna's tender mercy.

'The Dresden Madonna? Surely you mean the Sistine Madonna. *Chère* Varvara Petrovna, I spent two hours sitting in front of that painting and went away disillusioned. I didn't understand it at all and was greatly perplexed. Karmazinov also says it's hard to fathom. Nowadays nobody sees anything in it, neither the Russians nor the English. All this fuss was made by a bunch of old men.'

'A new fashion, I suppose?'

'Well, I think one mustn't dismiss the youth of today. People say they're communists; but in my opinion, one must protect them and appreciate them. I'm reading everything now—newspapers, communes, natural sciences—I get it all; one must know with whom one's living and dealing, mustn't one? One can't spend an entire life in the superior realm of one's own imagination. I've come to that conclusion and made it a rule to pamper our young people and thus keep them from going over the brink. Believe me, Varvara Petrovna, only we members of society, by our beneficial influence and kindness, can keep them from the abyss into which they're being pushed by those impatient old men. But I'm glad to have found out about Stepan Trofimovich from you. You've given me an idea: he may be of use to us at our literary gathering. You know I'm organizing a whole day of festivities on a subscription basis; the proceeds will be used to support poor governesses in our province. They're dispersed throughout Russia; why, we have six of them here in this district alone. Besides that, there are two women in the telegraph office and two in the academy; others would like to work, but lack resources. The lot of Russian women is appalling, Varvara Petrovna! This issue is now being discussed at our universities, and there was even a meeting of our government council about it. In this strange Russia of ours one can do anything one likes. Therefore, once again, it's only through the kindness and sympathy of all society that we can once again direct this great common cause back on to the right path. My goodness, don't we have any luminaries among us? Of course we do, but they're widely scattered. Gather them together and they'll be stronger. In short, first we'll have a literary matinée, a light lunch followed by intermission, and then a ball that same evening. We had wanted to start the evening with *tableaux vivants*, but apparently that would be too expensive; so there'll be one or two quadrilles danced in masks and costumes depicting various literary movements, for the public. It was Karmazinov who made this amusing proposal; he's providing tremendous assistance. You know, he'll be reading his latest work, one that no one's heard yet. He's putting down his pen and will be writing no more; this last piece is his farewell to the reading public. His splendid little speech is called 'Merci'. A French title, but he thinks it's more amusing and subtler that way. I do too, and even gave him some advice about it. I think Stepan Trofimovich might read something there too, if it's not too long and... erudite. Apparently Peter Stepanovich and someone else will be reading. He'll call on you to tell you about the programme; even better, if you'll permit me, I'll bring it to you myself.'

'And please let me sign your subscription list. I'll tell Stepan Trofimovich about it and will ask him myself.'

Varvara Petrovna went home completely enchanted; she was already won over to Yulia Mikhailovna's side and for some reason was very angry with Stepan Trofimovich; meanwhile he, poor man, knew nothing at all about it, and was sitting at home.

'I'm quite taken with that woman and don't understand how I could've been so mistaken about her,' she told Nikolai Vsevolodovich and Peter Stepanovich who dropped in that evening.

'But still you must make it up with the old man,' Peter Stepanovich suggested. 'He's in despair. You've sent him into exile. Yesterday he met your carriage and bowed, but you turned away. You know, we'll push him to the fore; I have some plans for him and he may yet prove useful.'

'Oh, he's going to read.'

'I didn't mean only that. I was going to drop in and see him today. Shall I tell him?'

'If you like. But I don't know how you'll arrange it,' she said indecisively. 'I intended to have it out with him and fix a time and place.' She frowned.

'Well, it's not worth fixing a time. I'll simply tell him.'

'Very well, tell him. But say I'll definitely fix a time. Be sure to add that.'

Peter Stepanovich ran off grinning. In general, as far as I can recall, he was being particularly nasty at the time, allowing himself to make extremely impatient remarks to almost everyone. It's odd, but somehow everyone forgave him. In general it seemed he was regarded in a special way. I must note that he received the news of Nikolai Vsevolodovich's duel with exceptional anger. It took him completely unaware; he even turned green when told about it. Perhaps it was his pride that suffered: he only found out about it the next day when everyone else already knew.

'But you had no right to fight a duel,' he whispered to Stavrogin five days later, meeting him by chance at the club. It's worth noting that during these last five days they hadn't met anywhere, even though Peter Stepanovich dropped in on Varvara Petrovna almost every day.

Nikolai Vsevolodovich glanced at him in silence in an absent-minded way, as if not really understanding what he was talking about, and then went by without stopping. He was on his way through the hall of the club towards the buffet.

'You've been to see Shatov as well... and plan to announce your marriage to Marya Timofeevna,' he said, running after him and grabbing him absent-mindedly by the shoulder.

Nikolai Vsevolodovich shook off his hand abruptly and turned on him swiftly, with a menacing frown. Peter Stepanovich looked at him and smiled a strange, prolonged smile. All this lasted only a moment. Nikolai Vsevolodovich walked on.

2.

From Varvara Petrovna's house he went straight to see his 'old man'; if he was hurrying, it was simply out of spite to revenge himself for a previous insult that I had no idea about at the time. The fact is that at their last meeting on Thursday of the week before Stepan Trofimovich had ended by driving Peter Stepanovich out of the house with a stick after an argument he himself had begun. He concealed this fact from me at the time; but now, as soon as Peter arrived with his usual smile, so innocently arrogant, and his unpleasantly inquisitive eyes peering into every nook and cranny, Stepan Trofimovich immediately made a secret signal indicating that I shouldn't leave the room. Thus the real nature of their relations was revealed to me, since on this occasion I overheard their entire conversation.

Stepan Trofimovich sat stretched out on the couch. Since that Thursday he'd grown thin and sallow. Peter Stepanovich was seated next to him in a most familiar manner, his legs casually tucked under him; he occupied much more space on the couch than respect for his father should have allowed. Stepan Trofimovich had made room for him in dignified silence.

A book lay open on the table. It was the novel *What is to be Done?** Alas, I must confess to a strange weakness in our friend: the idea that he must leave his seclusion and wage one last battle was exerting a stronger and stronger hold on his deluded imagination. I assumed he'd procured that novel and was now *studying* it so that if and when the inevitable confrontation with those 'shriekers' occurred, he'd know their arguments and methods in advance from their own 'catechism'; thus having prepared himself, he'd refute them triumphantly before *her very eyes*. Oh, how that book tormented him! Sometimes he tossed it aside in despair; jumping up from his seat, he'd rush around the room in a frenzy.

'I agree that the author's main idea is correct,' he declared once in a passion. 'But that only makes it worse! It's also our own idea, ours. We, we were the first to plant it, nurture it, prepare the way—what could they possibly say that was new after us? But good Lord, just look how all of it's expressed, distorted, twisted!' he exclaimed, rapping the book with his fingers. 'Were these the conclusions we were striving for? Who can even recognize our original idea in this?'

'Are you enlightening yourself?' asked Peter Stepanovich with a smirk, picking up the book from the table and reading its title. 'It's about time. I'll bring you something even better, if you like.'

Stepan Trofimovich lapsed into dignified silence once again. I was sitting on the sofa in the corner.

Peter Stepanovich quickly explained the reason for his visit. Of course Stepan Trofimovich was extremely upset; he listened with a combination of fear and indignation.

'Does Yulia Mikhailovna really think I'll come and read?'

'The fact is they have no real need of you. On the contrary, it's being done to flatter you and wheedle their way into Varvara Petrovna's good graces. But, it goes without saying, you won't dare refuse. I'll bet you even want to do it,' he smirked. 'All you old-timers have such infernal ambition. But listen, try not to be too boring. What do you have there, some Spanish history, or what? You'd better let me look it over a few days before the reading, or else you might put us all to sleep.'

The hasty and all-too-apparent rudeness of these caustic remarks was obviously premeditated. He was acting as if there were no other way of talking to Stepan Trofimovich, no way of using subtler words and concepts. Stepan Trofimovich was determined to ignore his insults. But the news his son conveyed produced a more and more overwhelming impression on him.

'And it was she, she *herself* who sent me this message through... *you?*' he asked, turning pale.

'Well, you see, she plans to fix a time and place for you to meet and reach a mutual understanding; it's the remnant of your little affair of the heart. You've been flirting with her for some twenty years now and you've taught her several ridiculous tricks. But don't worry, it's quite different now; she says repeatedly that only now has she begun to "see the light". I told her right to her face that this friendship of yours has been nothing more than a mutual outpouring of slops. She told me quite a bit, old boy; phew, you've been acting as her lackey for some time now. Why, I even blushed for you.'

'I've been acting as her lackey?' Stepan Trofimovich was unable to restrain himself.

'Worse, you were a sponger, that means, a voluntary lackey. Too lazy to work, but with quite an appetite for money. Now she understands it all; at least she's been saying terrible things about you. Well, old boy, I really laughed at your letters to her: so shameful and despicable. But you're so depraved, so very depraved! There's always something depraved in charity—and you're a clear example of it!'

'She showed you my letters to her!'

'The lot. But I couldn't possibly read them all. Phew, what a lot of paper you wasted; I think there were more than two thousand... And do you know, old man, I think there really was a time when she was ready to marry you? You let her go in the most inept way! I'm speaking from your point of view, of course; still, you'd have been better off than you are now, when you've almost been married off to cover up "another man's sins", or as a court jester for amusement, or for money.'

'For money! Did she tell you it was for money?' Stepan Trofimovich wailed in pain.

'What else? Don't worry, I defended you, of course. But that's really your only justification. She realized you needed money just like everyone else, and that from that point of view you might have been right. I proved to her, just as two times two makes four, that your living arrangements had been mutually advantageous: she was the capitalist and you were her sentimental court jester. She's not upset about the money, you know, even though you did milk her like a nanny-goat. What she's furious about is that she believed in you for twenty years, that you hoodwinked her with your noble sentiments and made her tell lies for so long. She'll never admit she told lies, but you'll suffer twice as much because of it. I don't understand how you never guessed that some day you'd have to pay for it. After all, you had a head on your shoulders. Yesterday I advised her to have you sent to a poorhouse—don't worry, a decent one—nothing degrading. That's probably what she'll do. Do you remember your last letter to me in Kh— province some three weeks ago?'

'You didn't show her that one?' cried Stepan Trofimovich, jumping up in horror.

'Of course I did! First thing. The one in which you said she was exploiting you, and envied your talent, and all that nonsense about "someone else's sins". Incidentally, old boy, your conceit knows no bounds. I laughed so much. Your letters are usually very boring; your style is terrible. Sometimes I didn't read them at all; there's one I still haven't opened; I'll send it back to you tomorrow. But your last letter—that one was the height of perfection! I laughed and laughed!'

'Monster, you monster!' Stepan Trofimovich wailed.

'Damn it, it's impossible to talk to you. Listen, you're not getting offended again as you did last Thursday, are you?'

Stepan Trofimovich drew himself up menacingly:

'How dare you speak to me like that?'

'Like what? Simply and clearly?'

'Tell me once and for all, you monster, are you my son or not?'

'You know that better than I. Of course, every father is inclined to blindness in such cases...'

'Shut up, shut up!' Stepan Trofimovich cried, trembling all over.

'You see, you're shouting and swearing at me just as you did last Thursday; you were even going to raise your stick against me, but then I found that document. Out of curiosity I turned my trunk inside out. It's true, there's nothing definite in it, so you can relax. It's merely a note from my mother to that Pole. But, judging from her character...'

'Another word out of you and I'll slap your face.'

'What people!' Peter Stepanovich said, turning to me all of a sudden. 'You see, this is the way it's been since last Thursday. I'm glad at least you're here today and can judge for yourself. First, a fact: he reproaches me for speaking like that about my mother. But wasn't he the first to bring it up? In Petersburg when I was still a student, wasn't he the one to wake me twice during the night, embrace me, and weep like an old woman? And what do you think he told me during those nights? Those modest tales about my mother, that's what! He was the one I heard it from!'

'Oh, but I meant it in the highest sense! You didn't understand me. You didn't understand a thing, not one thing.'

'Nevertheless, your action was more despicable than mine, admit it. You see, it really makes no difference to me at all. I'm looking at it from your point of view. Don't worry about mine: I don't blame my mother. If it was you, then it was you; if it was the Pole, then it was the Pole; it's all the same to me. I'm not to blame if things in Berlin turned out so stupidly. As if you could possibly have managed it better. Aren't you really ridiculous people after all! Do you really care whether I'm your son or not? Listen,' he said, turning to me again, 'he didn't spend one rouble on me all my life, he didn't know me until I was sixteen. Then he stole my money and now he's claiming his heart's been aching for me all his life; he's carrying on in front of me like an actor. I'm not Varvara Petrovna, you know!'

He stood up and took his hat.

'I curse you henceforth and for ever!' Stepan Trofimovich said, stretching his hand over him and turning as pale as death.

'Hey, the stupid things this man says!' Peter Stepanovich observed in genuine surprise. 'Well, goodbye, old man, I won't ever come see you again. But send me your article beforehand, don't forget. And try, if you can, to leave out all nonsense: facts, facts, and more facts. The main thing is, keep it brief. Goodbye.'

3.

But there were other factors involved here. Peter Stepanovich really did have designs on his father. In my opinion, he was hoping to drive his father to despair and thus involve him in some obvious scandal of a particular kind. All this was necessary for some distant, extraneous reason of his own which I'll explain in more detail later. He'd amassed a multitude of similar calculations and designs at the time—of course, almost all fantastic. He had yet another victim in mind in addition to Stepan Trofimovich. In general he had quite a few victims, as it turned out later; but he counted on this one particularly, and it was none other than Mr von Lembke himself.

Andrei Antonovich von Lembke belonged to a tribe* (favoured by nature) that in Russia numbers in the several hundred thousands according to the census, and which may, although it doesn't know it, constitute a closely organized union all on its own. It goes without saying this union isn't premeditated or fabricated; it exists as an independent tribal union, not dependent on agreements or the spoken word, as something morally obligatory, relying on the mutual support provided to all members in all places and under all circumstances. Andrei Antonovich had the honour to be educated in one of those better Russian academic institutions full of young men from families having either good connections or enormous wealth. Pupils from this institution, almost immediately upon completing their course, are appointed to rather important positions in some branch of government service. Andrei Antonovich had an uncle who was a colonel in the Corps of Engineers, and another who was a baker. Nevertheless, he'd managed to find his way into one of these better schools and there he encountered a fair number of kindred souls. He was a cheerful companion, a rather poor student, but one whom everyone liked. When in the upper grades many of his young schoolmates, especially the Russians, learned how to discourse about extremely lofty contemporary problems, their appearance suggesting that they were merely waiting to leave school to solve these problems—Andrei Antonovich continued to indulge in the most innocent schoolboy pranks. He amused everyone, by tricks that were not very clever, it's true, cynical at the most, but that was his aim. Sometimes, when the teacher turned to him with a question during a lesson, he would blow his nose in such an astonishing way that he'd make both his schoolmates and the teacher laugh; or else in the dormitory he'd act out some cynical *tableau vivant* to general

applause; or he'd play the overture from *Fra Diavolo**
entirely through his nose (rather skilfully). He was also
distinguished by a deliberate slovenliness which for some
reason he considered very clever. In his last year at school
he began to write Russian verse. He spoke the language of
his own tribe rather ungrammatically, like a great many
members of that tribe in Russia. His propensity for writing
verse drew him close to a schoolmate who was gloomy and
depressed, the son of a poor general, a Russian; at school
this lad was considered to have a great future ahead of him
as a man of letters. He took a patronizing interest in von
Lembke. But it transpired that three years after leaving
school this gloomy schoolmate, who'd given up his career
in the service to devote himself to Russian literature, and
who was consequently going about in torn boots, teeth
chattering from the cold, wearing only a light summer coat
in late autumn, suddenly encountered his former protégé—
'Lembka', as everyone in school used to call him, near the
Anichkov Bridge. And do you know what? He hardly recognized him at first glance and stood still in amazement.
Before him stood an irreproachably dressed young man,
with magnificently trimmed reddish sidewhiskers, wearing
a pince-nez and patent-leather boots, brand new gloves, a
bulky overcoat from Sharmer's, and carrying a briefcase
under his arm. Lembke was nice to his friend, gave him his
address, and invited him to drop in some evening. It also
turned out that he was no longer known as 'Lembka'; now
he was von Lembke. His friend did indeed drop in on him,
perhaps only out of spite. On the stairs, which were certainly
not very attractive, far from elegant, and carpeted in red
felt, he was stopped and questioned by the hall porter. A
bell rang loudly upstairs. But instead of the elegance the
visitor had expected to see, he found his 'Lembka' in a very
small side room, dark and dilapidated, divided in two by a
heavy, dark-green curtain, furnished with old, if comfortable
dark-green furniture, with dark-green blinds on the high,
narrow windows. Von Lembke was living in the house of a
distant relative, a general who was his patron. He greeted
his guest cordially; he was grave and exquisitely polite. They

chatted about literature, but kept within the bounds of decorum. A footman in a white tie served some weak tea with a few small, round dry biscuits. Out of spite his friend asked for a glass of seltzer water. They brought it to him, but only after a brief delay, and Lembke was embarrassed at having to summon the footman again and give him another order. Then he asked his guest if he would like something to eat and was obviously relieved when the visitor declined and finally departed. The simple truth was that Lembke was just embarking on his career, still sponging off his fellow-tribesman, the important general.

At the time he was also sighing for the general's fifth daughter, and, it seems, his feelings were reciprocated. But when the time came Amalia was married off nevertheless to an elderly German factory owner, the elderly general's old friend. Andrei Antonovich didn't shed many tears, but built himself a theatre out of cardboard. The curtain could be raised and actors came out and made gestures with their hands; the audience sat in boxes, the string-players moved their bows across their fiddles by some mechanism, the conductor waved his baton, and in the stalls cavaliers and officers clapped their hands. The whole thing was constructed of cardboard, everything invented and executed by von Lembke himself; he worked on the project for about six months. The general deliberately arranged an intimate get-together and the theatre was brought out for inspection; all five daughters were there, including the newly-wed Amalia, her factory owner, and many other ladies, both married and unmarried, with their German escorts, and they all carefully examined and admired the theatre; then they danced. Lembke was very pleased and quickly consoled.

Years passed and his career became more established. He regularly managed to secure prominent positions, always under the supervision of members of his own tribe; at last he worked his way up to a very high rank compared with his peers. He'd been wanting to get married for some time and had been looking around carefully. Without telling his superiors he sent a story off to the editor of a journal, but it wasn't accepted for publication. On the other hand, he made an entire model railway out of cardboard, and once again the result was a great success: passengers emerged from the station with suitcases and bags, children and puppydogs; they boarded railway carriages. Guards and porters walked around, the bell was rung, the signal given, and the train moved out. He spent a whole year working on this clever project. Still, he had to get married. His circle of acquaintances was rather large, particularly among Germans; but he also moved in Russian circles, especially in the line of duty. At last, when he'd reached the ripe old age of thirty-eight, he came into his inheritance. His uncle the baker had died and left him thirteen thousand roubles in his will. Now he needed a suitable position. In spite of the rather elevated style characterizing the world of the civil service he inhabited, Mr von Lembke was a very modest man. He would have been totally satisfied with some independent little government post, assigning him responsibility for purchasing firewood for government departments, or some other nice job of that sort, and he'd have been happy for the rest of his life. But then, instead of the expected Minna or Ernestine, all of a sudden Yulia Mikhailovna turned up. His career was immediately raised one full step on the ladder. The modest and diligent von Lembke realized that he too might have ambition.

According to the old way of calculating, Yulia Mikhailovna possessed some two hundred serfs; what's more, she had powerful friends. On the other hand, von Lembke was handsome, and she was already over forty. Remarkable as it is, he gradually fell genuinely in love with her as he became more and more used to the idea of being her betrothed. On his wedding day he sent her some verses. She liked every bit of it, even the verses: being forty is no joke. He soon got an important promotion and an impressive decoration; then he was appointed to a position in our province.

Before arriving in town, Yulia Mikhailovna worked very hard on her husband. In her opinion he was a man not without ability; he knew how to enter a room and show himself off to advantage; he knew how to listen thoughtfully and remain silent; he'd acquired some decent mannerisms, and could make a speech; he even had a few odds and ends of ideas, and had acquired the necessary gloss of contemporary liberalism. Nevertheless she was worried by the fact that he wasn't very receptive to new ideas; after a long, seemingly eternal search for a career, now he'd definitely begun to feel the need for peace and quiet. She wanted to instil her ambition into him, and he suddenly began to assemble a church* out of cardboard. The minister came out to deliver a sermon, worshippers listened with devoutly clasped hands, a woman wiped away her tears with a handkerchief, an old man blew his nose; finally a little organ, specially ordered and dispatched from Switzerland in spite of the expense, played a tune. Yulia Mikhailovna was quite alarmed and carried off the entire construction as soon as she found out about it; she locked it up in a trunk. In exchange, she allowed him to write a novel, if he agreed to keep it a secret. From then on she began relying on herself alone. Unfortunately this revealed considerable thoughtlessness and a lack of proportion on her part. Destiny had kept her an old maid for too long. One idea after another raced through her ambitious and rather excitable brain. She nurtured schemes; she desperately wanted to govern the province; she dreamed of becoming the centre of a circle and she chose a political tendency. Von Lembke was a bit frightened, but with his civil servant's tact soon guessed there was no reason to be afraid of governing the province. The first two or three months passed by very satisfactorily. But then Peter Stepanovich turned up and something odd began to happen.

The fact was that from the very first the young Verkhovensky manifested a flagrant lack of respect for Andrei Antonovich and assumed certain strange rights over him. Meanwhile, Yulia Mikhailovna, who was always so jealous of her husband's position, didn't care to notice anything at all; at least she didn't think it very important. The young man became her favourite: he ate, drank, and almost slept in their house. Von Lembke tried to defend himself, referring to him as the 'young lad' in front of other people, patting him on the shoulder in a patronizing manner, but all this was to no avail. Peter Stepanovich still seemed to be laughing right in his face, even while appearing to be talking seriously; he would say the most unexpected things in the presence of other people. Arriving home on one occasion, he discovered the young man asleep on the sofa in his study without invitation. The latter explained that he'd dropped in, but finding no one at home 'decided to catch up on his sleep'. Von Lembke was offended and complained to his wife again. After making fun of his irritability, she remarked pointedly that he seemed unable to make people respect him; at least 'the lad' never allowed himself such familiarity with her. Moreover, he was 'naïve and fresh, albeit beyond the social pale'. Von Lembke sulked. That time she was able to reconcile them. Peter Stepanovich didn't exactly apologize; he merely extricated himself with a crude joke, which could've been taken for another insult, but which in the present instance was taken as a sign of remorse. The weak spot in Andrei Antonovich's position was the fact that very early on he'd made a mistake and told him about his novel. Imagining that he'd met an ardent young man with poetic feeling, and having long dreamed of finding an audience, one evening during the early days of their acquaintance he'd read him two chapters. Peter listened, making no attempt to conceal his boredom, yawning impolitely, and offering not one word of praise; but as he left he asked to take the manuscript home to form an opinion of it at his leisure. Andrei Antonovich lent it to him. Since then he hadn't returned the manuscript, even though he called in every day, and replied with laughter to all enquiries. In the end he declared that he'd lost it somewhere in the street. When she found out about it, Yulia Mikhailovna was very angry with her husband.

'You didn't tell him about the cardboard church as well, did you?' she cried, almost in dismay.

Von Lembke decidedly began to brood, but brooding was bad for his health and had been forbidden him by his doctors. Besides the fact that there were numerous problems in the province—about which more later—this was a special case, one that wounded him in the heart, not just in his pride as governor. When he got married, Andrei Antonovich never conceived of the future possibility of family quarrels and disagreements. Or so he'd imagined all his life, dreaming of his Minna or Ernestine. He felt that he was unable to endure domestic storms. Yulia Mikhailovna finally decided to have a frank talk with him.

'You can't be angry with him because of that,' she said, 'if only because you're three times more sensible than he is and immeasurably higher on the social ladder. There are still many traces of his former free-thinking habits in the boy; in my opinion, it's simply mischief. But nothing can be done all of a sudden—one must proceed gradually. We must appreciate our young people; I respond to them with affection to prevent them from going over the top.'

'But he's saying the devil knows what,' von Lembke objected. 'I can't treat him tolerantly when in my presence and in front of other people he declares that the government deliberately gets common people drunk with vodka to brutalize them and keep them from rebelling. Imagine my position when I'm forced to listen to that in the presence of others.'

Saying this, von Lembke recalled a recent conversation with Peter Stepanovich. With the innocent aim of disarming him by displaying his own liberalism, he had shown him his private collection of diverse political pamphlets, both Russian and foreign, which he'd been assembling carefully since 1859, not so much as a hobby, but simply out of commendable curiosity. Peter Stepanovich guessed his intention and rudely replied that there was more sense contained in one line of some of the pamphlets than in some entire government departments, 'not excluding, perhaps, even your own'.

Lembke winced.

'But this is premature, much too premature,' he said almost beseechingly, pointing to the pamphlets.

'No, it's not premature; can't you see, if you're afraid, it's not premature.'

'But here, for example, there's a call to destroy churches.'

'And why not? You're a clever man; of course, you're not

a believer. You understand all too well that religion is needed to brutalize the common people. Truth is more honest than lies.'

'I agree, I agree, I agree with you completely, but it's premature, premature...' said von Lembke, knitting his brows.

'What kind of government official are you if you agree with the need to demolish churches, march on Petersburg armed with staves, and the whole question comes down to one of timing?'

Being caught so crudely, Lembke was sorely vexed.

'That's not it, not it,' he continued, his vanity more and more irritated. 'As a young man, and, this is the point, as one who's unfamiliar with our aims, you're making a big mistake. You see, dear Peter Stepanovich, you call us government officials? Correct. Independent officials? Correct. But allow me to enquire, how do we act? We bear the responsibility, and, as a result, we serve the common cause as much as you do. We merely try to keep together what you try to pull apart and it certainly would fall apart without us. We're not your enemies, not at all; we say, go forward, make progress, even pull it to pieces, that is, everything that's old and needs to be changed. But when necessary we'll keep you within bounds and save you from yourselves. Without us, you'll merely set Russia tottering, deprive her of her decent appearance; our task consists in worrying about that appearance. You must understand we're indispensable to one another. In England the Whigs and the Tories are also mutually indispensable. Well then: we're the Whigs and you're the Tories. That's how I understand it.'

Andrei Antonovich had even become emotional. He was fond of speaking in a clever and liberal style since he'd been in Petersburg, and the main thing here was, no one was eavesdropping. Peter Stepanovich remained silent and conducted himself in an unusually serious manner. But this inflamed the orator even more.

'Do you know,' he continued, pacing up and down his study, 'I'm "master of the province". Do you know, I have so many duties I can't carry out any one of them; on the other hand, I can say just as honestly, that I have nothing to do here. The whole secret is that everything depends on the government's views. Let the government decide to establish a republic, let's say, either for political reasons or to appease the mob, and on the other hand, simultaneously to strengthen the governor's power. If that should happen, we governors will have to swallow a republic. And not only a republic: we'll have to swallow anything you like. At least I feel I'm ready to... In a word, let the government demand *activité dévorante*[1] in a telegram, I'll provide *activité dévorante*. I've told them straight to their faces: "Gentlemen, one thing is essential to maintain the equilibrium and assure the well-being of all provincial institutions—namely, the strengthening of the governor's powers." You see, it's necessary for all institutions—both agricultural and legal—to lead a double life, so to speak; that is to say, it's necessary for them to exist (and I agree it's necessary), but, on the other hand, it's also necessary for them not to exist. It's all in accordance with the government's views. If it turns out these institutions are suddenly essential, I'll make sure they're immediately available. If this need passes, no one will be able to find them anywhere in my province. That's the way I understand *activité dévorante*, and it can't be achieved without strengthening the governor's powers. We're talking about this man to man. You know, I've already told them in Petersburg about the necessity of stationing a special guard at the door of the governor's house. I'm waiting for their answer.'

'You need two of them,' Peter Stepanovich replied.

'Why two?' von Lembke asked, stopping in front of him.

'One might not be enough to make people respect you. You should definitely have two.'

Andrei Antonovich grimaced.

'You... God only knows what you allow yourself to say, Peter Stepanovich. You take advantage of my kindness, make caustic remarks, and play the part of some *bourru bienfaisant*...'[2]

---

[1] furious activity
[2] well-meaning boor

'Just as you like,' Peter Stepanovich muttered. 'All the same, you're paving the way for us and promoting our success.'

'Who exactly is "us" and what success are you talking about?' von Lembke asked, staring at him in surprise; but he got no answer.

When Yulia Mikhailovna heard an account of this conversation she was greatly displeased.

'But', said von Lembke in his own defence, 'I can't pull rank with your favourite, especially when we're talking man to man... Perhaps I said too much... out of the goodness of my heart.'

'Out of too much goodness. I didn't know you had a collection of political pamphlets. Do me a favour, show them to me.'

'But... but he asked to borrow them from me for a day.'

'And you lent him something again!' Yulia Mikhailovna said angrily. 'What indiscretion!'

'I'll ask him for them back at once.'

'He won't give them back.'

'I'll demand them!' cried von Lembke, flaring up, and even leaping up from his seat. 'Who's he that I should be afraid of him, and who am I to sit here and do nothing?'

'Sit down and calm down,' Yulia Mikhailovna said, stopping him. 'I'll answer your first question: he came with the highest recommendations; he's a talented young man who sometimes says very clever things. Karmazinov has assured me he has connections everywhere and exerts a great deal of influence over young people in the capital. If I can succeed in attracting them through him and gathering them around me, I'll be able to save them from ruin by channelling their ambitions into a new outlet. He's devoted to me with all his heart and obeys me in all things.'

'But while you're pampering them... the devil only knows what they could do. Of course, it's only a thought,' said von Lembke, defending himself vaguely, 'but... but I've heard that pamphlets of some sort have been seen in one of our districts.'

'That rumour was making the rounds last summer—

pamphlets, counterfeit bills, who knows what else. Up to now not one thing has been found. Who told you?'

'I heard it from von Blum.'

'Ah, God preserve me from your Blum and don't ever mention his name again!'

Yulia Mikhailovna flew into a rage and was unable to speak for a minute. Von Blum was a clerk in the government office she particularly detested. More about him later.

'Please, don't be concerned about Verkhovensky,' she said, to conclude their conversation. 'If he's participated in any mischief, he wouldn't be talking to you or anyone else the way he does. Phrasemongers aren't dangerous; I might venture to say that even if something were to happen here, I'd be the first to find out through him. He's fanatically, quite fanatically devoted to me.'

I must observe, in anticipation of later events, that if it hadn't been for Yulia Mikhailovna's conceit and her vanity, all the trouble caused by these wretched little people might never have taken place. She was responsible for a great deal!

CHAPTER 5

Before the festivities

I.

THE DATE of the fête organized by Yulia Mikhailovna to benefit governesses in our province had been fixed several times and then postponed. Peter Stepanovich was continually bustling around her; the little clerk Lyamshin, who used to visit Stepan Trofimovich, suddenly found favour in the governor's house because he could play the piano and began running errands for the governor's wife. Liputin was there too; Yulia Mikhailovna planned to appoint him editor of a future independent newspaper in the province. There were also several ladies, both married and single. Finally, there was even Karmazinov, who, though he wasn't exactly bustling around, declared aloud with a satisfied look that he planned to astonish everyone when the literary quadrille began. There was a large number of subscribers and donors, including the most select society in town; but even the less select were to be admitted, as long as they had enough money. Yulia Mikhailovna observed that sometimes it was even incumbent on her to permit the mingling of social classes, 'otherwise who would enlighten them?' An unofficial domestic committee was formed and it resolved that the occasion would be a democratic one. The number of subscriptions tempted them to increase their expenditure; they wanted to stage something marvellous—that was why the fête kept being postponed. They couldn't decide where to hold the ball: at the home of the marshal of the nobility, which his wife had put at their disposal for the day, or at Varvara Petrovna's house in Skvoreshniki. It was a little too far to Skvoreshniki, but many members of the committee insisted it would feel 'more liberated' there. Varvara Petrovna would have loved her house to be chosen. It's difficult to say why this proud woman was trying to ingratiate herself with Yulia Mikhailovna. She probably liked it that the latter in her turn was almost fawning on Nikolai Vsevolodovich,

lavishing more attention on him than anyone else. I repeat:
Peter Stepanovich was constantly and continually, in a
whisper, attempting to promote an idea he'd already planted
in the governor's house, namely, that Nikolai Vsevolodovich
was a person with the most mysterious connections in a
most mysterious world, and that he had undoubtedly come
charged with some commission.

People were in a strange state of mind at the time. Among
the ladies especially, a sort of frivolous attitude prevailed
and it cannot be said it had come about gradually. It seemed
as though a number of extremely free-and-easy notions were
in the air. There was a mood of light-hearted merriment,
but I can't say it was always pleasant. A certain mental
disarray was in vogue. Afterwards, when everything was all
over, they blamed Yulia Mikhailovna, her circle and its
influence; but it was unlikely that it all originated in Yulia
Mikhailovna alone. On the contrary, many people at first
vied with each other in praising the new governor's wife for
trying to unite society and suddenly making things livelier.
There were even a few scandalous incidents for which Yulia
Mikhailovna couldn't be blamed at all; but at the time everyone
only laughed and was amused, and there was no one to stop
them. It's true that a rather large number of people stood to
one side with their own special outlook on events; but not
even they grumbled at the time; they even smiled.

I recall that, almost spontaneously, a rather large circle of
people had formed; its centre was probably to be found in
Yulia Mikhailovna's drawing-room. In the intimate circle
surrounding her it became acceptable, even the rule, especially among young people, to play various pranks, sometimes rather unruly ones. There were even some nice ladies
included in the circle. The young people organized picnics
and parties; sometimes they paraded through town in a
regular cavalcade of carriages and on horseback. They were
on the look-out for adventures, even deliberately organizing
and contriving them for themselves, simply to have an
amusing story to tell afterwards. They treated our town as
if it were the town of Glupov.* They were called 'scoffers'
or 'mockers' because they stopped at nothing. It happened,

for instance, that a lieutenant's wife from the local regiment, a brunette and still very young, though worn out by her husband's ill-treatment, sat down without thinking at a party to play whist for high stakes in the hope of winning enough money to buy herself a coat; but instead of winning, she lost fifteen roubles. Fearing her husband and having no money to pay her debt, she recalled her former audacity and resolved to ask for a loan on the sly, right there at the party, from our mayor's son, a repugnant creature, already dissipated in spite of his youth. He not only refused her, but laughed aloud and went to tell her husband. The lieutenant, who had trouble living on his meagre salary, took his wife home and had a whale of a time at her expense, in spite of her moans, cries, and entreaties on bended knee to be forgiven. This episode provoked nothing but laughter everywhere in town, and even though the lieutenant's poor wife didn't belong to the circle surrounding Yulia Mikhailovna, one of the ladies from this 'cavalcade', an eccentric and spirited woman somehow acquainted with the lieutenant's wife, went to visit her and simply brought her back to stay at her house. Our pranksters latched on to her, pampered her, showered her with gifts, and kept her there for four days without returning her to her husband. She stayed at the spirited lady's house and for a time went driving around town with her and the rest of her rowdy company, participating in their parties and dances. They kept urging her to take her husband to court and create a scandal. They assured her that everyone would support her and testify. The husband remained silent, not daring to protest. At long last the poor dear realized what a mess she'd got herself into and, nearly dead with fear, on the fourth day she ran away from her protectors and went home to her lieutenant. It's not altogether clear what transpired between husband and wife, but two shutters of the small wooden house in which they were renting an apartment remained closed for two whole weeks. Yulia Mikhailovna was angry with the pranksters when she found out about it, and was sorely vexed by the behaviour of the spirited lady, even though it was she who'd introduced her to the lieutenant's wife on the first day of her captivity. But the whole episode was soon forgotten.

Another time, a young petty official from a neighbouring district married the daughter of a petty official in our town, a respectable family man; the daughter was seventeen, very pretty, and acquainted with everyone in town. But it suddenly became known that on their wedding night the young groom had treated his new bride very badly, in revenge for his honour being insulted. Lyamshin, who was virtually a witness to the scene because he got drunk at the wedding and spent the night in their house, rushed around town as soon as it was light to spread the cheerful news. In an instant a posse of ten men was formed, all on horseback, some of them on hired Cossack mounts, including Peter Stepanovich and Liputin, who in spite of his grey hair took part in almost all the scandalous escapades of our frivolous young people. When the newly-weds appeared in the street to make their visits in a carriage drawn by a pair of horses, as is our local custom the day after a wedding, no matter what—the entire cavalcade surrounded the carriage and with raucous laughter accompanied them throughout town all that morning. It's true they didn't follow them into houses, but waited on their horses at the gates. They also refrained from hurling specific insults at the bride and groom; still, they created quite a scene. The whole town started talking. Naturally, everyone was laughing. Von Lembke got angry and once again had a heated discussion with Yulia Mikhailovna. She got angry too, and even considered shutting her door to the hooligans. But the next day she forgave them all as a result of Peter Stepanovich's exhortations and a few words from Karmazinov. He found the whole 'joke' rather amusing.

'It's in keeping with local customs,' he said. 'At least it's characteristic and... audacious. Besides, just look, everyone's laughing; you're the only one so indignant.'

But there were also some intolerable pranks which had a particular tenor.

In our town there appeared a book-pedlar selling Gospels, a respectable woman even though from the lower middle class. People started talking about her because some curious reports about book-pedlars had just appeared in the Moscow and Petersburg papers. Once again that rogue Lyamshin, assisted by a seminary student who was hoping for a teaching position in our school, while pretending to buy some books from the pedlar, secretly slipped into her bag a bundle of suggestive and obscene photographs from abroad, donated expressly for the purpose, as we later found out, by a venerable old man whose name I'll omit, but who wore an important decoration around his neck and who enjoyed, in his own words, 'hearty laughter and a good joke'. When the poor woman began taking her sacred books out of her bag in the Shopping Arcade, the photographs were suddenly scattered around. First there was laughter, then indignation; a crowd gathered and became abusive. It would have developed into a fight if the police hadn't arrived. The book-pedlar was locked up in gaol; only later that evening, thanks to the efforts of Maurice Nikolaevich, who learned the details of this despicable affair with indignation, was she released and escorted out of town. Yulia Mikhailovna would certainly have expelled Lyamshin from her house, but that same evening a group of young people brought him to her with the news that he'd composed a new piece for the piano and they prevailed upon her to hear it at least. The piece really turned out to be very amusing and bore the comic title, 'The Franco-Prussian War'. It began with the thunderous strains of the *Marseillaise*:

> *Qu'un sang impur abreuve nos sillons!*[1]

There followed a bombastic challenge, the thrill of future triumph. But suddenly, combined with masterly variations on the French national anthem, somewhere on the side, from underneath, in the corner, but very close by, were heard the vulgar strains of *Mein lieber Augustin*.* At first the *Marseillaise* doesn't notice a thing; it's reached a climax of intoxication with its own grandeur; but *Augustin* gains in power, becomes more insolent, and now the strains of *Augustin* unexpectedly begin to coincide with those of the

---

[1] May a tainted blood drench our furrows!

Marseillaise. The latter seems to get angry; it finally notices *Augustin* and wants to get rid of it, brush it off like an insignificant, but persistent fly, but *Mein lieber Augustin* holds on firmly; it's cheerful and self-confident, joyful and impudent. Suddenly the *Marseillaise* becomes terribly stupid: it no longer conceals its irritation and offended pride. Now it's a wail of indignation, tears and curses, with arms out-stretched to Providence:

Pas un pouce de notre terrain, pas une pierre de nos fortresses![1]

But it's already compelled to sing in time with *Mein lieber Augustin.* Its strains are stupidly merged with those of *Augustin*; it yields and dies away. Only from time to time, in snatches, the phrase '*qu'un sang impur...*' can be heard, but it skips ahead at once offensively to the vulgar waltz. The *Marseillaise* submits entirely: it's Jules Favre,* sobbing on Bismarck's bosom, surrendering everything, everything... But now *Augustin* grows fierce: hoarse sounds are heard, the consumption of vast quantities of beer, a frenzy of self-glorification, demands for billions, for fine cigars, cham-pagne, and hostages; *Augustin* becomes a ferocious roar... The Franco-Prussian War ends. Our young people applaud; Yulia Mikhailovna smiles and says, 'Well, how could I ever expel him?' A truce was declared. The scoundrel really did have talent. Stepan Trofimovich assured me once that the most sublime artists could also be the most terrible scound-rels, that the one thing has nothing to do with the other. Later it was rumoured that Lyamshin had stolen the piece from a modest and talented young man who happened to be passing through town and whose name is still unknown; but that's beside the point. This scoundrel, who for several years had hung around Stepan Trofimovich and at his parties would on demand impersonate all kinds of little Yids, a deaf peasant woman's confession, or a baby being born, now did a killingly funny caricature of Stepan Trofimovich himself, and sometimes by the way at Yulia Mikhailovna's, entitled 'A Liberal of the 1840s'. Everyone roared with

---

[1] Not an inch of our land, not a stone of our fortresses!

laughter. In the end it really was impossible to expel him: the man was indispensable. Besides, he fawned on Peter Stepanovich slavishly, and had in his turn by this time achieved a strange and powerful influence over Yulia Mikhailovna...

I wouldn't have begun talking about this scoundrel at all, and he really wouldn't be worth dwelling on, were it not for another disturbing incident in which he also played a role, or so I've been told; and I can't possibly exclude this incident from my chronicle.

One morning news of an outrageous and revolting sacrilege spread through town. At the entrance to our enormous market square stands the ancient church of Our Lady's Nativity, quite a remarkable piece of antiquity in our ancient town. Recently a large icon of the Virgin was placed in the wall behind a grating near the gates of the enclosure. Then one night this icon was stolen, the glass of the case broken, and the grating smashed; several stones and pearls, I don't know how valuable, were removed from the crown and setting. But the main thing was that in addition to the theft, an incomprehensible and mocking sacrilege was perpetrated: the next morning it was reported that a live mouse was found behind the broken glass of the icon. Now, four months later, it's positively been established that this crime was committed by the convict Fedka; but for some reason it was also said that Lyamshin had a part in it. No one said anything about Lyamshin at the time, and no one suspected him, but now everyone confirms that it was he who released the mouse. I recall that our authorities were somewhat at a loss. A crowd had been gathering at the scene of the crime since that morning. There was still a crowd, though not a very large one, only about a hundred people. Some arrived while others left. The ones who arrived crossed themselves and bowed down to the icon. They made contributions; a collection plate appeared, and with it, a monk. Only around three o'clock in the afternoon did the authorities realize that they could order the people not to stand around in a crowd; after saying their prayers, bowing to the icon, and making a contribution, they were supposed to move along. This unfortunate incident produced a very gloomy impression on von Lembke. As I was told afterwards, Yulia Mikhailovna said that from that ill-fated morning she'd begun to notice a strange dejection in her spouse which persisted until his departure from town some two months ago due to illness, and which, it seems, afflicts him even now in Switzerland, where he continues to recuperate after his brief career in our province.

I remember that at about one o'clock in the afternoon I went to the square; the crowd was quiet, their faces grave and gloomy. A fat, sallow merchant drove up in a carriage; he climbed out, bowed down to the ground, kissed the icon, made an offering of one rouble, got back in his carriage with a sigh, and then drove off. Another carriage drove up with two of our ladies accompanied by two of our pranksters. The young people (of whom one was no longer so young) climbed out of the carriage and crowded around the icon, pushing people away rather rudely. Both men failed to remove their hats and one set his pince-nez on his nose. A murmur arose among the crowd, subdued, it's true, but hostile. The young man wearing the pince-nez took a copper kopeck from his wallet stuffed with banknotes and tossed it into the plate; both men returned to their carriage, laughing and talking loudly. Then, all of a sudden Lizaveta Niko-laevna galloped up accompanied by Maurice Nikolaevich. She jumped down from her horse, tossed the reins to her companion who remained on his horse in accordance with her order, and went up to the icon precisely at the same time the kopeck had been tossed. A blush of indignation coloured her cheeks; she took off her round hat and gloves, fell on her knees before the icon straight on to the muddy pavement, and reverently prostrated herself three times. Then she took out her purse; since it contained only a few small coins, she instantly removed her diamond earrings and placed them on the plate.

'May I? May I? As an adornment for the setting?' she asked a monk in great agitation.

'You may,' he replied. 'Every contribution is welcome.'

The crowd remained silent, manifesting neither approval

nor disapproval; Lizaveta Nikolaevna mounted her horse in her muddy riding-habit and galloped away.

2.

Two days after the incident I've just described I met her with a crowd of people setting off in three carriages, surrounded by men on horseback. She beckoned to me, stopped the carriage, and insisted that I join their company. They made room for me in the carriage; with a laugh she introduced me to her companions, all elegant ladies, and explained that they were setting out on an extremely interesting expedition. She was laughing and already seemed a little overexcited. Recently she'd become cheerful to the point of skittishness. The expedition really was rather eccentric: they were heading across the river to the house of the merchant Sevostyanov, where for the last ten years or so, our saint and prophet, Semyon Yakovlevich, known not only among us, but also in the surrounding provinces and even in the capitals, had been residing in an annexe, living in peace, contentment, and comfort. Everyone used to visit him, especially people from other parts of the country, hoping to hear some wise words from this holy fool,* bowing down to him, bringing him offerings. These offerings, sometimes rather substantial, if not put to immediate use by Semyon Yakovlevich himself, would be piously dispatched to some church, principally to the Monastery of Our Lady; for that reason a monk from that monastery was always on duty near Semyon Yakovlevich. Everyone anticipated great merriment. Not one of this group had ever seen Semyon Yakovlevich before. Only Lyamshin had visited him once and assured everyone that the prophet had ordered him driven away with a broom and had thrown two large boiled potatoes at him with his own hand. Among the men I noticed Peter Stepanovich on a hired Cossack mount again, riding rather clumsily, and Nikolai Vsevolodovich, also on horseback. Stavrogin would sometimes participate in these merry excursions, and on such occasions would always have an appropriately cheerful expression, even though he spoke little and seldom. When, on its way to the bridge, the expedition approached the local hotel, someone announced that the body of a traveller who'd shot himself had just been discovered in one of the hotel rooms and the police had been sent for. At once it was suggested that they go and have a look at the body. This proposal was approved: our ladies had never seen a suicide. I recall one of them said aloud that 'she was so bored by everything she couldn't possibly be squeamish about any form of entertainment, as long as it was interesting.' Only a few people decided to wait outside near the stairs; the rest crowded into the dirty corridor. Among them to my astonishment I saw Lizaveta Nikolaevna. The door to the suicide's room was open; of course, they didn't dare refuse us entry. It was a young man, no more than nineteen, very handsome, with thick blond hair, a regular oval face, and a fine, high forehead. The body had already stiffened and its white face looked as if it were made of marble. A note lay on the table written in his own hand, asking that no one be blamed for his death, saying that he'd shot himself because he'd 'squandered' four hundred roubles. His note actually contained the word 'squandered': there were three grammatical mistakes in his four lines. One person was particularly distressed, apparently his neighbour, a corpulent landowner who was staying in another room of the hotel on business. From him we learned that the young man had been sent by his family, his widowed mother, his sisters and aunts, from the country to town to make some purchases under the supervision of an old female relative intended for the dowry of an elder sister who was getting married, and then he was to bring the purchases home. He was entrusted with four hundred roubles, accumulated over many decades, with sighs of apprehension, endless exhortations, prayers and blessings. Up to that time the young man had been modest and reliable. When he'd arrived in town three days ago he didn't seek out his old relative at all; he stopped at the hotel and went straight to the club—in the hope of finding in some back room a travelling banker, or at least a game of cards. But there was no game that evening, not even a banker. Returning to his hotel room around midnight, he ordered champagne, some Cuban cigars, and a supper consisting of six or seven courses. But he got drunk from the champagne and nauseous from the cigars, so he didn't even touch the food when it was served, and went to bed almost unconscious. When he awoke the next morning as fresh as a daisy, he set off at once for a gypsy camp in a section of town on the other side of the river, which he'd heard about the night before in the club; he didn't reappear in the hotel for two days. Finally, yesterday, at about five o'clock in the afternoon, he returned stone cold sober, went to bed immediately and slept until ten o'clock that evening. When he woke up he ordered a cutlet, a bottle of Château d'Yquem, some grapes, paper, ink, and the bill. No one noticed anything unusual about him; he was calm, quiet and polite. He must have shot himself around midnight, although it was odd that no one heard the shot; he was discovered the next day at about one o'clock in the afternoon when he failed to answer the door and it had to be broken down. The bottle of Château d'Yquem was half-empty and there were still some grapes left on the plate. The shot had been fired from a small three-barrelled revolver straight through the heart. There was very little blood; the revolver had fallen from his hand on to the rug. The youth himself was half-reclining on a sofa in the corner. Death must have occurred instantaneously. There was no trace of mortal agony on his face; his expression was serene, almost happy, without a care in the world. All the members of our party examined him with eager curiosity. In general there's always something diverting to the onlooker in a tragedy that befalls a person—whoever it might be. Our women looked on in silence; their escorts distinguished themselves with witty remarks and superb equanimity. One observed that it was clearly the best solution and that the young man could have conceived of nothing more sensible; another concluded that the young man had enjoyed himself, even if it had been very short-lived. A third suddenly blurted out a question: why had so many people taken to hanging themselves and shooting themselves of late—as if they'd been uprooted or the floor had given way beneath them? People shot the philosopher a glance of hostility.

Lyamshin on the other hand, who'd assumed the role of jester, helped himself to a bunch of grapes from the plate, and then, with a laugh, another person followed suit, and a third was about to reach for the bottle of Château d'Yquem. But the police chief arrived and stopped him, even requesting everyone to 'clear the room'. Since they'd all seen enough, they left immediately without argument, although Lyamshin started to pester the police chief about something or other. The general merriment, laughter, and playful banter were twice as lively during the remainder of the journey.

We arrived at Semyon Yakovlevich's precisely at one o'clock. The gates of the merchant's rather large house stood open, and we were free to enter the annexe. We were informed that Semyon Yakovlevich was having his dinner, but was still receiving guests. Our group entered at once. The room in which the holy man was dining and receiving was quite spacious; it had three windows and was divided into two sections by a waist-high wooden latticed partition running from one wall to the other. Ordinary visitors remained on the far side of the partition, while more fortunate guests were admitted by invitation of the holy man through the partition doors into his half of the room, where, if he so desired, he seated them on his old leather armchairs and sofa; he himself always sat on an old, worn-out Voltaire armchair. He was rather a large, bloated man with a sallow, clean-shaven complexion, about fifty-five years old, with thinning fair hair and a bald spot, a swollen right cheek, somewhat twisted mouth, a large wart near his left nostril, narrow little eyes and a serene, stolid, sleepy expression. He was dressed in German style in a black frock-coat, but without a waistcoat or a tie. A rather coarse white shirt peeked out from beneath his coat; he wore slippers (there seemed to be something wrong with his feet). I heard that at one time he'd been a civil servant and had held some rank. He'd just finished a bowl of fish soup and was setting to work on his second course—boiled potatoes in their skins with salt. He never ate anything else, but he drank a great deal of tea of which he was very fond. Three servants (provided by some merchant or other) were scurrying around him; one of them wore a frock-coat, another resembled a workman, the third a verger. There was also a lad of sixteen, a very lively fellow. In addition to the servants there was also a venerable, grey-haired monk with a collection mug; he was a little too fat. A large samovar was boiling on one of the tables where there was a tray stacked with almost two dozen glasses. On another table opposite lay the offerings: a few loaves and several pounds of sugar, two pounds of tea, a pair of embroidered slippers, a foulard handkerchief, a length of cloth, a piece of linen, etc. Almost all the cash offerings went into the monk's collection mug. The room was full of people—almost a dozen visitors, two of whom were sitting with Semyon Yakovlevich on the other side of the partition; one was a grey-haired old man, a pilgrim 'of the common folk', the other a dried-up little monk, newly arrived, sitting demurely with his eyes downcast. All remaining visitors stood on the other side of the partition, all mostly common folk, except for one fat merchant from the district town, a bearded man dressed in Russian style although he was known to be worth a hundred thousand roubles; one elderly, impoverished noblewoman, and one landowner. Everyone was awaiting his chance, but not daring to be the first to speak. Four people were on their knees, but the landowner was the one who attracted most attention. He was a corpulent man, about forty-five years old, down on his knees next to the partition, more conspicuous than anyone else, waiting reverently for a kind look or a kind word from Semyon Yakovlevich. He'd been there almost an hour and had yet to be noticed.

Our ladies crowded right up to the partition, whispering and giggling gaily. They pushed people aside or stood in front of those on their knees and other visitors, except for the landowner who stubbornly remained in full view and even grabbed hold of the partition. They directed their cheerful and curious glances at Semyon Yakovlevich, some through lorgnettes, pince-nez, and even opera glasses; Lyamshin, at least, was using opera glasses. Semyon Yakovlevich serenely and lethargically surveyed them all with his little eyes.

'What pulchritude! What pulchritude!' he deigned to utter in a hoarse bass voice with some slight surprise.

Our ladies started laughing: 'What does pulchritude mean?' But Semyon Yakovlevich sank into silence and finished his potatoes. At last he wiped his mouth with a napkin and was served tea.

He didn't usually have tea alone; he would offer it to his visitors, but by no means to all of them; he usually indicated those he wished to favour. These decisions of his were always strikingly unpredictable. He would pass over wealthy and powerful people, and sometimes serve tea to a peasant or some decrepit old lady; other times, he'd pass over poor beggars, and serve tea to some fat, wealthy merchant. The tea was also served in different ways: some got theirs already sweetened, others with sugar on the side, and some without any sugar at all. This time the newly arrived monk was favoured with a glass of sweetened tea, while the old pilgrim was given some without sugar. For some reason the fat monk with the collection mug was given no tea at all, even though he'd been served every day up to then.

'Semyon Yakovlevich, say something to me. I've been wanting to meet you for so long,' sang out the elegantly dressed lady from our carriage with a smile, screwing up her eyes. She was the one who'd observed previously that she wasn't fussy about the form of her entertainments, so long as they were amusing. The landowner on his knees sighed loudly and deeply, like the rising and falling of a huge pair of bellows.

'A glass of sweetened tea!' Semyon Yakovlevich declared suddenly, indicating the merchant worth a hundred thousand; he then stepped forward and stood next to the landowner.

'Give him more sugar!' ordered Semyon Yakovlevich, after they'd served him the tea; more sugar was added. 'More, give him more!' A third spoon was added, then a fourth. The merchant began drinking his syrup without demur.

'Good Lord!' people murmured, crossing themselves. The landowner sighed loudly and deeply once again.

'Father! Semyon Yakovlevich!' suddenly rang out the mournful, but unexpectedly shrill voice of the poor woman who'd been pushed over to the wall by our ladies. 'I've been waiting a whole hour for your blessing, dear Father. Speak to me. Advise me, mere wretch that I am.'

'Ask her,' said Semyon Yakovlevich to the servant who looked like a verger. He approached the partition.

'Have you done what Semyon Yakovlevich told you to do last time?' he asked the widow in low, measured tones.

'How could I, Father Semyon Yakovlevich, how could I do that?' the widow cried. 'They're cannibals! They're taking me to court; they're threatening to take it to the Senate. All this to their very own mother!'

'Give her some!' Semyon Yakovlevich said, pointing to the loaf of sugar. The boy jumped up, grabbed the loaf, and handed it to the widow.

'Oh, Father, you're very kind. What will I do with so much sugar?' the widow tried to protest.

'More, more!' Semyon Yakovlevich said.

They handed her another loaf. 'More, more,' the holy man urged; they brought her a third, then a fourth. The widow was surrounded on all sides by sugar. The monk from the monastery sighed: all that sugar might have made its way to the monastery, as it had on other occasions.

'What will I do with it all?' the widow moaned submissively. 'I'm only one person—it'll make me sick! Or is it some kind of prophecy, Father?'

'That's what it is, a prophecy,' said someone in the crowd.

'Give her another pound, more!' said Semyon Yakovlevich, without letting up.

There was one loaf of sugar left on the table; Semyon Yakovlevich indicated that she be given it and it was given to the widow.

'Lord, oh Lord!' the people sighed, crossing themselves. 'It must be a prophecy.'

'First sweeten your heart with goodness and loving kindness, and only then come running to complain about your own children, flesh of your flesh—that's what this sign must mean,' said the fat monk from the monastery in a soft, but complacent voice; he was the one who received no tea, but who now, in a fit of irritated vanity, had taken it upon himself to act as interpreter.

'How can you say that, Father?' the widow suddenly cried angrily. 'They dragged me with a rope into the flames when the Verkhishins' house caught fire! They put a dead cat in my trunk. They're capable of any outrage...'

'Away with her, away!' cried Semyon Yakovlevich all of a sudden, waving his arms.

The verger and the boy rushed behind the partition. The verger took the widow by the arm; she calmed down and was shuffled off to the door, glancing back at the sugar loaves that had been given to her which the boy was now carrying.

'Take one back!' Semyon Yakovlevich ordered the worker who stayed behind. He rushed out after them and in a few moments all three servants returned carrying one of the loaves that had been given to, then taken away from the widow; she did, however, carry off three loaves.

'Semyon Yakovlevich,' cried someone who was standing near the door. 'I saw a bird in my dream, a jackdaw, and it flew out of the water and into the fire. What does that mean?'

'Winter's coming,' said Semyon Yakovlevich.

'Semyon Yakovlevich, why haven't you said anything to me? I've been interested in you for a long time,' one of our ladies began again.

'Ask him!' Semyon Yakovlevich ordered suddenly, ignoring her, pointing to the landowner who was still on his knees.

The monk from the monastery, at whom this order was directed, slowly approached the landowner.

'How have you sinned? And what have you been ordered to do?'

'To refrain from fighting, to keep control of my hands,' the landowner replied hoarsely.

'Have you done so?'

'I can't; my strength gets the better of me.'

'Away with him! Away! Use the broom! The broom!'

Semyon Yakovlevich cried, waving his arms. The landowner didn't wait for his punishment to be administered; he jumped up and ran out of the room.

'He left behind a gold coin,' the monk announced, picking up a half-imperial from the floor.

'Give it to him!' Semyon Yakovlevich said, thrusting his finger in the direction of the rich merchant. The rich man didn't dare refuse and took it.

'Gold unto gold,' said the monk from the monastery, unable to restrain himself.

'And give that one some sweetened tea,' Semyon Yakovlevich said suddenly, pointing to Maurice Nikolaevich. The servant poured a glass of tea and was about to offer it to the dandy in the pince-nez by mistake.

'No, the tall one, the tall one,' Semyon Yakovlevich corrected him.

Maurice Nikolaevich took the glass, made a military half-bow, and began to drink. I don't know why, but our entire party burst out laughing.

'Maurice Nikolaevich!' said Liza, suddenly turning to him. 'The gentleman who was on his knees has left. Go take his place on your knees.'

Maurice Nikolaevich looked at her in astonishment.

'I beg you. You'll be doing me a great favour. Listen, Maurice Nikolaevich,' she said rapidly in an insistent, stubborn, emotional voice. 'You must kneel down, I must see you kneeling down. If you don't, you can't come to see me any more. I insist, absolutely insist on it!'

I don't know what she meant by it, but she kept demanding persistently, relentlessly, as if she were having a fit. As we'll see later, Maurice Nikolaevich interpreted these capricious impulses of hers, which had become especially frequent of late, as outbursts of blind hatred for him. It wasn't out of spite—on the contrary, she esteemed, loved and respected him; he himself knew that—but it was out of some strange, unconscious hatred which she was unable to control at times.

He silently handed his cup to an old woman standing behind him, opened the partition door, and without any

invitation entered the private section of Semyon Yakovlevich's room; he knelt down in the middle of the floor in
front of everyone. I think his simple and sensitive soul was
deeply shocked by Liza's crude, mocking gesture before the
whole company. Perhaps he thought she'd be ashamed of
herself, seeing the humiliation on which she'd insisted. Of
course, no one else would ever have dreamt of altering a
woman's behaviour by such a naïve and risky venture. He
knelt, and his face was imperturbably grave—he looked tall,
ungainly, ridiculous. But our party didn't laugh; his action
was so unexpected it made a painful impression. Everyone
looked at Liza.

'Anoint him, anoint him!' Semyon Yakovlevich muttered.

Liza suddenly turned pale, cried out, gasped for breath,
and rushed round the partition. There occurred a brief,
hysterical scene: with all her strength she tried to lift
Maurice Nikolaevich off his knees, pulling him by the elbow
with both her hands.

'Get up, get up!' she cried, beside herself. 'Get up at
once, immediately! How dare you kneel?'

Maurice Nikolaevich got off his knees. She squeezed his
arms above the elbow with her own two hands and looked
him intently in the eye. There was terror in her glance.

'Pulchritude, pulchritude!' Semyon Yakovlevich repeated
once again.

At last she dragged Maurice Nikolaevich back behind the
partition; a commotion arose among the members of our
group. The lady from our carriage, probably wishing to
break the tension, directed her question at Semyon Yakovlevich for a third time in a loud, shrill voice, with an affected
smile:

'Well, Semyon Yakovlevich, won't you "utter some
prophecy" for me as well? I've really been counting on you.'

'Up your——, up your——!' Semyon Yakovlevich said all
of a sudden, turning to her using an extremely indecent
expression. His words were uttered ferociously, with horrifying clarity. Our ladies shrieked and rushed for the door;
our gentlemen burst into Homeric laughter. Thus ended our
visit to Semyon Yakovlevich.

It was at this point that another extremely curious incident is said to have occurred; I must confess it was the main reason for describing this visit in such detail.

They say that as the whole crowd was rushing out Liza, supported by Maurice Nikolaevich, suddenly found herself face to face with Nikolai Vsevolodovich in the doorway. I must note that since her fainting fit that Sunday morning, although they'd met several times, they hadn't approached one another or exchanged a single word. I saw them bump into each other in the doorway: they both seemed to stop for a moment and stare at each other somewhat strangely. But it was hard to see in that crowd. They assured me, on the contrary, and completely in earnest, that Liza, after glancing at Nikolai Vsevolodovich, raised her hand rapidly to the level of his face and would certainly have struck him, if he hadn't managed to turn away in time. Perhaps she didn't care for the expression on his face or the way he smiled, especially at that moment, just after the episode with Maurice Nikolaevich. I must confess that I saw nothing myself, but everyone else assured me they'd seen it, even though they couldn't possibly have seen it because of all the confusion, although some of them might have. I didn't believe it at the time. But I remember that Nikolai Vsevolodovich looked rather pale all the way back to town.

3.

Almost at the same time and on the very same day, a conversation took place between Stepan Trofimovich and Varvara Petrovna at long last. She'd been thinking about it for some time and had announced it to her former friend a while ago, but for some reason had postponed it until now. The conversation took place at Skvoreshniki. Varvara Petrovna arrived at her country house all in a bustle: the day before it'd been decided once and for all that the fête was to take place at the marshal's house. But Varvara Petrovna was quick to realize that afterwards no one could prevent her from organizing her own special fête there at Skvoreshniki, and inviting the whole town once again. Then everyone would see which house was better, where the guests were received better, and where a ball was given in better taste. Altogether it was impossible to recognize her. She seemed to be reborn; from a previously unapproachable 'high society lady' (Stepan Trofimovich's expression), she was transformed into the most commonplace, whimsical society woman. But perhaps it only seemed so.

Arriving at her empty house, she toured all the rooms accompanied by her faithful old butler, Aleksei Yegorevich, and Fomushka, a man who'd been around a good while and was something of a specialist in decoration. They began discussing and deliberating: which pieces of furniture should be brought from the town house, which items and which pictures; where should they be put; how best to arrange the conservatory and flowers; where to hang new draperies, where to have the buffet, whether to have one or two, and so on and so forth. Then, right in the midst of all these exciting deliberations, she suddenly decided to send a carriage for Stepan Verkhovensky.

He'd been apprised some time before and was ready and waiting every day, expecting precisely this abrupt kind of invitation. After seating himself in the carriage, he crossed himself; his fate was to be decided. He found his friend in the large drawing-room, sitting on a small sofa in a recess, in front of a small marble table, with paper and pencil in hand: Fomushka was measuring the height of the gallery and windows, while Varvara Petrovna was jotting down the figures and making notes in the margins. Without interrupting her work, she nodded to Stepan Trofimovich; after he muttered some greeting, she extended her hand and without looking, motioned him to a seat next to her.

'I sat there and waited for five minutes, "controlling my emotions",' he told me afterwards. 'I saw a woman unlike the one I'd known for the past twenty years. The absolute conviction that everything was over gave me strength which surprised even her. I swear, she was astonished by my steadfastness in that last hour.'

All of a sudden Varvara Petrovna put her pencil down on the little table and turned to him quickly.

'Stepan Trofimovich, we must talk business. I'm sure

you've prepared some high-sounding words and fine phrases, but it would be much better to get right down to business, don't you think?'

He winced. She was in too great a hurry to establish the tone; what could possibly follow?

'Wait! Be quiet. Let me speak first, then you, although I really don't know what you can possibly say,' she continued very rapidly. 'I consider your pension of twelve hundred roubles as my sacred obligation until the end of your life; well, I mean, not a sacred obligation, but simply an agreement. That's more realistic, isn't it? If you like, we can write it all down. In case of my death, I've made special arrangements. But now in addition you'll receive from me your apartment, your servant, and your maintenance. If we calculate all this in cash, it comes to fifteen hundred roubles, isn't that so? I'll add an additional three hundred, making a grand total of three thousand roubles. Is that enough for you each year? I think it's sufficient. In extraordinary circumstances, of course, I can let you have more. So, take the money, send back my servants, and go live on your own, wherever you like, Petersburg, Moscow, abroad or in Russia, but not here. Do you understand?'

'Not so long ago those same lips made very different demands on me, though just as insistent and peremptory,' Stepan Trofimovich replied slowly and with melancholy precision. 'I submitted and... danced the *kazachok** to please you. *Oui, la comparaison peut être permise. C'était comme un petit cozak du Don, qui sautait sur sa propre tombe.*[1] Now...'

'Stop, Stepan Trofimovich. You're so long-winded. You didn't dance; you came out to meet me wearing a new cravat, clean linen and gloves, all pomaded and scented. I assure you, you wanted to get married; it was written all over your face. Believe me, your expression was most inappropriate. If I didn't mention it to you at the time, it was only out of delicacy. But you wanted it, you wanted to get married in spite of the disgusting things you were writing

---

[1] Yes, the comparison may be permitted. It was like a little Don cossack, dancing on his own grave.

about me and your fiancée. But that's not the point now. And why are you dragging in some *cozak du Don* over your grave? I don't understand that sort of comparison. On the contrary, don't die, but live on; live on as long as you like, I'll be delighted.'

'In the poorhouse?'

'The poorhouse? One doesn't wind up in the poorhouse with an income of three thousand roubles a year! Oh, I remember,' she said with a laugh, 'in fact Peter Stepanovich once made a joke about you going to the poorhouse. Well, there is actually this very special poorhouse that's worth thinking about. It's for the most distinguished people: there are colonels there, and even a general wants to live there. If you go there with all your money, you'll find peace, contentment, and servants, too. You'll have time for your studies and always be able to gather a group for a game of preference...'

'*Passons.*'

'*Passons?*' Varvara Petrovna winced. 'Well, in that case, that's all I have to say. You've been informed: from this time forth we'll live quite separately.'

'Is that all? All that's left after twenty years? Our final farewell?'

'You're certainly fond of flourishes, Stepan Trofimovich. It's no longer in fashion. Nowadays people speak crudely, but directly. You do go on about those twenty years! It was twenty years of mutual self-admiration, nothing more. Every one of your letters was not really written for me, but for posterity. You're a stylist, not a friend; friendship is merely a glorified word for it. In reality it was only a reciprocal outpouring of slops...'

'Good Lord, you've picked up so many phrases from other people! Lessons learned by heart! They've already put their uniform on you! You, too, are rejoicing; you, too, are basking in the sun; *chère, chère*, for what mess of pottage* have you sold them your freedom?'

'I'm not a parrot repeating other people's phrases,' Varvara Petrovna exploded. 'Rest assured I've stored up enough words of my own. What have you done for me in the last twenty years? You've even refused to let me see the books I ordered for you, books that would've remained uncut if it hadn't been for the bookbinder. What did you give me to read when I asked you to guide me during those early years? Always Capefigue and more Capefigue.* You were even jealous of my development and took appropriate measures. Meanwhile everyone was laughing at you. I confess, I've always considered you merely as a critic; you're a literary critic, nothing more. When I announced on the way to Petersburg that I intended to establish a journal and dedicate my life to it, you immediately looked at me ironically and suddenly became extremely supercilious.'

'That's not true, not at all... we were afraid of persecution...'

'It certainly is true, and you had no reason to fear persecution in Petersburg. Do you remember later, in February when the news arrived, you suddenly ran in to me terrified, demanding that I provide you with a letter testifying to the fact that the proposed journal had nothing whatever to do with you, that all those young people were visiting me, not you, and that you were merely a domestic tutor living in the house because you'd yet to receive your full salary. Isn't that so? Don't you remember? You've been leading quite a distinguished life, Stepan Trofimovich!'

'It was merely a moment of weakness, a moment when we were alone,' he exclaimed mournfully. 'Are you really going to end it all because of such trifles? Is there nothing more left between us after all these years?'

'You're terribly calculating; you keep trying to make me feel as if I'm in your debt. When you returned from abroad you looked down on me and wouldn't let me say a word. When I came and spoke with you later about my impressions of the Sistine Madonna, you wouldn't listen to me and started smiling superciliously into your cravat, as if I couldn't possibly have the same kind of feelings as you.'

'That's not true, it couldn't be true... *J'ai oublié*.'[1]

'Yes, it is true. What's more, there was nothing to be proud of since it was all nonsense and fantasy. Nowadays

---

[1] I've forgotten.

no one, no one gets excited about the Madonna, no one wastes any time over it, except for a few stubborn old men. It's been proven.'

'Proven, has it?'

'It serves no purpose whatever. This mug is useful because one can pour water into it; this pencil is useful because one can jot things down with it; but there you've got a woman's face that's inferior to any other face in nature. Draw an apple and then place a real one alongside—which one would you take? I'm sure you wouldn't make a mistake. That's what all your theories come down to, now that the first ray of free investigation has fallen upon them.'

'Is that so?'

'You're being sarcastic. What did you use to say about charity, for example? Yet the pleasure of bestowing charity is arrogant and immoral, a rich man's pleasure in his own wealth, power, and importance compared with that of a pauper. Charity corrupts both the giver and receiver; in addition, it doesn't achieve its purpose because it merely intensifies the poverty. Loafers who don't want to work crowd around those who give like gamblers around a gaming-table hoping to win. Meanwhile, the few wretched half-kopeck pieces thrown to them don't amount to anything. Have you given away much in your lifetime? Eight ten-kopeck pieces in all, not more, isn't that so? Try to recall when you last gave anything away—two years ago, or perhaps four? You declaim, but merely interfere with progress. Charity should even be forbidden by law in today's society. In the new order there won't be any poor people.'

'Oh, what a torrent of other people's words! You've even got as far as the new order? You poor creature! God help you!'

'Yes, I've got that far, Stepan Trofimovich. You carefully concealed all new ideas from me, though by now they're familiar to everyone. You did it merely out of jealousy, to have power over me. Why, even Yulia is a hundred miles ahead of me! But now my eyes have been opened. I have defended you, Stepan Trofimovich, as best I could; everyone attacks you, without exception.'

'Enough!' he said, starting to get up from his seat. 'Enough! And what else can I wish you, surely not repentance?'

'Sit down a minute, Stepan Trofimovich, I have something else to ask you. You received an invitation to read at the literary matineé; it was I who arranged it. Tell me, what do you plan to read?'

'Precisely about that queen of queens, that ideal of humanity, the Sistine Madonna, who in your opinion isn't even worth a glass or a pencil.'

'So you're not planning to read something historical?' Varvara Petrovna enquired in melancholy surprise. 'But they won't listen to you. You're obsessed with that Madonna of yours! Why do it if you'll put everyone to sleep? I assure you, Stepan Trofimovich, I'm saying this for your own good. The thing would be, wouldn't it, to choose some short, entertaining episode from medieval court life, from Spanish history, or even better, to tell some anecdote, and then pad it with other anecdotes and witty remarks of your own. They had such luxurious courts, such fine ladies, and poisonings. Karmazinov says it would be very odd if you couldn't find something entertaining to read from Spanish history.'

'Karmazinov, that idiot who's written himself out, is suggesting topics for me!'

'Karmazinov, that almost statesman-like intellect! You're being awfully free with your tongue, Stepan Trofimovich!'

'Your Karmazinov is a spiteful old woman who's written himself out. *Chère, chère*, how long have you been so enslaved to them, oh Lord?'

'Even now I can't stand him for the airs he puts on, but I must do justice to his intellect. I repeat, I defended you with all my might, as best I could. But why do you insist on being so boring and ridiculous? Instead, come out on stage with a respectful smile, as a representative of a past age, and tell a few anecdotes, with all your usual wit, as only you know how. So what if you're an old man, if you belong to a past age, if you've lagged behind them? You'll admit all that yourself, with a smile, in your preamble, and everyone will be surprised you're such a nice, kind, clever old relic... In a word, a man of the old school, but one sufficiently progressive to recognize the absurdity of all those ideas you used to believe in. Come, do me this favour, I beg you.'

'*Chère*, stop it! Don't ask, I can't. I'll talk about the Madonna, but I'll create quite a storm—one that will either crush all of them or destroy only me!'

'Undoubtedly only you, Stepan Trofimovich.'

'Then such be my fate. I'll tell them about that vile slave, that stinking, depraved lackey who'll be the first to mount the staircase, a pair of scissors in hand, to slash the divine countenance of the great ideal in the name of equality, envy and... digestion. Let my curse ring out, and then, then...'

'A lunatic asylum?'

'Perhaps. But in any case, whether I emerge the victor or the vanquished, that very same evening I'll take up my sack, a beggar's sack, leave all my belongings, all your gifts, pensions, and promises of future wealth, and I'll set off on foot to finish my life as a tutor in some merchant's family or else die of hunger in a ditch. I have spoken. *Alea jacta est*!'*

He stood up again.

'I've been convinced,' cried Varvara Petrovna, eyes flashing, rising to her feet, 'for years I've been convinced the only reason you have for living is to put both me and my house to shame with your slander! What do you mean, a tutor in some merchant's family or dying in a ditch? That's malice, slander, nothing more!'

'You've always despised me; but I'll end like a knight, faithful to my lady, for your opinion was always worth more to me than anything. From this moment forth I'll accept nothing from you, but will revere you without reward.'

'How stupid this all is!'

'You've never respected me. I may have many weaknesses. Yes, I sponged off you (I'm using the language of the nihilists); but sponging was never the guiding principle of my actions. It just happened like that, I don't know how... I've always thought there was something more important than food between us, and—never, never have I been a scoundrel! So, now I'll set out to make things right! It's late to begin, already late autumn; a mist lies over the fields, the hoar-frost of old age covers the road before me, and the wind howls around the yawning grave... But I'll set out, move forward, on a new path:

> Full of pure love,
> True to his sweet dream...*

Oh, farewell, my dreams! Twenty years! *Alea jacta est.*'

His face was sprinkled with the tears that had suddenly gushed from his eyes. He picked up his hat.

'I don't understand any Latin,' Varvara Petrovna said, trying very hard to control herself.

Who knows, perhaps she too wanted to weep, but indignation and caprice gained the upper hand.

'I only know one thing—all this is sheer naughtiness. You'll never be able to carry out your threats that are so full of egoism. You won't go anywhere, not to any merchant's family; you'll die very peacefully on my hands, still collecting your pension and receiving your insufferable friends here on Tuesdays. Farewell, Stepan Trofimovich.'

'*Alea jacta est*!' he said, bowing deeply to her, and returned home more dead than alive from emotional exhaustion.

CHAPTER 6

Peter Stepanovich gets busy

I.

THE DATE for the fête was agreed upon and von Lembke became even more depressed and pensive. He was filled with strange and sinister forebodings, and this disturbed Yulia Mikhailovna. True, not everything was quite right. Our former governor had left the administration of the province in some disarray; an epidemic of cholera was threatening; serious outbreaks of cattle plague had appeared in some places; fires had raged all that summer in towns and villages, and stupid rumours of arson were gaining strength among the people. The number of robberies had more than doubled. But all this, of course, would have been perfectly normal, had there not been other, weightier things disturbing the serenity of Andrei Antonovich, who up to then had been a happy man.

What struck Yulia Mikhailovna most of all was that with each passing day he was becoming more taciturn and, strange to say, more secretive. Indeed, why should he have anything to hide? It's true, he rarely opposed her; for the most part he obeyed her wishes entirely. At her insistence, for example, two or three very risky, almost illegal measures were implemented with the aim of strengthening the governor's powers. For the same purpose a number of sinister actions were condoned; for instance, certain people who deserved prison sentences or even exile to Siberia were recommended for decorations, purely at her insistence. In addition, some enquiries and complaints were systematically ignored. All this came to light afterwards. Von Lembke not only put his signature to everything, but never even questioned the role assumed by his wife in the execution of his official duties. On the other hand, he suddenly began to make a fuss over 'mere trifles', much to Yulia Mikhailovna's surprise. No doubt he felt the need to reward himself for his days of obedience by brief moments of rebellion.

Unfortunately, Yulia Mikhailovna, for all her perspicacity, was unable to fathom this subtlety in her husband's noble character. Alas! She had no time for it and that was the cause of many of their misunderstandings.

There are certain things which it is inappropriate for me to discuss; besides, there are some that I simply can't talk about. Nor is it my business to describe in detail administrative errors; therefore I will omit entirely that aspect of the affair. When I undertook this chronicle, I had a very different set of tasks in mind. Besides, a great deal will soon be brought to light by the Commission of Inquiry which has been appointed in our province—it's only a matter of waiting a little while. Some explanations, however, cannot possibly be avoided.

Now I'll return to Yulia Mikhailovna. The poor woman (I feel sorry for her) could really have achieved all that attracted and beckoned her (fame and so on), without any of the violent and eccentric efforts she decided on from the very beginning. But whether as a result of excessive poetic feeling or the sad and repeated failures of her youth, suddenly, with the change in her fortune, she felt specially selected, almost anointed, one of those 'upon whom a tongue of flame* had descended'; and all the trouble was in that tongue. After all, it wasn't like a chignon that could sit on any woman's head. But it's virtually impossible to convince a woman of the truth; on the other hand, anyone wanting to egg her on will always succeed, and people were falling over themselves to encourage her. The poor woman suddenly turned out to be the plaything of the most diverse influences, while at the same time imagining herself to be extremely original. Many experts feathered their nests and took advantage of her simplicity during her brief tenure as governor's wife. And what a mess she got herself into, all under the guise of independence! She favoured large agricultural estates, the aristocratic element, the strengthening of the governor's powers, the democratic element, new institutions, law and order, free-thinking, socialist notions, strict decorum in the aristocratic salon, and the free-and-easy, almost tavern-like manners of the young people surrounding her. She dreamt of *bestowing happiness* and reconciling the irreconcilable, or, to be more precise, unifying everything and everyone in adoration of her own person. She had her favourites; she was very fond of Peter Stepanovich, who, by the way, flattered her unabashedly. But she was fond of him for another reason as well, a bizarre reason, very characteristic of the poor woman: she kept hoping he'd reveal a conspiracy against the government to her! As difficult as it is to imagine, this was indeed the case. For some reason she believed a plot against the government was being hatched in our very own province. Peter Stepanovich, by his silence at certain moments and hints at others, encouraged this strange idea. She imagined he was in contact with everyone connected with the revolutionary movement in Russia, but at the same time, thought he was absolutely devoted to her to the point of adoration. The discovery of the conspiracy, gratitude from Petersburg, a future career, the influence of her 'kindness' on our youth, which would save them from the abyss—all these ideas coexisted quite happily in that fantasizing brain of hers. After all, she'd saved Peter Stepanovich, conquered him (for some reason she was absolutely certain of that), and she would save the others as well; she'd straighten them out; she'd report on them accurately; she'd act in the highest interests of justice, and perhaps even history; all of Russian liberalism would bless her name; and nevertheless the conspiracy would be discovered. All advantages in one fell swoop!

Still it was essential that Andrei Antonovich's mood improve before the fête. He must absolutely be cheered up and calmed down. With this aim in mind she sent Peter Stepanovich in to see him, in the hope that he'd relieve his depression by some reassuring means known only to him. Perhaps he'd even provide some special information, straight from the horse's mouth, so to speak. She had implicit faith in his ability. Peter Stepanovich hadn't been in von Lembke's study for some time. He dropped in on him just when the patient was in a rather difficult mood.

2.

There had occurred a particular combination of circumstances with which Mr von Lembke was quite unable to cope. In the district in which Peter Stepanovich had been having such a good time of late, a second lieutenant had been reprimanded by his superior officer. This took place in front of the entire company. The second lieutenant was a young man, recently arrived from Petersburg, taciturn and morose, of dignified appearance, although small, stout, and red-cheeked. He couldn't bear the reprimand; lowering his head in a savage way, he suddenly threw himself on his commander with an unexpected scream that astonished the entire company. He struck him with all his might and bit him on the shoulder; they had difficulty dragging him away. There was no doubt he'd gone mad; at least, it turned out that certain peculiarities in his behaviour had been observed during the last few weeks. For example, he'd thrown two of his landlady's icons out of his apartment and destroyed one of them with an axe; in his own room he'd placed on three lecterns the works of Vogt, Moleschott, and Büchner,* and in front of each he used to burn wax church tapers. From the quantity of books found in his apartment, it was clear he was well read. If he'd possessed fifty thousand francs he might have sailed to the Marquesas Islands like that 'cadet' whom Mr Herzen describes* with such good humour in one of his works. When he was arrested they found a large bundle of the most reckless political pamphlets in his pockets and in his apartment.

The political pamphlets in and of themselves were a trivial matter and, in my opinion, nothing to worry about. We've seen quite a few of them. Besides, they weren't even the latest ones: they were the same as those distributed in Kh— province, as we later learned, and Liputin, who'd been travelling in our district and the neighbouring province some six weeks earlier, assured us he'd seen the same ones there. But what most struck Andrei Antonovich was the fact that the manager of Shpigulin's factory had just handed over to the police two or three bundles of the same pamphlets found in the second lieutenant's apartment. They'd been left at the factory during the night and hadn't been opened yet, so not one of the workers had managed to read a word. The facts were ridiculous, but it made Andrei Antonovich reflect deeply. He felt the incident was unpleasantly complicated.

In the factory belonging to the Shpigulins the so-called 'Shpigulin affair' was just beginning; this occasioned a great deal of talk among us and in certain variants it even appeared in the Moscow and Petersburg papers. Three weeks before, one of the workers had fallen ill with Asiatic cholera and died; then a few more men became ill. Everyone in town was in a panic because cholera was moving in from the neighbouring province. I must note that satisfactory sanitary precautions had been taken, as far as possible, to meet this uninvited guest. But the factory belonging to the Shpigulins, millionaires and people with connections, had somehow been overlooked. And then, all of a sudden, came a hue and cry that it was the sole source and a hotbed of the infection, that the factory itself and especially the workers' quarters were so incredibly filthy that even had there been no cholera epidemic an outbreak would have occurred there anyway. Precautionary measures were adopted of course, and Andrei Antonovich energetically insisted on their immediate implementation. The factory was cleaned up within three weeks, but for some reason the Shpigulins closed it down anyway. One of the Shpigulin brothers had always lived in Petersburg; another left for Moscow after the authorities had ordered the factory cleaned up. The manager proceeded to pay off the workers and, as it now turns out, swindled them mercilessly. The workers complained and demanded a fair settlement; stupidly they went to the police, but without much fanfare or getting too agitated. It was just at that moment that Andrei Antonovich was handed the political pamphlets discovered by the manager.

Peter Stepanovich rushed into the study without being announced, just like an old friend of the family; besides, he had a commission from Yulia Mikhailovna. When he saw him, von Lembke frowned gloomily and stopped by the table in a most unfriendly way. He'd just been pacing up and down in his study discussing some private business with an office clerk named Blum, an extremely awkward and morose German he'd brought with him from Petersburg in the face of his wife's vehement opposition. At Peter Stepanovich's entrance, the clerk headed toward the door, but didn't leave. Peter Stepanovich thought he exchanged a meaningful glance with his superior.

'Aha, so I've caught you, the secretive town governor!' cried Peter Stepanovich, laughing and placing his hand on the political pamphlet lying on the table. 'This will be added to your collection, won't it?'

Andrei Antonovich flushed. His face suddenly seemed distorted.

'Stop it, stop it at once!' he cried, shaking with rage. 'How dare you, sir...'

'What's the matter? You seem angry!'

'Let me tell you, my good sir, I have no intention of putting up with your *sans façon*[1] any longer. I ask you to recall...'

'Well, I'll be damned! He really is angry!'

'Shut up, shut up!' von Lembke cried, stamping his feet on the carpet. 'How dare you...'

God knows how it all might have ended. Alas, there was another circumstance here in addition to all the others, known neither to Peter Stepanovich nor even to Yulia Mikhailovna. The unfortunate Andrei Antonovich had been so upset that during the last few days he'd even begun to be jealous of his wife's affection for Peter Stepanovich. In solitude, especially at night, he experienced some very unpleasant moments.

'Well, I thought that if a man reads you his novel in private for two days straight until long after midnight and wants to hear your opinion of it, then he's moved beyond official formalities at least... Yulia Mikhailovna receives me like a friend; what am I to make of you?' Peter Stepanovich asked, not without dignity. 'Incidentally, here's your novel

---

[1] off-hand manner

back,' he said, placing on the table a large, heavy, rolled-up notebook wrapped in blue paper.

Von Lembke blushed and looked embarrassed.

'Where did you find it?' he asked cautiously with a burst of joy he could not control, but attempted to with all his might.

'Just imagine, all rolled up as it is, it had slid under the chest of drawers. When I came in I must have tossed it down carelessly. It was found the day before yesterday when the floors were being scrubbed; you gave me quite a bit of work to do, though!'

Von Lembke dropped his eyes sternly.

'I haven't slept a wink the last two nights, all thanks to you. It was discovered the day before yesterday, and I held on to it, reading; I have no time during the day, so I read at night. Well, sir, it's not to my liking: not really my way of looking at things. But that doesn't matter. I've never considered myself much of a literary critic; but I couldn't tear myself away from it, my dear man, even though it really wasn't to my liking! The fourth and fifth chapters are... are... are... the devil knows what they are! And what humour you've crammed into it; I simply roared with laughter. How you've managed to make fun of things *sans que cela paraisse*![1] And then in the ninth and tenth chapters, all that stuff about love; it's not my cup of tea, but it's very effective. I almost started to snivel reading Igrenev's letter, though it's a very clever portrait.... You know, it's very moving, while at the same time you display his sort of false side, isn't that so? Have I guessed correctly? And I could simply give you a good beating for that ending. What are you trying to say? Why, it's the same old deification of domestic bliss, child-bearing, acquiring capital, and living happily ever after. Good Lord! You'll enchant your readers, since even I couldn't tear myself away from it, but that makes it worse. Readers are stupid as ever; that's why intelligent people have a duty to rouse them, while you... Well, enough is enough. Goodbye. Don't get angry again. I came to tell you a few important things, but you're in such a strange mood that...'

[1] without its being apparent!

Meanwhile Andrei Antonovich took his novel and locked it up in the oak book-case, managing incidentally to give Blum a wink, indicating that he should make himself scarce. He disappeared with a long, mournful face.

'My mood isn't all that strange, it's just that... all these unpleasantries,' he muttered, frowning but not angry, and sat down by the table. 'Have a seat and tell me what you came to say. I haven't seen you in a long time, Peter Stepanovich, but you can't come rushing in here with such bad manners... especially when I have business to attend to...'

'My manners never change...'

'I know that, sir, and I realize you didn't intend anything, but there are times when one has other worries... Have a seat.'

Peter Stepanovich sprawled on the sofa and in a flash tucked his legs up under him.

3·

'What other worries do you have? It's not this nonsense, is it?' he asked, nodding at the political pamphlets. 'I can bring you as many as you like; I first encountered them in Kh— province.'

'You mean when you were there?'

'Well, of course, not when I wasn't there. There was one pamphlet with a little illustration—an axe drawn on top. Allow me' (he picked up the pamphlet). 'Why, yes, there's an axe drawn here, too. It's the same one, the very same.'

'Yes, it's an axe. Look—an axe.'

'Well, does the axe frighten you?'

'It's not the axe, sir... and I'm not frightened, but this affair... this entire affair is so... there are certain circumstances.'

'What circumstances? That the pamphlets came from the factory? Ha, ha! You know, don't you, the workers in that factory will soon be writing their own pamphlets!'

'What do you mean?' von Lembke asked sternly.

'Just what I said. You'd better keep an eye on them. You're much too kind a man, Andrei Antonovich; you even write novels. You really should deal with it in the good, old-fashioned way.'

'What do you mean by that? What sort of advice are you giving me? The factory's been cleaned up; I gave the order and it was cleaned up.'

'There's a rebellion among the workers. You should have them all flogged; that would put an end to it.'

'A rebellion? Nonsense; I gave the order and it was cleaned up.'

'Hey, Andrei Antonovich, you're much too kind a man!'

'In the first place, I'm not all that kind; and in the second place...' von Lembke said, taking offence yet again. He was speaking to the young man without restraint, out of curiosity, to see if he'd learn something new.

'Aha, here's another old friend!' Peter Stepanovich said, interrupting him, seizing another document that lay under a paperweight. It was like a political pamphlet, apparently published abroad, but written in verse. 'Well, I know this one by heart: "A Noble Character"!* Let's see. Sure enough, "A Noble Character" it is. I first became acquainted with this character when I was living abroad. Where did you come across it?'

'You encountered it abroad?' von Lembke asked in astonishment.

'Indeed I did, four or even five months ago.'

'It seems you saw a great deal abroad,' von Lembke said, casting a shrewd glance at him. Without even listening, Peter Stepanovich unfolded the piece of paper and read the poem aloud:

A NOBLE CHARACTER

He was a man of common birth,
Raised by the humble, close to earth,
Of tsarist fury soon he knew,
Boyars' unfailing malice too;
He chose a life of suffering, grief,
Tortures fierce beyond belief,
In hope of making the people see:
All should be brothers, equal, free!

And when he had stirred a band to rise,
He managed to flee to foreign skies,
Escaping from under the bastions
Of the tsar, from knouts and chains and guns,
While from Smolensk to far Tashkent
The masses, awakened, fully bent
On ending a tyranny so malign,
Waited for the student's sign.

United now, they waited his call,
Waited his coming to lead them all
To put an end at last to tsars,
To do away with proud boyars,
To give the land back to the folk,
And smash that vilest triple yoke,
Family, Marriage, a Church that 'saves'—
Lies of the past that keep us slaves!

'You must have got it from that officer, didn't you?' Peter Stepanovich asked.

'So, you're also acquainted with that officer?'

'Of course I am. I spent two days carousing with him. He must have lost his mind.'

'Perhaps he didn't lose his mind.'

'Why, because he started biting people?'

'But, if you first saw these verses abroad and then, as it turns out, here in that officer's hands...'

'So what? Very mysterious! Andrei Antonovich, I can see you're interrogating me. You see, sir,' he began suddenly with unusual solemnity, 'when I returned from abroad I informed certain people about what I'd seen there. My explanations were deemed satisfactory, or else I'd never have honoured this town with my presence. I consider my duty in this matter has been done, and I owe no further explanations to anyone. And my duty was done not because I'm an informer, but because I could act in no other way. Those who wrote to Yulia Mikhailovna understood the matter and described me as an honest man... But to hell with all that! I've come to tell you something very serious and it's a good thing you sent away that chimney-sweep of yours. It's an important matter to me, Andrei Antonovich; I have a very great favour to ask of you.'

'A favour? Hmm, go on, I'm waiting and, I must confess, with considerable curiosity. In general I must admit you rather surprise me, Peter Stepanovich.'

Von Lembke was somewhat agitated. Peter Stepanovich crossed his legs.

'In Petersburg', he began, 'I spoke openly about many things, but about some, this one, for example' (he tapped 'A Noble Character' with his finger), 'I said nothing; in the first place, it wasn't worth talking about, and in the second place, because I answered only those questions I was asked. I don't like getting ahead of them in this regard; that's precisely how I see the difference between a scoundrel and an honest man who's simply compelled by circumstances... But that's neither here nor there. Well, sir, and now... now that these fools... well, since it's all come to light and is already in your hands, and, I can see, it can't be concealed from you—because you're a man with eyes in his head and it's impossible to know what you intend to do—while these idiots go on, I... I... well, in a word, I've come to ask you to save one man, he's an idiot, too, perhaps he's even insane, but to save him on account of his youth, his misfortune, in the name of your own humanity... Surely your humanity is not confined just to those novels you produce!' he said, suddenly breaking off with rude sarcasm and impatience.

In a word, here was a straightforward man, but awkward and tactless from an overflow of humane feelings and perhaps even an excess of sensitivity; above all, he appeared to be not all that clever, as von Lembke recognized at once with extraordinary shrewdness. He'd suspected this was true for some time, especially last week while sitting alone in his study, particularly late at night, cursing him inwardly with all his might for his inexplicable success in winning Yulia Mikhailovna's favour.

'For whom are you pleading and what does all this mean?' he asked in exalted fashion, trying to conceal his curiosity.

'It's... it's... damn it! It's not my fault I believe you! Is it my fault if I take you to be an honourable man and above all a sensible one... that is, able to understand... oh, damn it all.'

The poor fellow, apparently, couldn't gain control of himself.

'You must understand, of course,' he continued, 'you must understand that in telling you his name, I'll be betraying him to you. I am betraying him, isn't that so? Isn't it?'

'But how on earth can I possibly guess who it is, if you're not willing to say his name?'

'That's precisely what I mean. You can always lay a fellow low with that logic of yours, damn it... damn it all... the "noble character", the "student"—is Shatov... and that's all there is to it!'

'Shatov? What do you mean, Shatov?'

'Shatov is the "student" referred to in the pamphlet. He lives here; he's a former serf, the one who gave Stavrogin that slap.'

'I know, I know!' said von Lembke, screwing up his eyes. 'But what exactly, may I ask, is he accused of, and above all, what are you seeking from me?'

'I want you to save him, don't you see? I used to know him eight years ago; I might even have been his friend,' Peter Stepanovich cried, now beside himself. 'But I'm not obliged to give you an account of my past life,' he said, waving his arms. 'It's all so insignificant, a total of three and a half men, and if you include those living abroad, it doesn't even add up to ten. But the main thing is—I'm relying on your humanity, your intelligence. You'll understand and immediately see the matter in its true light as the absurd dream of someone who's insane, and not as God knows what... It's a result of misfortune, you see, prolonged misfortune, and not the devil knows what unheard of conspiracy against the government!...'

He was almost out of breath.

'Hmmm. I now see he's responsible for the pamphlets with the axe,' von Lembke concluded, almost majestically. 'But how, may I ask, if he was acting alone, did he manage to distribute them here, in the provinces, even in Kh— province and... and, above all, where on earth did he get them?'

'But I'm telling you there aren't more than five of them in all, well, maybe ten, how do I know?'

'You don't know?'

'How on earth would I know, damn it all!'

'But you knew Shatov was one of the conspirators, didn't you?'

'Oh!' cried Peter Stepanovich with a wave of his arm, as if fending off his interrogator's overwhelming perspicacity. 'Well, listen, I'll tell you the whole truth: I don't know anything about the pamphlets, that is, not one thing, damn it all, do you understand, not one thing!... Well, of course that second lieutenant, someone else, and another person here... well, maybe Shatov, and someone else as well, that's all—such a wretched lot! I came to plead for Shatov; he has to be saved because it's his poem, his own composition, and it was published abroad through him. That's what I know for sure; but I don't know anything about the pamphlets.'

'If the verses are his, surely the pamphlets are, too. What grounds do you have for suspecting Mr Shatov?'

With the look of a man who's lost all patience, Peter Stepanovich took out his wallet from his pocket and extracted a note.

'Here are the grounds!' he shouted, tossing the note on the table. Von Lembke unfolded it; it had been written about six months ago and sent abroad; it was very brief, consisting of only a few words:

I can't print 'A Noble Character' here; in fact, I can't do anything. Print it abroad.

I. Shatov

Von Lembke stared at Peter Stepanovich intently. Varvara Petrovna was right in saying he had the expression of a sheep, sometimes especially so.

'What I mean is', Peter Stepanovich burst out suddenly, 'he wrote these verses about six months ago, but he couldn't print them here at some secret printing press—therefore he asks to have them printed abroad... That's clear, isn't it?'

'Yes, it's clear, but who's he writing to? That's still not clear,' von Lembke observed with subtle irony.

'To Kirillov, of course; the note was written to Kirillov when he was living abroad... Didn't you know that? What's so annoying is you may be only pretending, and in fact you knew all about these verses some time ago, and about everything else as well! How did they turn up here on your desk? It happened somehow! And if so, why are torturing me like this?'

He feverishly wiped the sweat from his brow with a handkerchief.

'I may know a little something...' von Lembke conceded shrewdly, 'but who's this Kirillov?'

'An engineer who arrived here not long ago; he was Stavrogin's second. He's a maniac, a madman. That second lieutenant of yours may only be suffering from d.t.'s, but this fellow's completely insane—completely, I guarantee it. Oh, Andrei Antonovich, if the government only knew what sort of people they all are, it wouldn't need to take action against them. Every one should be locked up in an insane asylum; I had my fill of them at various congresses in Switzerland.'

'Is it from there they direct the movement over here?'

'Who directs it? Three and a half men. It's a crashing bore just to look at them. What movement here? Political pamphlets? What kind of people have been recruited: a second lieutenant with d.t.'s and two or three students! You're a clever man—so here's a question for you: why can't they win over more important people to their cause? Why only students and minors with an average age of twenty-two? And not even very many of them! There must be a million bloodhounds out looking for them. How many have been found? Seven. I tell you, it's a crashing bore.'

Von Lembke listened attentively, but with an expression that said, 'Don't expect me to believe these tall tales of yours!'

'But permit me... you just claimed this note was sent from abroad; there's no address. How do you know the note was addressed to Mr Kirillov, and above all, how do you know it was sent from abroad and... and... that it really was written by Mr Shatov?'

'Get a sample of Shatov's handwriting and compare it. You must have his signature on some document in your

office. As for the fact that it was addressed to Kirillov, he
himself showed it to me at the time.'

'Then you yourself must have...'

'Well, yes, of course. And that wasn't all I was shown
there. As for these verses, they're supposed to have been
written for Shatov by the late Herzen when he was still
wandering abroad, in commemoration of their meeting, by
way of praise, as a recommendation—damn it all... And now
Shatov circulates it among young people as if to say, "This
is what Herzen himself thought of me." '

'Aha, now I see,' said von Lembke, understanding at last.
'That's what I was wondering about: I understand about the
pamphlet, but why the poem?'

'Of course you understand! The devil knows why I've told
you so much. Listen, let me have Shatov, and to hell with
the rest of them, even Kirillov who's locked himself up and
is now hiding in Filippov's house where Shatov also lives.
They don't like me because I've made an about-face... but
promise me I can have Shatov and I'll serve you up all the
rest of them on a platter. I'll prove useful, Andrei Antonovich! I reckon the whole wretched lot of them numbers only
about nine or ten. I keep an eye on them myself, for my
own reasons. We know the identity of three of them already:
Shatov, Kirillov, and that second lieutenant. As for the
rest—I'm still only *keeping my eye on them*... but I have a
pretty keen eye. It's the same as in Kh— province—they
arrested two students with leaflets, one schoolboy, two
twenty-year-old noblemen, a teacher, and a retired major
aged sixty who was stupefied with drink. That was all there
was to it; and believe me, that *was* all. They were even
surprised there was no more than that. But we need six
days. I've got it all worked out—six days, no less. If you
want results—don't bother them for another six days, and
I'll wrap them all up in one bundle for you. If you make a
move before then—the birds will fly away. But hand Shatov
over to me. I've come for him... The best thing would be
to summon him secretly, in a friendly way, here to your
study, even, and interrogate him after letting him see you
know everything already... He'll probably throw himself at

your feet and burst into tears! He's an extremely nervous man and very unhappy; his wife is having an affair with Stavrogin. Be nice to him and he'll tell you everything; but we need six days... And above all, above all—not one word to Yulia Mikhailovna. It's a secret. Can you keep a secret?'

'What?' von Lembke said, his eyes bulging. 'You mean you've said nothing at all to Yulia Mikhailovna?'

'To her? Good Lord, no! You see, Andrei Antonovich, I value her friendship too much and have such high regard for her... and so on... but I won't make that mistake! I don't contradict her because, as you well know, it's dangerous to do so. I may have dropped a hint or two because she's so fond of it, but I certainly would never dream of providing her with a list of names or anything else, as I've just done for you, good Lord, no! Why have I turned to you now? Because you're a man after all, a serious person, with old-fashioned, reliable experience in the civil service. You've been around. I imagine that as a result of your Petersburg days you know by heart every step of the way in matters such as these. But if I were to mention these two names to her, she'd blurt them out all over the place... You know, then she'd really like to astonish all Petersburg. No, sir, she's too hot-headed, that's what.'

'Yes, there's something of that *fougue*[1] in her,' Andrei Antonovich muttered not without some satisfaction, at the same time finding it deplorable that this ignoramus dared express himself so freely about Yulia Mikhailovna. Peter Stepanovich, however, probably thought he hadn't gone far enough and needed to redouble his efforts both to flatter and vanquish von Lembke once and for all.

'That's it precisely: *fougue*,' he concurred. 'She may be a brilliant, cultured woman, but—she'll scare away the birds. She couldn't keep a secret for six hours, let alone six days. Hey, Andrei Antonovich, don't try to impose any six-day silence on a woman! You'll admit I have some experience, in this sort of thing, I mean; well, I know a thing or two about it and you know I do. I'm not asking for these six days just for fun, but because there's a good reason.'

---

[1] enthusiasm

'I've heard,' von Lembke said, uncertain whether to utter his thought, 'I've heard that when you returned from abroad, you expressed your... repentance in the appropriate places. Is that so?'

'Well, something of that sort may have occurred.'

'Of course, I wouldn't dream of prying... but you've always seemed to me to have been talking in quite a different style here, up to now—about Christianity, for example, social institutions, and even the government...'

'I've said quite a few things. I'm still saying some of them, but there's no reason to implement these ideas in the same way those idiots do—that's the whole point. What's the use of biting someone's shoulder? You agreed with me yourself, but you said it was too early.'

'That's not what I meant when I agreed with you or when I said it was too early.'

'You certainly weigh each and every word you say, don't you? You're a very cautious man!' Peter Stepanovich remarked cheerfully. 'Listen, old friend, I needed to get to know you; that's why I spoke like that. I get to know lots of people that way, not only you. Perhaps I needed to find out about your character.'

'Why did you need to find out about my character?'

'Well, how should I know,' he said, laughing again. 'You see, my dear, much esteemed Andrei Antonovich, you're a sly fellow, but it still hasn't come to *that* and probably never will, do you understand? Perhaps you do understand. Even though I provided explanations in the appropriate quarter when I returned from abroad, I still don't know why a person with certain convictions shouldn't act on the basis of those convictions to further certain ends... But no one *there* asked me to investigate your character; nor have I undertaken any such mission on my own. Consider the following: instead of revealing those two names to you as I just did, I could've gone straight to *them*, that is, where I first provided those explanations; and if I'd been trying to improve my own finances or gain any other advantage, of course it wouldn't really benefit me, since now they'll be grateful to you, not me. I've done it solely for Shatov,' Peter

Stepanovich added nobly, 'solely for Shatov, because of our previous friendship... Well, perhaps when you pick up your pen to write to *them*, you'll put in a kind word for me, if you like... I won't object, ha, ha! *Adieu*, though; I've stayed too long and shouldn't have said so much!' he added pleasantly, getting up from the sofa.

'On the contrary, I'm very glad this matter is being resolved, as it were,' said von Lembke, standing up, also with an amiable expression, obviously under the influence of Peter's last words. 'I'm most grateful for your services; rest assured I'll do everything in my power to draw attention to your zeal...'

'Six days, I need above all six days; don't make a move during the next six days, that's all I need!'

'So be it.'

'Of course, I can't tie your hands and wouldn't dare try. You'll need to keep an eye on them; but don't disturb the nest before it's time—that's where I'm relying on your intelligence and experience. I imagine you have plenty of bloodhounds and sleuth-hounds in reserve, ha, ha!' Peter Stepanovich blurted out cheerfully, without thinking (like a young man).

'Not exactly,' von Lembke said, amiably avoiding a direct answer. 'That's the sort of thing young people think—bloodhounds in reserve... Incidentally, allow me to add just this: if Kirillov was Stavrogin's second, then in that case Mr Stavrogin is...'

'What about Stavrogin?'

'I mean, if they're such good friends?'

'Oh, no, no, no! Clever as you are, you've missed the point. You surprise me. I thought you had certain information about that. Hmmm, Stavrogin—it's quite the opposite, I mean, quite... *Avis au lecteur*.'*

'Really? Is that so?' von Lembke asked in disbelief. 'Yulia Mikhailovna told me that according to her sources in Petersburg, he was a person with certain... instructions, so to speak.'

'I know nothing, nothing at all, absolutely nothing. *Adieu. Avis au lecteur*!' Peter Stepanovich said all of a sudden, obviously avoiding the question.

He rushed towards the door.

'Wait a minute, Peter Stepanovich, wait a minute,' cried von Lembke. 'There's one other little matter; then I won't keep you any longer.'

He took an envelope from his desk drawer.

'Here's a little example of the kind of thing we've been talking about. In showing it to you, I'm demonstrating the great trust I place in you. Here it is. What do you think of it?'

In the envelope was a letter—a curious, anonymous letter addressed to von Lembke, received only yesterday. To his intense annoyance, Peter Stepanovich read the following:

Your Excellency:
For that's who you are by rank. I hereby inform you that an attempt is being made on the lives of certain generals and against the fatherland; that's where it's all leading. I myself have been distributing things for many years. And then there's atheism. A rebellion is in the making; there are several thousand political pamphlets, and for each one of them, a hundred people will come running, their tongues hanging out, if it's not stopped in time by the authorities, since they've been promised great rewards. The common folk are stupid, and there's vodka besides. People are looking for the guilty party and are destroying both sides, afraid of both one and the other; I repent, but I haven't really participated in it, in view of my circumstances. If you'd like me to inform to save the fatherland, and the churches and icons as well, I'm the only one who can do it. But only on the condition I receive a pardon from the Third Section* by telegraph immediately, for me alone. Let the others answer for it. Place a candle every evening in the porter's window at seven o'clock as a signal. When I've seen it, I'll believe it and come and kiss the magnanimous hand from the capital city, but only on condition that I receive a pension, or else, how will I live? You won't regret it because they'll give you a medal. We must keep this a secret, or else they'll wring my neck.
Your excellency's desperate servant,
Falls at your feet

A repentant free-thinker *Incognito*

Von Lembke said the letter had turned up yesterday in the porter's lodge when no one was there.

'So what do you think?' Peter Stepanovich asked almost rudely.

'I'm assuming it's an anonymous lampoon, meant as a joke.'

'That's probably what it is. There's no hoodwinking you.'

'What makes me think so is that it's so stupid.'

'Have you received any other lampoons like this?'

'Twice, both anonymous.'

'Well, of course they wouldn't be signed. In a different style? Different handwriting?'

'Different style and handwriting.'

'As facetious as this one?'

'Yes, just as facetious, and, you know... quite contemptible.'

'Well, since there were others, this one must be the same thing.'

'What makes me think so is that's it's so stupid. Those people are educated and probably wouldn't write such nonsense.'

'Yes, indeed.'

'But what if there's someone who really wants to inform the authorities?'

'It's unlikely,' Peter Stepanovich said dryly, cutting him off. 'What does he mean by a telegram from the Third Section and a pension? It's obviously a lampoon.'

'Yes, yes,' von Lembke said, embarrassed.

'You know what? Leave it with me. I'll find out who wrote it. I'll find out before the others do.'

'Take it,' said von Lembke, agreeing, but with some hesitation.

'Have you shown it to anyone?'

'No, of course not. No one.'

'Not even Yulia Mikhailovna?'

'Oh, God forbid! And for God's sake, don't you show it to her!' cried von Lembke in a fright. 'She'd be so upset... and terribly angry with me.'

'Yes, you'd be the first to catch it; she'd say if people wrote such things, then you deserve it. We know what female logic is like. Well, goodbye. I might even present you with the author of this letter in two or three days. Above all, remember our agreement!'

4.

Peter Stepanovich might not have been a stupid man, but Fedka the convict was right when he used to say, 'First he gets his own picture of a man, then that's the man he sees.' He left von Lembke fully convinced he'd put the latter's mind at ease for the next six days at least, and he desperately needed that amount of time. But this idea was false and based solely on the assumption that he'd created for himself once and for all an Andrei Antonovich who was an absolute moron.

Like any other morbidly suspicious individual, Andrei Antonovich was always extremely and cheerfully trustful the moment he left uncertainty behind. This new turn of events appeared to him in a rather pleasant light at first, despite the return of certain bothersome complications. At least his old doubts had been laid to rest. Besides, he'd been feeling so tired the last few days, so exhausted and helpless, his soul involuntarily longed for peace and quiet. But alas, once again he was troubled. His prolonged residence in Petersburg had left indelible traces on his soul. The official, even confidential history of the 'new generation' was rather familiar to him—he was an inquisitive person and collected political pamphlets—but he never really understood anything about it. Now he felt he was lost in a forest: all his instincts told him that Peter Stepanovich's words contained something completely and utterly unintelligible—although 'the devil only knows what could happen with this "younger generation" and what's going on with them!' he mused, lost in perplexity.

Then, at that very moment, as if deliberately, Blum stuck his head in the door. Throughout Peter Stepanovich's visit he'd been waiting close by. Blum was actually a distant relative of von Lembke's, but this fact had been carefully and fearfully concealed. I must ask the reader's indulgence for wasting a few words on this insignificant character. Blum belonged to the strange class of 'unfortunate Germans'—not because he lacked talent, but for no good reason whatever. These 'unfortunate Germans' are no myth; they really do exist, even in Russia, and they are a special type. All his life Andrei Antonovich had the most touching sympathy for him and always, wherever he could, as he moved up in the civil service, promoted him to a subordinate post within his own jurisdiction; but Blum had no luck anywhere. Either the post was abolished or someone else was appointed as his superior; once he was almost put on trial with some other people. He was conscientious, but excessively gloomy, with no reason and to his own disadvantage. He had red hair and was tall, stooping, cheerless, even sensitive; but in spite of his low standing, he was insistent and stubborn as an ox, always on the wrong occasion. He and his wife and their numerous children had for many years felt a deep attach-ment for Andrei Antonovich. Except for Andrei Antonovich, no one had ever liked him. Yulia Mikhailovna had tried to get rid of him at once, but was unable to overcome her husband's resistance. It was the first quarrel of their married life and it occurred right after their wedding, during their honeymoon, when Blum suddenly showed up. He'd been carefully concealed from her up to then, along with the embarrassing secret of their relationship. Andrei Antonovich implored her with clasped hands, relating with emotion the whole story of Blum and of their friendship since childhood, but Yulia Mikhailovna felt humiliated for ever and even resorted to fainting. Von Lembke didn't yield an inch and declared he'd never abandon Blum for anything on earth and never part with him. She was very surprised and finally agreed to let Blum stay. But they resolved that the relation-ship should be concealed even more carefully than before, if that were possible, and that even Blum's first name and patronymic should be changed, since he was also called Andrei Antonovich. Blum knew nobody in our town except the German pharmacist, and he didn't visit anyone; as was his custom, he led a meagre and lonely existence. For a long time he'd known about Andrei Antonovich's literary pecca-dilloes. He was usually summoned to private readings from the novel, and would have to sit for six hours at a time; he perspired and expended great effort not to fall asleep and to keep smiling; upon returning home he'd complain to his long-legged, lanky wife about his benefactor's unfortunate proclivity for Russian literature.

Andrei Antonovich gave Blum an anguished look.

'I beg you to leave me in peace, Blum,' he began in agitated haste, obviously hoping to avoid any resumption of their previous conversation interrupted by Peter Stepanovich's arrival.

'But it could be arranged in a most delicate manner, with no publicity whatsoever; you have all the power you need,' Blum was insisting on something respectfully, but obstinately, bending forward, moving closer and closer to Andrei Antonovich with tiny steps.

'Blum, you're so devoted to me and so eager to serve that every time I look at you I'm overcome by panic.'

'You always say caustic things and then, feeling so pleased with yourself, you fall asleep peacefully; but by doing that you're only hurting yourself.'

'Blum, I've just become convinced that we've made quite a mistake, quite a mistake.'

'Surely not as a result of what that false, vicious young man just said to you, someone you yourself have been so suspicious about? He's won you over by flattering your literary talent.'

'Blum, you don't understand a thing; your idea is stupid, I'm telling you. We won't find anything; there'll be an awful outcry, then people will laugh, then Yulia Mikhailovna will...'

'We'll undoubtedly find everything we're looking for,' Blum said, advancing firmly towards him and placing his right hand over his heart. 'We'll conduct the search suddenly, early in the morning, maintaining utmost courtesy towards the person involved, observing the letter of the law precisely. The young men, Lyamshin and Telyatnikov, positively insist we'll find everything we want. They've been there many times. No one is well disposed toward Stepan Trofimovich. General Stavrogin's widow has openly refused to continue as his benefactress; every honest man, if there are any to be found in this vulgar little town, is convinced that the root and source of godlessness and social criticism has always been hidden there. He has all sorts of prohibited books, Ryleev's *Meditations*,* all Herzen's works... I've drawn up a rough list, just in case...'

'Good Lord! Everyone has those books. You're so naïve, my poor Blum!'

'And quite a few political pamphlets,' Blum went on without hearing his remark. 'We'll end by discovering the person who's been producing the pamphlets here. That young Verkhovensky looks extremely suspicious to me.'

'But you're confusing the father with the son. They're not on good terms; the son laughs openly at his father.'

'That's only a front.'

'Blum, you must have taken an oath to torment me! Just think, he's a prominent person around here. He was a professor; he's well known and will raise hell. People all over town will make fun of us and we'll lose everything... Just think what Yulia Mikhailovna will say!'

Blum carried on without listening.

'He was only a lecturer, a mere lecturer, and only a collegiate assessor when he retired from the civil service,' he said, striking his chest. 'He has no awards for distinction; he was dismissed from the service on suspicion of participating in plots against the government. He was placed under secret surveillance and probably still is. In view of the disorders which have recently come to light here, you're certainly obligated to act. In fact, you're missing a chance to earn yourself distinction by sheltering the real criminal.'

'Yulia Mikhailovna's coming! Get out of here, Blum!' von Lembke cried all of a sudden, hearing his wife's voice in the next room.

Blum gave a start, but didn't relent.

'Please, sir, allow me,' he persisted, pressing both hands even more firmly to his chest.

'Get out of here!' Andrei Antonovich cried, grinding his teeth. 'Do whatever you want... afterwards... Oh, my God!'

The curtain parted and Yulia Mikhailovna entered. She paused majestically at the sight of Blum, giving him a haughty, insulting glance, as if the man's presence alone offended her. Blum silently and respectfully made a deep bow and, stooping from respect, he headed for the door on tiptoe, holding his arms a little away from his body.

Whether he really took Andrei Antonovich's last hysterical exclamation as direct authorization to do as he asked, or whether he merely pretended to do so for his benefactor's own good, feeling all too certain that success would crown his efforts—still, as we'll see later, as a result of this conversation between the governor and his subordinate, a most unexpected event occurred. It amused many people, received considerable publicity, aroused Yulia Mikhailovna's wrath, and utterly disconcerted Andrei Antonovich, throwing him into a state of deplorable indecision at a most critical moment.

5.

It turned out to be a very busy day for Peter Stepanovich. After seeing von Lembke, he hurried off to Bogoyavlenskaya Street, but as he was going along Bykova Street past the place where Karmazinov* was staying, he suddenly stopped, smiled, and entered the house. He was informed that he was expected, a fact that interested him very much, since he'd never even indicated he might come.

But the great writer really was expecting him, and had been expecting him the day before and even the day before that. Three days earlier he'd entrusted him with the manuscript of 'Merci' (which he planned to read at the literary matinée on the day of Yulia Mikhailovna's fête); he'd done it out of generosity, certain the young man's vanity would be pleasantly flattered by the chance to read the great work in advance. Peter Stepanovich had long since noticed that this vain, spoiled gentleman, who held himself so offensively aloof from all but a few, this man of 'almost statesmanlike intellect', was simply trying to ingratiate himself with him, and was all too eager to do so. I think the young man finally guessed that even if Karmazinov didn't consider him to be the leader of the secret revolutionary movement in all Russia, then at least he considered him one of those most fully initiated into the secrets of that movement and possessing indisputable influence over the younger generation.

The state of mind of this 'cleverest man in all Russia' interested Peter Stepanovich, but up to then, for various reasons, he'd avoided any serious conversation with him.

The great writer was residing in the home of his sister, the wife of a court chamberlain and a landowner in our district. Both of them, husband and wife, stood in awe of their distinguished relative, but, to their great regret, at the time of this present visit they were both away in Moscow, and the honour of receiving him passed to an old woman, a very distant and poor relative of the court chamberlain's, who lived in their house and had been in charge of house-keeping for quite some time. After Karmazinov's arrival, the entire household moved about on tiptoe. The old woman reported almost daily to Moscow how well he slept and what he deigned to eat; once she'd even dispatched a telegram with the news that after a certain dinner party at the mayor's house, he was obliged to swallow a teaspoon of a particular kind of medicine. She entered his room only on very rare occasions when his manner to her was polite but dry, and he would speak to her only when absolutely necessary. When Peter Stepanovich arrived, Karmazinov was eating his morning cutlet and drinking half a glass of red wine. Peter Stepanovich had visited him before and every time found him partaking of his morning cutlet which he would consume in his presence, without ever offering him anything. After the cutlet he was brought a small cup of coffee. The footman who served the food was wearing a frock-coat, soft-soled boots, and gloves.

'Aha!' Karmazinov said, rising from the sofa, wiping his mouth with a napkin, and with an expression of pure joy came forward to exchange kisses—a characteristic habit of Russians if they're really very famous. But Peter Stepanovich recalled from his own experience that although Karmazinov would indicate a willingness to exchange kisses, he merely extended his own cheek to be kissed; so this time he did exactly the same thing. Their two cheeks met. Karmazinov gave no indication he noticed anything; he sat down on the sofa and gestured amiably to an armchair, into which Peter Stepanovich promptly slumped.

'Would you... you wouldn't like anything to eat, would you?' his host enquired, forsaking his usual practice this once, but with an air indicating that, of course, a polite refusal was clearly expected. Peter Stepanovich immediately expressed a desire to have lunch. A shadow of offended surprise flitted across the host's face, but only for a moment; he nervously summoned his servant, and, in spite of his good breeding, raised his voice disdainfully as he ordered another meal.

'What do you want, a cutlet or some coffee?' he asked again.

'A cutlet and some coffee, and tell him to bring some wine too—I'm famished,' Peter Stepanovich replied, scrutinizing his host's apparel with calm attention. Mr Karmazinov was wearing an indoor quilted jacket with mother-of-pearl buttons, but the jacket was too short and therefore most unbecoming to his rather prominent belly and well-padded hips; but tastes can certainly differ. A checkered woollen blanket covered his knees and hung down to the floor even though it was quite warm in the room.

'Are you ill, or what?' Peter Stepanovich enquired.

'No, I'm not ill, but I'm afraid of falling ill in this climate,' the writer replied in his shrill voice, though stressing each syllable very tenderly and lisping in a pleasant, aristocratic manner. 'I've been expecting you since yesterday.'

'Why? I made no promises.'

'Yes, but you have my manuscript. Have you... read it?'

'Manuscript? What manuscript?'

Karmazinov was terribly surprised.

'Surely you've brought it with you?' he asked, so disturbed all of a sudden that he actually stopped eating and stared at Peter Stepanovich with a look of alarm.

'Ah, you mean that "Bonjour" piece of yours...?'

' "Merci".'

'Well, whatever. I forgot all about it and haven't read it. I haven't had the time. Well, I don't know, it's not in any of my pockets... it must be at home on my table. Don't worry, it'll turn up.'

'No, I'll send someone to fetch it immediately. It might disappear, or even be stolen.'

'Oh, who'd want it? Why are you so worried? Yulia Mikhailovna says you always have several copies—one abroad with your notary, another in Petersburg, a third in Moscow, and you also send one to your bank, don't you?'

'But Moscow could burn down again, my manuscript with it. No, I'll send for it at once.'

'Wait a moment, here it is!' said Peter Stepanovich, pulling a bundle of paper from his back pocket. 'It got a little crumpled. Just think, ever since I took it from you it's been stashed away in my back pocket with my handkerchief; I forgot all about it.'

Karmazinov snatched the manuscript greedily, carefully examining it, counting the pages, and placing it with respect on a special little table next to him so he could keep his eye on it all the time.

'Apparently you don't do much reading,' he hissed, unable to restrain himself.

'No, not much.'

'And, as far as Russian literature is concerned—none at all?'

'Russian literature? Wait a moment, I did read some-thing... *Along the Road*, or *On the Road*, or *At the Cross-roads*,* I don't remember exactly what it was. I read it a long time ago, maybe five years. I don't have much time.'

A brief silence followed.

'As soon as I arrived I assured everyone here you were an extremely intelligent young man; now, it seems, they're all crazy about you.'

'Thank you,' Peter Stepanovich replied calmly.

His lunch was served. Peter Stepanovich pounced on the cutlet with great gusto, devoured it in an instant, drank the wine and gulped down the coffee.

'This boor,' thought Karmazinov, glancing at him as he finished off his own cutlet and swallowed the last of his coffee, 'this boor probably grasped the full meaning of my caustic remark... and I'm sure he read my manuscript eagerly; now he's lying just to show off. But what if he's not lying and really is quite stupid? I prefer men of genius to be a little stupid. Isn't he considered to be some sort of genius among them here?... But to hell with him.'

He got up from the sofa and began pacing the room from corner to corner, to aid digestion, as he did every day after lunch.

'Are you leaving soon?' asked Peter Stepanovich from his armchair, lighting a cigarette.

'I really came here to sell my estate and now everything depends on my manager.'

'Didn't you come here because they were expecting an epidemic over there after the war?'

'N-no, that's not entirely why,' Mr Karmazinov continued, emphasizing his words in a good-natured way, and giving a jaunty little kick with his right foot each time he rounded the corner as he paced the room. 'I really intend', he said with a laugh, not without venom, 'to go on living as long as possible. There's something in our Russian gentry that makes it wear out very quickly, in all respects. But I intend to wear out as late as possible and now I'm going to live abroad for good; the climate is better there, the buildings are made of stone, and everything is sturdier. I think Europe will last through my lifetime. What do you think?'

'How should I know?'

'Hmmm. If Babylon* really came crashing down there and its collapse was very great (I'm in complete agreement with you about that, although I think it'll last my lifetime), there's really nothing to come crashing down here in Russia, comparatively speaking. We have no stones to fall; everything will merely dissolve into dust. Holy Russia is less capable of offering resistance than any place on earth. Simple people still manage to carry on with their Russian God; but this Russian God, according to latest accounts, is extremely unreliable and has barely survived the emancipation of the serfs; He was badly shaken up, at least. And now there're railways, and here you are... I don't believe in the Russian God any more.'

'And in the European one?'

'I don't believe in any god. I've been slandered in the face of Russia's younger generation. I've always sympathized with all its movements. I've been shown the political pamphlets circulating here. People regard them with astonishment, because the form frightens them, but everyone's convinced of their power, even if they don't admit it. Everything's been going downhill for some time now, and everyone knows there's nothing to grab hold of. For that reason I'm already convinced of the success of the mysterious propaganda maintaining that for the most part Russia is now the only place in the whole world where anything at all can happen without any opposition. I understand all too well why wealthy Russians have been hastening to go abroad, and with every year the number grows larger and larger. It's merely a matter of instinct. If a ship starts to sink, the rats are the first to leave. Holy Russia is a land of wooden huts, a poor country and... a dangerous one, a country with ambitious paupers in its upper classes, while the majority of people live in ramshackle huts. Russia would welcome any way of escape—just show it to her. Only the government still tries to resist, but it merely waves its cudgel around in the darkness and strikes its own supporters. Everything here is doomed and condemned. Russia, as it is now, has no future. I've become a German and I'm proud of it.'

'But you started to say something about the pamphlets. Tell me everything: what do you think of them?'

'Everyone's afraid of them, so they must be very powerful. They openly expose deceit and prove there's nothing here to grab hold of and nothing to rely upon. They speak out, while everyone else remains silent. The most impressive thing about them (in spite of their form) is their unprecedented capacity to look truth straight in the eye. Only Russians of the younger generation have this ability. No, in Europe people aren't that bold: there, the kingdom is a rock and there's still something to rely on. As much as I can see and as far as I can judge, the essence of the Russian revolutionary idea consists in the negation of honour. I like the fact that it's expressed so boldly and fearlessly. No, in Europe it wouldn't be understood yet, but here it's just what we can latch on to. For Russians honour is merely an unnecessary burden. It always was a burden, throughout our history. The frank "right to dishonour" will attract Russians more than anything else. I belong to the older generation; I confess, I'm still in favour of honour, but only out of habit. I simply prefer old forms, let's say, out of cowardice; still, one must live out one's life.'

He stopped suddenly.

'But I'm doing all the talking,' he thought to himself, 'while he keeps silent and watches me. He came here so I'd ask him a direct question. I will.'

'Yulia Mikhailovna asked me to find out from you by using some subterfuge what sort of surprise you're planning for the ball the day after tomorrow?' Peter Stepanovich asked suddenly.

'Yes, it really will be a surprise, and I shall indeed astonish...' Karmazinov began with great dignity. 'But I won't tell you what the secret is.'

Peter Stepanovich didn't insist.

'A man by the name of Shatov lives around here, I believe?' the great writer enquired. 'Just think, I haven't seen him yet.'

'He's a very nice person. What of it?'

'Nothing. He's going around saying things. Wasn't he the one who slapped Stavrogin's face?'

'Yes.'

'And what do you think of Stavrogin?'

'I don't know; he's a womanizer, I hear.'

Karmazinov hated Stavrogin because he had the habit of taking no notice of him whatever.

'If what these political pamphlets predict ever happens here,' he said with a giggle, 'that womanizer will probably be the first to be strung up on a tree.'

'Perhaps even sooner than that,' Peter Stepanovich replied suddenly.

'Serve him right,' Karmazinov said, no longer laughing and agreeing rather too earnestly.

'You said that once before, you know, and I told him.'

'What? Did you really?' Karmazinov said, laughing again.

'He said that if he were to be hanged, it would suffice for you to be flogged, not merely as a formality, but so it really hurt, the way a peasant is flogged.'

Peter Stepanovich took his hat and stood up. Karmazinov held out both hands to him on parting.

'And what if,' he squeaked suddenly in a voice sweet as honey and with a special intonation, hanging on to Peter's hands, 'what if everything that's being planned... were to come about... when would it occur?'

'How should I know?' Peter Stepanovich answered somewhat rudely. They both looked intently into each other's eyes.

'Roughly? Approximately?' Karmazinov squeaked even more weakly.

'You'll have time to sell your estate and get out of here,' Peter Stepanovich muttered even more rudely. They were glaring at each other.

There was a moment of silence.

'It'll start at the beginning of May and will all be over by October,' Peter Stepanovich said all of a sudden.

'Thank you. Thank you very much,' Karmazinov said in an emotional voice, clasping his hands.

'You'll have time, you rat, to leave the ship!' Peter Stepanovich thought to himself as he reached the street. 'Well, if this "almost statesmanlike intellect" enquires so confidently about the day and hour, and then thanks me so respectfully for the information, there's no reason for us to doubt ourselves.' He smiled. 'Hmmm. And he really isn't all that stupid... he's merely an escaping rat; he won't inform on us!'

He ran over to Filippov's house on Bogoyavlenskaya Street.

6.

Peter Stepanovich went first to see Kirillov. He was alone, as usual, and doing his exercises in the middle of his room, that is, standing with his legs spread apart, waving his arms above his head in some special way. A ball lay on the floor. His morning tea stood on the table, cold and not yet cleared away. Peter Stepanovich paused on the threshold for a moment.

'I see you're very concerned about your health,' he said in a loud, cheerful voice as he entered the room. 'And what a fine, ball you have. Look at it bounce! Is it also part of your exercises?'

Kirillov put on his jacket.

'Yes, it's also for my health,' he muttered drily. 'Sit down.'

'I've only come for a minute. But I'll sit down. Your health is one thing, but I've come to remind you about our agreement. "In a certain sense" the time is approaching,' he concluded, making an awkward movement.

'What agreement?'

'What do you mean, what agreement?' Peter Stepanovich asked in dismay; he was quite alarmed.

'It's not an agreement and not an obligation; in no way am I obligated. That's a mistake on your part.'

'Look here, what are you doing?' Peter Stepanovich leapt to his feet.

'Just as I like.'

'Which is?'

'Just as before.'

'How am I supposed to take that? Does it mean you're still of the same mind?'

'Yes. But there's no agreement and never was, and I'm in no way obligated. It was my own free will then and it's my own free will now.'

Kirillov explained himself in a curt tones of disgust.

'I agree, I agree, your own free will, fine, as long as you don't change your mind.' Peter Stepanovich sat down again with a satisfied expression. 'You're getting angry over a word. You've become very bad-tempered lately, that's why I haven't been to see you. Besides, I was sure you wouldn't change your mind.'

'I don't like you at all, but you can be absolutely sure. Even though I really don't believe in betrayal or loyalty.'

'But look,' Peter Stepanovich said, alarmed once again, 'we must try to talk sense so nothing goes wrong. This matter demands precision, but you keep startling me. Can we talk about it?'

'Speak,' Kirillov snapped, looking away into the corner.

'Some time ago you decided to take your own life... that is, such was your idea. Am I expressing myself correctly? Am I mistaken?'

'I still have the same idea.'

'Splendid. Note: no one forced it upon you.'

'Of course not; now you're being stupid.'

'All right, I said something very stupid. Undoubtedly it would be stupid to force you to do it. I'll continue: you were a member of the Society under its old form of organization and you revealed this idea to one of its members.'

'I didn't reveal it, I merely told him.'

'All right. It would be funny to "reveal" it—it's no confession, is it? You merely told him. Fine.'

'No, it's not fine because you keep on mumbling. I'm not obliged to provide you with any explanation; besides you're incapable of understanding any of my ideas. I want to take my own life because that's my idea, because I don't want to be in fear of death, because... because it's none of your business... What do you want? Would you like some tea? That's cold. I'll get you another glass.'

Peter Stepanovich had actually picked up the teapot and was looking for an empty glass. Kirillov went to the cupboard and brought him a clean one.

'I just had lunch at Karmazinov's house,' the guest remarked. 'I listened to him talking, got in quite a sweat, and then came running over here. I got in a sweat again, and I'm dying for something to drink.'

'Go on then. Cold tea's nice.'

Kirillov sat down on the chair again and looked away into the corner.

'The idea has occurred to the Society', he continued in the same voice, 'that if I kill myself I could be useful to them: after you create a disturbance and they come looking for the guilty party, I'll suddenly shoot myself and leave a letter saying I did it and then they won't suspect you for a whole year.'

'For a few days at least; even one day is valuable.'

'Good. In that connection I was told that if I agreed, I

should wait. I said I'd wait until the time was determined by the Society because it makes no difference to me.'

'Yes, but remember, when you write your last letter, you're under an obligation to confer with me; since your arrival in Russia, you were to be... well, in short, at my disposal, I mean only in this respect, of course; in every other way you'd be free, naturally,' Peter Stepanovich added almost amiably.

'I'm not under any obligation, but I did agree because it makes no difference to me.'

'Fine, fine, I have no intention of wounding your pride, but...'

'It's not a matter of pride.'

'Remember that a hundred and twenty thalers was collected for your travel expenses, and you took the money.'

'Not at all,' Kirillov said, flushing. 'That's not what the money was for. People don't take money for that sort of thing.'

'Some do.'

'You're lying. I made a statement in a letter from Petersburg and gave you back the hundred and twenty thalers in Petersburg—right into your hands... the money was sent from there, if you didn't keep it all for yourself.'

'Fine, fine, I won't argue with you; the money was sent. The main thing is you're still of the same mind as you were then.'

'I am. When you come to tell me "It's time", I'll do it. Well, will it be soon?'

'Not long at all... Remember, we'll compose the note together, that very night.'

'Or that day. You said I'd have to claim responsibility for the political pamphlets, didn't you?'

'And something else as well.'

'I won't take responsibility for everything.'

'What won't you take responsibility for?' Peter Stepanovich looked startled again.

'Anything I don't want to; that's enough. I don't wish to talk about it any more.'

Peter Stepanovich took a grip on himself and changed the subject.

'There's something else,' he began. 'Will you be with us this evening? It's Virginsky's birthday and that's a pretext for gathering.'

'I don't want to.'

'Do me a favour and come. You must. We have to impress them with our number and the way we look... You have... well, in a word, you have a fateful face.'

'You think so?' Kirillov asked with a laugh. 'Fine, I'll come, but not because of the way I look. What time?'

'Oh, as early as possible—half-past six. And you know, you can come in and sit down; you don't have to talk to anyone, however many there are. But don't forget to bring paper and pencil.'

'What for?'

'It makes no difference to you, does it? It's my special request. You'll merely sit there, without talking to anyone, listen, and pretend to take a few notes now and then; you can even draw if you like.'

'What nonsense. What for?'

'Well, it makes no difference to you; you keep saying it makes no difference.'

'No, what for?'

'Here's why: one member of the Society, the inspector, remained in Moscow, but I told someone here that an inspector might come to visit. They'll think you're the inspector, and since you've already been here for three weeks, they'll be even more surprised.'

'Silly tricks. You have no inspector in Moscow.'

'All right, so we don't, to hell with him! What business is that of yours and what trouble is it to you? You're a member of the Society.'

'Tell them I'm the inspector; I'll sit there in silence, but I don't like the idea of the paper and pencil.'

'Why not?'

'I don't like it.'

Peter Stepanovich lost his temper, even turned green with anger, but he got control of himself again, rose and picked up his hat.

'Is *he* here?' he asked suddenly in a whisper.

'Yes.'

'That's good. I'll take him away soon, don't worry.'

'I'm not worried. He merely spends the night here. The old woman is in the hospital; her daughter-in-law died. I've been alone the last two days. I showed him the place in the fence where the board can be removed; he crawls through and no one sees him.'

'I'll take him away soon.'

'He says there are many places where he could spend the night.'

'He's lying. They're looking for him, but he won't be noticed here. You don't talk with him, do you?'

'Yes, all night. He abuses you a great deal. At night I read to him from Revelation and we drink tea. He listens very, very carefully, all night long.'

'Oh, hell, you'll turn him into a Christian!'

'He's already a Christian. Don't worry, he'll still slit throats. Whose throats do you want him to slit?'

'No, that's not why I want him; it's for something else... Does Shatov know about Fedka?'

'I don't talk to Shatov and don't see him.'

'Is he angry, or what?'

'No, we're not angry with one another, we just avoid each other. We lived together in America for too long.'

'I'm going to see him right now.'

'That's up to you.'

'Stavrogin and I might also come to see you later, some-time around ten o'clock.'

'All right.'

'I have to talk to him about some important... I say, can I have your ball? What use is it to you now? I'll use it for my exercises, too. I'll pay you for it, if you like.'

'Take it.'

Peter Stepanovich put the ball in his back pocket.

'I won't give you anything against Stavrogin,' Kirillov muttered as he showed his visitor out. Peter looked at him in astonishment, but said nothing.

Kirillov's last words troubled Peter Stepanovich a great deal; he still hadn't managed to make sense of them when he started up the stairs to Shatov's room, trying to replace his dissatisfied expression with a pleasant smile. Shatov was at home, not feeling very well. He lay on his bed, fully clothed.

'Oh, bad luck!' cried Peter Stepanovich from the threshold. 'Are you seriously ill?'

The pleasant smile suddenly disappeared from his face; a malicious gleam appeared in his eyes.

'Not at all,' Shatov replied, nervously jumping up. 'I'm not ill; a bit of a headache...'

He became quite flustered; the sudden appearance of such a visitor had definitely frightened him.

'I've come to see you about a matter that won't allow for any illness,' Peter Stepanovich began quickly and almost peremptorily. 'May I sit down.' He did so. 'You sit back down on the bed. That's it. Today, on the pretext of marking Virginsky's birthday, some of our group are meeting at his place. There won't be any hidden agenda; I've seen to that. I'm coming with Nikolai Stavrogin. Of course I wouldn't have dragged you there, knowing your present state of mind... wouldn't, I mean, have inflicted it on you, it's not that we think you might inform on us. But as it turns out, you need to be there. You'll meet the very people who have to decide how you can leave the Society and to whom you can turn over what you've got. We'll do it without being noticed; I'll take you off into a corner. There'll be a lot of people, and there's no reason for everyone to know. I must confess I had to do a lot of talking on your behalf; but now, it seems, they're all agreed, as long as you turn over the printing press and all the papers. Then you'll be free to go wherever you like.'

Shatov heard him out, frowning and resentful. His previous nervous alarm had left him entirely.

'I recognize no obligation whatever to account to you in any damned way,' he said abruptly. 'No one has any right to set me free.'

'Not exactly. You were entrusted with a great many things. You had no right to break with us like that. And, finally, you've never explained your position clearly; that put them into an ambiguous situation.'

'As soon as I came here I stated my position clearly in a letter.'

'No, not very clearly,' Peter Stepanovich calmly demurred. 'For example, I sent you "A Noble Character" to print here and asked you to keep the copies until they were needed; the same with those two political leaflets. You sent everything back to us with an ambiguous letter which didn't mean anything.'

'I simply refused to print it.'

'Yes, but not simply. You wrote, "I can't", but you didn't explain why. "I can't" doesn't mean "I don't want to." One might have concluded that you couldn't do it simply for financial reasons. That's how it was understood; they thought you were still willing to continue your association with the Society and they could entrust you with other matters. As a result, they might have compromised themselves. What they're saying here is that you simply meant to deceive them: you'd receive some important communication and would then inform on them. I defended you with all my might and showed them your brief letter as evidence in your favour. But, after rereading those two lines of yours, I had myself to acknowledge the letter was unclear and possibly misleading.'

'You've kept that letter so carefully all this time?'

'It makes no difference if I've kept it all this time; I still have it.'

'Well, the hell with it!' Shatov cried furiously. 'Let your friends think I informed on them! What do I care? I'd like to see what you can do to me!'

'Your name might be noted and when the revolution has its first success you could be hanged.'

'Will that be when you seize power and control all Russia?'

'No need to laugh. I tell you, I stood up for you. But whatever you think I'm still advising you to show up today. Why waste words from false pride? Wouldn't it be better to part as friends? In any case, you have to turn over the printing press, the type, and old papers—that's what we'll talk about.'

'I'll come,' Shatov muttered, head bent in thought. Peter Stepanovich looked askance at him from where he sat.

'Will Stavrogin be there?' Shatov asked suddenly, raising his head.

'He certainly will.'

'Ha, ha!'

They were silent for another moment. Shatov had a scornful, irritable grin on his face.

'And what about that disgusting "Noble Character" of yours—the thing I refused to print here? Has it been published?'

'Yes.'

'To make schoolboys think that Herzen himself wrote in your album?'

'Herzen himself.'

They were silent for about three minutes. At last Shatov got up from the bed.

'Get out of here! I don't want to be here with you any longer.'

'I'm going,' Peter Stepanovich replied, quite cheerfully even, standing up slowly. 'One thing more: does Kirillov live all alone in the annexe, without any servants?'

'All alone. Get out, I can't stand being in the same room with you.'

'Well, what a splendid fellow you are!' Peter Stepanovich mused cheerfully as he went out into the street. 'And you'll be just as splendid this evening, and that's just what I need; it couldn't possibly be better. The Russian God Himself must be helping us!'

7·

He'd probably been very busy that day running all sorts of errands—and, apparently, he'd been very successful, judging from the self-satisfied expression on his face when he arrived precisely at six o'clock that evening at Nikolai Stavrogin's house. But he was not admitted immediately; Maurice Nikolaevich had just entered and was closeted in the study with Nikolai Vsevolodovich. This bit of news disturbed Peter Stepanovich. He sat down very close to the door waiting for the guest to leave. They could be heard conversing, but it was impossible to make out what they said. The visit didn't last very long; soon a noise could be heard, then the sound of a very loud, sharp voice, after which the study door opened and Maurice Nikolaevich came out looking pale as a ghost. He didn't notice Peter Stepanovich and walked past him quickly. Peter rushed straight into the study.

I can't omit a fairly detailed account of this very brief encounter between the two 'rivals'—an encounter which seemed inconceivable in the circumstances, but which had nevertheless taken place.

This is what happened: Nikolai Vsevolodovich was dozing on the sofa in his study after dinner when Aleksei Yegorevich announced the arrival of an unexpected visitor. When he heard the visitor's name, Stavrogin jumped up from the sofa and could scarcely believe it. But a smile soon appeared on his lips—a smile of arrogant triumph and, at the same time, of vague, incredulous astonishment. As he entered, Maurice Nikolaevich was apparently struck by what this smile expressed; at least he stopped suddenly and froze in the middle of the room, as if unable to decide whether to proceed or turn back. His host then managed to alter his expression and went forward to greet him with an appearance of earnest wonder. The visitor didn't shake his host's outstretched hand, pulled up a chair awkwardly and without saying a word sat down before his host did, not waiting to be asked. Nikolai Vsevolodovich sat on the sofa half-facing him, and waited in silence.

'Marry Lizaveta Nikolaevna, if you can,' Maurice Nikolaevich said suddenly. He made this sudden offer, and what was so curious was that it was impossible to tell from his tone what he really meant: whether it was a request, a recommendation, a surrender, or a command.

Nikolai Vsevolodovich remained silent. Obviously the visitor hadn't said all he'd come to say; he looked straight at Stavrogin, waiting for an answer.

'If I'm not mistaken (and I'm sure I'm not), Lizaveta Nikolaevna is already engaged to you,' Stavrogin said at last.

'Promised and betrothed,' Maurice Nikolaevich attested firmly and clearly.

'Have you... quarrelled? Forgive my asking, Maurice Nikolaevich.'

'No, she "loves and respects" me, in her own words. Her words are more precious to me than anything.'

'No doubt about that.'

'But you should know that even if she were standing at the altar during our wedding, and you were to call her, she'd abandon me and everyone else and go running to you.'

'In the middle of your wedding?'

'And afterwards, even.'

'You're not mistaken?'

'No. Through her persistent, sincere, and intense hatred of you come frequent bursts of love and... madness... the most sincere and immeasurable love and—madness! On the other hand, through the love she feels for me, which is also sincere, come frequent bursts of hatred—such intense hatred! Never before could I have conceived of such... metamorphoses.'

'But I'm astonished you can come here and dispose of Lizaveta Nikolaevna's hand? Do you have any right to do so? Or has she authorized you?'

Maurice Nikolaevich frowned and looked down for a moment.

'You're just s ying that,' he said suddenly. 'Saying it in revenge and triumph. I'm sure you can read between the lines, and is this the place for petty vanity? Aren't you quite satisfied? Is it really necessary to spell it out and dot all the i's? I will dot them, if you so much need to humiliate me. I have no right whatever—there's no question of authorization. Lizaveta Nikolaevna knows nothing, but her fiancé has lost his mind and is ready for the lunatic asylum; to crown it all, he's come here to tell you that himself. You're the only one on earth who can make her happy, and I'm the only one who can make her unhappy. You run after her, pursue her, but won't marry her, I don't know why. If it's a lovers' quarrel you had abroad, and if you need to sacrifice me to end it—then do so. She's too unhappy, I can't stand it. What I said doesn't constitute permission or instruction, so there's no insult to your pride. If you wanted to take my place at the altar, you could've done so without my permission, and I wouldn't have come to you with my madness. All the more so since our wedding is no longer possible after these steps I'm now taking. I can't lead her to the altar if I'm a scoundrel, can I? What I'm doing here and the fact that I'm giving her to you, perhaps her worst enemy, is, in my opinion, such a despicable act that I'll never get over it.'

'Will you shoot yourself on our wedding day?'

'No, much later. Why should I soil her wedding dress with my blood? Perhaps I won't shoot myself at all, neither now, nor later.'

'I suppose you're saying that just to put my mind at ease.'

'You? What could shedding a few more drops of blood mean to you?'

He turned pale and his eyes glinted. There followed a moment of silence.

'Excuse me for asking you these questions,' Stavrogin began again. 'I had no right to ask some of them, but it seems to me I have every right to ask you one thing: tell me, what basis have you for coming to such a conclusion about my feelings for Lizaveta Nikolaevna? I mean your assumption about the strength of my feelings, such that you'd come and... risk making such a proposal.'

'What?' cried Maurice Nikolaevich with a slight shudder. 'Haven't you been trying to win her? Aren't you trying to win her now and don't you want her?'

'In general I don't discuss my feelings for one or another woman with anyone, whoever it might be, except the woman herself. Forgive me, but that's a peculiarity of my temperament. But I'll tell you the truth about everything else: I'm already married. Therefore it would be impossible for me to marry or even to try to "win" someone else.'

Maurice Nikolaevich was so astonished that he fell back in his chair and stared into Stavrogin's face for some time without moving a muscle.

'Imagine, I never thought of that,' he muttered. 'You said that morning you weren't married... so I took it that you weren't...'

He turned terribly pale; suddenly he banged his fist on the table with all his might.

'If, after such a confession, you don't leave Lizaveta Nikolaevna alone and if you make her unhappy, I'll beat your brains out with a stick, like a dog in a ditch!'

He jumped up and left the room quickly. When Peter Stepanovich came running in he found his host in a most unexpected frame of mind.

'Oh, so it's you!' Stavrogin cried and burst into loud laughter; he seemed to be laughing only at the sudden appearance of Peter Stepanovich, who'd come running in so full of curiosity.

'Were you eavesdropping at the door? Wait a moment, why have you come? I promised you something or other... Oh, yes! I remember: The meeting of "our" group! Let's go. I'm very glad. You couldn't have thought of anything more appropriate to the moment.'

He grabbed his hat and the two of them left the house at once.

'You're laughing in anticipation of meeting "our" group?' Peter Stepanovich cried cheerfully, fawning over him, first trying to keep pace beside his companion on the narrow brick pavement, and then even running alongside in the street, right in the mud, because his companion was completely unaware he was walking in the middle of the pavement and hogging it all to himself.

'I'm not laughing at all,' Stavrogin replied loudly and cheerfully. 'On the contrary, I'm sure they'll be very serious people there.'

' "Dismal dunces", as you were once kind enough to call them.'

'There's nothing more amusing than dismal dunces.'

'Ah, you must be thinking of Maurice Nikolaevich! I'm sure he came to cede his fiancée to you, right? It was I who urged him to do it, indirectly, of course. And if he doesn't give her up, we'll take her ourselves, won't we?'

Peter Stepanovich knew, of course, he was taking a risk by broaching such a subject, but once he was excited, he preferred to risk everything rather than remain in ignorance. Nikolai Vsevolodovich merely laughed.

'So you're still planning to help me out?' he asked.

'If you call on me. But you know there's a better way.'

'I know your way.'

'No, you don't, it's still a secret. But remember, the secret costs money.'

'I know how much it costs,' muttered Stavrogin, but he controlled himself and fell silent.

'How much? What did you say?' Peter Stepanovich asked with a start.

'I said, "The hell with you and your secret!" You'd do better to tell me who'll be there. I know we're going to a birthday party, but who exactly will be there?'

'Oh, all sorts of people! Even Kirillov will be there.'

'Are they all members of circles?'

'The devil take it, you're in such a rush! We've yet to form one circle here.'

'How did you manage to distribute so many pamphlets?'

'There are only four members of the circle where we're heading now. The rest are waiting to get in; they spy on one another and come running to me with their reports. They're a reliable lot. They're raw material that must be organized, and then we can clear out. But you wrote the rules yourself—there's no need to explain any of it to you.'

'Well, is it hard going? Any problems?'

'Hard going? Couldn't be better. Let me tell you something amusing: the first thing that impresses people is a uniform. There's nothing more powerful. I've devised titles and duties: we have secretaries, secret emissaries, treasurers, chairmen, registrars and their deputies—they like it and it's working very well. The next powerful force is, of course, sentimentality. In this country socialism spreads chiefly as a result of sentimentality, you know. The trouble is second lieutenants who bite; try as you may, you run up against them. Then there's the out-and-out swindlers; but they're not really such a bad lot. Sometimes it's even quite useful to have them around, but they take up so much time and require constant supervision. Last of all, the most important force—the cement that holds everything else together—is their being ashamed to possess their own opinions. Now that's a real force! And who's worked so hard, who's the "dear man"* who's laboured so diligently that not one single idea of their own has been left in their heads? They'd consider it a disgrace.'

'But if it's like that, why are you fussing around?'

'Well, if you see someone lolling around gaping, you've got to grab him! You don't seem seriously to believe we'll succeed? Oh, there's faith enough, but what's wanted is the will. Oh yes, it's precisely with people like that we *can* succeed. I tell you they'll go through fire for me, I only have to keep shouting at them that they're not sufficiently liberal. The fools reproach me with having deceived them about the central committee and its "innumerable branches". You blamed me for that once yourself: but I'm not deceiving them, am I? You and I are the central committee—and soon there'll be as many branches as you like!'

'They're all scum, nevertheless!'

'They're raw material. Even they will prove useful.'

'And are you still counting on me?'

'You're the head, you're a force; I'll merely be at your side, your secretary. We'll board our little boat, you know, oars of maple, sails of silk,* a fair maiden sitting at the helm, the lovely Lizaveta Nikolaevna... or however the hell that song goes...'

'You're stuck!' Stavrogin laughed. 'No, let me provide a little introduction for your tale. Are you counting up on your fingers all the forces that make circles? All your bureaucracy and sentimentality—it's all good cement. But there's one thing that's even better: persuade four members of a circle to finish off a fifth on the pretext that he's an informer, and you'll immediately bind them together with the blood that's been shed. They'll become your slaves; they won't dare rebel or call you to account. Ha, ha, ha!'

'Well, well, well,' thought Peter Stepanovich to himself, 'you'll have to pay for those words—perhaps as soon as this evening. You let yourself go too far.'

That's what, or approximately what, Peter Stepanovich must have been thinking to himself. But they were already approaching Virginsky's house.

'You've probably described me as some sort of member from abroad in contact with the *Internationale*, perhaps even as an inspector?' Stavrogin asked suddenly.

'No, not an inspector: you won't be the inspector. But you're a founding-member from abroad who knows the most important secrets—that's your role. You'll speak, won't you?'

'Where did you get that idea?'

'You're obliged to speak now.'

Stavrogin stopped in amazement in the middle of the street, not far from a street-lamp. Peter Stepanovich met his stare with brazen calm. Stavrogin spat and walked on.

'And are you going to speak?' he asked Peter Stepanovich suddenly.

'No, I'm going to listen to you.'

'Damn you! In fact you've given me a good idea!'

'What's that?' Peter Stepanovich cried in alarm.

'Perhaps I will speak, but afterwards I'll beat you up, and, I tell you, beat you up properly.'

'By the way, I told Karmazinov this morning that you said he should he flogged, and not merely for form's sake, but the way a peasant is flogged, so it hurt.'

'I never said anything like that, ha, ha!'

'Never mind. *Se non è vero...*'*

'Well, thank you. I'm very grateful.'

'Do you know what Karmazinov said? That our creed is essentially the negation of honour and that the surest way to get a Russian to follow you is to promise him the right to dishonour.'

'Splendid words! Golden words!' cried Stavrogin. 'It gets right to the heart of the matter! The right to dishonour— why, they'll all come running to us, not one would be left behind! Listen here, Verkhovensky, you're not working for the secret police are you?'

'Surely anyone who thinks of questions like that wouldn't dare utter them aloud.'

'I understand, but we're alone.'

'No, for the time being I'm not working for the secret police. Hold on, we're here. Compose yourself, Stavrogin; I always do before I enter. Look as gloomy as you can, that's all. You don't need to do anything else; it's really quite simple.'

CHAPTER 7

'Our group' meets

I.

VIRGINSKY lived in his own house, that is, his wife's house, on Muravinaya Street. It was a one-storey wooden building with no lodgers living there. Some fifteen guests had gathered on the pretext of celebrating the host's birthday; but the occasion was not at all like the usual provincial birthday party. At the beginning of their married life together the Virginskys had decided once and for all that it was stupid to invite guests to celebrate their birthdays since 'there was really nothing to rejoice about.' In just a few years they'd managed to cut themselves off from society completely. Although a man of ability and 'by no means poor', Virginsky struck everyone as somewhat eccentric, preferring his solitude and, what's more, 'arrogant' in his dealings with others. Madame Virginskaya, a midwife by profession, by virtue of that fact alone occupied a rung below everyone else on the social ladder; she was even lower than the priest's wife in spite of her husband's rank as an officer. But there was not a trace in her of the humility appropriate to her station. And after the ridiculous and unforgivably blatant affair she had had, on principle, with a scoundrel, Captain Lebyadkin, even the most indulgent of our ladies shunned her with notable contempt. But Madame Virginskaya took it as if that was precisely what she wanted. It's worth noting that those same stern ladies, whenever they found themselves in an interesting predicament, always turned to Arina Prokhorovna (that is, Madame Virginskaya), by-passing entirely the three other midwives in town. She was even sent for by the wives of landowners living out in the country—so great was everyone's faith in her knowledge, luck, and skill in critical cases. It ended up with her practising only in the wealthiest of homes; she had a passionate love of money. Once she realized the extent of her power, she made no attempt to curb her personality. Perhaps it was even for

good reason that in her practice she frightened nervous
patients in the best houses with incredibly nihilistic disregard for social decorum or by mocking 'everything holy',
precisely when the 'holy' might have proven most useful.
Our town doctor, Rozanov, who also delivered babies, tes-
tified that once, when a patient was howling in pain and
calling on the Almighty, Arina Prokhorovna suddenly, 'like
a pistol shot', let fire with a brace of free-thinking remarks
which so terrified the patient that it greatly accelerated her
delivery. Even though she was a nihilist, when the occasion
arose Arina Prokhorovna did not disdain certain social
prejudices, even quite old-fashioned ones, if they could
prove useful to her. For example, she'd never miss the
christening of a baby she delivered; she always arrived
wearing a green silk dress with a train, her hair arranged in
curls and ringlets, even though at all other times she seemed
to take special delight in her own slovenliness. And although
during the ceremony she always maintained a 'most impudent attitude' which embarrassed the officiating clergy, at
the end of the christening she invariably passed around the
champagne (which was really the reason she came and why
she got so dressed up), and heaven help anyone who took
a glass without leaving her a small consideration on the tray.

The guests gathered at Virginsky's house that evening—
almost all men—had a casual and unusual appearance. There
were no refreshments or card games. In the midst of the
large living-room, decorated with old blue wallpaper, two
tables had been pushed together and covered with a large,
not altogether clean tablecloth, on which stood two boiling
samovars. At the foot of the table was a huge tray holding
twenty-five glasses and a basket of French bread cut into a
number of small pieces, a bit like a boarding school for
upper-class boys and girls. Tea was poured by the hostess's
thirty-year-old spinster sister, a taciturn and venomous creature with no eyebrows and pale yellow hair, but who
believed in the new ideas and put the fear of God into
Virginsky in his domestic life. There were only three women
in the room: the hostess herself, the sister without eyebrows,
and Virginsky's sister, a young girl who'd just arrived from

Petersburg. Arina Prokhorovna, an imposing woman about twenty-seven years old, not bad-looking, a little dishevelled, wearing an ordinary greenish woollen dress, sat boldly surveying the guests, as if eager to say, 'You see I'm not afraid of anything.' The newly arrived Miss Virginskaya, a student and nihilist, also not bad-looking, rather short, well-fed, and round as a little ball, with very red cheeks, sat next to Arina Prokhorovna. She still had on her travelling dress, held a bundle of papers in her hand, and was examining the guests with impatient, roving eyes. That evening Virginsky himself was feeling somewhat indisposed, but he emerged to sit in an armchair next to the table. All the guests were seated and the orderly way in which they were arranged around the table suggested a formal meeting. Obviously everyone was waiting for something, and as they waited they carried on loud, somewhat irrelevant conversations. When Stavrogin and Verkhovensky appeared, everyone suddenly fell silent.

But let me provide some explanation to make things a little clearer.

I think all these people had really come together in the pleasant hope that they'd hear something particularly interesting, and had been so apprised in advance. They represented the flower of reddest liberalism in our ancient town and had been carefully selected by Virginsky to attend this 'meeting'. I must observe that several of them (though not very many) had never visited his house before. Of course, the majority of the guests had no very clear idea why they'd been summoned. True, at the time they all regarded Peter Stepanovich as an emissary and plenipotentiary from abroad; this idea had somehow taken root, and naturally flattered them. Meanwhile, among this small group of citizens who'd gathered under the guise of a birthday celebration, there were a few people who'd already received definite instructions. Peter Verkhovensky had managed to form a so-called 'group of five' in our town, similar to the one he'd already established in Moscow, and the one that, it now turns out, he'd formed among army officers in our district. It's said he also had one in Kh— province. The chosen members of this group now sat around the common table and skilfully managed to appear so ordinary that no one could pick them out. Since it's no longer a secret, they were: first, Liputin, then Virginsky himself, the long-eared Shigalyov, who was Mrs Virginskaya's brother, Lyamshin, and finally, a certain Tolkachenko—a strange character, a man of about forty, famous for his profound knowledge of the common people, primarily scoundrels and thieves, who made a point of frequenting taverns (though not merely to study the common people), and who prided himself on his poor apparel, greasy boots, shifty look, and his florid use of popular language. Once or twice before this Lyamshin had brought him to an evening at Stepan Trofimovich's house, where, however, he failed to create any particular impression. He would appear in our town on occasion, primarily when he was unemployed; he used to work on the railway. Each of these people had agreed to join the group of five in the firm belief that it was merely one among hundreds and thousands of such groups scattered throughout Russia, every one of which depended on some enormous, central, but secret power, that in turn was organically connected to the European revolutionary movement. Unfortunately, I must confess that at the time there was considerable dissension among them. The trouble was that although they'd been waiting for Peter Verkhovensky's arrival since spring, an event announced to them first by Tolkachenko, then by Shigalyov who'd just arrived in town, and although they were expecting extraordinary miracles from him and had all joined the group at his first summons, without the least objection, still, as soon as they'd constituted this group of five, they all felt somehow offended, I suspect because of the alacrity with which each had agreed to join. Each agreed, of course, out of a magnanimous embarrassment, lest it be said later that he didn't dare join the group; nevertheless, Peter Verkhovensky should have appreciated their noble deed, and at least should have rewarded them with some important bit of news. But Verkhovensky had no intention of satisfying their legitimate curiosity and gave them no extra information at all; in general he treated them with marked severity, even disregard. This was really irritating, and one member,

Shigalyov, was already inciting the group to 'demand an account', but not of course here at Virginsky's house, where so many outsiders were present.

Speaking of outsiders, I also have an idea that the above-mentioned members of the first group of five were inclined to suspect among the guests at Virginsky's house that evening the presence of members of other unknown groups, also formed in our town by the same Verkhovensky, and belonging to the same secret organization; the result was that in the end everyone present suspected everyone else and they struck a variety of poses—all of which imbued the meeting with a rather confusing, even slightly romantic character. However, there were some people quite above any suspicion. For example, one major on active service, a close relative of Virginsky's, an absolutely innocent man who hadn't even been invited, but who came to the party of his own accord, so that it was impossible not to admit him. But the host wasn't the least bit worried because the major 'couldn't possibly be an informer'; for in spite of his stupidity, all his life he had loved to frequent those places where extreme liberals congregated; and, while he himself didn't share their views, he loved to listen to them. Besides, he was already compromised: it happened that once in his youth whole bundles of *The Bell** and various political pamphlets had passed through his hands; although he was afraid even to open them, he considered it beneath contempt to refuse to distribute them—there are still Russians just like that to this very day. The remaining guests represented either a type of noble self-esteem, repressed and embittered, or they were still in the first flush of magnanimous youthful fervour. There were also two or three teachers, one of whom, lame and aged about forty-five, who taught at our local gymnasium, was a venomous and extremely vain man. There were also two or three officers. Of the latter, one was a young artillery officer who'd arrived a few days ago from his military training institution; he was a taciturn lad who'd yet to make many acquaintances, and had suddenly turned up at Virginsky's with a pencil in hand. He scarcely participated in the conversation, but constantly wrote things down in a little notebook. Everyone saw this, but for some reason pretended not to. There was also an idle divinity student, the same one who'd helped Lyamshin plant the indecent photographs in the book-pedlar's bag. He was a large lad with a free-and-easy, but at the same time mistrustful manner, and with a perpetual sarcastic smile on a face that radiated serene, triumphant superiority. I don't know why, but the son of our town mayor was also present—that nasty, prematurely dissipated lad about whom I spoke before in connection with the second lieutenant's wife. He sat in silence the entire evening. Finally, there was a gymnasium student, a temperamental, tousled lad of eighteen, who sat there with the gloomy look of a man whose pride's been hurt and who's suffering on account of his eighteen years. This little fellow, as was later discovered to everyone's astonishment, was already the head of an independent group of conspirators formed in the upper form of his gymnasium. I've made no mention of Shatov: he was sitting at the far end of the table, his chair pushed back away from the others, and was staring at the floor in grim silence. He refused both tea and bread, and held on to his cap the whole time, as if wishing to make clear he wasn't a guest, but had come on business, and would get up and leave whenever he wanted. Not far from him sat Kirillov who was also very quiet, but he wasn't staring at the floor; on the contrary, he fixed his steady, lustreless gaze on every speaker, and listened to everything without the least agitation or surprise. A few guests who'd never seen him before gave him stealthy, curious looks. It's not clear whether Madame Virginskaya herself knew anything about the existence of the group of five. I suspect she knew everything, probably from her spouse. Of course the female student was not party to anything, but she had her own worries. She was intending to spend only a day or two in town, and then travel through all university towns to 'take part in the sufferings of impoverished students and rouse them to protest'. She was carrying several hundred copies of a printed appeal, one she'd composed herself, apparently. It's curious, but the gymnasium student conceived a mortal hatred for her at first glance, although he'd never seen her before in his life; she felt the same about him. The major was an uncle of hers and was meeting her today for the first time in ten years. When Stavrogin and Verkhovensky arrived, her cheeks were as red as cranberries: she'd just quarrelled with her uncle on account of his views on the woman's question.

2.

Verkhovensky flung himself into the armchair at the head of the table with astonishing nonchalance and greeted hardly anyone present. His expression was disdainful, even arrogant. Stavrogin bowed politely to one and all but, in spite of the fact that they had been waiting for them, everyone, as if acting on orders, pretended not to notice their arrival. Their hostess turned sternly to Stavrogin as soon as he'd taken his seat.

'Would you like some tea, Stavrogin?'

'Please,' he replied.

'Some tea for Stavrogin,' she commanded her sister, who was pouring. 'Would you like some, too?' (This was directed at Verkhovensky.)

'Yes, of course. What a thing to ask your guests! And give me some cream in it. You always serve such filthy water instead of tea, and at a birthday party, too!'

'What? So you recognize birthdays, do you?' the female student asked with a laugh. 'We were just talking about that.'

'That's old hat,' muttered the gymnasium student at the other end of the table.

'What's old hat about it? It's not old hat to disregard superstitions, even the most harmless ones; on the contrary, it's still quite new, to everyone's shame,' the female student declared immediately, leaning forward in her chair. 'Moreover, there's no such thing as a harmless superstition,' she added bitterly.

'I merely wanted to say', the gymnasium student replied, getting terribly agitated, 'that although superstitions are old-fashioned of course, and must be eliminated, everyone already knows that birthdays are stupid, and it's very old hat to waste valuable time that's already been wasted enough all over the world; therefore, one ought to apply one's wits to more useful subjects...'

'You go on at such length, I can't understand a thing,' cried the female student.

'I think everyone has the right to express his views as well as the next person, and if, like everyone else, I want to state my opinion, then...'

'No one's taking away your right to express your opinion,' their hostess said, cutting him off abruptly. 'You're merely being asked not to ramble on, because no one can understand you.'

'Permit me to observe, however, that you have no respect for me; if I can't get my thoughts together, it's not because I don't have any, rather it's that I have an excess of them...' muttered the gymnasium student almost in despair, and he became very confused.

'If you don't know how to speak, then shut up,' the female student blurted out.

The gymnasium student jumped up from his chair.

'I merely wanted to state', he cried, burning with embarrassment and afraid to look around, 'that you only want to show off your intelligence because Mr Stavrogin came in—that's what!'

'That's a filthy and immoral thing to say and reveals the inadequacy of your intellectual development. I ask you not to address me again,' the female student rattled on.

'Stavrogin,' Madame Virginskaya began, 'before you came in everyone was arguing about the rights of families—including this officer right here.' She nodded at her relative, the major. 'Now, of course, I'm not going to bother you with nonsense like that, which was settled some time ago. But where could all these family rights and obligations have come from, in the sense of the superstition in which they appear to us now? That's our question. What's your opinion?'

'How do you mean, where could they have come from?' Stavrogin repeated the question.

'I mean, we know, for example, the superstition about God derived from thunder and lightning,' the female student broke in again suddenly, almost assaulting Stavrogin with her eyes. 'It's only too well known that primitive man, terrified by thunder and lightning, deified his invisible enemy, conscious of his own weakness with regard to them. But where did superstitions about the family come from? Where could the family itself have come from?'

'That's not quite the same thing...' said Madame Virginskaya, trying to stop her.

'I'm afraid the answer to your last question would be rather risqué,' replied Stavrogin.

'How so?' the student asked, leaning forward.

Titters arose from the group of teachers, echoed immediately by Lyamshin and the gymnasium student at the other end of the table; then the major laughed hoarsely.

'You ought to be writing vaudevilles,' Madame Virginskaya quipped to Stavrogin.

'A remark like that does you no credit, whatever your name is,' the female student snapped, now decidedly irritated.

'Don't you go attacking people like that, dear!' the major blurted out. 'You're a young lady; you should behave modestly. You're acting as if you just sat on a pin.'

'I'd appreciate it if you kept quiet and didn't address me in such a familiar way with your disgusting comparisons. I've never seen you before and prefer not to acknowledge you as a relative of mine.'

'But I'm your uncle, dear; I carried you in my arms when you were a baby!'

'What do I care what you carried in your arms. I didn't ask you to carry me; in other words, Mr Impolite Officer, you wanted to carry me. Let me remind you that you have no right to address me in a familiar manner, unless it's as a fellow citizen; I forbid it once and for all.'

'They're all like that!' the major cried, banging his fist on the table and turning to Stavrogin who was sitting across from him. 'Yes, sir, I must say, I love liberalism and contemporary ideas and I love to listen to intelligent conversation, but, I warn you, only from men. From women, from these modern blabbermouths—no, sir, it's too painful! Stop that wiggling!' he shouted at the female student who was bouncing about on her chair. 'No, I have the right to speak too; I've been offended.'

'You're merely interfering with others and you can't say anything yourself,' grumbled his hostess indignantly.

'No, I'll have my say,' the major cried heatedly, turning to Stavrogin. 'I'm counting on you, Mr Stavrogin, since you've just arrived, even though I haven't had the honour of knowing you. Without men, they'll perish like flies— that's what I think. The key to this entire woman's question of theirs is simply a lack of originality. I assure you the whole woman's question was thought up for them by men, out of sheer stupidity, to our own disadvantage. I only thank God I'm not married! They haven't the least sense of diversity, sir; they can't invent the simplest design; men have to create designs for them! Look at her: I used to carry her around in my arms; when she was ten I danced the mazurka with her; today, when she arrived here, I naturally rushed to embrace her, but the second thing she says to me is there's no such thing as God. I wouldn't mind if it had been the third thing, instead of the second, but she was in such a rush! Well, let's grant there are some intelligent people who don't believe in God; that's after all a result of their intelligence, but you, I tell her, you're just a kid, what do you know about God? Some boy, some student must have taught you; and if he'd taught you to light lamps in front of icons, you'd be doing that instead.'

'You're lying. You're a wicked man; I just pointed out how groundless your position was,' replied the female student disdainfully, as if unwilling to waste her breath explaining things to this man. 'I said earlier we were all instructed according to the catechism: "If you honour your mother and father, you'll enjoy long life and be rewarded with riches." That's what it says in the Ten Commandments. If God found it necessary to promise rewards for love, your God must be immoral. That's what I told you before. And it wasn't the second thing; I said it because you were asserting your rights. Whose fault is it you're stupid and still don't understand? You're offended and angry— that's the problem with your entire generation.'

'You silly goose!' said the major.

'And you're a fool.'

'Go on, call me names!'

'Wait a minute, Kapiton Maksimovich. You yourself told me you don't believe in God,' Liputin squeaked at the other end of the table.

'What if I did? That's a different matter altogether! Perhaps I do believe, but not entirely. And even though I don't believe entirely, I still don't say that God ought to be shot. When I was serving in the Hussars I used to think about God. There are lots of poems in which hussars drink and have a good time. Well, perhaps I used to drink too, but believe me, I'd also jump out of bed at night and stand in my socks crossing myself in front of the icons, asking God to give me faith because I could find no peace even then, not knowing if there was a God or not. I had a very rough time of it! In the morning, of course, I'd amuse myself, and once again my faith would seem to disappear; as a rule I've noticed that faith always disappears in the daytime.'

'You wouldn't have a pack of playing cards, would you?' Verkhovensky said, turning to Madame Virginskaya and yawning openly.

'I sympathize entirely with your question, entirely!' the female student burst out, flushing with indignation at the major's words.

'Precious time is being wasted listening to such stupid conversation,' their hostess snapped and looked at her husband severely.

The female student drew herself up:

'I'd like to report to this meeting on the sufferings and protests of students, but since time is being wasted in immoral conversation...'

'There's no such thing as morality and immorality!' said the gymnasium student, unable to restrain himself, as soon as the female student had begun.

'I knew that, Mr Gymnasium Student, long before it was ever taught to you.'

'And I maintain', he cried in a frenzy, 'that you're a child who's come from Petersburg to enlighten us, whereas we already know everything. As for the Commandment: "Honour thy father and thy mother" which you didn't even quote correctly, everyone in Russia since the time of Belinsky has known it was immoral.'

'Will this never end?' Madame Virginskaya asked her husband in a resolute voice. As the hostess, she blushed at the trivial nature of their conversation, especially when she noticed several smiles and even consternation among the new arrivals.

'Ladies and gentlemen,' said Virginsky, suddenly raising his voice, 'if someone wishes to begin talking about something more appropriate to our business or has anything to report, I propose he do so without wasting any more time.'

'I should like to pose one question,' said the lame teacher softly, who up to this point had sat very decorously in total silence. 'I'd like to know whether sitting here, now, we constitute some meeting, or whether we're merely a collection of ordinary mortals come together as guests at a party? I'm asking more for the sake of form and so as not to remain in ignorance.'

This 'clever' question created an impression: everyone exchanged glances, as if waiting for someone else to answer it; suddenly everyone, as if on command, turned to look at Verkhovensky and Stavrogin.

'I propose we vote on an answer to the following question: "Do we constitute a meeting, or not?"' said Madame Virginskaya.

'I second the motion,' Liputin replied, 'although the question is a bit vague.'

'I second it, too... Second,' other voices were heard.

'I think it would introduce some order into our proceedings,' Virginsky confirmed.

'Well, let's vote!' declared the hostess. 'Lyamshin, please sit down at the piano; you can cast your ballot from there when everyone starts to vote.'

'Again?' cried Lyamshin. 'Haven't I thumped enough for you?'

'I insist; sit down and play. Don't you want to serve the cause?'

'I can assure you, Arina Prokhorovna, no one's eavesdropping. It's your imagination. Besides, the windows are high and even if someone were listening in, he wouldn't understand anything.'

'We don't understand anything either,' someone muttered.

'I maintain that caution is always necessary. Just in case there are any spies,' she said, turning to Verkhovensky to explain. 'Let them listen out on the street and they'll hear us having a birthday party with music.'

'Oh, hell!' Lyamshin said. He sat down at the piano and began banging out some waltz, almost pounding his fists on the keys.

'Those in favour of having a meeting raise their right hands,' Madame Virginskaya proposed.

Some did, others didn't. Some people raised their hands and then lowered them. Then they reconsidered and raised them again.

'Damn it all! I don't understand a thing!' cried an officer.

'Nor do I!' said another.

'Well, I do understand,' cried a third. 'Raise your hand if you want to vote "yes".'

'What does "yes" mean?'

'We're having a meeting.'

'No, that we're not having a meeting.'

'I voted for having a meeting,' the gymnasium student cried, turning to Madame Virginskaya.

'Then why didn't you raise your hand?'

'I was looking at you; you didn't raise your hand so I didn't raise mine.'

'How stupid, I didn't raise my hand because I was making the motion. Ladies and gentlemen, I propose we do it another way: those in favour of a meeting sit still and keep their hands down. Those opposed to a meeting raise their right hands.'

'Those who oppose it?' the gymnasium student asked, repeating the question.

'Are you doing it on purpose?' Madame Virginskaya cried in a rage.

'No, wait a minute, those who favour it or oppose it, because it has to be specified,' chimed in two or three other voices.

'Those who oppose it, *oppose*.'

'Well, and what are they supposed to do? Raise their hands or not, if they *oppose* it?' cried the officer.

'Hey, we're still not used to a constitution!' observed the major.

'Mr Lyamshin, do me a favour, you're banging so loud no one can hear a thing,' said the lame teacher.

'I swear, Arina Prokhorovna, no one's eavesdropping,' Lyamshin cried, jumping up. 'I don't want to play! I came as a guest, not to thump on the piano!'

'Ladies and gentlemen,' Virginsky proposed, 'just speak up: is this a meeting or not?'

'Yes, it's a meeting, yes it is!' was heard on all sides.

'If that's the case, there's nothing to vote on. Enough. Are you satisfied, ladies and gentlemen, or do we need to vote?'

'No, no need, we understand!'

'Perhaps someone opposes a meeting?'

'No, no, we're all in favour.'

'But what does it mean to have a meeting?' cried one voice. No one answered him.

'We have to elect a chairman,' voices cried from different parts of the room.

'The host, the host, of course!'

'Ladies and gentlemen, if so,' the newly elected Virginsky began, 'I'd like to propose a motion: if anyone would like to speak about a subject more appropriate to our business or make a report, let him proceed without wasting any more time.'

General silence ensued. All eyes turned again to Stavrogin and Verkhovensky.

'Verkhovensky, don't you have anything to report to us?' Madame Virginskaya asked directly.

'Absolutely nothing,' he replied, yawning and stretching on his chair. 'I'd really like a glass of brandy, though.'

'Stavrogin, what about you?'

'No thank you, I don't drink.'

'I mean, would you like to speak or not? I wasn't talking about brandy.'

'Speak about what? No, I wouldn't.'

'They'll bring you brandy,' their hostess said to Verkhovensky.

The female student stood up. She'd already jumped up from her chair several times.

'I've come to report on the sufferings of unfortunate students everywhere and about ways to incite them to protest...'

She broke off; a rival had appeared at the other end of the table and all eyes were fixed on him. Long-eared Shigalyov, with a dark and gloomy expression, rose slowly from his place and, with a melancholy air, put a thick, closely written notebook on the table. He remained standing in silence. Many people looked at the notebook in consternation, but Liputin, Virginsky, and the lame teacher seemed pleased about something.

'I'd like to speak,' Shigalyov said grimly, but firmly.

'You have the floor.' Virginsky gave permission.

The speaker sat down. He was silent for about half a minute, then said in impressive tones:

'Ladies and gentlemen...'

'Here's the brandy!' snapped Madame Virginskaya's relative in contemptuous distaste. She'd been pouring tea, then gone to fetch the brandy, and now placed it in front of Verkhovensky with a glass she'd brought in her hand, without a tray or plate.

The interrupted orator paused with a dignified air.

'Never mind, go on, I'm not listening,' cried Verkhovensky, pouring himself a glass.

'Ladies and gentlemen, in asking for your attention,' Shigalyov began again, 'and, as you'll see later, in requesting your assistance on a matter of extreme importance, I must begin with an introduction.'

'Arina Prokhorovna, do you have a pair of scissors?' Peter Stepanovich asked suddenly.

'What do you need them for?' she asked, her eyes bulging.

'I forgot to trim my nails and have been meaning to do it for the last three days,' he replied, examining his long, dirty nails serenely.

Arina Prokhorovna flushed, but her young relative seemed to like this.

'I think I saw them over there on the window-sill earlier,' she said, getting up from the table. She went to find the scissors and brought them back. Peter Stepanovich didn't even look at her; he took the scissors and began fussing with them. Arina Prokhorovna realized there was a real reason for his request and was ashamed of her touchiness. Those present exchanged silent glances. The lame teacher regarded Verkhovensky with malice and envy. Shigalyov continued:

'Having devoted my energies to the question of social organization in any future society that will replace the present one, I've come to the conclusion that all creators of social systems, from ancient times down to our own in 187–, were dreamers, story-tellers and fools, who contradicted themselves and understood absolutely nothing about natural science or that strange animal called man. Plato, Rousseau, Fourier, aluminium columns*—all that is good only for sparrows, not human society. But since the future form of human society is needed right now, when we're finally ready to take action, in order to forestall any further thought on the subject, I'm proposing my own system of world organization. Here it is!' he said, tapping his notebook. 'I wanted to expatiate on my book to this meeting as briefly as possible, but I see it's necessary to provide a great deal of verbal clarification; therefore my entire explication will take at least ten evenings, corresponding to the number of chapters in my book.' (Laughter was heard.) 'Moreover, I must declare in advance that my system is not yet complete.' (Laughter again.) 'I became lost in my own data and my conclusion contradicts the original premiss from which I started. Beginning with the idea of unlimited freedom, I end with unlimited despotism. I must add, however, there can be no other solution to the social problem except mine.'

The laughter grew louder and louder, but mainly from the young people and the less committed guests, so to speak. Madame Virginskaya, Liputin, and the lame teacher looked annoyed.

'But if you yourself were unable to create a system and have begun to despair, what is there for us to do?' one officer enquired cautiously.

'You're right, Mr Officer,' Shigalyov said sharply, turning to him. 'All the more so since you used the word "despair". Yes, I've begun to despair; nevertheless everything my book says is irrefutable and there's no other solution; no one will ever conceive of one. Therefore, without losing any time, I hasten to invite all members of this society to express their opinions on ten consecutive evenings, following the reading of my work. If members wish not to listen, let's go our separate ways at the very beginning—men to perform government service and women, back to their kitchens, because if you reject my thesis, you'll find no other solution. None at all! If you miss this opportunity, you'll be doing yourselves an injury, since you're bound to come back to it sooner or later.'

People began to stir: 'Is he mad, or what?' voices were heard to say.

'So it all comes down to Shigalyov's despair,' Lyamshin concluded. 'And the essential question is this: should he or should he not despair?'

'Shigalyov's proximity to despair is a personal question,' declared the gymnasium student.

'I move we vote on the question of how much Shigalyov's despair affects our common concerns, and whether it's worth listening to him or not?' one officer suggested cheerfully.

'That's not the point,' broke in the lame teacher at last. As a rule he spoke with what looked like a sarcastic smile; consequently, it was difficult to determine whether he was sincere or joking. 'That's not the point, ladies and gentlemen. Mr Shigalyov is too earnestly devoted to the problem and therefore overly modest. I'm familiar with his book. As a final solution to the problem he proposes dividing humanity into two unequal parts. One-tenth will receive personal freedom and unlimited power over the other nine-tenths. The latter must forfeit their individuality and become as it were a herd; through boundless obedience, they will attain, by a series of rebirths, a state of primeval innocence, although they'll still have to work. The steps proposed by the author for depriving nine-tenths of humanity of their will and for transforming them into a herd through the re-education of entire generations are quite remarkable; they're founded on data from natural science and are quite logical. One may disagree with some of his conclusions, but it's hard to doubt the intelligence and knowledge of the author. It's a pity that his proposal to spend ten evenings listening to his book is so impractical, since we'd hear a great deal that's of interest.'

'Are you really serious?' Madame Virginskaya asked, turning to the lame teacher in some alarm. 'That man, not knowing what to do with people, relegates nine-tenths of them to slavery? I've been suspicious of him for some time.'

'You mean your younger brother?' asked the lame teacher.

'Kinship? Are you laughing at me or what?'

'Besides, to work for aristocrats and listen to them as if they were gods—why, it's disgusting!' the female student observed angrily.

'What I'm proposing is not disgusting; it's paradise, paradise on earth—there can be none other on earth,' Shigalyov concluded majestically.

'Instead of paradise,' cried Lyamshin, 'take nine-tenths of humanity and, if there's no place to put them, I'd blow them up and leave only a few handfuls of educated people who'd begin to live their lives in a scientific manner.'

'Only a fool would talk like that!' the female student cried, flaring up.

'He is a fool, but a useful one,' Madame Virginskaya whispered to her.

'Perhaps that would be the best solution to the problem!' Shigalyov cried heatedly, turning to Lyamshin. 'Of course, you don't understand what a profound thing you've just said, Mr Cheerful. But since your idea is almost impossible to carry out, we must limit ourselves to paradise on earth, if that's what it's called.'

'What awful nonsense!' Verkhovensky couldn't help saying. But he continued to trim his nails in absolute unconcern and didn't even look up.

'And, sir, why is it nonsense?' the lame teacher put in, as if he'd been waiting to attack the first thing the other said. 'Why do you consider it nonsense? Mr Shigalyov is rather a fanatical lover of humanity; but remember, Fourier, Cabet, and even Proudhon* proposed some of the most despotic and fantastic solutions to the problem. Mr Shigalyov may be solving the matter in a much more sober manner. I assure you that having read his book, it's almost impossible not to agree with him on several points. He may even be much more realistic than others and his paradise on earth may even be the real one, the very one, and the loss of which—if it ever actually existed—humanity has been lamenting.'

'Well, I knew I'd get into trouble,' muttered Verkhovensky again.

'Wait a minute,' cried the lame teacher, getting more and more excited. 'Discussions and arguments about the organization of future society are virtually an urgent necessity for all contemporary thinking people. Herzen spent his whole life on the subject. Belinsky, as I know for certain, spent entire evenings with friends, debating and solving the most trivial and so to speak domestic details of the organization of future society.'

'Some people even lose their minds over it,' the major interjected.

'Nevertheless, one's more likely to get somewhere by talking than by sitting there keeping silent like dictators,' Liputin hissed, as if daring to begin his attack at long last.

'I didn't mean that Shigalyov was talking nonsense,' Verkhovensky mumbled. 'You see, ladies and gentlemen,' he said, raising his eyes just a little, 'in my opinion all these books by Fourier and Cabet, all this "right to work" talk, this Shigalyov scheme—it's all like novels, of which you can write a hundred thousand. An aesthetic pastime. I understand why you're bored here in this ugly little town, and why you throw yourselves at any piece of paper with writing on it.'

'Wait just one minute, sir,' cried the lame teacher, wriggling in his chair. 'We may be provincials and, naturally, deserving of your pity, but still we know that nothing new has transpired in the world which we'd weep over had we missed it. In numerous pamphlets of foreign origin distributed around here we've been urged to close ranks and even form groups for the sole purpose of bringing about total destruction, on the pretext that however much you try to cure the world, you won't be able to do so entirely, but if you take radical steps and cut off one hundred million heads, thus easing the burden, it'll be much easier to leap over the ditch. It's a splendid idea, without doubt, but it's at least as incompatible with reality as Shigalyov's "theory" which you just referred to with such contempt.'

'Well, I didn't come here to debate,' Verkhovensky said, missing the mark with his significant little phrase; unaware that he missed, he moved the candle up closer for more light.

'It's a pity, a real pity you didn't come here to debate, and it's a real pity you're so preoccupied with your toilette.'

'What's my toilette got to do with you?'

'It's as difficult to cut off one hundred million heads as it is to change the world through propaganda. It might even be more difficult, especially in Russia,' Liputin ventured again.

'Now they're pinning all their hopes on Russia,' an officer remarked.

'We heard what they're pinning their hopes on,' the lame teacher replied. 'We know that a mysterious index finger is pointing at our magnificent fatherland as the country most capable of carrying out some great feat. But here's what: if the problem is to be resolved gradually through propaganda, at least I'll benefit personally, even if it's only pleasant chatter. I might receive a decoration from the government for service to social causes. On the other hand, in a rapid solution to the problem such as cutting off a hundred million heads, what benefit would I receive? If you start making that kind of propaganda, they might even cut your tongue out.'

'They'd certainly cut yours out,' said Verkhovensky.

'There, you see. And since, even in the most favourable circumstances, it would take at least fifty years, well, thirty, to complete such a slaughter—inasmuch as people aren't sheep, you know, and they won't submit willingly—then wouldn't it be better to pack up all your belongings and settle somewhere far away beyond the sea on some remote island and there close your eyes in peace? Believe me,' he said, tapping his finger significantly on the table, 'the only thing that kind of propaganda does is encourage emigration, that's all!'

He concluded in obvious triumph. He was clearly one of the district's intellectuals. Liputin smiled insidiously; Virginsky listened somewhat gloomily; the rest had followed the argument with great interest, especially the ladies and the officers. Everyone realized that he who advocated cutting off a hundred million heads had been pushed to the wall; they waited to see what would happen next.

'You put it very well,' Verkhovensky mumbled more apathetically than before, even sounding a bit bored. 'Emigration is a good idea. Nevertheless, if, in spite of all the obvious disadvantages you foresee, the number of soldiers ready to fight for the common cause increases with every passing day, we'll succeed even without you. You see, my good man, what's happening here is the replacement of the old religion by a new one; that's why so many soldiers are needed—it's a large undertaking. Go ahead and emigrate! You know, I advise you to go to Dresden, rather than to some remote island. In the first place, it's a town that's never experienced any epidemic; since you're a civilized man, you must be afraid of death. In the second place, it's not far from the Russian border, so you'll be able to receive income there quite easily from your beloved fatherland. Thirdly, it contains many so-called artistic treasures; it appears that as a former teacher of literature you have aesthetic sensibility. Finally, it even offers a pocket Switzerland*—that's for poetic inspiration, since you probably write verse. In a word, it's a treasure in a nutshell!'

There was a stir, especially among the officers. In another second they'd all have begun talking at once. But the lame teacher rose irritably to the bait.

'No, sir, perhaps we still won't run away from the common cause! You must understand, sir...'

'What? Would you really agree to form a group of five, if I proposed it to you?' Verkhovensky blurted out suddenly, laying the scissors down on the table.

Everyone seemed startled. The mysterious man had shown his hand too suddenly. He'd even uttered the words 'group of five'.

'Everyone considers himself an honest man and won't abandon the common cause,' said the lame teacher, trying to wriggle out of it, 'but...'

'No, sir, it's no longer a question of "but",' Verkhovensky interrupted him in a sharp, commanding voice. 'I declare, ladies and gentlemen, that I must have a straight answer. I understand all too well that having come here and called you all together, I'm obliged to provide some explanation' (another unexpected disclosure), 'but I can't give you any until I determine your true state of mind. Dispensing with all discussion—because we can't just go on talking for the next thirty years as people have done for the last thirty—I ask you which is nicer: the slow way consisting of writing social novels and predetermining the fate of mankind bureaucratically on paper for a thousand years in advance, while despotism continues to swallow the morsels of roast meat which would jump into your mouths of themselves and which you fail to catch; or, would you prefer a swift solution, whatever that may be, which would untie your hands at long last and provide humanity with ample opportunity to organize society for itself, not merely on paper, but in real life? They shout, "A hundred million heads"— that may be only a metaphor, but why should they be afraid, if despotism with its creeping paper dreams will devour in a hundred years or so not one hundred million, but five hundred million heads! And note that a man suffering from an incurable illness still won't be cured, whatever remedies are prescribed for him on paper; on the contrary, if there's any delay, he'll become so ill that he'll infect us too, ruining all the fresh reserves of strength we can still rely on, so in the end we'll all fail. I agree it's very pleasant to chat in an eloquent and liberal way, and that action is... a little risky. Well, I'm really not very good at speaking. I came here with certain information, and therefore ask the entire worthy assembly not to vote, but merely to declare which alternative you prefer: to proceed at a snail's pace into the swamp, or to cross the swamp full steam ahead?'

'I'm for crossing full speed ahead!' cried the gymnasium student in ecstasy.

'Me too,' echoed Lyamshin.

'Naturally there's no doubt about the choice,' muttered one of the officers, then another, and then someone else. What struck them all most was that Verkhovensky, who'd come with 'information', was promising to speak.

'Ladies and gentlemen, I see that almost everyone here has decided in favour of acting in the spirit of the pamphlets,' he said, eyeing the assembly.

'Yes, everyone,' cried a majority of voices.

'I must confess that I'm for a more humane solution,' said the major. 'But since everyone else agrees with you, I'll go along with the rest.'

'It appears you aren't opposed to it either?' Verkhovensky asked, turning to the lame teacher.

'It's not that I'm...' he said, blushing slightly, 'but if I agree with everyone now, it's simply not to destroy...'

'You're all the same! He's prepared to argue six months for liberal eloquence, but ends up voting along with everyone else! Ladies and gentlemen, think it over; is it true you're all ready?' (Ready for what?—it was such a vague question, but terribly appealing.)

'Everyone, of course...' they affirmed, but they were all looking at each other.

'Later perhaps you'll regret having agreed so quickly? That's almost always the way it is with you people!'

They became excited in a different sense, very excited. The lame teacher flew at Verkhovensky.

'I'd like to point out that answers to such questions are

conditional. If we've agreed now, you must agree that the question was posed in a very strange way...'

'What way?'

'A way in which such questions are not usually posed.'

'Explain, please. You know, I was sure you'd be first to take offence.'

'You've extracted from us an answer regarding our readiness to take immediate action; but what right have you to do that? What authority do you have to pose such questions?'

'You should've thought about asking that question sooner! Why did you answer? First you agreed, then you thought of that.'

'In my opinion the casually open way you put your main question suggests that you have no authority, no right, at all. You're merely asking out of your own curiosity.'

'What *are* you talking about?' cried Verkhovensky; he seemed a little disturbed.

'I'm talking about the fact that new members, whoever they may be, are supposed to be recruited in secret, not in the presence of twenty strangers!' the lame teacher declared. He'd spoken his mind, but was already much too agitated. Verkhovensky turned quickly to the assembled group with a splendidly counterfeit look of alarm.

'Ladies and gentlemen, I consider it my duty to announce to you that all this is nonsense and our conversation has gone rather astray. I've yet to recruit any members, and no one has the right to say I'm recruiting members; we're merely talking about opinions. Isn't that so? One way or another, you've caused me great alarm,' he said turning again to the lame teacher. 'I never thought such innocent matters would have to be discussed in such secrecy here. Are you afraid of an informer? Is it possible there's an informer here among us?'

The agitation became tremendous; everyone began speaking at once.

'Ladies and gentlemen, if that's true,' Verkhovensky continued, 'I've compromised myself most of all. Therefore I ask you all to respond to one question, only if you care to, of course. You're all completely free.'

'What question? What question?' they began to shout.

'The sort of question after which it'll become clear whether we should remain here together or pick up our hats in silence and go off in different directions.'

'The question, what's the question?'

'If one of us knew about an intended political murder, would he inform on us, knowing in advance all the consequences, or would he stay at home, awaiting developments? There could be differing views on this. The answer to this question will clearly indicate whether we should separate or stay together, not merely with reference to this one evening. Allow me to address you first,' he said, turning to the lame teacher.

'Why me?'

'Because you started it. Please don't try to avoid the question; cunning won't help. But, do as you like; you're completely free.'

'Excuse me, but even posing a question like that is offensive.'

'Come on, can't you be any more specific?'

'I've never been an agent for the secret police, sir,' he said, wriggling even more.

'Please, be more specific, don't keep us waiting.'

The lame teacher became so angry that he even stopped speaking. He looked at his tormentor in silence, glaring at him spitefully from under his glasses.

'Yes or no? Would you inform or not?' cried Verkhovensky.

'Of course I *wouldn't*!' cried the lame teacher twice as loud.

'No one would inform, no one, of course not,' many voices joined in.

'Let me address you, Mr Major. Would you inform or not?' Verkhovensky continued. 'Note that I've turned to you next intentionally.'

'I would not inform, sir.'

'Well, but if you knew that someone wanted to murder and rob someone else, an ordinary mortal, you would inform and turn him in, wouldn't you?'

'Of course, sir, but that's a civil case, while you're talking about political denunciation. I've never been a member of the secret police, sir.'

'No one here's ever been,' many voices resounded. 'It's an unnecessary question. Everyone will give the same answer. There are no informers here!'

'Why is that man standing up?' cried the female student.

'It's Shatov. Why have you stood up, Shatov?' cried Madame Virginskaya.

Shatov had in fact got to his feet; he held his hat in his hand and stared at Verkhovensky. He seemed to want to say something to him, but hesitated. His face was pale and angry, but he restrained himself; he said not a single word and left the room in silence.

'Shatov, acting like this will do you no good,' Verkhovensky shouted after him mysteriously.

'On the other hand, it will do you considerable good as a spy and a scoundrel!' Shatov shouted at him from the door and left.

Once again there were shouts and cries.

'There's the test for you!' cried one voice.

'It certainly was useful!' shouted another.

'Perhaps it was too late?' enquired a third.

'Who invited him? Who let him in? Who is he? Who is Shatov? Will he inform or not?' Questions came from all sides.

'If he's an informer, he'd have pretended not to be. But he didn't give a damn and just walked out,' someone remarked.

'Now Stavrogin's standing up; he hasn't answered the question either,' cried the female student.

Stavrogin indeed was on his feet, and with him, at the other end of the table, Kirillov stood up too.

'Excuse me, Mr Stavrogin,' said Madame Virginskaya, addressing him abruptly. 'All of us here have answered the question, while you're leaving without saying anything.'

'I see no need to answer the question that so interests you,' Stavrogin muttered.

'But we've compromised ourselves, and you haven't,' a few voices cried.

'What do I care if you've compromised yourselves?' Stavrogin said with a laugh, but his eyes glinted.

'What do you care? What do you care?' several voices exclaimed. Many people jumped up from their seats.

'Wait a minute, ladies and gentlemen, wait a minute,' cried the lame teacher. 'Mr Verkhovensky hasn't answered the question either; he merely posed it.'

This remark had a striking effect. They all exchanged glances. Stavrogin laughed right in the lame teacher's face and then left; Kirillov followed him. Verkhovensky ran out into the hallway after them.

'What are you doing to me?' he murmured, grabbing Stavrogin by the arm and squeezing it with all his might. Without a word Stavrogin freed his arm.

'Go straight to Kirillov's house; I'll be there soon... It's absolutely essential!'

'Not for me it isn't,' said Stavrogin, cutting him short.

'Stavrogin will be there,' Kirillov said to put an end to argument. 'Stavrogin, it *is* essential for you to be there. I'll tell you why when we get there.'

They went out.

CHAPTER 8

Ivan the Tsarevich

THEY went out. Peter Stepanovich was about to rush back to the 'meeting' to quell the chaos, but probably deciding it wasn't worth the trouble he left it all and two minutes later was already rushing down the street after the other pair. Along the way he remembered the short cut to Filippov's house; wading up to his knees in mud, he hurried along the lane, and indeed did arrive just as Stavrogin and Kirillov were entering the gates.

'You're here already?' Kirillov observed. 'That's good. Come in.'

'I thought you said you lived alone?' asked Stavrogin as he passed a boiling samovar in the hallway.

'You'll soon see who I live with,' Kirillov mumbled. 'Come in.'

As soon as they entered Verkhovensky pulled from his pocket the anonymous letter he'd taken from von Lembke and set it before Stavrogin. All three of them sat down. Stavrogin read the letter in silence.

'Well?' he asked.

'That scoundrel will do what he says here,' Verkhovensky explained. 'Since he's under your control, you must tell us what to do about him. I can assure you that tomorrow he may very well go to see von Lembke.'

'Well, let him go.'

'What do you mean, "Let him go"? Especially if we can prevent it.'

'You're making a mistake; he doesn't depend on me. Besides, I don't care; he poses no threat to me. He only poses a threat to you.'

'And to you.'

'I don't think so.'

'But others may not spare you, don't you understand? Listen, Stavrogin, you're merely playing with words. You don't begrudge the money, do you?'

'So it'll take money, will it?'

'Absolutely, two thousand roubles... fifteen hundred at least. Give it to me tomorrow or even today, and tomorrow evening I'll send him off to Petersburg, which is exactly what he wants. If you like, even with Marya Timofeevna—note that.'

There was something distracted about him; he was speaking somewhat carelessly, without weighing his words. Stavrogin looked at him in astonishment.

'I have no reason to send Marya Timofeevna away.'

'Perhaps you don't even want to?' Peter Stepanovich said with a sarcastic smile.

'Perhaps I don't.'

'In a word, will I get the money or not?' he shouted at Stavrogin in furious impatience and rather imperiously. Stavrogin stared at him gravely.

'There won't be any money.'

'Hey, Stavrogin! Do you know something or have you done something already? You're just fooling around!'

His face was distorted, the corners of his mouth quivered, and he suddenly burst out laughing in a strange, inappropriate way.

'But you just got some money from your father for your estate,' Nikolai Vsevolodovich observed serenely. '*Maman* just paid you six or eight thousand roubles for Stepan Trofimovich. You can pay the fifteen hundred out of your own funds. I don't want to pay for other people; I've given so much already, it's rather annoying...' he said, chuckling at his own words.

'Ah, now you're starting to make jokes...'

Stavrogin stood up; Verkhovensky jumped up at once and stood with his back against the door, as if trying to prevent him from leaving. Nikolai Vsevolodovich was about to push him away from the door and leave, but all of a sudden he stopped.

'I won't give you Shatov,' he said. Peter Stepanovich started; they stared at each other.

'I told you earlier why you need Shatov's blood,' said Stavrogin, his eyes flashing. 'You want it to cement your

little group together. Just now you managed very cleverly
to drive Shatov away. You knew only too well he wouldn't
say, "I won't inform", and he'd consider it beneath him to
tell you a lie. But me? What do you need me for now?
You've been pestering me since we met abroad. Everything
you've told me so far is pure nonsense. Meanwhile you
suggest I hand fifteen hundred roubles over to Lebyadkin
and provide Fedka with a reason to slit his throat. I know
you think I'd like him to slit my wife's throat, too. By
involving me in the crime, you hope to gain power over me,
isn't that so? What do you need that power for? What the
hell do you want me for? Once and for all have a good look
at me: am I your man? And leave me alone.'

'Did Fedka come to see you?' Verkhovensky asked breathlessly.

'Yes, he did; his price is also fifteen hundred roubles...
He'll tell you that himself, there he is...' Stavrogin said,
stretching out his hand.

Peter Stepanovich turned around quickly. On the threshold, out of the darkness, emerged a new figure—Fedka,
wearing a sheepskin coat, but without a hat, as if at home.
He stood there grinning, baring his even white teeth. His
black eyes with their yellowish gleam darted cautiously
around the room examining the gentlemen. There was something he didn't understand; Kirillov had obviously brought
him in just now and his questioning gaze returned to him.
He stood on the threshold, but didn't want to enter the
room.

'He's probably here to listen to our business deal or even
to see the money in our hands, isn't that so?' asked Stavrogin; without waiting for an answer, he left the house.
Verkhovensky caught up with him at the gate almost in a
mad frenzy.

'Stop! Not one step!' he cried, grabbing him by the elbow.
Stavrogin tried to shake off his arm, but couldn't. He was
overcome with fury: seizing Verkhovensky by the hair with
his left hand, he hurled him to the ground with all his might
and went out of the gate. But he hadn't gone thirty paces
before Verkhovensky caught up with him.

'Let's make up, let's make up,' he said to him in a convulsive whisper.

Stavrogin shrugged, but didn't stop or turn around.

'Listen, tomorrow I'll bring you Lizaveta Nikolaevna. Do you want her? No? Why don't you answer? Tell me what you want and I'll do it. Listen, I'll give you Shatov if you like.'

'Then it must be true you're planning to murder him?' cried Nikolai Vsevolodovich.

'Why do you want Shatov? What for?' the madman carried on, all out of breath and very rapidly, constantly running ahead and grabbing Stavrogin by the elbow, probably without noticing he did so. 'Listen: I'll give him to you. Let's make up. Your price is very high, but... let's make up!'

Stavrogin glanced at him at last and was astonished. This was not the same look, the same voice as Peter usually had, and had had back there in the room: now he saw a different face. The tone of the voice was different: Verkhovensky was imploring him, beseeching him. This was a man whose most precious possession was being taken away, or had been already, and he'd yet to recover from the shock.

'What's the matter with you?' cried Stavrogin. He didn't answer, but ran after him with the same imploring but at the same time relentless expression.

'Let's make it up!' he whispered once again. 'Listen, I have a knife hidden in my boot, just like Fedka, but I'll still make up with you.'

'What the hell do you need me for?' Stavrogin cried in positive rage and amazement. 'Is there some kind of mystery here or what? Am I to be your talisman?'

'Listen, we'll stir up trouble,' the other muttered rapidly, almost deliriously. 'You don't think we can do it? We'll stir up such trouble that everything will be shaken loose from its foundations. Karmazinov is right when he says there will be nothing to grab hold of. Karmazinov is very clever. Let there be only ten such groups in all Russia, and they can't touch me.'

'They're all such fools,' Stavrogin remarked involuntarily.

'Oh, try to be more foolish yourself, Stavrogin, try to be more foolish! You know, you're not so clever one can't wish you that: you're afraid, you lack faith, and you're frightened by the magnitude of it all. Why are they fools? They're not really such fools; nowadays no one has a mind of his own. There are very few original minds these days. Virginsky is a man with a pure heart, ten times purer than ours; well, so be it. Liputin is a scoundrel, but I know his weak spot. There's not one scoundrel who doesn't have a weak spot. Only Lyamshin has no weak spot; on the other hand, I hold him in my hand. A few more groups and I'll have passports and money everywhere. Isn't that good? Well, isn't it? And hiding places—let them look. They may uproot one group, but they'll miss others. We'll make trouble... Don't you really think two of us are enough?'

'Take Shigalyov and leave me in peace...'

'Shigalyov's a genius! You know he's a genius like Fourier? But he's bolder than Fourier, stronger. I'll look after him. He's discovered "equality".'

'He's feverish and raving; something very peculiar has happened to him,' Stavrogin thought, looking at him again. They both walked on without stopping.

'He's got it all just right in that notebook of his,' Verkhovensky continued. 'He has a system for spying. Every member of the society spies on every other one and is obliged to inform. Everyone belongs to all the others and the others belong to each one. They're all slaves and equal in their slavery. In extreme cases there's slander and murder, but for the most part—equality. In the first place the level of education, science, and accomplishment is lowered. A high level of science and accomplishment is accessible only to those possessing the highest abilities; and who needs those abilities? Those with higher abilities have always seized power and become despots. Those with higher abilities can't help being despots and have always done more harm than good; they'll either be banished or executed. Cicero's tongue will be cut out, Copernicus's eyes will be gouged out, Shakespeare will be stoned—there's Shigalyov's system for you! Slaves must be equal: without despotism there's never been any freedom or equality, but there must be equality in the herd. That's Shigalyov's system! Ha, ha, ha! Does it seem strange to you? I'm for Shigalyov!'

Stavrogin tried to quicken his pace and get home as soon as possible. 'If this fellow's drunk, how did he manage it?' he wondered. 'Surely not the brandy?'

'Listen, Stavrogin: it's a fine idea to level mountains—there's nothing ridiculous in that. I'm for Shigalyov! There's no need for education; we've had enough science! Even without science we have enough material for the next thousand years; but we must have obedience. The one thing the world needs is obedience. The desire for education is an aristocratic idea. As soon as a man experiences love or has a family, he wants private property. We'll destroy that want: we'll unleash drunkenness, slander, denunciation; we'll unleash unheard-of corruption; we'll suffocate every genius in its infancy. Everything will be reduced to a common denominator of complete equality. "We've learned a trade, we're honest men, and we need nothing more", that's the answer provided recently by English workers. Only what's necessary is necessary—that's the motto of the whole world from now on. But an upheaval is necessary, too; we rulers will take care of that. Slaves must have rulers. Complete obedience, total loss of individuality, but once in thirty years Shigalyov permits an upheaval and everyone starts devouring one another, up to a certain point, just to avoid boredom. Boredom is an aristocratic sensation; in Shigalyov's system there'll be no desires. Desire and suffering are for us, while Shigalyov's system is for slaves.'

'Do you exclude yourself?' Stavrogin asked, despite himself again.

'And you too. You know, I was thinking of giving the whole world to the pope. Let him come out barefoot and show himself to the crowd: "See what they've driven me to!" he'll say; everyone will follow him, even the army. The pope will be on top, we'll be around him, and under us—Shigalyov's system. All we need is for the *Internationale* to come to an agreement with the pope; that will happen, too. And the little old man will agree at once. He has no other choice; mark my words. Ha, ha, ha. Is it stupid? Tell me, is it stupid or not?'

'That's enough,' muttered Stavrogin in annoyance.

'Enough! Listen, I've given up the pope! And to hell with Shigalyov's system! To hell with the pope! What we need is something more topical, not Shigalyov's system, because it's too precious. It's an ideal, something in the future. Shigalyov is a jeweller and he's stupid, like any philanthropist. We need manual labour; Shigalyov despises manual labour. Listen: the pope will live in the West, while we here will have—you!'

'Get away from me; you're drunk!' Stavrogin muttered, quickening his pace.

'Stavrogin, you're a very handsome man!' cried Peter Stepanovich almost in ecstasy. 'Do you know how handsome you are? The best thing about you is you sometimes don't know it. Oh, I've studied you! Sometimes I look at you sideways on from the corner! There's even something sincere and naïve about you, do you know that? There is, really there is! You must suffer, suffer sincerely, as a result of that simplicity. I love beauty. I'm a nihilist, but I love beauty. Don't nihilists love beauty? It's only idols they don't love, but I even love idols! You're my idol! You never offend anyone, but everyone hates you; you regard everyone as your equal, but everyone's afraid of you, and that's good. No one ever comes to slap you on the shoulder. You're a terrible aristocrat. When an aristocrat goes in for democracy, it's irresistible. It means nothing to you to sacrifice life, whether yours or someone else's. You're just the sort of person needed. You're just the sort I need. I know of no one else but you. You're the leader, the sun, and I'm your worm...'

Verkhovensky suddenly kissed his hand. A chill ran down Stavrogin's back and he withdrew his hand in alarm. They stopped walking.

'You're mad!' whispered Stavrogin.

'Perhaps I'm raving, perhaps I am!' Verkhovensky said, speaking very quickly. 'But I've thought up the first step. Shigalyov could never think up the first step. There are lots of Shigalyovs! But there's only one man in all Russia who's discovered the first step and who knows how to take it. I'm that man. Why are you staring at me? I need you, you're necessary to me. Without you, I'm nothing. Without you I'm a fly, an idea in a glass bottle, Columbus without America.'

Stavrogin stood and stared intently into his mad eyes.

'Listen, first we'll stir up trouble,' Verkhovensky said in terrible haste, constantly clutching at Stavrogin's left sleeve. 'I've told you already. We'll get to the common herd. Do you know we're already very powerful? Our people aren't just those who slit throats and set fires, who use pistols in the classic manner and bite other people. Those people only interfere. I don't understand anything without discipline. I'm a scoundrel, after all, not a socialist, ha, ha! Listen, I've counted them all over: a teacher who laughs with his children at their God over their cradle is already one of us. A lawyer who defends an educated murderer by arguing he's more cultured than his victims, and couldn't help murdering to acquire money, is one of us already. Schoolboys who murder a peasant just to experience the sensation are already with us. Juries who acquit criminals right and left are with us. The public prosecutor who trembles in court because he's not sufficiently liberal is with us. Administrators, men of letters, oh, there are lots of them, lots, and they don't even know they're with us! On the other hand, the obedience of schoolboys and fools has reached the highest level; their teachers' gall bladders overflow with bile; vanity has spread everywhere and bestial appetites have grown to enormous proportions... Do you know, do you really know how many people we'll attract with our ready-made little ideas? When I went abroad, Littré's theory* that crime is insanity was all the rage; now I return home to find crime is no longer insanity, but some kind of common sense, almost an obligation, at least a noble protest. "How can a murderer refrain from committing murder if he needs money?" But that's only the beginning. The Russian God has already capitulated to cheap vodka. The common people are drunk, mothers are drunk, children are drunk, churches are empty, and in our courtrooms the choice is between "two hundred lashes or a bucketful of vodka". Oh, just wait until this generation grows up! It's a pity there's no time to wait, or we might've let them get even drunker! Ah, what a pity there's no proletariat! But there will be, there will be, it's coming to that...'

'It's also a pity we've grown more stupid,' Stavrogin muttered and resumed his way home.

'Listen, I myself saw a six-year-old child leading his drunken mother home, while she was swearing at him, using foul language. Do you think I'm happy about that? When she falls into our hands we'll cure her... if it's necessary we'll drive them into the desert for forty years... But one or two generations of vice are essential now; frightful, disgusting vice, turning man into filthy, cowardly, cruel, selfish scum—that's what we need! What's more, a little "fresh blood" so we can get used to it. What are you laughing at? I'm not contradicting myself. I'm merely contradicting the philanthropists and proponents of Shigalyov's system, not myself. I'm a scoundrel, not a socialist. Ha, ha, ha! It's a pity there's so little time. I promised Karmazinov it would begin in May and end in October. Is that too soon? Ha, ha! Do you know what I'll tell you, Stavrogin: although Russians use foul language, there's been no cynicism among them up to now. You know the peasant slave had more self-respect than Karmazinov? They may have beaten him up, but he always stood up for his gods; Karmazinov didn't.'

'Well, Verkhovensky, this is the first time I've listened to you, and I'm really astounded,' muttered Nikolai Vsevolodovich. 'You're not really a socialist at all, but some kind of ambitious... politician.'

'A scoundrel, a scoundrel. Are you worried about who I am? I'll tell you who I am; I was just coming to that. I had a reason for kissing your hand. People must believe we know what we want and that others are merely "swinging their cudgels and clubbing their own followers". Hey, if only there were more time! The great misfortune is there's no time. We'll proclaim destruction... why, why again is this little idea so fascinating? But we must get some exercise. We'll spread fires... We'll spread legends... Every mangy little group of five will prove useful. I'll find you such devoted followers in these groups that they'll be willing to shoot at anyone and will even be grateful for the honour. Well, sir, then the trouble will begin! There'll be an upheaval such as the world has never seen... Rus'* will be shrouded in mist and the land will weep for its old gods.... Well, sir, then we'll unleash... do you know who?'

'Who?'

'Ivan the Tsarevich.'*

'*Who*?'

'Ivan the Tsarevich; you, you!'

Stavrogin thought for a moment.

'The Pretender?' he asked suddenly, staring at the madman in astonishment. 'Ah, so that's your plan at last.'

'We'll say he's been "in hiding",' Verkhovensky said quietly in a tender whisper, as if really drunk. 'Do you know what that little phrase means, "He's in hiding"? But he'll appear, he will. We'll put about a legend even better than the one the Castrates have. He exists, but no one's ever seen him. Oh, what a fine legend we could put about! The main thing is—a new force is imminent. That's what they need, that's what they're weeping for. And what is there in socialism anyway? It destroyed the old forces, but failed to introduce any new ones. But here's a force, a tremendous, unbelievable force! We need only one lever to lift the earth. Everything will be moved!'

'So you've been counting on me in earnest,' Stavrogin said with a malicious laugh.

'Why are you laughing and why so maliciously? Don't frighten me. I'm like a child now and I can be scared to death by just one little smile like that. Listen, I'll show you to no one, no one: that's how it must be. He exists, but no one's seen him; he's in hiding. You know, it would be possible, even, to show him to one man, say, in a hundred thousand. And it would go all round the earth: "We've seen him, we've seen him." Ivan Filippovich, God of Sabaoth,* was seen too, ascending to heaven in a chariot before a multitude of his followers who saw him "with their own eyes". And you're no Ivan Filippovich; you're a handsome man, proud as a god, seeking nothing for yourself, with an aura of sacrifice, who's "in hiding". The main thing is the legend! You'll conquer them; you'll need only look, and you'll conquer them. He's bearing a new truth, but he's "in hiding". We'll hand down two or three judgements of Solomon at this point. Our little groups, our groups of five—we don't need any newspapers! If you grant only one petition out of ten thousand, everyone will come forward with them. In each district every peasant will know there's a hollow tree where petitions are to be deposited. The earth will resound with the cry: "A new, just law is coming." The oceans will seethe, the whole show will come crashing down, and then we'll plan to set up a stone structure. For the first time! *We* shall build it, we alone!'

'Madness,' said Stavrogin.

'Why, why don't you want it? Are you afraid? I've seized upon you because I thought you were afraid of nothing. Is that unreasonable? I'm still Columbus without America; is Columbus without America really reasonable?'

Stavrogin was silent. Meanwhile they'd come to his house and stopped at the front door.

'Listen,' said Verkhovensky, bending down to his ear. 'I'll do it for you without money. I'll finish with Marya Timofeevna tomorrow... without money; and tomorrow I'll bring you Liza. Do you want Liza tomorrow?'

'Has he really gone mad?' Stavrogin wondered with a smile. The front door opened.

'Stavrogin, is America ours?' Verkhovensky asked, seizing his sleeve for the last time.

'What for?' Nikolai Vsevolodovich replied earnestly and severely.

'You have no desire—I knew it!' he cried in a burst of furious spite. 'You're lying, you worthless, lecherous, perverted little aristocrat, I don't believe you, you've the appetite of a wolf!... You must know your bill's already been run up too high—I can't give you up now! There's no one else on earth like you! I invented you when I was abroad; looking at you, I invented it all. If I hadn't watched you from my corner, none of it would ever have come into my head!'

Stavrogin climbed the stairs without answering.

'Stavrogin!' Verkhovensky shouted after him. 'I'll give you a day... well, two days... three; I can't give you more than three. And then—your answer!'

At Tikhon's*

NIKOLAI VSEVOLODOVICH didn't sleep that night; he spent it sitting on the sofa, often turning his fixed gaze towards a point in the corner near the chest of drawers. A lamp burned in his room all night. Around seven in the morning he dozed off sitting up, and when Aleksei Yegorevich, following their well-established routine, came in precisely at nine-thirty with his morning cup of coffee, and in so doing woke him up, he opened his eyes and seemed to be unpleasantly surprised to find that he'd slept so long and it was already very late. He drank his coffee quickly, dressed quickly, and left the house in a rush. He made no reply to Aleksei Yegorevich's cautious question, 'Did he have any orders for him?' He walked along the street with his eyes fixed on the ground, deep in thought; only by lifting his head now and then did he suddenly reveal some vague, but intense anxiety. At one crossroads, still not far from his house, a crowd of peasants, some fifty or more, crossed his path; they walked sedately, almost in silence, in deliberate fashion. At a little shop where he had to wait for a minute or so, someone said these men were 'Shpigulin's workers'. He hardly paid any attention to them. At last, about ten thirty, he reached the gates of the Yefimovo Monastery of Our Lady at the edge of town near the river. Only when he got here did he suddenly seem to remember something; he stopped, feeling quickly and nervously for something in his side pocket and—smiled. After entering the enclosure, he asked the first lay brother he met how to find Bishop Tikhon, who was living in retirement within the monastery. The lay brother began bowing and immediately led the way. At a small staircase at the end of a long, two-storeyed monastery building, he was authoritatively and expeditiously handed over by the lay brother to a fat, grey-haired monk who met them; he conducted Stavrogin through a long, narrow corridor, also bowing all the time (although as a result of his obesity he couldn't bow very deeply, and merely jerked his head frequently and abruptly); he continually invited Stavrogin to follow him, even though he was following him anyway. The monk asked all sorts of questions and kept talking about the Father Archimandrite;* receiving no answers, he became even more respectful. Stavrogin noticed that he was known here, although, as far as he could recall, he'd only come here during his childhood. When they reached the door at the end of the corridor, the monk opened it with apparent authority and enquired familiarly of the lay brother who came running over whether they could go in. Not even waiting for a reply, he opened the door all the way and, with a bow, allowed his 'dear' visitor to enter. After receiving his thanks, he disappeared quickly, as if running away. Nikolai Vsevolodovich entered a small room; almost at the same time a tall, lean man, about fifty-five years old, appeared in the doorway of the adjoining room. He was dressed in a plain indoor cassock, and appeared somewhat sickly; he had a vague smile and a strange, seemingly bashful expression. This was none other than Tikhon, whom Nikolai Vsevolodovich had first heard of from Shatov, and whom he'd managed to collect some information about since then.

This information was varied and contradictory, but it had one element in common, namely, that both Tikhon's supporters and his detractors (and there were some), were somehow reluctant to talk about him—the detractors out of contempt, most likely, and the supporters, even the enthusiastic ones, out of modesty, as if they wanted to conceal something about him, some weakness of his, perhaps that he was a holy fool.* Nikolai Vsevolodovich learned that he'd been residing in the monastery for the last six years or so and that those who came to see him included both simple folk and people of high rank; that even in far-off Petersburg he had ardent admirers, especially female ones. On the other hand, he'd heard from a certain portly, elderly 'regular' member of our local club, a pious man to boot, that 'that Tikhon is almost insane; at least he's totally undistinguished and undoubtedly drinks heavily.' Let me add here, even though it's getting ahead of my story, that this last charge

is utter nonsense; he simply suffered from chronic rheumatism in his legs and occasionally from nervous convulsions.
Nikolai Vsevolodovich also found out that this retired bishop,
either because of some weakness of character or 'inexcusable
absent-mindedness, inappropriate in someone of his rank',
had been unable to inspire any special personal respect in
the monastery. It was said that the Father Archimandrite,
a stern and strict man in the performance of his supervisory
duties, and, in addition, a well-known scholar, even harboured what seemed to be a secret hostility to him, and
accused him (not to his face, but indirectly) of leading an
undisciplined life and, virtually, of heresy. The monastic
brotherhood also treated the sickly servant of God not
exactly in an offhand way, but, so to speak, in a familiar
one. The two rooms which made up Tikhon's cell were
furnished in a curious manner, too. Alongside some heavy,
old furniture covered in worn leather there stood three or
four elegant little pieces: a very expensive armchair, a large,
superbly crafted writing-desk, a magnificent carved bookcase,
tables, and shelves—all of them gifts. There was an expensive
Bukhara rug, and next to it little straw mats. There were
engravings depicting 'secular' motifs, as well as mythological
subjects, while nearby in a corner stood a large icon-case
with glittering gold and silver icons, one of which was very
old indeed and contained some relics. His library, they said,
was also too diverse and contradictory: alongside works of
great Christian saints and martyrs, there were theatrical
works, 'and perhaps even worse'.

After the initial greetings, exchanged for some reason with
evident awkwardness on both sides, hurriedly and even
indistinctly, Tikhon led the guest into his study and sat him
down on the sofa in front of the table, while he himself sat
nearby in a wicker chair. Nikolai Vsevolodovich was still
very preoccupied by some intense inner anxiety. He appeared to have decided on something extraordinary that
could not be gainsaid, and was at the same time almost
impossible for him. For a minute or so he looked around
the study, apparently unaware of what he was looking at;
he was thinking, but of course he didn't know what he was

thinking about. He was roused by the silence, and suddenly it seemed to him that Tikhon was lowering his eyes bashfully and even smiling in a silly, uncalled-for way. This immediately aroused in him a feeling of revulsion; he wanted to get up and leave, especially since he thought Tikhon was decidedly drunk. But the latter suddenly raised his eyes and looked at Stavrogin with such a steadfast and thoughtful gaze, together with such an unexpected and enigmatic expression that Stavrogin almost shuddered. He suddenly felt that Tikhon already knew why he'd come, that he'd been forewarned (even though no one in the whole world could have known the reason), and that if Tikhon hadn't spoken first, it was merely to spare him and to avoid humiliating him.

'Do you know who I am?' he suddenly asked abruptly. 'Did I introduce myself when I came in? I'm so absent-minded...'

'You didn't introduce yourself, but I had the pleasure of seeing you once before, some four years ago, here in the monastery... by chance.'

Tikhon spoke slowly and evenly, in a soft voice, clearly and distinctly pronouncing his words.

'I wasn't in this monastery four years ago,' Nikolai Vsevolodovich replied, actually rather rudely. 'I was here only as a child, before you came here.'

'Perhaps you've forgotten,' Tikhon observed cautiously, without insisting.

'No, I haven't forgotten. It'd be ridiculous if I didn't remember,' Stavrogin insisted somewhat unnecessarily. 'Perhaps you've only heard about me and formed some impression of me, and that's why you're confused and you imagine you've seen me here.'

Tikhon remained silent. Nikolai Vsevolodovich noticed that a nervous twitch sometimes flitted across his face, a symptom of his recent nervous illness.

'I can see that you're not well today,' he said. 'I think it would be better if I left.'

He was about to get up from his chair.

'Yes, yesterday and today I've had acute pains in my legs, and I got very little sleep last night...'

Tikhon stopped. Again his visitor suddenly lapsed into his previous vague pensiveness. The silence lasted for a long time, about two minutes.

'Have you been observing me?' he asked suddenly in alarm and suspicion.

'I was looking at you and remembering your mother's features. Although there's little external resemblance, there's a strong inner, spiritual likeness.'

'There's no likeness at all, especially not spiritual. None what-so-ev-er!' said Nikolai Vsevolodovich, growing anxious again for no reason and insisting excessively without knowing why. 'You're just saying that out of sympathy for my situation, and it's nonsense,' he blurted out suddenly. 'Why, does my mother really come to see you?'

'Yes, she does.'

'I didn't know that. I've never heard it from her. Does she come often?'

'Once a month or more.'

'I never heard that, never. I never did. Of course, you've heard from her that I'm insane,' he added suddenly.

'No, not that you're insane. But I've heard it from others.'

'You must have a good memory if you recall such nonsense. And have you heard about the slap in the face as well?'

'I've heard something about it.'

'You mean, all about it. You must have a great deal of free time. And about the duel?'

'About the duel, too.'

'You've heard quite a bit here. You don't need any newspapers. Has Shatov warned you about me? Well?'

'No. I do know Mr Shatov, but I haven't seen him for some time.'

'Hmmm.... What kind of map do you have over there? Why, it's a map of the last war!* What's that for?'

'I was using it while reading this book. It's a most interesting account.'

'Show it to me. Yes, it's not a bad exposition. But that's a strange choice of reading for you.'

He pulled the book towards him and glanced at it cursorily. It was a voluminous and well-written account of the circumstances of the last war, not so much from a military as from a purely literary point of view. After turning a few pages, he suddenly pushed the book away impatiently.

'I really don't know why I've come here,' he uttered in disgust, looking directly into Tikhon's eyes, as if expecting an answer from him.

'You don't seem too well, either.'

'No, I'm not well.'

And suddenly, putting it as briefly and abruptly as possible, so it was sometimes even difficult to understand, he explained that he was subject to hallucinations, especially at night; that he sometimes saw or felt next to him some malicious creature, sarcastic and 'rational', 'appearing in various guises, with different traits, but always one and the same, and I'm always furious...'

These revelations of his were wild and incoherent and indeed seemed to come from an insane person. All the same, Nikolai Vsevolodovich spoke with so strange a candour, such as had never been observed in him before, and with such completely uncharacteristic sincerity that it seemed as if his former self had suddenly and unexpectedly vanished once and for all. He was not in the least ashamed of revealing the fear with which he spoke about his apparitions. But all this took but a moment and disappeared as suddenly as it had come.

'This is all nonsense,' he said quickly, in awkward annoyance, recollecting himself. 'I'll go and see a doctor.'

'By all means,' Tikhon agreed.

'You speak so convincingly... Have you ever seen people like me, with this kind of apparition?'

'I have, but very rarely. I recall only one person like you in my whole life, an army officer, after the loss of his wife, his irreplaceable life's companion. I've only heard about one other one. Both went abroad to be cured... Have you been subject to this for very long?'

'About a year, but it's all nonsense. I'll go and see a doctor. It's all nonsense, terrible nonsense. It's all myself in different aspects, nothing more. Since I added that... last phrase just now, you probably think I'm still in doubt and not sure whether it's really me or it's the devil.'

Tikhon cast him an enquiring glance.

'And... do you really see him?' he asked, that is, dispelling any possibility that it was undoubtedly a false and morbid hallucination. 'Do you actually see some figure?'

'It's odd that you keep insisting on this, when I've already told you what I see,' Stavrogin said, once again growing more irritated with every word. 'Of course I see him; I see him as I see you... But sometimes I'm not sure what I see, and I don't know what's real: him or me... But it's all nonsense. Can't you even conceive that it's really the devil?' he added with a laugh, switching too abruptly into a sarcastic tone of voice. 'After all, it'd be more in keeping with your profession, wouldn't it?'

'It's more likely an illness, although...'

'Although what?'

'Devils undoubtedly exist and can be conceived of in very different ways.'

'You just lowered your eyes again,' Stavrogin interjected with an irritable sneer, 'because you're ashamed of me for believing in the devil; now you think I'm pretending I don't believe in him, and that I'm cunningly posing the question to you: does he really exist or not?'

Tikhon smiled vaguely.

'You know, it really doesn't suit you to lower your eyes: it's unnatural, ridiculous, and affected. And to compensate for my rudeness, I'll tell you boldly and in all seriousness: I do believe in the devil, I believe canonically in a personal devil, not in any allegory, and I have no need whatsoever to extract any secrets from anyone; that's all there is to it. You must be very glad...'

He emitted a nervous, unnatural laugh. Tikhon regarded him curiously, with a gentle and, as it were, timid glance.

'Do you believe in God?' Stavrogin blurted out suddenly.

'Yes.'

'Well, it's said if you believe and command a mountain to move,* it'll move... but that's nonsense. However, I'd still like to ask: could you move a mountain or not?'

'If God wills, I could move it,' Tikhon replied quietly, with restraint, starting to lower his eyes again.

'Well, that's the same as saying God himself would move it. No, I mean you, what about you, as a reward for your faith in God?'

'Perhaps I couldn't move it.'

' "Perhaps"? That's not bad. But why do you doubt it?'

'My faith is not perfect.'

'What? *Your* faith is not perfect? Not absolute?'

'No... perhaps my faith is not complete.'

'Well, at least you believe that with God's help you could still move it, and that's something. That's still more than the *très peu* of a certain archbishop,* although under threat of a sword. Of course, you're also a Christian?'

'May I not deny Thy Cross, O Lord,' Tikhon replied in almost a passionate whisper and bowed his head still further. The corners of his lips suddenly began to twitch nervously.

'But is it really possible to believe in the devil without believing in God?' Stavrogin asked with a laugh.

'Oh, altogether possible, it happens all the time,' Tikhon replied, raising his eyes and also smiling.

'And I'm sure you consider such faith more honourable than complete lack of faith... Oh, you priest!' said Stavrogin with a loud laugh. Tikhon smiled at him again.

'On the contrary, absolute atheism is more honourable than secular indifference,' he added cheerfully and ingenuously.

'Aha, so that's what you think.'

'The absolute atheist stands on the next to last rung of the ladder of perfect faith (whether or not he takes the next step); but the indifferent man has no faith whatever, except for an evil fear.'

'But have you... have you ever read the Book of Revelation?'

'Yes.'

'Do you recall: "Write to the Angel of the Laodicean Church..."?'*

'I do. Delightful words.'

'Delightful? That's a strange expression for a member of the clergy; but you're altogether something of an eccentric...

Where have you got that book?' Stavrogin asked, in something of a strange hurry and anxiety, searching for the book on the table. 'I want to read it to you... Do you have a Russian translation?'

'I know it, I know the place, I remember it very well,' said Tikhon.

'Do you know it by heart? Recite it!...'

He lowered his eyes quickly, placed the palms of his hands on his knees, and prepared to listen impatiently. Tikhon recited, recalling the passage word for word:

' "And unto the angel of the church of the Laodiceans write; These things saith the Amen, the faithful and true witness, the beginning of the creation of God; I know thy works, that thou art neither cold nor hot: I would thou wert cold or hot. So then because thou art lukewarm, and neither cold nor hot, I will spue thee out of my mouth. Because thou sayest, I am rich, and increased with goods, and have need of nothing; and knowest not that thou art wretched, and miserable and poor, and blind, and naked..." '

'Stop,' said Stavrogin, cutting him short. 'That's for the middle-of-the-road, the indifferent, isn't it? You know, I like you very much.'

'I like you too,' Tikhon answered in a low voice.

Stavrogin fell silent and suddenly lapsed into his former pensiveness. This seemed to occur in fits, here for the third time. When he told Tikhon that he liked him he was almost in one of these fits; at least he hadn't himself expected to say it. More than a minute passed.

'Don't be angry,' whispered Tikhon, almost touching Stavrogin's elbow with a finger, but appearing too timid to do so. Stavrogin jumped and knitted his brows wrathfully.

'How did you know I was angry?' he asked quickly. Tikhon was about to say something, but Stavrogin suddenly interrupted him in inexplicable anxiety:

'Why did you suppose I was absolutely bound to get angry? Yes, I was furious, you're right, precisely because I'd said I liked you. You're right, but you're a crude cynic; you look down on human nature. There might have been no question of anger, if it had been not I but someone else here... But we're not talking about someone else; we're talking about me. Nevertheless, you're an eccentric and a holy fool...'

He was becoming more and more irritated and, strange to say, he was not ashamed of his words:

'Listen, I don't like spies and psychologists, at least not the kind who pry into my soul. I don't invite anyone into my soul; I don't need any help; I can get along on my own. Do you think I'm afraid of you?' he said, raising his voice and looking up defiantly. 'You're absolutely certain I've come to reveal some "awful" secret to you and you're waiting for it with all the monkish inquisitiveness you're capable of. Well, I want you to know that I won't reveal anything to you, no secret at all, because I have no need of you whatsoever.'

Tikhon looked at him resolutely:

'You were struck by it saying the Lamb of God loves a man who is cold more than one who is merely lukewarm,' he replied. 'You don't want to be *merely* lukewarm. I feel that some extraordinary intention, perhaps even a dreadful one, is struggling inside you. If that's true, I implore you, don't torture yourself; tell me precisely why you've come here.'

'Why are you so sure I've come here about something?'

'I... guessed from your face,' whispered Tikhon, lowering his eyes.

Nikolai Vsevolodovich was rather pale, his hands trembling slightly. For several seconds he looked at Tikhon without moving and in silence, as if making up his mind once and for all. Finally he took some printed sheets from the side pocket of his jacket and placed them on the table.

'Here are some sheets intended for circulation,' he said in a breaking voice. 'If just one man should read them, I want you to know I won't conceal them; everyone will read them. That's been decided. I have no need for you whatever, because I've already decided it all. But read it... As you read, don't say anything; when you've read it, you'll tell me all that...'

'Shall I read it now?' Tikhon hesitated.

'Yes. I'm quite calm.'

'No, I can't make it out without my glasses. The print is so small, foreign.'

'Here are your glasses,' Stavrogin said, handing him a pair of glasses from the table, then leaning back on the sofa. Tikhon became absorbed in his reading.

2.

The print was indeed foreign—three small sheets of ordinary writing-paper, closely printed and stitched together. It must have been published secretly at some Russian printing press abroad, and at first glance the pages closely resembled a political pamphlet. The heading read: 'From Stavrogin'.

I shall insert this document verbatim in my chronicle. It must be assumed that by now it's quite well known. I've allowed myself to correct only the rather numerous spelling errors, some indeed quite surprising, since the author was an educated man after all, and even well read (relatively speaking, of course). I've made no changes in the style, in spite of irregularities and even some obscurities. In any case it's perfectly clear the author was above all not a man of letters.

From Stavrogin.

I, Nikolai Stavrogin, a retired army officer, lived in Petersburg in 186–, indulging in depravity in which I took no pleasure. During that time I occupied three separate apartments. I lived in one of them, furnished rooms with board and service, where Marya Lebyadkina, who is today my lawful wife, also lived. I rented the other two apartments by the month and used them for my amorous intrigues: in one I received a certain lady who loved me, in the other, I received her maid, and for some time I was preoccupied by the intention of bringing them together so the lady and her maid would meet in the presence of my friends and her husband. Knowing both their characters, I anticipated a great deal of pleasure from this stupid joke.

Making leisurely preparations for this meeting, I had to visit one of these apartments, in a large building on Gorokhovaya Street, more frequently, since that was where the maid used to come. I had only one room there, on the fourth floor, rented from lower middle class Russians. They themselves lived next door in another room that was even more crowded, so the door separating the two rooms always stood open, which was just what I wanted. The husband, who worked in some office, was away from morning to night. The wife, a woman about forty, used to cut up old things and fashion them into new clothes; she too used to leave the house fairly often to deliver her work. I would remain alone with their daughter, aged fourteen* I think, and still a child to all appearances. Her name was Matryosha. Her mother loved her, but often beat her and was in the habit of shouting at her cantankerously. This girl waited on me and straightened up my room behind the screen. I declare that I've forgotten the number of the house. Now, having made some enquiries, I know the old building has been demolished, and a very large, new house stands where two or three old ones were before. I've also forgotten the name of the family (perhaps I didn't even know it then). I remember that the woman was called Stepanida, Mikhailovna, I think. I don't recall his name. Who they were, where they were from, where they are now—I have no idea. I suppose if one were to initiate a search and make all possible enquiries of the Petersburg police, one might be able to trace them. All this happened in June. The house was light blue in colour.

One day my penknife was missing from the table. I really had no need for it; it had just been lying around. I told my landlady without ever thinking she'd give her daughter a beating for it. She'd been screaming at the child over the disappearance of some rag or other (I lived simply and they didn't stand on ceremony with me). When this same rag turned up under the tablecloth, the girl didn't utter one word in reproach and looked on in silence. I noticed and for the first time really took notice of the girl's face, since up to that time it had merely flashed by me. She was fair-haired and freckled, with an ordinary face, but very childlike and gentle, extremely gentle. The mother wasn't pleased the girl said nothing about having been beaten for nothing, and was just about to strike her again with her fist, but held back. Then the matter of my penknife came up. In fact, there was no one there except for the three of us, and the girl was the only one who came behind the screen into my room. The woman became furious because she'd beaten her unjustly the first time; she seized the broom, tore out all the twigs, and whipped the child until welts appeared, right before my eyes. Matryosha didn't scream from the beating, but gave a strange kind of sob at each blow. Afterwards she sobbed for a whole hour.

But this is what happened before that: at the very moment the landlady was rushing for her broom to pull out the twigs, I found the penknife lying on my bed where it had somehow fallen from the table. It occurred to me at once not to announce the discovery so the girl would be given a beating. I decided in an instant: at such moments I always catch my breath. But I intend to tell everything in the most definite terms so nothing remains concealed.

Each utterly disgraceful, immeasurably humiliating, despicable, and above all, ridiculous situation in which I have happened to find myself throughout my life has always aroused in me, together with immense anger, incredible pleasure. It's exactly the same at the moment of committing a crime or when one's life is in danger. If I were stealing something, at the very moment of the theft I'd experience ecstasy at the awareness of the depth of my vileness. It wasn't the vileness itself I liked (here my reason was totally intact); I liked the ecstasy residing in a tortured awareness of how low I had sunk. It was the same every time I stood at the barrier waiting for my adversary to fire his shot in a duel; I'd experience the same despicable, savage sensation, and on one occasion it was extraordinarily intense. I confess I often sought it out, because I found it stronger than anything else of that kind. When I got a slap in the face (I've had two in my entire life), this feeling was also present in spite of my terrible anger. But if one can restrain one's anger at the time, the rapture exceeds anything one could possibly imagine. I've never told anyone about this, not even hinted at it, I've concealed it as shameful and disgraceful. But once when I received a painful beating in a tavern in Petersburg and was dragged around by the hair, I didn't experience this sensation at all, only immense anger; since I wasn't drunk, I fought back. But if, while travelling abroad, I'd been seized by the hair and knocked down by the French vicomte who'd slapped me on the face and whose lower jaw I shot off in return, I'd have experienced this same ecstasy and, perhaps, wouldn't even have felt angry. That's how it seemed to me then.

I'm saying all this so that everyone will know this feeling never completely subjugated me; through it all there remained my awareness, total awareness (after all, everything depended on this awareness!). Although this feeling would possess me to the point of madness, it never did to the point where I forgot myself. Even when it was about to reach the flashpoint, I could still regain control over it, even arrest it at its climax; only I never wanted to stop it. I'm convinced I could live my whole life as a monk, in spite of the bestial sensuality with which I am endowed and which I have continual recourse to. Having indulged until the age of sixteen with unusual immoderation in the vice to which Jean-Jacques Rousseau confessed, I ceased doing so at the age of seventeen, just as soon as I so decided. I'm always master of myself when I want to be. And so, take it that I don't want to put the responsibility for my crimes either on my environment or my illness.

When the beating was over, I put the penknife into my waistcoat pocket, went out, and threw it on the street, far away from the house, so no one would ever know. Then I waited two days. The girl, after having a good cry, became even more taciturn; but I'm sure she harboured no ill will towards me. However, she must have felt some disgrace at having been punished that way with me there; she hadn't screamed when she was hit, only sobbed, no doubt because I was standing there watching it all. But like a child she blamed only herself for her disgrace. Up to this point she was probably still afraid of me, not of me personally, but as a lodger, a stranger; apparently she was also very shy.

And so, during those two days, I did actually ask myself the question: could I abandon a certain plan I had conceived? And I immediately felt I could—at any time and any moment. Just about then I was thinking of killing myself because of my morbid indifference; well, I'm not really sure why. During those two or three days (since it was absolutely necessary to wait until the girl had forgotten everything), probably to distract myself from a persistent fantasy or else just for the fun of it, I committed a theft in our apartment. It was the only theft I've committed in my whole life.

There was a large number of people living in the apartment. Among them was a civil servant who lived with his family in two furnished rooms; he was about forty, not altogether stupid, with a decent appearance, but rather poor. I didn't make friends with him and he was afraid of the company that surrounded me there. He'd just received his salary, about thirty-five roubles. The thing that goaded me on was that I actually needed some money then (even though I received some in the post four days later); so I stole out of necessity, as it were, and not for fun. It was done quite brazenly and openly: I simply went into his room when he was eating with his wife and children in another room. There on a chair near the door lay his crumpled uniform. The thought had suddenly flashed into my mind in the corridor. I thrust my hand into the pocket and pulled out his wallet. But the civil servant heard the rustling and glanced through from the other room. I think he actually saw at least something, but not everything, so of course he couldn't believe his eyes. I said I was passing through the corridor and had looked in to see what time it was on his clock. 'It's stopped,' he said, and I withdrew.

Then I drank rather heavily; there was a large crowd assembled in my room, including Lebyadkin. I threw away the wallet with the change but kept the bills. There were thirty-two roubles, three red bills and two yellow ones. I changed a red bill at once and sent out for some champagne; then I changed the second one, and finally the third. About four hours later, in the evening, the civil servant was waiting for me in the corridor.

'Nikolai Vsevolodovich, when you came into my room not long ago, did you by any chance happen to knock my uniform off the chair near the door that it was lying on?'

'No, I don't recall. Was it there?'

'Yes, it was.'

'On the floor?'

'At first on the chair, then the floor.'

'Did you pick it up?'

'Yes.'

'Well, what do you want then?'

'If that's the case, then nothing...'

He dared not speak out and dared not tell anyone else in the apartment—that's how timid these people are. Besides, everyone there was terribly afraid of me and respected me. Afterwards I enjoyed meeting his eye a few times in the corridor. Soon I grew bored with it.

After three days I returned to my lodgings on Gorokhovaya Street. The mother was carrying a bundle and about to go out; her husband was not at home, of course. Matryosha and I were left alone. The windows were open. There were many artisans living in the house, and the sound of hammers and singing went on all day long. We'd been there for about an hour. Matryosha sat on a bench in her little room with her back to me, poking at something with her needle. At last she suddenly began singing very, very softly; sometimes she used to do that. I took out my watch to see what time it was; it was two o'clock. My heart started to pound. But then I suddenly posed myself the question once more: 'Could I stop?' And answered at once, 'Yes, I could.' I stood up and started to sneak up on her. There were a lot of geraniums on the window-sill and the sun was shining very brightly. I sat down next to her on the floor very quietly. She started and was extremely frightened at first and jumped up. I took hold of her hand, kissed it gently, made her sit down on the bench again, and began to gaze into her eyes. My kissing her hand suddenly amused her like a little child, but only for a second because she soon tried to jump up again and was in such a fright that a tremor passed across her face. She looked at me in terror with staring eyes; her lips began to quiver, as if she were going to cry, but she still she didn't call out. I began kissing her hand again; I took her on to my lap and kissed her face and her feet. As I was kissing her feet, she drew right back and smiled as if in shame, but her smile was somehow crooked. Her whole face was flushed with embarrassment. I kept whispering something to her. Finally there occurred something so strange that I shall never forget it, something that quite astonished me: this little girl put her arms around my neck and suddenly began kissing me wildly. Her face expressed absolute rapture. I almost stood up and left out of pity—I found it so unpleasant in such a young creature. But I overcame this sudden feeling of fear and stayed.

When it was all over she was very embarrassed. I didn't try to reassure her and no longer caressed her. She stared at me, smiling timidly. Her face suddenly seemed stupid. Her feeling of embarrassment grew rapidly with every passing minute. At last she covered her face with her hands and stood in a corner motionless, her face to the wall. I was afraid she'd get frightened again as she had before, and I left the house in silence.

I suppose all that had happened must finally have seemed to her an immense abomination, a mortal horror. In spite of the Russian swear-words which she must have heard since she was a baby and all sorts of strange conversations, I'm absolutely convinced she still knew nothing. She probably felt in the end that she'd committed an enormous crime and was guilty of a mortal sin—she'd 'killed God'.

That night I had the brawl in the tavern which I mentioned in passing. But I awoke the next morning in my own room where Lebyadkin had brought me. My first thought on waking up was the following: had she told anyone or not? This was a moment of genuine fear, though not very intense. I was very cheerful that morning and very kind to everyone; my whole crowd seemed very pleased with me. But I left them all and returned to my lodging on Gorokhovaya Street. I encountered her downstairs in the entrance hall. She was coming home from a shop where she'd been sent for some chicory. When she saw me she shot upstairs in terror. When I came in her mother had already hit her twice across the face because she'd come running into the room 'at breakneck speed', and that concealed the real reason for her fear. And so, everything was calm for the moment. She hid away somewhere and didn't come in all the time I was there. I stayed for about an hour and then left.

Towards evening I began to feel afraid again, but this time the feeling was incomparably more intense. Of course, I could deny it all, but they might prove my guilt. I was haunted by the idea of imprisonment. I'd never felt fear, and except for this one episode in my life, neither before nor after was I ever afraid of anything. Especially not Siberia, even though I could have been sent there on more than one occasion. But this time I was frightened and felt genuine fear, I don't know why, for the first time in my life—a very painful feeling. Besides, that evening, in my own room, I conceived such a hatred for her that I resolved to kill her. The recollection of her smile was the main cause of my hatred. I conceived contempt mixed with intense loathing for her because, after it was all over, she had rushed off to the corner of the room and covered her face with her hands; I was overcome by inexplicable rage; then I suffered from a chill. When the fever began to increase towards morning, I was overcome by fear once again, but of such intensity that I'd never experienced anything so painful. But I no longer hated the little girl; at least, my hatred didn't reach the paroxysm it had the night before. I noticed that intense fear completely obliterates hatred and the desire for revenge.

I awoke up around noon much better, and was quite surprised by some of the things I had felt the day before. But I was in a bad mood and was compelled to return to Gorokhovaya Street once again, in spite of all my revulsion. I recall desperately wanting to have a quarrel, a really serious one, with anyone, right then. But when I arrived at my lodgings, there in my room I suddenly found the maid, Nina Savelievna, who'd been waiting for me for about an hour. I didn't like this woman at all, and she herself was a bit afraid I might be angry with her since she'd come without being asked. But I was suddenly very pleased to see her. She wasn't bad-looking, but was humble and had lower-middle class manners; my landlady had been singing her praises for some time. I found them having coffee together, and the landlady was delighted with their pleasant conversation. In the corner of their room I noticed Matryosha. She stood looking at her mother and the visitor without moving. When I came in she didn't hide as she had before, and didn't run away. I merely thought she'd grown very thin and had a fever. I caressed Nina and locked the door to the landlady's apartment, which I hadn't done for some time, so

Nina left feeling overjoyed. I escorted her out myself and didn't go back to Gorokhovaya Street for two days. I was bored with the whole affair.

I decided to put an end to it all, to give up the apartment and leave Petersburg. But when I came to give up the apartment, I found the landlady in a state of anxiety and grief: Matryosha had been ill for the last three days. Each night she had a fever and was delirious. Of course I asked what she said in her delirium (we spoke in my room in a whisper). She told me that her daughter uttered 'terrible things': ' "I killed God," she says.' I suggested she summon a doctor at my expense, but she refused. 'God willing, it'll pass. She won't stay in bed the whole time; she goes out during the day. She just ran down to the shop.' I resolved to see Matryosha alone; since the landlady blurted out that she'd have to go over to the Petersburg side* around five o'clock, I decided to come back later that evening.

I had dinner in a tavern. I returned at precisely quarter past five. I always used my own key to enter. No one was there besides Matryosha. She was lying on her mother's bed in her room behind the screen; I saw her look out at me, but I pretended I didn't notice. All the windows were open. The air was warm, it was even hot. I walked around the room and sat down on the sofa. I remember every moment of it. It afforded me distinct pleasure not to talk to Matryosha. I waited and sat there one whole hour, and suddenly she jumped up from behind the screen. I heard her two feet hit the floor as she jumped out of bed, followed by her rather quick footsteps; then she stood on the threshold of my room. She looked at me in silence. In these last four or five days, during which I hadn't once seen her very closely, she'd really grown very thin. Her face had a sort of drawn look and she was probably feverish. Her eyes appeared to have grown larger and stared at me motionlessly, as if with dull curiosity, or so it seemed to me at first. I sat there on the corner of the sofa, looked at her, and didn't move at all. Once again I suddenly felt that hatred. But soon I noticed she wasn't the least afraid of me, and might even have been delirious. But she wasn't in fact delirious. She suddenly began shaking her head at me, as people do when they're reproaching you, and she suddenly raised her tiny fist and began threatening me from where she stood. At first this gesture seemed ridiculous, then I couldn't bear it any longer: I stood up and approached her. There was a look of such despair on her face as was almost inconceivable in a child. She kept brandishing her little fist at me menacingly and shaking her head in reproach. I went up close to her and started speaking cautiously, but realized that she didn't understand. Then she suddenly covered her face impulsively with her hands as she'd done before, walked away, and stood by the window with her back to me. I left her, returned to my own room, and sat near the window. I don't understand why I didn't leave then and instead stayed there, waiting as it were. Soon I heard her hurried steps again; she went out through the door on to the wooden landing at the top of the stairs. I immediately ran to my door, opened it, and just caught a glimpse of Matryosha entering a tiny storeroom, no bigger than a chicken coop, next to the lavatory. A strange idea flashed into my mind. I opened the door—and returned to the window. Of course, I still couldn't believe the idea that had flashed into my mind, 'however'... (I remember everything.)

A minute later I looked at my watch and noticed the time. Evening was drawing on. A fly was buzzing around me and kept landing on my face. I caught it, held it in my hand, then let it out of the window. A cart of some kind drove noisily into the courtyard below. A workman, a tailor perhaps, was singing very loudly at a window in one corner of the courtyard (and had been doing so for some time). He was working and I could see him. It occurred to me that since no one had seen me as I'd entered the gates and climbed the stairs, of course it'd be better if no one met me now as I was going down the stairs; I moved my chair back from the window. Then I picked up a book, but laid it aside and began staring at a tiny red spider on one of the geranium leaves, and then dozed off. I remember everything down to the last moment.

Suddenly I grabbed my watch. Twenty minutes had passed since she'd gone out. My hypothesis reached the stage of probability. But I decided to wait another quarter of an hour. It also occurred to me that she might've returned and I simply hadn't heard her; but this was impossible: there was dead silence and I could hear the buzz of every tiny fly. All of a sudden my heart began to pound. I took out my watch: there were three minutes left, but I waited them out, though my heart was beating painfully. Then I stood up, put on my hat, buttoned my coat, and looked around the room to see if everything was in place—were there any signs that I'd been there? I moved the chair closer to the table where it had been before. At last I quietly opened the door, locked it with my own key, and went to the storeroom. The door was closed, but not locked; I knew that it didn't lock, but I didn't want to open it; I stood on tiptoe and looked through the chink. At this very moment, standing on tiptoe, I recalled that as I was sitting by the window, staring at the red spider, and had dozed off, I had thought about how I'd stand on tiptoe and put my eye to the chink in the door. By including this insignificant detail here I want to demonstrate clearly that I was in full possession of my mental abilities. I stared through the chink for some time; it was dark there, but not totally. At last I could discern what I needed to... I wanted to be completely sure.

At last I decided I could leave and went down the stairs. I didn't meet anyone. Around three o'clock we were sitting in our shirt-sleeves drinking tea in our rooms, playing a game with a deck of old cards, and Lebyadkin was reciting poetry. We were telling stories, and, as if on purpose, they were successful and amusing, not stupid as was so often the case. Kirillov was there too. No one was drinking, even though there was a bottle of rum, except for Lebyadkin who was helping himself. Prokhor Malov once observed that 'when Nikolai Vsevolodovich is content and not depressed, our whole circle is cheerful and witty.' I recalled his pronouncement at the time.

But around eleven o'clock the janitor's little girl came running in with the news from the landlady of the house on Gorokhovaya Street that Matryosha had hanged herself. I went back with the girl and realized that the landlady herself didn't know why she'd sent for me. She was howling and thrashing about; there was a great commotion, a large crowd of people, and a few policemen. I stood in the hall for a while and then left.

They hardly troubled me, although they asked me the usual questions. Except for saying that the girl had been ill and delirious during the last few days, and that I'd suggested sending for a doctor at my own expense, there was really nothing more that I could say. They also asked me about the penknife; I said the landlady had given her a beating, but that was nothing unusual. No one knew that I'd come earlier that evening. I heard nothing about the results of the post-mortem.

For a week or so I didn't go there. I dropped in to give notice long after they had buried her. The landlady was still weeping, even though she was busy with her rags and her sewing as before. 'It was me who upset her because of your penknife,' she told me, but without much reproach. I settled my account with her on the pretext that I could no longer stay in that apartment and receive Nina Savelievna. Once again she sang Nina Savelievna's praises at our parting. As I left I gave her a present of an extra five roubles in addition to what I owed her for the apartment.

In general I found life very boring at that time; I was sick to death of it. After the danger had passed I would've forgotten the events on Gorokhovaya Street, just as I did everything else at the time, if I hadn't kept recalling with considerable anger what a coward I'd been. I vented my anger on anyone I could. It was at that time, but for no reason in particular, that I conceived the idea of crippling my life in some way, in as vile a way as possible. For a year or so I'd been thinking about shooting myself; but then something even better occurred to me. One day, looking at the lame girl Marya Timofeevna Lebyadkina, who sometimes worked as a servant in my rooms and who was still not completely insane, merely an exalted idiot, and who was secretly head over heels in love with me (which my friends had discovered), I suddenly decided to marry her. The idea of a match between Stavrogin and such an outlandish creature made my nerves tingle. It was impossible to imagine anything more hideous. But I couldn't say for sure whether or not the anger at my own base cowardice that had overwhelmed me after the affair with Matryosha entered into my decision even unconsciously (of course, unconsciously!). In fact, I don't think it did; in any case, I didn't get married merely because of a 'bet over a bottle of wine after a drunken dinner'. The witnesses at our wedding were Kirillov and Peter Verkhovensky who just happened to be in Petersburg then, as well as Lebyadkin himself and Prokhor Malov (who's since died). No one else knew anything about it, and those present gave their word to keep silent. This silence always seemed somewhat disgusting to me, but hasn't been broken up to now, even though I've been intending to make it public; now I do make it public, along with all the rest.

After I got married I left to visit my mother in the provinces. I went for some distraction because the situation was intolerable. In our town I left behind the idea that I was insane—an idea that still persists to this day and undoubtedly continues to do me harm; I'll explain more about that later. Then I went abroad and lived there four years.

I went to the East, stood through eight hours of an all-night service at Mount Athos,* was in Egypt, lived in Switzerland, even visited Iceland; I sat through a whole year's course in Göttingen. During the last year I became very close to a family of Russian nobles in Paris and to two young Russian ladies in Switzerland. Two years ago, in Frankfurt, passing a stationery shop, I noticed among the photographs on sale a small picture of a little girl dressed in a splendid child's dress, but looking very much like Matryosha. I bought the picture immediately and when I got to my hotel, placed it on the mantelpiece. It remained there untouched one whole week; I didn't even glance at it. When I left Frankfurt I forgot to take it with me.

I mention this precisely to show to what extent I could control my recollections and how indifferent I'd become towards them. I used to reject them all *en masse*, and they would obediently disappear each time *en masse*, as soon as I wanted. I always found it boring to recollect the past, and could never talk about it, as most other people do. As far as Matryosha is concerned, I even forgot her picture on the mantel.

About a year or so ago in the springtime, as I was travelling through Germany, I absent-mindedly missed the station where I was supposed to change trains and found myself on a different line. I got off at the next stop; it was past two o'clock in the afternoon on a clear day. I was in a tiny little German town. They directed me to the hotel. I had to wait: the next train was due at eleven o'clock that evening. I was actually quite pleased with my adventure, since I was in no hurry to get anywhere in particular. The hotel turned out to be shabby and small, but surrounded by greenery and flower-beds. They gave me a very small room. I had an excellent meal; since I'd been on the road all the previous night, I fell fast asleep after dinner, somewhere around four o'clock in the afternoon.

I had a dream that was totally unexpected because I'd never had one like it before. In a gallery in Dresden there's a painting by Claude Lorrain, called I believe in the catalogue 'Acis and Galatea',* although I've always referred to it as 'The Golden Age', I don't know why. I'd seen it before, but just about three days earlier I'd noticed it once again in passing. It was this picture that appeared to me in my dream, not as a picture, but as if it were the real thing.

It was some little place in the Greek archipelago; there were gentle blue waves, islands and cliffs, a luxuriant shore, a fantastic panorama in the distance, a beckoning, setting sun—beyond description. One was reminded of the cradle of European civilization, the first scenes of mythology, of the earthly paradise... What a splendid race lived here! They woke up and fell asleep happy and innocent; the groves were filled with their merry songs; their abundant, untiring energy went into love and simple joys. The sun flooded the islands and sea with its rays, taking delight in its beautiful children. A wonderful dream, a lofty delusion! The most improbable fantasy ever conceived, to which all mankind has devoted its strength throughout its life, for which it's sacrificed everything, for which men have died on the cross and prophets have been killed, without which people do not wish to live but are unable even to die. I seemed to experience all these sensations in this dream; I don't know what it was that I dreamt precisely, but the cliffs and sea, the slanted rays of the setting sun—all this I still seemed to see, when I woke up and opened my eyes, for the first time in my life literally awash with tears. A feeling of happiness as yet unknown to me invaded my heart until it hurt. Evening had set in; into the window of my little room, through the greenery of the flowers standing on the sill, shone a whole cluster of the setting sun's bright, slanting rays, bathing me in light. I closed my eyes again quickly, as if yearning to recapture my passing dream, but suddenly, amidst the very bright sunlight, I noticed a very small spot. It acquired a shape, and all of a sudden I clearly saw a tiny red spider. At once I recalled the one on the geranium leaf, when the slanting rays of the setting sun were pouring down in the same way. Something seemed to pierce me; I raised myself and sat up in bed... (All, you see, just as it had happened the other time!)

I saw before me (Oh, not in reality! If only it had been real!), I saw Matryosha, emaciated, with feverish eyes, exactly as she was when she stood at my door shaking her head and raising her tiny little fist at me. Nothing had ever tortured me so! The pitiful despair of a helpless ten-year-old child with its undeveloped mind threatening me... (With what? What could she possibly do to me?), but blaming only herself, of course. Nothing like this had ever happened to me before. I sat there until nightfall, without moving, forgetting the time. Is this what's called remorse or repentance? I don't know and to this day can't tell. Perhaps it's not the recollection of the act that I find so loathsome even now. Perhaps even now that recollection contains something that appeals to my passions. No—what I find intolerable is solely this image, namely, her in the doorway, threatening me with her raised fist, just her appearance at that moment, that one minute, that shake of her head. That's what I can't stand because that's what I've been seeing ever since, almost every day. It doesn't come of its own accord; I summon it and can't help doing so, although I can't live with it. Oh, if only I could see her in reality, even in the form of an hallucination!

I have other memories of the past that perhaps go one better than this one. I treated a certain woman worse, and she died as a result. I took the lives of two innocent men in duels. Once I was mortally offended and didn't take revenge on my enemy. I have one poisoning to my credit—deliberate, successful, and completely undiscovered. (If necessary, I'm willing to make a full report.)

But why doesn't a single one of these memories make me feel anything similar? They make me feel only hatred, and that's inspired by my present situation, whereas at the time I would forget and dismiss it all cold-bloodedly.

After that I wandered around for almost an entire year and tried to find something to do. I know I could dismiss that little girl from my mind even now, if I wanted to. I'm in complete control of my own will, as always. But the whole point is that I never have wanted to do that, I don't want to now, and I never will want to; I know that by now. So it'll go on right up to the point where I go mad.

Two months later in Switzerland I was able to fall in love with a young woman, or, rather, I felt an access of passion, accompanied by a savage impulse such as I always used to have, to begin with. I felt a horrible temptation to commit another crime, bigamy I mean (because I was already married); but I fled on the advice of another young woman, to whom I had confessed almost everything. Besides, this new crime would in no way have spared me Matryosha.

Therefore I decided to have these pages printed and bring three hundred copies of them back to Russia. When the time comes I will send them to the police and the local authorities; at the same time I'll send them to the editors of all newspapers with a request to publish them, and to a large number of my acquaintances in Petersburg and throughout Russia. It will appear at the same time in translation abroad. I know that legally I may have nothing to fear, at least nothing major; I'm the only person to inform against me and there's no one to accuse me; besides, there's no evidence, or very little. Finally, there's the widespread idea that I'm not in my right mind, an idea that my family will try to use to quash any legal proceedings that might threaten me. I am declaring all this, by the way, as proof that I'm in my right mind and understand my situation. But as far as I'm concerned, there'll always be some people who know everything, who'll look at me, and I at them. And the more of these people there are, the better. I don't know if it'll be any help to me. For me it's the last resort.

I repeat: if a very thorough search were made by the Petersburg police, something might turn up. Her family may still be in Petersburg. The house, of course, will be remembered. It was light blue. I'm not going anywhere and will be at mother's estate in

Skvoreshniki for some time (a year or two). If required, I will come forward, anywhere.

Nikolai Stavrogin

Reading this lasted almost an hour. Tikhon read slowly and may have read several places a second time. All the while Stavrogin sat in silence, not stirring. It was strange but the signs of impatience, absent-mindedness, and as it were delirium evident in his countenance all that morning had almost disappeared, to be replaced by serenity and, as it were, by a kind of sincerity that lent him an almost dignified air. Tikhon took off his glasses and began to speak first with considerable caution.

'Might it be possible to make some changes in this document?'

'Why? I was writing sincerely,' Stavrogin replied.

'Maybe some of the style.'

'I forgot to warn you that anything you say will be in vain; I won't set aside my intention; don't bother trying to persuade me.'

'No, you didn't forget to warn me about this earlier, before I read it.'

'All the same, I'll say it again: whatever the force of your objections, I won't back down from my intention. Note that by this fortunate or unfortunate phrase—think what you will—I'm by no means trying to encourage you to make objections or attempt to prevail upon me,' he added, as if unable to control himself and suddenly returning for a moment to his previous tone, but then all at once smiling gloomily at his own words.

'I would not dream of objecting, let alone prevailing on you to forsake your intention. This idea of yours is a very fine one; the Christian idea could not find more complete expression. Repentance cannot go further than the astonishing feat you've conceived, only assuming...'

'Only assuming what?'

'Only assuming it is genuine repentance and a genuine Christian idea.'

'You seem to be splitting hairs. Isn't it the same thing? I wrote it in all sincerity.'

'It's as if you deliberately want to make yourself out worse than your heart would desire...' said Tikhon, growing bolder and bolder. Obviously the 'document' had made a strong impression on him.

' "Make myself out"? I repeat, I didn't "make myself out" anything and I certainly wasn't striking a pose.'

Tikhon quickly lowered his eyes.

'This document is the direct expression of a heart that's been mortally wounded—do I understand it correctly?' he persisted with unusual enthusiasm. 'Yes, it's repentance and the natural need for it that's overcome you; and you've entered upon a great path, an unprecedented path. But you seem to hate in advance all those who'll read what you've written, and you're summoning them to battle. You weren't ashamed to confess your crime; why are you ashamed of your repentance? Let them look at me, you say; well, but *you*, how will you look at them? Some parts of your statement are brought into relief by the style; it's as if you revel in your own psychology and latch on to every trivial detail merely to astonish the reader with an insensitivity you don't really have. What is this but the arrogant challenge of the guilty party to the judge?'

'Where's the challenge? I've kept any discussion of my own person out of it.'

Tikhon was silent. His pale cheeks had flushed.

'Let's leave this,' Stavrogin said sharply. 'Let me put you a question: five minutes have passed since that' (he nodded at the pages), 'yet I see no expression of disgust or shame in you... you can't be very squeamish!...'

He didn't finish and burst out laughing.

'You mean you would have liked me to express my contempt sooner,' Tikhon concluded resolutely. 'I won't conceal anything from you: I was horrified by so great an amount of idle energy intentionally wasted on filth.

'As for the crime itself, many other people sin the same way, but they live in peace and harmony with their consciences, regarding crimes of that sort as inevitable youthful peccadilloes. There are even elders of the church who sin the same way, even quite comfortably, frivolously. The whole world is filled with these horrors. But you've experienced the utter depths, and that very rarely happens to such a degree.'

'Surely you haven't begun to respect me after reading these pages, have you?' Stavrogin asked with a wry smile.

'I won't reply directly on that score. But of course there isn't and can never be a greater or more terrible crime than the one you committed against that little girl.'

'Let's stop measuring by yardsticks. I'm somewhat surprised by your mention of other people and the ordinariness of such a crime. Perhaps I've not suffered as much as I've described here, and perhaps I've really told a great many lies about myself,' he added unexpectedly.

Tikhon was silent once more. Stavrogin didn't even think of leaving; on the contrary, he began to lapse again into brief moments of deep thought.

'And this girl', Tikhon began again very timidly, 'with whom you broke off in Switzerland, if I may be so bold to ask... Where is she at the moment?'

'Here.'

Once again, silence.

'Perhaps I told you a great many lies about myself,' Stavrogin repeated insistently. 'Besides, what does it matter if I offer a challenge by the crudeness of my confession, given that you noticed the challenge? I'll force them to despise me even more, that's all. Then it'll be easier for me.'

'You mean, their hatred will arouse yours, and in hating, it'll be easier for you than if you had to endure their pity.'

'You're right. You know,' he said, laughing suddenly, 'they may call me a Jesuit and a sanctimonious hypocrite, don't you think? Ha, ha, ha. Don't you think?'

'Of course, there will be that reaction too. How soon do you plan to carry out your intention?'

'Today, tomorrow, the day after tomorrow, how should I know? But very soon. You're right. I think it'll happen just that way; I'll announce it all of a sudden, precisely at some vengeful, malicious moment, when I hate them most of all.'

'Answer me one question, but sincerely, to me alone: if someone forgave you for this' (Tikhon indicated the sheets of paper), 'not someone you respect or fear, but a stranger, a person you'll never know, someone who read your terrible confession to himself in silence—would the thought of that make it any easier for you, or would it be all the same?'

'It would make it easier,' Stavrogin replied in a low voice, dropping his eyes. 'If you were to forgive me, it would make it much easier for me,' he added unexpectedly and in a whisper.

'On the condition that you forgive me as well,' Tikhon replied in a voice full of emotion.

'For what? What have you done to me? Ah, yes, isn't that a monastic formula?'

'For the intended and the unintended. Having sinned, each man has sinned against all men, and each man is responsible in some way for the sins of others. There is no isolated sin. I'm a great sinner, perhaps even greater than you.'

'I'll tell you the whole truth: I want you to forgive me, and a second and third person, too, but not everyone—it'd be better if everyone else hated me. But I want it in order to suffer in humility...'

'But you couldn't suffer universal pity in that same kind of humility?'

'Perhaps I couldn't. You grasp all the subtleties. But... why are you doing this?'

'I sense the degree of your sincerity and, of course, I'm much to blame for not being able to get close to people. I've always felt this to be my great failing,' Tikhon said sincerely and intimately, looking Stavrogin straight in the eye. 'I'm doing it only because I'm terribly afraid for you,' he added. 'There's an almost impassable abyss before you.'

'You think I won't endure? I won't bear their hatred with humility?'

'Not only their hatred.'

'What else?'

'Their laughter.' Tikhon's half-whispered reply seemed dragged out of him.

Stavrogin was embarrassed; his face revealed anxiety.

'I knew you'd say that,' he replied. 'So, you must consider me a comic figure after reading my "document", in spite of all the tragedy? Don't be alarmed or disconcerted... I had a premonition this would occur.'

'The horror will be universal and, of course, more put on than genuine. People only fear what directly threatens their own interests. I'm not talking about good people: they'll be horrified and accuse themselves, but they'll go unnoticed. The laughter will be widespread.'

'And add the philosopher's comment that in another's woes there is always something gratifying.'

'That's a true thought.'

'However, you... you yourself... I'm surprised by the low opinion you have of other people, how loathsome you find them,' Stavrogin uttered with some bitterness.

'Believe me! When I said that I was judging by myself rather than talking about other people,' Tikhon exclaimed.

'Really? Don't tell me there's something in your soul which makes you rejoice in my misfortune?'

'Who knows, perhaps there is. Oh, perhaps there is!'

'Enough. Show me precisely how I appear ridiculous in my manuscript. I know, but I'd like you to show me. And tell me very cynically, with all the sincerity you're capable of. And I repeat, you're a terribly queer fellow.'

'Even the form you cast your great penance in has something ridiculous about it. Oh, don't believe you won't win!' he cried suddenly, almost in rapture. 'Even this form will triumph' (he indicated the sheets of paper), 'if you sincerely accept the insults and abuse. It's always been the way that the most ignominious cross ends by becoming a great glory and strength, if the humility of the deed is sincere. You may even find consolation during your own lifetime!'

'So you think what's ridiculous is just in the form, in the style?' Stavrogin insisted.

'And in the substance. The ugliness will kill it,' Tikhon whispered, lowering his eyes.

'What? The ugliness? What ugliness?'

'Of the crime. There are genuinely ugly crimes. Crimes, whatever they are, the more blood and horror, the more impressive they are, the more they are, so to speak, picturesque. But there are crimes that are shameful and infamous beyond any horror, so to speak, too inelegant...'

Tikhon didn't complete his thought.

'You mean,' Stavrogin interrupted him excitedly, 'you found me an extremely ridiculous figure when I kissed the little girl's dirty foot... and everything I said about my temperament... well, and everything else... I understand. I understand you very well. And you're in despair over me precisely because it's so ugly and loathsome; no, not loathsome, but shameful and ridiculous. And you think that's what I won't be able to bear?'

Tikhon remained silent.

'Yes, you do know people, that is, you know I won't bear it... now I understand why you asked if that young lady from Switzerland was here.'

'You're not prepared, not hardened,' Tikhon whispered timidly, lowering his eyes.

'Listen, Father Tikhon: I want to forgive myself; that's my principal aim, my entire aim!' Stavrogin said suddenly with gloomy rapture in his eyes. 'I know that only then will the apparition disappear. That's why I'm searching for immeasurable suffering, why I'm searching myself for it. Don't frighten me.'

'If you believe that you can forgive yourself and obtain that forgiveness for yourself in this world, then you already believe everything!' Tikhon cried in rapture. 'How can you say you don't believe in God?'

Stavrogin didn't answer.

'God will forgive you for your unbelief, since you honour the Holy Spirit without knowing it.'

'By the way, Christ won't forgive, will he?' Stavrogin asked, with a slight trace of irony in the tone of his question. For isn't it written: "Whoso shall offend one of these little ones"*—do you remember? According to the Gospel, there's no greater crime, nor can there be. Why, it's in that book!'

He pointed to the Gospel.

'I bring you joyful news in that regard,' Tikhon said with tender emotion. 'Christ will also forgive, if only you reach the point where you forgive yourself... Oh, no, no, don't believe it, I do Him wrong: even if you don't achieve reconciliation with yourself and forgiveness for yourself, even then He will forgive you for your intention and for your great suffering... for there is no word, no thought in human language to express *all* the ways and paths of the Lamb of God, "until His ways are revealed unto us".* Who can embrace Him, the boundless one? Who can fathom *everything*, the infinite?'

The corners of his mouth turned down as they had before, and a barely perceptible shudder crossed his face again. After regaining control of himself a moment later, he couldn't maintain it and dropped his eyes.

Stavrogin picked up his hat from the sofa.

'I'll come again sometime,' he said with an air of extreme exhaustion. 'You and I... I very much appreciate the pleasure of your conversation and the honour... and your feelings. Believe me, I understand why others love you so much. I ask for your prayers to Him, whom you love so much...'

'Are you leaving already?' Tikhon asked quickly and stood up, as if hadn't really expected such an immediate farewell. 'But I...' he seemed flustered. 'I was just about to make a request of you, but... I don't know how... and now I'm afraid.

'Oh I beg you, please do,' said Stavrogin, sitting down at once, his hat still in his hand. Tikhon observed his hat, and his demeanour—the demeanour of a man who'd suddenly assumed a certain urbanity, who was in turmoil and half-crazy, and was giving him five minutes to complete their business, and he became even more confused.

'My entire request is simply that you... but you're already aware, Nikolai Vsevolodovich (that's your name and patronymic, isn't it?), that if you publish these sheets of paper, you'll destroy your own future... in terms of a career, for example, and... in terms of everything else.'

'My career?' Nikolai Vsevolodovich replied, frowning unpleasantly.

'Why spoil it? Why such inflexibility?' Tikhon concluded, almost pleading, clearly aware of his own awkwardness. An expression of pain appeared on Nikolai Vsevolodovich's face.

'I've already asked you and I'll ask you again: whatever

you say will be to no avail... and I'm starting to find our conversation intolerable.'

He turned around in the armchair impressively.

'You don't understand me; hear me out and don't get irritated. You know my opinion: your deed, if performed out of humility, would constitute the greatest Christian feat, if you could endure. Even if you didn't, the Lord would still take into account your original sacrifice. Everything is taken into account: not a single word, not a single movement of the spirit, not a single thought is wasted. But I suggest you exchange one kind of heroic deed for another, even greater, something undoubtedly grand...'

Nikolai Vsevolodovich was silent.

'You're struggling with a desire for martyrdom and self-sacrifice; overcome this desire of yours, put aside those sheets of paper and your intention—then you'll overcome everything. You'll disgrace your own pride and your devil! You'll end up the victor and will achieve freedom...'

His eyes sparkled; he clasped his hands in front of him as if pleading.

'The simple truth is that you really don't want a scandal and you're laying a trap for me, good Father Tikhon,' Stavrogin mumbled carelessly and in annoyance, making as if to stand up. 'In brief, you'd like me to settle down, perhaps even get married, and end my life as a member of the local club, visiting your monastery on every holiday. Well now, that would be real penance! But as an expert on the human heart, perhaps you do anticipate that all this will actually come to pass, and all your sincere entreaties are merely for form's sake, since it is really what I myself desire. Am I right?'

He gave a self-conscious chuckle.

'No, not that kind of voluntary penance; I'm preparing another one for you!' Tikhon continued with ardour, not paying the least attention to Stavrogin's laughter or what he said. 'I know an elder, not here, but not far from here, a hermit and ascetic, in possession of such Christian wisdom that you and I cannot begin to understand. He'll honour my requests. I'll tell him everything about you. Go to him and become a novice; remain under his supervision for five or seven years, as long as you yourself find necessary. Take a vow, and by this greater sacrifice you'll get to possess everything you desire, beyond even what you expect, for you can't even imagine now what you'll gain!'

Stavrogin listened very, very gravely to this last proposition.

'You're simply suggesting I become a monk in that monastery? Much as I respect you, I should've expected this. Well, I must confess that in several pusillanimous moments the thought had already occurred to me that, once I'd published these pages for all to see, I'd hide away from people in a monastery, even if only for a little while. But I would immediately blush for such baseness. But to take the tonsure and become a monk—that idea never entered my head even in moments of the most extreme, pusillanimous fear.'

'You don't have to be in a monastery; you don't have to take the tonsure. You'd only be a novice in secret, in private; you could continue living in the world...'

'Stop it, Father Tikhon,' Stavrogin said, interrupting him in disgust, and he stood up. So did Tikhon.

'What's wrong with you?' he cried suddenly, looking at Tikhon almost in fear. The latter stood before him, his hands clasped in front of him, and a sickly shudder, as if he had some terrible shock, flickered across his face.

'What's wrong with you? What's wrong with you?' Stavrogin repeated, rushing forward to support him. He thought Father Tikhon was about to fall.

'I see... I see as if it were real,' Tikhon exclaimed in a voice that pierced the soul and with an expression of the most heartfelt grief, 'that you, you poor, lost young man, have never been so close to committing a most terrible crime as you are at this very moment!'

'Calm down!' Stavrogin repeated, really alarmed about him. 'Perhaps I can still put it aside... You're right; I may not be able to endure, and in my spite I'll commit some new crime... all that's true... you're right. I'll put it aside.'

'No, not after publishing these pages, but before, a day, an hour, perhaps, before taking this great step, you'll throw yourself into some new crime as a means of escape, simply to *avoid* publishing these pages!'

Stavrogin actually began to tremble with rage and, almost, from fear.

'You damned psychologist!' he said, cutting him short suddenly in a fury, and he left the cell without so much as a backward glance.

CHAPTER 9

The search at Stepan Trofimovich's

IN the meantime an incident occurred that surprised me and shocked Stepan Trofimovich. At eight o'clock in the morning his servant Nastasya came running over to tell me that her master had been 'raided'. At first I could make nothing of it: about all I could determine was that some officials had conducted the 'raid'—they'd arrived and taken away some papers; a soldier had tied them up in a bundle and 'carried them off in a wheelbarrow'. It was a bizarre story. I ran straight over to see Stepan Trofimovich.

I found him in an astonishing state of mind: distressed and extremely agitated, but at the same time, with a decided air of triumph about him. A samovar was boiling on a table in the middle of the room, next to which stood a glass of tea, poured but left untouched and now forgotten. Stepan Trofimovich was walking around the table, peering into every corner of the room, not really aware of what he was doing. He was wearing his everyday red knitted jersey, but upon seeing me, he hastened to put on his waistcoat and jacket, something he'd never done before when any of his close acquaintances had happened upon him in his jersey. He seized me warmly by the hand at once.

'*Enfin un ami*!'[1] (He heaved a deep sigh.) '*Cher*, I sent for you alone; no one else knows a thing. You must tell Nastasya to lock the door and let no one in, except, of course, for *them... Vous comprenez?*'

He looked at me uneasily, as if waiting for a reply. Naturally I began asking him all sorts of questions. Somehow from his incoherent speech, full of interruptions and unnecessary interpolations, I found out that at seven o'clock that morning a government official had come to see him 'all of a sudden'...

---

[1] A friend at last!

'*Pardon, j'ai oublié son nom. Il n'est pas du pays.* It seems,
Lembke brought him here, *quelque chose de bête et d'allemand
dans la physionomie. Il s'appelle Rosenthal.*'[1]

'You don't mean Blum?'

'Blum. That's precisely the name. *Vous le connaissez?
Quelque chose d'hébété et de très content dans la figure, pourtant
très sévère, roide et sérieux.* A sort of policeman, a submissive
subordinate, *je m'y connais.* I was still sleeping; just imagine,
he asked if he could "have a look" at my books and
manuscripts; *oui, je m'en souviens, il a employé ce mot.* He
didn't arrest me, only my books... *Il se tenait à distance,* and
when he began explaining why he'd come, he looked as if
I... *enfin il avait l'air de croire que je tomberai sur lui
immédiatement et que je commencerai à le battre comme plâtre.
Tous ces gens du bas étage sont comme ça,* when they're dealing
with a gentleman. Of course, I understood the whole thing
at once. *Voilà vingt ans que je m'y prépare.* I unlocked all
the drawers for him and handed over my keys; I gave them
to him myself, I gave him everything. *J'étais digne et calme.*
From my books he took away my editions of Herzen
published abroad, a bound volume of *The Bell,** four copies
of my poem, *et, enfin, tout ça.* Then some papers and letters
*et quelques-unes de mes ébauches historiques, critiques et po-
litiques.* They took it all away. Nastasya says they carried it
off in a wheelbarrow covered with an apron; *oui, c'est cela,*
with an apron.'[2]

He was raving. Who could make head or tail of it? I began
asking him more questions: had Blum come alone or not?
On whose authority? By what right? How did he dare? What
explanation did he offer?

---

[1] Sorry, I've forgotten his name. He's not from these parts. . . . something
stupid and German in his physiognomy. He's called Rosenthal.

[2] Do you know him? Rather a dull, self-satisfied look about him, but
very severe, stiff, and serious with it. . . . I know the type. . . . Yes, I
remember that's what he said. . . . He kept out of it . . . well, he looked as
if he thought I'd jump on him straight away and smash him to bits. All
those people of the lower orders are like that. . . . I've been expecting it for
twenty years. . . . I was dignified and calm. . . . well, and all that stuff. . . .
some of my historical, critical, political sketches. . . . yes, that's right . . .

'*Il était seul, bien seul,* but there was someone else *dans l'antechambre, oui, je m'en souviens, et puis...* There was someone else besides, I think, and there was a guard standing in the entry. You'd better ask Nastasya; she knows better than I do. *J'étais surexcité, voyez-vous. Il parlait, il parlait... un tas de choses.* But he said very little; it was I who did all the talking... I told him my life story, only one aspect, of course... *J'étais surexcité, mais digne, je vous assure.*[1] I'm afraid, however, that I burst into tears. They got the wheelbarrow from the shop next door.'

'Good Lord! How could it have happened? For heaven's sake, Stepan Trofimovich, be more precise! This sounds like a dream!'

'*Cher*, I feel as though it were a dream... *Savez-vous, il a prononcé le nom de Teliatnikoff*; I think he was the one hiding in the hall. Yes, I recall, he suggested calling the prosecutor, and, I think, Dmitry Mitrich... *qui me doit encore quinze roubles de* whist *soit dit en passant. Enfin, je n'ai pas trop compris.* But I outsmarted them; what do I care about Dmitry Mitrich anyway? I asked him to keep the whole thing quiet; I begged him to do so. I even humiliated myself, *comment croyez-vous? Enfin il a consenti.* Yes, I remember, it was he who asked; he said it would be better if I kept it quiet because he'd come only to "have a look around" *et rien de plus*, nothing more, nothing... and if they don't find anything, nothing will come of it. So we wound it all up *en amis, je suis tout-à-fait content.*'[2]

'But look here, he offered you the usual procedures and standard guarantees in such cases, and you yourself rejected them!' I cried in amiable indignation.

'No, it's better this way, without any guarantees. Who needs a public scandal? For the time being let it be *en amis...*

---

[1] He was on his own, quite on his own ... in the hall, I remember, yes, and then ... I was in a state, do you see. He was talking away... saying this and that.... I was in a state, but dignified, I assure you.
[2] Do you know, he mentioned the name Telyatnikov ... who, incidentally, still owes me fifteen roubles... In a word, I didn't understand too much.... what do you think? At last he agreed.... and nothing more ... as friends, I am completely satisfied.

You know, if... *mes ennemis* in town... find out, *et puis à quoi bon ce procureur, ce cochon de notre procureur, qui deux fois m'a manqué de politesse et qu'on a rossé à plaisir l'autre année chez cette charmante et belle* Nastasya Pavlovna, *quand il se cacha dans son boudoir. Et puis, mon ami,*[1] don't contradict me or discourage me, I beg you. There's nothing worse than when a man's distressed and a hundred of his friends point out what a fool he's been. Now sit down and have some tea; I'm really very tired... Perhaps I should lie down with a vinegar compress on my head. What do you think?'

'Absolutely,' I cried. 'With some ice even. You're very upset. You're pale and your hands are trembling. Lie down, have a little rest, and wait a bit before you tell me what happened. I'll sit here with you and wait.'

He couldn't make up his mind to lie down, but I insisted. Nastasya brought some vinegar in a cup; I moistened a towel and placed it on his forehead. Then Nastasya climbed on to a chair and lit the lamp in front of the icon. I noticed this with surprise; there'd never been a lamp before—it had suddenly appeared.

'I instructed her to hang it up this morning, just after they left,' Stepan Trofimovich mumbled, giving me a sly look. '*Quand on a de ces choses-là dans sa chambre et qu'on vient vous arrêter,*[2] it makes an impression, and they're sure to report having seen it...'

After dealing with the lamp, Nastasya stood in the doorway, pressing her right palm to her cheek and looking at him with a tearful expression.

'*Éloignez-la* on some pretext,' he said, nodding to me from the sofa. 'I can't stand that Russian pity of hers, *et puis ça m'embête.*[3]

But she left of her own accord. I noticed he kept looking at the door and listening for any sounds in the hallway.

[1] as friends ... my enemies ... and what use is our prosecutor, that swine of a prosecutor, who has been impolite to me on two occasions, and who received a sound thrashing last year at the home of the charming and lovely Nastasya Pavlovna, when he was hiding in her boudoir. And then, my friend

[2] When one has such things in one's room and they come to arrest you

[3] Make her go away ... besides, it annoys me.

'*Il faut être prêt, voyez-vous*,' he said, giving me a meaningful look, '*chaque moment...*¹ they come, they take you away, and phew... a man disappears!'

'Good Lord! Who'll come? Who'll take you away?'

'*Voyez-vous, mon cher*, I asked him directly as he was leaving what they would do with me.'

'You should've asked where they would exile you to!' I cried, still indignant.

'That's what I had in mind when I asked the question, but he went away without answering. *Voyez-vous*: regarding underwear and clothing, especially warm clothing, that's entirely up to them. If they say, take them, it's all right; otherwise, they'll send you away in a soldier's greatcoat. But I quietly hid thirty-five roubles' (he suddenly lowered his voice, glancing at the door through which Nastasya had just left) 'in the lining of my waistcoat, here, feel it... I don't think they'll make me take it off, and I left seven roubles in my purse for appearance's sake, "that's all I've got", so to speak. You see, there's some small change on the table. They'll never guess I hid some money. They'll think it's all I had. God knows where I'll have to spend the night.'

My head drooped at hearing such madness. Obviously a person couldn't be arrested or searched as he'd described; he was very confused, of course. It's true that all this happened before the most recent laws had been passed. It's also true they'd offered him more correct procedures (he said so himself), but he'd *outsmarted* them and refused... Previously, of course, that is, not so very long ago, under exceptional circumstances a governor could... But what kind of exceptional circumstances were there in this case? That's what was so baffling!

'They must've received a telegram from Petersburg,' Stepan Trofimovich said all of a sudden.

'A telegram! About you? Because of Herzen's works or that poem of yours? Have you gone mad? What is there to arrest you for?'

Now I was angry. He made a face and was obviously

¹ One has to be prepared, you see . . . at any moment

offended—not so much by my shouting at him but by the idea there was nothing to arrest him for.

'In this day and age who can tell what a man might be arrested for?' he mumbled enigmatically. A wild, absurd idea flashed through my mind.

'Stepan Trofimovich, tell me as a friend,' I cried, 'as a true friend; I won't ever betray you. Do you belong to some secret society or not?'

And, to my amazement, he wasn't quite sure whether or not he actually did belong to some secret society.

'That depends on what you mean, *voyez-vous...*'

'What do you mean "what you mean"?'

'When you support progress with all your heart and soul, who can vouch for a person? You think you don't belong to a society, but you look around and it turns out you do belong to something.'

'How is that possible? It's either yes or no!'

'*Cela date de Pétersbourg*[1] when she and I wanted to establish a journal. That's the origin of it. We managed to escape then and they forgot all about us; but now they've remembered us. *Cher, cher,* don't you see?' he cried in a pained voice. 'They'll take us away, stuff us into a covered cart, and send us to Siberia for the rest of our days, or else they'll forget about us in some prison...'

He suddenly burst out crying. Tears streamed from his eyes. He covered his face with his red silk handkerchief and wept convulsively for five minutes or so. I was racked with pain. This man who'd been a prophet among us for some twenty years, our preacher, teacher, patriarch, our Kukolnik,* who'd held himself so loftily and majestically above us, whom we'd worshipped with genuine reverence, considering it an honour—now all of a sudden this man was weeping, weeping like a naughty little boy in anticipation of the rod which the teacher had gone to fetch. I felt very sorry for him. Evidently he believed in that 'covered cart' just as firmly as he believed that I was now sitting next to him; and was expecting it that very morning, immediately,

---

[1] That began in Petersburg

that very minute, all because of Herzen's collected works and that poem of his! Such total and absolute ignorance of everyday reality was touching, but also somehow repellent.

He finally stopped weeping, got up from the sofa and began pacing around the room, resuming his conversation with me, but constantly glancing at the window and listening to every sound from the hall. Our conversation continued to be disjointed. All my assurances and attempts to calm him down rebounded like so many peas off a wall. He wasn't really listening, but he still desperately needed me to calm him down, and he continued talking without pause. I realized he couldn't get along without me now and wouldn't let me go for anything in the world. I remained with him; we sat together for over two hours. During our conversation he recalled that Blum had taken away two political pamphlets found among his papers.

'What political pamphlets?' I cried, foolishly frightened. 'Did you really...'

'Oh, they dropped ten off here,' he replied irritably (his tone when he spoke to me alternated between irritable and arrogant, and very plaintive and humble). 'But I got rid of eight, and Blum got his hands on only two...'

He suddenly went red in indignation.

'*Vous me mettez avec ces gens-là*! Do you really suppose I could be allied with those scoundrels, those cowards who circulate anonymous letters, with my son Peter Stepanovich, *avec ces esprits-forts de la lâcheté*![1] Oh, my God!'

'Why, perhaps they've mixed you up with someone else?... But that's nonsense, it's not possible!' I observed.

'*Savez-vous*,' he burst out suddenly, 'at times I feel *que je ferai là-bas quelque escalandre*. Oh, don't go, don't leave me alone! *Ma carrière est finie aujourd'hui, je le sens.*[2] You know, I might just hurl myself at someone there and bite him, like that second lieutenant...'

---

[1] You put me on the same level as those people! ... with those free-thinkers in cowardice!

[2] You know ... that I'll create a scandal there.... My career is finished today, I feel it.

He gave me a strange look—a look of fright, but at the same time trying to frighten me. He really was getting more and more irritated at someone and something, the more time passed and the 'covered cart' failed to appear; he even lost his temper. Suddenly Nastasya, coming from the kitchen into the hallway to get something, brushed against a coatstand and knocked it over. Stepan Trofimovich began to tremble and nearly fainted on the spot; but when the episode was explained, he almost screeched at Nastasya and stamping his feet chased her back into the kitchen. A minute later he looked at me in despair and cried:

'I'm done for! *Cher*,'—he suddenly sat down next to me and looked me straight in the eye with a pitiful expression. '*Cher*, I'm not afraid of Siberia, I swear to you, oh, *je vous jure* '(tears actually filled his eyes);' it's something else I'm afraid of...'

I guessed from his expression that he finally wanted to tell me something extraordinary, something he'd refrained from telling me up to now.

'I'm afraid of the disgrace,' he whispered mysteriously.

'What disgrace? On the contrary! Believe me, Stepan Trofimovich, everything that's happened today will be explained and will all turn out in your favour...'

'Are you so sure they'll pardon me?'

'What do you mean "pardon" you? What a thing to say! What on earth have you done? I assure you, you've done nothing!'

'*Qu'en savez-vous*; all my life has been... *cher*... They'll recall everything... and if they don't find anything, that's *even worse*,' he added all of a sudden, unexpectedly.

'Even worse?'

'Yes, worse.'

'I don't understand.'

'My friend, my friend, let them send me off to Siberia, to Archangel, let them take away my rights—if I'm to perish, let me perish! But... I'm afraid of something else.' He was whispering again, looking scared and with an air of mystery.

'What, what is it?'

'They'll flog me,' he said, looking at me with a desperate expression.

'Who'll flog you? Where? Why?' I cried, afraid he might be losing his mind.

'Where? Why, there... where it's done.'

'Where is it done?'

'Ah, *cher*,' he whispered almost into my ear, 'the floor suddenly opens up beneath you, you drop down halfway... Everyone knows it.'

'Fairy-tales!' I cried, having guessed what he meant. 'Old fairy-tales. Have you really believed them up to now?' I burst out laughing.

'Fairy-tales? Where do you think these fairy-tales come from? A man who's been flogged doesn't tell stories. I've pictured it all in my own mind some ten thousand times!'

'But why you? Why you? You haven't done a thing.'

'That's even worse! They'll realize I've done nothing, and they'll flog me anyway.'

'And you're sure that's what they're taking you to Petersburg for!'

'My friend, I've already said I regret nothing, *ma carrière est finie*. Ever since she bade me farewell in Skvoreshniki, I've cared nothing for my life... But the disgrace, the disgrace, *que dira-t-elle*,[1] if she finds out?'

He looked at me in despair; the poor man flushed completely. I too lowered my eyes.

'She won't find out a thing, because nothing is going to happen to you. I feel as though I were talking to you for the first time in my life, Stepan Trofimovich, you've astonished me so this morning.'

'My friend, it's not really fear. Even if they pardon me, even if they bring me back and do nothing to me—still I'm done for. *Elle me soupçonnera toute sa vie...*[2] me, me, the poet, the thinker, the man she worshipped for twenty-two years!'

'It'll never occur to her.'

---

[1] My career is finished.... what will she say
[2] She'll suspect me all her life

'It will,' he whispered with great conviction. 'She and I spoke about it several times in Petersburg, during Lent, before we left, when we were both very afraid... *Elle me soupçonnera toute sa vie...* and how can I disabuse her of the idea? It'll sound so unlikely. And who in this little town will believe, *c'est invraisemblable... Et puis les femmes...*[1] She'll be pleased. She'll be grieved, very much so, sincerely so, like a true friend, but in secret—she'll be pleased... I'm providing her with ammunition to use against me for the rest of my days. Oh, my life is over! Twenty-two years of complete happiness with her... and now this!'

He covered his face with his hands.

'Stepan Trofimovich, shouldn't you inform Varvara Petrovna at once about what's happened?' I suggested.

'God forbid!' he cried with a shudder and jumped to his feet. 'Absolutely not, never, not after what she said at our farewell at Skvoreshniki, no *never!*'

His eyes flashed.

We sat there for another hour or more, I think, still waiting for something—the idea had taken root. He lay down again, even closed his eyes, and remained still for some twenty minutes without saying a word, so that I actually thought he was asleep or unconscious. Suddenly he sat up impulsively, tore the towel off his head, jumped up from the sofa, rushed to the mirror, tied his cravat with trembling hands, and called to Nastasya in a thundering voice, demanding his coat, new hat, and walking-stick.

'I can't stand it any longer,' he said in a halting voice. 'I can't, I can't!... I'm going there myself.'

'Where?' I cried, also jumping up.

'To von Lembke. *Cher*, I must, I'm obliged. It's my duty. I'm a citizen and a man, not a chip of wood. I have rights and I want my rights... I haven't demanded my rights for the last twenty years; all my life I've neglected them criminally... but now I'll demand them. He must tell me everything, everything. He's received a telegram. He can't torment me; if so, let him arrest me, arrest me, arrest me!'

[1] it's improbable ... And besides, women

He was exclaiming, even screaming, and stamping his feet.

'I approve,' I said as calmly as possible, although I was very alarmed for him. 'True, it's better than remaining in such anxiety, but I don't approve of your frame of mind. Just have a look at yourself and see what you're like. *Il faut être digne et calme avec Lembke.*[1] You really might hurl yourself at someone now and bite him.'

'I'll give myself up. I'll walk straight into the lion's den...'

'I'll come with you.'

'I expected no less of you; I accept your sacrifice, the sacrifice of a true friend, but only as far as his house, only to his house. You mustn't, you have no right to compromise yourself by accompanying me inside. Oh, *croyez-vous, je serai calme*! At this moment I feel I'm *à la hauteur de tout ce qu'il y a de plus sacré...*'[2]

'I might even go inside with you,' I said, interrupting him. 'Yesterday I was informed by that stupid committee through Vysotsky that they were counting on me and had invited me to the fête tomorrow to act as one of the stewards, or whatever it's called... as one of the six young men supposed to see to the trays, wait on the ladies, show the guests to their seats, and wear a rosette of crimson and white ribbon on my left shoulder. I was going to refuse, but why shouldn't I enter his house now on the pretext of speaking to Yulia Mikhailovna about it... So we'll go in together.'

He was listening to me, nodding his head, but apparently not understanding a thing. We stood at the front door.

'*Cher*,' he said, extending a hand towards the icon lamp in the corner of the room. '*Cher*, I've never believed in it before, but... so be it, so be it!' He crossed himself. '*Allons!*'

'So much the better,' I thought, going out with him on to the porch. 'The fresh air will help along the way. He'll calm down, turn around, and go back home to lie down.'

But I miscalculated. Along the way an episode occurred that shocked Stepan Trofimovich even more and strengthened his

---

[1] You must be dignified and calm with Lembke.

[2] Oh believe me, I will be calm! . . . equal to all that is most sacred

resolve once and for all... I must confess, I never expected such energy from our friend as he suddenly displayed that morning. My poor, good friend!

CHAPTER 10

Filibusters. A fatal morning

I.

THE INCIDENT that occurred along the way was also rather remarkable. But I must relate everything in order. An hour before Stepan Trofimovich and I set out on the road, a crowd of workers from the Shpigulin factory, seventy or even more, had marched through town and been watched with curiosity by many people. They walked in a very orderly fashion, almost in silence. Later it was claimed that these seventy were chosen from all the workers at the Shpigulin factory, nine hundred in all, to go to the governor and, in the absence of the factory owners, to air their grievances against the arrogant manager who'd shut down the factory, dismissed the workers, and cheated them—a fact no longer in doubt. Some people refuse to believe there was ever any election, maintaining that seventy was far too many to be chosen; they say the crowd consisted merely of the most aggrieved parties who came to petition on their own behalf. Therefore there was never really any question of a factory 'revolt', concerning which there was such an uproar later on. A third group passionately maintains that these seventy men were not simply rebels, but definitely political rebels, that is, being among the most disruptive workers, they had been further stirred up by revolutionary pamphlets. In short, it's still not clear whether there ever was any outside agitation or incitement. My personal opinion is that the workers had never read the pamphlets; if they had, they'd never have understood a word of them because the authors of such materials write very obscurely, in spite of their bold style. But since the factory workers really were in a very difficult situation—and the police, to whom they'd turned, didn't want to get involved in their grievance—what could be more natural than the idea that they go in a group to the 'general himself', if possible, with petition actually in hand, to line up in orderly fashion in front of his house, and as soon as he emerged, to go down on their knees and cry out to him, as if to Providence itself? In my opinion, there was no need either for a revolt or for specially chosen workers, since this means of resolving grievances is both traditional and historical. From time immemorial Russians have always wanted to talk to the 'general himself', for the mere satisfaction of having done so, even if the conversation produces no tangible results.

Therefore I'm absolutely convinced that Peter Stepanovich, Liputin, and perhaps someone else, maybe even Fedka, had been sneaking around talking to the workers (there's rather conclusive evidence to support this view); probably they spoke with no more than two or three of them, perhaps even five, but just as an experiment, and nothing came of this conversation. And as far as a revolt is concerned, if the factory workers had understood anything of the propaganda, they'd have stopped listening at once, since they would've considered it ridiculous and entirely inappropriate. Fedka was another matter altogether; apparently, he had better luck than Peter Stepanovich. It's now known for a fact that two workers assisted Fedka in starting the fire that occurred three days later in town; a month after that, three more former factory workers in the district were apprehended and charged with arson and robbery. But if Fedka did manage to lure some workers into taking direct action, it was only those five; no charges were ever brought against any of the others.

Be that as it may, the crowd of workers finally arrived on the little square in front of the governor's house and lined up in silence in an orderly fashion. They stood on the steps waiting, their mouths gaping. I was told that as soon as they arrived, they doffed their caps, that is, perhaps half an hour before the governor's return; as if deliberately, he happened not to be at home when the crowd appeared. The police came immediately, at first in small groups, then in full force; they began, of course, by ordering the crowd to disperse in threatening tones. But the workers stood there stubbornly, like a herd of sheep gathered at a fence, and replied laconically that they'd come to see the 'general 'imself'; their determination was evident. The policemen's unnatural shouting ceased; it was followed by some discussion, mysterious, whispered orders, and stern, preoccupied anxiety which knit the brows of the authorities. The police commissioner proposed waiting for the arrival of von Lembke himself. It's pure nonsense to say that he came galloping up at full speed in a troika and was battling even before he got out. He was certainly fond of dashing through town and often did so in his carriage with its yellow back, and as his trace-horses, 'driven to debauchery', would gallop more and more frantically, to the great delight of the merchants in the Shopping Arcade, the governor would draw himself up to his full height, holding on to a strap specially attached to the side, and, extending his right arm, just like a monument, would thus survey the entire town. In the present instance, however, he didn't fight, and although he didn't refrain from using very strong language as he climbed out of his carriage, he did so merely to retain his popularity. It's even greater nonsense to say that soldiers were called in with bayonets and that a telegram was dispatched asking for reinforcements of artillery and Cossacks: these are mere fabrications which even the perpetrators themselves no longer believe. It's also nonsense that large barrels of water were brought by the fire brigade to spray the crowd. It was merely that in his excitement Ilya Ilyich had shouted that 'not one of them would get out of the water dry'. Probably it was from this remark alone that the barrels were invented which subsequently found their way into newspaper accounts in Moscow and Petersburg. The most reliable version, in all probability, is that at first the police did their best to form a cordon around the crowd. A messenger, the inspector of the first district, was dispatched to get von Lembke; he rushed off in the police commissioner's carriage down the road towards Skvoreshniki, knowing that von Lembke had set out in his own carriage about half an hour before...

I must confess, there's still one question that remains unanswered: how could they at first sight, from the very outset, have transformed an insignificant, that is, an ordinary

crowd of petitioners—true, there were seventy of them—
into a revolt threatening the very foundations of the state?
Why did von Lembke himself embrace this idea when he
arrived on the scene some twenty minutes after the messenger? I suppose (but again it's my personal opinion), it was
probably in the interests of Ilya Ilyich, an old friend of the
factory manager, to present the crowd to von Lembke in
this light, precisely because he didn't want him to look into
the matter any further; it was von Lembke himself who'd
given him this idea. In the last two days he'd had two
unusual and mysterious conversations with him—extremely
confused ones, by the way—but as a result of which Ilya
Ilyich concluded that the governor's mind was already made
up about the political pamphlets and the incitement of the
Shpigulin workers to some social revolt; his mind was made
up to such an extent that he might even have been sorry if
the whole thing turned out to be utter nonsense. 'He must
want to earn a decoration in Petersburg,' our clever Ilya
Ilyich concluded upon leaving von Lembke. 'What of it?
That'll suit me just fine too.'

But I'm convinced that poor Andrei Antonovich wouldn't
have favoured a rebellion, even to earn himself a decoration.
He was an extremely conscientious civil servant who'd
remained in a state of innocence until the time of his
marriage. Was it really his fault if instead of the blameless
firewood job and some equally innocent little Minnchen,
some forty-year-old princess had raised him up to her own
level? I know almost for sure that there first appeared on
that fateful morning unmistakable symptoms of the malady
which drove Andrei Antonovich into that well-known institution in Switzerland where even today he's still trying
to regain his strength. But if we acknowledge that the
unmistakable signs of *something* came to light that morning,
in my opinion it's also possible to recognize that similar
symptoms might have appeared the evening before, even if
not so unmistakable. I heard rumours from the most intimate sources (well, you may assume it was Yulia Mikhailovna who subsequently, not in triumph, but *almost* in
remorse—a woman never feels *complete* remorse—told me

some of it)—I heard that Andrei Antonovich had gone to his wife the evening before, very late at night, at three o'clock in the morning; he awakened her and demanded she hear 'his ultimatum'. He was so insistent that she was forced to get out of bed in indignation and in her curling papers; she sat down on the sofa to hear him out with a look of sarcastic contempt. This was the first time she realized how far gone Andrei Antonovich really was and she feared for herself. She ought finally to have come to her senses and relented, but instead she hid her horror and became even more stubborn than before. Like every other spouse, I suppose, she had her own way of dealing with Andrei Antonovich; she'd used it many times before and it had driven him to a frenzy more than once. Yulia Mikhailovna's way consisted of contemptuous silence for an hour, two hours, a day, even three days—silence no matter what, regardless of what he said and did, even if he climbed to the third-floor window to throw himself out—and this silence was intolerable for a sensitive man! Whether Yulia Mikhailovna was punishing her spouse for his blunders during the last few days or for the envy which, as governor, he felt for her administrative capabilities; whether she was indignant at his criticism of her behaviour among the young people or towards society as a whole, failing to understand her subtle and far-sighted political aims; whether she was angry at his obtuse and senseless jealousy of Peter Stepanovich—whatever the reason, she resolved not to relent, in spite of the fact that it was three o'clock in the morning and von Lembke was in a terrible state.

Pacing up and down her carpeted boudoir in a rage, he told her everything, absolutely everything, quite incoherently, but *everything* that had accumulated inside him because it'd gone 'beyond the limits of his endurance'. He began by saying that everyone was laughing at him and 'leading him around by the nose'. 'Damn that expression!' he cried shrilly when he noticed her smile. 'Yes, "by the nose"—it's the truth!' 'No, madam, the time has come; this is no time for laughter or feminine coquetry. We're not in the boudoir of some mincing society lady; rather we're two abstract creatures in a hot-air balloon who've met to tell each other the truth.' (Of course he was confused and unable to find the right words to express his thoughts, correct though they were.) 'It was you, madam, you, who drove me out of my previous position. I took this job solely for your sake, for the sake of your ambition... You're smiling sarcastically? Don't be so triumphant; don't be in such haste. You know, madam, you know that I could, I would have been able to cope with this job, and not only with this one, but with a dozen such jobs, because I'm a capable man; but with you, madam, with you around—I can't cope; with you around I am incapable. Two centres cannot co-exist, and you've built two of them—one in me, and the other here in your boudoir—two centres of power, madam, but I won't allow it, I won't!! In the civil service as in marriage, there can only be one centre, not two... How have you repaid me?' he cried. 'Our marriage has consisted merely in your demonstrating to me all the time how worthless I am, how stupid, even how despicable, while all the time I've been forced to demonstrate to you that I'm not worthless, not at all stupid, and that I astonish everyone with my nobility— well, isn't that humiliating for us both?' He began stamping his feet violently on the carpet; Yulia Mikhailovna felt compelled to rise with stern dignity. He calmed down quickly; but then he became very emotional and began weeping (yes, weeping), striking his chest, and for nearly five minutes he became more and more upset by Yulia Mikhailovna's silence. At length he made a terrible mistake: he let slip that he was jealous of Peter Stepanovich. Guessing that he'd made an utter fool of himself, he became absolutely furious and cried that 'he wouldn't allow anyone to deny the existence of God'; that he'd disperse her 'unforgivable salon of unbelievers'; that a governor was actually obliged to believe in God, and 'consequently, his wife was, too'; that he couldn't bear young people; that 'you, madam, you, for the sake of your own dignity, should've been concerned about your husband and have stood up for his intelligence, even if he were a man of little capacity (and by no means am I a man of little capacity!), meanwhile you are the reason that everyone here despises me, you put them up to it!...'. He shouted that he'd annihilate the woman question, smoke it out, that tomorrow he'd forbid and disband their idiotic fête in aid of the governesses (to hell with them!); that the next day he'd drive the first governess he met out of the province 'with his Cossacks!' 'To spite you, to spite you!' he screeched. 'Do you know,' he cried, 'do you know your scoundrels are inciting the men at the factory and that I'm well aware of it? Do you know they're deliberately distributing political pamphlets, de-lib-er-ate-ly! Do you know I have the names of four scoundrels and am losing my mind, completely, completely!!!...'

But here Yulia Mikhailovna suddenly broke her silence and declared sternly that she'd known for some time about these criminal intentions and that the whole thing was absurd; he was taking it all too seriously; and as far as these pranksters were concerned, she knew not only those four, but all of them (she was lying); but she had no intention whatever of losing her mind; on the contrary, she believed even more firmly in her own intelligence and hoped to bring the entire affair to a harmonious resolution: to encourage the young people, to bring them back to their senses, to show them unexpectedly and suddenly that their intentions were known, and then to provide them with new aims for rational and more rewarding activity.

Oh, the effect these words had on her husband! When he realized that Peter Stepanovich had duped him again and mocked him so rudely, that he'd actually told her a great deal more than he'd told him, and some time ago, and last of all, that Peter Stepanovich himself was the chief instigator of all these criminal intentions—he flew into a rage. 'I want you to know, you senseless, poisonous woman,' he cried, breaking all bonds at once, 'I want you to know that I shall arrest your unworthy lover at once, put him in chains, and lock him up in a dungeon or else—or else I'll throw myself out of the window before your very eyes!'

In response to this tirade Yulia Mikhailovna, turning green with anger, burst immediately into prolonged and resounding peals of laughter, complete with trills and tremolos, such as one hears in the French theatre when a Parisian actress, hired for a fee of a hundred thousand roubles to play a coquette, laughs in her husband's face when he dares be jealous of her. Von Lembke was about to head for the window, when suddenly he stopped dead, folded his arms across his chest, and as pale as a corpse, directed an ominous gaze at his hysterical wife. 'Do you know, Yulia, do you know...' he said in a breathless pleading voice, 'do you know I too can do something?' But at the fresh and even more violent burst of laughter that followed his last words, he clenched his teeth, moaned, and suddenly rushed—not to the window—but at his own wife, raising his fist at her! He didn't bring it down—no, never; but that was the end. Without knowing how he got there, he ran to his own study; dressed just as he was he threw himself face down on the bed, convulsively wrapping himself in a sheet, pulling it over his head, and lay there for two hours—without sleeping, without thinking, with a heavy stone weighing on his heart, and blank, immovable despair in his soul. Now and then a painful, feverish tremor shook his whole body. Disconnected fragments, unrelated to anything, kept crowding into his mind: he thought, for instance, about an old clock that used to hang on his wall fifteen years ago in Petersburg, which had lost its minute hand; then about the jolly civil servant Millebois with whom he'd once caught a sparrow in the Alexandrovsky Park, and how they'd laughed so loud they could be heard throughout the park, and that one of them was now a collegiate assessor. I think he fell asleep around seven o'clock in the morning, without being conscious of it; he slept very soundly and had pleasant dreams. He woke up around ten o'clock and suddenly jumped wildly out of bed, instantly recalling everything, and slapped himself soundly on the forehead. He turned down breakfast, refused to receive Blum, the police commissioner, and the official who came to remind him that the members of a certain committee were expecting him to chair a meeting that morning. He heard nothing and wanted to know nothing; like a madman he ran to Yulia Mikhailovna's rooms. There he was told by Sofya Antropovna, an elderly lady who'd lived with them for many years, that Yulia Mikhailovna had set off at ten o'clock that morning with a large group in three carriages to visit Varvara Petrovna Stavrogina at Skvoreshniki to inspect the site of the second fête scheduled to take place in two weeks, and that this visit had been arranged with Varvara Petrovna three days earlier. Struck by this piece of news, Andrei Antonovich went back to his study and impulsively ordered his own carriage. He could hardly stand the wait. His soul was yearning for Yulia Mikhailovna—merely to gaze at her, to be near her for five minutes; perhaps she'd glance at him, notice him, smile at him as she used to, forgive him—o-oh! 'What's taking so long?' Mechanically he opened a thick book lying on the table (sometimes he told his fortune using a book, opening it at random and reading the first three lines on the top of the right-hand page). What he found was: '*Tout est pour le mieux dans le meilleur des mondes possibles.*' Voltaire, *Candide*.* He spat in disgust and ran out to his carriage: 'To Skvoreshniki!' Afterwards the driver reported that his master had urged him on all along the way, but that as soon as they approached the manor house, he suddenly ordered the driver to turn around and take him back to town: 'Faster, faster, please.' But before reaching the town wall, 'he asked me to stop again. He got out of the carriage and walked across the road into a field, to relieve himself, I thought. But then he started looking at the flowers; he stood there for some time. It was very strange, really it was, and I began to wonder.' That was what the driver reported. I remember the weather that morning: it was a clear, cold, but windy September day; in front of Andrei Antonovich there stretched a harsh landscape of bare fields from which the crop had been harvested long ago; the howling wind was blowing some pitiful remnants of dying yellow flowers... Did he seek to compare himself and his fate to those wretched little flowers beaten down by the autumn and the frost? I think not. In fact, surely not; I think he was quite unaware of the flowers, in spite of reports by the driver and police inspector of the first district who arrived at that very moment in the commissioner's carriage and who maintained afterwards that he found the governor with a bunch of yellow flowers in his hand. That inspector—an ecstatic administrator, Vasily Ivanovich Filibusterov—was a relative newcomer in our town, but he'd already distinguished himself and had earned great renown by his extraordinary zest and zeal in carrying out all aspects of his duties, and by his inveterate drunkenness. Jumping down from the carriage, not in the least fazed by the governor's strange behaviour, he blurted out in one breath, looking crazy but sure of himself, that 'there was a disturbance in town.'

'Huh? What?' Andrei Antonovich turned to him with a stern face, but without the least surprise or any recollection of his carriage and driver, as if he were in his own study.

'I'm Police Inspector of the First District Filibusterov, your excellency. There's a revolt in town.'

'Filibusters?' Andrei Antonovich repeated thoughtfully.

'Exactly, your excellency. The Shpigulin men are rioting.'

'The Shpigulin men!'

The name Shpigulin seemed to remind him of something. He even gave a start and raised his index finger to his forehead: 'the Shpigulin men!' Silently, still deep in thought, he walked over to his carriage without hurrying, sat in it, and ordered his driver to take him to town. The inspector followed in his carriage.

I imagine many very interesting things must have vaguely occurred to him along the way, but he could scarcely have had any firm idea or definite intention when he arrived at the square in front of his house. As soon as he saw the crowd of 'rioters' drawn up in orderly fashion, the police cordon, the helpless police commissioner (perhaps even deliberately helpless), and the general expectation that he would take some action, all the blood rushed to his heart. He was very pale as he climbed out of his carriage.

'Hats off!' he said hardly audibly and somewhat breathlessly. 'On your knees!' he screeched unexpectedly, even to himself, and it was this unexpectedness that may explain the subsequent progress of the affair. It's like what happens during Lent in the countryside; is it possible for a sleigh to stop in mid-course once it starts rushing downhill? To his own misfortune all his life Andrei Antonovich had been known for his serene temperament; he'd never shouted at anyone or stamped his feet. It's much more dangerous dealing with such a person if ever, for any reason, his sleigh suddenly starts rushing downhill. Everything was whirling before his eyes.

'Filibusters!' he howled even more shrilly and absurdly, and his voice broke. He stood there, not knowing what he would do, but knowing and feeling with all his being that he would definitely do something.

'Oh, Lord!' came a voice from the crowd. One lad began crossing himself; three or four people tried to kneel, but the rest in one mass took three steps forward and suddenly began shouting: 'Your excellency... they hired us for a set term... the manager... you can't say...' and so on and so forth. It was impossible to understand anything.

Alas! Andrei Antonovich could make nothing out: he was still holding the flowers in his hand. The riot was as clear to him as the carts had been to Stepan Trofimovich. Among this crowd of 'rioters' who stood there staring at him, he kept seeing the figure of Peter Stepanovich 'inciting' them, a figure that had given him no peace since the day before— Peter Stepanovich, the detested Peter Stepanovich.

'Birch-rods!' he cried even more unexpectedly.

A deathly silence followed.

This is how it happened at the very beginning, according to the most reliable sources and my own surmises. But information about the ensuing events is less precise, as are my surmises. There are, however, a few facts.

In the first place, the birch-rods appeared all too quickly; apparently they'd been held ready in advance by the shrewd police commissioner. But only two men were actually flogged, not three; that much I insist on. It's utter nonsense to say that all the men were punished or even half of them. It's also nonsense to maintain that some poor gentlewoman who happened to be passing by was seized and flogged; yet I later read about this lady myself in a story appearing in a Petersburg newspaper. Many people in town talked about an old lady named Avdotya Petrovna Tarapygina, who lived in the poorhouse near the cemetery; they said she was returning home, crossing the square, making her way among the spectators out of natural curiosity, when she saw what was happening and exclaimed, 'What a shame!' and spat in disgust. For this she was supposedly apprehended and 'dealt with' accordingly. Not only did this episode find its way into print, it even resulted in the immediate organization of a subscription on her behalf. I myself contributed twenty kopecks. And then what? It now turns out there was no one by the name of Tarapygina living in our town! I myself went to the poor house near the cemetery to make enquiries: they'd never heard of any Tarapygina there. Moreover, when I told them about the rumours circulating, they were very offended. I mention this story of the non-existent Avdotya Petrovna because the same thing (if she actually existed) almost happened to Stepan Trofimovich; it's even possible that what happened to him was the source of the absurd rumour about Tarapygina, that is, as this rumour went the rounds he was somehow transformed into Tarapygina. What I chiefly don't understand is how he managed to slip away from me as soon as we reached the square. Sensing trouble, I wanted to escort him around the square directly to the governor's house, but I grew curious myself and stopped briefly to ask the first person I met. Suddenly I realized Stepan Trofimovich was no longer beside me. Instinctively I rushed off to look for him at once in the most dangerous place; I had the feeling that his sleigh too was heading downhill. And in fact he turned up in the very centre of the maelstrom. I remember seizing him by the arm; but he gave me a quiet, proud look of immense authority:

'*Cher*,' he uttered in a voice in which a taut string was trembling, 'if they deal with people so unceremoniously out here on the square, what can one expect from *that man*... if he has occasion to act independently?'

Trembling with indignation, and in an immense desire to challenge them, he pointed a menacing, accusatory finger at Filibusterov who was standing a few feet away and staring at us.

'*That man*!' cried the latter, blind with rage. 'What do you mean, *that man*? And who might you be?' he cried, rushing up with his fist clenched. 'Who are you?' he roared furiously, hysterically, desperately (I must observe that he knew Stepan Trofimovich perfectly well by sight). Another moment, of course, and he'd have seized him by the collar; fortunately, however, von Lembke turned his head at the sound of the shout. In perplexity he stared intently at Stepan Trofimovich, as if trying to understand something; suddenly he waved his arms. Filibusterov stopped short. I dragged Stepan Trofimovich away from the crowd. By that time, however, he may himself have been eager to get away.

'Home, home,' I insisted. 'If we didn't get a beating there, it was only thanks to von Lembke.'

'You go on, my friend. I'm to blame for involving you. You have a future and a career of a sort, while I—*mon heure a sonné*.'[1]

He resolutely climbed the steps of the governor's house. The porter knew me; I announced we'd both come to see Yulia Mikhailovna. We sat down in the hall and waited. I didn't want to leave my friend, but found it unnecessary to say anything to him. He had the look of a man who'd sworn to die for the sake of his country. We sat down not side by side, but in opposite corners; I sat closer to the inner door, he on the other side some distance away, his head lowered pensively, both hands resting lightly on his cane. He held his wide-brimmed hat in his left hand. We sat there like that for ten minutes.

2.

All of a sudden von Lembke came in with rapid steps, accompanied by the police commissioner; he looked at us absent-mindedly, without paying any attention, and was just about to enter his study when Stepan Trofimovich stood up and blocked his way. The tall figure of Stepan Trofimovich, so unlike other people, made its impression; von Lembke stopped.

[1] my hour has struck.

'Who's this?' he muttered in bewilderment, as if addressing his question to the police commissioner, but without turning his head and continuing to gaze at Stepan Trofimovich.

'Retired collegiate assessor Stepan Trofimovich Ver-khovensky, your excellency,' Stepan Trofimovich replied, with a dignified nod of the head. His excellency continued to stare at him with a blank expression.

'What is it?' he asked in the laconic tone of a man in authority, inclining an ear to Stepan Trofimovich with disdain and impatience, having finally taken him to be an ordinary petitioner with a written request.

'Earlier today my house was subjected to a search by an official acting in your excellency's name; therefore I should like...'

'Name? Name?' von Lembke asked impatiently, as if suddenly understanding something. Stepan Trofimovich repeated his name in an even more dignified manner.

'A-a-ah! It's... it's that hotbed... You, my dear sir, have shown yourself to be... You're a professor, aren't you? Aren't you a professor?'

'At one time I had the honour to give several lectures to the youngsters at a particular university.'

'Young-sters!' cried von Lembke with a sort of shudder, although I bet he understood very little of what was going on, perhaps not even with whom he was speaking. 'My dear sir, I won't allow it,' he said, suddenly becoming terribly angry. 'I won't allow those youngsters. It's all those political pamphlets. It's an attack on society, dear sir, it's piracy, those filibusters... What do you want?'

'On the contrary, your wife has asked me to read at tomorrow's fête. I'm not asking for anything; I've come to seek my rights...'

'The fête? There won't be any fête. I won't allow your fête, sir! Lectures? What lectures?' he cried furiously.

'I'd very much appreciate it if you would speak to me more politely, your excellency, without stamping your feet and shouting at me as if you were talking to a little boy.'

'Do you have any idea to whom you're speaking?' von Lembke asked, turning red in the face.

'Absolutely, your excellency.'

'I'm protecting society, while you're destroying it. Destroying it! You... I remember who you are: you served as a tutor in Mrs Stavrogina's household, didn't you?'

'Yes, I served·as... tutor... in Mrs Stavrogina's household.'

'And during the course of the last twenty years you've been the hotbed of all that's accumulated... all the fruits... I saw you just now in the square, didn't I? Beware, my dear sir, beware; your way of thinking is well known to me. You can be sure I'm keeping my eye on you. My dear sir, I can't permit you to give any lectures, I can't. Don't come to me with requests like that.'

Once again he was about to leave.

'I repeat, you're making a mistake, your excellency: it was your wife who asked me to read—not a lecture, but something literary, at tomorrow's fête. But now I refuse to read. I respectfully request that you explain to me, if you can, how and why my house was subjected to a search earlier today? Several of my books, papers, personal belongings, and private letters were taken and carried to town in a wheelbarrow...'

'Who conducted the search?' enquired von Lembke, startled, recovering his senses completely and blushing. He turned quickly to the police commissioner. At that moment the tall, stooping, awkward figure of Blum appeared in the doorway.

'That's the official,' Stepan Trofimovich said, pointing at him. Blum stepped forward with a guilty but unrepentant look.

'*Vous ne faites que des bêtises*,'[1] von Lembke said to him in anger and malice; he suddenly seemed transformed and completely returned to his senses. 'Excuse me,' he muttered in extreme confusion, turning as red as possible. 'It's all... this was all, undoubtedly, only a mistake, a misunderstanding... merely a misunderstanding.'

'Your excellency,' Stepan Trofimovich observed, 'in my youth I witnessed a characteristic incident. Once at the

---

[1] You always do such stupid things

theatre, in the corridor, a man went up to another man and gave him a resounding slap on the face. Realizing immediately that the face he'd slapped was not the intended one but a different one altogether that merely resembled it slightly, angry and in a hurry, like a man who can't afford to lose any precious time, he said exactly what your excellency just said: "I made a mistake... excuse me; it's all a misunderstanding, merely a misunderstanding." And when the insulted party continued to feel insulted and kept shouting, the first man observed in great annoyance: "But I said it was a misunderstanding. Why are you still shouting?"'

'That's... that's very amusing, of course,' von Lembke said with a wry smile, 'but... can't you see how miserable I am?'

He almost screamed and... seemed about to hide his face in his hands.

This unexpected and painful exclamation, almost a sob, was unbearable. It was probably his first moment since yesterday of clear, complete awareness of what was happening—followed immediately by complete, humiliating, unmistakable despair. Who knows, a moment more, and he might have filled the hall with the sound of tears. At first Stepan Trofimovich looked at him wildly; then suddenly he lowered his head and said in a profoundly sympathetic voice:

'Your excellency, don't trouble yourself with my peevish complaint any further; just tell them to return my books and letters...'

He was interrupted. Just at that moment Yulia Mikhailovna returned and entered noisily with the group that had accompanied her. But here I would like to describe what happened in as much detail as possible.

3.

In the first place, everyone, from all three carriages, entered the reception room in a large crowd. There was a separate entrance to Yulia Mikhailovna's rooms, directly from the steps on the left-hand side; but this time everyone filed through the hall, and I think it was because Stepan Trofimovich was there. Upon her return to town Yulia Mikhailovna had been informed about everything that had happened to him, just as she'd been told about the episode with the Shpigulin men. It was Lyamshin who had managed to inform her; he'd been left at home as a result of some misdemeanour and hadn't participated in the excursion; thus he knew everything before any of the others. With malicious glee he rushed off on a hired nag down the road to Skvoreshniki to meet the returning cavalcade with the glad news. I think that Yulia Mikhailovna, in spite of her lofty determination, must have been slightly disconcerted upon hearing such astonishing news, but probably only for a moment or so. The political side of the question, for example, couldn't have concerned her: Peter Stepanovich had impressed on her several times that those Shpigulin ruffians really should be given a good beating, and for some time he'd occupied a position of great authority in her eyes. 'But... he'll have to pay for this,' she probably thought to herself; 'he' referred to her husband, of course. I must observe in passing that Peter Stepanovich had taken no part in the general excursion this time, as if deliberately; no one had seen him anywhere since early that morning. By the way, I'll also mention that after receiving her visitors Varvara Petrovna returned to town with them (in the same carriage as Yulia Mikhailovna), intending to participate in the last committee meeting called to discuss tomorrow's fête. The news communicated by Lyamshin about Stepan Trofimovich must have interested her greatly, and perhaps even worried her.

The reckoning with Andrei Antonovich began at once. Alas, he sensed it from the moment he caught sight of his wonderful wife. With a candid expression and an enchanting smile she quickly approached Stepan Trofimovich, held out her elegantly gloved little hand, and showered him with the most flattering greetings—as if the only thing she'd been worrying about all morning was how to rush home and embrace him, because she'd finally have the chance to see him in her own house. There was no mention of the search that morning; she seemed to know nothing about it. Not a word to her husband, not a glance in his direction—just as if he weren't even in the room. What's more, she immediately and masterfully appropriated Stepan Trofimovich and led him off to the drawing-room—as if he had nothing at all to have out with von Lembke, and even if he had, it wasn't worth continuing with. Again I repeat: I think that in spite of her lofty tone, in this instance Yulia Mikhailovna was making a bad mistake. She was assisted by Karmazinov (who'd taken part in the excursion by her special request, and in that way had finally paid a courtesy call on Varvara Petrovna, though indirectly; because of her depression, Varvara Petrovna was absolutely delighted with the visit). While still standing in the doorway (he'd entered after the others) upon seeing Stepan Trofimovich he called out to him and ran to embrace him, interrupting even Yulia Mikhailovna.

'It's been ages since I've seen you! At long last... *Excellent ami.*'

He started kissing him, and naturally presented his own cheek. A disconcerted Stepan Trofimovich was forced to respond.

'*Cher,*' he told me later that evening, recalling the events of the day, 'I wondered at that moment which of us was most contemptible. He who embraced me to humiliate me, or I, who despised him and his cheek, but who kissed him, even though I could have turned aside... Damn it all!'

'Come, tell me, tell me everything,' Karmazinov drawled and lisped, as if Stepan Trofimovich should tell him the story of his life during the last twenty-five years. But this absurd gambit was considered to be 'good form'.

'You remember, we last saw each other in Moscow, at the dinner in honour of Granovsky.* That was twenty-four years ago...' Stepan Trofimovich began quite sensibly (therefore, not at all according to 'good form').

'*Ce cher homme,*' Karmazinov interrupted in a shrill, familiar manner, squeezing his shoulder in much too intimate a way. 'Yulia Mikhailovna, take us off at once to your rooms so he can sit down and tell us everything.'

'And yet,' Stepan Trofimovich said later that same evening, shaking with rage, as he continued complaining to me, 'I've never been very close to that irritable old bag. I started hating him when we were still young... just when he started hating me, of course...'

Yulia Mikhailovna's salon filled up quickly. Varvara Petrovna was particularly excited, although she tried to appear indifferent; but I caught two or three of her glances of hatred at Karmazinov and her angry looks at Stepan Trofimovich—she was angry in anticipation, and now from jealousy, and from love: if Stepan Trofimovich had somehow managed to blunder this time and be made a fool of by Karmazinov in front of everyone, I think she'd have jumped up and given him a sound beating. I forgot to say that Liza was also present; I'd never seen her more joyful, carelessly cheerful, and happy. Of course, Maurice Nikolaevich was there too. In the crowd of young ladies and rather undisciplined young men comprising Yulia Mikhailovna's usual entourage, among whom this lack of discipline was taken as a sign of animation, and cheap cynicism for intelligence, I noticed two or three new faces: an obsequious Pole who was passing through town and a German doctor, a robust old man who laughed loud and long at his own witty remarks, and finally, a very young princeling from Petersburg, somewhat of an automaton, but with the bearing of a statesman, wearing a terribly high collar. It was evident that Yulia Mikhailovna treasured this last visitor and worried about the impression her salon would make on him...

'*Cher monsieur Karmazinoff*,' Stepan Trofimovich began, assuming a picturesque pose on the sofa and suddenly beginning to lisp as much as Karmazinov did. '*Cher monsieur Karmazinoff*, the life of a man who belongs to the old days and holds certain convictions must appear monotonous, even after an interval of some twenty-five years...'

The German burst into loud, abrupt laughter, as if he were neighing, evidently supposing Stepan Trofimovich to have said something terribly amusing. The latter looked at him with studied amazement, which had no effect whatever on the German. The prince glanced at the German as well, turning his head and high collar, putting on his pince-nez, but without the least curiosity.

'... Must appear monotonous,' Stepan Trofimovich repeated deliberately, dragging out each word as long and nonchalantly as possible. 'Such has been my life for the last quarter of a century, *et comme on trouve partout plus de moines que de raison*,[1] and since I'm in complete agreement with that, it turns out that during this last quarter of a century...'

'*C'est charmant, les moines*,' Yulia Mikhailovna whispered, turning to Varvara Petrovna who was sitting behind her.

Varvara Petrovna replied with a proud glance. Karmazinov couldn't bear the success of this French phrase and interrupted Stepan Trofimovich quickly in a shrill voice.

'As for me, I've been feeling at ease on that score and have been living in Karlsruhe for the past seven years. Last year when the town council was proposing to install a new water main, I felt in my heart that the question of the Karlsruhe water main was dearer and more important to me than all the problems of my beloved homeland... during the entire period of the so-called local reforms.'

'I must sympathize with you, although it goes against the grain,' said Stepan Trofimovich with a sigh, inclining his head meaningfully.

Yulia Mikhailovna was triumphant: the conversation was becoming profound and taking on a political dimension.

'A drain for the sewage?' the doctor enquired loudly.

'A water main, doctor, a water main; I even helped them write the proposal.'

The doctor burst out laughing. Many people joined in, right in the doctor's face; he didn't notice, and was pleased everyone else was laughing.

'Permit me to disagree with you, Karmazinov,' Yulia Mikhailovna hastened to put in. 'Karlsruhe is all well and good, but you love to mystify, and this time we won't believe you. Who among Russian writers has created so many contemporary types, divined so many contemporary problems, put his finger on the contemporary features that make up a contemporary statesman? You, you alone, no one

[1] and since everywhere one encounters more monks than common sense

else. Now you assure us of your indifference to your homeland and of a terrific interest in the Karlsruhe water main! Ha, ha!'

'Yes, of course,' Karmazinov said, lisping, 'I've revealed all the faults of the Slavophiles in the figure of Pogozhev and all the faults of the Westernizers* in the figure of Nikodimov...'

'Was it really *all* the faults?' Lyamshin whispered quietly.

'But I do this in passing, merely to kill time... and to satisfy all those importunate demands of my fellow-countrymen.'

'No doubt you know, Stepan Trofimovich,' Yulia Mikhailovna continued rapturously, 'tomorrow we shall have the pleasure of hearing some splendid new lines... one of the most recent of Semyon Yegorevich's elegant artistic inspirations. It's called "Merci". In it he announces that he'll write no more, not for anything on earth, not even if some angel from heaven or, more likely, all high society were to beg him to change his mind. In a word, he's putting down his pen for the rest of his life; and this graceful "Merci" is addressed to the public as a token of his gratitude for the constant enthusiasm with which it's greeted his unswerving services to honest Russian thought.'

Yulia Mikhailovna was at a peak of ecstasy.

'Yes, I'm taking my leave; I'll say "Merci" and then depart. And there... in Karlsruhe... I shall close my eyes,' Karmazinov said, gradually becoming sentimental.

Like many of our great writers (and we have a great many great writers), he couldn't withstand flattery and began to weaken at once, in spite of his considerable wit. But I think it's forgivable. It's said one of our Shakespeares even blurted out in private conversation something to the effect that 'We *great men* can't do otherwise', and didn't even notice he'd said it.*

'There, in Karlsruhe, I shall close my eyes. For us great men, once our work is done, all that remains is for us to close our eyes as soon as possible, without seeking any reward. So too will I.'

'Send us your address and I'll come to Karlsruhe to visit your grave,' the German said with a resounding laugh.

'Nowadays they even transport corpses by rail,' one of the insignificant young men added suddenly.

Lyamshin positively squealed in delight. Yulia Mikhailovna frowned. In walked Nikolai Stavrogin.

'I was told you were taken off to the police?' he said loudly, addressing himself first to Stepan Trofimovich.

'No, a change of *policy* saved me from the police,' Stepan Trofimovich replied, making a pun.

'But I hope this incident won't have the slightest impact on my request,' Yulia Mikhailovna began again. 'I trust that in spite of this unfortunate unpleasantness which I still don't quite understand, you won't disappoint our eager expectations and deprive us of the pleasure of hearing you read at the literary matinée.'

'I don't know, now... I...'

'Really, I'm so unfortunate, Varvara Petrovna... imagine, just when I was so eager to make the personal acquaintance of one of Russia's most outstanding and original minds, all of a sudden Stepan Trofimovich declares his intention to desert us.'

'Your praise was uttered so audibly that I can't pretend not to have heard it,' Stepan Trofimovich replied gracefully. 'But I really don't believe that my humble self is so essential for your matinée tomorrow. Moreover, I...'

'You're spoiling him!' cried Peter Stepanovich, who came running into the room quickly. 'I've just managed to take him in hand; now, suddenly in one morning—a search, arrest, the police seize him by the scruff of the neck, and ladies sing him lullabies in the governor's drawing-room! Every single bone in his body must be aching in ecstasy; never in his wildest dreams did he imagine such a splendid scenario. Now he'll take to informing against the socialists!'

'That's impossible, Peter Stepanovich. Socialism is too grand an idea for Stepan Trofimovich not to realize that,' Yulia Mikhailovna interceded energetically.

'The idea is grand, but those advocating it aren't always giants, *et brisons-là, mon cher*,'[1] concluded Stepan Trofimovich, addressing his son and rising gracefully from his seat.

[1] and let us say no more about it, my dear

But at this point something completely unexpected occurred. Von Lembke had been standing in the salon for some time, apparently unnoticed by anyone, even though they'd all seen him come in. In accordance with her earlier scheme, Yulia Mikhailovna continued to ignore him. He stood near the door and listened to the conversation gloomily, with a stern expression. When he overheard allusions to the events of the morning, he began to stir uneasily. First he stared at the prince, obviously struck by his stiffly starched jutting collar; then he suddenly shuddered when he heard the voice of Peter Stepanovich and saw him run in. And as soon as Stepan Trofimovich had uttered his pronouncements about socialists, he suddenly went up to him, shoving aside Lyamshin, who immediately jumped back with an affected gesture of astonishment, rubbing his shoulder and pretending to have been gravely wounded.

'Stop it!' cried von Lembke, seizing the frightened Stepan Trofimovich by the arm and squeezing it with all his might. 'Stop, the filibusters of our age have been identified. Not one word more. Steps have been taken...'

He spoke in a loud voice that filled the room, and finished with a flourish. The impression he made was painful. Everyone knew something was wrong. I saw Yulia Mikhailovna turn pale. The effect was heightened by a stupid accident. After declaring steps had been taken, Lembke turned sharply and headed out of the room, but after only a couple of paces he tripped on the carpet, lurched forward, and almost fell flat on his face. For a moment he stopped, looked at the spot where he tripped, and said aloud: 'Fix it!' Then he left. Yulia Mikhailovna ran out after him. When she'd gone an uproar arose in which it was difficult to make sense of anything. Some said he was 'deranged', others, that he was 'susceptible'. Still others tapped their foreheads; over in the corner Lyamshin made a pair of horns above his head. They hinted at certain domestic events, all in whispers, of course. No one was in a hurry to leave; everyone waited. I don't know what Yulia Mikhailovna managed to do, but she returned a few minutes later, trying her best to look composed. She explained evasively that Andrei Antonovich was a little upset, but it was really nothing; such incidents had occurred since childhood and she knew 'much better'; finally, tomorrow's fête would cheer him up, of course. Then she paid a few more compliments to Stepan Trofimovich, merely out of politeness; in a loud voice she invited members of the committee to open their meeting right then and there. At that point those people who were not members of the committee got ready to leave; but the painful events of this fateful day were not yet over.

The moment Nikolai Vsevolodovich had entered the drawing-room, I noticed that Liza stared at him intently and that she was unable to take her eyes off him for a long time—so long, in fact, that at last she began to attract attention. I saw Maurice Nikolaevich lean over from behind; he looked as if he wanted to whisper something to her, but apparently changed his mind and quickly straightened up, glancing around guiltily at everyone. Nikolai Vsevolodovich aroused everyone's curiosity as well: his face was paler than usual, his expression extremely remote. After flinging his question at Stepan Trofimovich as he came in, he seemed to forget all about him straight away; indeed, I think he even forgot to greet his hostess. He didn't look at Liza even once—not because he didn't want to, but because, I believe, he didn't notice her either. Suddenly, after the silence following Yulia Mikhailovna's invitation to open the meeting without wasting any more time—suddenly Liza's ringing, deliberately loud voice rang out. She called to Stavrogin.

'Nikolai Vsevolodovich, there's a captain calling himself your relative, your wife's brother, named Lebyadkin, who keeps writing indecent letters complaining about you, who's offering to reveal certain secrets about you. If he's really related to you, order him to stop insulting me and spare me this unpleasantness.'

There was a terrible challenge in these words; everyone understood that. The accusation was unmistakable, although perhaps not quite even what she had expected to say. She was like a person who shuts his eyes, getting ready to jump off a roof.

But Nikolai Vsevolodovich's answer was even more astounding.

In the first place, it was odd that he was not at all surprised and listened to Liza with unruffled attention. His face reflected neither confusion nor anger. He replied to the fatal question simply, firmly, with a look of absolute readiness.

'Yes, I have the misfortune of being related to that man. I've been the husband of his sister, *née* Lebyadkina, for almost five years now. You may be sure I'll convey your request to him at the earliest opportunity. I promise he won't trouble you any further.'

I'll never forget the expression of horror on Varvara Petrovna's face. She got up from her chair with a frenzied look and raised her right hand as if to defend herself from a blow. Nikolai Vsevolodovich looked at her, at Liza, at the spectators, and then all of a sudden smiled with infinite arrogance; he left the room without hurrying. Everyone saw how Liza jumped up from the sofa as soon as Nikolai Vsevolodovich had turned to leave, and how she made as if to run out after him; but she came to her senses and didn't run; instead she went quietly, without saying a word, without looking at anyone, accompanied, of course, by Maurice Nikolaevich who went rushing out after her...

I won't mention all the commotion and conversation in our town that evening. Varvara Petrovna locked herself up in her town house; it was said that Nikolai Vsevolodovich went directly to Skvoreshniki without speaking to his mother. Stepan Trofimovich sent me over to '*cette chère amie*' to implore her to grant permission for him to call on her, but I wasn't received. He was terribly shocked and wept. 'What a marriage! What a marriage! What an awful thing to happen to the family,' he kept repeating. Then he remembered Karmazinov and abused him terribly. He was enthusiastically preparing for the next day's reading and—what an artistic temperament—he was rehearsing in front of a mirror, repeating all the witty remarks and puns he'd uttered in his entire life, all written down in a special notebook to insert in tomorrow's reading.

'My friend, I'm doing this for the sake of the great idea,' he said to me, obviously trying to justify himself. '*Cher ami*,

I've moved away from where I've been the last twenty-five years; suddenly I'm on my way—where to, I don't know, but I'm on my way...'

PART THREE

The fête. Part one

I.

THE FÊTE took place in spite of all the previous day's
confusion over the Shpigulin workers. I think even if von
Lembke had died during the night, the fête would still have
taken place the next morning—such was the particular
importance Yulia Mikhailovna attached to it. Alas, up until
the very last moment she remained completely blind and
had no real understanding of the prevailing mood in society.
In the end no one thought the triumphant day would pass
without some colossal scandal, some kind of 'denouement',
as people put it, rubbing their hands in anticipation. Many
people, it's true, tried to assume a most disapproving and
political demeanour; but in general a Russian derives inor-
dinate delight from any scandal. It's true we felt something
much more serious than mere longing for scandal: there was
a general sense of irritation, something implacably malevolent; everyone seemed to be terribly fed up. A general mood
of confused cynicism prevailed—a forced, strained kind of
cynicism. Only the ladies were in agreement and only on
one thing: their merciless hatred of Yulia Mikhailovna. All
feminine factions were unanimous on this point. And she,
poor thing, didn't even suspect it; right up until the last
moment she was convinced that she was 'surrounded' by
followers all still 'fanatically devoted' to her.

I've already alluded to the fact that all sorts of lower-class
types had made their appearance among us. In troubled

times of upheaval or transition various lower-class elements always turn up everywhere. I'm not talking about the so-called 'progressive' people, always in a rush (that's their main concern), often with an absurd, but more or less defined aim. No, I'm talking only about the scum. This scum, which exists in every society and rises to the surface during any transitional period, lacking not only a purpose, but any sign of rational activity, merely expresses unrest and impatience with all its might. Meanwhile, without even knowing it, this scum almost always falls under the control of a small group of 'progressives' acting with definite aims; this group directs the scum wherever it likes, so long as the group isn't composed of complete idiots, which, however, is sometimes the case. In our town it's said, now that everything is over, that Peter Stepanovich was controlled by the *Internationale*, Yulia Mikhailovna by Peter Stepanovich, and that she in turn, under his command, controlled the scum. The soundest intellects among us are now surprised at themselves: how could they have been so stupid at the time? What our time of troubles* consisted of and what kind of transition we were passing through I don't know, and I think no one does for sure—except for a few of those visitors of ours. In the meantime the most worthless creatures suddenly became the majority and began to criticize everything sacred, when previously they dared not open their mouths. The foremost people among us, who'd maintained the upper hand up until then, suddenly began listening to them and keeping silent themselves; some of them even tittered shamelessly in approval. People like Lyamshin or Telyatnikov or the landowner Tentetnikov, snivelling home-grown Radishchevs,* wretched little Yids with their mournful but arrogant smiles, scoffing travellers, poets from the capital with political tendencies, poets lacking tendencies and talent wearing peasant coats and tarred boots, majors and lieutenants laughing at their meaningless profession and ready, for an extra rouble, to remove their swords and become railway clerks; generals who'd become lawyers; trained arbitrators, merchants who were becoming educated, innumerable seminary students, women representing the woman question—all these people suddenly gained the upper hand among us, and over whom? Over the club, over venerable officials, over generals with wooden legs, over the most severe and unapproachable ladies in our society. If even Varvara Petrovna, right up until the catastrophe with her beloved son, was virtually at the beck and call of this scum, then our local Minervas can be forgiven their foolishness. Now, as I've already said, everything is attributed to the *Internationale*. This idea has become so entrenched that it is even conveyed to out-of-town visitors. Not long ago Councillor Kubrikov, aged sixty-two with the order of St Stanislav* around his neck, came forward without any prompting and in an emotional voice declared that for the last three months he'd undoubtedly been under the influence of the *Internationale*. When, with all due respect for his years and distinction, he was invited to be more explicit, despite the fact that he was unable to present any evidence except that he 'felt it in his bones', he nevertheless stuck firmly to his statement; he was interrogated no further.

I repeat: there was a small group of cautious people who remained aloof right from the start and who even locked themselves away. But what kind of lock can withstand the laws of nature? Young ladies grow up in the strictest of families, yet still feel the urge to dance. In the end all these people subscribed to the fund for our governesses. The ball was expected to be an absolutely splendid affair; marvellous stories were being told about it. There were rumours circulating about princes coming, with lorgnettes, about there being ten ushers, all young cavaliers with ribbons on their left shoulders; about Petersburg figures who were behind the whole event; about the fact that Karmazinov, in order to increase the amount of contributions, had agreed to read 'Merci' dressed as a governess of our province; about the 'literary quadrille', also to be danced in costume, each representing some literary tendency. Finally, some kind of 'honest Russian idea' would also dance in costume—which in and of itself would certainly constitute a complete novelty. How could one refuse to subscribe? Everyone subscribed.

2.

The festive day was divided into two parts: the literary
matinée, from noon until four o'clock, and then the ball,
from nine on. But in this very arrangement lay concealed
the seeds of disorder. In the first place, right from the start
a rumour was circulating among the public about a luncheon
immediately following the literary matinée or even during
it, in an intermission arranged for the purpose—a free
luncheon, of course, as part of the programme, to include
champagne. The enormous price of the ticket (three roubles)
contributed to the popularity of this rumour. 'Would I have
subscribed for nothing? The fête is supposed to last all day
and all night, they'll have to feed us. We'll starve.' That's
how people reasoned. I must confess that Yulia Mikhailovna
herself had provoked this disastrous rumour through her
own carelessness. A month back, while still under the initial
spell of her great project, she mentioned the fête to almost
everyone she met and said there'd be a series of toasts
proposed; she even sent a notice to one newspaper in the
capital. At the time she was fascinated by the idea of these
toasts: she wanted to propose them herself and was busy
composing them in anticipation. They were supposed to
clarify our primary purpose. (What was the purpose? I bet
the poor woman never composed a single toast.) They were
to be published in Moscow and Petersburg newspapers to
soothe and charm the higher authorities, and then were to
be distributed throughout the provinces to inspire wonder
and emulation. But toasts cannot be proposed without champagne, and since champagne cannot be consumed on an
empty stomach, naturally a luncheon would have to be
provided. Later, when thanks to her efforts a committee had
been formed and the affair was being considered more
seriously, it was quickly made clear that if they were to plan
for a feast, very little money would be left over for the
governesses, even if the subscription was hugely successful.
The question seemed to admit of only two solutions: either
Belshazzar's feast* with toasts, leaving only ninety or so
roubles for the governesses, or else a considerable sum of

money, while the fête remained a formality, so to speak.
The committee, however, merely wanted to frighten her a
little; by itself it came up with a third solution, a reasonable
compromise, that is, quite a decent fête in every respect,
but without champagne, still leaving a considerable sum for
the governesses, much more than ninety roubles. But Yulia
Mikhailovna didn't agree; her character despised the vulgar
mean. She proposed that if the first plan proved to be
unfeasible, they should immediately and whole-heartedly
embrace the opposite extreme, that is, raise such an enormous amount by subscription that they'd be the envy of
other provinces. 'The public must understand at long last',
she said, concluding her passionate speech to the committee,
'that the attainment of universal aims is incomparably more
sublime than a few moments of corporeal satisfaction. The
fête is essentially a means to propagate a great idea; therefore we must be content with the most economical little
German-style ball, merely as a symbol, and only because we
can't dispense with this insufferable ball altogether!' That's
how much she'd suddenly come to detest it! But they
pacified her at last. It was then, for example, they conceived
and proposed the 'literary quadrille' and other aesthetic
items, as substitutes for corporeal pleasures. It was then
Karmazinov agreed once and for all to read 'Merci' (up to
then he'd been procrastinating and tormenting them); thus
would they obliterate the very idea of food in the minds of
our incontinent public. So once again the ball was to become
a magnificent occasion, although of a different sort. But so
as not to disappear entirely into the ether, it was decided
to serve lemon tea and biscuits at the beginning of the ball,
followed by barley-water and lemonade, and at the end, even
ice cream, but nothing more. And for those who insist at all
times and places on being hungry and above all, thirsty—
a special buffet might be set up in the end room, to be
run by Prokhorych (the head chef from the club), and—
under the strictest supervision of the committee—they
could serve anything desired, but for an additional charge;
a notice would be prominently displayed at the entrance
indicating that the buffet was not included in the price of

admission. But the next morning they decided not to open the buffet after all, so as not to interfere with the reading, in spite of the fact that the buffet was to be located five rooms away from the large white hall in which Karmazinov had agreed to read his 'Merci'.

It's curious that the committee, including even some very practical people, had attached such enormous significance to this event, namely, to the reading of 'Merci'. As for the more poetic people such as the marshal's wife, for example, she told Karmazinov that immediately after the reading she would have a large marble plaque put up on the wall of her white hall with a gold inscription saying that on such and such a date, here, in this very place, the outstanding Russian and European writer put down his pen and read 'Merci', thus bidding a first farewell to the Russian public as represented by the leading citizens of our town; this inscription would be read by everyone at the ball, that is, only five hours or so after Karmazinov's reading of 'Merci'. I know for a fact that it was Karmazinov himself who demanded there be no buffet in any form whatever while he was reading, in spite of remarks by certain members of the committee that this was not really the way we did things in our town.

That was the state of affairs while people continued to believe they were to be provided with Belshazzar's feast, that is, a buffet by the committee; they believed it right up until the end. Even the young ladies dreamed about an assortment of condiments, preserves, and unheard-of delights. Everyone knew an enormous sum of money had been collected, the whole town was eager to attend, people were coming from outlying districts, and there weren't enough tickets to go round. It was also known that over and above the money collected from the sale of tickets, some significant contributions had been offered: Varvara Petrovna, for example, had paid three hundred roubles for her ticket and provided all the flowers to decorate the hall from her greenhouse. The marshal's wife (a member of the committee) had provided the house and lighting; the club had donated music and servants, and had lent them Prokhorych for one whole day. There were other contributions as well, though not quite as large, so the idea was even advanced of reducing the price of a ticket from three roubles to two. The committee was actually at first afraid that young ladies might not come if they had to pay three roubles, and they proposed selling special family tickets, so that each family would have to pay for only one young lady, while others in the same family, even if there were ten, would be admitted free of charge. But all their fears proved groundless: on the contrary, it was precisely the young ladies who came. Even the most impoverished civil servants brought along their girls, and it was all too clear that if they hadn't had any, it would never have occurred to them to subscribe. One low-ranking secretary brought his seven daughters, not to mention his wife, of course, as well as his niece; each one of these ladies held in her hand a ticket costing three roubles.

One can imagine the commotion all this caused in town! Consider, for instance: since the fête was divided into two parts, every lady needed two dresses for the occasion—a morning dress for the reading, and an evening dress for the ball. Many members of the middle class, as it later turned out, had pawned everything, even the family linen, including sheets and even mattresses, to some Yids who'd settled in our town some two years ago, as if on purpose, whose number had been increasing at an alarming rate as time went on. Almost all our civil servants had requested their salary in advance; some landowners sold their essential stock, all in order to bring their young ladies to the ball looking like marquises and to be no worse than anyone else. The splendour of the dresses on this occasion was unheard of in our district. For two weeks beforehand the town was filled with amusing domestic anecdotes brought immediately to Yulia Mikhailovna's court by our local gossips. Caricatures of certain families began to circulate among us. I myself saw several drawings in this spirit in Yulia Mikhailovna's album. All this became known to the people depicted in these caricatures; that's why, it seems to me, such a hatred of Yulia Mikhailovna had taken hold of certain families of late. Now everyone heaps abuse on her head and, recalling all the details, they grind their teeth. But it was quite clear in advance that if the committee were to displease people in some way, if something were to go wrong at the ball, the outburst of indignation would be quite astonishing. That's why everyone was expecting a scandal; and if they were all expecting one, how could it fail to happen?

At twelve noon the orchestra started playing. As one of the ushers, that is, one of the twelve 'young men wearing ribbons', I saw with my own eyes how this day of ignominy began. It began with an enormous crush at the entrance. How did it come about that everything went wrong from the very beginning, starting with the police? I don't blame the genuine public: fathers of families weren't pushed and didn't push anyone, in spite of their rank: on the contrary, I'm told that while still outside on the street they were taken aback by the unusual crush of people besieging the entrance and trying to take it by storm, instead of simply filing in. Meanwhile carriages continued to pull up and finally blocked the whole street. Now, as I write this, I have solid grounds for asserting that several of the lowest scum in our town were boldly escorted in without tickets by Lyamshin and Liputin, and by someone else as well, perhaps even one of the ushers. At any rate some total strangers showed up, people who'd come from surrounding districts and elsewhere. As soon as they were inside these savages immediately demanded to know where the buffet was (as if they'd been put up to it); when they discovered there was none, they began swearing with little finesse and an impudence hitherto unprecedented in our town. It's true some of them were already drunk. Several were stunned, like savages, by the magnificence of the marshal's hall, since they'd never seen anything like it before; upon entering, they were silent for a moment and stood there, mouths agape. The great White Hall really was rather splendid, though a little dilapidated: it was enormous, with two rows of windows, a ceiling painted in the old style with gilded mouldings, a mirrored gallery, red and white draperies, marble statues (not very exciting, but statues none the less), heavy antique furniture from the Napoleonic period painted gold and white, covered

with red velvet. At the time I'm describing a high platform
had been erected at one end of the hall for those who were
going to read, and the entire hall was filled with chairs
arranged like the stalls of a theatre, with wide aisles left for
the public.

But after the first few moments of surprise, there followed
the most senseless questions and remarks. 'Perhaps we don't
want to hear any readings... We paid our money... The
public has been impudently swindled... We're running this
show, not the Lembkes!...'. In a word, it was as if they'd
been admitted solely for this purpose. I remember one
encounter in particular which involved the princeling with
the stiff collar and look of a wooden doll who was present
at Yulia Mikhailovna's house the day before. He too, at her
urgent request, agreed to pin a ribbon on his left shoulder
and become one of our ushers. It turned out that this mute
wax figure on springs could take action in his own way,
even if he didn't know how to speak. When an enormous,
pock-marked retired captain accompanied by a whole crowd
of rabble demanded to know the way to the buffet, he
signalled to the policeman. The signal was promptly acted
upon: in spite of a stream of abuse from the drunk captain,
he was escorted out of the hall. Meanwhile the 'genuine'
public had finally begun to appear, and three long lines
stretched down the aisles between the chairs. The disorderly
element began to quiet down, but the public, even the most
'authentic' public, had a dissatisfied and perplexed look;
some of the ladies were quite simply frightened.

At last they took their seats; the music quieted down as
well. People began blowing their noses and looking around.
They waited with too solemn an air—which in itself is
always a bad sign. But the Lembkes still hadn't arrived.
Silks, velvets, and diamonds glowed and glittered on all
sides; a pleasant fragrance wafted through the air. The men
were wearing all their medals; some of the older ones were
even in uniform. At last the marshal's wife arrived, together
with Liza. Never had Liza looked so dazzling as that
morning in her splendid dress. Her hair was done up in
curls, her eyes sparkled, and her face wore a radiant smile.

She obviously created a sensation; people stared at her and whispered. They said she was looking for Stavrogin, but neither he nor Varvara Petrovna was there. At the time I didn't understand the expression on her face: why did it reflect so much happiness, joy, energy, and strength? I recalled the previous day's incident and felt at a loss.

But the Lembkes still weren't there. This was already a mistake. Later I found out that Yulia Mikhailovna had been waiting for Peter Stepanovich until the very last moment; recently she'd been unable to act without him, even though she never admitted it to herself. Let me add parenthetically that Peter Stepanovich, the night before at the last meeting of the committee, had refused to wear an usher's ribbon— something that upset Yulia Mikhailovna very much, even to the point of tears. To her surprise, and later even to her extreme embarrassment (here I'm anticipating), he disappeared for the whole morning and didn't even show up for the literary matinée; no one caught sight of him until later that evening.

At last the public began to display obvious signs of impatience. No one appeared on the stage either. In the back rows people started clapping, as in a theatre. Elderly gentlemen and ladies frowned. Obviously the Lembkes were putting on airs. Absurd whispers began even among the most respectable members of the audience to the effect that there might not even be a fête, that Lembke himself might really be indisposed, so on and so forth. Thank God Lembke appeared at last: he escorted his wife on his arm. I must confess that I myself had been terribly afraid they might not appear. But all fairy-tales came to nought; truth won out. The public seemed to relax. Lembke himself seemed perfectly fine; I recall that everyone reached this conclusion, since one could imagine how many pairs of eyes were fixed on him when he entered. As a matter of fact, very few members of our more respectable society had ever supposed he was ill; they considered his actions completely normal and even approved his handling of events on the square the previous morning. 'That's what he should've done right from the start,' said our higher officials. 'Otherwise you get a man coming here as a philanthropist and ending by acting in exactly the same way, not even noticing it's exactly what his philanthropy postulates'; at least that's what was said at the club. They blamed him only for losing his temper. 'He should have been more level-headed, but he's still new at the job,' said our experts.

All eyes turned to Yulia Mikhailovna with the same eagerness. Of course, no one has the right to demand from me, as narrator, too detailed an account of one point: that's a secret, a woman's secret. But I know only one thing: towards evening of the previous day she went into Andrei Antonovich's study and stayed there until well after midnight. Andrei Antonovich was forgiven and consoled. Husband and wife came to an agreement about everything, all was forgotten, and, at the end of the discussion, when von Lembke was still down on his knees, recalling with horror the central and final incident of the previous night, his wife's lovely little hand, then her lips, checked the passionate outpourings of penitent speech by a chivalrously sensitive gentleman, one weakened by emotion. Everyone saw the happiness reflected in her face. She had a frank, open air about her, and was wearing a splendid dress. It seemed as if she were at the pinnacle of her heart's desire; the fête—the object and crowning glory of her deep-laid plans—had been realized. As they made their way to their places in front of the stage, both Lembkes bowed and acknowledged greetings. They were surrounded at once. The marshal's wife stood up to meet them...

It was then that a nasty misunderstanding took place: for some reason or other the orchestra struck up a flourish—not a march, simply a flourish, the kind used in the club at the dinner-table when people rise to drink someone's health. I now know it was Lyamshin's doing, as one of the ushers; he intended to honour the Lembkes as they entered. Of course, he could always have excused himself by saying he'd done it out of stupidity or excessive zeal... Alas, I didn't know it at the time, but they weren't worrying about excuses and had finished with the events of that day. But this flourish wasn't the end of it: in addition to the annoying misunderstanding and the smiles of the public, suddenly at the end of the hall and in the gallery there was a shout of 'hurrah', also, it seems, in honour of the Lembkes. There were only a few voices cheering, but, I must confess, it continued rather a long time. Yulia Mikhailovna flushed and her eyes flashed. Lembke stood still at his place and, turning in the direction of the cheering, majestically and sternly surveyed the hall... They made him sit down at once. I observed once again on his face that dangerous smile with which he'd stood yesterday morning in his wife's drawing-room, looking at Stepan Trofimovich before going to speak to him. It seemed to me that his face now again wore a malevolent expression; what was even worse, it was also a comic one—the expression of a creature who had come to sacrifice himself, no matter what, to satisfy his wife's noble aims...

Yulia Mikhailovna quickly called me over and asked me in a whisper to run over to Karmazinov and beg him to begin. No sooner had I turned around than there occurred another vile incident, even more horrible than the first. On stage, on the empty stage where all eyes and hopes had been fixed, where there stood only a small table, chair, and a bottle of water on a silver tray—on the empty stage there suddenly appeared the enormous figure of Captain Lebyadkin in a frock-coat and a white tie. I was so astonished I couldn't believe my eyes. The captain, apparently, was embarrassed and paused at the back of the stage. All of a sudden a cry rang out from the audience: 'Lebyadkin! Is that you?' At the sound of this cry the captain's stupid red mug (he was dead drunk) broke into a broad, vacant grin. He raised his hand, wiped his forehead, shook his shaggy head, and, as if capable of anything, he took two steps forward; suddenly he snorted with laughter, not loud, but ringing, prolonged, joyful laughter, that made his whole stout figure heave and his little eyes screw up. At this sight almost half the audience began laughing, and twenty people or so started clapping. The more serious members of the public exchanged gloomy glances; everything happened in no more than half a minute. Liputin suddenly came running on to the stage wearing an usher's ribbon and accompanied by two servants; they cautiously took the captain by both arms and Liputin whispered something to him. The captain frowned and muttered: 'Well, all right.' He waved his arms, turned his huge back to the audience, and disappeared with the escort. But a moment later Liputin appeared on stage again. He wore the sweetest of his smiles, which usually put one in mind of vinegar and sugar, and in his hands he held a piece of notepaper. He approached the edge of the stage with short quick steps.

'Ladies and gentlemen,' he said, turning to the audience, 'As a result of a slight oversight there has occurred a comic misunderstanding which has now been eliminated; but in hope of success I've accepted a commission and a profound, most respectful request from one of our local poets... Moved by a humane and noble goal... in spite of his appearance... the same goal that's brought us all together... to wipe away the tears of the poor, educated young women of our province... this gentleman, that is to say, our local poet... in his desire to remain anonymous... would very much like to see his work read before the beginning of the ball... that is, I mean to say, before the formal reading begins. Even though this poem is not in the programme and wasn't included... because it was received only half an hour ago... it seemed to *us*' (us? I'm quoting his incoherent and confused speech word for word) 'that in view of its remarkable naïvety, combined with its extraordinary gaiety, this poem should be read, I mean, not as a serious work, but as something appropriate to the celebration... In a word, its basic idea... All the more so since it's only a few lines... so I should like to ask the audience's kind permission.'

'Read it!' boomed a voice from the far end of the hall.

'So, shall I read it?'

'Read it, read it!' cried many voices.

'I'll read it, then, with the audience's kind permission,' Liputin said with that same sweet smile on his face. He still seemed undecided and appeared even somewhat agitated. In spite of all their impudence these people still sometimes hesitate. On the other hand, a seminary student would never have hesitated, but Liputin still belonged to the older generation.

'I must warn you, that is, I have the honour of warning you that this work is not exactly the sort of ode that used to be written on festive occasions; it's almost a joke, so to speak, though it's replete with emotion combined with playful gaiety, and, so to speak, the most realistic truth.'

'Read it, read it!'

He unfolded a piece of paper. Of course, no one could stop him. Besides, he was wearing an usher's ribbon. In a resonant voice he declaimed:

'To the Local Governesses of the Fatherland from a Poet on the Occasion of the Fête.

     'Hail, governesses, here's your fête!
     Now it's time to celeberate.
     Reactionary or George Sand,
     Let us give you all a hand!'

'But that's Lebyadkin's work! Yes, it's Lebyadkin's!' several voices cried. Laughter broke out and even some applause, though not very much.

     'Now your job's to overlook
     The children with their grammar-book.
     But if you're quick, you'll wink an eye
     To catch the sexton passing by!'

'Hurrah! Hurrah!'

     'But in the great reforming fever
     The sexton may not have you either.
     You need a spot put by, you see,
     Or else it's back to ABC.'

'Precisely, precisely; now that's realism; nothing without a "spot put by" '!

     'But now that as we have a ball,
     We've made for you some capital.
     You'll have your dowry once for all,
     Sent by us from this very hall—
     George Sand or reactionary,
     Now it's time for making merry.
     Governess, you've got the cash—
     Spit on them, and have a bash!'

I confess I could scarcely believe my ears. This was such obvious impudence that it was impossible to forgive Liputin even on the grounds of stupidity. And Liputin wasn't stupid. His intention was clear, at least to me: to hasten the onset of disorder. A few lines of this idiotic poem, the very last one, for example, were so impudent no stupidity could possibly let it pass. It seems even Liputin felt he'd gone a bit too far: having performed this deed, he was so overcome by his own impudence that he didn't even leave the stage; he stood there as if wanting to add something. He probably expected it would end some other way; but even the small group of ruffians who'd applauded during the recitation suddenly fell silent, as if also overcome. The stupidest thing of all was that many of them took the whole episode seriously, that is, not as a parody, but as the real truth concerning the plight of governesses, as a poem with a political tendency. But the excessive informality of the verse struck even them at last. As regards our public, the entire hall was not only scandalized, but obviously insulted. I'm not mistaken in my impression. Yulia Mikhailovna said afterwards that one moment more and she would have fainted. One of our most respectable old gentlemen helped his lady to her feet and they both left the hall under the watchful gaze of the whole audience. Who knows, perhaps others might have followed their example if at that moment Karmazinov hadn't appeared on stage, in a frock-coat and white tie, holding a notebook in his hand. Yulia Mikhailovna turned her rapturous gaze on him as her saviour... But I was already behind the scenes; I wanted to get my hands on Liputin.

'You did that on purpose!' I cried, seizing his arm in indignation.

'I swear to God, I never thought,' he replied hurriedly, beginning at once to lie and pretend to be upset. 'They brought me the poem just a minute ago and I thought it would be a good joke...'

'You didn't think that at all. Do you really consider that untalented piece of trash a good joke?'

'Yes, sir, I do, sir.'

'You're simply lying, and they didn't bring it you just a minute ago either. You and Lebyadkin composed it together, perhaps yesterday even, to create a scandal. The last line is undoubtedly yours; the part about the sexton is, too. And why did he come on wearing a frock-coat? It must mean you meant him to read, if he hadn't gone and got so drunk.'

Liputin stared at me coldly and sarcastically.

'What business is it of yours?' he asked suddenly with strange composure.

'What do you mean? You're wearing an usher's ribbon too... Where's Peter Stepanovich?'

'I don't know; somewhere around here. What of it?'

'It's just that now I see it all clearly. It's simply a plot against Yulia Mikhailovna, to spoil the day with scandal...'

Liputin looked at me askance once again.

'And what's it to you?' he asked grinning. He shrugged his shoulders and moved away.

I was stunned. All my suspicions were warranted. I was still hoping I'd been mistaken! What could I do? First I thought of conferring with Stepan Trofimovich, but he was standing in front of a mirror, trying out different smiles, constantly referring to a piece of paper on which he'd made some notes. He was supposed to go on immediately after Karmazinov, and was no longer in any state to converse with me. Should I run to Yulia Mikhailovna? It was too soon to go to her: she needed a much harsher lesson to cure her of the conviction that she had a 'following' and everyone was 'fanatically devoted' to her. She'd never believe me and would have thought I was seeing things. And what could she do to help? 'Hey,' I thought, 'what business is it of mine really? *When it begins* I'll remove my usher's ribbon and go home.' I actually did say 'when it begins', that I recall.

But I had to go and hear Karmazinov. Taking a last look around behind the scenes, I noticed a large number of outsiders milling around, including some women, all coming and going. This area 'behind the scenes' was rather narrow, shielded from the audience by a thick curtain, and communicating with other rooms through a long corridor.

It was there our performers awaited their turn. I was
particularly struck at the time by one reader who was
supposed to follow Stepan Trofimovich. He was also a
professor (though even now I'm not quite sure where); he'd
voluntarily left his institution after an episode involving
students and he'd arrived in our town only a few days ago
with some purpose in mind. He too had been recommended
to Yulia Mikhailovna, and she received him with reverence.
I now know he'd been at her house only once before the
reading, and he'd been silent all that evening; he smiled
ambiguously at the jokes and the tone of the company
surrounding Yulia Mikhailovna, and made a rather unpleasant impression on everyone with his arrogant air and his at
the same time easily offended sensibilities. It was Yulia
Mikhailovna who had enlisted him to read. Now he paced
from corner to corner and, like Stepan Trofimovich, whispered to himself; but he looked down at the floor, instead
of at the mirror. And he wasn't trying out any smiles,
although he did smile frequently and rapaciously. Clearly it
was impossible to speak to him either. He was a smallish
man, about forty years old, bald, with a grey beard and
rather well dressed. But the most interesting thing about
him was that with every turn he raised his right fist, waved
it about in the air over his head, and suddenly brought it
down, as if smashing some opponent into the dust. He
performed this gesture continually. I began to feel uncom-
fortable. I hurried away to hear Karmazinov.

3.

Once again in the hall there was a feeling something was
wrong. I must declare in advance: I have great respect for
genius. But why is it that all our men of genius at the end
of their illustrious careers behave like little boys? What of
it if Karmazinov came out on stage looking like five court
chamberlains? Was it really possible to hold the audience's
attention for a whole hour with his article alone? In general
I've observed that even an extraordinary genius would have
difficulty holding the audience's attention with impunity for

more than twenty minutes at a light public literary reading. It's true the appearance of this great literary genius was received with the utmost respect. Even the sternest old men evinced approval and curiosity, and the ladies even manifested some enthusiasm. The applause, however, was short-lived, and somewhat unfriendly and sporadic. On the other hand, in the back rows, there wasn't a single disturbance until Mr Karmazinov began to speak; even then, nothing particularly bad occurred, only some misunderstanding, as it were. I've mentioned before that Karmazinov had a rather high-pitched voice, almost feminine in fact, and he spoke furthermore with a genuine, aristocratic lisp. He'd hardly uttered more than a few words when suddenly someone burst into loud laughter—probably some inexperienced fool who'd never seen much of the world and who was predisposed to such merriment. There was not the slightest indication of any demonstration; on the contrary, the audience shushed the fool and he fell silent. But then Mr Karmazinov announced, in his affected and mincing manner, that 'at first he hadn't wanted to read.' (What need was there to say that?) 'There are', he said, 'some lines which flow straight from the heart, such that one can't say them; it's quite impossible to utter such sacred things in public.' (Why then did he utter them?) 'But, since he'd been asked, he agreed, and since, in addition, he was laying down his pen for ever and had sworn never to write anything again, be that as it may, he'd written this last piece; and since he'd sworn never again to read anything in public, then, be that as it may, he'd read this last article', and so on and so forth—all in this vein.

All this wouldn't really have mattered; besides, who's not familiar with authorial introductions? Although I must observe that the low level of general education among our public and the widespread irritability of the back rows must have had an impact on the proceedings. Wouldn't it have been better to read a short story, a tiny little tale of the kind he used to write before—something I dare say highly polished and affected, but with some wit? It would have saved the day. But, no, sir, that was not to be! The oration* had begun! My God, what wasn't there in it! I can state categorically that even a crowd from the capital would've been stupefied, not just that audience. Imagine: almost thirty pages of the most affected and useless chatter. In addition, this gentleman recited as from on high, in melancholy tones, as if doing us all a favour; as a result our public felt actually somewhat offended. The theme... who could possibly discern the theme? It was an account of some impressions, recollections. But of what? About what? However much we knit our provincial brows during the first half of his reading, we could make nothing of it, so we listened to the second half merely out of courtesy. True, a great deal was said about love, the love of a genius for a particular person, but, I must confess, it all seemed a little awkward. In my opinion it wasn't at all appropriate for this short, plump figure of a great writer to be talking about his first kiss... And, what was also offensive, these kisses were somehow different from those exchanged by ordinary mortals. There was always a gorse bush around somewhere (it had to be gorse or some other plant one needed a botanical dictionary to identify). And there was always some violet tint in the sky, which, of course, no mortal had ever seen before; that is, everyone had seen it, but no one knew how to appreciate it, while 'I', he said, 'looked at it and describe it for you fools, as if it were the most ordinary thing.' The tree under which the fascinating couple sat had always to be of some orange hue. They are sitting somewhere in Germany. All of a sudden they behold Pompey or Cassius on the eve of a battle, and both experience a cold shudder of ecstasy. Some kind of water sprite begins squeaking in the bushes. Gluck* starts playing the violin among the reeds. The name of the piece is given *en toutes lettres*, but no one's ever heard of it, and one has to consult a musical dictionary. Meanwhile a mist billows; it billows and billows so much, it's more like a million pillows than a mist. Suddenly it all disappears and now the great genius is crossing the Volga during a thaw in winter. There are two and half pages of crossing; still he falls through a hole in the ice. The genius is drowning—do you think he drowns? Not on your life; all this shows that when he's nearly drowned and is gasping for breath, he catches sight of an ice floe, a tiny little ice floe no bigger than a pea, but pure and transparent, 'like a frozen tear', and in this ice floe all of Germany is reflected, or, to be more precise, the sky of Germany, and the iridescent sparkle reminds him of the same tear which, 'you recall, flowed from your eyes as we sat beneath that emerald tree and you joyfully exclaimed, "There is no crime!" "Yes," I replied through my tears, "but if that's true, there are no righteous men either." We burst into tears and parted for ever.'

She goes off somewhere to the seashore, he to some cave or other; he goes down, down, for three years he goes down beneath the Sukharyov tower in Moscow, and suddenly, in the very bowels of the earth, in the cave, he finds an icon lamp, and in front of the lamp sits a hermit. The hermit is praying. The genius presses his face against the iron grating on the little window and suddenly hears a sigh. Do you think it was the hermit who sighed? He doesn't care a bit about that hermit of yours! No, sir, the simple truth is that the sigh 'reminds him of her first sigh, some thirty-seven years ago', when, 'you recall, we were sitting under the tree of agate and you said to me, "Why love? Look, okra is growing all around and I'm in love, but when the okra stops growing, I'll stop loving."' Then the mist billows again, Hoffmann appears, a mermaid whistles a tune from Chopin, and suddenly from out of the mist, wearing a crown of laurels, Ancus Martius* appears above the roofs of Rome. 'A shudder of ecstasy ran up and down our spines and we parted for ever,' and so on and so forth.

In a word, perhaps I'm not conveying it all properly, and can't convey it all properly, but the theme of all that chatter was something of the sort. And really, what a disgraceful fondness all our great intellects share for word-play in the highest sense! The great European philosopher, the great scholar, the inventor, the toiler, the martyr—all those who labour and are burdened for the sake of our great Russian genius are really akin to so many cooks standing around in a kitchen. He's the master, and they come to him hat in hand awaiting his orders. True, he sneers scornfully at

Russia and likes nothing better than to declare the bank-
ruptcy of Russia in all respects before the great intellects of
Europe; but regarding his own intellect—no, sir, he's already
ascended to a much higher level than all the intellects of
Europe. They're merely material for his wit. He adopts
someone else's idea, interweaves it with its own antithesis,
and his witticism is complete. There's such a thing as crime;
there's no such thing as crime; there's no truth, there are
no righteous men; atheism, Darwinism, the bells of Moscow... Alas, he no longer believes in the bells of Moscow;
Rome, laurels... but he doesn't believe in laurels... Then
there's the required attack of Byronic spleen, a grimace from
Heine, something or other from Pechorin*—and he's off,
he's off, his engine roaring... 'But praise me, praise me, I
enjoy it so much. I'm only saying I'm laying down my pen.
Wait a while and I'll bore you three hundred times more.
You'll get tired of reading me...'

Of course, it didn't go very well; but worst of all, it was
his own fault. For some time people had been shuffling their
feet, clearing their throats, coughing, and doing everything
people do when a writer, whoever he is, keeps an audience
at a literary reading for more than twenty minutes. But our
writer of genius didn't notice a thing. He continued lisping
and mincing, without paying the least attention to his
audience; everyone was bewildered. Then all of a sudden in
the back row there rang out a solitary, but loud voice:

'Good Lord, what nonsense!'

This exclamation escaped quite involuntarily and, I'm
sure, was not intended as a demonstration. The man was
simply tired. But Mr Karmazinov stopped, looked at the
audience ironically, and with the bearing of an aggrieved
court chamberlain, suddenly lisped:

'It seems, ladies and gentlemen, I've bored you to tears?'

It was his own fault—he was the first to speak; by
provoking a reply, he made it possible for the rabble to
speak out and, as it were, to do so legally. If he'd restrained
himself, they'd have gone on blowing their noses, and it all
would have ended somehow... Perhaps he was expecting
applause in reply to his question; but there wasn't any

applause. On the contrary, they all seemed to be afraid, they shrank into themselves and fell silent.

'Why, you've never even seen Ancus Martius; that's just your style,' cried one irritated, even somewhat exasperated person suddenly.

'Precisely,' another chimed in at once. 'There're no ghosts nowadays, only natural science. Consult the natural sciences.'

'Ladies and gentlemen, least of all did I expect such objections,' said Karmazinov, terribly surprised. The great genius had lost all touch with his fatherland while living in Karlsruhe.

'In this day and age it's a disgrace to say that the world rests on the backs of three fishes,' one young lady chirped up suddenly. 'Besides, Karmazinov, you couldn't possibly have gone down into a cave and met a hermit. Who talks about hermits nowadays anyway?'

'Ladies and gentlemen, what surprises me most is that you take it all so seriously. But you're absolutely right. No one respects the real truth any more than I do...'

Although he was smiling sarcastically, he was considerably shaken. His face seemed to say: 'I'm not at all who you take me for; I'm on your side. But praise me, praise me more, as much as possible, I like it so much...'

'Ladies and gentlemen,' he cried at last, now genuinely aggrieved. 'I see my poor little poem is out of place here. It seems that I, too, am out of place here.'

'He aimed for a crow and hit a cow,' some idiot shouted as loud as he could; he must have been drunk, and no one should have paid him any attention at all. True, disrespectful laughter followed.

'Hit a cow, you say?' Karmazinov repeated at once. His voice was becoming shriller. 'I'll restrain myself, ladies and gentlemen, on the subject of crows and cows. I have too much respect for my audience to permit comparisons, however innocent. But I thought...'

'If I were you, sir, I'd be more careful...' cried someone from the back row.

'Here I thought that in laying down my pen and bidding farewell to my readers I would be listened to...'

'No, no, we want to hear you, we do...' a few brave voices cried out at last from the front row.

'Go on, go on!' cried a few ecstatic female voices; finally there was even some applause, though weak and scattered. Karmazinov smiled wryly and got up from his chair.

'Believe me, Karmazinov, we consider it a great honour...' even the marshal's wife couldn't refrain from saying.

'Mr Karmazinov,' one fresh, youthful voice cried suddenly from the back of the hall. It was the very young teacher from the local school, a fine young man, quiet and honourable, who'd just arrived in town. He got up from his seat. 'Mr Karmazinov, if I'd had the good fortune to fall in love as you just described, I certainly wouldn't have included it in an article read to the general public...'

He went quite pink.

'Ladies and gentlemen,' cried Karmazinov, 'I've finished. I'll skip the ending and leave now. But let me read just the last six lines.

'Yes, dear reader, farewell!' he resumed, reading his manuscript without sitting down in his chair. 'Farewell, reader. I won't even insist we part as friends: why should I trouble you? You may even abuse me; oh, abuse me as much as you like, if it pleases you. But it would be best if we merely forgot each other for ever. And if all of you, my readers, were suddenly to become so kind as to fall on your knees to implore me with tears: "Write something, oh, write something for us, Karmazinov—for the fatherland, for posterity, for the laurel wreath"—even then I'd reply, after thanking you very courteously, of course: "No, my dear fellow-countrymen, we've had quite enough of each other, *merci*! It's time for us to go our separate ways! *Merci, merci, merci*." '

Karmazinov bowed ceremoniously and, as red as if he'd been cooked, disappeared behind the scenes.

'No one's falling on his knees; that's pure fantasy.'

'What conceit!'

'It's merely his sense of humour,' someone more sensible corrected him.

'Well, spare us your idea of humour.'

'That's real impudence, ladies and gentlemen.'

'At least he's finished.'

'Ugh, what a boring programme!'

All these ignorant remarks from the back row (but not only from the back row) were drowned out by applause from another part of the audience. They called for Karmazinov. A few ladies led by Yulia Mikhailovna and the marshal's wife, crowded on stage. In her hands Yulia Mikhailovna held a sumptuous laurel wreath on a white velvet cushion inside a wreath of fresh roses.

'Laurels!' cried Karmazinov with a faint and slightly sarcastic smile. 'Naturally, I'm very moved; with deep emotion I accept this wreath which, though prepared in advance, has not yet faded. But let me assure you, *mesdames*, I've suddenly become such a realist that in this day and age I consider laurels much more appropriate in the hands of a skilful cook than in my own hands...'

'Yes, a cook is more useful,' cried the seminary student who was present at that 'meeting' at Virginsky's. There was a little disorder. In many rows, people jumped up to watch the presentation of the laurel wreath.

'I'd pay another three roubles for a good cook right now,' another voice said loudly, almost too loudly, insistently loudly.

'Me, too.'

'Me, too.'

'Is there really no buffet here?'

'Why, it's simply a swindle...'

It must be admitted, however, that all these unruly gentlemen were still very much afraid of our high officials and the police commissioner who was also present in the hall. After about ten minutes or so they took their seats again; but the previous sense of order was never re-established. It was into this incipient chaos that poor Stepan Trofimovich blundered.

4.

I ran to him behind the scenes once again and managed to warn him in some excitement that in my opinion the whole thing had fallen through and it was better not to appear on stage at all, but to leave and go home at once, pleading an upset stomach. I would remove my usher's ribbon and leave with him. At that moment he was on his way to the stage and suddenly stopped, looked me haughtily up and down, and enquired solemnly:

'Just why, my dear sir, do you consider me capable of such baseness?'

I retreated. I was convinced as two times two makes four that he wouldn't get out of there without catastrophe. Meanwhile as I stood there in utter despondency, there flashed before me once again the figure of the new arrival, the professor whose turn it was to read after Stepan Trofimovich and who earlier on had been raising and lowering his fist with all his might. He was still pacing up and down, absorbed in himself, muttering under his breath with a malicious but triumphant grin. Almost without meaning to (something impelled me again), I went up to him.

'Do you know,' I said, 'many examples have shown that if a reader holds his audience for longer than twenty minutes, it stops listening. Not even a celebrity can hold an audience for half an hour...'

He stopped short and seemed actually to shudder at the insult. His face took on a look of immense disdain.

'Don't worry,' he muttered contemptuously and went past me. At that moment Stepan Trofimovich's voice could be heard in the hall.

'Oh, to hell with the lot of you!' I thought and ran back into the hall.

Stepan Trofimovich sat himself down in the chair even before the disorder had died down. He was greeted in the front rows by some unfriendly looks. (Of late people at the club had stopped liking him and lost a good deal of their respect for him.) But just the fact that they didn't boo him was already something. I'd had a strange premonition since the day before: I expected them to boo him from the moment he appeared. Meanwhile, because of the disorder in the hall, they hardly noticed him at first. What could this man possibly hope for if they'd treated Karmazinov so badly? He was pale; he hadn't appeared in public for ten years. Judging from his agitation and signs I knew all too well, it was clear that he looked upon his appearance today on stage as a turning-point in his fate, or something like that. This man was dear to me. Imagine how I felt when he opened his mouth and I heard his first phrase!

'Ladies and gentlemen!' he said all of a sudden, as if resolved to go through with it, and, at the same time, in a voice that was almost breaking. 'Ladies and gentlemen! Only this morning I had before me one of the illegal pamphlets distributed here recently, and for the hundredth time I asked myself: "What's the big secret?" '

The entire hall fell silent immediately; all eyes were turned on him, some filled with alarm. There was no doubt he had got them interested right from the start. Even from behind the scenes heads poked out; Liputin and Lyamshin listened avidly. Yulia Mikhailovna waved her hand at me again:

'Stop him, stop him no matter what!' she whispered in alarm. I merely shrugged my shoulders; is it possible to stop a man once he's *resolved to go through with it*? Alas, I understood Stepan Trofimovich.

'Hey, he's going on about those pamphlets!' several people whispered in the audience; the entire hall was stirring.

'Ladies and gentlemen, I've solved the mystery. The whole secret of their effect is their stupidity!' His eyes were sparkling. 'Yes, ladies and gentlemen, if this stupidity had been intentional, fabricated—oh, then it would have been brilliant! But we must do them justice: they didn't fabricate anything. It's the barest, most naïve, silliest little stupidity—*c'est la bêtise dans son essence la plus pure, quelque chose comme un simple chimique.*[1] If it had been just a tiny bit cleverer, everyone would've seen the poverty of this silly stupidity at once. But now everyone stands perplexed: no one believes it was so genuinely stupid. "There can't possibly be nothing to it," everyone says to himself, hoping to discover the

---

[1] It's stupidity in its purest essence, something like a basic chemical element.

secret, wanting to read between the lines—and they've got the result they wanted! Oh, never before has stupidity been so triumphantly rewarded, in spite of the fact that it's so often deserved it... For, *en parenthèse*, stupidity, like the greatest genius, also serves to shape human destiny...'

'These are catch-phrases from the forties!' cried a rather modest voice, after which general commotion ensued with everyone shouting and yelling.

'Ladies and gentlemen, hurrah! I propose a toast to stupidity!' Stepan Trofimovich shouted, defying the audience in an absolute frenzy.

I ran up to him under the pretext of pouring him a glass of water.

'Stepan Trofimovich, stop now, Yulia Mikhailovna implores you...'

'No, you stop, you idle young man!' he shouted at me as loud as he could. I fled. '*Messieurs!*' he continued, 'why all this agitation, why these shouts of indignation? I've come with an olive branch. I've brought the last word, since in this matter I have the last word—and we'll make peace.'

'Down with him!' some people shouted.

'Quiet. Let him speak. Let him have his say,' cried others. The young teacher was especially agitated; having once dared to speak, he couldn't stop himself.

'*Messieurs*, the last word in this affair is universal forgiveness. As an old man I solemnly declare that the spirit of life still breathes in us, and the younger generation still possesses the life force. The enthusiasm of our youth is just as bright and pure as it was in our own day. Only one thing has happened: aims have changed, one kind of beauty has been replaced by another! The entire misunderstanding lies in the question of which is more beautiful: Shakespeare or a pair of boots, Raphael or petroleum?'

'Is he an informer?' wondered some.

'What compromising questions!'

'*Agent provocateur!*'

'But I declare,' Stepan Trofimovich screeched at the highest pitch of excitement, 'I declare that Shakespeare and Raphael are more important than the emancipation of the serfs, more important than nationalism, more important than socialism, more important than the younger generation, more important than chemistry, almost more important than humanity, because they are the fruit, the genuine fruit of humanity, and perhaps the most important fruit there is! The form of beauty already attained—without which I might not agree to live out my life... Oh, Lord!' he cried, clasping his hands, 'ten years ago I shouted these same words from a stage in Petersburg, the same words exactly, and they didn't understand a thing then either; they laughed and booed just as you're doing now. Silly people, why is it you still don't understand? Don't you know mankind can survive without your Englishman, without Germany, and certainly without Russians, without science, without bread—but not without beauty, for then there'd be nothing left to do on earth! The whole secret, the whole of history lies in that! Science itself won't stand up for one minute without beauty—don't you know that, you, who laugh at me—it will turn into a vulgar charade. You'll not even be able to invent so much as a nail!... I won't back down!' he shouted idiotically in conclusion and banged his fist down on the table with all his might.

While he was screeching without sense or order, the uproar in the hall increased. Many people jumped from their seats, others surged forward up to the stage. Altogether this took place much faster than I can describe, and there was no time to take appropriate steps. Perhaps no one even wanted to.

'It's fine for you to talk since you have everything you want, you spoilt creatures!' roared the seminary student, standing right next to the stage and grinning broadly at Stepan Trofimovich, who noticed him and rushed to the edge.

'I just said, didn't I, that enthusiasm in the younger generation is still as bright and pure as it was, but that it was perishing simply because it was mistaken about the forms of beauty. Isn't that enough for you? And if you consider that the person proclaiming this is a crushed and insulted father himself, then surely—oh, you petty little people—surely you can rise to greater heights of impartiality and detachment?... You ungrateful people... you unjust people... Why, why don't you want to make peace?'

He suddenly burst into hysterical sobs. He wiped away his streaming tears with his hands. His shoulders and chest were heaving from the sobs... He was oblivious to everything in the world.

The audience was seized with genuine panic and almost everyone got up from their seats. Yulia Mikhailovna jumped up quickly, seized her spouse by the arm and lifted him out of his chair... The affair had turned into an enormous public scandal.

'Stepan Trofimovich!' the seminary student roared gleefully. 'There's an escaped convict named Fedka roaming around in town and hereabouts. He robs people and not long ago committed another murder. Allow me to enquire: if you hadn't sold him into the army fifteen years ago to pay a gambling debt, or, more simply, if you hadn't lost him at cards, tell me, do you think he'd have landed in prison? Would he be slitting people's throats as he is now in his struggle to survive? What you do think, Mr Aesthete?'

I refuse to describe the ensuing scene. In the first place, there was a furious outburst of applause. Not everyone clapped, only about one-fifth of those present, but the applause was intense. The rest of the audience rushed for the exit, but since those who were clapping kept crowding forward to the stage, general confusion ensued. Ladies screamed, several young girls started to cry and asked to be taken home. Von Lembke was standing by his seat, gazing wildly around him. Yulia Mikhailovna was at an utter loss—for the very first time since she'd begun her career among us. As for Stepan Trofimovich, at first he seemed literally crushed by the seminary student's words; but all of a sudden he raised both his hands, as if extending them over the audience, and he shouted:

'I shake the dust from my feet and curse you... It's the end... the end...'

Turning around, he ran off the stage behind the scenes, waving his arms menacingly.

'He's insulted society!... Get Verkhovensky!' some people shouted furiously. They even wanted to go after him. It was impossible to dissuade them, at least at that moment, and suddenly the final catastrophe burst like a bomb over the gathering and exploded in its midst: the third reader, that maniac who kept waving his fist about behind the scenes, suddenly came out on to the stage.

He looked quite mad. With a broad, triumphant grin, full of immeasurable self-assurance, he scrutinized the agitated hall and seemed pleased by the disorder. He wasn't the least bit upset at having to read in the midst of such confusion; on the contrary, he was obviously delighted. This was so obvious that he immediately attracted attention.

'What's this now?' people started to ask. 'Who's this fellow? Shh! What does he want to say?'

'Ladies and gentlemen!' shouted the maniac with all his might, standing at the edge of the stage and speaking in the same shrill, feminine voice as Karmazinov had, but without the aristocratic lisp. 'Ladies and gentlemen! Twenty years ago on the eve of war with half of Europe, Russia represented as an ideal in the eyes of all state and privy councillors. Literature was controlled by censorship; military drill was taught in our universities; the army was turned into a ballet and people paid their taxes and kept silent under the yoke of serfdom. Patriotism had come to mean extorting bribes from the living and the dead. Those who didn't take bribes were considered rebels since they threatened the harmony of the existing order. Birch groves were destroyed to support the system. Europe trembled... But never before in all her one thousand years had Russia sunk to such infamy...'

He raised his fist, waved it enthusiastically and menacingly above his head, and suddenly brought it down violently, as if smashing his enemy to smithereens. A furious cry burst forth on all sides, drowned out by deafening applause. Almost half the people in the audience were clapping; the most innocent people were carried away. Russia was being dishonoured openly and publicly and how was it possible not to roar with delight?

'That's it! Now that's it! Hurrah! Yes, so much for aesthetics!'

The maniac continued rapturously:

'Twenty years have passed since then. Universities have been opened and have multiplied. Military drill has become a thing of the past; we're short of thousands of army officers. Railways have consumed all our resources and have covered Russia like a spider's web; the result is that fifteen years from now, perhaps, one may actually be able to get somewhere. Bridges catch fire only occasionally, but towns burn down frequently, in a well-established order, taking their turn, during fire season. In our courtrooms we get judgements of Solomon, while members of the jury take bribes simply in their struggle for existence, threatened as they are with starvation. Serfs have been liberated and now flog each other with cudgels instead of being flogged by their former owners. Seas and oceans of vodka are consumed to support the budget; in Novgorod, right opposite the ancient and useless Church of St Sofia, they're triumphantly erecting an enormous bronze globe* to commemorate one thousand years of disorder and confusion. Europe frowns and once again begins to be restless... Fifteen years of reform! Meanwhile, even during its most grotesque periods of reform, Russia has never sunk so low...'

His last words could hardly be heard in the roar of the crowd. He was seen to raise his fist and bring it down again triumphantly. The enthusiasm of the crowd knew no limits: people yelled, clapped their hands, even some women shouted, 'Enough! You can't do better than that!' They acted like drunkards. The orator looked out over the crowd and seemed to dissolve in his own triumph. I observed in passing that von Lembke, indescribably agitated, was pointing out something to someone. Yulia Mikhailovna, white as a sheet, was saying something hurriedly to the prince who'd come running up to her... But at that moment a crowd of about six people, more or less official, burst on to the stage from behind the scenes, seized the orator, and dragged him off into the wings. I don't understand how he could've got away from them, but he did, and once more he emerged, came to the edge of the stage, and managed to shout for all he was worth, waving his fist:

'But Russia has never sunk so low...'

Again he was dragged away. I saw about fifteen men rush off behind the scenes to rescue him; they didn't come across the stage, but from the side, knocking into the flimsy partition so it finally fell over... Then, unable to believe my own eyes, I saw a female student (Virginsky's relative) suddenly jump on the stage with the same bundle of papers under her arm, wearing the same dress, looking just as plump, surrounded by two or three women, two or three men, and accompanied by her mortal enemy, the gymnasium student. I even caught what she said:

'Ladies and gentlemen, I've come to describe the sufferings of unfortunate students and incite them to a general protest.'

But I ran off. I hid the usher's ribbon in my pocket, left by a rear door I knew about, and managed to get out of the house and on to the street. First of all, of course, I set out for Stepan Trofimovich's.

CHAPTER 2

The conclusion of the fête

I.

HE wouldn't see me. He'd locked himself in and was writing. To my repeated knocks and calls he answered through the door:

'My friend, I'm done with everything. Who can ask any more from me?'

'You're not done with anything; you've only helped make this mess of everything. For heaven's sake, Stepan Trofimovich, open up and no more jokes. We must take steps; they might still come over here and try to insult you...'

I thought I was entitled to be so severe with him, even insistent. I was afraid he might attempt to do something even more insane. But, to my astonishment, I encountered extraordinary determination:

'Don't you be the first to insult me. I'm very grateful for all you've done for me in the past, but I repeat, I'm done with everyone, both good and bad. I'm writing a letter to Darya Pavlovna, someone I've neglected unforgivably up to now. You may deliver it to her tomorrow, if you like, but for now, *merci*.'

'Stepan Trofimovich, I can assure you this is a more serious matter than you know. Do you think you demolished anyone over there? You didn't; you yourself were shattered like an empty glass jar.' (Oh, I really was so rude and impolite; I recall it now with regret!) 'This is certainly not the time to write to Darya Pavlovna... how can you possibly manage without me? What do you know about practical things? You're probably planning to do something foolish? You'll get into trouble again, if you're planning something...'

He got up and came to the door.

'You haven't spent much time with them, but you've been infected by their language and tone. *Dieu vous pardonne, mon ami, et Dieu vous garde.*[1] I've always noticed the makings of

---
[1] May God forgive you, my friend, and may God protect you.

a decent man in you; perhaps you'll reconsider—*après le temps* of course, just like all Russians. As for your comment about my impracticality, let me remind you of one of my cherished ideas: here in Russia we have an enormous number of people whose sole occupation it is to attack others for their impracticality. They do so with absolute ferocity and particular persistence, like flies in summer, accusing everyone except themselves. *Cher*, remember I'm very upset; don't torment me. Once again, *merci* for everything; let's part as Karmazinov did with his public, that is, let's forget each other as generously as possible. He was being insincere when he repeatedly asked his former readers to forget him; *quant à moi*, I'm not so vain; more than anything I'm relying on the youthfulness of your uncorrupted heart. Why should you remember a useless old man for very long? "Long life," my friend, as Nastasya wished me on my last birthday (*ces pauvres gens ont quelquefois des mots charmants et pleins de philosophie*).[1] I don't wish you much happiness—it'd bore you; I don't wish you misfortune; but in accordance with the philosophy of the people, I wish you simply: "Long life." Try somehow or other not to get too bored; this useless wish I add from myself. Well, goodbye then, good-bye for good. And don't stand there at my door; I won't open it.'

He went away and I could get nothing more out of him. In spite of his 'upset' he spoke smoothly, unhurriedly, and solemnly, obviously trying to impress me. Of course, he was a little irritated with me and was indirectly taking his revenge, perhaps even for yesterday's 'prison-carts' and 'trap-doors'. The tears he shed in public that morning, in spite of his triumph of a sort, left him, as he himself knew, in somewhat of an absurd position; there was no one who cared more about aesthetics and strict form in his relations with friends than Stepan Trofimovich. Oh, I'm not blaming him! But this fastidiousness of his and this sarcasm, maintained in the face of all these shocks, somewhat reassured me at the time. A man who, to all appearances, had changed

---

[1] (these poor people sometimes say charming things, full of philosophy)

so little from his ordinary self was certainly in no danger of doing anything tragic or extraordinary at that moment. That's how I reasoned at the time; my God, what a mistake I made! There were so many factors I failed to take into consideration...

Anticipating events somewhat, I'll quote the first few lines of the letter that Darya Pavlovna received the very next day:

Mon enfant, my hand is trembling, but I've done with everything. You weren't present at my last struggle with people; you didn't come to that 'reading' and it was a good thing you didn't. You'll be told that here in Russia, where men of character are so lacking, there arose one bold man and, in spite of death threats showered on him from all sides, he told these fools the truth, that is, that they were nothing but fools. *O, ce sont des pauvres petits vauriens et rien de plus, des petits* fools—*voilà le mot!*[1] The die is cast; I'm leaving this town once and for all and I don't know where I'm going. All those I once loved have turned away from me. But you, you, a pure and innocent creature, you, so meek, whose life was almost linked to mine at the whim of a capricious and imperious heart, you, perhaps, who looked at me with contempt as I shed tears of weakness on the eve of our wedding which never took place, you who cannot, whoever you are, regard me as anything but a ridiculous figure, oh, to you, to you alone goes out this last cry of my heart, my last duty is to you, to you alone! I can't leave you for ever with the thought that I'm an ungrateful fool, an ignoramus and an egotist as I am portrayed, no doubt, by a cruel and ungrateful heart, which, alas, I can never forget...

And so on and so forth, four rather large pages in all.

After banging my fist on his door three more times in reply to his 'I won't open it', and after shouting to him that he'd send Nastasya to fetch me at least three times that day, but that I wouldn't come, I left him and sped off to see Yulia Mikhailovna.

2.

There I witnessed a shocking scene: the poor woman was being deceived to her face, and there was nothing I could

---

[1] Oh, they are pitiful little scoundrels, and nothing more, little fools—that's the word!

do about it. Indeed, what could I say to her? I'd already managed to come to my senses and realize that all I had to go on were some vague feelings, suspicious intuitions, and nothing more. I found her in tears, almost hysterics, with eau-de-cologne compresses on her head and a glass of water in her hand. In front of her stood Peter Stepanovich who never stopped talking, and the prince, who never said a word, as if his lips had been sealed. With tears and lamentations she was reproaching Peter Stepanovich for 'deserting' her. I was immediately struck by the fact that she attributed the failure of the fête, the entire fiasco of that morning, in a word, absolutely everything, to Peter's absence.

I observed one important change in him: he appeared to be overly concerned about something, almost serious. Ordinarily he was never serious; he was always laughing, even when angry, and he was often angry. Oh, he was very angry now; he spoke rudely, carelessly, with irritation and impatience. He assured Yulia Mikhailovna he'd been suffering from a terrible headache and an attack of vomiting at Gaganov's apartment, where he'd dropped by early that morning. Alas, the poor woman desperately wanted to be deceived by him. The main question I found being debated was the following: would the second part of the fête, the ball, take place or not? Yulia Mikhailovna couldn't be persuaded to appear at the ball after all those 'earlier insults'; in other words, she desperately wanted to be persuaded to appear, and by none other than him, Peter Stepanovich. She regarded him as an oracle; it looked as though if he were to walk out on her at that moment, she'd immediately take to her bed. But he was not about to walk out on her; it was absolutely essential to him that the ball take place that very evening and that Yulia Mikhailovna should make an appearance there...

'Well, what's there to cry about? Must you absolutely make a scene? Must you vent your rage on someone? Well then, vent it on me, but be quick about it because time's running out and you must decide. They spoiled the reading, but we'll make up for it at the ball. The prince shares my opinion. Yes sir, if it hadn't been for the prince, who knows how it might have ended?'

At first the prince had been against the ball (that is, against Yulia Mikhailovna's appearing at it; the ball, in any event, had to take place), but after two or three such allusions to his opinion, he gradually began mumbling something as a sign of consent.

I was also struck by the unusual rudeness of Peter Stepanovich's tone. Oh, I absolutely reject the vile gossip spread around afterwards concerning an alleged liaison between Yulia Mikhailovna and Peter Stepanovich. There was nothing of the sort, nor could there be. From the very beginning he conquered her merely by supporting with all his might her dreams of having an influence on society and on the administration; he entered into her schemes, invented others for her, flattered her in gross ways, entangled her from head to foot, and became as essential to her as the air she breathed.

Her eyes flashed when she saw me and she cried:

'There now, ask him. Just like the prince he never left my side the whole time. Tell me, isn't it obvious this is all a conspiracy, a vile, cunning conspiracy, to do as much damage to me and Andrei Antonovich as possible? Oh, they arranged the whole thing beforehand! They had a plan. It's a group of conspirators, a whole group!'

'You're carrying it a little too far, as usual. You've always got some romantic notion in your head. But I'm very glad to see Mr...' (he pretended to have forgotten my name). 'He'll give us his opinion.'

'My opinion', I said hurriedly, 'is in complete agreement with Yulia Mikhailovna's. The conspiracy is all too obvious. I've brought you back these ribbons. Whether or not the ball takes place—of course, that's not my business because it's not within my power to decide—but my role as usher is at an end. Forgive my passion, but I can't act against the dictates of common sense and my own convictions.'

'Do you hear, do you hear?' she cried, throwing up her hands.

'I hear you, sir, and this is what I have to say to you,' he said, turning to me. 'I can only suppose that you've all consumed something or other that's brought on this delirium. In my opinion nothing whatsoever occurred, absolutely nothing that hasn't occurred before and that couldn't occur in any provincial town. What kind of conspiracy? It turned out rather badly, disgracefully stupidly. But where on earth is the conspiracy? Is it against Yulia Mikhailovna, against their own staunch supporter and protector, who forgives all their childish pranks? Yulia Mikhailovna! What have I been telling you over and over for the last month? What have I warned you about? Why, why on earth did you invite all those people? Why did you get involved with those creatures? Why, what on earth for? To unite society? But will it ever really be united, for heaven's sake?'

'When did you warn me? On the contrary, you encouraged me, you even demanded... I must confess, I'm pretty astonished that... You yourself introduced me to many peculiar characters.'

'On the contrary, I argued with you; I didn't encourage you. As for introducing you—that I did, but only after dozens of them had swarmed in on their own, and only recently, to fill out your "literary quadrille", because you couldn't complete it without those brutes. But today I bet another dozen or so managed to get in without tickets.'

'No doubt about it,' I agreed.

'There, you see, you're agreeing already. Just remember the mood that's been prevalent of late in this little town. Why, it's been nothing but shameless impudence, an uninterrupted scandal. And who encouraged it? Who used her authority to protect them? Who led them astray? Who incited the rabble? Why, in your album all their local family secrets are recorded. Wasn't it you who patted the heads of all those poets and artists? Didn't you allow your hand to be kissed by Lyamshin? Wasn't it in your presence the seminary student abused a state councillor and spoiled his daughter's dress with his tarred boots? Why are you so surprised now that the public is roused against you?'

'But it was all your doing, it was *you*! Oh, my God!'

'No, ma'am, I warned you, we quarrelled, do you hear, we quarrelled.'

'You're lying right to my face.'

'Of course it's easy for you to say that. Now you need a victim to vent your wrath; well then, vent it on me, as I've said. I'd do better to talk to you, Mr...' (He still couldn't remember my name.) 'Let's count up on our fingers: I maintain that apart from Liputin there was no conspiracy, none what-so-ever! I'll prove it; let's begin with an analysis of Liputin. He came out on stage with some verses by that idiot Lebyadkin—is that what you call conspiracy? Don't you think Liputin might simply have considered it all very amusing? Yes, seriously, seriously, merely amusing. He came on stage with a desire to amuse everyone, to entertain, first and foremost to amuse his own protectress Yulia Mikhai-lovna, and that's that. Don't you believe me? Doesn't that fit the spirit that's prevailed here the last month? If you like, I'll say it all: so help me God, in other circumstances he might even have pulled it off! It was a crude joke, a bit obscene, but it was amusing, wasn't it?'

'What! You consider Liputin's action amusing?' Yulia Mikhailovna cried in fearful indignation. 'Such stupidity, tactlessness, vileness, meanness; and his intention—you're saying it was done on purpose? Then you must be involved in the conspiracy with them!'

'Absolutely, I was sitting right behind them, hiding, pulling all the strings. Why, if I'd been participating in their conspiracy—you must understand this at least—it wouldn't have ended with Liputin alone! I suppose you think I'd arranged with my dear father that he would deliberately cause such a scandal? Well, madam, who was to blame for allowing my father to read? Who tried to stop you yesterday, only yesterday?'

'*Oh, hier il avait tant d'esprit*,[1] I was so counting on him; besides, he has such nice manners. I thought that both he and Karmazinov... and then!'

'Yes, ma'am, and then. But in spite of all his *tant d'esprit*, my dear father made quite a mess of it; if I myself had known in advance what a mess he'd make, then as a member

---

[1] Oh, he was so witty yesterday

of this indubitable conspiracy against your fête, I certainly
wouldn't have tried to dissuade you yesterday from letting
the billygoat into the vegetable garden, isn't that so? But I
did try to dissuade you yesterday—I tried because I had a
premonition of what might happen. Of course it was impossible to foresee everything: he himself probably didn't
know a minute beforehand what he was going to come out
with. These nervous old men hardly resemble real people!
But the situation can still be saved: to satisfy the public
send two doctors by administrative order to visit him tomorrow with all due ceremony to enquire about his health;
you can even do it today. Then have him sent straight to
hospital, to be treated with cold compresses. At least
everyone will laugh and see there's nothing to be offended
at. I could even announce it at the ball tonight, since I'm
his son. Karmazinov is another matter altogether; he made
a complete ass of himself and dragged out his article a full
hour—of course he must be part of the conspiracy with me!
"I'll make a mess of it," he must have thought, "just to
harm Yulia Mikhailovna!" '

'Oh, Karmazinov, *quelle honte*! I was burning with shame
for our public!'

'Well, ma'am, I wouldn't have burned, I'd have cooked
him instead. The public was right. And who was to blame
for Karmazinov? Did I foist him upon you or not? Have I
been one of his admirers or not? Well, to hell with him.
And as for the third maniac, the political speaker, now that's
a different matter. Everyone made a blunder there, not just
my conspiracy.'

'Oh, don't even mention it; it was awful, just awful! That
was my fault, all my fault!'

'Of course, ma'am, but I'll excuse you for that one. Why,
who's to keep an eye on them, those people who speak their
minds? Even in Petersburg you can't guard against them.
After all, he came to you well recommended; I'll say he did!
So you must agree that now you're actually obliged to make
an appearance at the ball. It's very important, since it was
you who put him on the platform. You must declare in
public that you don't share his opinions, that the fellow is

already in the hands of the police, and that you were deceived in some inexplicable manner. You must announce with indignation that you fell victim to a madman. After all, he is a madman, nothing more than that. That's the way you should refer to him. I can't stand these fellows who bite. I could say even worse things perhaps, but never from a platform. And now they're shouting about a senator.'

'What senator? Who's talking?'

'Look, I myself know nothing about it. You haven't heard anything about a senator, have you, Yulia Mikhailovna?'

'A senator?'

'You see, they're convinced a senator has been appointed from Petersburg to replace you here. I've heard that from many people.'

'I've heard it too,' I said in confirmation.

'Who said so?' cried Yulia Mikhailovna.

'You mean, who said it first? How should I know? It's just what they say. People are talking. Yesterday in particular they were talking about it. Everyone was being rather serious, although it was hard to make anything out. Of course, the more intelligent and competent people aren't talking, but even some of them are listening to what's being said.'

'What vileness! And... what stupidity!'

'Well, that's why you must appear in public now, to show those fools.'

'I must confess I do feel myself that I'm really obliged to, but... what if some further disgrace awaits me there? What if people don't show up? No one will come, no one, no one at all!'

'What a fuss! They won't come? What about all the new clothes and the girls' dresses? After that statement I simply refuse to recognize you as a woman. Such knowledge of human nature!'

'The marshal's wife won't come, she won't!'

'After all is said and done, what actually happened? Why won't they come?' he cried at last in bad-tempered impatience.

'Dishonour, disgrace—that's what happened. I don't know exactly what happened, but now I can't possibly go.'

'Why not? How was it your fault? Why are you taking the blame on yourself? Isn't the public more to blame, our elders, the heads of families? They should've restrained those scoundrels and sluggards—because that's what they were, scoundrels and sluggards, nothing more serious. There's no kind of society anywhere where the police alone can maintain order. Everyone here demands a special policeman assigned to protect him wherever he goes. People don't understand that society must protect itself. What do our heads of families do in comparable circumstances, our venerable elders, wives, and daughters? They keep silent and sulk. There's not even enough social initiative to restrain the pranksters.'

'Oh, that's absolutely true! They keep silent, sulk and... look about them.'

'Well, if it's true, you must say so now, aloud, proudly, sternly. Precisely to show them you aren't beaten. To show those old men and all those mothers. Oh, you can do it, you have the gift when your head is clear. You'll gather them around you and say it out loud. Then you'll send it to correspondents for the *Voice* and the *Financial Times*.* No, wait, I'll see to that myself; I'll arrange it for you. Of course, there must be more supervision, especially at the buffet; ask the prince, ask Mr... You can't possibly abandon us, *monsieur*, just when we have to start all over again. Well, last but not least, you and Andrei Antonovich, arm in arm. How is Andrei Antonovich?'

'Oh, you've always judged that angelic man so unfairly, so wrongly, so insultingly!' Yulia Mikhailovna cried suddenly with unexpected emotion; almost in tears she raised her handkerchief to her eyes. At first Peter Stepanovich was taken aback:

'Good Lord, I... but what have I... I've always...'

'Never, you've never! You've never given him what he deserved.'

'One can never understand a woman!' Peter Stepanovich muttered with a wry smile.

'He's the most righteous, most sensitive, most angelic of men! And the kindest of men!'

'Good Lord, but what have I ever said about his goodness... I've always acknowledged his goodness...'

'Never! But let's drop the subject. I haven't defended him very well. Earlier that little Jesuit, the marshal's wife, also made a few sarcastic remarks about what happened yesterday.'

'Well, now she has no time to be dropping hints about that; she has today to worry about. And why are you so concerned she might not come to the ball? Of course she won't come after getting herself involved in such a scandal. She may not be at fault, but she has her reputation to think about; her dainty little hands have been soiled.'

'What on earth? I don't understand: why are her hands soiled?' Yulia Mikhailovna asked in consternation.

'I mean, I'm not absolutely certain, but the whole town is saying it was she who brought them together.'

'What? Brought whom together?'

'Oh, you mean you still don't know?' he cried in well-simulated amazement. 'Stavrogin and Lizaveta Nikolaevna, of course!'

'What? How?' we all cried.

'Then you really don't know? Phew! Why, all sorts of tragic romances have taken place: Lizaveta Nikolaevna switched from the marshal's wife's carriage into Stavrogin's and then slipped off to Skvoreshniki with the "aforementioned gentleman" in broad daylight. Only an hour ago, less even.'

We were stunned. Of course we began showering him with questions, but to our surprise, even though he'd 'inadvertently' witnessed the scene, he really couldn't tell us very much about it. This is what seemed to have happened: when the marshal's wife was driving Liza and Maurice Nikolaevich from the 'reading' to Liza's mother's house (her legs were still aching), there was a carriage waiting to one side not far from the main entrance, only twenty-five paces or so. Liza jumped out and ran over to the other carriage; its door flew open and then slammed shut. Liza cried to Maurice Nikolaevich: 'Have mercy on me!' and the carriage headed off to Skvoreshniki at full speed. In reply to our insistent questions, 'Had it all been arranged?' 'Who was in the carriage?' Peter Stepanovich said he didn't know any-thing; of course it had all been arranged, but he didn't see Stavrogin in the carriage; it could've been his old footman Aleksei Yegorych. In reply to the questions, 'How did you happen to be there?' and 'How do you know they were heading to Skvoreshniki?' he said that he happened to be there simply because he was passing by, and, catching sight of Liza, he'd actually run over to the carriage (although he didn't make out who was sitting inside, for all his curiosity!), and that Maurice Nikolaevich not only failed to set off in pursuit, but didn't even try to stop Liza, and even restrained the marshal's wife who was shouting at the top of her lungs: 'She's going to Stavrogin, she's going to Stavrogin!' At that moment I suddenly lost all patience and shouted furiously at Peter Stepanovich:

'It was you, you villain, you who arranged it all! That's what you were doing all morning. You helped Stavrogin, you drove up in the carriage, you let her in... it was you, you, you! Yulia Mikhailovna, he's your enemy; he'll destroy you too! Beware of him!'

And I ran headlong out of the house.

To this very day I'm still astonished and don't understand how I could have shouted those words at him. But I'd guessed the truth: as it later turned out, everything occurred almost exactly as I'd described. The giveaway was the obviously contrived manner in which he announced what had happened. He hadn't blurted it out immediately upon entering the house, as his prime and most sensational item of news; instead he pretended we already knew without him—which was absolutely impossible in so short an inter-val. And if we had known, we couldn't have kept silent about it until he raised it. Nor could he have heard that the whole town was 'buzzing' about the marshal's wife, also because the interval was so short. Besides that, as he related what happened, he was grinning in a somewhat vulgar and frivolous way, probably because he considered us such fools and entirely deceived.

But I was no longer concerned about him; I believed the basic truth of his story and rushed away from Yulia Mikhailovna's house quite beside myself. The catastrophe had struck me to the very heart. I was wounded almost to the point of tears; yes, I may even have wept. I had no idea what to do. I rushed to Stepan Trofimovich, but the tiresome man still refused to see me. Nastasya assured me in a respectful whisper that he was having a rest, but I didn't believe it. I managed to interrogate the servants in Liza's house; they confirmed the fact of her flight, but didn't know any more about it. The house was in state of confusion; the ailing mistress was having fainting spells and Maurice Nikolaevich was attending her. It was impossible to summon him. As for Peter Stepanovich, in reply to my questions, I was informed that he'd been dropping in for the last few days, sometimes even twice a day. The servants were glum and spoke about Liza with special reverence; they were very fond of her. I had no doubt whatever that her reputation was ruined, absolutely ruined, but I was entirely unable to comprehend the psychological aspect of the affair, especially after yesterday's scene with Stavrogin. To run around town and make enquiries at the houses of malicious acquaintances where the news certainly must have spread by then seemed both repugnant to me and humiliating for Liza. Strange to say, I did go to see Darya Pavlovna where, by the way, I wasn't received (no one had been received at the Stavrogins' house since the day before). I don't know what I could have said to her or why I even went. From there I went to her brother. Shatov listened to me sullenly and in silence. I must note I found him in an unbelievably gloomy mood; he was terribly pensive and heard me out only with considerable effort. He said almost nothing and began pacing up and down, from corner to corner, around his little room, stamping in his boots even more than usual. When I was already on my way downstairs he shouted that I should go see Liputin: 'You'll find out everything there.' But I didn't go to Liputin; instead, having already gone some way, I turned and retraced my steps to Shatov's house. Pushing open his door halfway without entering, I asked him laconically and without any explanation, 'Would he be going to see Marya Timofeevna today?' In reply Shatov just swore, so I left. I'll note here, so as not to forget, that he deliberately went to the other side of town that evening to see Marya Timofeevna whom he hadn't seen for a long time. He found her in very good health and good spirits, but Lebyadkin was dead drunk, fast asleep on a sofa in the outer room. This was precisely at nine o'clock. He told me that himself the next day when we met briefly on the street. By ten o'clock that evening I'd decided to go to the ball, but not as a 'young usher' (since my ribbon had been left with Yulia Mikhailovna); I went simply out of an overwhelming curiosity to hear (without asking) what people were saying about these events in general. I also wanted to have a look at Yulia Mikhailovna, if only from a distance. I reproached myself a great deal for having run away from her house that afternoon.

3.

That entire night with all its almost absurd events and its horrible denouement toward morning still haunts me like a hideous nightmare and comprises—for me, at least—the most painful part of my chronicle. Even though I arrived at the ball late, I still got there before it was over—though it was destined to end so abruptly. It was past ten when I arrived at the entrance of the marshal's house where the White Hall, the same one in which the reading had taken place, in spite of the short time elapsed, had already been cleared and prepared for use as the main ballroom for the entire town, as was assumed. But, however much I'd opposed the ball earlier that morning, I still had no premonition of the full truth: not a single family from our high society showed up; even the more important civil servants absented themselves—and that was a very striking fact. As for the ladies and young girls, Peter Stepanovich's recent calculations (now known to be perfidious) turned out to be utterly incorrect: very few came. There was hardly one woman to every man, and what women they were! 'Certain' wives of regimental officers, post office employees or low-ranking civil servants; three doctors' wives with their daughters; two or three impoverished landowners' wives;

seven daughters and one niece of the secretary I mentioned earlier; merchants' wives—was this what Yulia Mikhailovna had expected? Even from among the merchants only about half came. As far as men were concerned, in spite of the absence of all our notables, there was still a rather large crowd of them in attendance, but this crowd produced an ambiguous and suspicious impression. Of course, there were a few quiet, respectable army officers with their wives, a few of the most obedient heads of families like the secretary, for example, with his seven daughters. All these humble, insignificant people had come because it was 'unavoidable', as one of these gentlemen had expressed it. On the other hand, the crowd of slick individuals, and, in addition, the crowd of people whom Peter Stepanovich and I had earlier suspected of having got in without tickets, seemed to have increased since that afternoon. So far they were all sitting in the buffet where they'd gathered soon after arriving, as if agreed upon beforehand. At least that's how it seemed to me. The buffet was located at the end of a long series of rooms in a spacious hall where Prokhorych had been installed together with all the delicacies of the club's kitchen, as well as a tempting display of hors d'œuvres and beverages. I noticed several people sitting there whose jackets were almost in tatters, wearing the most dubious attire, not at all appropriate for a ball, who'd obviously sobered up for the occasion with considerable effort and not for long, and heaven only knows where they'd sprung from, not from our town anyway. I knew, of course, it had been Yulia Mikhailovna's intention to make the ball as democratic as possible, 'admitting even tradesmen, if they had enough money to purchase tickets'. She could utter these words boldly at a meeting of her committee in full confidence that it would never occur to even one of our local shopkeepers, all of whom lived in poverty, to buy a ticket. Still, I doubted whether this gloomy and shabbily dressed crowd should have been admitted, in spite of the committee's democratic sentiments. But who let them in and for what purpose? Liputin and Lyamshin had already been deprived of their ushers' ribbons (even though they were present at the ball and particpated in the 'literary quadrille'); but to my amazement Liputin's place had been taken by the former seminary student who'd caused the biggest scandal at the 'literary matinee' by his tussle with Stepan Trofimovich, and Lyamshin's place had been taken by none other than Peter Stepanovich. Given these circumstances, what could one possibly expect? I tried to listen in on conversations. Some opinions astonished me by their eccentricity. For example, in one group it was maintained that Yulia Mikhailovna herself had arranged Liza's elopement with Stavrogin and had received money for her services. They even said how much. They said she'd even organized the entire fête with this very purpose in mind; that was why half the town had failed to appear—they'd discovered what was up. And Lembke himself was so overwhelmed that 'his reason had become deranged' and she was now 'leading him around like a madman'. There was also a great deal of laughter—hoarse, wild, sarcastic laughter. Everyone was terribly critical of the ball and Yulia Mikhailovna was abused without restraint. In general the babble was disorderly, incoherent, drunken, and very agitated, so it was hard to make anything out or reach any conclusions. At the buffet there were some cheerful people who were merely enjoying themselves; there were also some ladies of the sort who were never surprised or frightened by anything; they were nice, convivial ladies, most of them officers' wives, there with their husbands. They were seated at little tables, cheerfully drinking their tea. The buffet had turned into a cosy refuge for almost half the guests. But in a short time the entire mass of people would have to stream into the ballroom; it was a horrifying prospect.

Meanwhile in the White Hall three sparse quadrilles had been organized with the help of the prince. Some young ladies were dancing and their parents stood by admiring them. But even then many of the esteemed guests had begun to consider how, after providing a little amusement for their daughters, they could slip away quickly, well before 'the trouble started'. Everyone was absolutely convinced that it would. It's hard for me to depict Yulia Mikhailovna's state of mind. I didn't get a chance to chat with her, though I was able to get near her. She didn't respond to my bow as I entered, since she didn't notice me (she really didn't). Her face was sickly, her look contemptuous and arrogant, but unsettled and agitated. With obvious exertion she managed to control herself—but for whom and for what? She should have left immediately and, most importantly, taken her husband away with her; but she stayed! One could already see from the look on her face that her eyes had been 'opened entirely' and now there was nothing more for her to expect. She didn't even summon Peter Stepanovich to her side (he seemed to be avoiding her; I caught sight of him in the buffet and he was extremely cheerful). But she remained at the ball none the less and didn't let Andrei Antonovich out of her sight even for a minute. Oh, up to the last moment, even that very morning, she would've rejected with genuine indignation any hint about his health. But now her eyes were to be opened on this subject as well. As for me, from my first glance Andrei Antonovich looked to me worse than he had that morning. He appeared to be in a state of oblivion and didn't even know where he was. Sometimes he looked around suddenly with unexpected severity, twice at me, for example. Once he tried to talk. He began saying something very loudly, but didn't finish, giving a meek, elderly civil servant standing next to him a bit of a shock. But even this meeker half of the public in the White Hall avoided Yulia Mikhailovna glumly and timidly, while at the same time casting very strange glances at her husband, glances so frank and insistent as to be quite out of keeping with the timidity of these people.

'That was what struck me so forcefully and I suddenly began to guess the truth about Andrei Antonovich,' Yulia Mikhailovna herself admitted to me later.

Yes, once again it was all her own fault! Probably after my hasty departure from her house earlier that day she and Peter Stepanovich had decided the ball should take place and that they'd be there; she'd probably gone to his study to find Andrei Antonovich, utterly 'shattered' as he was by the matinée, had employed all her charm once again, and persuaded him to come with her. But how she must have been suffering now! And she still didn't leave! Was it pride tormenting her or had she simply forgotten where she was—I don't know. In spite of all her arrogance she tried with a smile and a feeling of humiliation to converse with some ladies, but they immediately became flustered and dissociated themselves with mistrustful monosyllables, 'Yes, ma'am', 'No, ma'am', obviously trying to avoid her.

The only person of indisputed consequence who showed up at the ball was that same pompous retired general whom I described above and who, at the marshal's house, after the duel between Stavrogin and Gaganov, 'opened the door to public impatience'. He paraded through the rooms with a dignified air, looking and listening and trying to pretend he'd come more to observe local customs than for his own amusement. He ended up by attaching himself to Yulia Mikhailovna and didn't leave her for a moment, evidently trying to soothe and reassure her. Without doubt he was a very kind man, dignified, and old enough for one to be able to tolerate even his compassion. But she was very annoyed at having to admit to herself that this old windbag dared pity and almost patronize her, realizing that he was honouring her by his presence. But the general didn't leave her side and kept talking without ever stopping.

'A town, they say, cannot exist without seven righteous men... seven is the number, I think, I don't remember ex-act-ly. I don't know how many of these seven men... the indisputably righteous men of our town... have the honour of attending your ball, but, in spite of their presence, I'm beginning to feel somewhat unsafe. *Vous me pardonnerez, charmante dame, n'est-ce pas?*[1] I'm speaking allegorically, but I stopped at the buffet and I'm glad to get back here safe and sound... Our inestimable Prokhorych is not quite in his proper place, and I'm afraid his booth may be destroyed by morning. But I'm only joking. I'm merely waiting to see how the "literary quadrille" turns out, then I'm going home to bed. You must forgive an old man who suffers from gout;

---

[1] You'll forgive me, charming lady, won't you?

I go to bed early, and advise you to go "beddy-bye" too, as they say *aux enfants*. I came for the pretty young ladies... whom I can never get to meet in such wide variety except at a place like this... They're all from the other side of the river, and I never go there. The wife of one officer... an infantry officer, I believe... isn't all that bad-looking, and she's very... and she knows it. I was talking to the mischievous little imp; she's very lively and... well, the young girls are fresh as well. But that's all; besides their freshness, there's nothing to them. Still, I'm enjoying myself. There are some fresh young buds here, but they all have thick lips. In Russian beauty generally there's little regularity to women's faces and... they even resemble pancakes... *Vous me pardonnerez, n'est-ce pas*... even though they have pretty little laughing eyes. These fresh buds are *enchanting* for two years or because of their youth, perhaps even three years... then they open out and are gone for ever... producing in their husbands that sad *indifference* which plays such an important role in the development of the woman question... if I understand that matter properly... Hmm. The hall is quite nice; the rooms aren't badly decorated. It could be worse. The music could be much worse... I'm not saying it should be. The fact that there are so few women in general makes a bad impression. I won't even comment on their attire. It's disgraceful how that fellow in grey trousers dares dance the cancan so openly. I could forgive him if were dancing from joy and since he's our local pharmacist... but eleven o'clock is still rather early, even for pharmacists... There in the buffet two men were fighting and weren't even thrown out. At eleven o'clock anyone fighting should have been thrown out, whatever the customs of our public... I'm not talking about two or three in the morning—then one has to make concessions to public opinion—if this ball lasts till three in the morning. But Varvara Petrovna didn't keep her word and failed to provide the flowers. Hmm, she had no time to think about flowers, *pauvre mère*! Have you heard about poor Liza? They say it's all rather mysterious and... once again Stavrogin is in the middle of it... Hmm. I should've gone home to bed... I can hardly keep my eyes open. When will the "literary quadrille" begin?'

At long last the 'literary quadrille' began. Lately whenever the subject of conversation in town was the forthcoming ball, the focus of attention was always this 'literary quadrille' since no one could imagine what form it would take; therefore it aroused immense curiosity. Nothing could be more hazardous to its success—and what a big disappointment it turned out to be!

The side doors of the White Hall opened and suddenly there appeared several figures wearing masks. The public surrounded them eagerly. Everyone at the buffet, to the last man, rushed into the hall at once. The masked figures took up their places for the dance. I managed to squeeze my way up to the front and I took up a position right behind Yulia Mikhailovna, von Lembke, and the general. Just then Peter Stepanovich, who'd so far been keeping out of sight, came running up to Yulia Mikhailovna.

'I've been in the buffet on watch,' he whispered with the look of a guilty schoolboy, a look he'd assumed just to irritate her even more. She flared up.

'I wish you'd stop deceiving me once and for all, you insolent creature!' she blurted out almost aloud; her remark was overheard by several people. Peter Stepanovich scurried away, looking very pleased with himself.

It would be difficult to imagine a more pitiful, vulgar, untalented and tasteless allegory than the 'literary quadrille'. It was impossible to conceive of anything more inappropriate for our public, although it was said to have been Karmazinov who thought it up. It's true that Liputin organized it, in consultation with the lame teacher who'd attended that evening gathering at Virginsky's. But Karmazinov had provided the inspiration; it's said he even wanted to dress up and play a special role in it. The quadrille consisted of six pathetic pairs of masked figures—it was almost as if they weren't masked at all because they were dressed in ordinary clothes, just like everyone else. Thus, for example, one elderly gentleman of average height was dressed in a frock-coat—in a word, like the rest of us—had a venerable grey beard (false, and this constituted his entire disguise); he danced by stamping up and down on the same spot with a very serious expression on his face, making rapid little steps and hardly moving from his place. He emitted some sounds in a low, husky bass voice; this huskiness was supposed to represent one of our best-known newspapers.* Opposite him two giants, X and Z, were dancing; these letters were fastened on to their frock-coats, but no one knew quite what the letters stood for. 'Honest Russian thought' was depicted in the shape of a middle-aged gentleman wearing glasses, a frock-coat, gloves and... handcuffs (genuine handcuffs). Under his arm this figure was carrying a briefcase with some important 'affair'.* An open envelope with a foreign post-mark was sticking out of his pocket, authenticating the honesty of 'honest Russian thought' to convince any scep-tics. All this was explained aloud by the ushers since it was impossible to read any words on the letter in his pocket. In his upraised right hand the figure of 'honest Russian thought' held a goblet, as if wishing to propose a toast. Flanking him on both sides two closely-cropped young nihilist women pranced, while *vis-à-vis* another middle-aged gentleman in a frock-coat was dancing. He held a heavy oak cudgel in his hand and was said to represent some formi-dable periodical published outside Petersburg:* 'I'll wipe you off the face of the earth.' But in spite of his cudgel he couldn't stand the bespectacled gaze of 'honest Russian thought' aimed at him, and tried to look away. When he danced his *pas de deux* he twisted and turned and didn't know what to do with himself—no doubt because his con-science was tormenting him... But I really can't recall every one of their obtuse inventions; it was all in the same style more or less and I felt terribly embarrassed by it. And it was precisely that impression, a sort of embarrassment, that was reflected in the entire public, even on the gloomiest of faces rushing in from the buffet. For a while everyone was silent and watched in hostile perplexity. Usually a person who's so embarrassed begins to get angry and finally becomes cynical. Gradually the audience began to stir:

'What's going on?' muttered one man who'd come from the buffet with his little group.

'Some kind of stupidity.'

'It's about literature. They're criticizing *The Voice*.'

'What do I care?'

From another group:

'Jackasses!'

'No, they're not jackasses, we are.'

'Why are you a jackass?'

'I'm not a jackass.'

'Well, if you're not a jackass, I'm certainly not one either.'

From a third group:

'We should beat the hell out of them and send them packing!'

'Tear down the whole hall.'

From a fourth group:

'The Lembkes should be ashamed to watch!'

'Why them, ashamed? Aren't you ashamed?'

'Even I'm ashamed, but he's the governor.'

'And you're a pig.'

'Never in my life have I seen such an uninteresting ball,' said one lady viciously who was standing next to Yulia Mikhailovna, obviously with a desire to be overheard. This lady was about forty years old, plump and heavily made-up, wearing a bright silk dress; she was known by almost everyone in town, but received by no one. She was the widow of a state councillor and had been left only a wooden house and a meagre pension; still she lived rather well and managed to keep some horses. About two months ago she'd been the first to pay a visit to Yulia Mikhailovna, who'd refused to receive her.

'It's just as I imagined,' she added, looking Yulia Mikhailovna right in the eye.

'If you imagined it, then why on earth did you come?' Yulia Mikhailovna couldn't resist asking.

'It was silly of me,' the bold lady replied at once, becoming very agitated (she was spoiling for a fight); but the general placed himself between them:

'*Chère dame*,' he said bending over Yulia Mikhailovna, 'you really ought to leave. We're only getting in their way; they'll have a fine time without us. You've done all you could; you opened the ball for them; well, leave them in peace... And it seems Andrei Antonovich doesn't quite feel sat-is-fac-to-ry... I hope there won't be any trouble.'

But it was already too late.

Throughout the quadrille Andrei Antonovich was looking at the dancers in a kind of angry perplexity; when the murmuring started in the audience, he began looking around uneasily. Then for the first time he caught sight of some of the characters in the buffet; his face expressed extreme astonishment. Suddenly raucous laughter burst out over one of the figures in the quadrille: the publisher of the 'formidable periodical published outside Petersburg', dancing with the cudgel in his hands, feeling once and for all that he could no longer stand the bespectacled gaze of 'honest Russian thought', but not knowing how to get away, suddenly, in the last figure, went to meet him walking on his hands, which, by the way, was supposed to represent how this 'formidable periodical published outside Petersburg' constantly turned good common sense on its head. Since only Lyamshin could walk on his hands, it was he who'd been chosen to play the part of the publisher with the cudgel. Yulia Mikhailovna had no idea he would walk on his hands. 'They kept that from me, kept it from me,' she repeated afterwards in despair and indignation. The raucous laughter from the crowd was occasioned not by the allegory, of course, since no one gave a damn about that, but simply by the spectacle of someone walking on his hands wearing a frock-coat with tails. Von Lembke flew into a rage and started to shake.

'Scoundrel!' he cried, pointing at Lyamshin. 'Seize that rascal, turn him over... grab his legs... his head... so the head is on top... on top!'

Lyamshin jumped to his feet. The laughter grew even louder.

'Throw out all the rascals who are laughing!' von Lembke suddenly ordered. The crowd started to murmur and roared with laughter.

'That's impossible, your excellency.'

'You shouldn't abuse the public, sir.'

'He's a fool!' one voice cried out from the corner.

'Filibusters!' someone cried from the other end.

Von Lembke turned quickly at this last cry and went pale. A dumb smile appeared on his face, as if he suddenly remembered something and understood.

'Ladies and gentlemen,' said Yulia Mikhailovna, turning to the advancing crowd while she drew her husband along behind her, 'ladies and gentlemen, you must excuse Andrei Antonovich. He's not feeling well... excuse him, forgive him, ladies and gentlemen!'

I heard it quite clearly: she said 'forgive him.' The whole scene occurred very quickly. But I distinctly remember that one part of the audience was already heading for the door, as if in alarm, right after hearing those words from Yulia Mikhailovna. I even recall one woman's hysterical cry through her tears:

'Oh, it's just like what happened before!'

All of a sudden another bomb burst in the midst of this crush heading for the door, in this 'just like before':

'Fire! The whole river bank's in flames!'

I don't remember where that terrible cry first arose: whether it came from one of the rooms or someone came running upstairs from the entry, but it was followed by such a commotion as I can't begin to describe. More than half the people in attendance at the ball came from the other side of the river—they were proprietors or inhabitants of the wooden houses there. They rushed to the windows, pulled back the curtains in an instant, and tore down the blinds. The river bank was in flames. It's true, the fire had just started, but it was blazing in three separate spots—that's what was so frightening.

'Arson! The Shpigulin men!' people in the crowd shouted.

I recall several typical exclamations:

'In my heart and soul I knew they'd set something on fire; I've felt it coming for a long time.'

'The Shpigulin men, Shpigulin men, no one else!'

'They got us all here deliberately so they could set the fires.'

This last, most astonishing cry came from a woman; it was the unpremeditated, involuntary cry of a Korobochka,* all of whose possessions were on fire. Everyone rushed towards the exit. I won't begin to describe the crush in the entry as people grabbed their coats, shawls, and cloaks, or the shrieks of frightened women and cries of young ladies. I don't think there were any deliberate thefts, but it wasn't surprising that in such disorder several people left without their coats because they were unable to find them; this fact was much talked about afterwards and grew into a legend with considerable embellishment. Von Lembke and Yulia Mikhailovna were almost crushed by the crowd in the doorway.

'Stop them all! Don't let any of them leave!' screamed von Lembke, waving his arms menacingly at the people. 'Search everyone, without exception, immediately!'

A violent storm of protest arose from the crowd.

'Andrei Antonovich! Andrei Antonovich!' cried Yulia Mikhailovna in utter despair.

'Arrest her first!' he cried, pointing a menacing finger at his wife. 'Search her first! This whole ball was organized for the purpose of setting fire to...'

She cried out and fainted (oh, this time it was a genuine faint, of course). The prince, the general and I all rushed to her aid; there were others who helped us at that terrible moment, even some ladies. We carried the poor woman out of that inferno to her carriage; she came to her senses only as they approached their own house and her first utterance was again about her husband. With the destruction of all fantasies right before her eyes the only thing she had left was Andrei Antonovich. The doctor was sent for. I waited there at the house for an hour as did the prince; in a burst of generosity (even though he himself was very frightened), the general insisted on remaining at the 'poor woman's bedside' throughout the night, but ten minutes later, even before the doctor arrived, he fell asleep on an armchair in the hall just where we'd deposited him.

The police commissioner, who'd hastened from the ball to the fire, had managed to drag Andrei Antonovich behind him and had hoped to install him next to Yulia Mikhailovna in their carriage, trying his best to persuade his excellency to 'get some rest'. I don't understand why he didn't insist on it. Of course Andrei Antonovich didn't want to hear anything about 'rest' and was anxious to get to the fire; but that wasn't a good enough reason. It ended with the police commissioner escorting the governor to the fire in his own carriage. It was later reported that von Lembke gesticulated wildly all the way there and 'kept shouting bizarre orders that were impossible to follow'. It was subsequently reported that at the time his excellency was suffering from delirium as a result of his 'sudden fright'.

There's no need to describe how the ball ended. A few dozen merrymakers together with several ladies remained behind in the halls. There were no police. They wouldn't release the orchestra and beat up any musician who tried to leave. Towards morning they pulled down 'Prokhorych's booth', drank themselves into a stupor, danced the Komarinsky with wild abandon, defiled the rooms, and only at daybreak did a part of this rabble, completely drunk, arrive at the scene of the fire in time to create additional disturbances... The other half, dead drunk, remained to spend the night in the halls, with the usual traces left on the velvet divans and the floor. In the morning at the earliest possible moment, they were dragged by the feet on to the street. Thus ended the fête organized for the benefit of governesses in our province.

4·

The fire alarmed the residents of the other side of the river precisely because it was so obviously a case of arson. It's worth noting that the first cry of 'Fire!' was followed immediately by the assertion that 'the Shpigulin men had set the fire.' By now it's already a well-established fact that three of Shpigulin's men did indeed take part in setting the fire, but no more; all the rest of the factory workers were fully exonerated both officially and by public opinion. Besides those three scoundrels (one of whom was caught and confessed, while the other two are still at large), Fedka the convict undoubtedly had a hand in setting the fire. That's all we really know for sure about the fire's beginning; conjectures are another matter altogether. What inspired these three scoundrels? Were they acting on someone's orders or not? It's very hard to answer these questions even now.

Owing to the strong wind, the fact that almost all the houses on the other side of the river were wooden, and finally, the fact that fires had been set in three separate places, the conflagration spread quickly and enveloped the entire quarter blazing furiously (actually fires were set in only two spots; the third was stopped and extinguished almost immediately, but more about that later). But the accounts published in all the Moscow and Petersburg newspapers greatly exaggerated the disaster: not more than (and perhaps even less than) approximately one quarter of the entire town on the other side of the river was consumed by fire. Our brigade, even though inadequate relative to the size of our town and its population, responded in a very prompt and selfless manner. But it could have done very little, in spite of all the help it received from the inhabitants, if it hadn't been for the change in the wind which suddenly died down just before dawn. No more than an hour after our flight from the ball, when I made my way to the river bank, the fire was already blazing away furiously. The entire street parallel to the river was in flames. It was as bright as day. I won't begin to describe in detail the scene of the conflagration: who in Russia is unfamiliar with such a sight? The commotion and crush in the side streets adjacent to the one in flames was huge. The residents were certainly expecting the fire to spread and were dragging their possessions outside, yet were still not abandoning their houses; they sat waiting on top of trunks and feather-beds, each under his own windows. A part of the male population was engaged in hard labour, ruthlessly chopping down wooden fences, even razing entire huts which were standing closer to the fire and downwind from it. Only the children who'd been woken up were crying; women who'd already dragged their worldly goods out were howling and wailing. Those who hadn't finished were silently and energetically at work. Sparks and embers were flying in all directions; they were extinguished as quickly as possible. Spectators crowded around the fire itself, having come from all parts of town. Some helped to put it out, others stood around gazing at the sight. A large conflagration at night always produces an exciting and exhilarating impression; this explains the attraction of fireworks. But there you have fire displayed in graceful, controlled forms and, what with the absence of danger, it creates a pleasant, playful impression, like a glass of champagne. But a real fire is something different: the horror and vague feeling of personal danger, added to the thrilling effect of a night fire, produce in the spectator (not, of course, in those whose houses have gone up in flames) a certain shock to the system and as it were a challenge to the destructive instincts which, alas, lie buried within each and every soul, even that of the meekest and most domestic civil servant... This grim sensation is almost always intoxicating. 'I really don't know whether it's possible to watch a fire without a certain enjoyment.' That's word for word what Stepan Trofimovich said to me once after returning from a night fire he'd come upon by chance while still under the initial impression the spectacle made on him. Needless to say, that same admirer of nocturnal conflagrations would rush into the flames to save a child or an old woman from burning; but that's a different matter altogether.

Following close behind the curious crowd, without having to make any enquiries, I managed to reach the most central and dangerous spot where at long last I caught sight of von Lembke whom Yulia Mikhailovna had asked me to find. He was in an astonishing and extraordinary position. He stood astride the remains of a wooden fence; on his left, some thirty paces away, rose the blackened skeleton of a two-storey wooden house that had burned almost entirely; it had holes instead of windows on both floors, the roof had caved in, and flames were still creeping among the charred beams. At the end of the courtyard, some twenty paces away from the burnt-out house, a two-storey wooden annexe had also started to smoulder, and firemen were trying to save it with all their might. On the right the firemen and the crowd were trying to preserve a rather large wooden building which wasn't engulfed in flames yet, but had caught fire several times, and was doomed to burn inevitably. Facing the annexe, von Lembke shouted and gesticulated, giving orders that no one carried out. He seemed to have been deposited there and left to his own devices. At least, in the vast and diverse crowd surrounding him, composed of people of all classes including some gentlemen and even the priest from our cathedral, although they were listening to him with curiosity and amazement, no one was talking to him or trying to lead him away. Von Lembke was pale, his eyes gleaming, and he was uttering the most astonishing words; in addition he was standing there bareheaded, having lost his hat some time ago.

'It's all arson! It's nihilism! If anything is burning, it's nihilism!' I heard almost in horror. Although there was nothing to be surprised at, still there's always something shocking about reality when it stares you right in the face.

'Your excellency,' said a policeman, popping up next to him, 'perhaps you ought to go home and get some rest, sir... It's dangerous even for your excellency to be standing here.'

This policeman, as I later found out, had been dispatched by the commissioner to keep watch over Andrei Antonovich and try his best to get him home; in the event of danger, he was even supposed to employ force. The task was obviously beyond the man's power.

'They'll wipe away the tears of those whose houses have been destroyed, but they'll burn down the whole town. It's those four scoundrels, four and a half. Arrest that scoundrel! It's all his doing; the other four and a half were slandered by him. He insinuates himself into the honour of families. They used the governesses to set fire to our houses. It's disgraceful, disgraceful! Hey, what's he doing over there?' he cried, suddenly noticing a fireman on the roof of the burning annexe; the roof was already in flames and the fire was flaring up. 'Pull him down, pull him down! He'll fall in! He'll catch fire! Extinguish him... What's he doing there?'

'He's putting out the fire, your excellency.'

'Not likely. The fire is in the minds of men and not on roofs of houses. Pull him down and give it all up! It's better to give it up, give it up! Let it put itself out somehow! Hey, who's that crying? An old woman! An old woman is crying. Why have they forgotten the old woman?'

And, in fact, on the lower floor of the burning annexe an old woman was standing shouting; she was the eighty-year-old relative of the merchant who owned the burning house. But she hadn't been forgotten; she herself had returned to the annexe while she still could with the insane idea of rescuing her feather-bed from the corner room still untouched by the fire. Choking from smoke and screaming from the heat, because now her little room had caught fire, she still persisted with all her might in trying to squeeze her feather-bed through the broken window pane with her feeble hands. Lembke rushed to help her. Everyone saw him run up to the window, seize the end of the feather-bed, and begin to pull it through with all his might. As bad luck would have it, a rafter from the roof caved in at that very moment and struck the wretched man. It didn't kill him; it merely grazed his neck as it fell, but it ended Andrei Antonovich's career, at least in our town; the blow knocked him off his feet and he fell down unconscious.

At last the gloomy, dismal day dawned. The fires diminished; after the wind died down silence descended, followed by a light drizzle, as fine as if it came through a sieve. I was already in the another part of the burned area, far from the place where von Lembke had fallen, and there I overheard some rather strange conversations among the crowd. One curious fact was discovered: at the very edge of the district, on a piece of wasteland beyond the allotments, no less than fifty paces from other buildings, there stood one small recently built wooden house; this little house had caught fire at the very beginning of the conflagration, almost before all others. If it had burnt down, it couldn't have set fire to any other buildings in town because of its distance from them; the opposite was also true—if the entire part of town on that side of the river had burnt, this one house would have remained untouched, no matter how strong the wind. It turned out it had caught fire separately and independently from all the rest, and so there had to be some reason for it. But the point was it didn't burn down completely, and towards dawn some astonishing things were discovered in it. The owner of this new house, a tradesman who lived not far away, as soon as he noticed the fire raging, rushed to it; with the help of his neighbours, he managed to halt its progress by scattering logs which had been placed against the side wall and set on fire. But there were lodgers in the house—the captain, well-known in our town, his sister, and their elderly servant, and all three, the captain, his sister, and the servant had been murdered and apparently robbed that very night. (That was where the police commissioner had got to when von Lembke was trying to rescue the feather-bed.) By morning the news had spread and a large crowd of all sorts of people, even some whose houses had burnt down, flocked to the piece of wasteland in the direction of the new house. It was difficult to move, given the mass of people. I was informed immediately that the captain had been found with his throat cut, lying on a bench, fully clothed; he must have been dead drunk when killed, so he didn't feel a thing; he'd bled profusely, 'like a bull'. His sister Marya Timofeevna had been 'stabbed repeatedly' with a knife and lay on the floor in the doorway; she must have been awake and had fought and struggled against her assailant. The servant, who'd probably been awake too, had had her skull completely crushed. According to the owner's account, the captain was drunk the morning before when he'd come to call, bragging and displaying a considerable sum of money, some two hundred roubles. The captain's old torn green wallet was found empty on the floor; but Marya Timofeevna's trunk had not been opened, and the silver setting on the icon hadn't been removed; the captain's clothes hadn't been touched. It was obvious the thief was in a hurry and was also familiar with the captain's affairs; he'd come for the money alone and knew exactly where to find it. If the owner hadn't come running to the house in time, the smouldering logs would've burned the house down, and 'it would've been difficult to learn the truth from charred corpses.'

That's how the story went. One other bit of information was added: this apartment had been rented for the captain and his sister by Mr Stavrogin, Nikolai Vsevolodovich himself, the son of the general's widow; he'd come in person to rent the house, and had had to insist because the owner didn't want to rent it, since the house was built as a tavern; but Nikolai Vsevolodovich was prepared to meet any terms and paid the rent for six months in advance.

'There's more to this than meets the eye,' someone in the crowd was heard to utter.

But most people remained silent. Their faces were glum, but I saw no signs of indignation. All around I continued to hear stories about Nikolai Vsevolodovich: the fact that the murdered girl was his wife; that the previous day he'd 'dishonourably' abducted a young lady from one of our leading families, the daughter of General Drozdov; that complaints were going to be lodged against him in Petersburg; that his wife had been murdered so now he could marry the young lady. Skvoreshniki was no more than two and a half miles away, and I remember wondering whether I shouldn't go there and let them know what was happening. But I didn't notice anyone trying to incite the crowd against them; I don't want to make false accusations, but I did recognize two or three faces from the buffet; towards morning they turned up at the fire and I knew them at once. I especially remember one tall, thin fellow, a tradesman, a confirmed drunkard, curly-haired, with a face as dark as if blackened with soot; later I found out he was a locksmith. He wasn't drunk then, but, in contrast to the glum crowd, he seemed beside himself. He kept addressing the crowd, although I don't recall his exact words. He said nothing more coherent than, 'Well, lads, what's all this? Is it going to go on like this?' He kept waving his arms around as he spoke.

CHAPTER 3

The end of a romance

1.

FROM the large drawing-room at Skvoreshniki (the one in which the last meeting between Varvara Petrovna and Stepan Trofimovich had taken place) the fire could be seen very clearly. At daybreak, around six in the morning, Liza was standing at the furthest window on the right-hand side, staring at the fading reddish glow. She was alone in the room. She still had on the dress she was wearing yesterday for the matinée—a splendid dress, bright green, covered with lace, now crumpled, thrown on quickly and carelessly. Suddenly noticing her bodice was not completely fastened, she blushed, made haste to adjust it, picked up her red shawl from the armchair where it had been thrown yesterday when she arrived, and tossed it over her shoulders. A few curls of her luxuriant hair crept out from under the shawl over her right shoulder. Her face was tired and careworn, but her eyes shone under her knitted brows. She went up to the window again and leaned her warm forehead against the cold pane of glass. The door opened and Nikolai Vsevolodovich came in.

'I sent a messenger on horseback,' he said. 'In about ten minutes we'll find out. Meanwhile the servants say that part of town on the other side of the river has burned down, near the river bank on the right side of the bridge. The fire started around midnight; now it's dying down.'

He didn't approach the window, but stopped about three paces behind her; she didn't turn around to face him.

'According to the calendar it should've been light an hour ago,' she said irritably, 'but it's still almost dark as night.'

'Calendars are full of lies,'* he replied with a gentle smile, but then feeling embarrassed, hastened to add: 'It's boring to live according to calendars, Liza.'

He fell silent, annoyed to have said something so trite; Liza gave a wry smile.

'You're in such a gloomy mood you can't even find the right words to say to me. Don't be concerned, you do have a point: I always live by the calendar; every step I take is calculated according to it. Are you surprised?'

She turned quickly from the window and sat in an armchair.

'Please take a seat as well. We don't have much time left together and I'd like to say everything I want... you too should say everything you want.'

Nikolai Vsevolodovich sat down next to her and took her hand quietly, almost timidly.

'What do these words mean, Liza? Where have they come from so suddenly? What do you mean, "We don't have much time left together"? That's the second enigmatic phrase you've used, my darling, in the last half hour since you woke up.'

'You've taken to counting my enigmatic phrases?' she said with a laugh. 'Do you remember yesterday when I came in I called myself a corpse? That's one you thought it best to forget. Forget or ignore.'

'I don't recall, Liza. Why a corpse? You must live...'

'And now you've fallen silent? Your eloquence has vanished entirely. I've spent my hour on the earth; that's enough. Do you remember Christopher Ivanovich?'

'No, I don't,' he said, frowning.

'Christopher Ivanovich, in Lausanne? You got terribly bored with him. He used to open the door and say, "I've come for only a minute or two", and then he'd stay all day. I don't want to be like Christopher Ivanovich and stay all day.'

An anxious expression crossed his face.

'Liza, it hurts me to hear such tormented words. This pose must cost you dearly, too. What purpose does it serve? What's it for?'

His eyes glowed.

'Liza,' he cried, 'I swear I love you more today than I did yesterday when you came to me!'

'What a strange confession! Why speak about today and yesterday and make comparisons?'

'You won't leave me,' he went on almost in despair. 'We'll go away together, today, won't we? Won't we?'

'Ow, don't squeeze my hand like that! Where are we to go away together to? Somewhere "to be resurrected" again? No, we've tried that too many times... it's too slow for me. I'm not capable of it; it's too noble for me. If we leave, let it be to Moscow, to visit people and be received—that's my ideal, you know. I've never hidden from you, even in Switzerland, the kind of person I am. Since it's impossible for us to go to Moscow and visit people because you're already married, there's nothing more to talk about.'

'Liza! What about what happened yesterday?'

'What happened, happened.'

'That's impossible! It's cruel!'

'So what if it's cruel; you'll bear it even if it's cruel.'

'You're paying me back for yesterday's fantasy...' he muttered, grinning maliciously. Liza blushed.

'What a mean thought!'

'Then why did you grant me... "so much happiness"? Don't I have the right to know?'

'No, somehow you'll get by without having any rights; don't aggravate the meanness of your suggestion with stupidity. You're out of luck today. By the way, aren't you afraid of public opinion and the fact that you'll be condemned for "so much happiness"? Oh, if that's true, for heaven's sake don't trouble yourself. You're not the cause of it and you don't have to answer to anyone. Yesterday when I opened your door, you didn't even know who'd come in. All this was my own fantasy, as you just said, nothing more. You can look everyone in the face boldly and triumphantly.'

'Your words, that laughter of yours—have been causing me such cold terror for the last hour. That "happiness" of which you speak so frantically is worth... everything to me. Can I really lose you now? I swear, I loved you less yesterday. Why are you trying to take it all away from me today? Do you know how much it's cost me, this new hope? I've paid for it with my life.'

'Your life or someone else's?'

He got up quickly.

'What do you mean by that?' he asked, casting a steady glance at her.

'Did you pay for it with your life or mine—that's what I meant. Or don't you understand anything any more?' Liza flushed. 'Why did you suddenly jump up? Why are you looking at me like that? You're frightening me. What are you so afraid of? I noticed some time ago that you're afraid, right now, this very minute... Good Lord, how pale you've become!'

'If you know something, Liza, I swear to you *I* know nothing... and it wasn't *that* I was talking about at all just now when I said I've paid with my life...'

'I don't understand you at all,' she said, faltering timidly.

At last a slow, pensive smile formed on his lips. He sat down quietly, rested his elbows on his knees, and covered his face with his hands.

'It's a nightmare and delirium... We were talking about two different things.'

'I don't know what you were talking about... Didn't you really know yesterday that I'd leave you today? Did you know or not? Don't lie, did you or didn't you?'

'I knew,' he replied softly.

'Well, then, what do you want? You knew it and reserved a "moment" for yourself. Aren't we even now?'

'Tell me the whole truth,' he cried in anguish. 'Yesterday when you opened my door, did you know you were opening it for only one hour?'

She glared at him with hatred.

'Honestly, the most serious person can pose the most astonishing questions. What are you so upset about? Is it really your vanity—a woman is leaving you and not the other way around? You know, Nikolai Vsevolodovich, since I've been here, I've discovered how very generous you've been to me, and it's precisely that I can't bear.'

He stood up and took a few steps around the room.

'Fine, let it end as it should... But how could it all have happened?'

'Why worry about that? The thing is you know perfectly well how; you understand it better than anyone on earth and were counting on it. I'm a young lady of the nobility; I was brought up on opera—that's how it all started, that's the whole explanation.'

'No.'

'There's nothing here to injure your vanity; it's all absolutely true. It began with a beautiful moment that was too much for me to bear. The day before yesterday when I "insulted" you in front of everyone and you responded like a true cavalier, I returned home and immediately guessed you were running away from me because you were already married, not because you despised me, which, as a young lady in high society, I dreaded most of all. I realized that by escaping you were protecting me, fool that I was. You see how I appreciate your generosity. Then Peter Stepanovich came and immediately explained everything to me. He told me you were inspired by some great idea, in the face of which he and I meant nothing at all, but that I still represented an obstacle on your path. He said he was involved in it too; he insisted the three of us work together and said some fantastic things about a wooden boat with oars made of maple from a Russian folksong. I complimented him, told him he was a poet, and he took my praise at face value. But since I knew long ago, apart from him, that I'd have the strength to last only a minute or so, I decided to go through with it. Well, that's all there is to it. That's enough; no more discussion, please. We might end up quarrelling. Don't be afraid of anyone; I'll bear all the responsibility. I'm a bad girl, capricious, seduced by that operatic boat; I'm a young lady... But you know, I still thought you were in love with me. Don't despise a foolish girl and don't laugh at the tear rolling down my cheek. I love to cry when I feel sorry for myself. Well, enough, enough. I'm good for nothing, and you're good for nothing; two insults, one from each side, now we can be consoled. At least we each have our vanity intact.'

'Nightmare and delirium!' cried Nikolai Vsevolodovich, wringing his hands, pacing around the room. 'Liza, you poor girl, what have you done to yourself?'

'I've burnt my finger in the candle flame, nothing more.

You're not crying too, are you? Observe the proprieties; be less sensitive...'

'Why, why did you come to me?'

'Don't you understand the ridiculous position where you've put yourself in public opinion by asking such questions?'

'Why did you ruin yourself so monstrously and stupidly, and what's to be done now?'

'This is Stavrogin, the "vampire Stavrogin", as one lady here says who's fallen in love with you! Listen, I've told you already: I've compressed my entire life into one hour and I'm content. You should do the same with yours... but there's no need for you to do so; you still have many different "hours" and "moments" ahead of you.'

'As many as you have; I give you my solemn word, not one more hour than you have!'

He continued to pace about and didn't see her rapid, penetrating glance, which suddenly seemed to brighten with hope. But the ray of light went out almost instantly.

'If you only knew the price I'm paying, Liza, for my present *impossible* sincerity. If I could only reveal to you...'

'Reveal? You want to reveal something to me? God preserve me from your revelations!' she said, interrupting him almost in alarm.

He stopped and waited uneasily.

'I should confess to you that ever since those days in Switzerland I began to suspect that there was something awful, loathsome, and bloody on your conscience, and... at the same time, something that put you in a ridiculous position. Be careful of revealing anything to me if it's the truth: I'll laugh at you. I'll be laughing at you for the rest of your life... Oh, have you turned pale again? I won't, I won't, I'll leave right away,' she cried, jumping up from the chair with a gesture of scorn and contempt.

'Torment me, punish me, vent your spite on me,' he cried in desperation. 'You have every right to do so! I knew I didn't love you, I ruined you. Yes, "I reserved a moment for myself"; I had hope... for a long time... one last hope... I couldn't withstand the bright light flooding my heart when you came to me yesterday all on your own, alone, first. All of a sudden I believed... Perhaps I still believe even now.'

'I'll repay such noble frankness with the same: I don't want to be your sister of mercy. Perhaps I really will become a nurse if I don't manage to die this very day; but if so, it won't be to nurse you, even though you deserve a nurse as much as any creature lacking arms and legs. It always seemed that you'd take me off to some place where an enormous, man-sized evil spider lived and we'd gaze at him for the rest of our lives and be afraid of him. That's how we'd spend our mutual love. You'd be better off going to Dashenka; she'll go with you wherever you want.'

'Did you really have to bring her up now?'

'Poor little puppy dog! Give her my regards. Does she know that even when you were in Switzerland you settled on keeping her for your old age? What solicitude! What farsightedness! Oh, who's this?'

At the far end of the room the door opened slightly; someone's head became visible and then disappeared hurriedly.

'Is that you, Aleksei Yegorych?' Stavrogin enquired.

'No, it's only me,' said Peter Stepanovich, thrusting himself halfway in again. 'How do you do, Lizaveta Nikolaevna? In any case, good morning. I knew I'd find you both here in this room. I've only come for a moment, Nikolai Vsevolodovich—I came as fast as I could to have a few words with you... it's essential... only a very few words!'

Stavrogin headed towards the door, but after several steps turned back to Liza.

'If you hear something in a moment, Liza, I want you to know I'm guilty.'

She shuddered and looked at him fearfully; but he left the room hurriedly.

2.

The room from which Peter Stepanovich had peeked in was a large oval vestibule. Before Peter came in, Aleksei Yegorych had been sitting there, but he sent him away. Nikolai Vsevolodovich closed the door to the drawing-room behind him and stood waiting. Peter Stepanovich shot him a rapid, searching glance.

'Well?'

'If you know already', Peter Stepanovich hastened to say, as if trying to peer into Stavrogin's soul, 'then none of us is to blame in any way, least of all you, because it was such a confluence of circumstances... such a coincidence... in a word, no legal case could be brought against you, and I've come here to inform you.'

'Have they been burnt? Murdered?'

'Murdered, but not burnt, that's the bad part, but on my word of honour, I'm not to blame for it, whatever you suspect—since you suspect me, right? Do you want the whole truth? You see, the idea did really occur to me—you yourself suggested it, not in earnest, but as a tease (you couldn't have suggested it in earnest)—but I couldn't make up my mind, and I wouldn't have for anything, not for a hundred roubles—there was nothing in it, that is, for me, for me...'. He was talking very rapidly, rattling on. 'But then, what a coincidence of circumstances: the day before yesterday, in the evening, I gave that drunken fool Lebyadkin two hundred and thirty roubles (of my own money, you hear, none of yours; but the thing is, you know that, too). Listen, it was the day before yesterday, not yesterday after the matinée, note that: it's a very important coincidence because at the time I didn't know for sure whether Lizaveta Nikolaevna would come to you or not; I provided my own money simply because the other day you distinguished yourself by taking it into your head to tell everyone your secret. Well, I won't meddle in that... it's your own business... you're such a cavalier... but, I confess, I was as astonished as if you'd hit me over the head with a cudgel. I tell you in very truth I'm sick and tired of these tragedies—note I'm completely in earnest, despite the high style—since ultimately all this interferes with my plans, I promised myself, without telling you, to get rid of Lebyadkin at all costs by packing him off to Petersburg, especially since he was hoping to go there himself. I made one mistake: I gave him the money in your name. Was it a mistake or not? Perhaps it wasn't such a mistake, eh? Now listen to me and hear how it all turned out...' In his excitement he came quite close to Stavrogin and began reaching for his jacket lapels (it might even have been deliberate). Stavrogin struck his hand with a strong blow.

'What are you doing? That's enough. You'll break my arm like that. The main thing is how it all turned out,' he said, rattling on again, in no way surprised by the blow. 'In the evening I gave him the money so he and his sister could leave at dawn the next day; I entrusted this little matter to that rascal Liputin—to accompany them and see them off. But that scoundrel Liputin decided he had to play a trick on the public—perhaps you've heard about it? At the matinée? Listen to me, listen: so they both had something to drink; they compose some verses—half of them were Liputin's; he dresses Lebyadkin up in a frock-coat; he assures me he's sent him off early that morning. Meanwhile he keeps him hidden in a back room somewhere to push him out on stage. But Lebyadkin rapidly and unexpectedly gets drunk. Then the scandal we know about ensues, after which he's carted off home dead drunk, and Liputin quietly makes off with the two hundred roubles, leaving him only small change. Unfortunately, however, it turns out that Lebyadkin had taken the two hundred roubles out of his pocket that morning, bragged about it, and flashed the money around where he shouldn't have. Since Fedka was expecting it, having overheard something at Kirillov's (you remember your hint?), he decides to take advantage of it. That's the whole truth. I'm glad at least that Fedka didn't find the money, since that scoundrel was counting on a thousand! He was in a hurry and it seems as if he was afraid of the fire... Would you believe it, that fire came like a bolt from the blue. Yes, the devil only knows what to make of it! It's just mob rule... You see, I expect so much of you that I keep nothing from you: well, yes, I've been cherishing the idea of a fire for some time now, since it has such popular and earthy appeal; but I was keeping it for a critical hour, a precious moment when we'd all rise up and... But all of a sudden they took it into their own heads to do it, now, without orders, just when we should be lying low and holding our breath. No, it's mob rule! In a word, I still don't know anything; there's talk about two Shpigulin men... but if *our men* are involved in it, if even one of them is implicated—heaven help him! You see what happens when you relax discipline even a little! No, this democratic rabble with its groups of five gives lousy support; what's needed is one magnificent, despotic will, an idol resting on something solid and standing apart... Then the groups of five would cringe in obedience and be prepared to serve when the occasion arises. In any case, even though they're going about town now saying that Stavrogin wanted his wife burnt to death and that's why fires were set in town, still...'

'Are they really saying that?'

'Well, not exactly; I must confess, I've heard nothing of the kind, but what can one do with the common people, especially those who were burnt out: *Vox populi vox dei.** How long would it take a stupid rumour like that to spread?... In fact, there's absolutely nothing for you to be afraid of. Legally you're completely in the clear, your conscience is clean—you didn't want it to happen, did you? You didn't want it. There's no evidence, only coincidence... Unless of course Fedka remembers your careless words at Kirillov's (why did you say that?), but it really doesn't prove anything, and we can shut Fedka up. In fact I'll shut him up today...'

'So the bodies weren't burnt at all?'

'Not a bit; that scoundrel can't do anything properly. At any rate, I'm glad you're so calm... because even though you're not guilty of anything, not even in thought, nevertheless... Still you must admit this solves all your problems splendidly: suddenly you're a free widower. Whenever you like you can marry a beautiful young woman with lots of money, who, furthermore, is already yours. That's what simple, crude coincidence can do, right?'

'Are you threatening me, you idiot?'

'Come, come now. An idiot, am I? What kind of attitude is that? You ought to rejoice, but you... I rushed over here specially to inform you as soon as possible... Why would I threaten you? What good could come of anything I get by threats? I need you to help me from goodwill, not from fear. You're the light and the sun... It's I who am thoroughly afraid of you, not the other way around! I'm no Maurice Nikolaevich... Just imagine, as I was rushing over here in a carriage, Maurice Nikolaevich was already here, standing near the fence at the bottom of your garden... in his greatcoat, soaked through; he must have spent the whole night there! Wonder of wonders! Crazy people go to such lengths!'

'Maurice Nikolaevich? Really?'

'Oh yes. He's sitting by the fence. No more than three hundred paces away. I walked right past him, but he didn't see me. You didn't know? In that case I'm very glad I didn't forget to tell you. That sort of fellow can be very dangerous if he happens to have a revolver with him; and then there's the night, the slush, his natural exasperation—just think about his position, ha, ha! What do you think, why is he sitting there?'

'He's waiting for Lizaveta Nikolaevna, of course.'

'Aha! Why should she go to him? And... in such rain... what a fool he is!'

'She'll be going to him very soon.'

'Oho! That's a bit of news! So then... But listen, her position is completely changed now: why does she need Maurice? You're a free widower and could marry her to-morrow, couldn't you? She still doesn't know—allow me, I'll arrange everything for you. Where is she? Let me tell her and make her happy too.'

'Make her happy?'

'I'll say, let's go.'

'Do you think she won't start wondering about those corpses?' Stavrogin asked, screwing up his eyes in a peculiar way.

'Of course she won't,' replied Peter Stepanovich, like a genuine idiot, 'because legally... Oh, you! What if she does work it out? Women are excellent at ignoring such things; you still don't understand them! Besides, it's to her advant-age to marry you now because she's disgraced herself; in addition, I told her about that "boat": I knew she'd be affected by it, naturally, that's the sort of girl she is. Don't worry, she'll step over those corpses with no trouble at all! All the more since you're absolutely, completely innocent, isn't that right? She'll merely put those corpses by to use against you later, maybe in the second year of your marriage. Every woman about to get married puts something of this sort aside from her husband's past, and afterwards... who knows what a year will bring? Ha, ha, ha!'

'If you came here in a carriage, take her to Maurice Nikolaevich right now. She just said she couldn't stand me and was leaving; of course, she won't accept my carriage.'

'Oho! Are you serious about her leaving? How could this have happened?' Peter Stepanovich asked, staring at him stupidly.

'Last night she guessed somehow that I don't love her at all... it's something she knew all along, of course.'

'Is it true you don't love her?' Peter Stepanovich exclaimed with a look of extreme surprise. 'If that's so, then yesterday when she came to you, why did you let her stay instead of behaving honourably and informing her you didn't love her? That was quite vile of you; and what sort of awkward position have you left me in now?'

Stavrogin suddenly burst out laughing.

'I'm laughing at my pet monkey,' he explained at once.

'Ah, so you've guessed I was playing the fool,' Peter Stepanovich said, bursting into horribly hearty laughter. 'I did it to make you laugh! You know, as soon as you came to meet me, I guessed from your expression that you had some "bad luck". Perhaps even a complete failure, right? Well, I bet', he cried, almost choking with ecstasy, 'all night you sat side by side on chairs in this room wasting valuable time debating some abstract, noble subject... Well, forgive me, forgive me; what business is it of mine? Yesterday I knew for sure it'd end up stupidly. I brought her here simply to amuse you and to show you won't grow bored with me; I'll prove useful to you in that way three hundred times; in general I love to be nice to people. If she's no longer needed, just as I expected when I came here, then I'll...'

'So you brought her here just for my amusement, did you?'

'Of course, why else?'

'Not to force me to kill my wife?'

'Oho, was it you who killed her then? What a tragic figure you are!'

'Makes no difference. You killed her.'

'*I* killed her? I tell you I wasn't involved in the least. But you're beginning to upset me...'

'Go on. You said, "If she's no longer needed, then..."'

'Then I'll deal with her, of course! I'll marry her off without any difficulty to Maurice Nikolaevich; by the way, I didn't station him at the end of your garden, so don't get any ideas about that. *I'm* afraid of him now. You just said: deliver her in my carriage, but I just came rushing past him... what if he does have a revolver?... It's a good thing I brought mine with me. Here it is' (he took a revolver out of his pocket, showed it and put it away again) '—I brought it along because it was such a long way to come... But I can fix everything for you in an instant: now her little heart is aching for Maurice Nikolaevich... it should be aching, at any rate... and you know, so help me God, I'm even beginning to feel a little sorry for him myself! I'll take her to Maurice, and she'll start thinking about you immediately—praising you and abusing him—that's a woman's heart for you! You're laughing again, are you? I'm glad you've cheered up. Well then, let's go. I'll start with Maurice right away, and about those... those who were murdered... you know, it might be better not to say anything about that right now. She'll find out later anyway.'

'What will she find out about? Who's been murdered? What did you say about Maurice Nikolaevich?' Suddenly Liza opened the door.

'Oh! Were you eavesdropping?'

'What did you just say about Maurice Nikolaevich? Has he been murdered?'

'Oh! So you didn't really hear! Don't worry, Maurice Nikolaevich is alive and well; you can satisfy yourself on that score in an instant since he's here, standing at the garden fence by the road... he was there all night it seems; he's soaked, in his greatcoat... I came past him and he saw me.'

'That's not true. You said "murdered"... Who's been murdered?' she insisted in a torment of suspicion.

'Only my wife was murdered, her brother Lebyadkin and their servant,' Stavrogin announced firmly.

Liza shuddered and grew very pale.

'It was a monstrous, strange case, Lizaveta Nikolaevna, an absurd case of robbery,' Peter Stepanovich rattled on at once, 'robbery under cover of the fire. It was all the work of that criminal Fedka the convict and that idiot Lebyadkin who showed his money to everyone... that's why I came rushing over here... it was such a terrible blow. Stavrogin could hardly take the news when I told him. We were conferring on whether to tell you or not.'

'Nikolai Vsevolodovich, is he telling the truth?' Liza just managed to ask.

'No, it's not the truth.'

'Not the truth?' cried Peter Stepanovich with a start. 'What do you mean?'

'God in heaven, I'm going out of my mind!' shrieked Liza.

'You must understand at any rate that right now he's off his head!' yelled Peter Stepanovich. 'After all, his wife's been murdered. Look how pale he is... He spent the whole night with you; he didn't leave you for an instant. How could anyone suspect him?'

'Nikolai Vsevolodovich, before God, tell me the truth: are you guilty or not? I'll believe you, I swear it, so help me God, and I'll follow you to the end of the earth, yes, I will! I'll follow you like your little dog...'

'Why are you tormenting her, you bizarre creature, you?' Peter Stepanovich cried furiously. 'Lizaveta Nikolaevna, I swear to you, do as you like with me, he's innocent; on the contrary, it's nearly killed him; you can see he's raving. In no way is he guilty, no way at all, not even in his thoughts!... It's all the doing of thieves, who in a week or so will undoubtedly be caught and punished... It was Fedka the convict and the Shpigulin men; the whole town is talking about it, and that's what I'm on about too.'

'Is that so? Is it?' Liza asked, trembling all over, awaiting her final sentencing.

'I didn't kill them and was against it, but I knew they'd be murdered and I didn't stop the murderers. Leave me, Liza,' said Stavrogin and went into the drawing-room.

Liza covered her face with her hands and left the house. Peter Stepanovich was about to go rushing out after her, but he turned and came back into the room.

'So that's it? That's it, is it? You're not afraid of anything?' he hurled at Stavrogin in an absolute fury, muttering incoherently, hardly finding his words, foaming at the mouth.

Stavrogin stood in the middle of the room and said not a word in reply. With his left hand he tugged gently at a lock of hair and smiled forlornly. Peter Stepanovich pulled him violently by the sleeve.

'You've had it, have you? So that's what you're up to! You'll inform on the others, then you'll go off to a monastery or to hell... But I'll get rid of you all the same, even though you're not afraid of me!'

'Oh, it's you rattling on, is it?' Stavrogin said, seeing him at last. 'Run,' he said, suddenly coming to his senses, 'run after her, order the carriage, don't leave her... Run, run after her! Take her home so no one knows and she doesn't go there... to see the bodies... the dead bodies... Make her get into the carriage. Aleksei Yegorych! Aleksei Yegorych!'

'Stop it, don't shout! She's already in Maurice's arms. He won't get into your carriage... Stop it! There's something even more important than your carriage!'

He took out his revolver again; Stavrogin looked at him in earnest.

'Well, go on, kill me,' he said softly, almost in a conciliatory tone.

'Damn it, what lies people tell about themselves!' Peter Stepanovich said, shaking with fury. 'So help me, I should kill you! She ought to have spat in your face!... What kind of "boat" are you? Just some old, broken-down, leaky wooden barge!... You ought to come to your senses now, if only out of spite, only from spite! Oh, it's all the same to you, isn't it, if you get a bullet between the eyes?'

Stavrogin gave a strange laugh.

'If you weren't such a joker I might've said just now: yes... If you were only tiny bit more intelligent...'

'I may be a joker, but I don't want you, my better half, to be a joker! Do you understand me?'

Stavrogin understood; perhaps he was the only one who did. Shatov was astonished later when Stavrogin told him Peter Stepanovich had this capacity for profound emotion.

'As for now, you can go to hell; by tomorrow I may have come up with something. Come back tomorrow.'

'Really? Really?'

'How should I know?... Go to hell, go to hell!'

And he left the room.

'Well, perhaps it's all for the best,' Peter Stepanovich muttered under his breath as he put away his revolver.

3.

He rushed to catch up with Lizaveta Nikolaevna. She hadn't got very far, only a few steps from the house. She'd been detained by Aleksei Yegorych who was following her now, in his frock-coat, without a hat, one step behind her, his head bent respectfully. He was entreating her to wait for the carriage; the old man was frightened and almost in tears.

'You go back, the master's asking for his tea and there's no one to serve him,' Peter Stepanovich said, pushing him away and taking Liza by the arm.

She didn't pull her arm away, but seemed not to know what she was doing; she still hadn't recovered her senses.

'In the first place, you're not going the right way,' Peter Stepanovich began to prattle. 'We have to go that way, not past the garden; in the second place, it's impossible to go on foot. It's three miles to your house and you're not properly dressed. If you'd just wait a little while, I came in a carriage, it's in the courtyard. I can fetch it in an instant, put you in it, take you home and no one will see you.'

'How kind you are...' Liza said sweetly.

'For heaven's sake, any humane person would do the same in my place...'

Liza looked at him and was surprised.

'Oh my goodness, I thought you were that old man!'

'Listen, I'm awfully glad you're taking it like this, because it's all stupid convention; come to think of it, it might be better if I ordered the old man to get the carriage ready. It'd only take ten minutes; meanwhile, we'll turn around and wait on the porch. Agreed?'

'First I want to... where are those murdered people?'

'Oh, you and your whims! I was afraid of this... No, it's better to leave that well alone; there's no reason for you to see.'

'I know where they are, I know the house.'

'So what if you do? For goodness sake, it's raining, and it's foggy... (Why on earth did I agree to take on this sacred obligation?) Listen, Lizaveta Nikolaevna, you have one of two choices: either come with me in my carriage, in which case, wait here and don't take another step. If you go another twenty paces, Maurice Nikolaevich is sure to see us.'

'Maurice Nikolaevich? Where? Where?'

'Well, if you want to go with him, I'll take you a little further, show you where he is, and bid you farewell; I don't want to meet him right now.'

'He's waiting for me, oh God!' she stopped suddenly, her face filled with colour.

'Good Lord, he's a man without prejudices! You know, Lizaveta Nikolaevna, none of this is any of my business. I'm a complete outsider; you know that yourself. Nevertheless, I still wish you well... If your "boat" didn't succeed because it turned out to be a broken-down, rotting old barge...'

'Oh, that's wonderful!' cried Liza.

'It may be wonderful, but tears are streaming down your cheeks. You must have courage. You must be strong as a man. In our day and age when women... Oh, the hell with it!' (Peter Stepanovich was almost ready to spit.) 'The main thing is, not to have any regrets: it may all turn out for the best. Maurice Nikolaevich is a man who... in a word, he's a sensitive man, even though he's not very forthcoming, which is also fine, in certain circumstances, if he's a man without prejudices...'

'That's wonderful, wonderful!' Liza cried, bursting into hysterical laughter.

'Oh, hell... Lizaveta Nikolaevna,' Peter Stepanovich cried, suddenly feeling exasperated. 'I'm here just for you... What do I have to do with it? I was of service to you yesterday when you wanted to come here, and now again today... Well, you can see Maurice Nikolaevich from here; there he is, but he doesn't see us. Lizaveta Nikolaevna, have you ever read *Polinka Saks*?'*

'What's that?'

'There's a story called *Polinka Saks*. I read it when I was a student... There's a civil servant named Saks—a very wealthy man—who arrests his own wife at his dacha for infidelity... Oh, well, to hell with it; what does it matter? You'll see, Maurice Nikolaevich will propose to you even before you get home. He still doesn't see us.'

'Oh, don't let him see us!' Liza cried all of a sudden like a madwoman. 'Let's run away, far away! To the forest, to the fields!'

And she turned and ran back.

'Lizaveta Nikolaevna, what a failure of courage!' said Peter Stepanovich, running after her. 'Why don't you want him to see you? On the contrary, look him straight in the eye, proudly... If you're thinking about *that*... about your virginity... it's merely a prejudice, an old-fashioned convention... Where are you going, where are you going? Oh, she's running away! Let's go back to Stavrogin's house, we'll take my carriage... Where are you going? That's the fields over there... well, now she's fallen down!...'

He stopped. Liza was flying like a bird, not knowing where she was running, and Peter Stepanovich was already fifty paces or so behind her. She fell, stumbling on a hummock. At that very moment, off to the side, a dreadful cry was heard; it was Maurice Nikolaevich who had seen her running and watched her fall. Now he was running across the field towards her. In an instant Peter Stepanovich retreated to the gates of Stavrogin's house to get into his own carriage as quickly as possible.

Meanwhile Maurice Nikolaevich, in a terrible fright, was already standing beside Liza who'd managed to sit up; he was leaning over her, holding her hand in both of his. All the improbable circumstances of this meeting had shaken his sanity and tears were streaming down his face. To see the woman he adored running insanely across a field at that hour, in such weather, wearing only a dress, the same splendid one she'd worn yesterday, now all crumpled, muddied from her fall... He couldn't say a word; he took off his greatcoat and with trembling hands placed it over her shoulders. All of a sudden he cried out, having felt her lips pressing against his hand.

'Liza!' he cried. 'I'm good for nothing, but don't drive me away!'

'Oh, yes, let's get out of here. Don't leave me!' she cried; seizing him by the hand, she dragged him along behind her. 'Maurice Nikolaevich,' she said, lowering her voice in fear, 'I was so brave there, but now I'm afraid of death. I'm going to die, I'm going to die very soon, but I'm afraid of dying, very afraid...' she whispered, squeezing his hand firmly.

'Oh, if only there were someone here!' he said, turning around desperately, 'someone passing! You'll get your feet wet, you'll... lose your reason!'

'Never mind, never mind,' she said, trying to reassure him. 'It's all right; I'm not so afraid with you here. Hold my hand, lead me... Where are we going now? Home? No, first I want to see the people who were killed. They say his wife was murdered, but he says he murdered her. That's not true, is it? I want to see the people who were murdered... for myself... it's because of them that he stopped loving me last night... I'll see and find out everything. Quickly, quickly, I know the house... the fire was over there... Maurice Nikolaevich, my friend, don't ever forgive me, a dishonoured woman! Why should you forgive me? Why are you crying? You should strike me and kill me here in the fields like a dog!'

'No one can judge you now,' Maurice Nikolaevich said firmly. 'God will forgive you. I have no right to judge you!'

It would be difficult to describe their conversation. Meanwhile they walked quickly arm in arm, hurrying along as if they were mad. They were heading straight towards the scene of the fire. Maurice Nikolaevich still hadn't despaired of meeting a cart along the way, but none came by. A fine, light drizzle enveloped the countryside, swallowing each ray of light and every shade of colour, transforming everything into a smoky, leaden, indistinguishable mass. Although day had broken some time ago, it was still very dark. All of a sudden out of the smoky, cold haze there emerged a single figure, a strange, absurd figure walking towards them. Trying to imagine it now, I think had I been in Lizaveta Nikolaevna's place, I wouldn't have believed my eyes; but she cried out joyfully and recognized the person at once. It was Stepan Trofimovich. How he'd departed, in what manner his insane idea of flight had been put into practice—more about that later. I mention only that he'd been in a fever all that morning, but his illness hadn't stopped him: he strode firmly along on the damp ground. Clearly he'd planned this undertaking to the best of his ability, all on his own, in spite of his lack of practical experience. He was dressed 'for the road', that is, in a greatcoat with long sleeves, a broad patent-leather belt fastened around his waist with a buckle, a pair of tall shiny boots like a hussar, trousers tucked in. No doubt he'd entertained the image of a traveller for some time. Several days in advance he'd outfitted himself with the belt and those tall shiny hussar's boots in which he could hardly walk. A broad-brimmed hat, a knitted scarf wrapped tightly around his neck, a walking-stick in his right hand, and an extremely small but very tightly packed travelling bag in his left hand completed his costume. In addition, he held an open umbrella in that same right hand. These three objects—umbrella, walking-stick and travelling bag—were awkward for him to manage during the first mile, and heavy too during the second.

'Is it really you?' cried Liza, looking at him in sorrowful amazement that replaced her initial burst of spontaneous joy.

'Lise!' Stepan Trofimovich exclaimed, rushing towards her, also almost deliriously. '*Chère, chère*, is it really you... in such a fog? Do you see the glow from the fire! *Vous êtes malheureuse, n'est-ce pas?* I see, I see, don't tell me, but don't ask me anything either. *Nous sommes tous malheureux, mais il faut les pardonner tous. Pardonnons Lise*, and we'll be free for ever. To forsake the world and become totally free—*il faut pardonner, pardonner et pardonner!*'[1]

'But why are you kneeling?'

'Because in bidding farewell to the world I want to take leave of my entire past as well, in your person!' He burst into tears and held both her hands up to his tear-stained eyes. 'I kneel before all that was beautiful in my entire life; I kiss it and give thanks for it! Now I've torn myself in two: there—a madman who dreamt of soaring into the heavens, *vingt-deux ans!* Here—a broken, shivering old man and tutor... *chez ce marchand, s'il existe pourtant ce marchand...*[2] But Lise, you're drenched!' he cried, jumping to his feet, feeling his knees also had got soaked on the wet ground. 'How can you be wearing a dress like that?... and you're on foot, in country like this... You're crying? *Vous êtes malheureuse?* Why, I did hear something or other... But where are you coming from now?' The questions came faster and faster; his face was fearful and he regarded Maurice Nikolaevich in great bewilderment. '*Mais savez-vous l'heure qu'il est?*'[3]

'Stepan Trofimovich, have you heard anything back there about people being murdered... Is it true? Is it?'

'Those people! I saw the red glow of what they'd done all night long. They couldn't end up any other way...' His eyes were gleaming again. 'I'm running away from delirium, from a feverish dream; I'm running in search of Russia, *existe-t-elle la Russie? Bah, c'est vous, cher capitaine!*[4] I never

---

[1] You're unhappy, aren't you?... We're all unhappy, but one must forgive them all. Let us forgive, Lise... one must forgive, forgive, and forgive!

[2] at that merchant's house, if he exists, that merchant

[3] But do you know what time it is?

[4] does it exist, Russia? Why, it's you, my dear captain!

doubted for a moment I'd meet you somewhere performing a heroic deed... But take my umbrella and tell me—why are you on foot? Take my umbrella, for heaven's sake, and I'll hire a carriage somewhere. You see, I'm on foot because Stasie (that is, Nastasya) would've shouted it to everyone in the whole street if she'd found out I was leaving; but I slipped away, as *incognito* as possible. I don't know—in the *Voice* they write about robberies happening all over the place, but surely, I thought, I wouldn't meet a robber the moment I came out on the road. *Chère Lise*, I thought I heard you say someone murdered somebody? *O mon Dieu*, you're ill!'

'Let's go, let's go!' Liza cried, almost in hysterics, once again dragging Maurice Nikolaevich along behind her. 'Wait a minute, Stepan Trofimovich,' she said, turning to him suddenly, 'wait a minute, you poor man. Let me make the sign of the cross over you. It might be better to restrain you physically, but I prefer to make the sign of the cross over you. Pray for "poor" Liza, will you—but not too often, don't burden yourself. Maurice Nikolaevich, give the child back his umbrella, give it to him at once. That's right... Let's go! Let's go!'

Their arrival at the fatal house took place at the same time as a large crowd gathered in front of the house had already heard a fair amount about Stavrogin and how advantageous it was for him to murder his wife. Nevertheless, I repeat, the overwhelming majority continued to listen without speaking or moving. The only people who'd lost control of themselves were brawling drunkards and some 'crazies' such as the tradesman who was waving his arms around. Everyone knew him to be a quiet man, but if something struck him in a particular way, he'd suddenly break loose and go flying off the handle. I didn't witness the arrival of Liza and Maurice Nikolaevich. I saw Liza first, petrified with amazement, standing some distance away from me in the crowd, and I didn't even make out Maurice Nikolaevich at first. Apparently there was a moment when he fell back a few steps behind her because of the crush, or else he was pushed. Liza, forcing her way through the crowd, seeing and hearing nothing around her as if she were delirious and fleeing a hospital ward, drew attention to herself all too quickly: people started to speak up loudly and, suddenly, to yell. Then someone shouted: 'It's Stavrogin's woman!' Then from the other side: 'It isn't enough they murdered them, now they've come to have a look!' All of a sudden I saw someone's arm raised above her head from behind and then come down on top of it; Liza fell. Maurice Nikolaevich gave a dreadful shout, rushed to her aid and with all his might struck the person standing between himself and Liza. But at that very moment the tradesman grabbed him with both arms from behind. For a while it was impossible to make out what was happening in the ensuing mêlée. It seems that Liza managed to get up, but after another blow she fell again. Suddenly the crowd parted and a small empty space was left around Liza prostrate on the ground, while the bloodied, enraged Maurice Nikolaevich stood over her, yelling, wailing, wringing his hands. I don't recall exactly what happened next: I remember only that Liza was suddenly carried away. I ran after her; she was still alive, perhaps even still conscious. The tradesman and three other men from the crowd were seized. To this day these three deny having had any role in the criminal act, and stubbornly maintain they were arrested by mistake; perhaps they're even right. The tradesman, even though he was clearly implicated, has been unable to this very day to explain coherently what actually happened, because he had taken leave of his senses. I too, as an eyewitness, even though at some distance, was required to testify at the inquest: I declared that everything had occurred entirely by accident, through the actions of people who, while they might have been incited, were not really aware of what they were doing. They were drunk and not in control of themselves. I stand by that opinion even today.

CHAPTER 4

The final decision

I.

MANY people saw Peter Stepanovich that morning; those who did reported him to be in a state of extreme agitation. At two o'clock he went to see Gaganov, who had arrived from the country only the day before and whose house was full of guests hotly debating recent events. Peter Stepanovich did most of the talking and made them listen to him. He'd always been considered 'a very talkative student with nothing between the ears'; but now he was going on about Yulia Mikhailovna, and in all the general confusion, the topic was fascinating. In his capacity as her recent and intimate confidant, he reported many new and extremely unexpected details; incidentally (and, of course, inadvertently) he repeated several personal remarks she'd made about important figures in town, and by so doing wounded their vanity. What he said was unclear and confused; he seemed to lack guile; he was an honest man placed in the difficult position of having to clear up at one fell swoop an enormous number of misunderstandings; and in his simple-minded, straightforward way, he didn't even know where to start or stop. He also let slip rather carelessly that Yulia Mikhailovna knew Stavrogin's entire secret and it was she who was masterminding the whole intrigue. Why, she'd even taken him for a ride as well, him, Peter Stepanovich, because he too had fallen in love with the unfortunate Liza; meanwhile he'd been so 'hoodwinked' that he *almost* delivered her to Stavrogin who was waiting in a carriage. 'Yes, yes, it's all right for you to laugh, gentlemen, but if I'd only known, if I'd only known how it would all turn out!' he concluded. In reply to various agitated questions about Stavrogin, he declared openly that in his opinion the tragedy befalling the Lebyadkins was purely an accident; Lebyadkin himself was to blame for it, since he showed people the money he'd received. Peter Stepanovich explained this part especially

well. One of his audience observed that it was no good his
'pretending'; he'd eaten, drunk, and almost slept in Yulia
Mikhailovna's house, yet now he was the first to blacken
her reputation, and that doing so was by no means as fine
a thing as he supposed. But Peter Stepanovich defended
himself: 'I didn't eat and drink there because I had no
money; I'm not to blame if they invited me. Let me be the
judge of how grateful I'm to feel.'

In general he made a favourable impression. 'Granted he's
an absurd fellow, even, of course, an empty-headed one, but
why should he be blamed for Yulia Mikhailovna's stupidity?
On the contrary, he even tried to stop her...'

Around two o'clock news arrived that Stavrogin, of whom
there'd been so much talk, had unexpectedly left for Petersburg on the afternoon train. This interested everyone very
much; many people frowned. Peter Stepanovich was so
stunned that he was reported to have blanched and shouted
strangely: 'Who let him go?' He rushed out of Gaganov's
house immediately. But he was seen in two or three other
houses afterwards.

Towards dusk he found it possible to get in to see Yulia
Mikhailovna, although only with great difficulty because
she'd decided that she didn't want to receive him. I found
out about it from her only three weeks later, just before her
departure for Petersburg. She didn't convey all the details;
she merely observed with a shudder that 'at the time he
astonished her beyond belief.' I assume he merely frightened
her by threatening to name her an accomplice, if she should
ever take it upon herself to 'spill the beans'. The need to
frighten her was closely connected to his plans at the time,
plans about which she was naturally unaware; only afterwards, some five days later, did she guess why he doubted
her ability to keep silent and why he feared new outbursts
of her indignation...

At about eight o'clock that evening, when it was already
dark, 'our group' met, the full complement, five of them,
gathered on the edge of town in Ensign Erkel's apartment
in a crooked little house on Fomin Lane. This general
meeting was called by Peter Stepanovich himself; but he

was unforgivably late, and the others had been waiting for him for over an hour. Ensign Erkel was the very same officer, newly arrived in our town, who, at Virginsky's house, had sat there the whole evening pencil in hand and notebook open in front of him.

He'd arrived in town recently, rented a room in a house on a lonely lane from two sisters, elderly tradeswomen, and was supposed to leave town soon; a gathering at his place would be less likely to draw attention. This strange young man was distinguished by unusual reticence; he could sit for ten evenings in a row in noisy company listening to the most extraordinary conversations without ever saying one word; on the contrary, he'd listen carefully and follow everything that was being said with childlike eyes and great attention. His face was handsome and seemed actually rather intelligent. He didn't belong to the group of five; we assumed he had some special orders of a purely executive kind from somewhere or other. Now we know he had no orders whatsoever; he himself hardly understood his own position. He merely worshipped Peter Stepanovich whom he'd encountered not long ago. If he'd met some prematurely depraved monster who incited him on some romantic social pretext to form a band of brigands and ordered him to murder and rob the first peasant they came across as a test, he'd undoubtedly have gone and done just that. He had an ailing mother living somewhere to whom he sent half his meagre earnings—how she must have kissed that poor little blond head of his, how she must have trembled over it, prayed for it! I'm going into all this detail about him because I feel so sorry for him.

The members of the group were very excited. The events of the previous evening had made quite an impression, and they seemed scared. The simple, albeit systematic public scandal in which they'd played such an active part, had unexpectedly unravelled. The fire last night, the murder of the Lebyadkins, the mob violence done to Liza—all this came as quite a surprise; nowhere was it anticipated in their programme. They passionately accused the hand that guided them of despotism and duplicity. In a word, while they were waiting for Peter Stepanovich, they worked themselves into such a state that they resolved again, once and for all, to demand a categorical explanation from him; and if he were to refuse again, as he had done in the past, they were even prepared to disband the group with the stipulation that in its place a new secret society for the 'propagation of ideas' be formed, on their own initiative, based on principles of equal rights and democracy. Liputin, Shigalyov, and the expert on the people supported this plan; Lyamshin remained silent, although he seemed to be in agreement. Virginsky hesitated and first wished to hear what Peter Stepanovich had to say. They proposed listening to him, but he still hadn't arrived. Such disregard on his part added fuel to the fire. Erkel said absolutely nothing and made arrangements for the tea which he himself carried in from the landlady on a tray with glasses, without bringing in the samovar and not allowing the servant to enter the room.

Peter Stepanovich only appeared around half-past eight. With rapid steps he approached the round table in front of the sofa where the company was seated; he held his cap in his hand and refused the offer of tea. He looked angry, stern, and haughty. He must have noticed at once from the look on all their faces that they were 'rebelling'.

'Before I even open my mouth, you must tell me everything; you're hiding something,' he observed, gazing at each countenance with a malicious grin.

Liputin began 'in the name of all those assembled'; in a voice trembling with offence, he declared that 'if things were to continue in the same way, they might as well blow their own brains out.' Oh, they weren't afraid of blowing their own brains out, and were even prepared to do so, but only for the common good. (There was a general stir of approval.) Therefore, he must be honest with them so they'd always know what v   what beforehand, in advance, 'or else, then what?' (Once more, a stir and a few guttural sounds.) It was humiliating and dangerous to proceed in such a manner... It wasn't at all because we were afraid; but, if one person was doing all the acting and the rest of them were mere pawns, the one might make a mistake and the rest would all be lost. (Exclamations: 'Yes, yes!' Universal support.)

'Damn it all! Then what do you want?'

'What connection is there', Liputin burst out, 'between Mr Stavrogin's sordid little intrigues and our common cause? Even if he's linked to the centre in some mysterious way, and even if this fantastic centre really exists, we have no desire to know anything about it. But in the meantime, a murder has been committed and the police have been alerted; if they follow the thread, they're bound to get to us.'

'If you and Stavrogin are caught, they'll catch us too,' added the expert on the people.

'And it'll be of no use whatsoever to the common cause,' Virginsky concluded gloomily.

'What nonsense! The murders were accidental, committed by Fedka during a break-in.'

'Hmm. But it's a strange coincidence,' Liputin remarked, writhing.

'Or, if you like, it all happened because of you.'

'What do you mean, because of us?'

'In the first place, you, Liputin, took part in this intrigue yourself; in the second place and most important, you were ordered to send Lebyadkin away and provided with the necessary funds. And what did you do? If you'd sent him away, nothing would've happened.'

'But wasn't it you who gave me the idea to turn him loose on stage to read his poem?'

'An idea isn't an order. Your order was to send him away.'

'My order. It's a pretty funny business... On the contrary, you ordered me to delay sending him away.'

'You're mistaken and exhibiting stupidity and wilfulness. As for the murders—they were Fedka's doing; he acted alone and his motive was robbery. You listened to what people were saying and believed it. You lost heart. Stavrogin isn't that stupid; the proof is he left at twelve noon, after meeting with the vice-governor. If anything was amiss, they'd never have let him go off to Petersburg in broad daylight.'

'We're not arguing that Mr Stavrogin committed murder himself,' Liputin said maliciously and unceremoniously. 'He might not even have known, just like me. You yourself know all too well that I knew nothing, even though I'm in it up to my ears now.'

'And just who are you accusing?' Peter Stepanovich asked, looking at him grimly.

'Those who find it necessary to set towns on fire, sir.'

'Worst of all is that you're trying to wriggle out of it. Perhaps you ought to read this and share it with the others; it's just for your information.'

He pulled out of his pocket Lebyadkin's anonymous letter to von Lembke and gave it to Liputin. The latter read it, was obviously surprised, and handed it thoughtfully to his neighbour: the letter quickly made its way around the circle.

'Is it really Lebyadkin's handwriting?' asked Shigalyov.

'Yes,' declared Liputin and Tolkachenko (that is, the expert on the people).

'I'm showing you this just for your information, knowing how sentimental you all feel about Lebyadkin,' Peter Stepanovich repeated, taking the letter back. 'Thus it seems, gentlemen, that a certain Fedka has rid us of a very dangerous man totally by chance. That's what chance can sometimes do! It's instructive, isn't it?'

The members quickly exchanged glances.

'And now, gentlemen, it's my turn to ask you some questions,' said Peter Stepanovich, sententiously. 'Allow me to enquire how it was you came to set fire to the town without permission?'

'What's that? We, we set fire to the town? You must be mad!' several people exclaimed.

'I understand you were carried away by the game,' Peter Stepanovich continued stubbornly, 'but this is not exactly silly little scandals with Yulia Mikhailovna. I've gathered you all here, gentlemen, to inform you of the danger you've stupidly incurred which threatens much more than you yourselves.'

'Excuse me; on the contrary, we were just about to inform you about the degree of despotism and inequality which led to such serious and extraordinary steps being taken, without any consultation,' Virginsky, who'd been silent up to this point, said almost indignantly.

'So, you deny it? I maintain it was you who set the fire, you yourselves and no one else. No, don't lie, gentlemen, I have accurate information. In your wilfulness you subjected the common cause to grave danger. You're only one in an endless network of knots and you're obliged to obey the centre without question. Meanwhile three of you, lacking any instructions whatsoever, incited the Shpigulin men to arson, and the fires occurred.'

'Three? Which three of us?'

'The day before yesterday at three in the morning, you, Tolkachenko, incited Fomka Zavyalov in the Forget-Me-Not Tavern.'

'For pity's sake,' cried the other, jumping up, 'I hardly said more than a word or two, and even that was unintentional—merely because he'd been flogged that morning. I dropped it at once when I saw he was too drunk. If you hadn't reminded me, I'd never have remembered it. The town couldn't have caught on fire from that one word.'

'You're like a man who's amazed when a whole powder factory explodes from one tiny spark.'

'I spoke to him in a whisper in the corner, right into his ear. How did you find out?' Tolkachenko wondered suddenly.

'I was sitting there under the table. Don't worry, gentlemen, I know every move you make. Do I see you grinning nastily, Mr Liputin? I know, for example, that three days ago at midnight, in your own bedroom, just as you were going to bed, you pinched your wife all over until she was black and blue.'

Liputin gaped and went pale.

(Later we learned that he'd found out about Liputin's heroic deed from Agafya, Liputin's maid, who was being paid from the very beginning to spy on him; this came to light only afterwards.)

'May I establish one fact?' Shigalyov asked, standing up all of a sudden.

'Go ahead.'

Shigalyov sat down and braced himself:

'As far as I understand—and it's impossible not to understand—you yourself, to begin with, and then once again, very eloquently—although much too theoretically—painted us a picture of Russia covered with an endless network of knots. In turn, each of these active groups was to proselytize, branch out endlessly in all directions, and, by engaging in systematic propaganda, undermine continually the prestige of local authorities, cause confusion in villages, foster cynicism, scandals, and disbelief in all things, a thirst for something better, and last of all, by means of fires (which have such great impact on the common people), reduce the whole country, at any given moment if need be, to a state of utter desperation. Aren't these your own views that I've tried to reproduce word for word? Isn't this your plan of action, communicated by you as an authorized representative of the central committee, which body remains to this day completely unknown to us and something of a chimera?'

'That's correct, but you've dragged it out considerably.'

'Everyone has the right to express himself in his own way. Having given us to understand that this network of separate knots covering Russia now consists of several hundred groups and, propounding the proposition that if each group does what it's supposed to successfully, then all Russia, at a given moment, at a pre-arranged signal...'

'Oh, to hell with you! I've got enough to do without you!' Peter Stepanovich said, turning around in his armchair.

'Very well, I'll be brief and end with a question. We've already witnessed scandals, noted the people's discontent, been present at and participated in the downfall of the local administration, and, last of all, we've seen the fires with our own eyes. Why are you so dissatisfied? Isn't this your programme? What can you accuse us of?'

'Wilfulness!' Peter Stepanovich cried furiously. 'When I'm around, you've no right to act without my permission. Enough. Someone is about to inform on us; perhaps tomorrow or even tonight you'll all be arrested. That's how it is. I have reliable information.'

Now everyone gaped at him.

'You'll be arrested not only as instigators of the fire, but as members of a group of five. The informer knows all the secrets of the network. That's the sort of mess you've made!'

'It must be Stavrogin,' cried Liputin.

'What... why Stavrogin?' Peter Stepanovich cried, suddenly stopping short. 'Oh, hell,' he continued immediately. 'It's Shatov! I trust you all know that at one time Shatov belonged to our group. I must report that by following his movements through people he never suspected, I was amazed to discover that the organization of the network was no secret to him and... in short, he knows everything. To save himself from being accused of his previous involvement, he's planning to inform on all of us. Up to now he's been hesitating, so I've spared him. But this fire of yours has caused him to make up his mind: he was quite shaken and is no longer hesitating. Tomorrow we'll be arrested as arsonists and political offenders.'

'Is that true? How does Shatov know?'

The agitation was indescribable.

'It's all perfectly true. I have no right to reveal my sources or tell you how I learned about it, but this is what I can do for you in the meantime: through a certain person I can influence Shatov so, without his suspecting why, he'll delay informing on you—but for no more than twenty-four hours. I can't do any more than that. So you can consider yourselves safe until tomorrow morning.'

Everyone was silent.

'Let's dispatch him to the devil!' Tolkachenko was the first to exclaim.

'We should've done it a long time ago!' Lyamshin put in maliciously, banging his fist on the table.

'But how can we do it?' muttered Liputin.

Peter Stepanovich took up this question immediately and explained his plan. It consisted of the following: the next day, at nightfall, they were to lure Shatov to a secluded spot where the secret printing press (which had been in his keeping) was hidden away, and—'deal with him right then and there'. He went into all the necessary details which we'll omit now, and thoroughly explained Shatov's present ambivalent attitude to the central society, which is already known to the reader.

'That's all well and good,' Liputin observed uncertainly,

'but once more... since it'll be a new adventure of a similar sort... won't it cause too great a sensation?'

'Without doubt,' Peter Stepanovich replied, 'but that's been foreseen. There are ways of evading suspicion.'

And, with his earlier precision, he told them all about Kirillov, his intention to commit suicide, how he promised to wait for their signal and leave a note that they'd dictate in which he'd take all the blame on himself. (In a word, everything the reader knows already.)

'They got to know *there* about his steadfast intention to take his own life—a philosophical and, in my opinion, an insane intention.' (Peter Stepanovich continued his explanation.) 'Not one strand of hair, not one speck of dust is overlooked *there*; everything is done for the good of the cause. Having foreseen how useful it could be, and having convinced themselves his intention was entirely serious, they offered him the means of coming to Russia (for some reason he was set on dying here); they gave him a commission he was obliged to carry out (and did); in addition, they bound him by a promise already known to you, to take his life only when they told him to do so. He agreed to everything. Note his membership in the organization is on special terms and he wishes to be useful to it; I can't tell you any more. Tomorrow, *after we deal with Shatov*, I'll dictate him a note in which he'll admit he's responsible for Shatov's death. That will sound very credible: they were friends and travelled to America together where they quarrelled; all of this will be explained in the note... And... it might even be possible, judging from the circumstances, to dictate something more to Kirillov, for example, something about the proclamations, maybe even the fire. But I'll have to think some more about it. Don't worry, he has no prejudices; he'll sign anything.'

Doubts were expressed all around. The story sounded fantastic. But everyone had heard something about Kirillov, Liputin more than the rest.

'He'll change his mind all of a sudden and decide not to do it,' said Shigalyov. 'Any way you look at it, he's still crazy; therefore, the plan is unreliable.'

'Don't worry, gentlemen, he'll do it,' Peter Stepanovich said, cutting him short. 'According to our agreement I'm supposed to tell him the evening before, that is, tonight. I'm inviting Liputin to come with me right now to see him and make sure; then he'll return to you, gentlemen, even tonight if you wish, to report whether I've told you the truth or not. However,' he said suddenly, breaking off in extreme irritation, as if he suddenly felt he was doing these creatures too great an honour and was wasting time trying to convince them, 'however, you may do as you wish. If you decide not to do it, our bond is severed, but only because of your disobedience and treachery. In that case, we'll go our separate ways from now on. But then you must understand that in addition to the unpleasant fact of Shatov's betrayal and its consequences, you'll be bringing yet another little unpleasantness upon yourselves, one you were definitely warned about when this bond was formed. As far as I'm concerned, gentlemen, I'm not really frightened... Don't think I'm all that closely connected to you... But that doesn't matter.'

'No, we'll do it,' Liputin replied.

'There's no other way out,' Tolkachenko muttered. 'And if Liputin comes back and confirms what you've said about Kirillov, then...'

'I'm against it; with all my heart and soul I protest against such a bloody solution!' Virginsky said, rising from his seat.

'But?' asked Peter Stepanovich.

' "But" what?'

'You said "but"... and I'm waiting.'

'I don't think I said "but"... I only wanted to say that if it's decided, then...'

'Then?'

Virginsky fell silent.

'I think one may disregard the threat to one's personal safety,' said Erkel, opening his mouth all of a sudden. 'But if the common cause suffers, then I think one shouldn't disregard the threat to one's personal safety...'

He got confused and blushed. For all that each was preoccupied with his own thoughts, they all looked at him

in amazement; it was so unexpected that he too could have
something to say.

'I'm for the common cause,' Virginsky uttered all of a
sudden.

Everyone stood up. It was decided to communicate once
more tomorrow at noon, although without gathering everyone together for a meeting, and to make final arrangements.
The place where the printing press had been hidden was revealed; each person was assigned his role and duties. Liputin
and Peter Stepanovich set off together to see Kirillov at
once.

2.

All the members of the group were convinced that Shatov
would betray them; but they also believed that Peter Stepanovich was using them as pawns. Still they knew that
tomorrow they would all appear at the appointed place and
Shatov's fate had been sealed. They felt like flies suddenly
caught in a web by an enormous spider; they were furious,
but quaking with fear.

Peter Stepanovich was undoubtedly guilty in their eyes:
everything would have gone much more smoothly and *easily*,
if he'd tried in the least to make reality more palatable. But
instead of presenting the facts in a decent light, befitting
citizens of ancient Rome or something of that sort, he
merely appealed to their animal instinct and emphasized the
risk to their own skins; that was simply discourteous. Of
course, there's a struggle for existence in everything;*
there's no other principle, everyone knows that; nevertheless...

But Peter Stepanovich had no time to inspire the Romans;
he himself was thrown off his stride. Stavrogin's flight had
both shocked and depressed him. He was lying when he
said that Stavrogin had been seen with the vice-governor;
in fact, Stavrogin left without seeing anyone, not even his
mother—and what was really odd, no one even tried to
detain him. (Subsequently the authorities had to explain this
particular circumstance.) Peter Stepanovich had been making enquiries all day long, but hadn't found out a thing;

never before had he been so upset. Could he, could he really give Stavrogin up just like that? That was why he couldn't be any nicer to the members of the group. Besides, they'd tied his hands: he'd already decided to gallop off after Stavrogin but meanwhile he'd been detained by Shatov. He had to cement the group of five together once and for all, just in case. 'They can't be tossed away just like that; they might come in handy.' I suppose that's what he thought.

And as far as Shatov was concerned, Peter Stepanovich was absolutely convinced he'd betray them. Everything he said to the members of the group about him betraying them was a lie: he'd never seen any denunciation or even heard of one, but he was as sure about it as he was that twice two makes four. He felt that Shatov couldn't possibly endure the present situation—Liza's death, Marya Timofeevna's death—and that now he would make up his mind once and for all. Who knows, perhaps he even had some grounds for supposing that. It's also known that he hated Shatov personally; there'd been some kind of quarrel between them at one time, and Peter Stepanovich was never able to forgive the insult. I'm actually convinced this was his main motive.

The pavements in our town are narrow and made of brick; in some places there are only raised wooden planks. Peter Stepanovich walked in the middle of the pavement, occupying it entirely, paying not the least attention to Liputin, and leaving him no room to walk alongside; he either had to hurry on ahead, walk a step behind, or, if they were to converse, run alongside in the muddy street. Peter Stepanovich suddenly recalled how he'd had to wade through mud to keep up with Stavrogin, who also strode down the middle, occupying the whole pavement. He remembered the entire scene and was almost overcome with rage.

Liputin, too, was choking with resentment from a sense of insult. Peter Stepanovich might treat *other* members of the group like that, but not him. Why, he *knew* more than the others, he stood closer to the affair, he was more intimately involved with it, and had been so continuously, although his participation had been indirect up to now. Oh, he knew Peter Stepanovich could destroy him even now *if the worst occurred*. But he'd conceived a hatred for Peter Stepanovich some time ago, not because of any dangers involved, but because of his arrogant manner. Now, when it was time to take action, he was angrier than all the others put together. Alas, he knew that tomorrow, like a slave, he'd be the first to arrive at the appointed place; he'd even lead the others there; he also knew that if now, before tomorrow, he could somehow kill Peter Stepanovich, he'd certainly do so.

Immersed in these thoughts, he trotted alongside his tormentor in silence. Apparently Peter Stepanovich had forgotten all about him; from time to time he bumped him carelessly and rudely with his elbow. Suddenly Peter Stepanovich stopped on one of the broadest streets and ducked into a tavern.

'Where are you going?' cried Liputin. 'This is a tavern.'

'I feel like having a steak.'

'For pity's sake, it's always full of people.'

'So what?'

'But... we'll be late. It's already ten o'clock.'

'We can't get there too late.'

'Then I'll be late! They're waiting for me to return.'

'So what? It'd be stupid for you to hurry back to them. What with all your fussing I haven't had my dinner today. Besides, the later we get to Kirillov's, the better.'

Peter Stepanovich took a private room. Liputin sat in an armchair to one side and watched angrily and resentfully as Peter ate. More than half an hour passed. Peter Stepanovich didn't hurry; he ate with gusto, summoned the waiter, asked for a different kind of mustard, then a beer, all the time saying not one word to Liputin. He was deep in thought. He could do two things simultaneously—eat with gusto and be deeply absorbed in thought. Liputin came to hate him so intensely he was totally unable to tear himself away. It was akin to a nervous seizure. He counted every piece of steak Peter put into his mouth; he hated him for the way he opened his mouth, chewed his food, and smacked his lips over the fattier morsels; he hated the steak itself. At last things began to swim before his eyes; his head began to spin; hot and cold shivers ran up and down his spine.

'You're not doing anything. Read this,' said Peter Stepanovich, tossing him a piece of paper. Liputin drew near the candle. The paper was covered with scribbles; the handwriting was awful and there were corrections on every line. By the time he mastered it, Peter Stepanovich had already paid his bill and was just leaving. On the pavement Liputin handed him back the paper.

'Hold on to it; I'll explain it later. By the way, what do you think?'

Liputin shuddered.

'In my opinion... pamphlets like that are... just stupid nonsense.'

His anger surfaced: he felt as if something had caught him up and was carrying him along.

'If we decide', Liputin said, shivering all over, 'to distribute pamphlets like that, we'll make people despise us for our stupidity and incompetence.'

'Hmm. I don't think so,' Peter Stepanovich replied, walking on resolutely.

'Well I do. Did you write it yourself?'

'That's none of your business.'

'I also think that poem "A Noble Character" was the most absurd thing imaginable and could never have been written by Herzen.'*

'You're lying; it was a good poem.'

'I'm also surprised, for example,' Liputin went on, still bounding along in high excitement, 'we're being told to behave so as to make everything collapse. In Europe it's only natural to hope that everything collapses, because there's a proletariat; but here we're only amateurs and, in my opinion, merely raising a lot of dust.'

'I thought you were a Fourierist.'*

'That's not what Fourier says, not at all.'

'I know it's nonsense.'

'No, Fourier isn't nonsense... Excuse me, I just don't believe there'll be an uprising in May.'

Liputin even unbuttoned his coat, he was feeling so heated.

'Well, enough of that, but now, before I forget,' said Peter Stepanovich, jumping to another subject with fearful composure, 'you'll have to set and print this leaflet with your own hands. We'll dig up Shatov's printing press and you'll get it tomorrow. You must print as many copies as you can as soon as possible and then distribute them throughout the winter. The means will be provided. You must make as many copies as you can because they'll be needed in other places as well.'

'No sir, excuse me. I can't take on such a... I refuse.'

'You will take it on though. I'm acting on orders of the central committee and you must obey.'

'I think that our centres abroad have forgotten what Russian reality is like and have broken their links with it; that's why they're talking such nonsense... I also think that instead of several hundred groups of five in Russia, we're the only one there is and there's no network whatsoever,' gasped Liputin in conclusion.

'All the more contemptible on your part: you chase after the cause without believing in it... now you're chasing after me like a mangy little cur.'

'No sir, I'm not. We have a perfect right to leave you and establish a new society.'

'*Idiot!*' Peter Stepanovich bellowed suddenly, his eyes flashing menacingly.

They both stood facing each other for a while. Peter Stepanovich turned and continued on his way confidently.

An idea flashed through Liputin's mind like lightning: 'I'll turn around and go back: if I don't turn around now, I'll never go back.' That's what he thought for exactly ten paces, but on the eleventh a new and desperate idea occurred to him: he didn't turn around and didn't go back.

They approached Filippov's house, but instead of going in, they turned down a side street, or rather an inconspicuous path along the fence. For a while they had to walk along the steep bank of a ditch on which it was difficult to keep their footing so they had to hold on to the fence. In the darkest corner of the slanting fence Peter Stepanovich removed a plank; a gap appeared through which he slipped immediately. Liputin was surprised, but followed him; then they replaced the plank. This was the secret entrance through which Fedka used to visit Kirillov.

'Shatov mustn't know we're here,' Peter Stepanovich whispered sternly to Liputin.

3.

Kirillov, as always at this hour, was sitting on his leather sofa having tea. He didn't come to meet them, but he did jump up and look at them anxiously.

'You're not mistaken,' said Peter Stepanovich, 'that's exactly why I've come.'

'Today?'

'No, no, tomorrow... around this time.'

And he sat down hurriedly at the table, taking note of Kirillov's agitation with some anxiety. But Kirillov had already recovered his composure and looked his usual self.

'These people still refuse to believe it. You're not angry I've brought Liputin along?'

'I'm not angry today, but tomorrow I want to be alone.'

'But not before I come, and therefore in my presence.'

'I'd prefer not in your presence.'

'You remember you promised to write and sign everything I dictate?'

'It's all the same to me. Are you going to stay here much longer?'

'I have to see someone in about half an hour, so whatever you say, I'll have to spend the next half hour here.'

Kirillov fell silent. Meanwhile Liputin sat down to one side under the portrait of the bishop. His last desperate idea was taking possession of him more and more. Kirillov hardly noticed him. Liputin had known about Kirillov's theory earlier and had always laughed at him; but now he was silent and looked around gloomily.

'I wouldn't say no to a cup of tea,' Peter Stepanovich said, pulling up his chair. 'I've just had a steak and was hoping to have some tea here with you.'

'Go ahead.'

'You used to offer it to me,' Peter Stepanovich observed sourly.

'It doesn't matter. Give Liputin some too.'

'No, sir, I... I can't.'

'You don't want it or you can't?' Peter Stepanovich asked, turning to him quickly.

'I'm not going to here,' Liputin said expressively. Peter Stepanovich frowned.

'That smacks of mysticism; the devil only knows what sort of people you are!'

There was no reply; everyone was silent for a minute or two.

'But I know one thing,' he added abruptly all of a sudden, 'no prejudices will stop each one of us from fulfilling his obligations.'

'Did Stavrogin leave?' asked Kirillov.

'Yes.'

'He was wise to do so.'

Peter Stepanovich's eyes flashed, but he controlled himself.

'I don't care what you think, as long as each person keeps his word.'

'I'll keep my word.'

'I've always been sure you'll do your duty like an independent and progressive fellow.'

'You're very amusing.'

'That may be; I'm glad to entertain you. I'm always pleased to be of service.'

'You want me to shoot myself, but you're afraid I might suddenly decide not to do it.'

'Well I mean, don't you see, it was you who linked your plan to our activities. Reckoning on your plan, we've already done certain things; you really can't refuse now because you'd be letting us down.'

'You have no claim whatsoever.'

'I understand, I understand; it's entirely your own decision, and we don't mean a thing. Just as long as you make the right decision.'

'And must I take on myself all the filthy things you've done?'

'Listen, Kirillov, you're not losing heart, are you? If you want to refuse, tell me at once.'

'I'm not losing heart.'

'I asked because you've got too many questions.'

'Are you going to leave soon?'

'Another question?'

Kirillov looked at him with contempt.

'Look here,' Peter Stepanovich went on, getting more and more angry, upset, and unable to find the appropriate tone, 'you want me to leave so you'll have solitude and be able to concentrate; but those are bad symptoms in you, you most of all. You like to think too much. In my opinion, it's better not to think, just do it. In fact, you're worrying me.'

'The only thing that distresses me is that a reptile like you should be near me when the moment comes.'

'Well, I don't mind about that. Perhaps when the moment comes I'll go outside and stand on the porch. To be going to die and worry about things like that... that's a very bad symptom. I'll go out on the porch; you can assume I understand nothing and am infinitely beneath you as a human being.'

'No, not infinitely; you have talents, but there's a great deal you don't understand because you're so despicable.'

'Fine by me, fine by me. I've already said I'm happy to entertain you... at such a time.'

'You don't understand anything.'

'Well, I... in any case, I'm listening respectfully.'

'You can't do anything; you can't even conceal your petty spite at this moment, even though it's not in your interest to display it. You're starting to make me angry and I may suddenly decide to wait another six months.'

Peter Stepanovich looked at his watch.

'I've never understood anything about your theory, but I know you didn't come up with it on our account, and therefore you'll carry it out without us too. I also know you haven't swallowed the idea—the idea's swallowed you; therefore you won't postpone it.'

'What? The idea's swallowed me?'

'Yes.'

'And I didn't swallow the idea? That's good. You've a grain of intelligence. Only you're teasing me, but I'm proud of it.'

'Splendid, splendid. That's just what we need, for you to be proud of it.'

'Enough; you've finished your tea, now leave.'

'Damn it, I suppose I must,' Peter Stepanovich said, getting up. 'But it's a little early. Listen, Kirillov, will I find the person I'm looking for at Myasnichikha's, you understand. Or was she lying?'

'You won't find him because he's here, not there.'

'What do you mean here, damn it, where?'

'Sitting in the kitchen, eating and drinking.'

'How dare he?' Peter Stepanovich said, blushing angrily. 'He was supposed to wait... what nonsense! He has no passport and no money!'

'I don't know. He came here to say goodbye; he's dressed and ready to go. He's leaving and won't come back. He says you're a scoundrel and he doesn't want to wait for your money.'

'Aha! He's afraid I'll... well, even now I could, if... Where is he? In the kitchen?'

Kirillov opened a side door into a tiny dark room; three steps led down into the kitchen, straight to the partitioned section where the cook's bed was usually placed. There in the corner, under the icons, sat Fedka at a bare deal table. In front of him on the table stood a pint bottle, a plate with some bread, and a piece of cold beef with some potatoes in an earthenware dish. He was eating listlessly and was already half-drunk, but was wearing his sheepskin coat and was obviously ready to leave on his journey. A samovar was boiling on the other side of the partition, but not for Fedka, although he himself had been lighting it every evening for more than a week and had been fanning the coals for 'Aleksei Nilych Kirillov, since he so liked drinking tea at night'. I'm convinced that since there was no cook, Kirillov himself had prepared the beef and potatoes for Fedka that morning.

'What have you done now?' cried Peter, bursting into the room. 'Why didn't you wait where you were supposed to?'

And he banged his fist down on the table.

Fedka assumed an air of dignity.

· 'Wait a minute, Peter Stepanovich, wait just one minute,' he began, enjoying the way he articulated each and every word. 'First of all you'd better realize you're here paying a nice visit to Mr Kirillov, Aleksei Nilych, what's boots you could clean any day you like because he's an educated man; beside him, you're not worth a damn!'

He pretended to spit ostentatiously to the side. His arrogance and determination were evident, as well as a dangerous calm argumentativeness threatening to explode. But Peter Stepanovich had no time to notice this danger; besides, it didn't fit with his view of things. His head was spinning from all the events and failures of the day... From the top of the three steps Liputin peered down inquisitively into the dark little room.

'Do you or don't you want a real passport and enough money to get you to where you were told to go? Yes or no?'

'See here, Peter Stepanovich, you've been fooling me from the start, and it looks to me like you're a real scoundrel. No different from a filthy human louse—that's what I thinks of you. You promised to pay me a lot of money for shedding innocent blood and you swore it was for Mr Stavrogin, though it turns out to be just a case of your incivility. I didn't get nothing out of it, let alone fifteen hundred roubles, and Mr Stavrogin smacked you in the face—we heard all about that. Now you go threatening me again and promising me money—but you don't say what it's for. I think you're sending me off to Petersburg to get back at Mr Stavrogin somehow, at Nikolai Vsevolodovich I mean, counting on my gullible nature. And that shows you're the real murderer. You know what you deserve for no longer believing, in your depravity, in God Himself, in the true Creator? You're no better than a heathen, you're on the same level as a Tatar or a Mordva.* Aleksei Nilych, him what's a real philosopher, has explained to you more than once the meaning of the true God, the real Creator, the creation of the world, our future fate, and the transformation of all creatures and every beast in the Book of Revelation. But you, like a heathen idol, keeps on in your deaf and dumb state and you've brought Ensign Erkel to the same point, just like that wicked tempter, they call the atheist...'

'Oh, you drunken sot! You steal settings from icons and go about preaching the word of God!'

'Look, Peter Stepanovich, I'm telling the truth that I robbed those settings; but I only took the pearls. And how do you know, maybe a tear of my own was changed into a pearl at that very moment in the furnace of the Almighty for some insult I'd suffered, like that orphan what lacks even daily shelter. You know, don't you, from all your books that once upon a time a merchant, with just the same tearful lamentation and prayer, stole a pearl from the halo of the Mother of God and afterwards, for all to see, he put the money he got for it at the feet of the blessed Virgin, and the Holy Mother of God protected him with her mantle before all the people, so that a great miracle was proclaimed and the authorities had it written down in official books just like it happened. But you put a mouse inside; what means, you insulted the very hand of God. If you wasn't my own master by birth what I carried around in my own arms as a young lad I'd have finished you off right now, and right here!'

Peter Stepanovich became absolutely furious.

'Tell me, did you see Stavrogin today?'

'Don't you dare to go interrogating me. Mr Stavrogin is certainly surprised at you and didn't have any part in it, neither wishing it, nor ordering it, nor providing the money. You dared me.'

'You'll get your money and another two thousand in Petersburg when you get there, all of it, even more.'

'You're lying, dear sir, and it's very funny to see how gullible you are. Mr Stavrogin stands miles above you, and you stand there below, barking like a stupid cur, and Stavrogin, he considers it a great honour even to spit on you from above.'

'Do you know,' cried Peter Stepanovich in a rage, 'that I won't let you take one step out of here, you scoundrel! I'll take you right to the police.'

Fedka jumped to his feet, his eyes gleaming in fury. Peter Stepanovich grabbed his revolver. Then there rapidly occurred an extremely nasty scene: before Peter Stepanovich could aim the revolver, Fedka swung around and struck him in the face with all his might. There followed the sound of a second terrible blow, then a third, a fourth, across the face. Peter Stepanovich was dazed, his eyes bulged, he muttered something and suddenly came crashing down full length on to the floor.

'There you are, take him away!' Fedka cried triumphantly; a moment later he grabbed his cap, seized his bag from under the bench, and off he went. Peter Stepanovich lay gasping, unconscious. Liputin even thought a murder had been committed. Kirillov rushed headlong into the kitchen.

'Water!' he cried. Dipping an iron ladle into a bucket, he poured some water over his head. Peter Stepanovich stirred, raised his head, sat up, and stared blankly in front of him.

'Well, how do you feel?' asked Kirillov.

Peter Stepanovich stared back at him intently, not yet recognizing him; but, when he saw Liputin coming back from the kitchen, he broke into a repulsive grin and suddenly jumped up, snatching his revolver from the floor.

'If you decide to run away tomorrow like that scoundrel Stavrogin,' he said, pouncing furiously on Kirillov—he was pale, stuttering and slurring his words—'I'll follow you to the ends of the earth and kill you like a fly... I'll crush you... understand?'

He pointed the revolver right at Kirillov's forehead; but, coming completely to his senses at almost the same time, he lowered his arm, put the revolver back in his pocket, and, without one more word, ran out of the house. Liputin went after him. They slipped through the same gap in the fence and made their way along the top of the slope, clutching on to the fence. Peter Stepanovich strode along the lane so rapidly that Liputin could scarcely keep up. At the first crossroads he stopped suddenly.

'Well?' he asked, turning to Liputin with a challenge.

Liputin remembered the revolver and was still trembling from the previous scene; but an answer suddenly slipped out of his mouth all by itself:

'I think... I think they're not waiting for the student from

Smolensk to far Tashkent* with such great impatience.'

'Did you see what Fedka was drinking in the kitchen?'

'What he was drinking? Vodka.'

'Well, that's the last time he'll be drinking vodka. I want you to remember that for future reference. As for now, you can go to hell; you're not needed until tomorrow... But listen to me: don't do anything stupid!'

Liputin rushed off home as fast as he could.

4.

He even had a passport in a false name hidden away. It's bizarre to think that this careful little man, petty tyrant to his family, civil servant none the less (even though a Fourierist), and, last but not least, capitalist and moneylender, had long ago conceived the fantastic idea of procuring himself a passport in case of emergency, so that with its help he might escape abroad *if*... he allowed for the possibility of this *if*!... even though, of course, he himself was unable to formulate what this *if* could possibly mean...

But now this *if* had suddenly formulated itself in the most unexpected way. The desperate idea that he carried with him to Kirillov's after Peter Stepanovich had called him an 'idiot' on the pavement, was to drop everything and go abroad the first thing tomorrow morning! If someone doesn't believe that such fantastic things can occur in everyday Russian life, let him investigate the biographies of Russian emigrants living abroad. Not one of them escaped in a more intelligent or realistic way. It's always been the unbridled reign of phantoms and nothing more.

When he arrived home he began by locking his door, taking out his travelling bag, and beginning to pack feverishly. His chief concern was money, how he could manage to salvage it, and how much. *Salvage* precisely, since he thought he hadn't a moment to spare; at first light he'd have to set out along the high road. He had no idea where to board the train; he vaguely decided to get on at the second or third large station away from town and make his way to that station on foot, if necessary. Thus, instinctively and mechanically, with thoughts whirling in his head, he was packing his bag when all of the sudden he stopped, gave it all up, and with a deep sigh, stretched out full length on his sofa.

He clearly felt and suddenly realized that he might run away—he probably would—but he was no longer strong enough to resolve the question whether to leave *before* or *after* the business with Shatov; now he was no more than a crude, lifeless body, an inert mass, someone moved by some awful external force; even though he had a passport to travel abroad and could run away from Shatov (why else should he be in such a hurry?), he wouldn't run away either before Shatov or from Shatov, but precisely *after* Shatov; this was already decided, signed and sealed. In intolerable distress, trembling constantly and astonished at himself, moaning and holding his breath in turn, he somehow managed to survive, locked in and lying on the sofa, until eleven o'clock the next morning. Then there suddenly occurred an unexpected shock that suddenly determined his future course of action. At eleven o'clock when he unlocked his door and went out to greet the members of his household, he suddenly learned from them that the robber and escaped convict Fedka, who'd been terrorizing the area, that looter of churches recently turned murderer and arsonist, whom the police had been searching for but had been unable to arrest, was found murdered early that morning about seven miles from town, at the place where the main road takes a turn towards the village of Zakharino and that the whole town was talking about it. He rushed headlong out of the house at once to learn all the details and found out, first of all, that Fedka had been found with his skull smashed, to all appearances robbed, and secondly, that the police already had strong suspicions and even good grounds for believing the murderer to be one of the Shpigulin men, a certain Fomka, the man who'd served as his accomplice in killing the Lebyadkins and setting fire to their house; there had been a quarrel between them along the road concerning a large sum of money stolen from Lebyadkin which Fedka was supposed to have hidden away... Liputin also ran to Peter Stepanovich's and managed to learn on the sly at the back door that Peter Stepanovich had returned home the night before after midnight and had slept soundly until eight o'clock that morning. There was of course no question of anything unusual in the circumstances of Fedka's death; careers like his frequently end like that. But the coincidence of the fatal words, 'that Fedka was drinking vodka for the last time', with the immediate fulfilment of the prediction was so remarkable that Liputin suddenly ceased wavering. The shock had come; it was as if a stone had fallen on him and crushed him once and for all. Returning home, he silently pushed his travelling bag under the bed. That evening he was the first to appear at the appointed place for the meeting with Shatov, although he still had his passport in his pocket...

CHAPTER 5

A female traveller

I.

THE CATASTROPHE with Liza and the death of Marya Timofeevna made an overwhelming impression on Shatov. I mentioned earlier that I'd met him that morning in passing; he seemed not to be in his right mind. He told me, incidentally, that the previous evening around nine o'clock (that is, three hours before the fire), he'd been to see Marya Timofeevna. The next morning he went to have a look at the bodies, but, as far as I know, made no official statement anywhere that morning. Meanwhile, towards the end of that day, a veritable storm had arisen in his mind and... it seems I can now state with certainty, there came a moment just around twilight when he was ready to get up, go out, and—tell everything. Exactly what this *everything* was—he himself didn't quite know. Of course he would have achieved nothing except to give himself away. He had no evidence whatever that could expose the crime that had just been committed; he himself had mere vague conjectures about it to go on, only enough to convince himself alone with absolute certainty. But he was prepared to ruin himself if he could but 'crush the scoundrels'—in his own words. Peter Stepanovich had fairly correctly divined this impulse in him and knew he was taking a big risk in putting off the execution of his terrible new plan until the next day. On his side, as usual, he showed great self-confidence and contempt for all these 'insignificant little creatures', Shatov in particular. For some time he'd despised Shatov for his 'snivelling idiocy', as he himself had expressed it during his time abroad; he confidently hoped to be able to deal with such a simple creature, namely by not letting him out of his sight the whole of that day, and intercepting him at the first sign of danger. But what saved the 'scoundrels' for a little while longer was an entirely unexpected circumstance, something not one of them had foreseen...

At about eight o'clock in the evening (precisely when the members of the group were gathering at Erkel's awaiting Peter Stepanovich, indignant and agitated), Shatov was lying stretched out on his bed in the darkness without a candle, suffering from a headache and a slight chill. He was tormented by uncertainty; he was angry; he kept trying to make up his mind, but was unable to do so; cursing himself, he felt that nothing would come of it. Gradually he slipped into a light sleep and had something like a nightmare; he dreamt he was tied to his bed with ropes, totally bound and unable to move, and all the while he heard someone pounding at the fence, at the gate, at his door, at Kirillov's door, so furiously that the whole house was shaking. Some distant, familiar voice that tormented him was calling to him plaintively. He suddenly came to and sat up in bed. To his astonishment the pounding at the gate continued, although not nearly as loudly as it had seemed in his dream; still it was repeated and persistent, and the strange, 'tormenting' voice, yet not at all plaintive, on the contrary, impatient and irritable, was heard down at the gate alternating with someone else's voice, more restrained and ordinary. He jumped up, opened the window, and stuck out his head.

'Who's there?' he asked, literally petrified with fear.

'If that's Shatov,' came the curt, firm reply from below, 'be so good as to tell me directly and honestly whether you'll agree to let me in or not?'

So it was true; he had recognized the voice!

'Marie!... Is that you?'

'Yes, it's me, Marya Shatova. I assure you I can't keep the driver here a moment longer.'

'At once... I'll get a candle...' Shatov cried weakly. Then he rushed to find matches. As usual in such cases, the matches were nowhere to be found. He dropped the candlestick and the candle on the floor, and as soon as he heard the impatient voice calling from below once more, gave it all up and rushed down the steep staircase as fast as he could to open the gate.

'Do me a favour, hold my bag while I settle with this blockhead,' was the greeting he received from Mrs Marya

Shatova. She thrust into his hands a rather flimsy cheap canvas bag made in Dresden and studded with brass nails. She pounced angrily on the driver:

'I can assure you, you're asking too much. If you spent an extra hour dragging me around through muddy streets, it's your own fault because you didn't know where the stupid street was or how to get to this idiotic house. Be so kind as to take your thirty kopecks and understand that you won't get anything more.'

'Come on, lady, you kept telling me Voznesenskaya Street, but this is Bogoyavlenskaya*: Voznesenskaya is a long way from here. You've just got my gelding in a sweat.'

'Voznesenskaya, Bogoyavlenskaya—you ought to know these stupid street names better than me since you live here. Besides, you're being unfair: the first thing I said was Filippov's house, and you told me you knew where it was. In any case you can take me to court tomorrow if you like; as for now, I beg you to leave me in peace.'

'Here's another five kopecks!' said Shatov, impetuously taking a five-kopeck piece from his pocket and handing it to the driver.

'I must ask you not to do that!' Madame Shatova cried, flaring up, but the driver had urged his gelding on and Shatov, taking Marya by the hand, led her in through the gate.

'Hurry, Marie, quickly... that doesn't matter—you're soaking wet! Here, this way—what a pity there's no light— the stairs are steep. Hold tight. Well, here's my little room. Excuse me, I have no light... One minute!'

He picked up the candlestick, but it was still a while before any matches could be found. Madame Shatova stood waiting in silence in the middle of the room and didn't move.

'Thank God, at last!' he cried gleefully, lighting up the room. Marya Shatova quickly surveyed the place.

'I heard you were living in squalor, but I didn't think it would be like this,' she said in disgust and moved towards the bed.

'Oh, I'm so tired!' she said, sitting on the hard bed with an exhausted air. 'Please put down the bag and sit down on that chair. Oh well, do as you like, but you're getting in the way. I've come to stay with you for a while, until I find work, because I know nothing about things here and don't have any money. But if I'm in your way, please tell me at once, as you must do if you're an honest man. I could sell something tomorrow and stay in a hotel. You could take me there yourself... Oh, I'm so very tired!'

Shatov trembled all over.

'There's no need, Marie, no need for a hotel! What hotel? Why? Why?'

He clasped his hands, imploring her.

'Well, if we can do without a hotel, I still have to explain the situation. You remember, Shatova, we lived together as a married couple in Geneva for a little over two weeks; it's been three years since we parted, without any particular quarrel though. Don't think I've come back to resume anything from our stupid past. I've come back to find work, and if I've returned to this town, it's only because it's all the same to me. I haven't come to apologize for anything; please don't get any stupid ideas about that.'

'Oh, Marie! That's not necessary, not at all!' Shatov muttered vaguely.

'Well, if that's so, if you're so civilized that you understand the situation, let me add that if I've turned to you now and come straight to your place, it's partly because I've always considered you to be no villain, and perhaps much better than the others... those scoundrels!'

Her eyes flashed. She must have endured a great deal from those 'scoundrels'.

'I do assure you I wasn't laughing at you just now when I said you were kind. I was speaking plainly, without eloquence, which I can't bear. But this is all nonsense. I've always hoped you would have enough intelligence not to annoy me... Enough, I'm tired!'

She gave him a long, weary, harassed look. Shatov stood in front of her, about five paces away, on the other side of the room, listening to her timidly, but with a sense of renewal, with unwonted radiance in his expression. This strong, rough man, whose exterior was so prickly, had suddenly softened completely and was now radiant. Something extraordinary and completely unexpected stirred in his soul. Three years of separation, three years of broken marriage had driven nothing whatever from his heart. Perhaps he'd dreamt about her every day for the last three years, about this dear creature who'd once told him 'I love you.' Knowing Shatov, I can say for certain that he never even allowed himself to dream of the possibility that one day a woman would say 'I love you' to him. He was chaste and incredibly bashful; he considered himself a terrible monster; he hated his own face and character; he compared himself to a freak that could be carted around and exhibited at fairs. As a result he valued honesty above all else, and was fanatically devoted to his own convictions; he was gloomy, proud, easily angered and taciturn. Yet here was this unique being who'd loved him for two weeks (he always believed that, always!)—a being he'd always considered immeasurably higher than himself, in spite of a quite clear-eyed understanding of all her mistakes; a being he could forgive *everything*, absolutely everything (there could be no question about that whatsoever; in fact, even the opposite was true; as it turned out, he considered he had wronged her); and now, all of a sudden, this woman, this Marya Shatova was back in his house, once again standing before him... it was almost inconceivable! He was so overcome, there was so much that was terrible in this event, and at the same time so much happiness that he couldn't, perhaps didn't even want to, perhaps was afraid to understand it all. It was a dream. But when she looked at him with her tormented eyes, he suddenly realized this dear being was suffering and perhaps had been wronged. His heart froze. He looked at her features with anguish: the first bloom of youth had long since disappeared from the exhausted face. True, she was still attractive—in his eyes just as beautiful as ever. (In fact, she was about twenty-five years old, quite strongly built, above average height (she was taller than Shatov), with a full head of dark brown hair, a pale oval face and large dark eyes that glittered now with a feverish brilliance.) But the earlier light-hearted, innocent, good-natured energy that he had known so well had been replaced by sullen irritability, disenchantment, almost cynicism to which she herself had not grown accustomed and which she actually resented. But the main thing was, she was ill, that he saw clearly. In spite of his fear of her, he went up to her abruptly and took hold of both her hands.

'Marie... you know... you may be very tired, for God's sake, don't be angry... Would you like some tea, for example? It might make you feel better, don't you think? If you'd only agree!...'

'What's to agree with? Of course I agree! What a baby you are. Give me some tea, if you can. It's so cramped in here! And very cold!'

'Oh, I'll get some logs, logs... I have some logs!' said Shatov, pacing around the room. 'Logs... that is, but... I'll get the tea first,' he said, waving his arm in desperate determination and grabbing his cap.

'Where are you going? Don't you have any tea here?'

'I will, I will, I will, soon I'll have everything here... I...'. He seized a revolver from the shelf.

'I'll sell this revolver at once... or I'll pawn it...'

'That's stupid and will take too long! Here, take some of my money if you don't have any. There's eighty kopecks, I think. That's all. This place is like a madhouse.'

'No, no, I don't need your money. I'll be right back, in a minute, I can manage without the revolver...'

He went straight to see Kirillov. This was probably about two hours before Peter Stepanovich and Liputin paid him the visit. Although Shatov and Kirillov lived in the same yard, they scarcely saw each other. When they met they never greeted or spoke to each other: they'd 'lain' side by side in America for too long.

'Kirillov, you always have tea. Do you have any now and a samovar?'

Kirillov was pacing around the room (as was his custom, from one corner to another, all night long). He suddenly stopped and stared intently at this man who'd come rushing in, though without any particular surprise.

'Yes, I have tea, I have sugar, and I have a samovar. But

you don't need a samovar since the tea is still hot. Sit down and have some.'

'Kirillov, in America we lay side by side... My wife has come back to me... I... Give me some tea... I need a samovar.'

'If your wife's come back, you need a samovar. But take it later. I have two of them. For now take the teapot from the table. It's hot, very hot. Take everything, take the sugar; everything. Bread... Lots of bread, take it all. There's some veal. I've a rouble in money.'

'Give it to me, friend. I'll give you it back tomorrow! Oh, Kirillov!'

'Is it the same wife who was in Switzerland? That's good. And the fact you came running in here is also good.'

'Kirillov!' cried Shatova, putting the teapot under his arm, taking the sugar and bread in both hands. 'Kirillov! If... if only you'd renounce your terrible fantasies and stop your atheistic ravings... oh, what a fine person you'd be, Kirillov!'

'Clearly you love your wife even after Switzerland. That's good —if even after Switzerland. When you need more tea, come back. Any time of night, I never sleep. I'll have a samovar. Take the rouble, there. Go back to your wife; I'll stay here and think about you and your wife.'

Marya Shatova was obviously satisfied with the speed of it and sipped the tea almost greedily; but there was no need to go back for the samovar. She drank only half a cup and ate only a tiny piece of bread. She refused the veal irritably and with disgust.

'You're ill, Marie, this all shows you're not well...' Shatov observed timidly, waiting on her timidly.

'Of course, I'm not well; please sit down. Where did you get the tea since you had none?'

Shatov told her briefly about Kirillov. She'd heard something about him.

'I know he's insane; that's enough, thanks. Aren't there enough idiots? So you were in America? I heard, you wrote.'

'Yes, I... I wrote to Paris.'

'Enough, and please talk about something else. Are you a Slavophile* by conviction?'

'I... it's not that I... I became a Slavophile because it was impossible to be a Russian,' he said with a wry smile and with the effort of a man who's made an inappropriate and ill-timed witticism.

'You're not a Russian?'

'No, I'm not.'

'Well, that's stupid. Sit down, I beg you, once and for all. Why are you wandering around? You think I'm delirious? Perhaps I will be. You said only two of you live in this house?'

'Two... downstairs...'

'And both so clever. Downstairs? You said downstairs?'

'No, nothing.'

'How do you mean, nothing? I want to know.'

'I was only going to say that now there are only two of us living in this house, but the Lebyadkins also used to live downstairs before...'

'That's who was murdered last night?' she shot back suddenly. 'I've heard. I'd just arrived when I heard. You had a fire?'

'Yes, Marie, yes, and perhaps I'm doing a despicable thing this minute by forgiving those scoundrels...' he said, standing up suddenly, pacing around the room and waving his arms almost in a frenzy.

But Marie didn't quite understand him. She was listening absent-mindedly; she asked questions, but didn't listen to his replies.

'Nice goings-on around here. Oh, it's so disgusting! They're all scoundrels! Sit down, I beg you, once and for all. Oh, how you irritate me!' she said, dropping her head on the pillow in exhaustion.

'Marie, I won't... Maybe you should have a bit of a lie down, Marie?'

She didn't answer and closed her eyes in exhaustion. Her pale face resembled a corpse. She fell asleep almost immediately. Shatov looked around, put out the candle, once again glanced uneasily at her face, clasped his hands tight in front of him, left the room on tiptoe and went out into the passage. At the top of the stairs he pressed his face into the corner and stood there for about ten minutes, in silence, without moving. He would have stood there longer, but suddenly from below he heard quiet, cautious footsteps. Someone was coming up the stairs. Shatov remembered he'd forgotten to lock the gate.

'Who's there?' he asked in a whisper.

The unknown visitor kept climbing the stairs without hurrying or replying. When he got to the top he stopped; it was impossible to get a good look at him in the darkness. Suddenly he asked cautiously:

'Ivan Shatov?'

Shatov identified himself but then quickly held out his hand to stop him; but the stranger took Shatov's hand—Shatov recoiled as if he'd touched a horrible reptile.

'Stay here,' he whispered quickly. 'Don't go in. I can't receive you now. My wife has come back to me. I'll bring a candle.'

When he returned with a candle, he saw it was a young officer; he didn't remember his name, but he'd seen him somewhere before.

'Erkel,' the man introduced himself. 'You saw me at Virginsky's.'

'I remember; you sat there and kept writing. Listen,' Shatov cried suddenly, going up to him frantically, but still speaking in a whisper, 'You gave me a signal just now when you took my hand. I don't give a damn about all these signals! I don't acknowledge them... I don't want to... I can throw you downstairs right now, do you know that?'

'No, I don't know that and have no idea why you're so angry,' the guest replied without malice, almost good-naturedly. 'I've merely come to give you a message and have no desire to waste any time. You have a printing press that doesn't belong to you and you're responsible for, as you yourself know. I've been ordered to ask you to hand it over to Liputin at seven o'clock tomorrow evening. Furthermore, I've been instructed to tell you that nothing more will be required of you.'

'Nothing?'

'Absolutely nothing. Your request is being granted; you're

being released. I've been told to relay that message to you definitely.'

'Who ordered you to tell me?'

'Those who gave me the signal.'

'Have you come from abroad?'

'That... I think, should make no difference to you.'

'Oh, damn you! Why didn't you come earlier if you were ordered to?'

'I was following instructions and wasn't alone.'

'I understand, I understand you weren't alone. Oh... hell! Why didn't Liputin come himself?'

'So, I'll call for you at six o'clock tomorrow evening and we'll proceed on foot. Besides the three of us, no one else will be there.'

'Will Verkhovensky be there?'

'No, he won't. Verkhovensky is leaving town tomorrow morning at eleven o'clock.'

'Just as I thought,' Shatov whispered furiously and struck his fist against his hip. 'He's running away, the scoundrel.'

He sank into agitated reflection. Erkel stared at him intently, remaining silent, waiting.

'How will you take possession of it? You can't just pick it up and carry it away.'

'That won't be necessary. You'll simply show us where it is and we'll make sure it's really buried there. We know only approximately where it is; we don't know exactly. Have you ever shown anyone the place?'

Shatov looked at him.

'You, you, you're such a little boy—such a silly little boy—you're up to your ears in it too, like a stupid sheep. Oh, that's just what they need—young blood like yours! Well, go on! Ugh! That scoundrel has deceived all of you and now he's run off.'

Erkel gave him a clear, calm look, but seemed not to understand.

'Verkhovensky's run off, Verkhovensky!' Shatov cried furiously, grinding his teeth.

'But he's still here, he hasn't left yet. He's going tomorrow,' Erkel replied softly and persuasively. 'I invited him to be present as a witness; all my instructions made reference to him.' He confided everything like an inexperienced young boy. 'Unfortunately, he couldn't agree because of his impending departure; he's really in something of a hurry.'

Shatov once again glanced pityingly at the young simpleton, but suddenly made a gesture of dismissal as if thinking: 'It's not even worth pitying them.'

'Fine, I'll come,' he said abruptly all of a sudden. 'As for now, go away, off with you!'

'I'll call for you at six o'clock sharp,' Erkel said, bowing politely and descending the stairs without hurrying.

'You little fool!' Shatov cried after him from the top of the stairs, unable to restrain to himself.

'What's that?' Erkel called up from below.

'Nothing, keep going.'

'I thought you said something.'

2.

Erkel was the sort of 'little fool' who lacks only the higher form of reason that controls man's head; but he had plenty of inferior, subordinate reasoning powers, even to the point of cunning. Fanatically, childishly devoted to 'the cause', but in fact devoted to Peter Verkhovensky, he acted on the instructions given him during the meeting of the group of five at Virginsky's when roles were being decided and distributed. Peter Stepanovich, when assigning him the role of messenger, managed to take him aside and talk with him for about ten minutes. Carrying out orders was a necessity for this shallow, unthinking creature, who always yearned to submit to someone else's will—oh, not, of course, for any reason other than the good of the 'common' or 'noble' cause. But even that didn't make any difference, since little fanatics such as Erkel can never conceive of serving an idea other than by identifying it with the person who according to their conception expresses the idea. The sensitive, affectionate, and kind-hearted Erkel was perhaps the most callous of the murderers planning to kill Shatov; he would be present at the execution without blinking an eye, without feeling the least bit of personal guilt. For example, he'd been ordered to get a good look at Shatov's surroundings while carrying out his orders; when Shatov met him at the top of the stairs and blurted out (probably without thinking) that his wife had come back to him, Erkel had enough instinctive cunning to evince not the least bit of curiosity, in spite of the fact that it immediately occurred to him that the return of Shatov's wife could have a significant impact on the success of their undertaking...

And so it did: that fact alone saved the 'scoundrels' from Shatov's carrying out his intention and, at the same time, helped them 'get rid of him...'. In the first place, it rattled Shatov, threw him off track, deprived him of his usual perspicacity and caution. Any idea of his personal safety was the last thing that could have struck him when he was so preoccupied with something else. On the contrary, he was eager to believe that Peter Verkhovensky really would run away tomorrow: that coincided with all his suspicions! Returning to his room, he sat down in the corner again, rested his elbows on his knees and covered his face with his hands. He was tormented by bitter thoughts...

Then he'd lift his head again and tiptoe in to have a look at her. 'Good Lord! She'll have a fever by tomorrow morning; she may even have one now! Of course she's caught a cold. She's not used to this awful climate; then that railway carriage, third class, snowstorm, rain, and all she was wearing was that thin cloak, no other clothes... How could anyone leave her like that, abandon her without help? And that bag of hers, it's so tiny, light, crumpled—weighing only about ten pounds! The poor thing, she's worn out! She's been through so much! She's proud, that's why she doesn't complain. But how irritable, how very irritable she is! That's her illness: even an angel becomes irritable when ill. What a dry forehead, feverish no doubt; her skin is so dark around the eyes... and yet, how beautiful the oval shape of her face is, and her rich hair, how...'

He quickly averted his eyes, walked away in haste, as if afraid of seeing something in her other than an unhappy, exhausted creature in need of help—'how could he even think about *hopes*? Oh, how base man is, how vile a beast!'

And he went back to his corner, sat down, covered his face with his hands, and once more started dreaming, reminiscing... Once more he was haunted by those hopes.

'Oh, I'm so tired, so very tired'; he recalled her exclamations, her weak, broken voice. 'Lord! Abandon her now, when all she has is eighty kopecks; she'd even held out her purse, that tiny old thing! She's come back to find a position—well, what does she know about positions? What do they know about Russia? Why, they're just like capricious children; it's their own fantasies they've created themselves. And she's angry, poor thing, because Russia isn't anything like their foreign fantasies! Oh, you unfortunate creatures, you innocent babes!... But it really is quite cold in here.'

He remembered her complaint and his promise to light the stove. 'I have some logs; I could bring them in, but I don't want to wake her. Still, I could. And what about the veal? She might want something to eat when she wakes up... Well, later; Kirillov doesn't sleep all night. I should cover her; she's sound asleep, but she's probably very, very cold!'

He went in to have another look at her; her dress had got rucked up a little and half her right leg was exposed to the knee. He turned away suddenly, almost in alarm, took off his own warm coat and, left in his old threadbare jacket, covered her up, trying not to look at her bare leg.

Lighting the logs, walking around on tiptoe, inspecting the sleeping woman, dreaming in the corner, another inspection—all this took a great deal of time. Two or three hours passed. It was during this time that Verkhovensky and Liputin paid their visit to Kirillov. At long last Shatov dozed in the corner. Then he heard her groan; she awoke and called to him; he jumped up like a criminal.

'Marie! I must have dozed... Oh, what a scoundrel I am, Marie!'

She sat up, looked around with wonder as if not recognizing where she was, and suddenly jumped up in indignation and fury:

'I've taken your bed; I was dead tired and fell asleep. Why didn't you wake me? How dare you think I came to be a burden to you?'

'How could I wake you, Marie?'

'You could have. You should have! There's no bed for you here, since I took yours. You shouldn't have put me in such an awkward position. Do you think I've come to take advantage of your generosity? You must take your own bed right now and I'll lie down on some chairs in the corner...'

'Marie, I don't have enough chairs and there's nothing to make a bed.'

'Well, then, I'll simply lie down on the floor. Otherwise you'll have to sleep there. I want to lie on the floor, right now, right now!'

She stood up, went to take a step, but suddenly a violent spasm of pain took away all her strength and resolution; she fell back on the bed with a loud groan. Shatov ran over to her but, hiding her face in the pillow, Marie seized his hand and squeezed it with all her might. This lasted about a minute.

'Marie, my dear, if necessary, there's a Doctor Frenzel who lives nearby; he's a friend of mine, a close friend... I could fetch him.'

'Nonsense!'

'Why nonsense? Tell me, Marie, what's hurting? We could try some compresses... on your stomach, for instance... I could do that even without a doctor... Or mustard plasters.'

'What's this?' she asked strangely, lifting her head and looking at him in fear.

'What's what, Marie?' Shatov asked, not understanding her. 'What are you talking about? Oh God, I'm completely lost, Marie. Forgive me, I don't understand a thing.'

'Oh, leave me alone. It's not for you to understand. It would even be ridiculous...' she said, smiling bitterly. 'Talk to me about something. Walk around the room and talk to me. Don't just stand there next to me and don't look at me: I ask you for the five-hundredth time!'

Shatov began to walk around the room, looking at the floor, trying with all his might not to look at her.

'There's—don't be angry, Marie, I beg you—there's some veal, just right here, and some tea... You ate so little before...'

She waved him away angrily and in disgust. Shatov bit his tongue in desperation.

'Listen, I plan to open a bookbinding shop* here, organized on rational principles. Since you live here, what do you think: will it succeed or not?'

'Oh, Marie, books aren't read much here, and there simply aren't any around. Do they really need them bound?'

'Who's "they"?'

'Local readers and inhabitants in general, Marie.'

'Well, speak more clearly. He says "they", and who does he mean by "they"? You don't know any grammar.'

'It's in the spirit of the language, Marie,' Shatov muttered.

'Oh, get away with your spirit, I'm sick of it. Why won't the local inhabitants or readers need their books bound?'

'Because reading books and having them bound represent two enormously different stages of development. First, people gradually get used to reading, over centuries naturally, but they don't take care of their books and toss them around. Having books bound signifies respect for the book; it indicates that people not only love to read, but they view it as an important occupation. Nowhere in Russia has that stage been reached. Europe has been binding its books for some time.'

'Even though pedantically put, that's at least not stupid and reminds me of three years ago; you were sometimes rather clever three years ago.'

She said this with the same disgust as she had all her previous capricious utterances.

'Marie, Marie,' Shatov said, turning to her with deep emotion. 'Oh, Marie! If you only knew how much has happened during these last three years! I heard later that you despised me for changing my convictions. But who was it I deserted? Enemies of real life; antiquated little liberals afraid of their own independence; lackeys of thought, enemies of personality and freedom, decrepit preachers of death and decay! What do they have? Old age, the golden mean, base philistine mediocrity, envious equality, equality with no sense of dignity, equality as understood by lackeys or Frenchmen in 1793... But the main thing is, they're all scoundrels, scoundrels, and more scoundrels.'

'Yes, there are a lot of scoundrels,' she replied abruptly and as if in pain. She lay there stretched out, not moving, as if afraid to stir, her head thrown back on the pillow, resting on her side, directing her exhausted but proud gaze at the ceiling. Her face was pale, her lips dry and parched.

'You understand, Marie, you understand!' Shatov cried. She tried to shake her head in disagreement, but suddenly another spasm of pain overcame her. Once again she hid her face in the pillow and with all her might gripped Shatov's hand until it hurt. He'd rushed over to her and was beside himself with fear.

'Marie, Marie! This may be very serious, Marie!'

'Be quiet... I won't have it, I won't,' she cried, almost in frenzy, turning her face upwards again. 'Don't you dare look at me with that compassion of yours! Walk around the room, say something, talk...'

Shatov, like one distraught, began muttering something.

'What kind of work do you do here?' she asked, interrupting him with contemptuous impatience.

'I work in the office of a local merchant. If I really wanted to, Marie, I could earn good money here.'

'So much the better for you...'

'Oh, don't misunderstand me, Marie. I merely said it as...'

'What else do you do? What are you preaching? You have to be preaching something; that's your nature!'

'I'm preaching God, Marie.'

'But you don't believe in Him. I never could understand that idea.'

'Let's leave that until later, Marie.'

'What sort of person was Marya Timofeevna?'

'Let's leave that until later, too.'

'Don't you dare say things like that to me! Is it true her death was caused by the wickedness of... those people?'

'Absolutely,' Shatov said, grinding his teeth.

Marie suddenly raised her head and cried out in pain:

'Don't you ever talk about that again, never again, never!'

She fell back on the bed in a spasm of the same terrible

pain; this was the third time, but now her groans were louder and had become screams.

'Oh, you intolerable man! You unbearable man!' she cried, tossing about, no longer sparing herself and shoving Shatov away as he stood over her.

'Marie, I'll do whatever you want... I'll walk around and talk to you...'

'Can't you see it's begun?'

'What's begun, Marie?'

'How do I know? How do I know anything about it?... Oh, damn it! Damn it all from the very beginning!'

'Marie, if you'd tell what's begun... or else I... how can I understand?'

'Oh, you abstract, useless windbag. Damn everything on earth!'

'Marie! Marie!'

He seriously thought she was going insane.

'Can't you see I'm in labour?' She sat up and looked at him with terrible, acute malice distorting her whole face. 'Curse this child, even before it's born!'

'Marie,' Shatov cried, finally realizing what it was all about. 'Marie... Why didn't you tell me before?' he cried, pulling himself together suddenly and grabbing his cap with energetic decisiveness.

'How could I know when I came in here? Would I really have come to you? They told me it would be another ten days! Where are you going? Where? Don't you dare!'

'To fetch a midwife! I'll sell my revolver; first thing we need now is money!'

'Don't you dare, don't you *dare* go for a midwife. Fetch any old woman, an old peasant woman; I have eighty kopecks in my bag... Peasant women give birth without midwives... And if I croak, so much the better...'

'You'll have a midwife and an old peasant woman. But how can I leave you alone, Marie?'

Realizing it was better to leave her alone now without help, rather than later, in spite of her frantic state, he paid no attention to her moans and angry exclamations, and rushed downstairs as fast as he possibly could.

3.

First he went to see Kirillov. It was already almost one o'clock in the morning. Kirillov was standing in the middle of his room.

'Kirillov, my wife's having a baby!'

'What do you mean?'

'A baby, she's having a baby!'

'You're... not mistaken?'

'Oh, no, no, she's having contractions!... We need a woman, some old woman, right away... Can we get one now? You used to have so many old women around...'

'I'm sorry I don't know how to give birth to babies,' Kirillov replied thoughtfully. 'I mean, not that I don't know how to give birth, I don't know what to do to give birth to them... or... No, I don't know how to say it.'

'You mean you don't know how to help someone in labour; but that's not what I'm asking. I'm asking for a woman, an old woman, a peasant woman, a nurse, a servant!'

'You'll get an old woman, but perhaps not right away. If you like, I could come instead...'

'Oh, that's impossible; I'll go to Mrs Virginskaya, the midwife.'

'She's horrible!'

'Oh, yes, Kirillov, yes, but she's the best of the lot! Oh, no, there won't be reverence, or joy, only disdain, abuse, blasphemy—and in the presence of so great a mystery, the arrival of a new being!... Oh, she's cursing it already!...'

'If you like, I'll...'

'No, no, but while I'm running to fetch her (I'll drag Mrs Virginskaya there), you can go to the bottom of our staircase and stand there quietly listening, but don't dare go in, you'll frighten her; don't go in under any circumstances; just listen... in case of any emergency. And only if there's an emergency, then go in.'

'I understand. I have another rouble. Here. I was going to buy a chicken tomorrow, but I'm not going to now. Hurry up, go as fast as you can. There'll be a samovar here all night.'

Kirillov knew nothing about the plans for Shatov, nor was he aware of the danger the man was in. He knew only that he had some old score to settle with 'those people'. Even though he himself was partly implicated in the affair as a result of instructions from abroad (which, by the way, were very vague, since he wasn't too closely involved with them), lately he'd given it all up, all instructions; he'd distanced himself from everything, from the 'common cause' in particular, and had been devoting himself to a life of contemplation. Although at the meeting Peter Verkhovensky had invited Liputin to go with him to Kirillov's house to make sure the latter would, at the right moment, take the 'Shatov affair' upon himself, still during the interview with Kirillov he said not one word about Shatov, he didn't even hint at it. He probably thought it impolitic and considered Kirillov unreliable, and so decided to leave it until the next day when it would all be over and really wouldn't make any difference to Kirillov. At least that's what Peter Stepanovich thought about Kirillov. Liputin also noted there'd been no mention whatever of Shatov, in spite of Verkhovensky's promise; but Liputin was too agitated to protest about that.

Shatov ran like a whirlwind to Muravinaya Street, cursing the distance and seeing no end to it.

He had to knock for some time at Virginsky's house: everyone had gone to sleep a while ago. But that didn't keep Shatov from pounding at the shutters with all his might. The dog chained in the yard rushed around barking at him ferociously. All the dogs in the street followed suit; a canine bedlam ensued.

'Why are you knocking and what do you want?' asked Virginsky at the window at long last, but in a gentle tone, quite different from what one would expect in response to such an 'outrage'. The shutters were thrown back and the little ventilation pane opened.

'Who's there? What scoundrel?' a woman's voice shrieked with all the anger one would have expected in the circumstances. It was Virginsky's relative, the old maid.

'It's me, Shatov. My wife's come back to me and now she's giving birth...'

'Well, let her give birth. Go away!'

'I've come for Arina Prokhorovna and won't leave without her!'

'She can't take care of everyone. Night deliveries is a special practice... Go to Maksheeva's and stop making so much noise!' the angry female voice rattled on. Shatov heard Virginsky try to stop her, but the old maid pushed him aside and wouldn't give way.

'I won't leave!' Shatov shouted again.

'Wait a bit, just wait a bit!' Virginsky cried at last, having dealt with the old woman. 'I beg you, wait five minutes, Shatov. I'll wake Arina Prokhorovna. Please don't knock and don't shout... Oh, how terrible this all is!'

After five interminable minutes Arina Prokhorovna appeared.

'So your wife has come back to you?' her voice asked from the window. To Shatov's surprise she didn't sound angry at all, just peremptory as usual; but that was the only way Arina Prokhorovna knew how to speak.

'Yes, my wife, and she's in labour.'

'Marya Ignatievna?'

'Yes, Marya Ignatievna. Of course, Marya Ignatievna!'

There was a moment's silence. Shatov waited. He heard whispering inside the house.

'Has she been back long?' Madame Virginskaya enquired again.

'She arrived at eight o'clock this evening. Hurry, please.'

Again he heard whispering, as if they were conferring.

'Listen, you're not making a mistake, are you? Did she send you to me?'

'No, she didn't send me to you. She wanted an old woman, any old woman, so as not to burden me with the expense. But don't worry, I'll pay you.'

'Fine, I'll come whether you pay or not. I've always valued Marya Ignatievna's independent attitude, even though she may not remember me. Do you have the most essential things?'

'I don't have anything, but I'll get it, I'll get it...'

'There's generosity even in these people!' Shatov thought

as he headed for Lyamshin's. 'Convictions and human feeling—it seems they're two very different things. Perhaps I've been unfair to blame them!... We're all to blame, all of us... if only everyone could be convinced of that!...'

He didn't have to knock very long at Lyamshin's; to his surprise, Lyamshin opened the window at once, having jumped out of bed in his night-shirt and bare feet, running the risk of catching a cold. He was very cautious and always worried about his health. But there was a special reason for his alertness and haste: Lyamshin had been trembling all evening and was unable to fall asleep as a result of his agitation after the meeting of the group; he was haunted by fear of a visit from uninvited and entirely unwanted guests. Most of all he was tormented by news of Shatov's denunciation... And now, all of a sudden, as if on purpose, someone was pounding at his window incredibly loudly!...

He was so terrified when he saw Shatov that he immediately slammed the window shut and jumped back into bed. Shatov began pounding ferociously and shouting.

'How dare you knock like that so late at night?' Lyamshin shouted menacingly, though quaking with fear, at least two minutes later when he decided to open the window again and make sure Shatov had come alone.

'Here's your revolver back. Take it and give me fifteen roubles for it.'

'What's going on? Are you drunk? This is highway robbery; I'm going to catch cold. Wait a minute, I'll get a blanket on.'

'Give me fifteen roubles right now. If you don't, I'll knock and shout until dawn; I'll break your window-frame.'

'And I'll get the police and have you locked up.'

'Think I'm dumb, do you? Think I won't get the police? Who has more to fear from them, you or me?'

'How can you harbour such contemptible beliefs?... I know what you're hinting at... Stop it, stop it, for heaven's sake, stop knocking! Who on earth can get hold of any money at night? What do you need the money for if you're not drunk?'

'My wife has come back to me. I'm letting you have this

revolver for ten roubles less than I paid for it and I've never even fired it; take the revolver, take it immediately.'

Lyamshin stuck his hand out mechanically through the open window and took the revolver; he waited and suddenly, thrusting his head rapidly out of the window, muttered, as if beside himself, with a chill running up and down his spine:

'You're lying, your wife hasn't come back to you at all. You... you just want to run away.'

'You idiot, where can I run to? Let your Peter Verkhovensky run away, not me. I was just at the midwife Virginskaya's house and she's agreed to come. Ask her. My wife is suffering. I need money; give it to me!'

An elaborate firework display of ideas exploded in Lyamshin's devious mind. Suddenly everything appeared in a different light, but fear still prevented him from thinking clearly.

'But how can that be... you're not even living with your wife?'

'I'll smash your skull for asking questions like that.'

'Oh, my God, forgive me, I understand, I was simply so surprised... I understand, I understand. But... but—will Arina Prokhorovna really come? Did you just say she'd gone? You know that's not true. You see, you see, you see, you're lying to me at every stage.'

'She's probably with my wife right now; don't delay me. It's not my fault you're so stupid.'

'That's not true, I'm not stupid. Excuse me, I can't possibly...'

And now, absolutely distraught, he began to close the window for the third time, but Shatov let out such a yell that he stuck his head back out at once.

'But this is absolutely personal assault! What on earth do you want from me? What? Tell me! Formulate it! And think, just think, it's the middle of the night!'

'I want fifteen roubles, you blockhead!'

'But I might not want my revolver back at all. You have no right. You bought it from me—now it's over and done with; you have no right. There's no way I can come up with that kind of money in the middle of the night. Where can I get that sum?'

'You always have money. I've taken ten roubles off the price already, but you're well-known as a moneygrubbing little Yid.'

'Come back the day after tomorrow—listen, in the morning the day after tomorrow, precisely at twelve o'clock, and I'll let you have it all, all of it, you hear?'

Shatov pounded ferociously on the window-frame for the third time:

'Give me ten roubles, and tomorrow, as soon as it's light, another five.'

'No, another five the day after tomorrow; tomorrow, I swear, I won't have it. Don't even think of coming.'

'Give me ten roubles; oh, you scoundrel!'

'What are you insulting me for? Wait a moment, I have to get some light; you've broken the window here... Imagine going round swearing at people in the middle of the night. Here!' he said and thrust a banknote out through the window.

Shatov grabbed it—it was a five-rouble note.

'I swear to you, I can't do any more, you can slit my throat but I can't. I can give you the rest the day after tomorrow, but I can't give you any more now.'

'I won't leave,' Shatov bellowed.

'Well, here, take this, here, this as well, see, but I won't give you any more. Even if you yell your head off, I won't give you any more, no matter what, I won't, I won't, I won't!'

He was in a frenzy, in despair, in a cold sweat. The two bills he'd just handed over were one-rouble notes. Shatov now had a total of seven roubles.

'Well, damn you; I'll come back tomorrow. I'll beat the hell out of you, Lyamshin, if you don't have the other eight roubles.'

'You won't find me at home, you fool!' flashed through Lyamshin's mind.

'Wait a minute, wait!' he shouted frantically to Shatov who was already running away. 'Wait a minute, come back.

Tell me, please, were you telling me the truth? Has your wife really come back to you?'

'Idiot!' Shatov cried, spat in disgust, and ran home as fast as his legs could carry him.

4.

I must mention that Arina Prokhorovna knew nothing about the resolutions adopted at yesterday's meeting. When Virginsky had returned home feeling weak and stunned, he didn't dare tell her about the decision that had been taken; but he was unable to restrain himself completely and told her half of it—that is, Verkhovensky's announcement of Shatov's intention to inform on them; but even then he said he didn't really believe it. Arina Prokhorovna was terribly frightened. That explains why, when Shatov came running to fetch her, even though she was exhausted from having spent the previous night attending another labour, she decided to go with him at once. She'd always been sure that 'a piece of trash like Shatov was capable of committing any sort of despicable political act'; but the arrival of Marya Ignatievna put things in an entirely different light. Shatov's fear, the desperate tone of his request, and his entreaties for help all signified a change in the traitor's feelings: a man who had decided to betray himself merely in order to destroy others would have had a very different look and tone. In a word, Arina Prokhorovna decided to see for herself, with her own eyes. Virginsky was very pleased with her decision—it was as if a large weight had been lifted from him! He even began to feel somewhat hopeful: Shatov's appearance seemed utterly incompatible with Verkhovensky's conclusion...

Shatov was not mistaken; upon his return he found Arina Prokhorovna already with Marie. She'd just arrived and had contemptuously dismissed Kirillov, who was hanging around at the foot of the staircase. She quickly introduced herself to Marie who failed to recognize her as a previous acquaintance. She found her in a 'very bad way', that is, spiteful, distraught, in a state of 'the most cowardly despair'; within five minutes she managed to overcome all resistance.

'Why do you insist you don't want an expensive midwife?' she was asking just as Shatov came in. 'That's pure nonsense, spurious notions resulting from your present abnormal condition. With the help of just any old woman, a peasant woman, there's a fifty-fifty chance something would go wrong; then the trouble and cost would be even greater than with an expensive midwife. How do you know I'm an expensive midwife? You'll pay me later; I won't charge more than necessary, and I guarantee success. You won't die with me; I've seen worse cases. If you like, I can send the child off tomorrow to an orphanage, then to be brought up in the country, and that will be that. You'll recuperate, take up some reasonable work, and in a very short time you'll pay Shatov back for the room and board, which won't be that much anyway...'

'It's not that... I have no right to burden...'

'Those are very rational and civic feelings, but believe me, Shatov will hardly spend anything if he's willing to transform himself from a creature of fantasies into a man with even a drop of common sense. He merely has to refrain from doing anything stupid, beating a drum, running around with his tongue wagging. If we don't take him firmly in hand by morning he'll have roused all the doctors in town; he woke all the dogs on my street. You don't need a doctor, I've already told you I can answer for everything. You could still hire an old woman as a servant, that won't cost much. But he might prove useful too himself, instead of just doing stupid things. He has two hands and two legs; he could run to the chemist's without offending your feelings by his charity. To hell with his charity! Wasn't it he who brought you to this position? Wasn't it he who caused all the trouble in that family where you were a governess when he came up with the selfish idea of marrying you? We heard all about it... Though just now he came running to fetch me like a madman, shouting up and down the whole street. I won't force myself on anyone; I've come for your sake alone, on principle, because we should stick together. I told him that even before I left the house. If you think I'm not needed here, I'll say goodbye; I only hope there won't be any trouble which could easily be avoided.'

She even rose from the chair.

Marie was so helpless, in such suffering and, truth be told, so afraid of what lay ahead of her, that she dared not let her go. But this woman suddenly became hateful to her: she was talking at complete cross-purposes, that wasn't what Marie had in mind! But the prediction about death in the hands of an incompetent midwife overcame her aversion. On the other hand, from then on she became more demanding of Shatov, even merciless. It finally reached the point where she forbade him not only to look at her, but even to stand near her. Her suffering increased. Her curses, even her abuse, became more ferocious.

'Ach, we'd better send him away,' snapped Arina Prokhorovna. 'He looks terrible, he's only scaring you; he's as a pale as a corpse! Tell me, please, you odd creature, what's up with you? What a performance!'

Shatov made no reply; he decided not to answer.

'I've seen stupid fathers in such cases who go off their heads too. But at least they...'

'Stop it, or leave me here to die! Don't say another word, not another word! I won't have it, I won't!' Marie screamed.

'No question of not saying another word, unless you've lost your reason; that's what I think has happened with you in your condition. We must at least talk about the business in hand: tell me, has anything been prepared? You tell me, Shatov, since she can't.'

'Tell me what you need.'

'So nothing's been prepared.'

She listed everything she needed; to be fair to her, she limited herself only to what was absolutely essential, the bare necessities. Shatov managed to find some of them. Marie took out a key and offered it to him so he could look inside her travelling bag. Since his hands were trembling it took him longer than necessary to open the unfamiliar lock. Marie was beside herself, but when Arina Prokhorovna jumped up to grab the key away from him, Marie wouldn't permit her to look inside the bag on any account and insisted, screaming and shrieking wilfully, that only Shatov was allowed to open it.

It was necessary to run to Kirillov to fetch some other things. As soon as Shatov turned to go, Marie began to call him back frantically and calmed down only when Shatov came rushing back from the stairs to assure her he'd only be gone a minute or so to fetch the necessary items and he'd be right back.

'Well, my lady, it's certainly hard to please you,' Arina Prokhorovna said with a chuckle. 'First you tell him to stand there facing the wall and not dare look at you, then you tell him he can't leave you, even for a minute, or else you'll start crying. Why, he might begin to imagine all sorts of things. Come, come, don't be silly, don't fuss, I was only teasing.'

'He won't dare imagine anything.'

'My, my, my, if he didn't love you like a sheep he wouldn't be running all over town with his tongue hanging out and wouldn't be waking up all the dogs. He even broke my window-frame.'

5.

Shatov found Kirillov still pacing up and down in his room, so preoccupied that he'd quite forgotten about the arrival of Shatov's wife; he listened, but didn't understand.

'Oh, yes,' he remembered suddenly, as if tearing himself away from some absorbing idea with great effort and only for a moment. 'Yes... an old woman.... Your wife or an old woman? Wait a minute: both your wife and an old woman, right? I remember. I did go; the old woman will come, but not right away. Take a pillow. Anything else? Yes... Wait a minute. Shatov, do you ever experience moments of eternal harmony?'

'You know, Kirillov, you really shouldn't stay up every night.'

Kirillov came to his senses and—strange to say—began speaking much more coherently than usual; it was obvious he'd formulated these thoughts some time ago, perhaps even jotted them down:

'There are seconds, usually no more than five or six at a time, when you suddenly feel the presence of eternal harmony, completely attained. It's not an earthly feeling; I'm not saying it's heavenly, but in his earthly form man is unable to endure it. He must be physically transformed or else die. This feeling is clear and unmistakable. It's as if you suddenly sensed the whole of nature and said: Yes, it's true. When He created the world, God said at the end of every day of creation: "Yes, it is true, it is good." It's... it's not a flood of tender emotion, it's simply a sense of happiness. You don't have to forgive anything because there's no longer anything to forgive. It's not that you feel love, oh—it's much higher than that! What's most terrifying is that it's so awfully clear and there's such a feeling of happiness. If it were to last for more than five seconds—the soul couldn't endure it and would have to disappear. In these five seconds I live a lifetime and I'd give my whole life for them because it'd be worth it. To withstand ten seconds one must be transformed physically. I think that man must stop having children. Why have children? What's the use of development if the goal's already been achieved? In the Gospel it says that at the Resurrection people will no longer bear children, but will be like angels of God.* That's a hint. Is your wife giving birth?'

'Kirillov, does this occur often?'

'Once every three days, once a week.'

'Do you have epilepsy?'

'No.'

'Well, you will. Watch out, Kirillov, I've heard that's just the way epilepsy begins. An epileptic once described in detail his sensation before a seizure just the way you did; he said it lasted five seconds and he couldn't endure any more. Remember Mohammed's pitcher* from which not one drop of water spilled while he circled paradise on his steed? The pitcher—that's your five seconds; it's too much like your eternal harmony, and Mohammed was an epileptic. Watch out, Kirillov, it's epilepsy!'

'It won't have time,' Kirillov said, laughing softly.

6.

The night was passing. Shatov was summoned, abused, and sent on errands. Marie reached an extreme stage of fear for

664 Devils. Part Three

her life. She screamed that she wanted to live 'absolutely, absolutely!' and was afraid to die. 'I don't want to, I don't want to!' she kept repeating. If Arina Prokhorovna hadn't been there, things would have gone very badly. She gradually gained complete control of her patient. Marie began to obey her every word and order, like a little child. Arina Prokhorovna ruled by sternness, not kindness, but it worked brilliantly. It began to grow light. Suddenly Arina Prokhorovna got the idea that Shatov had just run out on to the stairs to pray to God, and she began laughing. Marie also began laughing maliciously, sarcastically, as if she experienced some relief from that laughter. They finally chased Shatov away altogether. The morning was cold and damp. Shatov stood in the corner pressing his face against the wall, just as he had the evening before when Erkel arrived. He trembled like a leaf, afraid to think, but his mind clung to every image as it emerged, just as it does in our dreams. He was preoccupied with fantasies which continually broke apart, like rotten threads. At last the moans coming from the room were replaced by horrible animal cries, unbearable, impossible. He wanted to cover his ears, but couldn't; he fell to his knees, repeating unconsciously, 'Marie, Marie!' At last a cry was heard, a new cry that made Shatov shudder and jump up from his knees; it was a baby's cry, weak and discordant. He made the sign of the cross and went rushing into the room. In her arms Arina Prokhorovna held a small, pink, wrinkled creature that was crying and moving its tiny arms and legs; it was terrifyingly helpless and, like a speck of dust, at the mercy of the first breath of wind. But it was crying and proclaiming that it too had every right to exist... Marie lay there almost unconscious, but in a minute she opened her eyes and looked at Shatov in a very, very strange way: it was an entirely new look. He wasn't yet able to understand it, but he'd never seen it before or remembered anything like it.

'Is it a boy? A boy?' she asked Arina Prokhorovna in a feeble voice.

'A little boy!' she shouted in reply, swaddling the infant.

For a moment, after swaddling him and before laying him across the bed between two pillows, she gave him to Shatov to hold. Marie, as if afraid of Arina Prokhorovna, quietly signalled to him. He understood at once and lifted the baby up to show her.

'How... pretty...' she whispered weakly with a smile.

'My word, look at him staring!' the triumphant Arina Prokhorovna replied, laughing cheerfully, looking right into Shatov's face. 'What a face he's making!'

'Rejoice, Arina Prokhorovna... It's a great joy...' muttered Shatov with an expression of idiotic bliss, radiant after Marie's two words about the child.

'What kind of great joy is it?' Arina Prokhorovna asked good-naturedly, bustling about, cleaning up, and working as hard as a convict.

'The mystery of the appearance of a new being; it's a great and inexplicable mystery, Arina Prokhorovna. What a pity you don't understand!'

Shatov mumbled incoherently, stupefied and enraptured. It was as if something was reeling around inside his head and, of itself, beyond his control, was flowing from his soul.

'There were two people, and all of a sudden there's a third being, a new spirit, whole and complete, such that no human hands could ever create; new thought and new love; it's frightening, actually... There's nothing greater on earth!'

'Ach, what nonsense! It's simply a new stage of organic development and nothing more, no mystery at all,' Arina Prokhorovna replied, laughing sincerely and cheerfully. 'Your way, every fly is a mystery. But here's what: unnecessary people should never be born. First remake the world so they won't be unnecessary, then give birth to them. As it is, we'll have to take him off to the orphanage the day after tomorrow... But, that's how it should be.'

'I'll never let him go to any orphanage!' Shatov announced resolutely, staring at the floor.

'Adopting him as your son are you?'

'He is my son.'

'Of course, he's a Shatov, legally he's a Shatov, but there's no reason for you to pose as some great benefactor of all humanity. He can't ever manage without grand phrases. Well, well, all right, but listen here, good people,' she said, finally finishing her cleaning up, 'it's time for me to go. I'll come again in the morning and in the evening if I need to, but now, since everything's turned out so well, I have to attend to some others who've been waiting for me for quite a while. Shatov, I hear you've got an old woman somewhere; well, an old woman's all well and good, but you, her husband, shouldn't leave her; sit by her, in case you're needed. Marya Ignatievna won't chase you away... Now, now, I'm only teasing...'

Shatov accompanied her to the gate and she added to him alone:

'You've given me something to laugh at for the rest of my life. I won't take any money from you; I'll be laughing even in my sleep. I've never seen anything funnier than you last night.'

She left entirely satisfied. From Shatov's appearance and his utterances it was as clear as day that this man 'was intending to become a father and was an absolute ninny'. She ran home on purpose to tell Virginsky all about it, even though it was more direct and closer for her to drop in on her next patient.

'Marie, she told you to wait a bit before you go to sleep, though I can see it's terribly difficult...' Shatov began timidly. 'I'll sit here by the window and watch over you, all right?'

He sat down near the window behind the sofa so she couldn't possibly see him. But even before a minute had gone by she called him over and asked him irritably to adjust the pillow for her. He started to do so. She looked at the wall in anger.

'Not like that, oh, not like that... How clumsy you are!'

Shatov adjusted the pillow again.

'Bend down to me,' she suddenly said wildly, trying as hard as she could not to look at him.

He shuddered, but bent down.

'More... not like that... closer,' and suddenly her left arm went rapidly round his neck and he felt a firm, moist kiss on his forehead.

'Marie!'

Her lips trembled; she tried to regain control of herself, but suddenly lifted herself up and, with eyes flashing, pronounced:

'Nikolai Stavrogin is a scoundrel!'

And she fell back on the bed helplessly, like a blade of grass mown down, her face buried in the pillow, sobbing hysterically, clasping Shatov's hand tightly in her own.

From that moment on she wouldn't let him leave her side; she demanded he sit near the bed. She couldn't say much, but kept looking at him, smiling blissfully. It was as if she'd become a silly little girl. Everything seemed to have been reborn. First Shatov cried like a little boy, then he talked about God knows what, in a wild, stupefied, inspired way; he kissed her hands; she listened to him in ecstasy, perhaps not even understanding, but affectionately touching his hair with her feeble hand, stroking it, admiring it. He told her about Kirillov, how they'd begin to live now, 'anew and for ever', the existence of God, how good everyone was... In rapture they lifted up the child to have another look at him.

'Marie,' he cried, holding the child in his arms. 'The old delirium, disgrace, and death are over! Let's work and begin a new life—all three of us. Yes, yes!... Oh, yes: what shall we name him, Marie?'

'Him? What shall we name him?' she repeated in surprise. Suddenly her face expressed terrible grief.

She clasped her hands, looked at Shatov with reproach, and buried her face in the pillow.

'Marie, what's the matter?' he cried in grief-stricken alarm.

'How could you, how could you...? Oh, you ingrate!'

'Marie, forgive me, Marie... I merely asked what we'd name him. I don't know...'

'Ivan, Ivan,' she said, lifting her flushed, tearstained face. 'Did you really suppose we could call him any other *horrible* name?'

'Marie, calm down, you're so distraught!'

'There you go again; you think it's because I'm so distraught? I bet if I'd said we should call him... that horrible name, you'd have agreed at once, and wouldn't even have noticed! Oh, you're ungrateful, mean creatures, all of you!'

A minute later they made it up, of course. Shatov persuaded her to get some rest. She fell asleep, but didn't let
go of his hand; she woke frequently, looked at him as if she
was afraid he might leave, then went back to sleep again.

Kirillov sent an old woman over to 'congratulate them',
in addition, he sent some hot tea, a fresh cutlet, some
bouillon, and some white bread for 'Marya Ignatievna'. The
patient sipped the bouillon eagerly, the old woman changed
the baby's nappy, and Marie forced Shatov to eat the cutlet.

Time passed. Shatov fell asleep in exhaustion on the chair,
his head resting on Marie's pillow. That's how they were
found by Arina Prokhorovna, who kept her promise; she
cheerfully woke them, spoke to Marie about important
matters, examined the child, and once again ordered Shatov
to stay there. Then, after making fun of the 'happy couple'
with a shade of contempt and scorn, she went away, as
satisfied as she'd been before.

It was already quite dark when Shatov woke up. He lit a
candle quickly and went to fetch the old woman; but he'd
scarcely started downstairs when he was met by the sound
of someone's soft, unhurried footsteps coming up towards
him. It was Erkel.

'Don't go in!' whispered Shatov. Seizing him impetuously
by the arm, he pulled him back toward the gate. 'Wait here,
I'll be right out, I forgot about you, forgot all about you!
Oh, you've certainly reminded me, though!'

He was in such a hurry that he didn't even stop to see
Kirillov, and merely called the old woman. Marie was in
despair and indignation that 'he could even think of leaving
her alone.'

'But,' he cried ecstatically, 'it's the very last step! Then
we'll embark on a new path, and never, never again will we
have to recall the old horrors!'

Somehow or other he convinced her and promised to
return precisely at nine o'clock; he kissed her firmly, kissed
the baby, and quickly went out to meet Erkel.

Both set off to the Stavrogin park at Skvoreshniki where
a year and a half ago, in a deserted place at the edge of the

park where the pine forest begins, he had buried the printing press entrusted to him. It was a wild and deserted place some distance from the Skvoreshniki mansion and not visible from it. It was a walk of three or even four miles from Filippov's house.

'Are we going on foot? Let's take a cab.'

'No cab, please,' objected Erkel. 'They insisted on that. A cab driver would be a witness.'

'Oh... hell! Never mind, only I want to get it over and done with!'

They walked very quickly.

'Erkel, you're still such a young boy!' cried Shatov. 'Have you ever been happy?'

'You seem to be very happy just now,' Erkel observed with curiosity.

CHAPTER 6

A full night's work

I.

DURING the course of that day Virginsky spent two hours running around to all the members of the group to tell them Shatov certainly wouldn't inform because his wife had come back to him and had given birth to a baby, and no one 'possessing any knowledge of the human heart' could possibly suppose that he could be dangerous at such a time. But to his annoyance he found almost no one at home, except for Erkel and Lyamshin. Erkel heard him out without saying a word, looking him straight in the eye; in answer to the direct question, 'Would he go at six o'clock or not?' Erkel replied with the brightest of smiles that 'of course he'd go'.

Lyamshin was lying down, apparently seriously ill, his head tucked under the quilt. He was frightened at the sight of Virginsky, and as soon as the latter began speaking, still under his quilt he abruptly waved him away, imploring him to leave him in peace. But he listened to everything Virginsky had to say about Shatov; and for some reason Lyamshin was very struck by the fact that he'd found almost no one at home. It also turned out that he already knew all about Fedka's murder (from Liputin); he told Virginsky about it himself in a hurried, incoherent manner, which in turn struck Virginsky. In answer to Virginsky's direct question, 'Should they go or not?' he began imploring him once again, waving his arms around, that 'it didn't concern him directly; he knew nothing about it, why didn't they go away and leave him in peace?'

Virginsky returned home depressed and deeply disturbed. He found it difficult, too, to hide all this from his family; he was used to sharing everything with his wife, and if a new idea hadn't been hatching in his feverish brain at that very moment, a new reconciliatory plan of future action, he might very well have taken to his bed like Lyamshin. Not only did this new idea give him a boost, he even began to look forward to the appointed hour with impatience, even headed for the appointed spot earlier than he needed to.

It was a very dark spot at one end of the enormous Stavrogin park. I went there deliberately to have a look at the place afterwards; it must have seemed very gloomy on that bleak autumn evening. The old forest reserve began just there; huge, ancient pine trees towered in the darkness as dark, indistinct shapes. The darkness was such that they could scarcely see each other at a distance of two paces, but Peter Stepanovich, Liputin, and subsequently Erkel brought along lanterns. It isn't known why or when, in the unrecorded past, a rather ridiculous grotto was built there out of rough, unhewn stone. The table and benches in the grotto had long since decayed and crumbled into dust. About two hundred paces on the right was the third pond in the park. The three ponds, beginning at the house itself, stretched one after another for more than a mile, to the very edge of the park. It was hard to imagine that any noise, shout, or even a shot could reach the inhabitants of the deserted Stavrogin mansion. With Nikolai Vsevolodovich's departure yesterday and Aleksei Yegorych's absence, that left no more than five or six people in the house, all of them more or less invalids. In any case, one could be virtually sure that even if any cries or shouts for help had been heard by the isolated inhabitants, they might have felt scared, but not one would have left his warm stove or cosy bench to come to the rescue.

At twenty minutes past six all of them, except Erkel who'd been ordered to fetch Shatov, were there. This time Peter Stepanovich wasn't late; he came with Tolkachenko. The latter was sullen and preoccupied; all his assumed, arrogantly boastful determination had disappeared. He hardly left Peter Stepanovich's side and seemed to have suddenly become inordinately attached to him; he rushed up frequently to whisper something fussily to him, but Peter hardly answered him or else uttered some gloomy reply just to get rid of him.

Shigalyov and Virginsky had arrived even a little earlier than Peter Stepanovich; when he appeared they moved quickly to one side, in profound and obviously premeditated silence. Peter Stepanovich lifted his lantern and scrutinized them all in an unceremonious and offensive manner. 'They want to talk,' flashed through his mind.

'Isn't Lyamshin here?' he asked Virginsky. 'Who said he's ill?'

'I'm here,' Lyamshin replied, suddenly emerging from behind a tree. He was wearing a heavy coat and was wrapped tightly in a blanket, so it was hard to discern his features even with a lantern.

'So only Liputin's missing?'

Then Liputin emerged silently from the grotto. Peter Stepanovich lifted his lantern again.

'Why were you hiding in there? Why didn't you come out?'

'I assume we all keep our freedom of... movement,' muttered Liputin, though probably not quite understanding what he wanted to express.

'Gentlemen,' said Peter Stepanovich, abandoning the half-whisper and raising his voice for the first time, which produced quite an effect. 'I believe you all appreciate that now is not the time to go over everything once again. Yesterday everything was stated, and restated, directly and definitively. But, as I can see from your faces, some of you may still want to say something; in that case I ask you to make haste. There's not much time, damn it, and Erkel could bring him here any minute...'

'He's sure to bring him,' Tolkachenko added for some reason.

'If I'm not mistaken, the transfer of the printing press will take place first?' asked Liputin, once again not quite understanding why he put the question.

'Well, of course; we don't want to lose the thing,' Peter Stepanovich said, bringing the lantern closer to Liputin's face. 'But yesterday everyone agreed it wasn't really necessary to take possession of it immediately. He can merely point to the place where it's buried; we can dig it up later. I know it's here somewhere about ten paces from one corner of the grotto... But damn it, Liputin, how could you have forgotten it all? It was agreed you'd meet him alone; then we'd all come out later... It's strange you're asking now, or is it just to fill the time?'

Liputin lapsed into gloomy silence. Everyone fell silent. The wind rustled the tops of the pine trees.

'But I hope, gentlemen, that each of you will do his duty,' Peter Stepanovich snapped impatiently.

'I know Shatov's wife has come back to him and has given birth to a child,' Virginsky began suddenly, agitated, hurriedly, barely getting out the words and gesticulating. 'Knowing the human heart... we can be sure he won't inform on us now... because he's so happy... I tried to tell everyone but didn't find anyone at home... so now, perhaps, there's no need to do it...'

He stopped: he'd run out of breath.

'If you, Mr Virginsky, had suddenly become so happy,' Peter Stepanovich said, taking a step towards him, 'would you put off—not informing, since no one's talking about that—some dangerous, heroic deed you'd planned before you'd become happy, one you considered your duty and obligation to perform, in spite of the risk and possible loss of your happiness?'

'No, I wouldn't put it off! Under no circumstances would I put it off!' Virginsky replied with terribly absurd passion, moving forward.

'Wouldn't you rather be unhappy again than be a scoundrel?'

'Yes, yes... On the contrary... I'd even rather be a complete scoundrel... no, that is... not a scoundrel, but, on the contrary, become completely unhappy, rather than be a scoundrel.'

'Well, then, you must realize that Shatov considers informing on us his civic duty, a matter of cherished conviction; the proof is he's exposing himself to some risk *vis à vis* the government, although, of course, in return for informing they'll pardon him. That kind of man will never give up. There's no happiness will get the better of him; in a day or two he'll return to his senses, reproach himself, and carry out his intention. Besides, I don't see anything happy in the fact that after three years his wife's come back to him to bear Stavrogin's child.'

'But no one's ever seen the denunciation,' Shigalyov shouted insistently all of a sudden.

'I've seen the denunciation,' cried Peter Stepanovich. 'It exists, and this is all terribly stupid, gentlemen.'

'But', shrieked Virginsky suddenly, 'I protest... I protest with all my might... I want... Here's what I want: when he comes here I want all of us to come out and ask him. If it's true, we'll make him repent, and if he gives us his word of honour, we'll let him go. In any case—we'll have a trial; we'll act according to the law. We shouldn't hide and then jump out on him.'

'Putting the common cause at risk on the basis of his word of honour—that would be the height of stupidity! Damn it, that's so stupid, gentlemen, especially at a time like this! And exactly what role are you taking upon yourself at this moment of danger?'

'I protest, I protest,' Virginsky persisted.

'Stop shouting at least, or we won't hear the signal. Shatov, gentlemen... (Damn it, this is so stupid now!) I've already told you that Shatov is a Slavophile, that is, as stupid as they get. But damn it, that doesn't make any difference either, and to hell with it! You're only mixing me up!... Shatov was an embittered man, gentlemen; but he belonged to our group, whether he wanted to or not. Up to the last moment I'd hoped that, embittered as he was, he might have proved useful to our common cause... I protected him and spared him, in spite of receiving the most precise instructions... I spared him a hundred times more than he was worth! But he ended up by informing on us. Well, to hell with him! What does it matter? Don't any of you try to weasel out of this now! Not one of you has the right to abandon this affair! You can embrace and kiss him, if you like, but you have no right to stake the common cause on his word of honour! That's the way swine behave and those being paid by the government!'

'Who here's being paid by the government?' Liputin asked, screening his words carefully.

'You, perhaps. You'd better keep quiet, Liputin. You're talking only out of habit. Gentlemen, a person being paid by the government is anyone who loses heart at a moment of danger. There'll always be some fool who, in panic at the last minute, will run and cry, "Oh, forgive me, I'll sell them all out!" But you must know, gentlemen, that by now you won't be pardoned for any denunciation. Even if your sentence were to be reduced by two counts, it'd still mean Siberia for each one of you; what's more, there's no escaping another sword. And that other sword is even sharper than the government's weapon.'

Peter Stepanovich was furious and said more than he needed to. Shigalyov took three steps towards him resolutely.

'I've been thinking over this matter since yesterday evening,' he began confidently and methodically, as always. (I believe if the earth were caving in beneath him he wouldn't have changed his intonation or altered his methodical exposition even one iota.) 'Having thought about it, I've concluded that the projected murder is not only a waste of valuable time that could be better employed on more essential and pressing business, but, in addition, represents the sort of pernicious deviation from the normal path that has always done most harm to our cause and has delayed its success for decades, subjecting it to the influence of men who are not serious and primarily politicians, rather than uncorrupted socialists. I've come here solely in order to protest against this projected enterprise, for general edification, and them—to dissociate myself from the present moment which you, why I don't know, call *your* moment of danger. I'm leaving—not because I'm afraid of the danger or because I feel sorry for Shatov, whom I have no wish to embrace, but solely because this entire affair, from beginning to end, is in direct contradiction to my programme. As for my informing on you or my being paid by the government, you can feel completely secure: there'll be no denunciation.'

He turned and walked away.

'Oh hell, he'll meet them and warn Shatov!' cried Peter Stepanovich, grabbing his revolver. They heard him cock it.

'You can be sure', said Shigalyov, turning again, 'if I meet Shatov along the way, I may greet him, but I won't warn him.'

'You know you may have to pay dearly for this, Mr Fourier?'

'I ask you to remember I'm not Fourier. By confusing me with that sentimental, abstract mumbler you're merely demonstrating that even though my manuscript was in your hands, it's still completely unfamiliar to you. As for your revenge, I can say it's useless to cock your gun; it's totally against your own interests at the present moment. If you threaten to shoot me tomorrow or the day after, you'll gain nothing from it but unnecessary trouble; you may kill me, but sooner or later you'll come over to my system. Goodbye.'

At that moment, at a distance of some two hundred paces there came from the park, in the direction of the pond, the sound of a whistle. Liputin responded immediately, still according to the previous day's agreement, with a whistle (to do so, rather than rely on his somewhat toothless mouth, he'd bought a child's clay whistle in the market that morning for a kopeck). Erkel had warned Shatov along the way there'd be whistles, so he wasn't suspicious in the least.

'Don't worry, I'll keep to one side and they won't even see me,' Shigalyov assured them in an impressive whisper; then, without hurrying or going out of his way, he resolutely headed home through the gloomy park.

By now everything is known down to the most minute detail about this horrible event. To begin with Liputin met Erkel and Shatov at the grotto; Shatov didn't greet him and didn't extend his hand, but immediately said hurriedly and in a loud voice:

'Well, where's your shovel? Don't you have another lantern? Don't be afraid; there's no one here. Even if you fired a cannon, they wouldn't hear it at Skvoreshniki. It's over here, right here, in this spot...'

He stamped his foot ten paces from the far corner of the grotto nearest the forest. At that very moment Tolkachenko came rushing out of the woods and threw himself on him, while Erkel grabbed him from behind by the elbows. Liputin attacked from the front. The three of them knocked him off his feet and pinned him to the ground. Then Peter Stepanovich came running out with his revolver. The story goes that Shatov had time to turn towards him and was able to make out his features and recognize him. Three lanterns lit the scene. Shatov gave a sudden short, desperate cry; but they didn't let him go on. Peter Stepanovich placed the revolver firmly and accurately against his forehead, pressed hard—then pulled the trigger. The shot wasn't very loud; at least nothing was heard at Skvoreshniki. Shigalyov heard it, of course; he'd scarcely managed to get more than three hundred paces away. He heard both the cry and the shot, but according to his own subsequent testimony, he didn't turn around and didn't even stop. Death occurred almost instantaneously. Peter Stepanovich was the only one who managed to keep his head, though I don't think he remained altogether cool. He squatted down and with a quick determined hand searched the victim's pockets. There was no money to be found (he'd left his wallet under Marya Ignatievna's pillow). They found two or three bits of paper, of no importance: one note from the office, the title of some book, and one old bill from a restaurant abroad which he'd kept in his pocket, goodness knows why, for over two years. Peter Stepanovich transferred the papers to his own pocket; suddenly noticing that all the others were standing around looking at the body and not doing anything, he started hurling coarse abuse at them and urging them back to work. Tolkachenko and Erkel came to their senses and ran at once to fetch two big stones from the grotto that had been placed there earlier that morning, weighing some twenty pounds each, and already prepared, that is, firmly and securely tied with ropes. Since they proposed to carry the body to the closest pond (the third one) and dump it, they began tying the stones to it, at the neck and feet. Peter Stepanovich did the tying, while Tolkachenko and Erkel merely held the stones and handed them to him in turn. Erkel handed over the first one, and while Peter Stepanovich, grumbling and cursing, bound Shatov's legs with the rope and tied the first stone to them, all this rather long time Tolkachenko held out the second one at arm's length, bending forward with his whole body deferentially in order to hand over his load without delay as soon as asked; not once did he think of resting it on the ground. When at last the two stones were fastened, Peter Stepanovich stood up and looked into the faces of those assembled; then a rather strange thing occurred, something totally unexpected that surprised almost everyone there.

As I've already said, except for Tolkachenko and Erkel, virtually everyone was standing around doing nothing. Although Virginsky had rushed towards Shatov when all the others did, he didn't grab him or help hold him down. Lyamshin joined the group only after the shot had been fired. Then, during the course of what might have been ten minutes of fussing over the body, all of them seemed to have lost control of part of their faculties. They stood around in a group and experienced only a sense of surprise, rather than any upset or alarm. Liputin stood in front, closest to the body. Virginsky was behind him, peering over his shoulder with a peculiar, as it were detached curiosity, even standing on tiptoe to get a better look. Lyamshin hid behind Virginsky, only occasionally and furtively peeking out from behind to take a look, then quickly ducking back again. When the stones had been fastened and Peter Stepanovich had got up, Virginsky suddenly began trembling all over, flung up his hands and cried out plaintively at the top of his lungs:

'It's not right, not right! No, it's not right at all!'

He might have added something to this belated exclamation, but Lyamshin didn't allow him to finish: he seized him from behind suddenly, squeezed him with all his might, and uttered the most uncanny scream. There are moments of violent panic, when a man for instance will suddenly cry out in a voice quite unlike his own, in a voice no one suspected him of even having before; such moments can sometimes be very terrifying. Lyamshin screamed in a voice that was more animal than human. Squeezing Virginsky harder and harder from behind with convulsive strength, he kept screaming without pausing or stopping, his eyes popping out of his head, his mouth hanging open, stamping his feet gently on the ground, as if beating a rhythm on a drum. Virginsky was so frightened that he himself started screaming like a madman, and in a frenzy so vindictive one would never have expected it in Virginsky, began to tear away from Lyamshin's grip, scratching and pounding him as best he could, given he had his arms behind him. Erkel finally helped him drag Lyamshin off. But when Virginsky in his fright jumped some ten paces to the side, Lyamshin, catching sight of Peter Stepanovich, suddenly started screaming again and then rushed at him. Tripping on Shatov's body, he fell over it on to Peter Stepanovich and wrapped him so tightly in his arms, pressing his head against his chest, that neither Peter Stepanovich, nor Tolkachenko, nor Liputin was able to do anything at first. Peter Stepanovich yelled, cursed, and pounded him on the head with his fists; at last, somehow freeing himself, he seized his revolver and aimed it right into Lyamshin's open mouth; Lyamshin kept screaming, even though he was now being held by Tolkachenko, Erkel, and Liputin. But he continued to scream, in spite of the revolver. Finally Erkel, rolling his handkerchief into a ball, shoved it skilfully into Lyamshin's mouth and thus ended the screaming. Meanwhile Tolkachenko tied his hands with a left-over piece of rope.

'Very odd,' said Peter Stepanovich, scrutinizing the madman in alarmed amazement.

He was clearly taken aback.

'I would've expected something quite different from him,' he added thoughtfully.

Meanwhile they left Erkel in charge of him. They had to hurry with the body: there had been so much screaming someone might have heard them. Tolkachenko and Peter Stepanovich raised their lanterns and took hold of the head; Liputin and Virginsky picked up the feet and off they went. With the two stones their load was very heavy, and the distance was more than two hundred paces. Tolkachenko was the strongest of the lot. He advised them to march in step, but no one answered so they went on as best they could. Peter Stepanovich walked on the right, leaning forward, carrying the dead man's head on his shoulder and supporting the stone from below with his left hand. Since Tolkachenko didn't offer to help carry the stone during the first half of the trip, Peter Stepanovich ended by shouting a curse at him. His cry was sudden and solitary; everyone continued carrying the load in silence. Only when they reached the pond Virginsky, stooping under the burden and as if exhausted by its weight, suddenly exclaimed once again in the same loud and plaintive voice:

'It's not right, no, no, it's not right at all!'

The place where the third, rather large Skvoreshniki pond ended and where they'd brought their victim was one of the most desolate and least frequented parts of the park, especially that late in the season. At this end the pond was overgrown with weeds along its banks. They put down the lantern, swung the corpse, and threw it into the water. There was a long muffled splash. Peter Stepanovich raised the lantern and the others all craned their necks behind him, watching curiously to see the body sink, but nothing at all was visible. The body with the two stones had sunk immediately. Wide ripples spread over the surface of the water and died away quickly. It was all over.

'Gentlemen,' said Peter Stepanovich, turning to all of them. 'Now we must go our separate ways. You will doubtless be experiencing the unfettered pride that accompanies the fulfilment of an obligation freely undertaken. If, unfortunately, you're still too upset at the present to enjoy this feeling, you'll undoubtedly experience it tomorrow when you'll be ashamed not to feel it. I'll consent to regard Lyamshin's disgraceful outburst as an instance of delirium, all the more so since he's said really to have been ill since this morning. And you, Virginsky, one moment of unfettered reflection will show that for the sake of the common cause, one can't possibly act on the basis of someone's word of honour, and we had to do precisely what we did. Subsequent events will indicate that a denunciation did in fact exist. I'll consent to forget all your protests. As for any danger, I anticipate none whatsoever. It won't occur to anyone to suspect you, especially if you can behave yourselves; the whole thing depends on you and the complete conviction which, I hope, you'll share fully tomorrow. That, by the way, was why you were made into a separate branch of a free organization of like-minded men, in order to at any given moment combine your efforts in the common cause and, if necessary, to observe and supervise one another. Each of us is obligated to give a full account. You have now been called to renew the enterprise which has grown old and rotten with stagnation; keep this in mind always to give you courage. At the present time all your efforts should be directed towards bringing the whole thing down, both the government and its morality. Only we will be left, we who have prepared ourselves to assume power: we'll attract the clever people to our side and ride roughshod over the fools. You mustn't back off from this. We must re-educate a whole generation to make it worthy of freedom. There are still thousands of Shatovs ahead of us. We'll organize ourselves to seize control of the movement; it'd be a shame not to take control of what's lying idle, gaping at us. Now I'm going to Kirillov, and by morning we'll have the document in which, as he dies, he'll take responsibility for everything by way of an explanation to the authorities. Nothing could be more plausible than the two things together. In the first place, he was on bad terms with Shatov; they lived together in America and had plenty of time for disagreement. It's well known that Shatov betrayed his convictions; in other words, the hostility between them arose both from conviction and fear of denunciation—which is the most implacable kind. All this will be put on paper. Finally, it will be mentioned that Fedka was staying with Kirillov in Filippov's house. In that way all suspicion will be removed from you because these blockheads will be thrown off the track. We won't be seeing each other tomorrow, gentlemen; I'm going off to the country for a short time. But you'll receive word from me the day after tomorrow. I'd advise you to spend the day at home. Now we'll separate and proceed in groups of two along different paths. Tolkachenko, I'd like you to look after Lyamshin and take him home. You have some influence over him and perhaps can make him understand he'd be the first to suffer from his own cowardice. Mr Virginsky, I don't want to have any doubts about you or your relative Shigalyov: he is not going to inform on us. What he did was regrettable; still, he hasn't yet said he plans to leave our society, so it's premature to bury him. Well—let's go, gentlemen; blockheads as those fellows are, caution would still be advisable…'

Virginsky set off with Erkel. Before handing Lyamshin over to Tolkachenko, Erkel managed to lead him up to Peter Stepanovich and report that Lyamshin had come to his senses, regretted his action, and asked for forgiveness; he couldn't even remember what had come over him. Peter Stepanovich set off alone, walking around the far shore of the ponds through the park. This was the longest route. To his surprise about halfway home Liputin caught up with him.

'Peter Stepanovich, now Lyamshin will inform on us!'

'No, he'll come to his senses and realize he'd be the first to be sent to Siberia if he informs. Now no one will inform. You won't either.'

'What about you?'

'Undoubtedly I'd get you all put away if you make the slightest move to betray us; you know that. But you won't betray us. Was that why you came running after me for two miles?'

'Peter Stepanovich, Peter Stepanovich, we might never see each other again?'

'What makes you think that?'

'Tell me just one thing.'

'Well, what is it? But I wish you'd just go away.'

'One thing, but it must be the truth: are we the only group of five on earth or is it true there are several hundreds of these groups? I'm asking because it's of utmost importance for me to know, Peter Stepanovich.'

'I can see that by the terrible state you're in. You know, Liputin, you're more dangerous than Lyamshin?'

'I know, I know, but—the answer, your answer!'

'You're a stupid fellow! After all, what difference does it

make to you now whether there's one group of five or a thousand?'

'That means there's only one! I knew it!' cried Liputin. 'All along I knew there was only one, I knew it all along.'

And without waiting for any further answer, he turned and quickly vanished into the darkness.

Peter Stepanovich stood there thinking for a while.

'No, no one will inform,' he said decisively. 'No, the group has to remain a group and obey, or else I'll... But what scum these people are!'

2.

First he went home and packed his suitcase carefully, in no hurry. The express train left at six o'clock in the morning. This early train ran only once a week and had been added to the schedule quite recently, only as a trial run. Although Peter Stepanovich had warned the members of the group that he planned to leave for the country, as it turned out later, his intentions were entirely different. After he finished packing, he settled the bill with his landlady, having notified her previously, and took a cab to Erkel's apartment, not far from the station. Then, just about one o'clock in the morning, he set off to Kirillov, again using Fedka's secret route.

Peter Stepanovich was in a dreadful mood. In addition to other very serious reasons for his dissatisfaction (he still couldn't find anything out about Stavrogin), it seems, since I can't establish it for sure, that during the course of that day he received from somewhere or other (most likely Petersburg) secret information about some danger awaiting him in the near future. Of course now there are many legends circulating in our town about this period; but if anything was known for sure, it was limited to the immediate participants. For my part, I can only assume that Peter Stepanovich could have been involved in similar affairs elsewhere, aside from in our town, so he might really have received such information. I'm even convinced, in spite of Liputin's cynical and desperate doubts, that there might have been a few other groups of five besides ours, in the capitals, for instance; and if not exactly groups of five, then he had contacts and connections—perhaps even very curious ones. Not more than three days after his departure, an order came to our town from the capital for his immediate arrest—I don't know whether it was because of his activities here or elsewhere. This order succeeded in intensifying the overwhelming feeling of fear, almost mystical in nature, that had suddenly overtaken our local authorities, and our hitherto so singlemindedly frivolous society, on the discovery of the mysterious and ominous murder of the student Shatov— a murder seen as the climax of many senseless acts—and attended by a number of extremely suspicious circumstances. But the order came too late: Peter Stepanovich was already in Petersburg under an assumed name where, having got wind of what had happened, he speedily managed to slip away and go abroad... But I've gone far ahead of my story.

He went to Kirillov looking angry and irritable. In addition to his main business, he seemed to want to get something else out of him, to take revenge on him for something. Kirillov appeared glad to see him; it was clear he'd been waiting a very long time and in great impatience. His face was paler than usual; the gaze of his dark eyes was heavy and fixed.

'I thought you weren't coming,' he said slowly from one end of the sofa where he was sitting, but without rising to meet him. Peter Stepanovich stood in front of him and before uttering a word, stared intently into his face.

'Then everything's in order, and we won't be going back on our promise, will we, my fine fellow?' said Peter, smiling with offensive condescension. 'Well, then,' he added with a nasty jocularity, 'if I was late, there's no reason for you to complain: I've given you a present of three more hours.'

'I don't want any extra hours from you, and you can't give me any presents... you fool!'

'What?' Peter Stepanovich asked, somewhat startled, but then gained control of himself. 'How touchy you are! Hey, are we in a temper then?' he asked with the same offensively arrogant look. 'It would be much more appropriate at a time like this to keep calm. The best thing would be to consider yourself like Columbus, look upon me as a mouse, and not be offended by me. I gave you this advice yesterday.'

'I don't want to look upon you as a mouse.'

'Is that a compliment, or what? Oh, but even the tea's cold—that means everything is topsy-turvy. There's something suspicious going on here. Why, I see something over there on the window-sill, on a plate' (he went towards the window). 'Oho, boiled chicken with rice!... But you haven't touched it yet? That must mean we're in a certain mood where even chicken can't...'

'I had some, and it's none of your business. Shut up!'

'Oh, certainly, besides, it doesn't matter. But it does matter to me: just think, I've hardly had any dinner. So if, as I assume, this chicken is no longer needed... then?'

'Eat it, if you can.'

'Thank you, and I'll have some tea.'

He sat down on the other end of the sofa at the table and set about eating the food with extraordinary gusto; but at the same time he kept constant watch over his victim. Kirillov stared at him in ill-tempered aversion, as if unable to tear himself away.

'However,' Peter Stepanovich suddenly burst out while continuing to eat, 'let's get down to business. We're not backing out, are we? What about the document?'

'This evening I decided that it's all the same to me. I'll write it. Am I to say about the pamphlets?'

'Yes, about the pamphlets too. But I'll dictate it to you. After all, it's all the same to you. Surely the content couldn't upset you at a moment like this.'

'That's none of your business.'

'Of course not. But we only need a few lines: say that you and Shatov distributed the pamphlets with Fedka's help, who, by the way, was hiding in your apartment. This last point about Fedka is very important, the most important even. You see, I'm being perfectly open with you.'

'Shatov? Why Shatov? I won't say a thing about Shatov.'

'What's up with you now? You can't possibly do him any harm.'

'His wife's come back to him. She woke up and sent to ask where he is.'

'To ask where he is? Hmm, that's awkward. She might send over again; no one must know I'm here...'

Peter Stepanovich began to worry.

'She won't find out; she went back to sleep. She has the midwife there, Arina Virginskaya.'

'So that's how it is... she won't hear us, will she? Look, we'd better close the door.'

'She won't hear a thing. And if Shatov comes, I'll hide you in the other room.'

'Shatov won't be coming; you'll write that you quarrelled with him over his betrayal and denunciation... this very evening... and you are responsible for his death.'

'He's dead!' cried Kirillov, jumping up from the sofa.

'At eight o'clock this evening, or to be more precise, at eight o'clock last night, since it's now already after midnight.'

'You murdered him!... And I foresaw it yesterday!'

'So you did! With this revolver' (he took out his revolver as if to show him, but didn't put it away again, keeping it in his right hand, just in case). 'But you're a strange fellow, Kirillov, you knew yourself it would have to end like this for that stupid man. What was there to foresee? I made it as plain as day on several occasions. Shatov was preparing to inform on us: I was keeping an eye on him; it was unthinkable to let him go through with it. And you'd been given instructions to watch him; you told me some three weeks ago that...'

'Shut up! You did it to him because he spat in your face in Geneva!'

'Both for that and other reasons. For many other reasons; but without malice. Why are you jumping up? Why make such faces? Oho! So that's it, is it?'

He jumped up and raised his revolver. What happened is that all of a sudden Kirillov had grabbed his own gun from the window-sill where it had been ready and loaded since that morning. Peter Stepanovich took up his position and aimed his weapon at Kirillov, who gave a nasty laugh.

'Confess, you scoundrel, you brought your revolver because you thought I might shoot you... But I won't shoot you... although... although...'

Once more he aimed his revolver at Peter Stepanovich as if trying it out, as if incapable of denying himself the pleasure of imagining what it would be like to shoot him. Peter Stepanovich, still in position, waited, waited until the last moment, without pulling the trigger, risking the possibility of receiving a bullet in the head first: anything could happen with such a 'maniac'. But the 'maniac' finally lowered his arm, gasping for breath, trembling, unable to speak.

'You've had your fun,' said Peter Stepanovich, also lowering his weapon. 'I knew you were playing a game; but, you know, you were taking a risk: I could've fired.'

He sat down on the sofa fairly calmly and poured himself some tea, though his hand was shaking slightly. Kirillov laid his revolver on the table and began pacing up and down.

'I won't write that I killed Shatov... now I'm not going to write anything. There won't be any document.'

'There won't?'

'No, there won't.'

'How mean and stupid!' Peter Stepanovich went green with fury. 'I suspected as much. You've not taken me by surprise, you know. But as you like. If I could force you, I'd do so. You're a scoundrel, though,' said Peter Stepanovich, increasingly unable to control himself. 'You asked us for money then and promised us all sorts of things... But I won't leave here empty-handed; at least I'll watch you blow your brains out.'

'I want you to leave here right now,' Kirillov said, stopping firmly in front of him.

'No, that's not on,' said Peter Stepanovich, grabbing his revolver once again. 'Now, maybe, out of spite and cowardice, you might decide to postpone the whole thing and tomorrow go and inform on us to get some more money; they pay, you know. The hell with you—people like you are capable of anything! But don't worry, I've foreseen everything: I won't leave here before I've blown your brains out with this revolver, just like I did to that scoundrel Shatov, if you're afraid to do it yourself and put off your plan. Damn you!'

'You've got to see my blood too, have you?'

'Not out of malice, do you understand; it's all the same to me. It's just that I need to feel secure about our cause. You can't rely on people, you can see that yourself. I don't at all understand where you got your fantastic plan of taking your own life. It wasn't my idea; you told the members of the group about it abroad even before you told me. No one wormed it out of you; no one even knew you. You came forward with it yourself, sensitive creature that you were. Well, what's to be done now if a certain scheme of local activity has been built on it with your consent and at your own suggestion (note that carefully, at your own suggestion!)—a scheme that cannot possibly be altered. Now you've put yourself in a position where you know too much. Tomorrow if you decide to talk and go off to inform the police, that might not be very helpful to us, don't you agree? No, sir; you're obligated, you gave your word, you took the money. You can't deny that...'

Peter Stepanovich had become very angry, but Kirillov hadn't been listening to him for some time. He was pacing up and down the room again, lost in thought.

'I feel sorry for Shatov,' he said, stopping in front of Peter Stepanovich again.

'Well I do, too, but surely...'

'Shut up, you scoundrel!' roared Kirillov, making a terrible and unambiguous gesture. 'I'll kill you!'

'All right, all right, all right, so I lied, I agree, I don't feel sorry for him. All right, enough, enough!' Peter Stepanovich said, jumping up apprehensively and putting a hand out in front of him.

Kirillov quietened down abruptly and resumed his pacing.

'I won't postpone it; I want to put an end to myself right now: everyone's a scoundrel!'

'Now, that's the idea! Of course everyone's a scoundrel, and since life on earth is so contemptible to any decent man, then...'

'Fool, I'm a scoundrel too, just like you and everyone else, I'm not a decent man. There's never been a decent man anywhere.'

'At last he's guessed it. Can you really have failed to understand up to now, Kirillov, with your intelligence, that everyone's the same, no one's any better or worse, there are only more intelligent and less intelligent people, and if everyone's a scoundrel (which, by the way, is nonsense), then, of course, there can't be anyone who isn't one?'

'Ah! So you're really not laughing at me?' Kirillov asked, looking at him in some surprise. 'You're speaking heatedly and plainly... Is it possible people like you have convictions?'

'Kirillov, I could never understand why you wanted to kill yourself. I only know it's because of some conviction... some strong conviction. But if you feel the need to pour out your heart, so to speak, I'm at your service... But we must keep track of the time...'

'What time is it?'

'Oho, two o'clock sharp,' Peter Stepanovich said, looking at his watch and lighting a cigarette.

'It looks like we can still reach an agreement,' he thought to himself.

'I have nothing to tell you,' Kirillov muttered.

'I recall something about God... you once explained it all to me; even twice. If you shoot yourself, you'll become God, isn't that right?'

'Yes, I'll become God.'

Peter Stepanovich didn't even smile; he waited. Kirillov looked at him shrewdly.

'You're a political impostor and an intriguer; you want to get me talking about philosophy, make me enthusiastic, then bring about a reconciliation to disperse my anger; and, when we've made up, you'll ask me to sign a document saying I killed Shatov.'

Peter Stepanovich replied with almost natural artlessness:

'Well, supposing I am such a scoundrel... does it really matter to you, Kirillov, in your last moments? What, pray, are we arguing about? You're one sort of person, I'm another. So what? Besides, we're both...'

'Scoundrels.'

'Yes, perhaps even scoundrels. You know it's only words.'

'All my life I've wanted it to be more than only words. I've gone on living because of that. Even now every day I want it to be more than just words.'

'Well, everyone looks for something better. A fish... I mean, everyone looks for his own comfort; that's all. It's been known for ages.'

'Comfort, you say?'

'Well, it's not worth arguing over words.'

'No, that was well said; let's say comfort. God is necessary; therefore, He must exist.'

'Well, that's splendid.'

'But I know He doesn't exist and can't exist.'

'That's more likely.'

'Don't you understand that a person holding two such ideas can't go on living?'

'And has to shoot himself, right?'

'Don't you understand a person might shoot himself solely because of that? You don't understand that such a man can exist, one out of your thousands of millions, one who doesn't want it and won't endure it.'

'I understand only that you seem to be hesitating... That's very bad.'

'Stavrogin was also swallowed by an idea,' Kirillov said, pacing gloomily around the room, not picking up on Peter's last remark.

'What?' Peter Stepanovich asked, pricking up his ears. 'What idea? Did he tell you something himself?'

'No, I guessed it myself: if Stavrogin believes, he doesn't believe he believes. If he doesn't believe, he doesn't believe he doesn't believe.'

'Well, Stavrogin has something else, much wiser than that...' Peter Stepanovich muttered cantankerously, following with some alarm this turn in their conversation and Kirillov's pallor.

'Damn it, he won't shoot himself,' he thought. 'I knew it all along; his brain is warped, that's all. What scum these people are!'

'You're the last man to be with me: I wouldn't want to part with you on bad terms,' Kirillov said gratuitously.

Peter Stepanovich didn't reply at once. 'Damn it, what's this all about?' he wondered again.

'Believe me, Kirillov, I have nothing against you personally, and have always...'

'You're a scoundrel, and yours is a false kind of intelligence. But I'm the same as you are, and I'm going to shoot myself, while you'll remain alive.'

'You mean, in other words, I'm so base I'll want to remain alive.'

He still couldn't decide whether or not there was any point in continuing the conversation at this time, and resolved to 'be guided by circumstances'. But Kirillov's tone of superiority and his undisguised contempt had always irritated him, now more than ever. Perhaps that was because Kirillov, who was to die in less than an hour (Peter Stepanovich always kept this in mind), appeared to him a sort of half-person, a creature that could not be allowed to be arrogant.

'You seem to be boasting to me about shooting yourself?'

'I've always been surprised other people go on living,' Kirillov said, not hearing this last remark.

'Hmmm, it's an idea, I suppose, but...'

'You're an ape. You're agreeing with everything I say, just to get the better of me. Shut up! You don't understand a thing. If there's no God, then I am God.'

'I never could understand that point of yours: why are you God?'

'If God exists, then everything is His will, and I can do nothing of my own apart from His will. If there's no God, then everything is my will, and I'm bound to express my self-will.'

'Self-will? And why are you bound to?'

'Because all will has become my own. Can it possibly be that no one on the whole planet who's finished with God and has come to believe in himself wouldn't dare express his self-will on the most important point? It's as if a poor man received an inheritance and felt afraid, didn't dare approach the bag of gold, considering himself too weak to possess it. I want to express my self-will. Even if I'm alone, I'll do so.'

'Do it, then.'

'I'm obligated to shoot myself because the greatest degree of self-will is to take my own life.'

'But you're not the only person ever to kill himself; there's been a great many suicides.'

'Each one had a reason. But to do it without any reason, simply out of self-will—I'm the only one.'

'He's not going to shoot himself,' flashed once more through Peter Stepanovich's mind.

'You know,' he observed irritably, 'if I were in your shoes I'd have killed someone else beside myself to express my self-will. You might prove useful. I'll tell you who, if you're not afraid. Then you won't have to shoot yourself today. We could come to terms.'

'To kill someone else would represent the lowest degree of self-will; that's you all over. I'm not you: I want the highest degree and will kill myself.'

'He got there by his own intelligence,' Peter Stepanovich muttered spitefully.

'I'm obliged to declare my unbelief,' Kirillov said, pacing the room. 'There's no idea greater than the fact that God doesn't exist. Human history supports me. The only thing man has done is to keep inventing God to go on living and not kill himself; this alone constitutes global history up to now. During the entire course of global history I alone am the first person who doesn't want to invent God. Let everyone know this once and for all.'

'He's not going to shoot himself,' Peter Stepanovich thought in alarm.

'Who is there to know it?' he asked, goading him on. 'There's only you and me here. Do you mean Liputin?'

'Let everyone know; they'll all find out. There's no secret that won't be made known. That's what *He* said.'

With feverish ecstasy he pointed to the image of the Saviour, in front of which a lamp was burning. Peter Stepanovich grew furious.

'So, you still believe in *Him*, do you? You even lit the

icon lamp; that wouldn't be "to be on the safe side", would it?'

Kirillov remained silent.

'You know, I think it's possible you believe more than any priest.'

'In whom? In *Him*? Listen,' said Kirillov, stopping and gazing ahead with a fixed, frenzied look. 'Listen to this great idea: there was one day on earth and in the middle of the earth stood three crosses. One man on the cross believed so much that he said to another: "Thou shalt be with me in paradise today." The day ended, they both died and departed, but found neither paradise nor salvation. That which had been promised did not come true. Listen: that man was the greatest of all men on earth; he provided a reason to live life. The whole planet with everyone living on it is sheer madness without that one man. There's never been a man like *Him* before or since, and never will be, even with a miracle. For that is the miracle, that there never was or ever will be one like *Him*. And if that's true, if the laws of nature didn't spare even *Him*, even their own miracle, but forced *Him* to live among lies and to die for a lie, then the entire planet is a lie and rests on lies and stupid mockery. In that case the laws of the planet are mere lies, and a devils' vaudeville. What's the purpose of living? Tell me, if you're a man.'

'That's another matter. It seems to me you've confused two different causes; that's a dangerous thing to do. But wait a moment; what if you are God? What if the lie's ended and you've guessed that all lies come from belief in a former God?'

'At last you've understood!' cried Kirillov ecstatically. 'It must be possible to be understood if a person like you can understand! Now you realize that salvation for everyone lies in proving this idea. Who will prove it? I will. I don't understand how up to now an atheist could know there was no God, yet still not kill himself immediately. To realize there's no God, but at the same time not to realize that one's become God oneself is absurd, or else one would certainly kill oneself. If you realize it—you're sovereign and won't kill yourself; you'll live in great glory. But one person, he who comes first, must certainly kill himself, or who'll make a start and prove it? So I must certainly kill myself to make a start and prove it. I'm still only God against my will and I'm unhappy since I'm *obligated* to express my self-will. Man's been unhappy and impoverished up to now because he's been afraid to express the essence of his self-will; he's expressed it only in peripheral pursuits, like a schoolboy. I'm terribly unhappy because I'm terribly afraid. Fear is man's curse... But I'll express my self-will, I'm obliged to believe I don't believe. I'll begin and end, thus opening the door. And I'll save. That alone will save all people and will physically transform the next generation; for in his present state, as far as I can see, man cannot possibly exist without his former God. For three years I've been seeking the attribute of my own divinity and now I've found it: the attribute of my own divinity is—Self-Will! That's all I can do to demonstrate in the highest degree my own independence and my terrifying new freedom. For it is very terrifying. I shall kill myself to show my independence and my terrifying new freedom.'

His face was unnaturally pale, his expression, unbearably sad. He seemed delirious. Peter Stepanovich thought he might collapse at any moment.

'Give me a pen!' Kirillov shouted all of a sudden, completely unexpectedly, in positive inspiration. 'Dictate; I'll sign anything. I'll even say I murdered Shatov. Dictate while it still amuses me. I'm not afraid of what supercilious slaves may think! You'll see for yourself: the whole mystery will be revealed! And you'll be crushed... I believe! I believe!'

Peter Stepanovich jumped up and instantly brought him an inkstand and paper and began to dictate, seizing the moment and trembling in his success.

'I, Aleksei Kirillov, declare....'

'Wait! No, no! To whom do I declare?'

Kirillov shook as if in a high fever. This declaration of his and the peculiar, unexpected idea of making it so suddenly seemed to engulf him entirely, as though it were some escape desperately sought by his tormented spirit, if only for a single moment.

'To whom do I declare? I want to know.'

'To no one, to everyone, to the first person who reads it. Why limit it? To the whole world!'

'The whole world? Bravo! And there's no need for repentance. I don't want to repent, and I don't want to address the authorities.'

'No, of course not, to hell with the authorities! Now write, if you're in earnest!' Peter Stepanovich cried hysterically.

'Wait! I want to draw a face at the top with its tongue sticking out.'

'Oh, what nonsense!' Peter Stepanovich said angrily. 'You can express all that by the tone without a picture.'

'The tone? That's good. Yes, by the tone, yes! Dictate the right tone.'

'I, Aleksei Kirillov,' Peter Stepanovich dictated forcefully and peremptorily, leaning over Kirillov's shoulder and following the formation of each letter made by a hand trembling with excitement. 'I, Kirillov, declare that today, the —th day of October, at eight o'clock in the evening, I killed the student Shatov for his treachery, in the park, and for his denunciation concerning the pamphlets, and Fedka as well who was secretly staying with both of us at Filippov's house where he'd been for ten days. I'm also killing myself today with a revolver not because I repent or am afraid of you, but because when I was abroad I conceived the intention of taking my own life.'

'Is that all?' Kirillov exclaimed in surprise and indignation.

'Not one word more!' said Peter Stepanovich with a wave of the hand, attempting to snatch the document away from him.

'Wait!' Kirillov cried, firmly placing his arm on the piece of paper. 'Wait! That's nonsense! I want to say who helped me kill him. Why Fedka? And the fires? I want to say everything and also to abuse them in the tone, the tone!'

'It's enough, Kirillov, I assure you, enough!' Peter Stepanovich said, almost imploring him, afraid he might tear up the piece of paper. 'For them to believe you, you must make it as obscure as possible, just like that, by hints. You must show only a corner of the truth, just enough to tease them. They'll create a story for themselves even better than ours, of course; they'll believe it more than ours and that'll be better than anything else, much better! Give it to me; it's splendid just as it is. Give it to me, give it to me!'

He tried to snatch the piece of paper. Kirillov listened to him, eyes popping out of his head, as if trying to make sense of what was being said, but, apparently no longer understanding.

'Oh, hell!' Peter Stepanovich said, suddenly in a rage. 'He hasn't signed it yet! What are you staring at me for like that? Sign it!'

'I want to abuse them...' Kirillov muttered, though taking the pen and signing the document. 'I want to abuse them...'

'Write: "*Vive la république*", and that's enough.'

'Bravo!' Kirillov almost roared with ecstasy. ' "*Vive la république démocratique, sociale et universelle ou la mort!*"... No, no, not that. "*Liberté, égalité, fraternité ou la mort!*"[1] That's better, that's better.' He wrote with glee under his signature.

'Enough, enough,' Peter Stepanovich kept repeating.

'Wait, a little more... You know what, I'll sign it again in French: "*de Kiriloff, gentilhomme russe et citoyen du monde*" Ha, ha, ha!' he said and burst out laughing. 'No, no, no, wait, I've found the best one of all. Eureka! "*Gentilhomme-séminariste russe et citoyen du monde civilisé!*"[2] That's best of all,' he said jumping up from the sofa. With a rapid movement he suddenly seized his revolver from the window-sill, ran into the next room, and shut the door tightly behind him. Peter Stepanovich stood there thoughtfully for a moment, looking at the door.

'If he does it at once, he may actually shoot himself, but if he begins thinking—nothing will come of it.'

Meanwhile he took the piece of paper, sat down, and read it through. The wording of the declaration pleased him once again.

---

[1] Long live the democratic, social, and universal republic, or death!... Liberty, equality, fraternity, or death!

[2] *de Kiriloff*, Russian gentleman and citizen of the world... Russian gentleman-seminarist and citizen of the civilized world!

'Now what do I need to do? I have to confuse them for a while, divert their attention. The park? There's no park in town, so they'll work out it's at Skvoreshniki. While they're working that out, time will pass; while they're searching—more time. And then, when they find the body—it'll mean the document was telling the truth; it'll mean it was all true, even the part about Fedka. And what about Fedka? Fedka explains the fire and the Lebyadkins: that means, it all started from here, at Filippov's house. And they didn't see anything, they missed it all—that'll certainly make their heads spin! They'll never even think about our group; Shatov, and Kirillov, and Fedka, and Lebyadkin. And why did they kill each other—that'll be another question for them to answer. Damn it, I still haven't heard a shot!...'

Although he'd been reading and admiring the wording of the document, all the while he'd been listening in agonizing anxiety and—suddenly he flew into a rage. He glanced uneasily at his watch; it was getting late. Ten minutes had already passed since Kirillov had left the room... Seizing a candle, he headed for the door of the room he had shut himself into. At the door it occurred to him that the candle was about to burn out—it would last only another twenty minutes or so, and there wasn't another one. He grabbed hold of the handle and listened carefully; not the slightest sound could be heard. He unlocked the door suddenly and lifted his candle: something let out a roar and hurled itself upon him. With all his might he slammed the door shut and pressed all his weight against it; but everything had become quiet—once again deathlike stillness prevailed.

He stood there indecisively for a long time with the candle in his hand. During the split-second the door was open, he'd been able to see very little, but caught a glimpse of Kirillov standing on the other side of the room near the window, and saw the savage fury with which he'd suddenly hurled himself at him. Peter Stepanovich shuddered, quickly placed the candle on the table, took out his revolver, and withdrew on tiptoe to the opposite corner of the room, so that if Kirillov opened the door and rushed toward the table with his revolver, Peter would still have time to aim and fire before he did.

By now Peter Stepanovich no longer believed at all in the possibility of Kirillov's suicide! 'He was standing in the middle of the room thinking,' swept through Peter's mind like a whirlwind. 'And the room was dark and terrifying... He let out a roar and hurled himself at me. There are two possibilities: either I interfered with him at the moment he was planning to pull the trigger, or... or he was standing there thinking about how to kill me. Yes, that's it, he was thinking... He knows I won't leave without killing him, if he fails to shoot himself—that means, he has to kill me first so I won't kill him... And it's so still again in there, so very still! It's terrifying: all of a sudden he'll open the door... The most swinish thing is that he believes in God more than any priest... He won't shoot himself for anything!... There are so many of these characters nowadays who "get there by their own intelligence". Scum! Oh, hell, the candle, the candle! It'll certainly burn down in the next quarter of an hour... We must be done with it; no matter what, we must be done with it.... Well, I could kill him now... With this piece of paper no one will ever think I killed him. I could arrange his body on the floor with the discharged revolver in his hand, so everyone will think he did it himself... Oh, hell, how can I kill him? If I open the door, he'll throw himself at me again and fire before I do. Damn it, he's sure to miss!'

He was in agony, trembling at the necessity of taking action and at his own indecisiveness. At last he took the candle and went up to the door once again, raising and aiming his revolver; he placed his left hand in which he was holding the candle on the door handle. But he made a mess of it: the handle clicked and squeaked. 'He'll fire at once!' flashed through Peter's mind. With all his might he pushed the door open with his foot, raised the candle and stuck out his revolver; but there was no shot, no scream... There was no one in the room.

He shuddered. The room was not a passageway and led nowhere, with no way to escape. He raised the candle a little higher and looked carefully: there was no one there at all. In a whisper he called Kirillov's name—then once again, a little louder; no one replied.

'Could he possibly have escaped through the window?'

One of the small ventilation panes was in fact open. 'How stupid, he couldn't squeeze through there.' Peter Stepanovich crossed the room to it: 'There's no way he could have.' All of a sudden he turned around and was shaken by an extraordinary sight.

On the wall opposite the windows, to the right of the door, stood a cupboard. On the right side of the cupboard, in the corner formed by the wall and the cupboard, stood Kirillov; he stood there in a horribly strange way—motionless, erect, hands at his sides, his head held high and the back of it pressed hard against the wall right in the corner, as if he wanted to efface and conceal himself. To all appearances, he was hiding, but that was somehow hard to believe. Peter Stepanovich was at an angle to the corner and could see only the salient parts of the figure. He couldn't make up his mind to move to the left to get a better view of Kirillov and thus solve the mystery. His heart began to beat wildly... All of a sudden he flew into a mad rage: with a dash and a shriek, stamping his feet, he hurled himself ferociously at the horrible place.

But just before he reached it, he stopped once again as if rooted to the spot, even more overcome with horror. What struck him most was that the figure, despite his cry and his manic attack, didn't even stir, didn't move so much as one limb—just as if it were made of stone or wax. The pallor of the face was unnatural, the fixed black eyes gazed off at some point in the distance. Peter Stepanovich moved the candle lower and then higher again, lighting the figure from all sides and staring into its face. He suddenly noticed that even though Kirillov was looking straight ahead, he could still see Peter out of the corner of his eye, and perhaps was even watching him. Then the thought occurred to him to hold the candle right up to scorch the face of 'the scoundrel', and see what he'd do. Suddenly he fancied that Kirillov's jaw twitched and a sarcastic smile seemed to cross his lips—just as if he'd guessed Peter's thought. He began to tremble and, unaware of what he was doing, gripped Kirillov firmly by the shoulder.

Then something so hideous happened so quickly that afterwards Peter Stepanovich could never quite sort out his impressions and fully understand it. Barely had he touched him when Kirillov ducked sharply and with his head knocked the candle out of his grasp; the candlestick went flying on to the floor with a ringing sound and the flame went out. At the same instant he felt a terrible pain in the little finger of his left hand. He cried out and only remembered in his frenzy bringing his revolver down three times hard on the head of Kirillov, who had bent down and bitten his finger. At last he managed to get his finger away and went rushing out of the house as fast as he possibly could, looking for the way in the darkness. Terrible shrieks came bursting out of the room after him:

'Now, now, now, now...'

Ten times. But Peter kept running and had just made it to the front hall when suddenly he heard a loud shot. Then he stopped in the darkness and deliberated for five minutes; at last he went back inside. But he had to find a candle. He could look on the floor to the right of the cupboard for the candlestick that had been knocked from his grip; but how would he light the candle? Suddenly an obscure recollection flashed into his head: he remembered the day before, as he ran down into the kitchen to attack Fedka, noticing in passing a big red box of matches on a shelf in the corner. He groped his way to the left towards the kitchen door, found it, went through the passage, and started down the stairs. On the shelf exactly where he remembered it he hit in the dark on the full, unopened box of matches. Without striking one, he quickly went back up the stairs, and only when he got near the cupboard where Kirillov had bitten him and he'd struck him with his revolver did he suddenly remember his hurt finger and instantly became aware of the almost unbearable pain. Clenching his teeth, he somehow lit the candle, put it back in the candlestick, and looked around; near the open window-pane, with his feet pointing towards the right-hand corner of the room, lay Kirillov's body. The shot had been fired into his right temple, and the bullet had come out at the top of his head on the left, shattering the skull. He could see splashes of blood and brains. The revolver was still in the suicide's hand on the floor. Death must have occurred instantáneously. After examining everything with his usual thoroughness, Peter Stepanovich stood up and went out on tiptoe, closed the door, placed the candle on a table in the first room, thought and decided not to blow it out, realizing that it couldn't possibly cause a fire. Glancing once more at the document on the table, he grinned mechanically and then, still on tiptoe for some reason, left the house. He slipped out through Fedka's secret passage again and carefully replaced the loose board behind him.

3.

At precisely ten minutes to six Peter Stepanovich and Erkel were walking up and down the platform at the railway station beside a rather long line of carriages. Peter was leaving and Erkel was saying goodbye to him. The luggage had been loaded and a small bag reserved his seat in a second-class compartment. The first bell had already rung; they were waiting for the second. Peter Stepanovich was looking around boldly, scrutinizing the passengers as they boarded the train. But he didn't see any close acquaintances; twice only he nodded his head—once to a merchant he knew slightly, the other time to a young village priest returning to his parish only two stations away. Erkel evidently wanted to talk about something important during these last few moments, although, perhaps, he himself didn't know what; but he didn't dare begin. It seemed to him that Peter Stepanovich felt burdened by his presence and was waiting impatiently for the last bells to ring.

'You look at everyone so boldly,' Erkel observed with a certain timidity, as if wanting to warn him.

'Why not? I don't have to go into hiding just yet. It's still early. Don't worry. I'm only afraid that the devil might send Liputin this way; he'll sniff me out and come running over.'

'Peter Stepanovich, they're unreliable,' Erkel declared decisively.

'Who, Liputin?'

'All of them, Peter Stepanovich.'

'Nonsense; now they're all tied down by yesterday's events. Not one of them will betray us. Who would risk certain ruin, except someone who's lost his reason?'

'But, Peter Stepanovich, they will lose their reason.'

This thought, apparently, had also occurred to Peter Stepanovich; therefore Erkel's remark irritated him even more:

'You're not getting cold feet too, are you, Erkel? I've been relying on you more than any of the others. Now I've seen what each of them is worth. Convey everything to them today by word of mouth; I hand them all over to you. Go and see them all this morning. Tomorrow or the day after you'll get them together and read them my written instructions, when you find them capable of listening... but believe me, they will be by tomorrow because they'll be terrified and they'll be obedient and soft as wax... The main thing is you mustn't lose heart.'

'Oh, Peter Stepanovich, I do wish you weren't leaving!'

'But it's only for a few days; I'll be coming straight back.'

'Peter Stepanovich,' said Erkel cautiously, but firmly, 'even if you're going to Petersburg, don't you think I know you're doing only what's necessary for the common cause?'

'I expected no less of you, Erkel. If you've guessed I'm going to Petersburg, you can understand I couldn't tell them yesterday, at that moment, that I was going so far away, for fear of frightening them. You saw yourself what they were like. But you know I'm doing it for the cause, for the primary and most important cause, for the common cause, not just to get away, as Liputin thinks.'

'Peter Stepanovich, even if you were going abroad, I'd understand; I'd understand you have to take care of yourself because you are everything, while we are nothing. I'd understand, Peter Stepanovich.'

The poor lad's voice was trembling.

'Thank you, Erkel... Ow, you've squeezed my bad finger'

(Erkel was clumsily shaking his hand; Peter's bad finger was elegantly bound in black silk). 'But I tell you once more positively, I'm going to Petersburg only to sniff around, perhaps only for a day, and then I'll come straight back here. On my return I'll stay at Gaganov's place in the country for the sake of appearances. If there's any risk of danger, I'll be the first to take the lead and share it. If I'm delayed in Petersburg, I'll let you know at once... in the way we agreed upon, and you'll tell the others.'

The second bell rang.

'That means not more than five minutes till the train leaves. You know, I didn't want this local group to break up. I'm not afraid; don't worry about me. I have lots of these groups in the general network, and no one of them is all that important; but there's nothing wrong in having an extra group. Besides, I feel happy about you, even though I'm leaving you all alone with these monsters: don't worry, they won't inform, they wouldn't dare... Aha, so you're travelling today, too?' he shouted suddenly in a totally different, altogether cheerful tone of voice to a very young man who'd come up to say a cordial hello to him. 'I didn't know you were taking the express too. Where're you going? To visit your mother?'

The young man's mother was a wealthy landowner in the next province; the young man was a distant relative of Yulia Mikhailovna and had been her guest in town for the last two weeks.

'No, I'm going further, to R—. I have to survive eight hours in the train. Are you going to Petersburg?' the young man asked with a laugh.

'Why did you suppose I was going to Petersburg?' Peter Stepanovich asked, laughing even more boldly.

The young man wagged a gloved finger at him.

'Well, yes, you guessed right,' Peter Stepanovich whispered to him mysteriously. 'I'm carrying letters from Yulia Mikhailovna and have to call on three or four important people there, damn them all, frankly. Hell of a job!'

'Why, pray tell, is she so frightened?' asked the young man, now also in a whisper. 'Yesterday she didn't even allow me in to see her; in my opinion, she has no reason to fear for her husband; on the contrary, he fell so elegantly at the fire, so to speak risking his own life.'

'Well, there it is,' said Peter with a laugh. 'You see, she's afraid some people may have written from here already... that is, certain gentlemen... In a word, the point is Stavrogin; that is, Prince K.—oh, it's quite a long story. I could tell you some of it along the way—as much, that is, as chivalry permits... This is my relative, Ensign Erkel, from the next province.'

The young man, who'd been looking sideways at Erkel, doffed his hat; Erkel responded with a bow.

'Look, Verkhovensky, eight hours in a railway carriage is a horrible fate. Berestov, a very amusing colonel whose estate's next to ours, is travelling with us in first class; he's married to a Garin (*née* de Garine), and you know, he's a very decent fellow. Even has a few ideas. He's been here only about two days. He's terrifically keen on cards; what do you say we organize a game? I've already spied a fourth—Pripukhlov, our bearded merchant friend from T—, a millionaire, that is, a genuine millionaire, I tell you... I'll introduce you; he's a most interesting moneybags; you'll be amused.'

'I'd be delighted to have a game of cards with you, but I'm travelling second class.'

'Oh, nonsense, certainly not! You'll sit with us. I'll have you transferred to first class at once. The chief conductor will do anything I ask. What luggage do you have? A bag? A rug?'

'Splendid, let's go!'

Peter Stepanovich picked up his bag, rug, and book and moved immediately with the greatest enthusiasm into first class. Erkel assisted in the move. The third bell sounded.

'Well, Erkel,' Peter Stepanovich said, hurriedly and with a preoccupied look extending his hand for the last time from the train window. 'Here I am sitting down to a game of cards with them.'

'Why explain, Peter Stepanovich? I understand, I quite understand it all, Peter Stepanovich!'

'Well then, in that case, all the best,' Peter Stepanovich said, suddenly turning away in answer to a call from the young man who wanted to introduce him to the other players. And that was the last Erkel ever saw of his Peter Stepanovich!

He returned home very depressed. It wasn't that he was afraid Peter Stepanovich had suddenly abandoned them all, but... but he'd turned away from him so quickly when that young dandy had called him, and... he certainly could have said something else to him besides 'all the best' or... or even shaken hands more warmly.

This last thing was the most painful. Something else was beginning to gnaw at his poor heart, something he himself didn't quite understand, something connected with the events of the previous evening.

CHAPTER 7

Stepan Trofimovich's last journey

I.

I'M convinced that Stepan Trofimovich was terribly afraid when he felt the approach of the time fixed for his insane undertaking. I'm convinced that he suffered greatly from fear, especially the night before, that awful night. Nastasya recalled afterwards that he'd gone to bed late and slept soundly. But that doesn't prove anything; they say people sentenced to death sleep very soundly the night before their execution. Even though he set off at first light when a nervous man is always a little more confident (the major, Virginsky's relative, used to stop believing in God once night had passed), I'm convinced that never without horror could he have imagined himself travelling all alone along that highway and in such a state. Naturally, a certain feeling of desperation probably mitigated at first the full force of the terrible abrupt sensation of solitude he suddenly experienced as soon as he left Stasie and the cosy place where he'd spent the last twenty years. But that didn't matter: even if he'd clearly foreseen all the horrors awaiting him, he'd still have set out on his journey along the highway! There was an element of pride in his undertaking that fascinated him in spite of everything. Oh, he could have accepted Varvara Petrovna's luxurious conditions and remained dependent on her generosity '*comme un* ordinary hanger-on'! But he didn't accept her charity and didn't stay. Now he was leaving her, raising the 'banner of a great idea', setting out to die for it on the great highway! That's precisely what he must have been feeling; that's precisely how his action must have struck him.

The question has occurred to me more than once: why was it he ran away, that is literally ran on foot, and didn't ride away in a carriage? At first I explained this as the impracticality of his fifty years and the fantastic twist to his thinking produced by violent emotion. It seemed to me that

the idea of ordering fresh post-horses (even if they came
with harness bells) must have occurred to him as too simple
and prosaic; on the other hand, a pilgrimage, even with an
umbrella, was much more colourful and expressive of love
and revenge. But now that everything is over, I suppose it
was a much simpler affair at the time: in the first place, he
was afraid to take horses because Varvara Petrovna might
have found out and forcibly prevented him from leaving,
something she certainly would have done, and he would
certainly have submitted, and—then farewell to his great
idea for ever. In the second place, to order fresh post-horses
he had to know at least where he was going. But not
knowing that was precisely what caused him most distress
at that moment: he was absolutely incapable of specifying
any destination. Deciding on a particular place would immediately have rendered the entire enterprise ridiculous and
impossible in his own eyes; he felt this very clearly. After
all, what exactly would he do in that place, and why there,
and not some other place? Seek out *ce marchand*?[1] But what
marchand? A second question trotted out again, the most
terrible of all. In fact, there was nothing he was more
terrified of than this *marchand* whom he'd suddenly set out
to find at breakneck speed, and whom, naturally enough, he
was afraid of finding more than anything. No, the highway
was much better; he'd just set off and go along without
thinking about anything for as long as he could. The
highway—very, very long, with no end in sight—just like
human life, human dreams. The highway comprised an idea;
but what sort of idea was there in post-horses? There was
merely the end of an idea... *Vive la grande route*,[2] and leave
the rest to God.

After the sudden and unexpected meeting with Liza previously described, he continued in a state of even greater
oblivion. The highway passed within half a mile of Skvoreshniki and—strange to say—initially he didn't even notice
when he reached it. At that moment logical reasoning, even

[1] that merchant?
[2] Long live the highway

distinct perception was intolerable to him. A light rain stopped and started again; but he didn't even notice it. Nor did he notice how he'd tossed the bag over his shoulder and how much easier it was to walk that way. He must have gone on a mile or two like that, when all of a sudden he stopped and looked around. The old, black road, rutted by wheels and bordered by willows, extended before him like an endless thread; to the right lay a bare field where the grain had long since been harvested; to the left—bushes and a wood beyond. And in the distance—in the distance lay the scarcely visible line of the railway running off at a slant, with smoke rising from a train; but no sound could be heard. Stepan Trofimovich grew a little nervous, but only for a moment. He sighed vaguely, deposited his bag beside a willow, and sat down for a rest. As he sat, he felt a chill and wrapped himself up in his blanket; noticing the rain at the same time, he opened his umbrella over his head. He sat there for a while like that, occasionally moving his lips, keeping a firm hold on the umbrella handle. Various images swept by in a feverish array, rapidly following one another in his mind. 'Lise, Lise,' he thought, 'and *ce Maurice* with her... Strange people... And what strange kind of a fire was that, and what were they talking about? Who was murdered?... I daresay Stasie still hasn't been able to find out anything and is waiting for me with some coffee... Cards? Did I really lose someone at a game of cards? Hmmm... here in Russia, during the time of so-called serfdom... Oh, my God, what about Fedka?'

He trembled all over in fear and looked around: 'Why, what if Fedka is sitting somewhere here behind a bush? They say he has a whole band of robbers out here along the highway! Oh, my God, then I'll... I'll tell him the whole truth, I'm to blame... and because of him I suffered *for ten years*, more than he ever suffered in the army, and... and I'll give him my wallet. Hmmm, *j'ai en tout quarante roubles; il prendra les roubles et il me tuera tout de même.*'[1]

---

[1] I have altogether forty roubles; he'll take the roubles and then kill me all the same.

In his fear he for some reason closed his umbrella and placed it next to him. In the distance, coming from town, appeared some sort of cart. He began to watch it in some anxiety:

'*Grâce à Dieu*, it's a cart and it's approaching slowly; it can't be dangerous. Those are just broken-down local nags... I've always said about that breed... It was Peter Ilych, wasn't it, who talked about that breed in the club, but I got the better of him, *et puis*. But what's that behind... and it looks like a woman in the cart. A peasant woman and a peasant— *cela commence à être rassurant*. The woman's behind, the peasant up front—*c'est très rassurant*. And they have a cow tied to the cart by its horns, *c'est rassurant au plus haut degré*.'[1]

The cart drew level with him; it was rather a solid, decent-looking one. The woman sat on a tightly stuffed sack, while the peasant was up front, his legs hanging down sideways towards Stepan Trofimovich. A reddish cow was in fact trudging along behind, tied to the cart by its horns. The peasant and the woman stared at Stepan Trofimovich, their eyes bulging; Stepan Trofimovich stared back at them exactly the same way. But after he let them get about twenty paces or so past him, he suddenly stood up and ran to catch up with them. It was only natural he should feel safer near the cart, but by the time he caught up with it, he'd already forgotten everything and had withdrawn once more into fragmented thoughts and images. He walked on, having no suspicion, of course, that at that moment he was in the eyes of the peasant and the woman the most mysterious and fascinating thing that could possibly be encountered along the highway.

'And just who might you be, if you don't mind my asking?' the peasant woman said at last, unable to restrain herself, when Stepan Trofimovich suddenly looked up at her absent-mindedly. The woman was about twenty-seven years old, solidly built, with black brows, rosy cheeks, and

[1] that's beginning to reassure me. . . . that's very reassuring. . . . that's reassuring in the highest degree.

a friendly smile on her red lips, between which shone even, white teeth.

'Are you... are you talking to me?' muttered Stepan Trofimovich in mournful surprise.

'He must be a merchant,' the peasant observed with confidence. He was a large man, about forty, with a broad, intelligent-looking face and a full, reddish beard.

'No, I'm not exactly a merchant, I... I... *moi c'est autre chose*,'[1] Stepan Trofimovich parried the question somehow. He managed to drop back a step or two, just in case, to the rear of the cart, so he was now walking alongside the cow.

'Must be from the gentry,' the peasant decided, hearing the foreign words, and tugged at his horse.

'That's what we were looking at you for, wondering if you was out for a walk?' the woman asked, full of curiosity.

'Are you... are you asking me a question?'

'Foreigners sometimes come here on the train, and your boots don't look like they're made round here...'

'Them's army boots,' the peasant explained complacently and significantly.

'No, I'm not exactly in the army, I...'

'What an inquisitive woman she is,' Stepan Trofimovich thought to himself in annoyance. 'And how she's looking at me... *mais, enfin*.... In a word, it's odd but I feel guilty about them. But I've done nothing to them to feel guilty about.'

The woman whispered something to the man.

'If you won't take offence, we'd be glad to give you a ride, if you'd like to, that is.'

Stepan Trofimovich suddenly roused himself.

'Yes, yes, my friends, with great pleasure, because I'm very tired. Now, how do I get up?'

'How astonishing it is,' he thought to himself, 'I've been walking alongside this cow for so long but it never occurred to me to ask them for a ride... This "real life" has something absolutely characteristic to it...'

But the peasant still didn't stop his horse.

'And where might you be going?' he asked in some uncertainty.

[1] I'm something else

Stepan Trofimovich didn't understand at once.

'You must be going to Khatovo?'

'To Khatov's? No, not exactly to Khatov's... I'm not sure I even know him, although I've heard of him.'

'The village of Khatovo, it's a village, about nine miles from here.'

'A village? *C'est charmant*, I'm sure I've heard of it...'

Stepan Trofimovich kept walking; they still hadn't helped him into the cart. A brilliant idea flashed through his mind:

'Perhaps you think I'm... I have a passport and I'm—a professor, a teacher, if you like... a head teacher. I'm a head teacher. *Oui, c'est comme ça qu'on peut traduire.*[1] I'd really like to sit down, and I'll buy you... I'll buy you half a litre of wine in return.'

'This'll cost you half a rouble, sir; it's a bad road.'

'Or else it wouldn't be fair on us,' the woman added.

'Half a rouble? Well, fine, half a rouble. *C'est encore mieux, j'ai en tout quarante roubles, mais...*[2]

The peasant stopped his horse; with their joint efforts they managed to pull Stepan Trofimovich up and seat him on the sack next to the woman. A whirlwind of ideas still went on in his head. At times he was aware of feeling terribly confused and thinking about quite the wrong thing, and this surprised him. Being conscious of the morbid weakness of his own mind was very hard for him to bear at times, humiliating even.

'Why... why is there a cow behind the cart?' he asked the woman suddenly.

'Like as if you've never seen a cow before, sir?' the woman replied with a laugh.

'We bought her in town,' the peasant explained. 'Our own cattle died last spring, see; plague, it was. All around us cattle died, all around us; not half of them left, a shame it was.'

His horse had become stuck in the mud and he lashed it again.

---

[1] Yes, one could translate it like that.

[2] That's even better, I've forty roubles in all, but

'Yes, that sometimes happens here in Russia... in general we Russians... well, yes, it does happen,' Stepan Trofimovich didn't finish what he was saying. .

'If you're a teacher, what are you going to Khatovo for? Or are you going further?'

'I'm... I'm not exactly going further... *C'est-à-dire*, I'm going to visit a merchant.'

'You'll be going to Spasov,* then?'

'Yes, yes, that's it precisely, Spasov. But it really doesn't matter.'

'If you're going to Spasov and on foot, it'll take you a week to get there in those boots of yours,' said the woman with a laugh.

'Well, well, that doesn't matter either, *mes amis*, it doesn't matter,' Stepan Trofimovich said, interrupting them impatiently.

'What awfully inquisitive people; but the woman speaks better than he does, and I note that since the 19th of February* their style has changed somewhat, and... and what business is it of theirs whether I'm going to Spasov or not? Besides, I'm going to pay them, so why are they pestering me?'

'If you're going to Spasov, you take the steamer,' the peasant persisted.

'That's right,' the woman added with animation, 'because if you go round by the shore, it's an extra thirty miles.'

'Forty.'

'You'll just be able to catch the two o'clock steamer at Ustievo tomorrow,' the woman said, settling the matter. But Stepan Trofimovich remained stubbornly silent. His interrogators were silent as well. The peasant tugged at his horse; the woman occasionally exchanged brief remarks with him. Stepan Trofimovich dozed. He was awfully surprised when the woman roused him with a laugh and he found himself in quite a large village at the entrace to a hut with three windows.

'You had a little sleep, sir?'

'What's this? Where am I? Ah, well! Well... it doesn't matter,' Stepan Trofimovich said with a sigh and climbed down from the cart.

He looked around gloomily; the village seemed strange and somehow horribly unfamiliar.

'But I've forgotten the half rouble!' he said, turning to the peasant with an unnecessary haste; he was evidently already afraid of parting with them.

'You can settle up inside, if you please,' the peasant said, inviting him in.

'It's nice in there,' the woman said, reassuring him.

Stepan Trofimovich climbed the shaky steps.

'But how is this possible?' he whispered in profound and frightened consternation, though he still entered the hut. '*Elle l'a voulu.*'[1] Something pierced his heart; once again he was oblivious of everything, even that he had entered the place.

It was a bright, rather clean peasant hut with three windows and two rooms; it wasn't really an inn, but a house where people who knew it used to stop on their way through the village. Stepan Trofimovich, not in the least embarrassed, went to the corner of the room reserved for visitors, forgot to greet anyone, sat down and sank into thought. Meanwhile after three damp hours on the road an extremely pleasant feeling of warmth suddenly spread through his body. Even the chill that shuddered up and down his spine, common during bouts of fever in specially sensitive people, struck him as strangely agreeable as he made the abrupt transition from cold to warmth. He raised his head, and the appetising aroma of hot pancakes, which the woman of the house was busy making on the stove, began to titillate his sense of smell. Beaming childishly, he leaned over to the woman and suddenly babbled:

'What's that? Pancakes? *Mais... c'est charmant.*'

'Would you care for some, sir?' the woman politely offered at once.

'I would, I certainly would, and... I'd also like some tea,' Stepan Trofimovich said, reviving.

'Shall I fetch the samovar? With greatest pleasure.'

The pancakes were served on a big plate with a crude

[1] She wanted it.

blue pattern—typical peasant pancakes, thin, made half from wheat-flour, drenched in hot fresh butter, the tastiest of pancakes. Stepan Trofimovich tried them with delight.

'They're so rich and tasty! If I could only have *un doigt d'eau de vie*.'[1]

'Is it a little vodka you'd like, sir?'

'Precisely, precisely, just a little, *un tout petit rien*.'

'About five kopecks' worth, then?'

'Yes, five—five—five—five—*un tout petit rien*,' agreed Stepan Trofimovich with a blissful smile.

Ask a man of the common people to do something for you, and, if he can and wants to, he'll serve you conscientiously and cordially; but ask him to fetch you some vodka— and his customary serene cordiality is suddenly transformed into hasty, joyful eagerness, almost familial solicitude. Fetching vodka—even though only you, not he, will be drinking it, and he knows that beforehand—he still senses something of your future satisfaction... Not much more than three or four minutes later (a tavern stood only a few steps away) a small bottle and a large greenish glass appeared on the table in front of Stepan Trofimovich.

'Is that all for me?' he asked, extremely surprised. 'I've always drunk vodka, but I never knew you got so much for five kopecks.'

He poured a glass, stood up, and with a certain solemnity crossed the room to the far corner where his travelling companion, the woman with black eyebrows, was sitting on the sack—the one who pestered him so with her questions along the way. The woman was embarrassed and about to decline, but after she said everything required by propriety, she finally stood up, drank the vodka politely in three sips as women do, and with an expression of intense suffering on her face, returned the glass and bowed to Stepan Trofimovich. He bowed solemnly and went back to his table looking rather pleased with himself.

All this took place on the spur of the moment: he himself, a moment before, had had no idea of offering the woman vodka.

---

[1] a nip of vodka

'I deal extremely well with the common people, extremely well, and I've always told them that,' he thought complacently, pouring himself the remaining vodka from the bottle. Even though less than a glass was left, the vodka warmed and revived him and even went to his head a little.

'*Je suis malade tout à fait, mais ce n'est pas trop mauvais d'être malade.*'[1]

'Would you care to make a purchase?' enquired a woman's soft voice next to him.

He raised his eyes and, to his astonishment, beheld a lady—*une dame et elle en avait l'air*[2]—over thirty years old, very modest in appearance, dressed like a townswoman, in a dark dress with a large grey shawl over her shoulders. There was something pleasant about her face, something that appealed to Stepan Trofimovich immediately. She'd just come back to the hut where she'd left her things on a bench, right next to the place occupied by Stepan Trofimovich—among those things was a briefcase which, he recalled, he'd noticed with some interest when he came in, as well as a small oilskin bag. From her bag she took two beautifully bound books with crosses engraved on their covers and offered them to Stepan Trofimovich.

'*Eh... mais je crois que c'est l'Évangile*; with the greatest pleasure... Ah, now I understand... *Vous êtes ce qu'on appelle*[3] a gospel woman; I've often read about you... Half a rouble?'

'Thirty-five kopecks each,' the gospel woman replied.

'With the greatest pleasure. *Je n'ai rien contre l'Évangile, et...*[4] I've been wanting to reread it for some time now...'

The thought flashed through his mind at that moment that he hadn't read the Gospel for at least thirty years; some seven years ago he'd recalled a few passages from it while reading Renan's *Vie de Jésus.** Since he had no small change he pulled out his four ten-rouble notes—that was all he had. The woman of the house went to change one of them, and only then did he notice, upon looking around, that a rather

---

[1] I'm quite ill, but it's not such a bad thing to be ill.
[2] a lady and she looked like a lady
[3] Why, I believe it's the Gospel . . . You are what's called
[4] I have nothing against the Gospel, and

large crowd of people had gathered in the hut; they were staring at him and, apparently, talking about him. They were also commenting on the recent fire in town, the owner of the cart and the cow most of all, since he'd just come back from town. They were discussing arson and the Shpigulin affair.

'He said nothing about the fire when they picked me up, though he did talk about everything else,' Stepan Trofimovich thought for some reason.

'Stepan Trofimovich, sir, is it really you? I never expected it!... Don't you know me?' cried an elderly man who looked like a house serf from the old days. He was clean-shaven and wore an overcoat with a long, turned-down collar. Stepan Trofimovich was frightened when he heard his name.

'Excuse me,' he muttered, 'I don't remember you at all...'

'You've forgotten! Why, sir, I'm Anisim, Anisim Ivanov. I used to be in the service of the late Mr Gaganov; I've seen you, sir, with Varvara Petrovna many times at the late Avdotya Sergeevna's. I used to bring you books from her and twice I brought you sweets from Petersburg from her...'

'Oh, yes, I do remember you, Anisim,' Stepan Trofimovich said with a smile. 'Do you live here now?'

'I live near Spasov, sir, in V— Monastery, in the service of Marfa Sergeevna, Avdotya's Sergeevna's sister. Do you remember her? She's the one who broke her leg getting out of her carriage on the way to a ball. She lives near the monastery, and I live there with her, sir; and now, as you see, I'm on my way to town to visit my relatives...'

'Oh, yes, yes.'

'I'm glad to see you, sir; you used to be so kind to me,' Anisim said, smiling ecstatically. 'But where are you going, sir, all on your own, it seems?... You never went anywhere alone before, did you, sir?'

Stepan Trofimovich looked at him in alarm.

'You aren't coming to see us in Spasov, are you, sir?'

'Yes, I'm going to Spasov. *Il me semble que tout le monde va a Spassof...*'[1]

---

[1] It seems to me that everybody is going to Spasov

'To Fyodor Matveevich, is it? He'll be so glad to see you. He used to respect you so in the old days; even now he often talks about you...'

'Yes, yes, to Fyodor Matveevich.'

'Of course, sir, of course. That's why the peasants seem so surprised, sir; they're saying they met you walking along the highway. They're foolish people, sir.'

'I... I... I, you see, Anisim, like an Englishman I bet I'd get there on foot, and I...'

Beads of sweat stood out on his forehead and temples.

'Of course, sir, of course,' said Anisim, listening to him with merciless curiosity. But Stepan Trofimovich couldn't stand any more. He was so embarrassed that he wanted to get up and leave the hut. But the samovar was brought in and then the gospel woman returned from wherever she'd gone off to. Like a drowning man he turned to her and offered her some tea. Anisim gave up and went away.

The peasants really were, in fact, in a state of perplexity: 'What sort of man is he? They found him walking along the highway; he says he's a teacher, he's dressed like a foreigner, but he has the mind of a child. He gives absurd answers, as if he's running away from someone, and he has money!' The idea arose that they ought to inform the authorities—'since things haven't been all that quiet in town lately'. But Anisim managed to calm them down. He went into the passage and told everyone who'd listen that Stepan Trofimovich wasn't exactly a teacher, but 'a very great scholar who studied important subjects. He was a landowner in their district who'd lived for twenty-two years in the house of General Stavrogin's widow. He was the most important person in that house, and was held in great respect by all the townsfolk. He used to lose fifty and hundred-rouble notes at cards in an evening; he held the rank of councillor, equal to lieutenant-colonel in the army, only one rank lower than a full colonel. As for his having so much money, he gets more from General Stavrogin's widow than you can even count', and so on and so forth.

'*Mais c'est une dame, et très comme il faut*,'[1] Stepan Trofimovich said, recovering from Anisim's assault and regarding his neighbour, the gospel woman, with agreeable curiosity, as she drank tea from a saucer and nibbled at a lump of sugar. '*Ce petit morceau de sucre ce n'est rien....*'[2] There's something noble and independent about her, and at the same time, something gentle. *Le comme il faut tout pur*,[3] but only in a different sense.'

He soon found out she was Sofya Matveevna Ulitina,* lived in K—, and had a sister living there, a tradesman's widow; that she herself was also a widow; her husband had been killed at Sevastopol after being promoted from sergeant to second lieutenant for meritorious service.*

'But you're still so young, *vous n'avez pas trente ans*.'[4]

'I'm thirty-four, sir,' Sofya Matveevna smiled.

'So, do you understand French, too?'

'A little, sir; I spent four years in a gentleman's house and learned some there from the children.'

She told him that after being left a widow at the age of eighteen, she spent some time in Sevastopol as a nurse and then lived in various places; now she went around selling the Gospel.

'*Mais mon Dieu*, wasn't it you who were involved in some strange episode, some very strange episode in our town?'*

She blushed; it turned out that it was.

'*Ces vauriens, ces malheureux!...*'[5] he began in a voice quivering from indignation; a poignant and hateful recollection stirred painfully in his heart. For a moment he seemed to lose himself in it.

'Why, she's gone away again,' he recollected himself with a start, noticing that she was no longer next to him. 'She keeps going out and fussing with something; I see she's actually upset... *Bah, je deviens égoiste...*'[6]

---

[1] Why, she's a lady, and very ladylike
[2] The sugar lump doesn't matter
[3] Absolutely ladylike
[4] You're not even thirty
[5] These scoundrels, these wretches
[6] Bah, I'm becoming selfish

He looked up and once again saw Anisim, but this time in the most threatening circumstances. The whole hut was filled with peasants; apparently Anisim had brought them along with him. There was the owner of the hut, the peasant with the cow, and two other peasants (who turned out to be cab drivers); another small man, half-drunk, dressed like a peasant but clean-shaven, resembling a tradesman who drank too much, was now doing most of the talking. All of them were discussing him, Stepan Trofimovich. The peasant with the cow insisted that to drive around the shore of the lake would be forty miles out of the way and he should take the steamer. The half-drunk tradesman and the owner of the hut objected heatedly:

'Because, old pal, for his excellency, of course it'd be closer to cross the lake by steamer; that's for sure; but maybe these days the steamer isn't going there.'

'Yes is, it is, it'll be going there for another week,' Anisim said, more heatedly than the rest.

'Well, all right then! But it doesn't arrive on time because it's so late in the season. Sometimes it stays in Ustievo three days.'

'It'll be here tomorrow, two o'clock sharp tomorrow. You'll get to Spasov before evening, sir,' Anisim said, beside himself.

'*Mais qu'est ce qu'il a cet homme*,'[1] Stepan Trofimovich wondered in alarm, awaiting his fate in fear.

The cab drivers came forward and began joining in; they'd take him to Ustievo for three roubles. The rest added that three roubles wasn't too much to ask; they'd been driving to Ustievo all summer for that price.

'But... it's nice here too... And I don't want to go,' Stepan Trofimovich mumbled.

'Nice, sir, you're right, it's very nice in Spasov now, and Fyodor Matveevich will be so glad to see you.'

'*Mon Dieu, mes amis*, this is all so unexpected for me.'

At last Sofya Matveevna came back. She sat down on the bench looking very sad and dejected.

[1] But what's the matter with that man?

'I'll never get to Spasov!' she said to the woman of the house.

'So, you're going to Spasov, too?' Stepan Trofimovich asked with a start.

It turned out that a certain landowner, Nadezhda Yegorovna Svetlitsyna, had promised to take her to Spasov the day before and told her to wait in Khatovo, but then never showed up.

'What am I going to do now?' Sofya Matveevna repeated.

'*Mais, ma chère et nouvelle amie*, I could take you, like that lady, to that village, whatever it's called, I've hired a carriage to, and tomorrow—well, tomorrow we'll go to Spasov together.'

'You're not going to Spasov, too, are you?'

'*Mais que faire, et je suis enchanté!*[1] I'll take you along with the greatest pleasure; you see, they want to take me and I've already hired someone... Which one of you have I hired?' Stepan Trofimovich asked, now feeling desperately eager to go to Spasov.

In a quarter of an hour they were already seated in a covered cart: he very animated and completely satisfied, she next to him with her bag and a grateful smile on her face. Anisim helped them in.

'Have a good journey, sir,' he said, bustling around the cart for all he was worth. 'It's been very good to see you again!'

'Goodbye, goodbye, my friend, goodbye.'

'You'll see Fyodor Matveich, sir...'

'Yes, my friend, yes... Fyodor Petrovich... but goodbye for now.'

2.

'You see, my friend, you'll permit me to call you that, *n'est-ce pas?*' Stepan Trofimovich began hurriedly, as soon as the cart started moving. 'You see, I... *J'aime le peuple, c'est indispensable, mais il me semble que je ne l'avais jamais vu de près. Stasie... cela va sans dire qu'elle est aussi du*

---

[1] Why, no help for it, and I'm delighted!

peuple... mais le vrai peuple,[1] that is, the real people, the ones on the highway, it seems to me all they care about is where I'm going... But let's leave insults aside. I seem to be spewing out nonsense, but that's because I'm talking so fast.'

'It seems you're not quite well, sir,' Sofya Matveena said, regarding him closely but respectfully.

'No, no, all I have to do is wrap myself up; the wind *is* a bit fresh, a bit too fresh, but we'll forget about that. That's not what I really wanted to say. *Chère et incomparable amie*, it seems I'm almost happy, and you're the reason for that. Being happy doesn't do me any good because immediately I want to go and forgive all my enemies...'

'But that's a good thing, sir.'

'Not always, *chère innocente. L'Évangile... Voyez-vous, désormais nous le prêcherons ensemble*, and I'll gladly help you sell those beautiful little books. Yes, I feel it may be an idea, *quelque chose de très nouveau dans ce genre.* The common people are religious, *c'est admis*, but they still don't know the Gospel. I'll explain it to them... In my oral presentation I can correct all the mistakes in that remarkable book which I'm naturally prepared to treat with the utmost respect. I'll prove useful along the highway, too. I've always been useful, I've always told *them* so *et à cette chère ingrate...*[2] Oh, we'll forgive, we'll forgive, we'll begin by forgiving everyone, always... We hope they'll forgive us. Yes, because each and every one of us is guilty towards one another. We're all guilty!...'

'I think you put that very well, sir.'

'Yes, yes... I'm speaking very well. I will speak to them very well, but... but what was the main thing I meant to say? I keep losing the thread and forgetting... Will you let me stay with you? I feel that the way you look at me and...

[1] I love the people, that's essential, but it seems to me that I've never seen them close up. Stasie... it goes without saying that she is also from the people... but the real people
[2] dear innocent. The Gospel... Look, from now on we'll preach it together ... something really new of its kind ... we know that ... and that dear, ungrateful woman.

I'm actually quite surprised by your manners. You're simple-hearted; you call me 'sir' and turn your cup upside-down on your saucer... with that horrid lump of sugar. But there's something charming about you; I can see by your features that... oh, don't blush, and don't be afraid of me as a man. *Chère et incomparable, pour moi une femme c'est tout.*[1] I can't live except near a woman, but only near her... I've become confused, very confused... I can't even remember what I was going to say. Oh, blessed is he to whom God always sends a woman, and... I think actually I'm in some sort of ecstasy. Even on the high road there are higher thoughts! There—that's what I wanted to say—about the idea; now I've remembered, but I kept losing the thread before. Why have they taken us away? It was so nice there, but here—*cela devient trop froid. A propos, j'ai en tout quarante roubles et voilà cet argent,*[2] take it, take it, I'm incapable, I'll lose it and they'll take it away from me, and... I feel I'd like to go to sleep; my head is spinning. It's spinning, spinning, spinning all around. Oh, you're so kind. What's that you're covering me with?'

'You've got a fever, sir, and I'm covering you with my blanket. As for the money, sir, I'd rather...'

'Oh, for heaven's sake, *n'en parlons plus, parce que cela me fait mal,*[3] oh, you're so kind!'

He stopped talking abruptly and very quickly fell into a feverish, shivery sleep. The country road on which they travelled those seventeen miles was not one of the smoothest, and the carriage bounced along mercilessly. Stepan Trofimovich woke up often, raised his head from the small pillow which Sofya Matveevna had managed to slip under it, clutched her by the hand and asked, 'Are you still here?'—as if afraid she'd leave him. He also told her that in his dream he'd seen a gaping mouth filled with teeth and felt revolted by it. Sofya Matveevna was very worried about him.

---

[1] Dear and incomparable lady, for me a woman is everything.

[2] it's becoming too cold. By the way, I have altogether forty roubles, and here it is

[3] let's not talk of it any more, because it pains me

The cab driver brought them to a large hut with four windows flanked by smaller buildings in the courtyard. Stepan Trofimovich awoke and made haste to enter; he went right into the second, most spacious, best room in the house. His sleepy face assumed a very fussy expression. At once he explained to the landlady, a tall and stout woman about forty with very dark hair and a slight moustache, that he needed the whole room to himself: 'the door was to be closed and no one should be admitted, *parce que nous avons à parler*.'[1]

'*Oui, j'ai beaucoup à vous dire, chère amie.*[2] I'll pay you, I'll pay you!' he cried, waving his hand at the landlady.

Although in a hurry, he seemed to be having difficulty speaking. The landlady listened to him in an unfriendly manner, but remained silent as a sign of her consent, though there was a feeling of something menacing in her response. He didn't notice anything and hurriedly (he was in a terrible hurry) demanded she leave and serve dinner as soon as possible, 'without a moment's delay'.

The woman with a moustache could stand no more.

'This isn't an inn, sir. We don't serve dinner to travellers. We can boil up some crayfish or put on the samovar, but we have nothing else to offer you. There won't be any fresh fish until tomorrow.'

But Stepan Trofimovich waved his hand and repeated in angry impatience: 'I'll pay, but hurry, hurry.' They settled on fish soup and roast chicken; the landlady declared there was not a chicken to be had in the whole village; she agreed to look for one, but only as if doing him an immense favour.

As soon as she left Stepan Trofimovich sat down on the sofa and settled Sofya Matveevna next to him. There were a sofa and armchairs in the room, but they were in poor condition. In general the entire room, though rather large (there was a bed behind a partition), with its old, torn yellow wallpaper, its ugly prints of mythological figures on the walls, its long row of icons set in brass frames in the nearest

---

[1] because we have to talk.
[2] Yes, I have a great deal to say to you, my friend.

corner, its strange assortment of furniture—presented altogether a most unattractive combination of urban style and traditional peasant life. But he didn't notice any of this; he didn't even glance out the window at the enormous lake which began only twenty yards from the house.

'At last we're alone and we won't let anyone in! I want to tell you everything, everything from the very beginning.'

Sofya Matveevna stopped him with great anxiety:

'Are you aware, Stepan Trofimovich...'

'*Comment, vous savez déjà mon nom?*[1] he asked with a delighted smile.

'I heard Anisim Ivanovich say it earlier, when you were talking with him. But here's what I wanted to say...'

And she told him in a rapid whisper, with a glance at the closed door, fearing someone might overhear, that it was simply awful here in this village. Although all the local peasants were fishermen, they earned their living by charging travellers as much as they possibly could every summer. The village wasn't on the main road, but out of the way, and people only came here because it was where the steamer stopped, and when it didn't arrive—in bad weather it never did—people were stranded here for several days, and all the huts in the village were occupied and that was just what the villagers were waiting for; they charged three times the regular rate for everything; and the local landlord was proud and arrogant because he was the richest man around; he owned one fishing net that cost a thousand roubles alone.

Stepan Trofimovich looked into Sofya Matveevna's animated face with something like reproach and made an attempt to stop her several times. But she stood her ground and had her say: according to her own words she'd been here once before during the summer with 'a very wealthy lady' from town, spent the night waiting for the steamer to come, two whole days actually, and he couldn't possibly imagine what they had to put up with. 'Now, Stepan Trofimovich, you've asked for this room for yourself, sir... I only wanted to warn you, sir... There are already a few

---

[1] What, you know my name?

travellers in that room, an older man, a young man, and a woman and children. By two o'clock tomorrow the whole hut will be full because the steamer hasn't been here for two days and it'll certainly come tomorrow. So for a separate room and for asking to have dinner served, sir, and for all the trouble this causes other travellers, they'll charge you a price unheard-of even in the capitals, sir...'

But he was suffering, really suffering.

'*Assez, mon enfant*, I beg you; *nous avons notre argent, et après—et après le bon Dieu.* I'm even surprised that you, with your lofty ideals... *Assez, assez, vous me tourmentez*,'[1] he said hysterically, 'the whole future lies before us, but you... you're making me afraid of the future...'

He began immediately telling her the story of his life, so hurriedly that at first it was quite hard to understand him. He went on for rather a long time. The fish soup was served, then the chicken, finally the samovar, and he was still talking... A somewhat strange and morbid account emerged, but then again, he was ill. It was a sudden exertion of his intellectual faculties that of course—as Sofya Matveevna foresaw with alarm throughout his narrative—was bound to produce extreme exhaustion in his disordered system immediately afterwards. He began with his childhood, when 'with a strong, young heart he ran through the fields'; only an hour later did he reach his two marriages and his life in Berlin. But I hesitate to laugh. There was really something sublime in it for him, to use contemporary language, almost a struggle for existence.* He saw before him the woman he'd selected to share his future life's path and hastened to initiate her, as it were. His genius must no longer be kept secret from her... Perhaps he was exaggerating Sofya Matveevna's worth, but he had already chosen her. He couldn't live without a woman. By the look on her face he realized that she hardly understood a word he was saying, even the most fundamental parts.

---

[1] Enough, my child . . . we have our money, and afterwards—afterwards God will help us. . . . Enough, enough, you're tormenting me

'*Ce n'est rien, nous attendrons,*[1] meanwhile she can understand me with her intuition.'

'My friend, the only thing I need is your heart!' he cried, interrupting his story, 'and that kind, charming way you're looking at me now. Oh, don't blush! I've already told you that...'

A great deal remained obscure to poor, entrapped Sofya Matveevna, especially when the story became a lengthy dissertation on the fact that no one had ever been able to understand Stepan Trofimovich, and how 'true talents are wasted in Russia.' It was all 'so terribly intellectual' she reported later sadly. She listened in evident distress, her eyes bulging slightly. When Stepan Trofimovich resorted to humour and sarcastic wit at the expense of our 'progressive and governing circles', she tried desperately on two occasions to respond to his laughter with a laugh, but the result was worse than tears, so that even Stepan Trofimovich was finally embarrassed, and attacked the nihilists and the 'new people' with even greater passion and spite. At this point he simply frightened her; she felt relieved only when he embarked on the story of his great romance, but her relief was short-lived. A woman is always a woman, even if she's a nun. She smiled, nodded her head, even blushed and dropped her eyes, which brought Stepan Trofimovich to the pitch of ecstasy and inspiration, so that he began telling quite a lot of lies. Varvara Petrovna appeared in his tale as an enchanting brunette ('the rage of Petersburg and many European capitals'); her husband had died, 'felled by a bullet at Sevastopol', solely because he felt himself unworthy of her love and had yielded his place to a rival, that is, to none other than Stepan Trofimovich... 'Don't be embarrassed, gentle lady, my good Christian woman!' he cried to Sofya Matveevna, almost believing the story he was telling her. 'It was something sublime, so subtle that neither one of us ever spoke about it during our life together.' The reason for this state of affairs later turned out to be a certain blonde (if not Darya Pavlovna, then I don't know who Stepan

[1] It's nothing, we'll wait

Trofimovich had in mind). This blonde owed everything to the brunette and, as a distant relative, had grown up in her household. The brunette, finally noticing the blonde's love for Stepan Trofimovich, locked her secret away in her heart. All three of them, pining in mutual generosity, remained silent for twenty years, locking their secrets away in their hearts. 'Oh, what passion this was, what passion!' he exclaimed, sobbing with genuine ecstasy. 'I saw the full bloom of her beauty (the brunette's), watched "with aching heart" as she passed me every day, as if ashamed to be so fair.' (At one point he said: 'ashamed to be so fat' by mistake.) At long last he ran away, casting aside this feverish dream of twenty years—'*Vingt ans!*' Now he was on the broad highway... Then, in an overwrought state of mind, he began to explain to Sofya Matveevna the meaning of their encounter that day, 'so fortuitous and fateful an encounter for ever and ever.' At last Sofya Matveevna rose from the sofa in terrible embarrassment; he attempted to fall on his knees, and she started to cry. It was beginning to grow dark; they'd spent several hours together in that locked room...

'No, you'd better let me go into the other room, sir,' she muttered, 'or else, what will people think, sir?'

She finally tore herself away; he let her go, giving her his word that he'd go straight to bed. In bidding her farewell, he complained of a bad headache. When she'd first come in, Sofya Matveevna had left her bag and other things in the outer room, intending to spend the night there with the owners of the hut; but she had no time to rest.

That night Stepan Trofimovich had one of his bilious attacks—so familiar to me and all his friends. It was the usual outcome of nervous distress and moral upheaval. Poor Sofya Matveevna didn't get any sleep the whole night. Since she was attending the patient, she had to enter and leave the hut fairly frequently through the owners' room; both the travellers sleeping there and the landlady complained loudly and then even began to abuse her when, towards morning, she decided to put on the samovar. Throughout the attack Stepan Trofimovich was in a state of semi-consciousness; sometimes it seemed to him the samovar was being put on, he was being given something to drink (raspberry tea), and his stomach and chest were being covered. But most of the time he felt _she_ was right there next to him; that it was she who was coming and going, lifting him out of bed, and helping him back in again. Around three o'clock in the morning he felt a little better; he sat up, put his legs down, and without thinking, fell flat on the floor in front of her. This was no longer the kneeling before her of the previous evening; he simply fell at her feet and kissed the hem of her dress...

'Stop, sir, I don't deserve it at all, sir,' she muttered, trying to lift him back into bed.

'My saviour,' he said, clasping his hands reverently before her. '_Vous êtes noble comme une marquise!_[1] I'm—I'm a scoundrel! Oh, all my life I've been so dishonest...'

'Calm down,' Sofya Matveevna implored him.

'It was all lies I told you last night—vainglorious, self-indulgent frivolous lies—all lies, every last word. Oh, I'm a scoundrel, such a scoundrel!'

His fit of biliousness thus turned into another fit, one of hysterical self-accusation. I've mentioned these fits before when I spoke about his letters to Varvara Petrovna. He suddenly remembered Lise, his meeting with her the previous morning: 'It was so awful and—there must have been some tragedy, but I didn't ask, I didn't find out! I was thinking only about myself! Oh, what's wrong with her, don't you know, what's wrong with her?' Stepan Trofimovich implored.

Then he swore he'd 'never betray _her_', he'd return 'to _her_' (that is, Varvara Petrovna). 'We'll go to her house every day' (that is, with Sofya Matveevna), 'just as she's getting into her carriage for a morning outing, and we'll watch quietly... Oh, I want her to slap my other cheek; how I'll enjoy it! I'll offer her my other cheek to slap _comme dans votre livre!_[2] Now, only now have I understood what it means to "turn the other cheek". I never understood it before!'

---

[1] You are as noble as a marquise!
[2] like in your book!

For Sofya Matveevna the two days that followed were the worst days of her life; even now she shudders at the memory of them. Stepan Trofimovich got so sick he was unable to travel on the steamer that arrived on time at two o'clock the next day; since she was unable to leave him there alone, she didn't go to Spasov either. According to her own account, he was actually glad the steamer left.

'Well, that's fine, that's splendid,' he muttered from his bed, 'because I've been so afraid we'd leave. It's so nice here, better than anywhere else... You're not leaving me, are you? Oh, you haven't left me!'

But it wasn't really all that nice 'here'. He didn't want to hear anything about her difficulties; his head was filled solely with fantasies. He looked upon his illness as transitory, trifling, and thought little of it; he thought only of how they'd go off and begin selling 'those little books'. He asked her to read him the Gospel.

'It's been a long time since I read it... in the original. Someone might ask me something, and I'd make a mistake; one must prepare oneself.'

She sat down next to him and opened the book.

'You read beautifully,' he said, interrupting her after the first line. 'I see, I see I wasn't mistaken!' he added mysteriously, but ecstatically. In general he was in a state of constant exaltation. She read him the Sermon on the Mount.

'*Assez, assez, mon enfant*, enough... Don't you think *that's* enough?'

And he closed his eyes in exhaustion. He was very weak, but still hadn't lost consciousness. Sofya Matveevna tried to get up, thinking he wanted to sleep. But he stopped her:

'My friend, I've lied my whole life. Even when I was telling the truth. I've never spoken for the sake of truth, only for my own sake. I knew that before, but only now do I see... Oh, where are those people I've offended with my friendship all my life? All of them, all of them! *Savez-vous*, I may be lying even now; certainly I'm lying even now. In life the hardest thing of all is to live and not tell lies... and... not believe in one's own lies, yes, yes, precisely that! But wait, all that later... We're together, together!' he added with enthusiasm.

'Stepan Trofimovich,' Sofya Matveevna enquired timidly, 'shouldn't we send to town for the doctor?' He was awfully surprised.

'What for? *Est-ce que je suis si malade? Mais rien de sérieux.*[1] Why do we need any outsiders? They'll find out and—then what will happen? No, no, no outsiders, we're together, together!'

'Won't you', he said after a pause, 'read me something else, anything you like, whatever strikes your eye.'

Sofya Matveevna opened the book and started to read.

'Wherever it opens, wherever it happens to open,' he repeated.

' "And unto the angel of the church of the Laodiceans write...." '

'What's that? What? Where's that from?'

'It's from the Book of Revelation.'

'*O, je m'en souviens, oui, l'Apocalypse. Lisez, lisez,*[2] I'm trying to tell our future from the book, I want to know what turns up. Read about the angel, the angel...'

' "And unto the angel of the church of the Laodiceans write; These things saith the Amen, the faithful and true witness, the beginning of the creation of God; I know thy works, that thou art neither cold nor hot; I would thou wert cold or hot. So then because thou art lukewarm, and neither cold nor hot, I will spue thee out of my mouth. Because thou sayest, I am rich, and increased with goods, and have need of nothing; and thou knowest not that thou art wretched, and miserable, and poor, and blind, and naked." '*

'That... that's in your book!' he exclaimed, his eyes gleaming, raising his head from the pillow. 'I never knew that wonderful passage! Hear that: better cold, cold, than lukewarm, than *only* lukewarm. Oh, I'll prove it. But don't leave me, don't leave me alone! We'll prove it, we'll prove it!'

'I won't leave you, Stepan Trofimovich, I'll never leave you, sir!' she cried, grabbing hold of his hand, squeezing it,

---

[1] Am I as ill as that? But it's nothing serious.

[2] Oh, I remember, yes, the Apocalypse. Go on, read.

and pressing it to her heart; she looked at him with tears in her eyes. ('I felt so very sorry for him at that moment,' she recounted later.) His lips trembled, as if in a spasm.

'But what are we going to do, Stepan Trofimovich? Shouldn't we let some of your friends or relatives know about you?'

He was so alarmed at this idea that she was sorry she'd brought it up again. Shivering and trembling, he implored her to call no one, to do nothing; he made her promise. He urged her: 'No one, no one! The two of us, just the two of us, *nous partirons ensemble*.'[1]

Even worse, the landlord and landlady began to be uneasy, grumble and pester Sofya Matveevna. She paid them and allowed them to get a good look at her money; this placated them for a while, but then the landlord demanded to see Stepan Trofimovich's papers. The sick man pointed to his small bag with a condescending smile; in it Sofya Matveevna found the certificate of resignation from the university, or something of the sort, that had served as his passport all his life. The landlord wasn't satisfied and said 'he should be taken somewhere else because this isn't a hospital; if he were to die, there'd be trouble—they'd never hear the end of it.' Sofya Matveevna would have tried to talk him into calling a doctor, but it turned out it would be too expensive if they sent to town so she had to give up that idea. Feeling rather dejected, she returned to the sick man. Stepan Trofimovich was getting weaker and weaker all the time.

'Now read me one more passage... about the swine,' he said all of a sudden.

'What, sir?' Sofya Matveevna asked, terribly frightened.

'About the swine... that's in there too... *ces cochons*... I remember the devils entered the swine and were all drowned. You must read me that passage; I'll tell you why later. I want to recall it word for word. It has to be word for word.'

Sofya Matveevna knew the Gospel well and quickly found the passage in Luke, the one I have used as the epigraph to my chronicle. I'll quote it again here:

---

[1] we'll set out together.

'And there was there an herd of many swine feeding on the mountain: and they besought him that he would suffer them to enter into them. And he suffered them. Then went the devils out of the man, and entered into the swine: and the herd ran violently down a steep place into the lake, and were choked. When they that fed them saw what was done, they fled, and went and told it in the city and in the country. Then they went out to see what was done; and came to Jesus, and found the man, out of whom the devils were departed, sitting at the feet of Jesus, clothed, and in his right mind: and they were afraid.'*

'My friend,' Stepan Trofimovich said in great agitation, '*savez-vous*, this wonderful and... all my life this extraordinary passage has been a stumbling block for me... *dans ce livre*... so that I remember this passage from my childhood. Now an idea has occurred to me; *une comparaison*.[1] A great many ideas keep occurring to me now: you see, this is exactly like our Russia. These devils who go out of the sick man and enter the swine—they're all the plagues, all the miasmas, all the filth, all the devils, and all the demons who have accumulated in our great, our dear, sick Russia for centuries, for centuries! *Oui, cette Russie, que j'aimais toujours*.[2] But a great idea and a great will protect her from on high, just as they did that madman possessed by devils, and all the devils will leave, all the filth, all the abominations festering on the surface... they themselves will ask to enter the swine. They may even have entered them already! It's we, we and they, and Petrusha... *et les autres avec lui*,[3] and I, perhaps, first of all, at the head of them; we'll cast ourselves, all the insane and possessed, from the cliffs into the sea and we'll all drown, and it'll serve us right, because that's all we're really good for. But the sick man will be healed and "will sit at the feet of Jesus"... and everyone will look upon him in astonishment... My dear, *vous comprendrez après*, meanwhile it excites me greatly... *Vous comprendrez après*... *Nous comprendrons ensemble*.'[4]

[1] a comparison.
[2] Yes, this Russia that I've always loved.
[3] and the others with him
[4] you'll understand later... You'll understand later... We'll understand together.

He became delirious and finally lost consciousness. This situation continued for the whole next day. Sofya Matveevna sat beside him and wept, scarcely sleeping for three nights; she avoided meeting the landlord, who, she suspected, had begun to do something about them. Deliverance came only on the third day. In the morning Stepan Trofimovich regained consciousness, recognized her and stretched out his hand towards her. She crossed herself hopefully. He wanted to look out the window: '*Tiens, un lac*,'¹ he said. 'Good heavens, I hadn't noticed it before...' At that moment there was a rumble of a carriage at the door of the hut and great confusion arose inside.

3.

It was Varvara Petrovna herself, who'd arrived in a four-seater carriage drawn by four horses, accompanied by two footmen and by Darya Pavlovna. This miracle had been accomplished very simply: Anisim, dying of curiosity, arrived in town and called at Varvara Petrovna's house the next day. He blurted out to all the servants that he'd met Stepan Trofimovich all alone in the village, that some peasants had seen him going along the highway alone, on foot, and he was headed to Spasov by way of Ustievo, accompanied by Sofya Matveevna. Since Varvara Petrovna, for her part, was already terribly worried and was doing her best to locate her fugitive friend, the servants informed her about Anisim immediately. She heard him out, especially the details concerning his departure for Ustievo in a cart together with a certain Sofya Matveevna, and she set out at once in hot pursuit and turned up in Ustievo herself. She had as yet no idea whatever that he was ill.

Her stern and commanding voice resounded through the hut; even the landlord and landlady were frightened. She had stopped only for information and to make enquiries, convinced that Stepan Trofimovich had got to Spasov long ago; when she found out he was still there and was ill, she entered the hut in a state of great agitation.

¹ Look, a lake

'Well, where is he? Ah, so it's you!' she cried, spotting Sofya Matveevna, as soon as she appeared at the doorway of the other room. 'I can guess by your shameless face it's you. Away, you hussy! Don't let me see her in this house again! Out of here with her, or else, my good woman, I'll have you put away for the rest of your life. Keep her safe meanwhile in another house. She's been in gaol in town once already, and she'll be there again. And, landlord, I ask you not to let anyone else in while I'm here. I'm the widow of General Stavrogin and I shall occupy the whole house. And you, my dear, will have to answer to me for everything.'

The familiar voice startled Stepan Trofimovich. He began to tremble. But she'd already stepped behind the screen. Eyes flashing, she dragged up a chair with her foot, and leaning back in it, shouted at Dasha:

'Get out of here for a little while; stay with the landlord. What's all this curiosity? And close the doors firmly behind you.'

For some time she looked at his frightened face in silence with a sort of predatory gaze.

'Well, and how are you, Stepan Trofimovich? Are you enjoying yourself?' she blurted out suddenly with vicious irony.

'*Chère*,' Stepan Trofimovich began muttering, not knowing what he was saying, 'I've discovered real Russian life... *Et je prêcherai l'Évangile...*'[1]

'Oh, you shameless, ungrateful man!' she cried suddenly, throwing up her hands. 'Wasn't it enough to disgrace me the way you did? And now you've taken up with... Oh, you shameless, depraved old man!'

'*Chère*...'

His voice failed and he could say nothing; he merely looked at her, eyes popping in fear.

'Who on earth is *she*?'

'*C'est un ange... C'était plus qu'un ange pour moi*,[2] all night she... Oh, don't keep shouting, don't frighten her, *chère, chère*...'

---

[1] And I'll preach the Gospel
[2] She's an angel... She was more than an angel to me

All of a sudden Varvara Petrovna jumped up from her chair with a crash and cried out in fright: 'Water! water!' Even though he'd recovered his senses, she was still trembling with fright; her face was pale as she looked at his distorted features. Only now for the first time did she realize how sick he really was.

'Darya,' she whispered suddenly to Darya Pavlovna, 'have the doctor fetched immediately, Dr Salzfisch. Get Yegorych to go at once; tell him to hire horses here and take another carriage from town. The doctor must be here by evening.'

Dasha rushed to carry out her orders. Stepan Trofimovich stared at her with wide, frightened eyes; his pale lips trembled.

'Wait a bit, Stepan Trofimovich, wait a bit, my dear!' she said, coaxing him like a little child. 'Now, just wait a bit, wait a bit, Darya will come back and... Oh, my God, landlady, landlady, come here, my good woman!'

In her impatience she herself ran out to fetch the landlady.

'This very minute, at once, bring *that woman* back. Get her back, get her back!'

Fortunately Sofya Matveevna hadn't had time to get away from the house and had only just reached the gate with her bag and sack. She was brought back. She was so frightened that even her arms and legs were shaking. Varvara Petrovna grabbed her by the hand as a hawk pounces on a little chick, and dragged her headlong to Stepan Trofimovich.

'Well, here she is. I didn't eat her up. You thought I'd eaten her up, didn't you?'

Stepan Trofimovich grabbed Varvara Petrovna by the hand, raised it to his eyes, and burst into tears, sobbing violently and convulsively.

'There, there, calm down, my dear, calm down. Oh, my goodness, calm down, won't you?' she shouted furiously. 'Oh, you tormentor, tormentor, my eternal tormentor!'

'My dear,' Stepan Trofimovich muttered at last, addressing Sofya Matveevna, 'stay out there, my dear, I want to say something here...'

Sofya Matveevna made haste to leave the room.

'*Chérie, chérie...*' he gasped.

'Wait before you try to speak, Stepan Trofimovich, wait a bit until you've had some rest. Here's some water. Do wait, please!'

She sat down again on the chair. Stepan Trofimovich kept firm hold of her hand. For a long time she didn't let him speak. He raised her hand to his lips and began kissing it. She clenched her teeth, looking away into the corner.

'*Je vous aimais*!' he blurted out at last. She'd never heard him say those words in that way.

'Hmmm,' she muttered in reply.

'*Je vous aimais toute ma vie... vingt ans*!'[1]

She remained silent—two or three minutes.

'But when you were getting ready to receive Dasha you sprinkled yourself with scent...' she said suddenly in a terrible whisper. Stepan Trofimovich was dumbfounded.

'You put on a new cravat...'

Once more there was silence for two minutes.

'Do you remember the cigar?'

'My friend,' he started to mumble, horrified.

'The cigar, in the evening, at the window... the moon was shining... after the summerhouse... at Skvoreshniki? You do remember, don't you?' she said, jumping up, grabbing the two corners of his pillow and shaking it with his head on it. 'You remember, you shallow, shallow, disgraceful, cowardly, irredeemably shallow man?' she hissed in her vicious whisper, restraining herself from shouting. At last she left him alone, fell into her chair, and covered her face with her hands. 'Enough!' she cried, straightening up. 'Twenty years have passed and can't be brought back; I'm a fool as well.'

'*Je vous aimais*,' he said, folding his hands again.

'Why do keep on with *aimais* and *aimais*? Stop it!' she cried, jumping up again. 'And if you don't go to sleep right now, I'll... You need peace and quiet; now sleep, sleep, close your eyes. Oh, my goodness, perhaps he wants some lunch. What are you eating? What does he eat? Oh, my goodness, where did she go? Where is she?'

Uproar was about to ensue. But Stepan Trofimovich

---

[1] I loved you!... I loved you all my life... twenty years!

muttered in a weak voice that he'd really like to go to sleep for *une heure*, and then—*un bouillon, un thé... enfin, il est si heureux.*[1] He lay down and really did seem to fall fast asleep (he was probably pretending). Varvara Petrovna waited and then tiptoed out from behind the screen.

She sat down in the other room, drove away the landlord and landlady, and ordered Dasha to bring *her* in. A serious interrogation followed.

'Now, dear, tell me all the details; sit down over here, next to me. Well?'

'I met Stepan Trofimovich...'

'Stop. Silence. I warn you if you tell lies or conceal anything, I'll dig up your bones from under the earth. Well?'

'Stepan Trofimovich and I... as soon as I arrived in Khatovo, ma'am,' Sofya Matveevna began, almost gasping...

'Stop. Silence. Wait. Why are you babbling like that? In the first place, tell me what sort of creature you are.'

She told her something about herself, though in very few words, beginning with Sevastopol. Varvara Petrovna listened in silence, sitting erect in her chair, staring sternly straight into the speaker's face.

'Why are you so frightened? Why are you staring down at the ground? I like it when people look straight at me when they're arguing with me. Go on.'

She told about their meeting, about the books, about how Stepan Trofimovich treated the peasant woman to vodka...

'Good, good, don't leave out the slightest detail,' Varvara Petrovna said encouragingly. Finally she told how they'd arrived here, how Stepan Trofimovich kept talking, 'though he was already very sick, ma'am,' and how he'd told her his life story from the very beginning, going on for several hours.

'Tell me about his life.'

Sofya Matveevna stopped suddenly and was completely at a loss.

'I can't tell you anything about that, ma'am,' she said, almost in tears, 'I hardly understood anything.'

[1] Some bouillon, some tea... really, he was so happy.

'You're lying—you must have understood something.'

'He went on about some noble lady with black hair,' Sofya Matveevna said, blushing terribly, but noticing Varvara Petrovna's blond hair and the total lack of any resemblance between her and the 'brunette'.

'Black hair? What exactly did he say? Well, tell me!'

'He said that this noble lady was very much in love with him, ma'am, all her life, for twenty long years; but she dared not speak about it and was ashamed because she was very fat, ma'am...'

'He's a fool!' Varvara Petrovna cut her off pensively, but resolutely.

By now Sofya Matveevna was weeping.

'I can't tell you any of it properly because I was very worried about him and couldn't understand, since he's such a clever man...'

'A goose like you has no business to judge his intelligence. Did he offer you his hand?'

The woman trembled.

'Did he fall in love with you? Tell me! Did he offer you his hand?' Varvara Petrovna shouted.

'It was almost like that, ma'am,' she replied in tears. 'But I didn't take it seriously because he was ill,' she added firmly, lifting her eyes.

'What's your name?'

'Sofya Matveevna, ma'am.'

'Well, then, Sofya Matveevna, you should know that he is the most worthless, most trivial little man... Good Lord! Do you consider me a villain?'

Sofya Matveevna's eyes bulged.

'A villain? A tyrant? Who's ruined his life?'

'How could that be, ma'am, since you're weeping yourself?'

Varvara Petrovna really did have tears in her eyes.

'Well, sit down, sit down, don't be afraid. Look me straight in the eye again. Why are you blushing? Dasha, come here, look at her: what do you think, is her heart pure?...'

To Sofya Matveevna's amazement, perhaps even to her

great consternation, Varvara Petrovna suddenly patted her on the cheek.

'It's a pity you're such a fool. A fool beyond your years. Well, my dear, I'll take care of you. I can see it's all nonsense. Stay here for the time being; they'll find a place for you. You'll get your board and everything else from me... until I send for you.'

Sofya Matveevna muttered in alarm that she had to hurry on.

'There's nowhere for you to hurry to. I'll buy all your books; you stay here. Silence, no excuses. After all, if I hadn't come, you wouldn't have left him here, would you?'

'Not for anything would I have left him, ma'am,' Sofya Matveevna replied softly and firmly, wiping her eyes.

Dr Salzfisch was brought late that night. He was a respectable old man and quite an experienced practitioner who'd only recently lost his post in the civil service as a result of a quarrel with his superiors over a point of honour. From then on Varvara Petrovna had begun to 'protect' him with all her might. He examined the patient carefully, questioned him, and cautiously informed Varvara Petrovna that the condition of the 'sufferer' was extremely dubious, as a result of certain complications from the illness, and said that one must expect anything, 'even the very worst'. Varvara Petrovna, who for twenty years had become unaccustomed to the very idea of anything serious and decisive in connection with Stepan Trofimovich, was profoundly shaken and even turned pale:

'Is there really no hope?'

'One can never say there's absolutely no hope at all, but...'

She didn't go to bed all night and could hardly wait for morning. As soon as the patient opened his eyes and regained consciousness (he was still conscious, though growing weaker by the hour), she approached him with a most decided air.

'Stepan Trofimovich, we have to be ready for anything. I've sent for a priest. You must do your duty...'

Knowing his convictions, she was afraid he might refuse. He looked at her in surprise.

'Nonsense, nonsense!' she cried, thinking he was already refusing. 'There's no time for any of your pranks. You've played the fool long enough.'

'But... am I really that ill?'

He consented thoughtfully. And in general, I learned from Varvara Petrovna afterwards, he was not the least bit afraid of death. Perhaps he simply didn't believe it and continued to regard his illness as insignificant.

He confessed and took the sacrament quite willingly. Everyone, including Sofya Matveevna and even the servants, came in to congratulate him on receiving the sacrament. They all wept softly to see his emaciated, exhausted face and his pale, trembling lips.

'*Oui, mes amis*, and I'm just surprised you should... go to so much trouble. Tomorrow I'll probably get up and we'll... set off... *Toute cette cérémonie*... to which, naturally, I pay deep respect, was...'

'I beg you, father, to remain here with the patient,' Varvara Petrovna said, hurriedly stopping the priest who'd already begun to remove his vestments. 'As soon as they bring in some tea, I'd like you to start talking about religious matters, to support his faith.'

The priest began talking; everyone sat or stood around the patient's bed.

'In our sinful time,' the priest began in an even tone of voice, with a cup of tea in his hand, 'faith in the Almighty is mankind's sole refuge from all the trials and tribulations of life, as well as the only hope for eternal bliss, promised to the righteous...'

Stepan Trofimovich seemed to come back to life; a sly smile passed over his lips.

'*Mon père, je vous remercie, et vous êtes bien bon, mais...*'[1]

'There's no *mais* about it, no *mais* at all!' cried Varvara Petrovna, jumping up from her chair. 'Father,' she addressed the priest, 'he's, he's the sort of man, he's the sort of man... in an hour you'll have to hear his confession again! That's the sort of man he is!'

[1] Father, I thank you and you're very kind, but

Stepan Trofimovich smiled faintly.

'My friends,' he said, 'God is necessary to me now if only because He's the only being whom one can love eternally...'

Whether he really had converted or whether the majestic ceremony attendant on the administration of the sacrament had impressed him deeply and aroused his artistic sensibility, still, firmly and, it's said, with great emotion, he uttered several things in direct contradiction to many of his former convictions.

'My immortality is necessary if only because God will not want to commit an injustice and smother once and for all the flame of love for Him that's been kindled in my heart. And what's more precious than love? Love is higher than being, love is the crown of being; how is it possible that being should not be subordinate to love? If I've come to love Him and rejoice in my love—is it possible He would extinguish me and my joy and turn us both into nothing. If there is a God, then I am immortal! *Voilà ma profession de foi.*[1]

'There is a God, Stepan Trofimovich, I assure you there is,' Varvara Petrovna implored him. 'Renounce your convictions, abandon all your foolishness even once in your life!' (It looks as if she didn't quite understand his *profession de foi.*)

'My friend,' he said, becoming more and more animated, although his voice broke frequently, 'my friend, when I understood... this turning of the other cheek, I... I came to understand something else as well... *J'ai menti toute ma vie,*[2] my whole life! I'd like... but tomorrow... tomorrow we'll all set off.'

Varvara Petrovna started weeping. He was looking for someone.

'Here she is, she's here!' she said, taking Sofya Matveevna by the hand and drawing her close to him. He smiled tenderly.

'Oh, how I should like to live all over again!' he cried with a great burst of energy. 'Every minute, every moment

---

[1] There's my profession of faith.
[2] I've lied all my life

of life must be a blessing to man... must be, absolutely must be! It's the duty of man himself to make that so; it's the law—hidden, but absolutely essential... Oh, how I'd like to see Petrusha... and all of them... even Shatov!'

I must mention that neither Darya Pavlovna, nor Varvara Petrovna, nor even Salzfisch, who'd just come from town, knew anything about Shatov.

Stepan Trofimovich was getting more and more agitated, morbidly so, beyond his strength.

'The eternal idea alone that there is something immeasurably more just and happier than I am fills me with boundless joy and—pride,—oh, whoever I may be, whatever I may have done! Much more essential to man than his own happiness is to know and to believe at every moment that somewhere there exists perfect and serene happiness, for everyone and everything... The whole law of human existence is that a man should always be able to bow down before what's immeasurably great. If you deprive people of what is immeasurably great, they won't be able to live, and they will die in despair. The infinite and the eternal are as essential to man as this small planet where we live... My friends, all of you, everyone: long live the Great Idea! The eternal, infinite Idea! Every man, whoever he is, must bow down before the Great Idea. Even the most foolish man must have something great. Petrusha... Oh, how I'd like to see them all again! They don't know, don't know that the same eternal Great Idea also dwells in them!'

Dr Salzfisch wasn't present during the ceremony. Coming in suddenly, he was horrified and dispersed the crowd, insisting that the sick man be left in peace.

Stepan Trofimovich died three days later, but by then he was completely unconscious. He passed away quietly, like a candle that burns down. Varvara Petrovna had a funeral service performed at the hut and transported her poor friend's body to Skvoreshniki. His grave stands in the churchyard there and is already covered with a marble slab. An inscription and a railing will be added in the spring.

Varvara Petrovna's absence from town lasted eight days in all. Sofya Matveevna returned to town seated next to her in the carriage, and she seems to have settled down with her for good. I must mention that as soon as Stepan Trofimovich lost consciousness (that very morning), Varvara Petrovna immediately dismissed Sofya Matveevna, sending her out of the hut altogether, while she herself looked after the patient, all alone to the very end; only after he'd passed away did she summon her back at once. She didn't want to hear any objections whatever from the terrified Sofya Matveevna to her proposal (rather, her command) that Sofya settle at Skvoreshniki.

'That's nonsense! I myself will go with you to sell the Gospel. Now I have no one at all left on earth!'

'But you have a son,' Salzfisch observed.

'I have no son!' Varvara Petrovna cut him short and—it was as if she'd uttered a prophecy.

CHAPTER 8

Conclusion

ALL the crimes and outrages committed came to light with extraordinary rapidity, much faster than Peter Stepanovich had expected. To begin with, the unfortunate Marya Ignatievna Shatova woke up before dawn the night of her husband's murder, looked for him, and became indescribably agitated when she saw he wasn't there beside her. The servant woman hired by Arina Prokhorovna Virginskaya to spend the night there with her was unable to calm her down and, at first light, ran to fetch Arina Prokhorovna, who, she convinced the sick woman, would know where her husband was and when he'd come back. Meanwhile Arina Prokhorovna was also quite worried: she'd already heard from her husband about the nocturnal adventure at Skvoreshniki. He'd returned home after eleven in a terrible state; wringing his hands, he threw himself face down on the bed and, shaking with convulsive sobs, kept repeating: 'It wasn't right, not right; it wasn't right at all!' Naturally, he ended up confessing everything to Arina Prokhorovna—but to her alone of the whole household. She left him in bed with a stern warning that 'if he was going to whimper, he'd better do so into his pillow, so no one would hear him, and he'd be a fool if he showed any traces of it the next day.' Still, she thought more about it and immediately began to clear things away, just in case: she managed to conceal or destroy extra papers, books, and even, perhaps, some pamphlets. All the while she realized that she herself, her sister, her aunt, the female student, and perhaps even her long-eared brother really had nothing to be afraid of. When the nurse came to fetch her in the morning, she went to see Marya Ignatievna without hesitation. She was however terribly anxious to find out as soon as possible whether it was true what her husband had told her last night in such a terrified and frantic whisper, as if almost delirious—about Peter Stepanovich's relying on Kirillov to serve the common cause.

But she arrived at Marya Ignatievna's too late: having dispatched the servant, left all alone, Marya Ignatievna couldn't bear it; she got out of bed, threw on the first thing to hand, something very light and not at all right for the season, and set off to find Kirillov, thinking that perhaps he'd be the one to reveal her husband's whereabouts. One can well imagine the effect of what she saw there on a woman who'd just given birth. It's remarkable but she didn't read Kirillov's last letter, lying there in full view on the table; no doubt in the shock she overlooked it. She ran back to her room, snatched up her baby, left the house and ran out into the street. The morning was damp and foggy. There was no one at all to be seen along the deserted street. She kept running, gasping for breath, through the cold, thick mud and finally began knocking at various houses. At one, they wouldn't open the door; at another, they took a long time to do so. Losing patience, she ran off to a third house and began knocking. That was the home of our merchant Titov. There she created a huge commotion, wailing and declaring incoherently that 'they'd murdered her husband'. Something about Shatov and his fate was already known in Titov's house; they were horror-stricken that she who, according to her own account, had given birth only the day before, could now be running through the street in such clothes and such cold, with a barely covered baby in her arms. At first they thought she was delirious, especially since they couldn't work out who'd been murdered: Kirillov or her husband? Concluding that they didn't believe her, she was about to run on further, but was forcibly restrained; they say she screamed and put up a terrible struggle. They went over to Filippov's house, and within two hours the news of Kirillov's suicide and his last letter was known to the whole town. The police came to question Marya Ignatievna who was still conscious; here it became clear she hadn't read Kirillov's note, but why precisely she should have concluded that her husband had been murdered they were unable to discover from her. She only shouted that 'if Kirillov were dead, her husband was also dead; they were together!' Towards noon she became unconscious and never recovered; she died three days later. The baby had caught cold and died even before she did. When Arina Prokhorovna was unable to find Marya Ignatievna and the baby, she suspected something was amiss; she wanted to run home, but stopped at the gate and sent the nurse to 'enquire from the gentleman at the cottage whether Marya Ignatievna was there or if he knew where she was.' The messenger returned, screaming at the top of her lungs. Having prevailed upon her to stop screaming and refrain from telling anyone with the well-known argument that 'she'd get into trouble', she slipped out of the courtyard.

It goes without saying that she too was questioned that same morning, since she'd been Marya Ignatievna's midwife. But they didn't get much out of her: she gave them a very cool, composed account of all that she'd seen and heard at Shatov's, but as to what had happened, she said she knew nothing and understood nothing about it.

One can imagine the uproar that arose in town. A new 'episode', another murder! But there was something else: it became clear that there existed, there really existed a secret society of murderers, arsonists, revolutionaries, and rebels. Liza's terrible death, the murder of Stavrogin's wife, Stavrogin himself, the arson, the ball for the governesses, the dissolute crowd surrounding Yulia Mikhailovna von Lembke... People insisted on seeing some mystery even in the disappearance of Stepan Trofimovich. There was a great deal of whispering about Nikolai Vsevolodovich. Towards the end of the day they found out about Peter Stepanovich's departure, and strange to say, had the least of all to say about that. But most of all that day they talked about 'the senator'. A crowd was gathered at Filippov's house almost all that morning. The police had in fact been led astray by Kirillov's letter. They also believed both that Kirillov murdered Shatov and that the 'murderer' committed suicide. However, though the authorities were somewhat at a loss, they were not entirely in the dark. The word 'park', for example, such a vague indication of location in Kirillov's letter, didn't confuse anyone as Peter Stepanovich had hoped it would. The police rushed to Skvoreshniki at once, not only because it contained a park, the only one in the vicinity, but from instinct, since all the recent horrors were either directly or indirectly connected with Skvoreshniki. In any case, that's my theory. (I should mention that early that morning Varvara Petrovna, who knew nothing of all this, set out in pursuit of Stepan Trofimovich.) The evening of that same day, they found the body in the pond by following several leads. Shatov's cap was discovered at the site of the murder; it had been overlooked by the murderers in their extreme carelessness. A visual inspection and medical examination of the body as well as certain preliminary deductions aroused suspicion that Kirillov must have had some accomplices. It became clear there really was a secret society to which Shatov and Kirillov belonged, and that this society was connected to the pamphlets. Who were these accomplices? There was no thought of the members of 'our' group as yet that day. They found out Kirillov had lived like a hermit, in such complete seclusion that, as described in the letter, Fedka could be harboured there for many days while a general search for him was being conducted... The thing that mainly confounded everyone was that in all this confusion, there was nothing to connect or explain these events. It's difficult to imagine what conclusions and absurd theories our panic-stricken society might have arrived at, if everything hadn't suddenly been explained all at once, the very next day, thanks to Lyamshin.

He couldn't stand it. What happened was precisely what even Peter Stepanovich had begun to foresee towards the end. Entrusted to Tolkachenko, and then to Erkel, he spent the whole next day in bed, apparently quite calm, turned to the wall, saying nothing, hardly replying when spoken to. Thus the whole day he learned nothing at all about what was happening in town. But Tolkachenko, who was well-informed about everything, decided that evening to abandon the task of watching Lyamshin imposed on him by Peter Stepanovich and leave town for the country, that is, to put it simply, to escape. The fact is, they lost their heads, just as Erkel had predicted they would. By the way, I must note that Liputin also disappeared from town that day, and before noon. But it so happened that the authorities didn't learn about his disappearance until the evening of the following day, when they went directly to interrogate members of his family who had become thoroughly scared by his absence, but who were afraid to speak out. But now to get back to Lyamshin. As soon as he'd been left alone (Erkel, relying on Tolkachenko, had gone home earlier), he rushed out of the house and, of course, soon learned what had happened. Without even returning home, he started running with no idea where he was going. But the night was so dark, and what he meant to do so terrible and arduous, that after running down two or three streets, he went home and locked himself in for the night. He apparently attempted suicide towards morning; it was unsuccessful. He sat there, however, locked in almost until noon and then—all of a sudden, ran to the authorities. They say he crawled on his knees, sobbed and wailed, kissed the floor, crying that he was unfit even to kiss the boots of the officials standing before him. They calmed him down and even treated him kindly. The interrogation is said to have lasted three hours. He told them everything, absolutely everything, the whole truth, everything he knew, all the details; he jumped ahead, was quick to confess, told them many unnecessary things without waiting for their questions. He turned out to know rather a lot and did a fairly decent job of describing the whole thing: the tragedy with Shatov and Kirillov, the fire, the Lebyadkins' death, and so on, were all relegated to secondary importance. Most important of all was Peter Stepanovich, the secret society, the organization, the network. In reply to the question: 'Why were so many murders, scandals, and outrages committed?' he replied in ardent haste that it was to promote 'the systematic undermining of every foundation, the systematic destruction of society and all its principles; to demoralize everyone and make hodge-podge of everything, and then, when society was on the point of collapse—sick, depressed, cynical, and sceptical, but still with a perpetual desire for some kind of guiding principle and for self-preservation—suddenly to gain control of it, raising the banner of rebellion and relying on a whole network of groups of five, which meanwhile were actively recruiting new members, discovering weak spots in the system to be attacked, and determining the best ways of proceeding.' In conclusion he said that here in our town Peter Stepanovich had organized the first attempt at such systematic disorder, the programme for future action, so to speak, for all groups of five; this was only his own (Lyamshin's) idea, his theory; he hoped 'they would be sure to remember and bear in mind how frankly and amenably he'd explained it all to them and, of course, he might prove to be of even greater use to the authorities in the future.' In reply to the definitive question: 'Are there many groups of five?' he replied there was an enormous number of them, that Russia was covered with a network, and although he couldn't provide any evidence, I think he was totally sincere. He could offer them only the printed programme of the society, published abroad, and a project for developing a system of future activities, which, though only a rough copy, was written in Peter Stepanovich's own hand. It turned out that as regards 'the undermining of every foundation' Lyamshim was quoting word for word from this pamphlet, including even periods and commas, even as he assured them it was all just his imagination. Concerning Yulia Mikhailovna, he expressed himself in an extremely amusing fashion, even without their having to ask; skipping ahead of himself he said that 'she was innocent and had been made a fool of.' But the remarkable thing was that he totally exonerated Nikolai Stavrogin from playing any role in the secret society or from participating in any agreement with Peter Stepanovich. (Lyamshin had no idea whatever of Peter Stepanovich's secret and rather ridiculous hopes for Stavrogin.) The death of the Lebyadkins, according to him, was arranged by Peter Stepanovich acting alone, without any assistance from Nikolai Vsevolodovich, with the insidious intention of involving Stavrogin in the crime and thereby making him dependent on Peter Stepanovich; but instead of gratitude, on which he was undoubtedly and carelessly reckoning,

Peter Stepanovich aroused only complete disgust and even despair in the 'noble' Nikolai Vsevolodovich. Still going at top speed, and without being asked, he finished with Stavrogin by throwing out an obviously disingenuous hint to the effect that he was extremely important, but there was some kind of mystery here; he had lived among us *incognito*, so to speak, he had some sort of commission, and it was very possible he'd soon come back to us from Petersburg (Lyamshin was sure Stavrogin was in Petersburg), only in a completely different guise, in a different setting, with a group of people about whom we might soon be hearing, and he'd heard all this from Peter Stepanovich, 'the secret enemy of Nikolai Vsevolodovich'.

I must add a note here. Two months later Lyamshin confessed to having exonerated Stavrogin deliberately, hoping for his protection and that in Petersburg Stavrogin would obtain a reduced sentence for him on two counts and would provide him with money and letters of recommendation to go into exile with. This confession made it evident that he really did have an extremely exaggerated conception of Nikolai Stavrogin.

Naturally Virginsky was also arrested the same day, together, in the heat of the moment, with his whole household. (Arina Prokhorovna, her sister, her aunt, and even the female student were released a long time ago; they say even Shigalyov will be set free very soon, since he doesn't fit into any category of plaintiff; however, that's only what I've heard.) Virginsky admitted everything immediately: he was ill and feverish when arrested. They say he was almost glad: 'A load has been lifted from my heart,' he's supposed to have said. I heard he's now providing evidence freely, but even with a certain dignity, and he hasn't renounced any of his 'bright hopes', even though at the same time he's condemning the political path (as opposed to the social one) on to which he was drawn, accidentally and unwittingly, by a 'whirlwind of associated circumstances'. His behaviour at the time of the murder has now been put in a mitigating light and it seems he can also count on a certain mitigation of his sentence. At least that's what they say in town.

But it's very unlikely Erkel's sentence will be reduced. From the moment of his arrest he's either remained silent or distorted the truth as much as possible. They haven't been able to exact a single word of repentance from him up to this point. However, he's aroused a certain sympathy even in the severest of his judges—for his youth, his helplessness, and the obvious fact that he was merely the fanatical victim of a political seducer; and most of all by his conduct towards his mother, to whom he used to send almost half his small salary. His mother is now living in our town; she's a weak, sickly woman, prematurely aged; she weeps and literally grovels at our feet seeking mercy for her son. Whatever happens, many people in our town feel sorry for Erkel.

They arrested Liputin in Petersburg where he'd been for two weeks. An almost inconceivable thing happened to him there, one that's even difficult to explain. They say that even though he had a false passport, a good chance to slip abroad, as well as a significant amount of money, he still remained in Petersburg and didn't go anywhere. For some time he hunted for Stavrogin and Peter Stepanovich; then he suddenly went in for drinking and debauchery beyond all measure, like a man who's lost all good sense and any idea of his own predicament. He was arrested in Petersburg, dead drunk in a brothel. There's a rumour circulating to the effect that he hasn't lost heart, is presenting false evidence, and is preparing for the coming trial with a certain sense of triumph and optimism(?). He even intends to make a speech at the trial. Tolkachenko, arrested somewhere in the provinces about ten days after his escape, is behaving himself incomparably better; neither lying nor distorting the truth, but telling everything he knows, without trying to justify himself; he takes blame on himself with all modesty, but is also inclined to make eloquent speeches; he talks a great deal and quite willingly, but when it comes to knowledge of the common people and its revolutionary(?) elements, he strikes poses and is eager to produce an effect. I've heard that he too hopes to speak at the trial. In general he and Liputin are not too scared, and that seems somewhat strange.

I repeat, the business is not yet over. Now, three months later, our society has rested, recovered, recuperated, and formed its own opinions to such an extent that some people consider Peter Stepanovich a genius, or at least someone 'possessing the abilities of a genius'. 'Organization, sir!' they say in the club, raising a finger. But this is all quite innocent, and only a few people talk like that. Others, on the contrary, while not denying him acuteness of perception, cite his total ignorance of reality, his terrible penchant for abstraction, and his grotesque and narrow development in one direction, resulting in extreme shallowness. Everyone is agreed about his moral qualities; no one has any argument on that score.

I really don't know who else I should mention here if I'm not to forget anyone. Maurice Nikolaevich has gone away somewhere for good. Old Mrs Drozdova has sunk into senility... But there's one very grim story left to tell. I'll restrict myself to the facts alone.

Upon her return Varvara Petrovna stopped at her town house. All at once the accumulated news burst in upon her and gave her a terrible shock. She shut herself up all alone. It was evening; everyone was tired and went to bed early.

In the morning the maid handed Darya Pavlovna a mysterious-looking letter. According to her, the letter had arrived the day before, but very late, when everyone was asleep, and she didn't want to disturb them. It didn't come in the post, but was delivered to Skvoreshniki by some unknown person and handed to Aleksei Yegorych. He in turn had delivered it into her hands last evening, and then went straight back to Skvoreshniki.

Darya Pavlovna, her heart pounding, looked at the letter for some time and dared not open it. She knew who it was from: Nikolai Stavrogin. She read the inscription on the envelope: 'To Aleksei Yegorych to be given secretly to Darya Pavlovna.'

Here's the letter, word for word, without correcting a single mistake in the style of this Russian gentleman who, in spite of his European education, still hadn't quite mastered Russian grammar:

Dear Darya Pavlovna,

You once said you wanted to be my 'nursemaid' and made me promise to send for you when it became necessary. I'm leaving in two days and won't return. Do you want to come with me?

Last year, like Herzen, I registered as a citizen in the Swiss canton of Uri* and no one knows about it. I've already bought a small house there. I still have twelve thousand roubles; we'll go and live there for ever. I don't want to go anywhere else ever again.

The place is very boring, a narrow valley; mountains restrict one's view and one's thoughts. It's very gloomy. I chose it because there was a little house for sale. If you don't like it, I'll sell it and buy another one in a different place.

I'm not well, but I hope the air there will rid me of hallucinations. That's the physical side; as for the moral side, you know it all. But is it all?

I've told you a great deal about my life. But not everything. I haven't told even you everything! By the way, I admit that in my conscience I feel responsible for the death of my wife. I didn't see you after the event, and that's why I'm confirming it now. I've wronged Lizaveta Nikolaevna too, but you know that; you foresaw almost all of it.

It'd be better if you didn't come. My asking you to come is really despicable. Why should you bury your life with mine? You're dear to me and for me, bored as I was, it was good to be near you: only in your presence could I speak about myself out loud. Nothing will come of this. You described yourself as a 'nursemaid'—it's your own phrase; why sacrifice so much? You must also realize I don't spare your feelings in asking you, nor do I respect you, in expecting you. However I do ask you and expect you. In any case, I need a reply from you since I must leave very soon. Otherwise I'll go alone.

I don't expect anything from the canton of Uri; I'm simply going there. I didn't choose a gloomy place intentionally. I'm not attached to anything in Russia—everything is as alien to me here as elsewhere. True, I've liked living here less than any other place; but even here I was incapable of finding anything I could hate!

I've tested my strength everywhere. You advised me 'to get to know myself'. In tests for myself and for others it seemed unlimited, just as it had during my entire previous life. Before your eyes I endured a slap in the face from your brother; I admitted my marriage publicly. But how to apply my strength—that's what I never could see, what I don't see even now, in spite of your encouragement in Switzerland, in which I believed. Just as before I'm still capable of wishing to do a good deed and taking pleasure in doing so; but at the same time I wish to do evil and also take pleasure in that. But just as before both feelings are always too trivial and never very powerful. My desires are too weak; they can't be a guide to me. It may be possible to cross a river on a log, but not on a splinter of wood. This is just so you don't think I'm going to Uri with any hopes.

As always I blame no one. I tried wild debauchery and wasted my strength; but I don't like debauchery and didn't really want it. You've been watching me lately. You know, I regarded all our iconoclasts with spite, out of envy for their hopes. But you were afraid for no good reason: I couldn't become their comrade because I had nothing in common with them. Nor could I do it just for fun, out of spite; not because I was afraid of the ridiculous—I can't be afraid of the ridiculous—but because I still have the habits of a decent man and found it disgusting. But if I'd felt more spite and envy, I might have joined them. Judge for yourself how easy it's been for me and how I've been tossed about!

Dear friend, you tender and generous creature whose heart I've divined! Perhaps you dream of giving me so much love and lavishing so much of the beauty of your splendid soul upon me that you hope finally to give me some purpose? No, you must be more careful: my love will be just as petty as I myself am, and you won't be happy. Your brother used to tell me that he who loses touch with his own land loses his own gods, that is, his every purpose in life. One can argue endlessly about everything, but the only thing to emanate from me is negation without magnanimity, without power. Not even negation has come from me. Everything seems always so trivial and stale. Kirillov was magnanimous and couldn't bear an idea and—he shot himself; but I can see he was magnanimous because he lost his reason. I can never lose my reason and can never believe in an idea to the extent he did. I can't even get interested in an idea to that extent. Never, never could I shoot myself!

I know that I ought to kill myself, wipe myself off the face of the earth like an insect. But I'm afraid of suicide because I'm afraid to show any magnanimity. I know it'll be another delusion— the last in an endless series of delusions. What's the use of deceiving myself merely to feign greatness of soul? I could never experience indignation or shame, therefore, not despair either.

Forgive me for writing so much. I've come to my senses now, and it happened by accident. A hundred pages would be too little, ten lines about enough. Ten lines to ask you to be my 'nursemaid'.

Since I left Skvoreshniki I've been living at the stationmaster's house at the sixth station away from town. I got to know him five years ago during my binge in Petersburg. No one knows I'm here. Write to me in his name. I'm enclosing the address.

Nikolai Stavrogin

Darya Pavlovna went to show the letter to Varvara Petrovna at once. She read it and asked Dasha to leave the room so she could read it again alone; but she called her back very soon.

'Are you going?' she asked almost timidly.

'Yes,' Dasha replied.

'Get ready! We'll go together!'

Dasha looked at her questioningly.

'What's there for me to do here now? What difference does it make? I'll register in the canton of Uri and live in the valley too... Don't worry, I won't interfere.'

They began packing quickly to catch the midday train. But before half an hour had passed Aleksei Yegorych returned from Skvoreshniki. He announced that Nikolai Vsevolodovich had arrived 'suddenly' that morning, on the early train, and was now at Skvoreshniki, but 'in such a state he won't answer any questions, he went all round the house and shut himself up in his part of it...'

'I decided to come and tell you, even though I received no orders,' Aleksei Yegorych added with a very significant expression.

Varvara Petrovna gave him a penetrating glance and asked no further questions. The carriage was brought around at once. She set out with Dasha. She's said to have crossed herself frequently all along the way.

In 'his part of the house' all the doors stood open and Nikolai Vsevolodovich was nowhere to be found.

'Could he be up in the attic, ma'am?' Fomushka enquired cautiously.

It's worth nothing that several servants followed Varvara Petrovna into 'his part of the house'; the rest waited in the hall. Never before had they let themselves violate the rules of etiquette. Varvara Petrovna noticed, but said nothing.

They went upstairs to the attic. There were three rooms, but no one was to be found in any of them.

'Would he have gone up there, ma'am?' someone asked, indicating a door to the loft. And in fact the door to the loft that was always locked was now unlocked and stood wide open. The little room was just under the roof and could be reached only by climbing a long, very narrow, terribly steep wooden staircase. There was a tiny cubicle located up there.

'I'm not going up there. Why would he go up there?' Varvara Petrovna asked, turning terribly pale as she looked at the servants. They looked back at her and said nothing. Dasha shuddered.

Varvara Petrovna rushed up the stairs; Dasha followed her; but as soon as she entered the loft, she screamed and fell in a faint.

The citizen of the canton of Uri was hanging behind the door. On the little table lay a scrap of paper with some words scribbled on it in pencil: 'No one is to blame, I did it myself.' Also on the table lay a hammer, a piece of soap, and a large nail, obviously a spare in case it was needed. The strong silk cord from which Nikolai Vsevolodovich hung, evidently put by and selected well in advance, had been amply smeared with soap. Everything indicated premeditation and consciousness up to the very last minute.

At the post-mortem our medical experts absolutely and emphatically rejected the possibility of insanity.

EXPLANATORY NOTES

2 *Pushkin*: Dostoevsky uses as an epigraph excerpts from a lyrical ballad entitled 'Devils' (*Besy*, 1830) by the Russian poet and prose writer Alexander Pushkin (1799–1837), and borrows the title of the poem for his novel (which has also been translated *The Possessed*).

4 *Chaadaev, Belinsky, Granovsky, and Herzen*: P. Ya. Chaadaev (1794–1856) was a philosopher and writer whose 'First Philosophical Letter' (pub. 1836) created a storm of protest in Russian culture. *V. G. Belinsky* (1811–48) was a radical social and literary critic in early 19th-century Russia. *T. N. Granovsky* (1813–55) was a liberal historian and professor of history at Moscow University. (Several details of Stepan Trofimovich Verkhovensky's academic career are based on Granovsky's life.) *Alexander Herzen* (1812–70) was a leading left-wing Russian writer, journalist, editor and social critic.

5 *Slavophiles*: Slavophilism was an intellectual and political movement in the 19th century which emphasized the national identity of Russia, idealized the Russian past, and opposed westernization.

a progressive monthly journal: during the 1840s the liberal journal *Notes of the Fatherland* published translations of several novels by Charles Dickens and George Sand.

6 *Fourier*: Charles Fourier (1772–1837) was a French social philosopher who devised a scheme for communal harmony based on the 'phalanstery', a type of socialistic community.

Faust: Goethe's dramatic poem, the first part of which was published in 1808. The actual details of Verkhovensky's literary work are taken from a trilogy by the young Russian poet V. S. Pecherin (1807–85) entitled 'Pot-Pourri' published in *The Polar Star* in 1861.

9 *the people's poet*: N. A. Nekrasov (1821–77), poet, writer, and publisher, was the leading representative of the 'realist school' in Russian poetry. He was preoccupied with his country's ills which he ascribed chiefly to serfdom.

10 *Maecenas*: Gaius Maecenas (d. 8 BC) was a Roman statesman and munificent patron of letters who enjoyed a close association with the Emperor Augustus.

13 *rumours*: rumours about the government's intention to end serfdom began circulating in the mid-1850s. The edict was finally issued by Alexander II on 19 Feb. 1861.

14 *tax-farmer*: individuals hired by the state to collect taxes on liquor. They frequently managed to increase their personal wealth during the performance of their official duties.

17 *Kukolnik*: N. V. Kukolnik (1809–68) was a dramatist and novelist known primarily for his patriotic plays on historical themes. The portrait in question was an engraving by K. P. Bryullov made in 1836.

de Tocqueville . . . Paul de Kock: Alexis de Tocqueville (1805–59) was a French social philosopher and liberal thinker. *Paul de Kock* (1793–1871) was the author of extremely popular French sentimental and sensual novels about Parisian life under Louis-Philippe.

19 *Radishchev*: A. N. Radishchev (1749–1802) was a writer, social critic, and early opponent of serfdom and unlimited autocracy.

21 *a superfluous letter in the alphabet*: the hard sign (*tverdyi znak*) was finally abolished after the Revolution of 1917.

22 *Kraevsky*: A. A. Kraevsky (1810–89) was the publisher of the liberal journal *Notes of the Fatherland*.

24 *Vek and Vek . . .* : these lines parody popular satiric verse published in literary journals of the 1860s.

31 *chez ces séminaristes*: the word 'seminarists' became a term of abuse for members of the radical intelligentsia in the 1860s, since many of them were educated in seminaries.

32 *now I respect you*: this is a parody of a similar confession made in N. G. Chernyshevsky's (1828–89) revolutionary novel *What is to be Done?* (1863).

33 *Caesarism*: a reference to Napoleon III (1808–73), nephew of Napoleon I; he reigned as Emperor of France (1852–70) and wrote a book about Caesar with whom he strongly identified.

34 *the 19th of February*: the date of the emancipation of the serfs in Russia (1861).

The peasants . . . about to happen: from an anonymous poem entitled 'Fantasy' published in *The Polar Star* (1861).

35 *some noteworthy thoughts*: these thoughts parody several utterances on the subject by the liberal Russian novelist I. S. Turgenev (1818–83).

the great Rachel: the French actress Eliza Rachel (1821–58); *bouquet de l'impératrice* was a popular French perfume.

Anton Goremyka: a powerful tale by the novelist D. V. Grigorovich (1822–99) written in 1847 portraying the plight of the Russian peasant in poignant terms.

Anton Petrov: a peasant from the village of Bezdna who organized a rebellion in 1861 to claim rights to the land; the rebellion was suppressed and Petrov was shot.

36 *Peterschule*: a German middle school established on the Nevsky Prospect in Petersburg during the 18th century.

Pan-Slavism: an extension of mid-19th-century nationalism that emphasized political as well as cultural solidarity among Slavic peoples; it attracted numerous followers in Russia, especially among the Slavophiles.

Igor: the Russian prince (1150–1202) who was defeated in battle against the Cumans and became the hero of a medieval epic, *The Tale of Igor's Campaign*. See n. to p. 74 below.

37 *George Sand . . . novels*: a reference to *Lélia* (1833) by the French novelist and feminist George Sand (1804–76).

Belinsky . . . letter to Gogol: in 1847 Belinsky wrote a passionate appeal to the Russian writer N. V. Gogol in protest at the latter's reactionary views as expressed in his *Selected Passages from Correspondence with Friends* (1847). The letter was widely circulated and later published by Herzen in *The Bell*.

38 *Krylov's fable*: a reference to I. A. Krylov's (1768–1844) fable entitled 'The Inquisitive Fellow' (1814). The 'French social insects' refer to Fourier's disciples and other representatives of utopian socialist thought.

42 *1863*: that is, in reward for his participation in the suppression of the Polish uprising.

44 *marshal of the nobility*: a representative of the nobles of a certain province or district, elected for three years to manage the nobles' affairs, represent their interests, and perform several state functions.

45 *Nicolas*: the use of French names was quite common among the Russian gentry; cf. Maurice, Lise, etc.

51 *The Voice*: a moderately liberal newspaper published in Petersburg from 1863 to 1883 by A. A. Kraevsky.

54 *Considérant*: Victor Considérant (1808–93) was a French socialist, a disciple of Charles Fourier, and author of *Destinée sociale* (1834–8).

55 *phalanstery*: see n. to p. 6 above.

58 *administrative ecstasy*: in Russian, *administrativniy vostorg*, a phrase that came into the language from the satirical works of Saltykov-Shchedrin (see also p. 505, and n. to p. 337 below).

63 *Pascal said it*: a quotation from *Lettres provinciales* (1656–7) by Blaise Pascal (1623–62), French scientist and religious philosopher.

74 *The Tale of Igor's Campaign*: the most famous example of medieval Russian literature—a 12th-century epic poem (although some scholars have questioned its authenticity).

83 *Badinguet*: a stonemason whose name and clothes were borrowed by the future Emperor Napoleon III in 1846 during his escape to England.

89 *a journal article*: Karmazinov is a caricature of I. S. Turgenev. The article in question is most likely his sketch entitled 'The Execution of Troppmann' (1870).

93 *Teniers*: David Teniers the Younger (1610–90) was a Flemish painter best known for his scenes of daily life.

L'homme qui rit: a novel by the French writer Victor Hugo (1802–85), written in 1869.

94 *Mr G—v*: the narrator's name is spelled out in full as 'Govorov' in Dostoevsky's notebooks. The name is derived from the Russian root *govor*—'to say, speak, tell'.

99 *the last peace congress*: the International League for Peace and Freedom met in Geneva in September 1867.

108 *Pechorin*: the protagonist of *A Hero of Our Time* (1840) by the romantic poet and novelist M. Yu. Lermontov (1814–41).

114 *like a Kalmuck's*: the Kalmucks (or Kalmyks) are an Asian people belonging to one branch of the Oirat Mongols.

115 *Circassian*: a Muslim people inhabiting the Krasnodar region of Russia.

118 *Emperor Nikolai Pavlovich*: Tsar Nicholas I (1796–1855) who ruled Russia from 1825–55.

124 *Sevastopol*: the city on the Crimean peninsula besieged for almost a year during the Crimean War (1853–6) between Russia and the allied powers of Turkey, England, France, and Sardinia.

126 *Korobochka*: one of the provincial landowners satirized by Gogol in his comic novel *Dead Souls* (1842): she is a narrow-minded old miser.

134 *the 'new people'*: a reference to the younger generation of radical intellectuals; the formulation is borrowed from the subtitle of Chernyshevsky's novel *What is to be Done?*, 'From Tales About New People'.

144–5 *servility of thought*: Dostoevsky's notebooks for his earlier novel *Crime and Punishment* (1866) contain the following entry: 'N.B. Nihilism is servility of thought. The nihilist is a lackey of thought.'

152 *Mount Athos*: a religious community located on a peninsula in north-east Greece, the site of Eastern Orthodox monasteries of the order of St Basil founded in 963.

155 *For me no need . . .* : lines from a Russian folksong describing Yevdokia Lopukhina, the first wife of Peter the Great (1672–1725), forced by him to enter a convent.

156 *I have come to welcome you . . .* : Lebyadkin's 'verses' parody a well-known lyric poem by A. A. Fet (1820–92) entitled 'I have come to you with a welcome' (1843).

162 *the last famine*: presumably the one that occurred in 1867–8.

176 *this 'holy fool'*: 'fools for the sake of Christ' (*yurodivye*) were men and women who wandered the countryside behaving in strange, sometimes irrational ways.

183 *Yermolov*: A. P. Yermolov (1772–1861) was the general who served as commander-in-chief of Russian forces in the Caucasus (1817–27).

184 *the Moscow News*: a conservative newspaper published by M. N. Katkov (1818–87).

185 *Be still, my despairing heart*: an inaccurate quotation from a lyric entitled 'Doubt' (1838) by N. V. Kukolnik. The original line reads 'Sleep, my despairing heart.'

186 *Montbart*: the name is probably borrowed from the famous French pirate Montbars or Monbars (1645–?), leader of a band of buccaneers.

'*The Cockroach*': a general parody of Krylov's fables written in a grotesque style.

187 *a monument*: in 1855 a monument to Krylov was erected in the Summer Garden in Petersburg. The subscription had been organized by the minister of education, S. S. Uvarov.

188 *Davydov*: D. V. Davydov (1784–1839) was a poet, memoirist, and military theorist best remembered as the 'hussar-poet', creator of a lyrical hero who celebrates wine, women, and song on the eve of battle.

197 *Sodom*: the city destroyed by fire because of the sinfulness of its people in Genesis 18–19.

216 *the Decembrist L—n*: M. S. Lunin (1787–1845) was a participant in the Decembrist Rebellion on the Senate Square in Petersburg in 1825.

217 *Lermontov*: Lermontov (see n. to p. 108) fought several duels and was finally killed in one in 1841.

221 *zemstvo*: a locally elected council established to administer a district or province; they became most active in the 1880s.

225 *Bazarov*: the nihilist protagonist of Turgenev's novel *Fathers and Sons* (1861).

226 *Nozdryov*: another of the provincial landowners in Gogol's *Dead Souls* (1842): an outright and imaginative liar.

227 *Sistine Madonna*: the best-known painting by the Italian Renaissance painter Raphael (1483–1520).

238 *Balzac's Women*: presumably an illustrated album of heroines from Honoré de Balzac's interlocking series of novels and short stories *La Comédie humaine* (1831–50).

Castrates: a fanatical sect of Russian schismatics formed in the late 18th century who became eunuchs.

239 *the Internationale*: the International Workingmen's Association, later called the First International, organized in 1864 in London by Karl Marx. Its goal was to unify workers of all countries to promote socialist revolution.

Sharmer's: E. F. Sharmer was a well-known tailor in Petersburg from whom Dostoevsky ordered his own clothes.

246 *Pushkin wrote one to Heeckeren*: before fighting his last duel with D'Anthès, Pushkin wrote a letter to Baron Louis van Heeckeren dated 26 Jan. 1837 in which he insulted both the baron and his adopted son D'Anthès.

249 *the angel swears*: in Revelation 10: 6.

262 *a Slavophile idea*: see above, n. to p. 5.

264 *threatened in Revelation*: in Revelation 8: 10–11 and 16: 4.

267 *Nozdryov*: see above, n. to p. 226

Stenka Razin: a Cossack leader who organized a rebellion against the tsar in 1670. He was defeated, turned over to the government, and beheaded. His exploits have been celebrated in song and legend.

268 *the Marquis de Sade*: (1740–1814) was a French soldier, libertine, and author of licentious novels that challenged official morality in the name of authentic desire.

273 *like Martin with soap*: this popular saying of unknown origin was recorded by Dostoevsky in his Siberian notebooks.

277 *At night I'd wander . . .*: a quotation from a poem by P. A. Vyazemsky (1792–1878) entitled 'To the Memory of the Painter Orlovsky' (1838).

280 *Gogol's 'Last Story'*: in his *Selected Passages from Correspondence with Friends* (1847) Gogol referred to a future work to be called 'Farewell Story'.

285 *Derzhavin*: an inaccurate quotation from a poem by the classical writer G. R. Derzhavin (1743–1816) entitled 'God' (1784). The original line reads: 'I'm a tsar,—I'm a slave, I'm a worm,—I'm a god.'

291 *Grishka Otrepiev*: the most famous impostor and claimant to the Russian throne during the Time of Troubles (1598–1613). He reigned briefly as Tsar Dmitry 1605–6.

320 *What is to be Done?*: see above, n. to p. 134

325 *a tribe*: Germans first settled on what is now Russian territory in the late 12th–early 13th century when the Teutonic Order conquered the Baltic Provinces. A considerable number of these Baltic Germans were drawn into the ranks of the imperial administration in Petersburg.

326 *Fra Diavolo*: a comic opera written in 1830 by the French composer Daniel Auber (1782–1871).

329 *a church*: the Russian word *kirka* indicates that it is a Lutheran church rather than an Orthodox one.

337 *Glupov*: the name of a fictional town ('Stupidville') depicted in a satire of the Russian past called *The History of a Town* (1869) by the novelist M. E. Saltykov-Shchedrin (1826–89).

340 *the Marseillaise ... Mein lieber Augustin*: the French national anthem is contrasted with a popular German waltz in Lyamshin's improvisation of 'The Franco-Prussian War'.

341 *Jules Favre*: a French statesman (1809–80) who resigned his position in government service in 1871 because of the harsh conditions imposed on France by Germany at the end of the Franco-Prussian War.

344 *holy fool*: see above, n. to p. 176.

356 *the kazachok*: a lively Ukrainian folk dance.

357 *mess of pottage*: in Genesis 25: 29–34 Esau sells his birthright to his brother Jacob for some bread and a 'mess of pottage' (lentil soup).

358 *Capefigue*: Batiste Capefigue (1802–72) was a popular, second-rate French historian and man of letters.

361 *Alea jacta est*: 'The die is cast' (Lat.): the words Julius Caesar is supposed to have said before crossing the Rubicon into Italy to begin the civil war (49 BC).

362 *Full of pure love ... sweet dream*: a quotation from Pushkin's lyric poem, 'There once lived a poor knight' (1829).

364 *tongue of flame*: a quotation from Pushkin's lyric poem 'The Hero' (1830).

366 *Vogt, Moleschott, and Büchner*: Karl Vogt (1817–95) was a German naturalist, supporter of Darwin, and author of textbooks and other works on natural science. *Jacob Moleschott* (1822–93) was a Dutch physiologist and philosopher, often regarded as the founder of materialism. *Ludwig Büchner* (1824–99) was a German physician, philosopher of materialism, and a popularizer of science.

   that 'cadet' whom Mr Herzen describes: a reference to Herzen's account of P. A. Bakhmetev in his memoirs *My Past and Thoughts* (1855).

371 *A Noble Character*: parody of a poem entitled 'The Student' (1868) by N. P. Ogaryov (1813–77), poet, essayist and co-editor with Herzen of the radical journal *The Bell*.

380 *Avis au lecteur*: (Fr.) The phrase is used to indicate a foreword or prefatory note in a book. Here it carries a note of caution, 'A word to the wise'.

381 *Third Section*: the Russian secret police reorganized under Count A. K. Benckendorff (1783–1844) as part of the tsar's Chancery.

386 *Ryleev's Meditations*: K. F. Ryleev (1795–1826) was a romantic poet and Decembrist, best known as the originator of a verse genre, the *duma* or 'meditation'—short historical poems glorifying the Russian past.

387 *Karmazinov*: The portrait of the 'great writer' is a caricature of I. S. Turgenev; 'Merci' is a parody of several of his works including 'Apropos of Fathers and Sons' (1868–9), 'Spectres' (1863), and 'Enough' (1865).

390 *Along the Road . . . At the Crossroads*: these titles are humorous inventions.

391 *Babylon*: the catastrophe predicted in Jeremiah 51: 6 and Revelation 14: 8.

408 *'dear man'*: a reference to Chernyshevsky's *What is to be Done?* in which the heroine Vera Pavlovna constantly refers to her first husband as 'that dear man'.

   oars of maple, sails of silk: a paraphrase of a folksong from the Volga region.

409 *Se non è vero*: this Italian expression continues: '. . . è ben trovato.' ('Even if it's not true, it's well conceived.')

415 *The Bell*: a periodical edited by Herzen and published in London by the first free Russian press abroad (1857–62). Although it was banned in Russia, it still circulated and was read widely.

426 *aluminium columns*: a reference to the utopian vision in Vera Pavlovna's fourth dream in Chernyshevsky's *What is to be Done?*

429 *Cabet . . . Proudhon*: Étienne Cabet (1788–1856) was a French utopian socialist and reformer. *Pierre Proudhon* (1809–65) was a French social theorist and radical thinker.

431 *a pocket Switzerland*: the area around Dresden, the capital of Saxony, has often been compared to Switzerland for its natural beauty. Originally a Slavic settlement, it was settled by Germans in the 13th century.

445 *Littré's theory*: the name of the French positivist E. Littré (1801–81) is used in error. The thesis under consideration actually belongs to the Belgian mathematician A. Quetelet (1796–1874) and was popularized in Russia by V. A. Zaitsev.

447 *Rus*: the ancient name used to describe the territory inhabited by Eastern Slavs in general, and Russians in particular.

Ivan the Tsarevich: another pretender to the Russian throne (see above, n. to p. 291); he first appeared in 1845 and claimed to be the son of Constantine (Nicholas I's elder brother).

Ivan Filippovich, God of Sabaoth: one of the legends believed by the sect of Castrates in which their faith would be propagated in the West.

450 *At Tikhon's*: see above, Note on the text, p.xiv

451 *Archimandrite*: the head of an Orthodox monastery.

a holy fool: see above, n. to p. 176

454 *last war*: presumably the Crimean War (1853–6). See above, n. to p. 124

456 *mountain to move*: a test of faith described in Mark 3: 13.

457 *the très peu of a certain archbishop*: an incident at the beginning of the French Revolution described by Dostoevsky in 1873 concerning a Parisian archbishop who, under duress, confessed his faith in God (*très peu*—'very little'), and who was subsequently beheaded.

Angel of the Laodicean Church: from Revelation 3: 14–17.

461 *their daughter, aged fourteen*: note the discrepancy in the girl's age; below, on p. 472, we're told she's ten years old.

467 *the Petersburg side*: one section of the town located on a large island in the Neva estuary.

470 *Mount Athos*: see above, n. to p. 152.

471 *Acis and Galatea*: a composition by the French landscape painter Claude Lorrain (1600–82) on display in the Dresden Gallery. The subject was borrowed from Book XIII of Ovid's *Metamorphoses*.

479 *Whoso shall offend* . . . : from Matthew 18: 6.

480 *until His ways* . . . : the source of this quotation is unknown.

485 *The Bell*: see above, n. to p. 415.

489 *Kukolnik*: see above, n. to p. 17.

504 *Candide*: 'Everything is for the best in the best of all possible worlds': the famous pronouncement by the philosopher Pangloss, the hero's mentor, whose optimism is satirized by Voltaire in his novel *Candide* (1759).

513 *Granovsky*: see above, n. to p. 4.

516 *Westernizers*: a current in 19th-century thought maintaining that there were no fundamental differences between Russia and the West, that Russia was merely less developed and should strive to imitate Western models as closely as possible. The Westernizers were the opponents of the Slavophiles (see above, n. to p. 5).

'We great men ... didn't even notice he'd said it': another of Dostoevsky's vicious swipes at Turgenev.

524 *our time of troubles*: The Time of Troubles was a period of unrest and civil strife between the death of Tsar Fyodor (1598) and the establishment of the Romanov dynasty (1613).

Tentetnikov ... Radishchevs: Tentetnikov was a young, enlightened liberal landowner in the second, unfinished volume of Gogol's *Dead Souls*. Radishchev, see above, n. to p. 19.

525 *the order of St Stanislav*: one of the orders or decorations awarded for meritorious service in Imperial Russia.

526 *Belshazzar's feast*: the 'great feast' given by the king in Daniel 5: 1–4.

540 *the oration*: see above, n. to p. 387.

541 *Pompey or Cassius ... Gluck*: Pompey (106–48 BC) was a Roman general and great rival of Julius Caesar. *Cassius* (85–42 BC) was the leader of the successful conspiracy to assassinate Caesar in 44 BC. *Christoph von Gluck* (1714–87) was a German-born operatic composer whose work had a major impact on French operatic tradition.

542 *Ancus Martius*: the semi-legendary fourth king of Rome (640?–616? BC).

543 *Pechorin*: see above, n. to p. 108.

553 *an enormous bronze globe*: to commemorate Russia's Anniversary of One Thousand Years in 1862 a large monument was erected in Novgorod.

564 *the Voice... the Financial Times*: two widely distributed liberal newspapers in the 1870s.

575 *one of the best-known newspapers*: a reference to A. A. Kraevsky and his newspaper *The Voice* published in Petersburg 1863–83.

some important 'affair': a reference to the radical journal *The Affair* or *The Cause* (*Delo*), published in Petersburg 1866–88 and connected to the revolutionary movement in Europe.

periodical . . . published outside Petersburg: a reference to the reactionary journal *Moscow News* published by M. N. Katkov.

578 *Korobochka*: see above, n. to p. 126.

587 *Calendars are full of lies*: a quotation from Act III, sc. 21 of A. S. Griboedov's (1795–1829) verse comedy *Woe from Wit* (1825).

596 *Vox populi vox deï*: 'The voice of the people is the voice of God' (Lat.).

604 *Polinka Saks*: an epistolary novel written in 1847 by A. V. Druzhinin (1824–64) that traces the development and resolution of a love triangle.

621 *struggle for existence*: a reference to Charles Darwin's *Origin of Species* (1859) which set forth a theory of evolution including the idea of natural selection.

624 *written by Herzen*: see above, p.377 and n. to p. 4.

a Fourierist: see above, n. to p. 6.

630 *Tatar or Mordva*: the Tatars are a Turkic-speaking people who came originally from Central Asia or Siberia in the 13th century. The Mordva (or Mordvinians) are a Finnic-speaking people who inhabit a region in central European Russia.

632–3 *waiting for the student . . . Tashkent*: see above, p. 372.

638 *Voznesenskaya Street . . . Bogoyavlenskaya*: Marya Shatova has confused the streets named for two different holidays in the Orthodox church calendar: Voznesenskaya is Ascension, while Bogoyavlenskaya is Epiphany.

642 *Slavophile*: see above, n. to p. 5.

650 *a bookbinding shop*: a reference to the co-operative economic enterprise organized by Chernyshevsky's heroine Vera Pavlovna in *What is to be Done?*

663 *angels of God*: a reference to Matthew 22: 30 and Mark 12: 25.

Mohammed's pitcher: according to Muslim legend Mohammed was once awakened by the archangel Gabriel whose wing brushed against a pitcher of water. Mohammed managed to complete a journey to Jerusalem and have a conversation with God, His angels and prophets in heaven in so short a span of time that he returned home to catch the falling pitcher before even one drop of water had spilled.

712 *Spasov*: the word *Spas* in Russian means 'Saviour'; hence, Spasov connotes 'place of salvation'.

19th of February: see above, n. to p. 34.

715 *Renan's Vie de Jésus*: a reference to the first volume of *A History of the Origins of Christianity* (8 vols, 1863–83) by the French historian Ernest Renan (1823–92). The book attempts to retell Jesus' life by removing all supernatural events and making him into an ordinary man.

718 *Ulitina*: 'Sofya' means wisdom and Ulitina is derived from the word *ulitka*, 'snail', referring perhaps to the pace of redemption.

Sevastopol: see above, n. to p. 124.

some very strange episode: see above, p. 339–40.

725 *struggle for existence*: see above, n. to p. 621.

730 *And unto the angel ... and naked*: Revelation 3: 14–17.

732 *And there was ... they were afraid*: Luke 8: 32–5.

753 *Herzen ... Uri*: when Alexander Herzen was stripped of all rights in 1851 and denied permission to return to Russia, he became a Swiss citizen and registered in the canton of Freiburg.

THE WORLD'S CLASSICS

A Select List

SERGEI AKSAKOV: A Russian Gentleman
Translated by J. D. Duff
Edited by Edward Crankshaw

JANE AUSTEN: Emma
Edited by James Kinsley and David Lodge

ROBERT BAGE: Hermsprong
Edited by Peter Faulkner

KEITH BOSLEY (Transl.): The Kalevala

GEORGE BÜCHNER:
Danton's Death, Leonce and Lena, Woyzeck
Translated by Victor Price

THOMAS CARLYLE: The French Revolution
Edited by K. J. Fielding and David Sorensen

GEOFFREY CHAUCER: The Canterbury Tales
Translated by David Wright

ANTON CHEKHOV: The Russian Master and Other Stories
Translated by Ronald Hingley

CHARLES DICKENS: Christmas Books
Edited by Ruth Glancy

FËDOR DOSTOEVSKY: Crime and Punishment
Translated by Jessie Coulson
Introduction by John Jones

MARIA EDGEWORTH: Castle Rackrent
Edited by George Watson

SUSAN FERRIER: Marriage
Edited by Herbert Foltinek

GUSTAVE FLAUBERT: Madame Bovary
Translated by Gerard Hopkins
Introduction by Terence Cave

ELIZABETH GASKELL: Cousin Phillis and Other Tales
Edited by Angus Easson

ANTHONY TROLLOPE: The American Senator
Edited by John Halperin

Dr. Wortle's School
Edited by John Halperin

The Last Chronicle of Barset
Edited by Stephen Gill

IVAN TURGENEV: First Love and Other Stories
Translated by Richard Freeborn

VIRGIL: The Aeneid
Translated by C. Day Lewis
Edited by Jasper Griffin

HORACE WALPOLE: The Castle of Otranto
Edited by W. S. Lewis

IZAAK WALTON and CHARLES COTTON:
The Compleat Angler
Edited by John Buxton
Introduction by John Buchan

OSCAR WILDE: Complete Shorter Fiction
Edited by Isobel Murray

ÉMILE ZOLA:
The Attack on the Mill and other stories
Translated by Douglas Parmeé

A complete list of Oxford Paperbacks, including The World's Classics, OPUS, Past Masters, Oxford Authors, Oxford Shakespeare, and Oxford Paperback Reference, is available in the UK from the Arts and Reference Publicity Department (RS), Oxford University Press, Walton Street, Oxford OX2 6DP.

In the USA, complete lists are available from the Paperbacks Marketing Manager, Oxford University Press, 200 Madison Avenue, New York, NY 10016.

Oxford Paperbacks are available from all good bookshops. In case of difficulty, customers in the UK can order direct from Oxford University Press Bookshop, Freepost, 116 High Street, Oxford, OX1 4BR, enclosing full payment. Please add 10 per cent of published price for postage and packing.